CHARLES C. CROM
KENNETH W. CROMWELL

THE TOMB OF THERAGAARD

✜ NEW PALADIN ORDER ✜
BOOK I

The Tomb of Theragaard
Copyright © 2018 by Charles C. Cromwell and Kenneth W. Cromwell. All rights reserved.

No part of this book may be used or reproduced in any manner whatsoever without written permission except in the case of brief quotations embodied in critical articles or reviews.

This book is a work of fiction. Names, characters, businesses, organizations, places, events and incidents either are the product of the author's imagination or are used fictitiously. Any resemblance to actual persons, living or dead, events, or locales is entirely coincidental.

For information contact :
Kenneth Cromwell - Author on Facebook
@kcromwellauthor
www.newpaladinorder.com

ISBN: 978-1-718122-77-2

Printed in the United States of America.

The New Paladin Order

by Kenneth and Charles
Cromwell

The Tomb of Theragaard

The Siege of Tryon Keep

Descent to the Sunken Cathedral

Contents

Prologue. The Dark Pact 1
Chapter 1. The Acolyte 5
Chapter 2. The Apprentice. 11
Chapter 3. The Lords of the Graveyard 17
Chapter 4. A Plague upon Arkos. 23
Chapter 5. The Visitor 28
Chapter 6. A Wolf among Sheep 38
Chapter 7. Darkness and Light in the Vaults 46
Chapter 8. Point of Departure 59
Chapter 9. The Fire Inside 62
Chapter 10. Refusal of the Call 72
Chapter 11. Revelations 76
Chapter 12. Tryam's Unanswered Questions 82
Chapter 13. Telvar's Test of Fire 85
Chapter 14. The New Beginning. 90
Chapter 15. The Gigantic Hand 99
Chapter 16. A Blow to Tryam's Plans 106
Chapter 17. An Unwelcome Discovery. 113
Chapter 18. The Last Normal Morning 117
Chapter 19. The Tournament 125
Chapter 20. Tryam at the Crossroads. 147
Chapter 21. Telvar at the Crossroads. 151
Chapter 22. Dementhus at the Crossroads 155

Chapter 23. Departure 161
Chapter 24. Beyond the Threshold. 170
Chapter 25. Puzzle Pieces 184
Chapter 26. Interrogation 188
Chapter 27. Endless Vistas. 193
Chapter 28. Remorse and Return 201
Chapter 29. The Trial of Blood. 209
Chapter 30. The Sacrifice of Blood. 212
Chapter 31. The Cave in the Mountain 218
Chapter 32. The War Machine. 220
Chapter 33. The Hound of Fenrir 222
Chapter 34. Clan Ulf on Fire 228
Chapter 35. A Duel to the Death 233
Chapter 36. The Expedition 236
Chapter 37. The Flames in Which They Burn 242
Chapter 38. Pursuit into the Coronas 248
Chapter 39. A Sleeping Giant 260
Chapter 40. Doors Deep. 265
Chapter 41. Off the Path. 273
Chapter 42. The Barge 282
Chapter 43. The Summoning 284
Chapter 44. The Hideout 290
Chapter 45. Banging Heads into Walls. 306
Chapter 46. Unexpected Visitors. 311
Chapter 47. The Confession 317
Chapter 48. Another Point of Departure. 320
Chapter 49. Alive and Alone 324
Chapter 50. Ocean of Blood 330
Chapter 51. The Red Cloud 332
Chapter 52. Eternal Loyalty 339
Chapter 53. Assault 350
Chapter 54. Back to the Mountain. 362

Chapter 55. The Summit in Shadow. 368
Chapter 56. Heads Shall Roll! 372
Chapter 57. Caged Wolf 375
Chapter 58. In the Cave 378
Chapter 59. The Guardians and Escape 382
Chapter 60. The Shambling Mound 395
Chapter 61. An Old Acquaintance 399
Chapter 62. Meeting in the Blue Room 413
Chapter 63. The Gem 419
Chapter 64. Ardrah 425
Chapter 65. Birth 436
Chapter 66. Hell's Fires 438
Chapter 67. The Final Lesson 453
Chapter 68. The Binding Spell. 461
Chapter 69. Negotiations with the Commander 463
Chapter 70. The Invocation of the Golem 467
Chapter 71. Rallying the Brothers 470
Chapter 72. War of Wills 476
Chapter 73. A Day for Diplomacy 478
Chapter 74. Gathrey. 482
Chapter 75. The Last Game 485
Chapter 76. The First Wave 491
Chapter 77. The Return of Abbaster 494
Chapter 78. Lord Dunford's Arrival 502
Chapter 79. Preparations and the Wedding 505
Chapter 80. Fight, Part, and Retreat 512
Chapter 81. Welcome Whispers 518
Chapter 82. The Battle for Arkos 522
Chapter 83. The Golem versus the Cavalry Charge . . . 530
Chapter 84. Iscandious's Gambit 533
Chapter 85. The Defense of the Keep 537
Chapter 86. The Markswoman. 542

Chapter 87. Starting Her Journey Alone 546
Chapter 88. Yearning for Theragaard. 554
Chapter 89. Negotiations for Peace 556
Chapter 90. Retreat 565
Chapter 91. Answering Theragaard's Call 567
Chapter 92. Vengeance. 570
Chapter 93. Dementhus versus Rax Partha. 573
Chapter 94. Dawn. 576
Chapter 95. The Paladin 581
Chapter 96. Out of the Pit 584
Epilogue. Her Home. 589

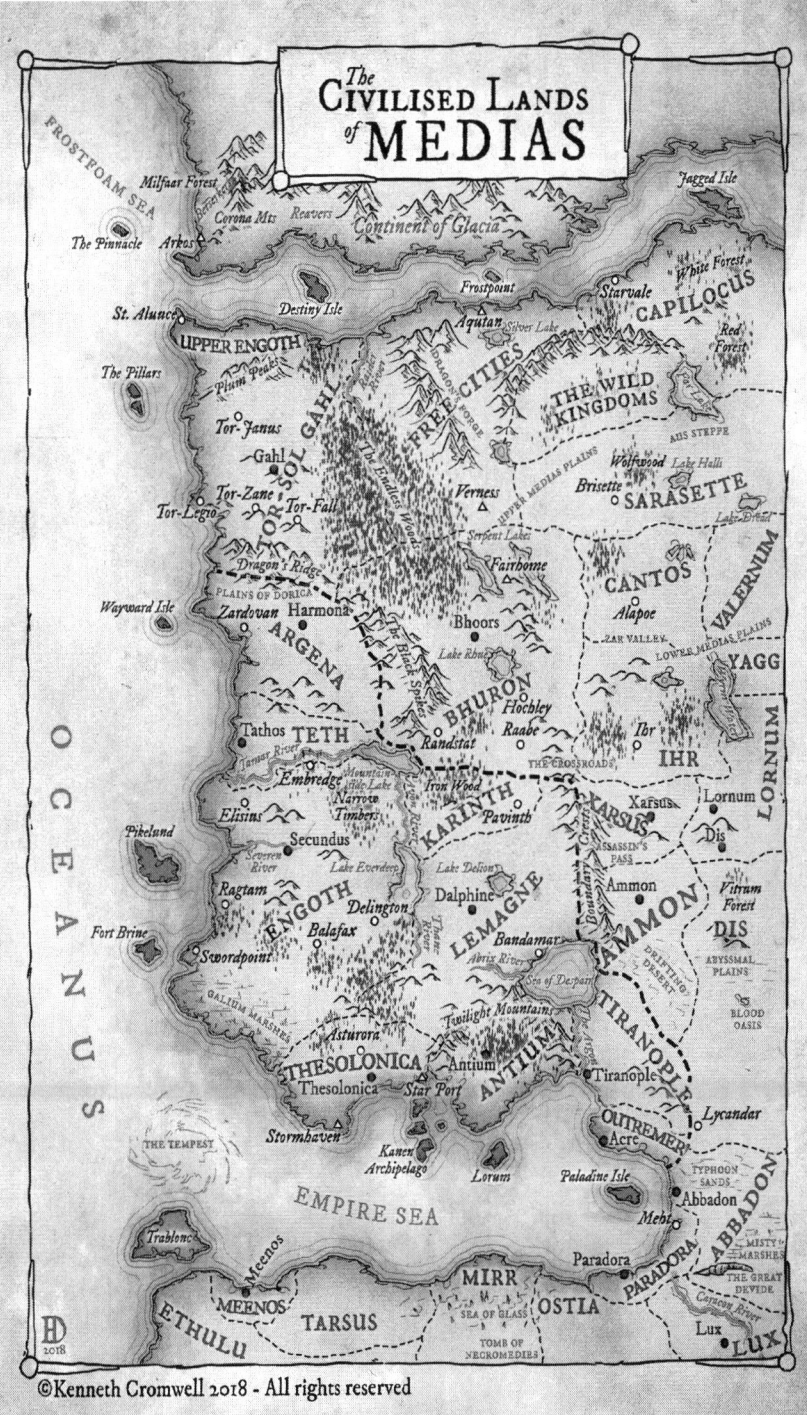

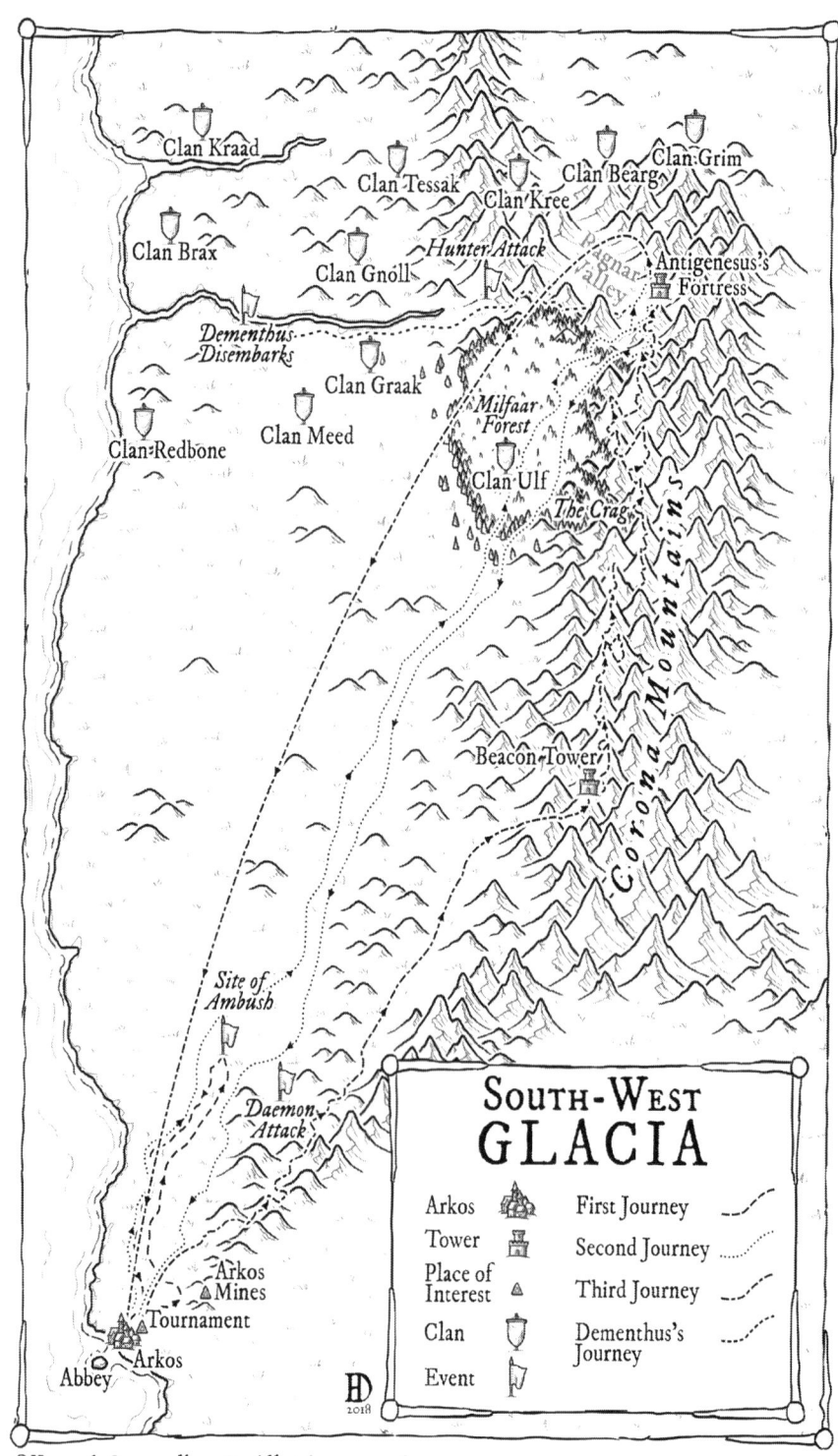

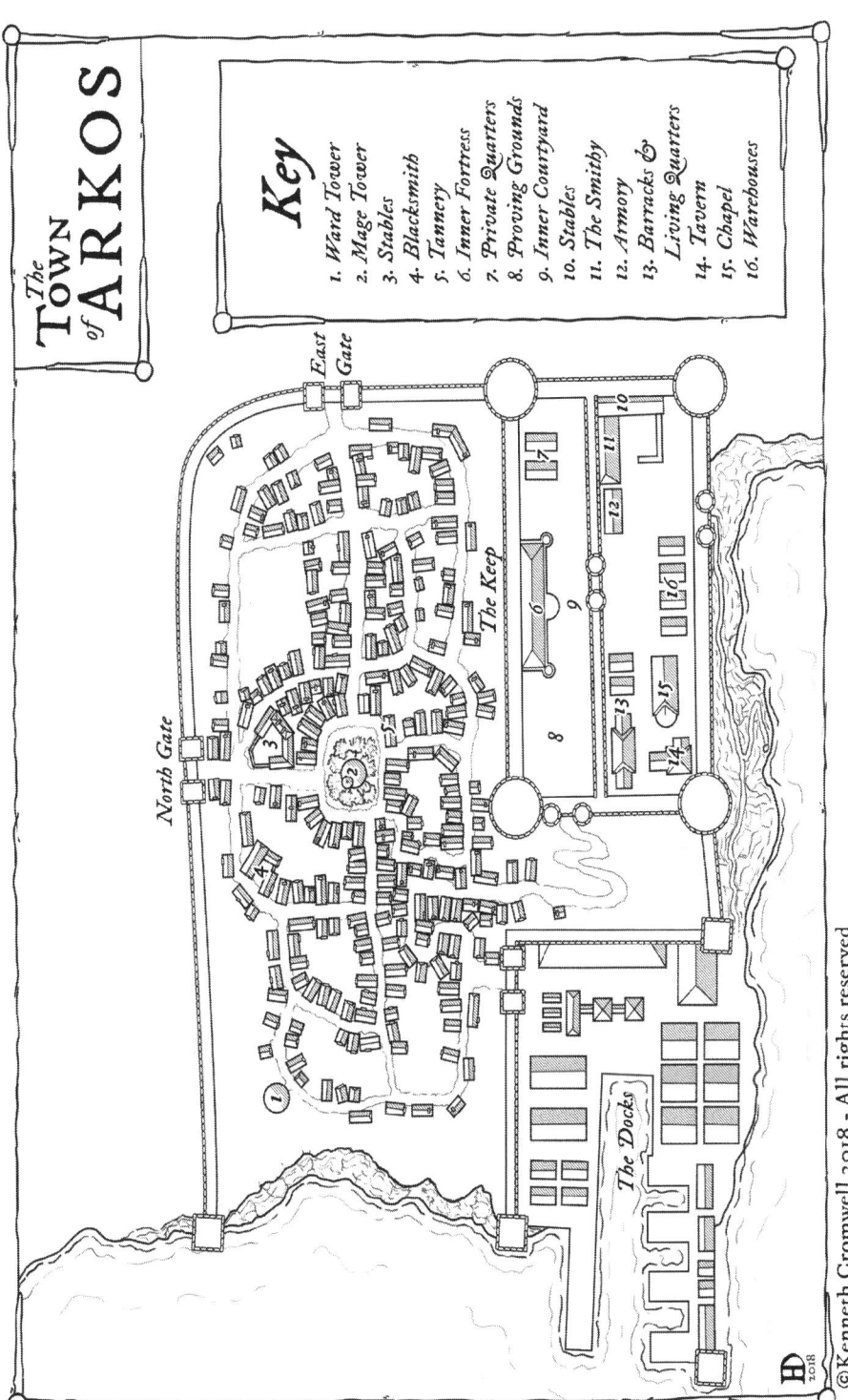

PROLOGUE
THE DARK PACT

As he moved toward the fresh corpse on the obsidian slab, Dementhus felt flowing from his outstretched hands the power of necromancy. As he laid his hands upon the body, he uttered the black tongue in a fevered pitch: "*Semetnus Ra, Thumpus Ra, Lorith Nadar!*" His mind channeled the dark forces of un-life into the remains, and he watched with fiendish eyes the thing convulse back into a crude form of existence, birthed in blood and offal.

The creature, who in life had been his apprentice, struggled to rise from the black stone slab. Dementhus addressed his former student: "Do you know who I am?"

The thing's milky eyes moved toward the Necromancer's voice. It took a step forward. Its tongue lolled inside its ruined mouth like that of a rabid dog's. It spoke, and the voice that emerged was that of a whisper: "My master."

The wizard smiled at the abomination and said a prayer of thanks to the Dark God, Terminus. Dementhus wondered why it had taken him this long to turn against his former colleagues. *This is the true power of magic, not the illusions and cantrips allowed by the Wizard Council of the Western Kingdoms!*

Dementhus took a long dagger from his robes and cast another spell. The dagger glowed red hot. He plunged the burning blade into the undead thing's rib cage. Flames engulfed the creature, and it crumpled to the floor, lifeless again. His apprentice had served him well in both life and death. Dementhus did not regret what he had done.

He was cleaning the scorched blood off the dagger when his heart jolted within his chest. The amulet he wore around his neck was glowing a dark crimson. It was the same amulet he had received when he'd converted to the worship of Terminus. Its activation meant that Bafomeht, the priest king of Lux, was summoning him. The Prophet was the only person said to have survived a journey through the perpetual storm that surrounded the doomed city of Antium, a feat those on the Wizard Council had thought impossible. Dementhus knew it was true. Not only had Bafomeht survived, he had returned with the ultimate prize: the Words of Terminus, directly from the Dark God's lips.

The wizard gathered his wits and headed out of the summoning chamber. He took the steps to his quarters two at a time, ignoring the pain in his hands and feet, the price he'd paid for his newfound skill. He reached for his staff but decided against it; Bafomeht might take offense at the sight of a tool Western wizards had used for centuries as a weapon in conflicts with those of the East. He instead headed out into the blinding light and blistering heat with no magical power save what he had stored in his mind.

The Prophet lived in the Great Ziggurat, situated at the heart of the city. Dementhus did not have to go far. His own quarters were in the city's religious district—the most heavily guarded section in Lux, a city of sand-colored pyramids, silver-domed buildings, and ancient marble temples.

The wizard had been inside the Great Ziggurat one time before, when, on bended knee, he had pleaded with the shamans of Lux to allow his conversion to the cult of Terminus, something unheard of being requested by a wizard from the Western Kingdoms. It was only after having been tortured to the brink of madness to test his sincerity that Dementhus had been allowed to read the Words of Terminus and learn of the dark magic they possessed.

The Ziggurat was gargantuan, blocking out the sun, and Dementhus soon found himself in the cool comfort of its imposing shadow. If the stories whispered by the shamans were true, buried beneath the black stone pyramid was a meteorite that had fallen to Medias thousands of years before. It was with weapons forged from that same meteorite that the first great empire of Lux had risen to power. Now it was with the newly discovered Words of Terminus that Lux was rising again.

Once at the entrance, a featureless ten-foot-wide gap along the south wall, Dementhus displayed the glowing amulet to the black-robed guards. Without delay, the guards parted their curved scimitars to allow him passage. The wizard strode down the sloped corridor, his heart pounding harder the

THE TOMB OF THERAGAARD

deeper into the massive stone structure he ventured. *Does Bafomeht know I've mastered the skill of necromancy? Are his agents watching my every move?*

A strong pull, like that of a great yearning, guided him through the unfamiliar corridors. His journey through a twisted maze of passages ended in an arched entranceway carved in obsidian. He entered without hesitation. In the center of the spacious room beyond, on a simple stone throne, sat Bafomeht. A shaft of light from high overhead illuminated the robed Prophet, but harsh shadows kept his features hidden.

"Come closer," commanded the seated figure, "and kneel before me."

Dementhus hesitated a moment to enable his eyes to adjust to the bright light before Bafomeht beckoned him forward with a pale, skeletal hand. The wizard rushed to the raised dais and fell to his knees. "How may I serve you?"

Bafomeht leaned forward and snatched the wizard's head with a speed and strength that belied his withered form. "Release your will," he whispered, "and allow me to share a vision."

Before Dementhus could offer resistance, daggers of energy drove into his skull. As the Prophet's grip grew stronger, the wizard's body contorted and writhed. His sight dimmed, and his eyes rolled back into his head. As the pain intensified, images of the past replaced the darkness. He saw large battles raging and great men dying.

Dementhus's heart threatened to burst through his chest, but his desire to see the visions overpowered his fear, and he opened his mind to enable greater amounts of energy to stab deep into his brain. "More! I want to see more!"

Visions played before Dementhus's mind: a struggle on a twin-peaked mountaintop between an archmagus in white robes and a holy knight in gleaming silver armor, a battle between armies on a frost-covered battlefield where blood had turned the snow crimson, and a Golem—an ancient magical construct fifty feet tall—wielding a giant steel sword slashing unopposed through a line of men.

The scenes changed as time flowed forward: the knight buried in a dusty tomb, a wizard burnt and his ashes scattered over a barren landscape, and a tribe of bearskin-clad primitives sacrificing a man held to a behemoth metal hand reaching out from thick glacial ice.

Bafomeht's hands released their hold, and the wizard slumped to the floor, his own red robes pooled around him like spilt blood. He took a moment to recover before crawling his way back to his feet.

His face still hidden in the shadows of his cowl, the Prophet leaned forward and stared into the Western wizard's eyes. Bafomeht spoke with a strong and youthful voice incongruous with his advanced age:

"We must spread the Words of Terminus, and to do so, we need powerful magic. I am sending forth my most devout followers on quests to the distant reaches of Medias to find artifacts lost during the chaos that followed the fall of the great kingdom of Antium." The Prophet again snatched Dementhus's head, and his voice again became an intense whisper. "The vision I have shown to you comes from Terminus Himself. Follow the visions and find the lost Golem you have seen."

Grasping at Bafomeht's skeletal hands, Dementhus smiled up at the hidden face. "O Bafomeht, I am ready. I would crawl to the ends of Medias for our great cause. I shall leave at once, for I know where I must go and what I must do!"

Bafomeht pushed Dementhus away and leaned back on his throne. "Two devout followers will go with you. I urge you to use their skills."

"Yes, my master."

The Prophet dismissed him with a wave of his hand.

Dementhus bowed. He turned to leave, but before he passed through the obsidian archway, he took one last look back. Something behind the throne loomed over Bafomeht. He was sure of it. Something blacker than the gloom of the chamber, something perhaps more powerful than the Prophet himself. Whatever it was chilled Dementhus to his soul.

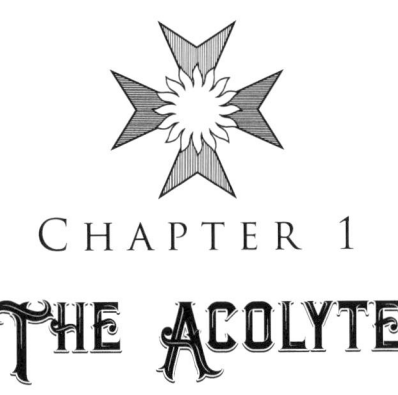

Chapter 1
The Acolyte

"Make haste, boy!" The command came from the head of the abbey, Abbot Monbatten, a man with harsh features and unyielding principles. "If these supplies are not unpacked by the end of the day, you shall be scrubbing the cloister floor from now until spring."

"Yes, Father," responded Tryam meekly, returning from his daydream.

Tryam stood before the ward tower, an imposing thirty-foot-high stone structure resembling a lighthouse in design but with two major differences: Its strong granite shaft supported a translucent blue crystal instead of a great fire, and its purpose was not as a beacon to draw others in but as a ward against malevolent creatures from the Abyss called Daemons, who ravaged the world at night.

The supplies the acolyte was tasked to unload were meant for the monks responsible for illuminating the crystal in time of need. Tryam envied these men. Though undoubtedly dangerous, their job was much more meaningful than his: being stuck inside the abbey doing repetitive chores. Tryam was strong of faith but was never allowed to shine Aten's light in any substantial way.

But as a ward of the abbey, he was obliged to live under abbey rules and had always done so. In fact, his earliest memory was of waking up in the gloom of the infirmary with Monbatten staring down at him. The abbot had said, "I understand you have no memory of those dark events that brought you here today. You need only know that the evil of war has taken your parents and that we at the Abbey of Saint Paxia have taken a vow of peace above all else." His face was expressionless, his voice cold. "Obey me, Father Monbatten, obey our rules, and you will be content living among us."

5

Tryam was not content, however. Looming on the horizon was his eighteenth birthday. Once reaching adulthood, he would be forced to choose: Either take a vow and become a member of the order for life, or head out into the dangerous world alone with nothing but his faith.

Turning from his introspective thoughts, Tryam resigned himself to his lot in life and set himself to work. By noontime, he had unloaded four wagons' worth of goods, but the crates still needed to be carried down the steep steps into the tower's storage room. He would be on this chore all day, but at least the abbot had wandered off on another errand. Hours later, after what felt like his thousandth trip to the basement and back, he was stopped in his tracks by two figures wearing warm smiles and quizzical looks.

"What the devil are you doing?" asked a brawny youth well over six feet tall. "Moving in?"

The youth's companion, a slight, beautiful girl with gold hair and ice-blue eyes added, "Anyplace would be better than living in that gloomy abbey."

"I wish I were moving into this tower," lamented Tryam, "but I'm afraid not." He pointed to the stack of crates. "I am bringing my brothers their winter supplies. The tower is vital to the defense of Arkos."

Glad for the excuse to rest, Tryam dried his sweaty hands on his white robes. It was always a pleasure to speak with someone outside of the abbey. Wulfric and Kara, Berserkers from the Ulf clan, were natives to this region, whereas the monks and the inhabitants of the mining town of Arkos came from the civilized lands on Medias's largest continent. Arkos was a long-established colony of the kingdom of Engoth, across the treacherous Frostfoam Sea.

"We guard our villages with steel," stated Wulfric, gripping the hilt of his sword. "I would not put much faith in the light from a crystal, especially if an army of bloodthirsty Reavers approached."

"The walls protect us from any invaders," informed Tryam. "The light is to save us from creatures from the Abyss."

Wulfric shrugged his broad shoulders. "If you say so, but it is our experience that Daemons come and go as they please, take or kill whatever they want. You Engothians are a fearful lot."

Wulfric and Kara were the only Berserkers who regularly ventured into town. They even traded goods, an activity foreign to most of their kind. Tryam had met the pair when he was looking to help supply the abbey's infirmary with warmer blankets. Although their existence was harsh, their freedom to go wherever they wanted and do whatever they desired made Tryam envious. "Your life is so different from mine. I can't imagine living with such independence. Being so carefree."

"While it is true I have seen the sun rise and set from a hundred different mountaintops, I still must answer to my father, the leader of my clan. I can't imagine what it must be like to always have a full stomach or have the time to read books."

Blood rushed to Tryam's face in shame. He cast his eyes downward. "I did not mean to sound callous to the struggles of your people. It is just that I have seen the world only from the view out of my cell."

The big Berserker responded by playfully punching Tryam in the shoulder. "Do not look so glum. Your path is not set. I don't think you are fated to spend your entire life locked away in an abbey."

"I shall if I listen to Father Monbatten."

"You should listen to your gut," offered Kara. "Not that curmudgeon."

Kara, with the restless spirit common among the Berserkers, stepped on the stack of crates and jumped up and down, threatening to break the contents inside. "Enough talk! Can we help? We have no plans today."

"Sure, but we can't damage anything. Father Monbatten would have my head for it. He knows the count of every spoon and dish."

Wulfric offered his hand to Kara, but she brushed it away and made a face before jumping to the ground on her own. Tryam was fascinated by Kara and felt awkward and clumsy in her presence. The order forbade female monks.

After only a minimal delay when Tryam and Wulfric had to stop Kara from sneaking upstairs to "light" the crystal, the trio made quick work with the supplies. Exhausted, they rested on the steps at the base of the tower, enjoying the rare warm autumn evening, the sky a dark blue.

Not wishing to return to the abbey right away, Tryam was happy for the respite. When a patrolling squadron of Engothian knights passed by, he nudged Wulfric. "I wonder what it must be like to be a knight and wear all that armor."

Wulfric shrugged. "My father wears only the hides of animals he has slain, but I have tried armor and find it useful."

Before the knights marched off, a redheaded squire nailed a sign to a wooden post. Kara sprinted over to look. She read the sign over a couple of times; then she ripped it down and ran back to the steps. With a mischievous smile on her face, she thrust the sign in front of Tryam. "This says the knights are holding a tournament," she said, not able to contain her excitement. "The victor will be trained and accepted into their ranks. This is your opportunity to leave the dusty monks behind. A chance to see the world!"

Tryam had seen the announcements around town but had never considered entering the tournament. He stood and took the poster from Kara's hands. He read it again, scrutinizing every sentence. The wording was vague about what the tournament would entail, but he felt something inside him stir. Maybe it was the talk with Wulfric, or maybe it was Kara's soul-shaking smile, but a jolt of boldness overrode his caution. "You know what? I think I shall enter the tournament."

"That's the spirit!" Kara laughed as she slapped him on the back.

"Hey!" teased Tryam in feigned agony. "Don't injure me before the contest even starts!"

Tryam was about to tease Kara some more when he noticed the smile disappear from Kara's face. Before he could figure out why, a hand struck his ear.

"Stop this foolishness! You will not be allowed to disrespect every pacifistic principle Saint Paxia espoused by entering a tournament glorifying violence." Monbatten's glare was enough to dissipate all of Tryam's newfound boldness. "If you are done here, I believe there are more duties for you to perform back at the abbey."

Monbatten turned his wrath toward Wulfric and Kara. "I trust you two are done distracting Tryam from his duties? You both should return to your people, and I shall thank you to leave Tryam alone in the future."

Kara looked ready to spit fire, but Wulfric covered her mouth with one of his large hands. "We were only trying to help," the Berserker snarled.

"Father, let me at least thank them before I return to the abbey." Tryam knew it would be unwise to discuss the tournament with the abbot now—or at any time.

"Very well, but make it quick. I expect to see you back on the island shortly."

With that, the abbot left, heading toward the harbor, leaving the trio to exchange expressions of relief mixed with dismay.

Kara, now free to speak again, said, "What a mean old goat! You aren't going to listen him, are you?"

THE TOMB OF THERAGAARD

"I am still under the guidance and protection of the order, and members are expected to do as Father Monbatten commands." Tryam hesitated as he watched Kara's face frown in disappointment. When he continued, he surprised himself with the words that came out of his mouth. "But since I have not yet taken the oath, I am not bound by his wishes. I *will* defy the abbot and enter the tournament!"

Kara unleashed a wild yelp and jumped up and down. "But you'd better win!"

Wulfric nodded his head. "You are nearly as tall as I am, but while I have spent my youth swinging swords and axes, you have spent yours swinging a mop. You will need to learn how to handle a weapon and build up your muscles. I can teach you that." He thumped his chest. "The knights have a contingent of archers, so I am sure they will also test your skill with a bow. You are in luck, since Kara is a master!" He turned to her. "Kara, would you be willing to teach this mild-mannered monk the way of combat?"

"Of course!" she responded without hesitation, patting the quiver on her back. "I don't want to see Tryam bending his knee to that ogre for the rest of his life. Plus, it sounds like fun!" Kara gave Tryam a hug. "But when could you train? Those sneaky monks watch you more than a mother does her babe."

As Tryam pondered the reality of what he was proposing to do, he became concerned. "Kara is correct. I have little free time."

"Are you ever left alone?" asked Wulfric.

"After the evening meal, we are required to do private meditation. I usually do so in my cell, but I could probably leave the abbey without anyone noticing."

Kara's smile returned. "But where could we go to practice? We need enough room to swing swords and shoot arrows." To emphasize her point, she attacked Wulfric with an imaginary weapon.

Tryam thought for a moment, ignoring Kara's swings, which were now aimed at *his* head. "We can meet by the old graveyard outside the church grounds. No one goes there anymore."

Wulfric brought up a problem Tryam hadn't considered. "Are you forgetting the abbey is on an island and not in Arkos? The knights won't be willing to ferry two Berserkers to the island after dark. How shall we get there?"

A solution came to Tryam's mind. "There is a hidden tunnel that links the town to the abbey. I doubt anyone else knows it exists. I can show it to you."

Kara's face fell in shock. "A secret tunnel, and you never told me?"

"Sorry," explained Tryam, "I never thought you would have cause to need it."

"That's okay," replied Kara after some delay. "I forgive you." The Berserker girl then quickly aimed a pretend thrust at Tryam's head. When the young acolyte didn't duck in time, she said to Wulfric, "We do have a lot of work to do on this one."

Chapter 2
The Apprentice

Telvar leaned over the edge of the starboard railing, emptying his lunch into the rough waves of the Frostfoam Sea. It was the young wizard's first overseas voyage, and it was an experience he quickly wanted to forget. Still, he understood it came with his chosen vocation. He would travel to the ends of Medias for his magic. When the ship made a course correction toward the inlet where the town of Arkos stood, he gathered his strength and wits.

Upon entering the calmer waters of the harbor, he was initially unimpressed by what he could see of the small walled town. He had grown up in the city of Secundus, the capital of Engoth, a former colony of the once-flourishing Antium Empire when it still encompassed half of Medias. Secundus housed hundreds of thousands of people and contained large amphitheaters, glittering domes, and spires that stretched into the heavens. Telvar's only knowledge of the piddling town of Arkos came from the captain of the *Ice Warrior*. The man claimed the town had expanded in recent years, thanks to the discovery of a new vein of coronium ore after other veins had been mined out years before. Telvar was aware of coronium. The ore, when refined, yielded a rare metal that could be used to make magically imbued artifacts. Most of the population of Arkos worked in the mines or in their support.

Before heading to the docks, the *Ice Warrior* passed by an island crowned by a church. Underneath the church were the remnants of a multitiered fortification. The sizable ruins brought to mind a more intriguing past. *Why did the Ancients have cause to build a fortress in these remote lands? Perhaps there is more to Arkos than I imagined.*

The captain called for oars, and the *Ice Warrior* eased toward an open pier as cloak-shrouded knights in small vessels rowed out to meet her. Telvar moved to the bow to give Arkos a better look. Three significant structures dominated this town of single-story stone buildings. In the north Telvar recognized the outline of a ward tower, a necessary protection in a place so isolated from civilization; in the south sat a squat keep, the familiar banners of Engoth fluttering in the wind; and in the town's center he saw, with ambitious eyes, the fifty-foot-tall mage tower, which was his destination.

After watching the sailors on board moor the ship with hawser lines, Telvar retired back to his cabin. Secluded from the others, he practiced over and over in his mind what he would say when he reached the mage tower, before a knock on the door told him he could depart. He retrieved his leather satchel and grabbed his long metal staff. Without bothering to say goodbye to the captain or crew, he strode down the wobbly plank to the pier. He looked around for someone to acknowledge him but saw no one save knights and dock workers going about their normal daily routines. *Surely, Lord Dunford must know about my arrival, so where are his escorts? The Wizard Council sent a letter to the commander months ago about my apprenticeship with Myramar. What gross incompetence from these metal-plated dunces!*

Sighing and shrugging his shoulders, Telvar headed deeper into the rather busy harbor, where a dozen or more ships of various sizes were either taking on ore and passengers or unloading large sacks of foodstuffs and barrels of ale. A wall and gate separated the harbor from the town, and right before the gate was the harbor office.

Telvar saw a mustachioed knight coming out of the building and hailed him. "Hello, sir. I have just disembarked from the *Ice Warrior*, and I can't seem to find my escort. I am Myramar's apprentice, and I need assistance."

The knight did not bother to stop or even acknowledge the request.

Does this fool think me some commoner?

Telvar resisted the temptation to cast a spell that would send the man flying across the harbor and instead entered the building through a door that had a symbol over its lintel of crossed anchors on a shield. Inside the office, a plump knight sat behind a large oak desk. The man looked up from the parchment he held in his hand and creased his brow.

"Hello, sir knight," said Telvar. "I have just arrived."

The man dropped the parchment and crossed his arms over his bulging breastplate. "I can see that! What do you want? This is a busy time."

Telvar was accustomed to people, even knights, being deferential to his standing as a wizard. All spellcasters were required by the Wizard Council to wear a metallic band with a colored gem around their head as a way to identify themselves to the public. Even though he was only of the first rank—called the Red, or the Rutilus, rank—his status gave strangers pause and sometimes fear.

Telvar adjusted his wizard band before replying. "A letter was sent about my arrival from the Wizard Council months ago. My name is Telvar. I am here to work with Myramar."

The slow-witted knight stared back blankly and then reluctantly opened a desk drawer. From inside he retrieved and then unfolded a piece of parchment. His small round eyes darted back and forth as he read the words. Telvar resisted the urge to ask the man if he needed assistance.

After a few moments, almost as if the knight were disappointed, it became evident that the words on the parchment indicated that Telvar had spoken the truth. He put down the letter. "Everything appears to be in order," he said. "You are free to enter the town."

"That's it? Nothing more?"

"No."

"Then good day, sir."

Telvar did not need an escort to find the mage tower. Though the streets were maze-like, the tower was visible from any vantage point. He passed through the harbor gate and down the streets, avoiding eye contact with Arkos's dirt-covered citizens.

The closer he came to his destination, the more he thought about what it would mean to have a tower of his own, with the resources to learn new spells and create new magic. Of course, he would have to wait until Myramar's death to become the tower master, but from what he knew of the old wizard's health, that time would not be long in coming. The only regret Telvar had was that the tower stood in the middle of absolutely nowhere. But this was just a first step. As soon as he rose higher in the ranks of wizards, he planned on challenging for a more prestigious tower.

A ten-foot-tall circular fence surrounded the tower, which itself was enveloped by soaring trees and numerous gardens. Telvar walked the perimeter to examine the building from all sides. He was most curious about the lens, which stood affixed to one side of the tower's domed top. The two most important parts of any mage tower were its lens, which focused mana from the stars, and the gem located beneath the lens, which stored the energy collected. The wizard who controlled the tower controlled all the energy the lens and gem had gathered. This tower's lens looked well crafted. Telvar could hardly wait to get inside to examine the gem.

After a couple of rounds, he made his way to the gate, an ornate but curiously unlocked affair that swung inward when pushed on. *Does Myramar know I am here?* Telvar was unsure how the old mage accomplished it, but the air inside the grove was warmer than outside, and most of the plants were still in full bloom. He closed the gate behind him and started down a hewn stone path that led directly to the tower's front door. Telvar identified dozens of different species of plants and trees along the way.

A fist-shaped knocker hung invitingly from the door. Telvar took a deep breath and rapped the bronze metal against the strong oak. When there was no immediate answer, the young wizard paced back and forth. *Once beyond this threshold, I shall begin my ascendency, becoming the greatest wizard since Necromedes the Thrice-Reborn!*

After a few moments of anxiety, the door creaked inward, and from the shadows a raspy voice queried: "For what purpose do you impose on me?"

Telvar took a step forward only to be warded off with a gnarled hand pointing an equally gnarled staff at his chest.

"It is Telvar, sir!" answered the young mage. "The new apprentice."

Enough light shone on the band around the aged man's head to reveal the red gem of a Rutilus wizard, the same rank Telvar had just attained, but whereas Telvar was of the first level of the rank, the script around the band he was gazing at indicated the wearer was of the eighth level. *This has to be Myramar!*

"Yes. Telvar. That's right. The Council felt I needed to train a possible successor." Myramar straightened his back, then shook his fist. "I tried to tell them I'm not yet ready for the tomb."

Telvar again tried to step inside the tower. "It is an honor—"

Before he had made an inch's worth of progress, the gnarled staff poked him in the chest. "They also told me you burned the magic laboratory in Secundus completely to the ground!"

"Not completely," Telvar hurried to explain. "Only a small part of one of the labs. It was—"

"Ha! You'll not be burning down this tower if I have my way!"

This old fool is testing me. "It was only because I lacked superior tutelage. Training that I can get from you, good sir!"

THE TOMB OF THERAGAARD

"Training, bah! You are like all wizards nowadays. You want instant gratification!" Myramar tapped his staff on the ground. "Such gratification rarely happens, and when it does, it is never for something that matters. Anything important comes from hard work and patience. Patience!"

Telvar was unsure of how to respond and was wary of taking another step.

After scratching his thick white hair, Myramar said, "You may as well come in. I'd rather not spend my last moments arguing."

Fearing the mage might change his mind, Telvar entered the tower with alacrity. "Thank you, sir," he added when safely inside, bowing to the older wizard.

The door led directly into the grand entrance hall. Being the son of a merchant, for which he had been ridiculed during his schooling from fellow students from noble families, Telvar was delighted by the quality of furniture and other trappings. He saw velvet tapestries, gold sconces, and other expensive trinkets from across Medias. The tower was round, and this room was a half circle. A stairway leading up was along the side of the wall, stairways leading down were to the left and right, straight ahead was a fireplace with two comfortable-looking cushioned chairs. To the side of the fireplace was a door that led to the other half of the tower's ground floor.

"Your specialty is elemental magic?" Myramar asked, moving stiffly as he placed his staff carefully atop the mantel of the fireplace. "Is that so?"

"Yes. I thought it to be the most practical area of magic to study. Elemental magic gives a solid foundation upon which to build other skills." Telvar cleared his throat and straightened his wizard band. "It is the most difficult of all magics to learn, and I welcome challenges."

The old mage nodded his head. "Elemental magic was my foundation magic as well. Summoning the elements is difficult, but controlling what you have brought forth to this realm is another level of difficulty entirely."

Myramar slumped into one of the armchairs. He beckoned the young wizard to sit on the matching chair opposite him. Once Telvar was seated, the mage continued.

"The ground floor is for the public's eyes. No one but you and I shall go above or below this level. This area is to stay spotless. My dear, sweet maid passed on a few months ago, and I have not had the heart to replace her. Lord Dunford, the commander of Arkos, often meets with me in the dining area, so we must keep up appearances." The old man stroked his beard as his eyes scanned the room. "You are to sweep and dust the floors each morning, shake out the rugs once per week, make sure the sconces are lit at sundown and extinguished after I retire to my bedchamber, and keep the fireplace lit at all times." He pointed his staff at Telvar. "Also, I hope you know how to cook, for you shall prepare meals. The door next to the fireplace leads to the kitchen."

Telvar's head was spinning. *Shake out rugs? Dust floors? Cooking!*

Oblivious to Telvar's reaction, Myramar continued. "There are two access ways to the underground areas of the tower. I would show them to you now, but I am too weary at the moment. The stairway to your left leads to my subterranean laboratory. I have not used that research lab for years." He pointed to the other stairway. "The stairway to your right takes you to the food and supply rooms. There is an underground entrance to the tower in one of the storage areas. We use this when we need discretion for certain visitors or dangerous reagents."

Myramar paused to catch his breath. "The central staircase takes you to the other floors. The second floor is the library. There are two sections to this library. One section you can use to do your research, and another area is locked behind a red door. You are not ready to go beyond the red door until I say you are!" He emphasized his point by waving his index finger. Then, after a pause: "There is a small guest room on this floor, which you may use as your own. It used to be my maid's."

After a coughing fit, the old wizard continued. "My research laboratories are on the third floor. There I have rooms assigned for the testing of spells, the mixing of potions, and the imbuing of items with magic. When the time comes, I shall allow you limited access to this area."

"The fourth floor is the gem room," the old mage went on. "It is also where my sleeping chambers are located. I see no good reason for you to ever venture there unless I summon you." He crinkled his brow. "Do you have questions?" Not waiting for the young wizard to respond, he continued. "Good. I am feeling peckish. Prepare something from whatever you find in the kitchen, and be quick about it."

Telvar cursed under his breath as he got to his feet. "Yes, master."

If he is teaching me patience, he had better hope I pass. I shall not be any old fool's maid!

He headed for the kitchen without delay.

Chapter 3

The Lords of the Graveyard

The centuries-old cemetery was frequented rarely, and those buried within its confines had long been forgotten. It was a dark and quiet place. Tryam affixed a torch inside a bronze bracket atop a crumbling tomb, mindful of any watchers from the abbey. A chilly breeze caused the flame to flicker, making shadows play on the lonely graves. Though it was not ideal, Tryam was satisfied that this place could serve as a sparring ground.

Since his talk with Wulfric and Kara, the young acolyte had been coming to the graveyard every evening looking for his friends, but they had yet to show. He hoped nothing serious had delayed them, but he understood that a Berserker's life was chaos compared with the lives of the monks of Saint Paxia. Since arriving at the monastery as an orphan, Tryam had lived under a strict regimen: prayer, breakfast, mass, instruction, chores, evening meditation, then sleep. Repeated the next day. The monotony was its own prison.

Despite the absence of his friends, Tryam did not waste the time he had available. In his hand he held a wooden practice sword he had found many years before when exploring the ruins that encircled the lower part of the island. He had kept it mostly for curiosity's sake and had hid it in his chambers. Father Monbatten did not approve of any weapon of war, even a practice sword.

As he dodged the tombstones, Tryam used the sword to slash at the shadows. He was not even sure how to grip the "weapon," so he held it in his right hand in the most comfortable position he could figure. He stabbed and twirled while doing his best not to trip over his long white robes.

The sword felt comfortable in his hands, even though blisters had formed and threatened his grip. After an hour of shadow swordplay, he succumbed to fatigue and settled on the ground, leaning against a half-buried tombstone.

Tryam's thoughts wandered to his surroundings. He felt a connection with the dead he did not fully understand and at peace among the slumbering souls. *I wonder what lives were led by those whose graves I rest beside. Would they approve of my decision to defy the abbot?* He stood up and walked among the ancient stones, reading their epitaphs.

> Jan ex Ulter — Protector of the Fallen, Defender of the Weak
> Slan ex Retam — Warrior, Priest, and Friend
> Elas ex Modrain — Forever Free
> Dadula ex Fromon — Asleep in the Sleep of the Saved
> Jarond ex Praeor — Giving Life from Death
> Erlim ex Laabs — From Failing Hands He Passes the Sword

The simple markers belied the status of the men whose bodies rested in the cold ground below. *These men were paladins! Knights in the service of Aten!*

Tryam was familiar with the history of these holy warriors, but only from books he had secreted from the library when the abbot was not looking. Paladins served no king but God Himself. These men dedicated their lives for the grace of Aten, not for gold or fame.

Tryam looked at the toy in his hand, imagining it as a great broadsword. He then imagined adversaries lurking in the shadows. He gave a great roar and leapt at his phantom foes. "Fight me!" he said to the ghosts.

A voice from the dark mocked: "Does a great warrior challenge me?"

Tryam whirled around, tripping over his robes. It was Kara's gentle laughter that calmed his nerves when he saw it was only his overdue friends.

"Your battle cry may have awakened the dead," Wulfric teased.

"Or the monks," added Kara.

Tryam's embarrassment faded in the excitement at seeing the Berserkers. "You've both come! I was worried something may have happened back home. I practiced my sword work, but I need a lot of help," he admitted sheepishly.

"The key to wielding a sword is having a proper grip." Wulfric drew his blade. "Once you master that, all you have to do is aim for your enemy's head and then unleash a blow with all your might!"

Tryam looked at Wulfric askance. "Really?"

Wulfric laughed. "Well, perhaps there is a little more to it. If you have a short sword, you must learn to block and stab. With a longer blade, you must be able to parry and slash. Blunt weapons are great for crushing skulls and breaking bones. All of these skills require both strength and dexterity. But without power behind your attacks, you won't be able to best anyone."

As Tryam compared his slim and awkward form to that of the barrel-chested Berserker youth, doubt filled his mind.

Kara swatted Wulfric's big head. "Don't listen to this brute. A skilled swordsman can defeat the strongest of men. I've seen it many times. Being big and strong can lead to overconfidence."

As he checked his head for injury, Wulfric raised his voice. "I can teach skill as well. But first, you must start with the basics, and that means simple slashes and thrusts." He then thrust the hilt of his sword toward Tryam. "Here, take my sword."

The two exchanged weapons. Tryam imitated the grip he had seen Wulfric use. "Like this?"

Wulfric grinned. "That's the grip. You're a born warrior. We shall spar a little. Watch my footwork. Don't worry about hurting me. Come at me strong!"

"Are you sure?"

"Yes, don't worry. Attack as with purpose!"

Tryam thrust the heavy metal sword toward Wulfric's hide-protected left leg. Wulfric shifted his feet, then deflected the attack with the wooden sword. "Did you see how I moved? Try again!"

Tryam attempted another slash but made no progress in connecting. He wanted to curse but kept his tongue. He charged recklessly at Wulfric and struck at his torso. Wulfric dodged the move with the grace of a mountain lion. Tryam stumbled and struggled to keep upright. This time, despite his best efforts, a mild curse escaped the young acolyte's lips.

"Don't get frustrated," encouraged Wulfric. "Use your anger to focus on your opponent!"

Taking his friend's words under advisement, Tryam cleared his head of distractions and thought only of the blade in his hand. He circled around the big Berserker and looked for an opening. He tried a feint and then a quick thrust, but Wulfric brushed aside the intended blow. He made repeated attempts but did not get any closer.

"I might as well try striking at the wind!" Tryam conceded, letting his sword drop to his side.

"Remember, I was born with a blade in my hand. Let me show you step by step. That way you may learn to anticipate how a battle-tested warrior will react to your attacks."

Wulfric showed moves and countermoves in precise steps. Once he demonstrated a move, and its counter, he made Tryam act it out, albeit at a reduced speed, only increasing the pace when Tryam had it memorized. Whenever the young acolyte's concentration lapsed, Wulfric's wooden sword helped him focus, his bruises a reminder of all he had learned.

The two continued until exhaustion wore Tryam down. "I think I have had enough," admitted Tryam as he fell to his knees. "I am too tired to hold the sword anymore."

Disappointment showed on the Berserker's face; he still looked as fresh as when they had started. "This was only a first step on a long journey. Do not look too far in the distance and think you will never make it to the end." He smiled. "Besides, swordplay is likely only one trial you will go through during the tournament."

Tryam was glad to put his sword down. For the moment at least. "What else should I be preparing for?"

"From what I have heard in town, perhaps feats of strength, working in a team, skill with a longbow," listed Wulfric.

With a shout loud enough that Tryam had to cover his ears, Kara jumped off the tomb she was observing from and landed in front of Tryam. "Target shooting with a longbow! I can teach you that. Even Wulf would admit that I have the best shot in the clan!" She clapped her hands. "Here, stand up, I shall set up a target for you. Oh, and take my bow and quiver, marksman!"

Too exhausted to protest, Tryam watched as the lithe girl scavenged for a target. When she picked up a fallen urn, he was about to protest, but after seeing how big Kara's smile was, he kept his mouth closed; he could pray for that person's immortal soul once practice was over. Tryam found Kara's casualness amusing and refreshing. *Father Monbatten would not approve of Kara!*

Kara returned and maneuvered Tryam's hands upon her longbow. She instructed him as she did so. "I am a much better teacher than Wulf. You want your dominant hand to be the one to pull back the string. Here, take one of my arrows."

For as long as Tryam had known Kara, she carried distinctive red arrows in a quiver that was forever slung over her shoulder. She painted her arrows red so that on a hunt there would be no disputes over who had made the killing shot. That she would give him one of her arrows made Tryam nervous. He did not want to disappoint her.

Kara placed the urn precariously on top of a cross-shaped tombstone fifty paces away. The number of blasphemies that Tryam was engaged in were quickly placed to the back of his mind as he prepared to shoot. He listened to her instructions on aiming as if Aten Himself were giving them to him.

"Fire!" Kara commanded.

Tryam heard more than saw the arrow fly out of his bow. In the torchlight, he strained to watch it cover the distance to the target. The arrow swiped the side of the urn with enough force to cause it to fall and crash to the ground.

"I hit it!" rejoiced Tryam.

The smile on Kara's face was from ear to ear as she rushed to give the nascent marksman a congratulatory hug. Kara then ran to retrieve the broken urn, and, with no concern for the dead person's ashes she was spreading to the winds, she flashed the broken shard in front of Wulfric's face. "Ha, I told you I was a better teacher."

Wulfric brushed her aside and grasped Tryam's forearm. "Nicely done. But don't think, based on one lucky strike, you are a true marksman."

"I shan't."

"We have six weeks to get you ready for the tournament," reminded Kara as she retrieved her arrow and took back her longbow. "Wulfric and I can be here for you every night unless we have more trading to do. Wulfric is working on something, but I can't tell you what just yet. Anyway, you will do well. I just know it. Then we shall have to start calling you Sir Tryam!"

Tryam thanked Kara for her encouraging words. "I wish we had more time tonight, but the sun threatens to reveal us to the early risers at the abbey. I don't think I've ever stayed up this late."

Wulfric gathered his sword and then held Kara in his arms. "We should leave then. I have a deal with a sailor about delivering a few wolf pelts. Get rest, and take two helpings at breakfast, lunch, and dinner. Your body will need the fuel."

"I shall."

"And don't forget what you learned here tonight," Kara added.

"I shan't."

Tryam watched the two walk down to the ruins, where the entrance to the secret tunnel between Arkos and the island lay hidden. After they disappeared from view, he picked up his wooden sword and took a final practice swing. It felt more natural. Before retiring to bed, he prayed over the broken urn and asked for forgiveness.

Chapter 4

A Plague Upon Arkos

Inside his cabin, Dementhus unlocked an iron-bound oak chest. Beads of sweat bubbled on his brow as he struggled with aching hands to lift the lid and retrieve a bottle from inside. He opened the vial, and its contents frothed when the air touched them. He took a sniff to check the potency. He then took a sip. As the foul liquid slid down his throat and into his gut, his breathing became easier, and sensation returned to his extremities. He took one swig and then another. When he finally corked the potion and returned it to the chest, only a small amount of liquid remained. A semblance of life was restored to his necrotic flesh, a painful reminder of the cost of the black arts.

Dementhus started to walk away before remembering something else he needed but was loath to touch. With an ease impossible only a few moments before, he flung open the chest's lid in search of the amulet he had received after his conversion to the Dark God. Now the jewel was something much more than a sign of his fealty. Bafomeht had altered the crystal, and beneath the jewel's flawless facets something inside stirred. Without daring to stare inside the crystal too deeply, he took the amulet in his hands and placed it around his neck; then he concealed it underneath his red robes. He closed and locked the chest, running his hand over his balding scalp. Dementhus tossed the last strands of his hair onto the ground, briefly lamenting the days when his vigor had been as natural as his magic.

Even though it had been many months since his encounter with the Prophet, the visions burned into Dementhus's brain were still quite clear. And while it was said that Terminus's patience was limitless, that of His messenger on Medias was not. As each day passed, Dementhus felt the pressure to find the Golem growing and the glances from the two men Bafomeht had sent along to aid in his search more suspicious.

But as his ship neared its destination, he felt he was now close, and he reflected on the progress he had made. He had traveled first on camel to the city Abbadon to seek out the pirates at that great southern port and probe them about the places and people he had seen in his vision. It became clear that where he needed to go was far from the deserts. On leaving the sandstorms and blistering heat of Lux and then departing from Abbadon for his long voyage back to the Western Kingdoms, the Necromancer used his newly mastered dark magic to birth a crew of the undead.

He and his companions first sailed across the sea to ancient Tiranople. That great city, with its palaces of white marble, was the last living appendage of the great Antium Empire. There he resumed his guise as a loyal member of the Wizard Council, and under the pretense of studying lore, he gained access to the city's library. However, as with most documents written about the era when the wizards of the world had colluded to challenge Aten for supremacy over Medias and created such wonders as the Golem, what had been preserved was either inaccurate or unhelpful.

But he had found one clue. The twin white-capped peaks were the clearest images from his vision, and the maps he examined indicated that only one such mountain range was likely to contain such massive peaks: the Corona Mountains. He provisioned his ship and set sail for the north, making way for the continent of Glacia, where the Corona peaks stood.

The Coronas crowned the ice continent. Dementhus had spent months exploring the rugged coastline. It was only now, when the ship sailed into a remote inlet where the small mining town of Arkos sat, that he felt he was getting close.

Dementhus returned to the deck of the galley. As he gazed out over the town, the Necromancer drew upon his knowledge of the War of the Broken Spire. He knew of the mission to kill the last great archmagus, Antigenesus. The paladins of Antium had located his tower somewhere in the crags of these very mountains. *Could Antigenesus be the wizard in the vision? Could the artifact I seek be his attempt to create life? The most powerful of all Golems?*

One of Aten's greatest warriors, Theragaard, had built a fortress from which to gather his men and hold the line. The battle between the wizard's army and the forces of Aten had raged for years.

The larger of the Necromancer's two companions, a brute named Abbaster, interrupted his thoughts. "Are you sure this is the place, wizard?"

Irritated at the tone of Bafomeht's agent, Dementhus took the time to cover his hands in velvet gloves before responding. "Yes, the ruins on the island match those of Theragaard's fortress." He gestured to the island. "It appears that a church now stands in its place. To be absolutely certain, we must investigate."

Abbaster grunted in acknowledgment. The swarthy man paced the deck like a trapped beast, his massive hands never wandering far from the two scimitars strapped to his waist by a red sash. The warrior, a native of Lux, was unabashedly cruel and ruthless, qualities Dementhus had already used to his advantage. It was Abbaster who had provided him with the corpses for his crew.

Emerging from belowdecks was Bafomeht's other agent, Gidran. More talkative and inquisitive, he was harder for Dementhus to read. The faithful shaman, a cleric of Terminus, strode to the bow of the ship and pointed to Arkos. "The town is well garrisoned. I see the banners of Engoth flying over a small stronghold. They will not tolerate our presence for long."

"Gidran, you worry too much." Dementhus despised the shaman, for he had no doubt that the man would turn against him at the first sign of trouble.

"What is our plan, then, to avoid conflict with the Engothians?" asked Gidran. "We cannot simply announce to the garrison that a ship of the dead with a necromancer and a shaman of Terminus is here. The knights may be fools, but they are not entirely witless."

Dementhus pointed to the metal band around his bald skull with its white diamond badge of office. "I am an Albus mage. I shall tell them I am on urgent business from the Wizard Council. No one would dare question me." He clenched his jaw and looked straight ahead. "But we shall act discreetly nonetheless, as one would on a mission from the Council."

Removing a two-foot metal rod from his robes, Dementhus closed his eyes and uttered a phrase in the language of magic. After a moment, the gem affixed to the top of the rod glowed a pale green. Dementhus held the rod in his outstretched arm and pointed it skyward. A thin beam issued forth into the gray morning clouds above. The clouds agitated as if in a storm, then descended as if weighted down. Soon, fog shrouded the galley and then slowly drifted into the harbor.

Dementhus secreted the rod back into his robes and pointed toward the warrior Abbaster. "I want you to guard the ship in my absence. You have my authority to kill anyone who tries to board."

Abbaster was pleased with this command and smiled. "You have my word that no one will step foot on this deck without your permission."

Gidran glared at the wizard. "How may I assist?"

"I have an important mission for you. After we dock, I shall tell the knights we have a very sick crew. The threat of a plague will put energy in their steps. I shall tell them that you, as a brother in Aten, have contained the outbreak but are in desperate need of supplies. You will ask the knights to take you to the abbey, on the island where the ruins to Theragaard's fortress lie. The monks there will welcome you as a brother."

"What will be my true purpose?"

"You must investigate the ruins of that fortress and learn the history of the abbey that now stands upon it. If that is indeed the fortress of Theragaard, then his tomb may lie somewhere in its depths. Theragaard was favored by Aten, and thus his spirit may very well seek to thwart our master's plan. You must find Theragaard's tomb, defile it, and call upon Terminus to banish Theragaard's spirit from this world."

"I have no badge of office. How shall I get the monks at the abbey to give me aid?"

"Tell them you are a monk from Tiranople. They will not question it and must give you food and shelter as a fellow brother of Aten."

"As you wish. But what shall you do?"

"I shall make my way to the mage tower and ask the town wizard for help in searching its archives for any clues as to the location of Antigenesus's tower."

The sounds of the harbor reached Dementhus's ears. He commanded the undead to stow the sails and to row the ship into position alongside an ancient wooden pier. He then commanded Abbaster to secure the ship with ropes. By this time, the fog limited visibility to only a few feet. When the ship was secure, the Necromancer ordered the undead belowdecks.

Out of the mist, Dementhus could see a knight in frost-covered armor emerging on the pier. "I want to speak to the fool of a captain who docks a boat under heavy fog!" the knight shouted. "Where is your manifest? Why does this ship carry no ensigns upon its mast?"

Ignoring the bluster, Dementhus smiled and waved at him from the ship's railing. "Apologies, good knight. My name is Dementhus, and this is my ship. I am responsible for this unexpected interruption."

"Come down! I shall not be shouting!"

Dementhus stepped off the ship's plank onto the dock. He casually dropped his cowl. Gazing at the exposed Albus mage badge of office, the knight softened his expression dramatically. Dementhus continued smiling. "Is this better?"

The knight bowed his head. "Apologies, sir. This is a busy time for us. The last supplies before winter are arriving, and the last ships filled with ore are departing for Engoth."

"No need for apologies, but I am in need of expediency. I am on an urgent mission for the Wizard Council. I desire to speak to the town mage at once."

"Myramar? Yes, sir." The knight cleared his throat and shifted nervously on his feet. "But we still need to examine your ship."

"You are free to do so, but I must warn you: The plague struck my crew. We lost many fine sailors on our journey here."

"The plague?" The knight's eyes widened. "You must depart at once!"

"Fear not. Those who remain on board are no longer contagious."

The knight took a step toward the ship but then recoiled from the stench, an unintended benefit of having a crew made from rotting flesh. The knight staggered back. "Perhaps, an inspection is not necessary," he said. "As a precaution, we shall instead isolate your ship." His eyes watered. "Will you be the only one departing?"

"No. Could you escort my companion—Gidran here—over to the abbey? He requires supplies from his brothers in Aten."

"Why, of course. We can take your companion at once. We have a skiff we use to bring men and supplies to and from the island."

"Superb." Dementhus bowed to the knight, who quickly disappeared back into the mist.

Dementhus glanced around the bustling port. He felt closer to his vision now than ever before.

Chapter 5
The Visitor

Telvar had worn his fingers to the bone. He had mended his master's clothes, reorganized the kitchen cabinets, cleaned out the cellar storage rooms, dusted the great hall, and shaken out more rugs than he thought any single wizard could possibly possess. But in all that time, he had not lifted a single finger in the practice of his magical arts. *Magic is a muscle that needs to be flexed, or it withers away!*

The frustrated young wizard mused that if commoners only knew how much research, memorization, calculation, and practice was involved in casting even the simplest cantrip, they would not consider a career as a wizard so very enticing. His current menial task was putting away the research books Myramar had failed to reshelve from the night before. *At least, I have progressed from cleaning the kitchen to cleaning the library.*

Picking up the last book, Telvar glanced at its title, *The Effects of the Sun on the Subterranean Grub Worm*. As he tried to contain his disappointment in his master's reading selection, Telvar sighed; then a sneezing fit beset him. He sighed again. *More dusting needs to be done.*

Before Telvar could reach for his rag, a rapping from the tower's front door caught his attention. Myramar had not had any visitors since his arrival. Grateful for the break in routine, Telvar scrambled down the ladder he used to reach the upper shelves and rushed down the stairs to the first-floor entrance.

Mage towers had many defenses, the most basic of which was the ability to see who was at the front door without the use of an ordinary peephole. At this early hour, the old wizard would still be in bed, and Telvar imagined his master would not mind if he activated the door's eyeglass. *Why disturb an old man's sleep?* The young mage pictured in his mind the magic-imbued glass that was hidden above the door's frame. He uttered the words of activation and reached out into the astral plane for the device. He smiled as he felt himself make the connection.

Standing before the door, in the dim light of dawn, was a red-robed figure. The man was of average height and had plain features, but his eyes burned with intelligence. In a move that startled Telvar, the visitor looked directly into the eyeglass, lowered his cowl, and revealed the white wizard band around his bald head. *An Albus mage here? But why?*

A cold chill ran down his spine, and Telvar withdrew his connection to the eyeglass. He did not recognize the wizard, but that was not unusual. The higher-status wizards lived, worked, and socialized among themselves, and the Albus wizards were of the highest rank. Telvar straightened out his robes, brushing as much dust from himself as possible; then he plastered a smile on his face, unlatched the lock, and pulled on the door handle.

"Please, come in. Sorry for keeping you waiting." Telvar bowed as low as he could manage without tipping over. "How can I be of service to you this morning?"

The red-robed mage nodded his head slightly in response, then casually entered the tower. "Are you the tower mage?" Telvar felt the stranger's eyes on his low-level wizard band. "I thought he would be a much more experienced man."

"Well, no, I am not," admitted Telvar awkwardly. "But I am sure I can help you."

"Unless you are the tower mage, I don't see how you could. Where is Myramar?"

"I am here," said the old mage, emerging from the shadows. "I apologize. My young apprentice did not inform me we had a visitor and took it upon himself to let you in." Myramar brushed past Telvar. "Why are we graced with a visit from an Albus mage? Apologies, sir. I have been away from the Council for so long, I do not even know your name."

This time the red-robed wizard bowed deeply. "My name is Dementhus. I apologize for not making arrangements to have my visit known in advance to you, but I am afraid the Council requested that I travel with a certain anonymity and haste. May we talk in private?"

"Of course." Myramar turned to his apprentice. "Telvar, please … uh … escort Dementhus to the second-floor antechamber. I shall be there momentarily."

Telvar detected a change in his master's demeanor: The old man was flustered. Myramar awkwardly excused himself and then headed to the kitchen. Telvar took a deep breath and directed the inscrutable Albus mage to the steps that hugged the tower wall. "Please," he said in his most charming voice. "Follow me."

Seeking an opportunity to ingratiate himself with a member of the Wizard Council, Telvar tried to engage Dementhus in conversation as they slowly progressed up the stairs, but the visitor left his queries frustratingly unanswered. When Telvar showed him into the antechamber, the red-robed wizard settled into a chair with the same calm command a king does his throne and asked to be left undisturbed.

Shutting the double doors behind him, Telvar went back down to look for Myramar. He found the old man in the kitchen preparing the noxious-smelling drink he used to ease the pain of aching joints. Telvar questioned his master: "An Albus mage here? Isn't this exciting? Do you know what this is all about?"

"One day you will learn," said Myramar warily, "that visits from the Wizard Council are something to be feared and avoided at all costs." The old man then wagged his finger in Telvar's direction. "You wonder why I have been at this same remote tower for fifty years? I shall answer you. It's the ability to do research without interference from meddling wizards on the Council!"

After Myramar finished mixing the drink, he poured the liquid into two glasses and placed them on a tray. Before he left, he looked into Telvar's eyes. "The sooner this man leaves, the sooner we can start your training. I think you have learned enough about patience."

Now he speaks of training? The Albus mage does have him spooked!

☩ ☩ ☩

The wait for the old tower wizard seemed interminable. Dementhus filled the time by plotting the various methods in which to kill Myramar and his apprentice without compromising his plans. He was weighing the consequences of such actions when the door to the antechamber opened.

Myramar entered, carrying a tray with two silver drinking vessels. He placed the tray on the carved table in front of him.

"Sorry for the delay. At my advanced age, I cannot function without my morning remedies. Would you like a try? It is my own concoction.

THE TOMB OF THERAGAARD

It's best to down the drink in one gulp. What it lacks in taste, however, it makes up for in potency."

Curious if the liquid could aid his own physical ailments, Dementhus accepted a cup. He sniffed the potion to determine what ingredient gave the liquid its pungent aroma but to no avail. He took a small taste to see if his tongue could do any better. Failing at this too, he downed the rest of the liquid in a single gulp to measure any effect on his body. The old wizard waited for his reaction.

Dementhus felt a warmth spreading throughout his body almost like a narcotic but with no disruption to his mental prowess. "I can feel its soothing effects already. May I inquire what is it made from?"

"Of course," the tower mage said, smiling. "The drink is derived from one of the local herbs, a hardy little plant the natives call warroot. The barbarian women pulp the plant into a liquid and give it to their warriors to imbibe before battle, in order to increase their strength and endurance. I added my own ingredient, ice worm extract, to increase its potency. I let the mixture sit in the sunlight for two weeks to ferment."

The mixture eased the pain in Dementhus's extremities, but it could not replace his own potion, which was formulated to stop the spread of decaying flesh that resulted from his necromancy. Such spreading of decay would escalate until he could no longer function. "Interesting," Dementhus replied politely. "I shall make note of it for future reference."

"Excellent." The old wizard smiled, sat down in the opposite chair, and downed his drink in one gulp. The liquid appeared to relax the old man, and he leaned back more comfortably in the chair. "It has been over a decade since I've met with a member of the Council. Have you just obtained the Albus?"

"This past year. Once I'd achieved that rank, I was voted onto the Council."

"Do you mean to challenge for the White Tower?"

"Me? Challenge for the White Tower? No." Dementhus feigned laughter at the question, as if the notion were absurd. However, after he recovered the Golem and destroyed Arkos, it was the first thing he planned to do.

Images of the White Tower filled his mind. Before turning against the Council, Dementhus had believed the White Tower in Secundus to be his ultimate destiny. It wasn't until he'd discovered a tome of necromancy under the ruins of a crumbling pyramid in the high Eastern deserts that he learned how weak Western magic truly was. The Council controlled the spread of magic and banned certain knowledge altogether. Since then, Dementhus had spent his efforts in expanding his mastery of these forbidden magics. He now believed that the Prismatic Tower—the most powerful of all towers—had not been destroyed during the War of the Broken Spire but still existed somewhere on Medias. It was only reputed to have been destroyed, in order to keep a single wizard from becoming the master of all the others. He vowed he would become the first Prismatic Mage in half a millennium.

"I think venerable Domedian shall die in the White Tower of old age," said Dementhus. "I have no desire for such a lofty position," he lied, "and no wizard is brave enough to challenge him."

"You are ambitious, though," pressed Myramar, "to have made it to the Albus at your age."

"Yes, I am driven, but only to serve the Wizard Council as best I can," lied Dementhus. "And as an emissary of the Wizard Council, I have a matter of importance to discuss with you."

"I hope I may be of service. My body may not look it, but I am as capable a wizard as ever."

Dementhus leaned in close to Myramar, hoping to appear sincere. "I believe you can be of service, but it is not your magic I require. Instead, I need access to this tower's archives."

Myramar raised his bushy eyebrows. "The archives? For what purpose?"

"A young mage has gone rogue and turned against the Council."

"Rogue mage?" Myramar reacted with disbelief. "When will the young ever learn? Defying the mage hierarchy can bring only death and sorrow." Myramar briefly held his head in his hands. After he regained his composure, he continued: "The young want power, power, power! Yet all they accomplish is destruction." He sighed in disgust. "Who is this rogue wizard?"

"His name is Adra," Dementhus improvised. "A recent graduate to the Puteulanus. He tried for a Blue Tower but was unsuccessful. Adra then attempted to murder a Blue Tower mage with a company of sellswords but failed. He fled Engoth, scarred, bloody, but with an appetite for—as you said—more power. I've been tasked to find this mage, and I believe him to be somewhere in the Corona Mountains."

Myramar stroked his beard. "Why do you believe he has fled to this inhospitable land? I doubt even a Blue mage could survive this continent

THE TOMB OF THERAGAARD

without considerable help. If the cold does not kill him, the wildlife or the natives would. The Reavers ravage the eastern part of this continent, while the native Berserkers here are in a constant state of war. If he were to be caught in a tribal fight, he would be cut to shreds before uttering the first syllable of a spell. If he is searching for sanctuary, he would not find it this far north."

"I don't believe he is here in search of sanctuary. I believe he knows the location of the tower of Antigenesus."

"That's ridiculous!" Myramar jumped up from his chair. Flustered, he took a moment to recover. "Everybody knows the history. Antigenesus's tower was destroyed, and the archwizard himself burnt to ashes."

Dementhus rose from his chair. "Apparently, this wizard does not think that is the case. I was the one who searched his chambers at the Veneficturis. He had maps of this region. He even had one of Antigenesus's old spell books." Dementhus placed his hands on the venerable wizard's shoulders. "This is why I need access to your magic library."

Shaking his head in disbelief, Myramar asked softly, "How can my archives be of use?"

"I am interested in the journals of the previous tower mages. They may contain clues to the events that led to Antigenesus's demise five hundred years ago and the true location of his fortress."

Dementhus waited for Myramar's reaction. He prepared a spell in case the old man rejected the request. For a wizard to grant a stranger unfettered access to a tower's magic library, even if that stranger were from the Wizard Council, took a great deal of faith.

The old wizard looked down at his wrinkled hands and paused in thought before replying. "I shall make my archives available to you at once. Although, sadly, upon their arrival in Arkos, the Order of Saint Paxia demanded every record from the period of the War of the Broken Spire to be burned. At the time, the Church had dominion over this land, and the tower wizard was at their mercy."

The news of the destroyed records stunned Dementhus. "How unfortunate and how shortsighted of them!" He placed his hands behind his back and exhaled slowly. "In any case, I thank you. I shall let the Wizard Council know of your generosity. I can only hope that not all the records were destroyed."

"Let us hope so," agreed Myramar.

Dementhus reached inside his robes and produced the amulet he had taken from the chest aboard the galley. "I have something to present to you. You might consider it as payment for being such a gracious host. It is more of an enigmatic puzzle then a keepsake. Please, take a look." He showed Myramar the amulet. "This is an ancient elemental artifact of fire. None of us on the Council has been able to solve how it works or what it does. Since you are an elemental mage, I figure this conundrum would especially interest you."

The tower wizard took the proffered amulet and turned it over in his hands; then he held it up to a nearby candle. "One is never too old for a good mystery. I shall endeavor to get answers for the Council." Myramar tucked the amulet into his robes. "I suppose you would like to get started right away?"

"If that would be possible, yes."

Myramar led Dementhus toward the magic library's outer red door. The old wizard pushed the door open without having to unlock it.

"Before I begin my search, I beg one more accommodation," Dementhus said as he crossed the threshold into the magic library. "I ask not to be disturbed."

"Of course," agreed Myramar. "But if there is anything you desire, I shall be available at any time. And feel free to call upon my apprentice for all menial tasks. He is also young and ambitious and in desperate need of discipline." The old wizard bowed, then closed the magic library door, leaving Dementhus alone in the archives.

The old fool is gone. But it will not be too long before he will become an important player in my schemes.

The magic library was circular in shape, with crumbling parchments and leather-bound tomes crammed into every conceivable space. No windows were present, and the only light came from the domed ceiling twenty feet above, where a glowing multifaceted gem dangled.

Dementhus doubted that all the old texts had been destroyed. No mage would succumb to the pressure of a mob of radical monks, especially when it concerned his magic library. A wizard would use magical means to hide the records in a method that the monks could not detect. Undaunted by the challenge before him, Dementhus lit a small candle and went about scanning the library's archives.

Newer works lined the shelves nearest the door. Most of these works were written by Myramar himself and on very obscure subjects. Dementhus found tomes ranging from the study of the arctic wind patterns to anatomical examinations of hundred-foot-long ice worms whose tunneling threatened workers in the coronium mines.

Pressing forward, he found the tower mage journals easily; they were in a bookshelf in the center of the library. The journals confirmed what Myramar had said: The records included only the last hundred years' worth of history, even though the tower itself was more than four hundred years old.

Nonetheless, he gleaned one important fact: The offending mage who had burned the records was a man name Korddainer. The journals of Korddainer failed to mention the incident, however, a fact Dementhus found peculiar. *Was there a reason, besides shame, that Korddainer did not mention the monks and their demands?*

Dementhus needed to learn more about this wizard, and he began to look for any other parchments written in Korddainer's hand. After a few hours of searching, he located a bound copy of pages that related to Korddainer: his correspondence. Perusing the fragile parchment, he learned that most of the missives were exchanges between Korddainer and a wizard in Tiranople concerning the mage's fear of a challenge being made on his tower. It was not uncommon for a wizard to die during such an attempt. But no challenge ever appeared to have occurred.

The correspondence did hold one clue that piqued the Necromancer's interest: Korddainer mentioned his thaumaturgical specialty: the magic of illusions. *If an illusionist could not find a method to hide the tower's records, then he is either brainless or gutless.*

Dementhus placed his candle on a writing desk he found buried beneath a stack of old maps. He pulled out the desk's chair and sat down to sort his racing mind. He took deep breaths. With his mind clear, he tried to imagine himself in Korddainer's position. *What would I have done to save the old archives?*

Drawing on a broad range of magical knowledge, illusions being one of them, Dementhus imagined making a grand spectacle for the monks' benefit. He would have poured a dozen amphorae of oil on the offending texts and set them ablaze. Right in front of their eyes. Once the texts were ashes and scattered in the wind, he would have bowed to the monks in humility, begging that they forgive any transgression past or future, before returning to the tower, knowing the whole thing had just been an illusion.

Retrieving pouches from inside his robes, the Necromancer placed the small velvet bags on the desk before him. He sifted through the assortment of reagents until he found the two samples he was looking for: finely ground iron fragments and spores from a plant known to be highly corrosive to metal.

Thinking of a spell that could detect concealed compartments, he placed the two components in a larger leather bag, while he opened a connection to the astral plane, the vortex of residual energy left behind when Aten had created the universe.

Once he had channeled enough power into his body, he broke off his connection to the astral plane and spoke the arcane words of magic that would enable the two reagents to interact. The wizard let the magic flow through his body and into the reagent bag. He stopped the flow after only a few moments and then opened the bag to examine its contents. Satisfied with the results, he emptied a portion of the now-sparkling powder mixture into his hand. Taking a deep breath, he blew the new substance into the air. He then uttered the command word "Seek." In response, the glistening dust shot into the air.

Dementhus repeated the process, taking a small sample and blowing the magical dust into the air, until he observed the dust settling in a rectangular pattern on the floor opposite of the magic library's entrance. *There it is! A hidden compartment!*

The wizard wiped his hands clean of the powder and put the reagent pouches back into his robes. He went to his knees to examine how to open the concealed door, but he found no hinges or any other physical way of doing so. *Korddainer must have used a magical lock.*

Dementhus took a step back. He concentrated and brought into his mind a spell that would reveal such a device. He uttered the words and made the complex hand gestures necessary and soon sensed the other wizard's handiwork. As he struggled to assert his will over the spell that Korddainer, a capable illusionist, had left behind, beads of sweat formed on his brow. To supplement his own power, Dementhus drew out his charged rod and drained into his body some of the magic stored within the rod's gem. The more magic that flowed, the clearer the lock came into focus. Once he could see the device's layout, it was easy for him to manipulate the spell so it would respond to his commands.

"Reveal!"

The floor of the library vibrated, and where the dust had settled, a two-foot-square section of the floor slid sideways, revealing a compartment containing a stack of old parchments. Dementhus reached inside and grabbed the top text. He recognized the handwriting as that of Korddainer. The text itself was a report on the tower lens and the former tower mage's experiments with various angles and the resulting energy fluctuations. He went through more of the texts; they were all standard summations of the workings of the tower lens.

Taking all the suspect texts, he went back to his desk. He took the first parchment and held it up to the candle to see if it contained hidden writing. However, it was so thick he could not even see the flame's light behind it. It was when he tried to tear a piece from the corner that he learned what Korddainer had done.

A smirk appeared on the Necromancer's face as he peeled off the top layer to reveal an ancient scrap of parchment beneath. He delicately removed that parchment and placed it on the desk.

Upon reading the first few lines, he could tell that the writing style dated to the period of Antigenesus. His heart raced as he read further and noticed the flourishes and notations unique to the hand of the great archmagus. Dementhus needed no further evidence. *I hold in my hands the very words of Antigenesus!*

He gathered sixty-four inner pages that had been concealed within the enclosing pages of the tower observations. He read the texts thoroughly, looking for any information that would prove useful in determining where the Golem might be and the location of the tower.

The first page detailed how a thousand slaves had been necessary to construct the fortress in the inhospitable lands up north. Another text detailed the long march the slaves had been forced to take to reach the stronghold and that it was a ten-day journey from the coast. The last account stole the breath from Dementhus. It stated the final obstacle to overcome had been carrying the lens to the top of a distinctive twin-peaked, white-capped mountain. *The mountain from my vision!*

As the Necromancer read further, his excitement grew. While the exact location was never revealed, the defenses for the fortress were laid out, including the spell needed to lock and unlock the entrance to the tower. Though this was a significant accomplishment, he would have to look elsewhere for the current location of the Golem, the archmagus's greatest achievement.

Dementhus committed the entry spell to memory.

Chapter 6
A Wolf Among Sheep

The absence of Dementhus's suspicious gaze relieved Gidran. The shaman respected the Necromancer's skills in magic but did not trust the man's fealty to the Dark God. Dementhus was ambitious, and ambition was a selfish attribute. If Bafomeht commanded him to turn against the foreign wizard, this self-important Albus mage from Secundus, Gidran would not hesitate to act.

Moments after Dementhus left for the mage tower, two cloaked knights approached the pier in a shallow skiff. After they made room for him in the bow, Gidran, who despised any environment outside of his sacred deserts, cautiously stepped foot into the small craft. Wordlessly, the three made their way through the supernatural fog toward the island where the abbey stood. The closer the skiff approached the shrouded ruins, the more uncertainty crept into the shaman's head. He said a silent prayer to Terminus.

The suddenness with which the island emerged from the thick fog startled the shaman into cutting his prayer short. The enormity of the ice-covered battlements that ringed the bottom of the island soon filled his field of vision and loomed over the boat like a legendary frost giant leaning out over the water. Dark windows on the crumbling gate towers straight ahead stared down at him like enormous sunken eyes. He sensed that the place was ancient, its secrets deep, and the scent of Aten was strong.

One knight secured the boat to a wooden pier jutting out from a stone landing at the base of the ruined gatehouse. The other knight rang a large brass bell situated outside the twisted metal gate. The mist muffled the clank of the bell. Gidran doubted if any of the monks atop the island could hear it, and he suggested that they proceed past the gate, when a figure in

THE TOMB OF THERAGAARD

white robes appeared from the mist. The man ducked under the inoperable portcullis, then stepped onto the landing and revealed his wrinkled face.

"Good morning, lads," said the elderly monk with a bright smile that belied a stern, gravelly voice. "Or else it would be if it weren't for this confounded fog!" When he realized the others greeted him with somber faces, however, the monk's smile faded. "I hope nothing's the matter."

"It's the plague, Brother Emil," said one of the knights.

The monk's face went pale. "The plague! Dear Aten, I shall get Father Monbatten immediately!"

Before the monk could flee, Gidran rushed forward. He bowed before the old man. "Do not be alarmed. There is no immediate threat. My name is Gidran, and as a fellow brother in Aten, I humbly seek your aid. My companions and I are on an important mission for the Wizard Council. An Albus wizard named Dementhus is our leader. On our way here, our crew showed signs of a serious illness. Regretfully, before I could stop the disease from spreading, most of the brave sailors died. We have unfortunately exhausted all our supplies in tending to the sick, and our journey is still long."

Before Emil could respond, a stentorian voice sounded from the gate's threshold: "You are not from Engoth."

Searching for his inquisitor's face, Gidran addressed the observation. "No, as you can discern from my accent, I am from Tiranople. I am functioning as a representative of the Church on a critical mission for the Wizard Council."

"And what is this urgent matter that the Church of Aten would send a monk alongside an Albus mage?"

"Unfortunately, as with most matters involving the Council, their mission is secret. However, the matter was urgent enough that the Church called for a representative to go along." Gidran shook his head in feigned exasperation, and let a frown cover his face. "I wish I could divulge our purpose, but I have taken a vow to not do so."

"And why, pray tell, would the Church want a representative on a matter involving wizards?"

Whoever this inquisitor was, he sounded accustomed to others yielding to his will. Gidran tested his theory: "I think it would be prudent to have that information divulged in a more private setting."

"No! I insist you answer me now. Explain why the Church wanted a representative to go along."

Gidran paused as he considered what he could say that would best convince the man that his lying tale was true. "We seek a rogue mage. A mage involved in the unholy practice of necromancy."

"Necromancy!"

The man stepped forward. The faint light revealed an aged monk with silver hair in gold robes. Around his neck was a symbol of his order, a dove in flight, and in his hand was an antique wooden staff, appearing otherwise like a shepherd's staff. "Necromancy!" repeated the man. "May Aten preserve us!" He pointed his staff at Gidran. "What order are you from? Are you skilled enough to complete this task? Necromancy is an abomination!"

"I am a member of the Order of Saint Alikey. I regret I do not bear the symbol of my order, but it was a necessary precaution to keep the mission secret."

Gidran quickly prepared a backstory for his lies, cursing Dementhus for putting him in such a delicate situation. On a previous mission for Bafomeht, he had witnessed Abbaster torture a monk from the Order of Saint Alikey outside the ancient city of Acre. Thanks to Abbaster's skill with sharp instruments, the man revealed every fact about his life, including details of the secretive order.

"It is time I introduce myself, Brother. My name is Father Monbatten. I am the abbot here. This church and all those who live within are brothers of the Order of Saint Paxia. Who is the abbot of your order? I may have met him at the last Church conclave."

"I have been abroad a long time," lied Gidran as his brain searched for the name that the tortured monk's bloodied lips had revealed long before. "But the last I knew, Father Fritzal led my order."

The wizened abbot furrowed his brow and then nodded his head. "Yes, that's he. I had almost forgotten his name."

Gidran noticed that the abbot now assumed a less confrontational posture. The lies were working.

Monbatten pointed toward the open gate. "It is almost time for our communal breakfast. Join us, and we can see about aiding your mission. It is rare that we get visitors."

"I thank you," Gidran said, still quite leery of Monbatten's generosity.

Before departing, the shaman bid farewell to the two knights who had escorted him to the island. Then he followed Monbatten and Emil through the broken portcullis. The courtyard beyond was narrow, only twenty feet wide. Gidran discerned that this had once been the lower entrance to an ancient fortress. Murder holes dotted the walls of the gate towers, and crenellated parapets crowned the fortification.

The monks led Gidran on a narrow road that sloped up the island. The side of the path facing the water held a high wall, while crumbling moss-covered buildings lined the other side.

After fifty feet, the path led under an archway. Gidran recognized the structure as a victory arch. Ordinarily, the denizens of a castle would decorate such an arch with sculpted reliefs, intricate carvings, and chiseled dedications; however, all of these had been obliterated, and the top of the structure was devoid of statues of any heroes or depictions of conquest.

"Father Monbatten, why was this arch desecrated so?" the shaman asked as innocently as he could.

Monbatten scowled. "When the Order of Saint Paxia was granted possession of this island from the Church, the ghostly ruins here were scarred with reminders of dark and violent times. In those early days, our brothers removed as many of those images as possible. Our order believes in peace above all else. Let's not linger in this dark place."

"Of course," said Gidran to the impatient monk.

The path followed the side of the island for three quarters of its length until a cliffside acted as a natural barrier. From there, the path doubled-back to form a second tier and a second line of defense from any invader.

They passed abandoned barracks, stables, a cemetery, and a dilapidated inner keep until they wound their way to another unguarded gate. This final gate led out past the ruins and up to a hill, the highest point on the island, where the new church and its associated buildings stood, surrounded by an ancient wall. They followed a worn stone path up the hill, through a gap in that wall, and past a bell tower. There, Gidran saw the church of Saint Paxia. It was quite small and shaped like the cross of Aten. To the right was the cloister, with beautiful, well-maintained gardens within; smaller buildings led off from the church, connected by covered walkways.

Monbatten led Gidran past the church and into a side building, which turned out to be the monks' dim dining hall. Inside, the monks, as tradition demanded, ate in silence, so the only sound was that of spoons scraping on wooden trenchers. Gidran sat between Monbatten and Emil, at the head of the main table, and was given a bowl containing a pleasant-smelling herbal soup, a piece of fresh bread, and a cup of watery beer. The dining hall itself was austere; the only decorations were intricately shaped green metallic crosses over the exits. Carved in green metal above the head table was a picture of a dove in flight. The monks were half a hundred strong, most of them middle-aged or over.

While he ate, Gidran prepared his story. He needed to ingratiate himself with these monks so they would give up secrets of the island's past.

When the church bell signaled the end of the breakfast meal, Monbatten broke the silence. All eyes were fixed on the abbot as he introduced the stranger to their home. It was apparent by the curious looks he received that this was a very rare occurrence. When Monbatten was done with his introduction, the monks pestered Gidran for news from the outside world.

The shaman answered their inquiries, and as he told them about the political disputes in the capital, Secundus, and in far-off Tiranople, he was at his charming best. All seemed well until a youth tasked with cleaning the tables asked a question that drew ire from Monbatten, though the question seemed innocent enough to Gidran. The youth inquired about the wars in the province of Outremer, a disputed land between Lux and Tiranople, a place where many holy sites of Aten were under attack by Gidran's fellow believers of Terminus.

Gidran answered, giving details of how the city of Acre was holding firm, when Monbatten interrupted: "There will be no discussion of war at this table. Let me remind you all: The Order of Saint Paxia holds the spiritual life to be above all else. We do not glorify the baser acts of men, such as war. Ours is a contemplative life, a life of peace, healing, and proselytizing." He slammed a fist on the table. "Do you understand? Leave war to those secular leaders who wage it. God willing, let it never touch us here in our sanctuary of peace."

Momentarily forgetting his purpose for being there, Gidran prodded the pompous abbot to see if he could determine how zealous the man was to his cause. "My order also despises war, but we recognize the necessity of righteous self-defense. Do you not praise those who use the sword to help the cause of Aten?"

Monbatten stood up from the table and walked among the monks who now gathered around Gidran. He pointed at the stranger and let out a dismissive chuckle as would one amused by a small child.

"Do you hear this, my brothers? Gidran here thinks one can spread the Word of Aten by the sword!"

Most of the monks laughed.

Monbatten walked over to a lectern near the end of the head table and retrieved a book resting upon it. "It is not just our dear friend Gidran who would have you believe that. There are many deserts, marshes, and ravaged cities littered with the bones of men who died thinking they could spread the Word of Aten that way. They all left the world more beholden to the dark forces in the Abyss."

The abbot laid down the book in front of Gidran. "This is the written word of God, as interpreted by Saint Paxia. Inside this book, he proves that the only way to spread the Word of Aten is through devotion, prayer, and proselytizing."

When Gidran took a quick survey of the faces of the monks before him, the abbot's hold over his flock was evident; they were all in thrall of his every word.

Monbatten looked at him, awaiting his reply.

Gidran smiled, answering, "Devotion, prayer, and proselytizing are all noble pursuits, and I do not disagree about their worth. To distrust wars of conquest is understandable, but do you believe in self-defense?"

Before the abbot could respond, the youth who had asked the question earlier interrupted. "Brother Gidran asks an important question. With all due respect to Saint Paxia, isn't the use of force sometimes defensible, such as for the brave warriors who fought off the Daemons during the Abyssal War?"

Monbatten shook his head. "Tryam, do not interrupt your betters. You are not yet a full member of the brotherhood. You have not had the time to study the works of Saint Paxia from a historical perspective." The clang of the bell tower interrupted the abbot. "Let us take that as a sign from Aten to leave our arguments behind us."

Turning to the assembled monks, Monbatten continued: "We thank Brother Gidran for giving us a chance to reaffirm the founding principles of Saint Paxia. Please, everyone, head to the church, so we may contemplate what we have learned this morning."

The assembled monks followed the abbot's command and headed out of the dining hall, bowing in respect to Gidran as they left. Monbatten stepped aside to speak to Emil in private. After he was done, he returned to Gidran's side. "Brother Emil will procure all the supplies you need to help the sick men on board your ship. Despite our differences, we both are still brothers of Aten."

Gidran bowed to the abbot. "Yes, praise Aten. Thank you for your hospitality and your wisdom. I hope I did not overstep my bounds here in your sanctum."

"Not at all," the abbot said bloodlessly. "Will you join us for mass?"

"I have grown weary from my journey and feel the need to meditate. Can you show me to a cell?"

"Perhaps you have grown weary from our debate as well?" Monbatten snapped his fingers, and the youth who had posed the provocative question stepped to attention. "Tryam, show Brother Gidran to the guest chambers."

After bowing to Monbatten, Gidran followed the young acolyte as he led him out the back entrance of the dining hall. The enclosed walkways between buildings were narrow and dark but unusually warm despite the absence of any braziers. The architecture impressed Gidran, and he saw this as an opportunity to engage the young man. "I noticed during our meal that though no fires burned, the room was quite comfortable. What keeps the abbey so warm?"

"I'm not sure I want to tell you," said the boy with no hint of humor. "You might be frightened if I did!"

Gidran could not help but laugh and was glad the youth appeared to be willing to speak to an outsider. "My son, I have seen too many frightening things in my life to be scared anymore. Please tell me. I have traveled the world and enjoy learning about the wonder of it all."

"Well," said Tryam hesitantly, "the church and everything on this island rests on a volcano! From what I have learned, the monks who built the abbey many years ago discovered a system of pipes from ancient times that led to volcanic vents. These pipes carry heat to clay tiles underneath the flooring. It is quite an elaborate system. I doubt anyone alive now could replicate the design."

"It sounds as if you are familiar with the church and its history. How did you come about such information?"

"I do the upkeep for the church grounds, so I've been everywhere around here."

Stopping the youth, Gidran pulled Tryam aside, and before he spoke again, he made sure no monks were lurking about. "Your asking that question of Father Monbatten impressed me. He is an imposing figure."

The youth seemed apprehensive, and his eyes darted about. "Sometimes, despite all my reading and training as an acolyte, I still have questions."

"Using violence to defend yourself is not a sin. Violence is a tool. As with any tool, it is the cause in which it is used that makes it evil or not." Gidran watched the youth's face for signs of approval and saw it when the dark-haired lad nodded his head. Once the shaman felt the boy's trust in him grow, he continued: "When I walked the winding path to the abbey, I noticed something peculiar. I observed what appeared to be a vandalized victory arch. Who were the original occupants of this island?"

"Maybe we should speak of this when we get to your cell," whispered Tryam. "These hallways echo, and you can never be sure who might be listening."

"Oh, understood," said Gidran, grinning.

The two passed a scriptorium, an indoor garden, and a library before reaching a lone tunnel that ended in a square room with multiple cells. None of the rooms were occupied, much to Gidran's relief.

Tryam led Gidran to the cell nearest the entrance along the west wall. Inside was a writing desk with an oil lamp, a window with its shutters closed, and a small cot. Inside a nook in the corner was a shrine, where unlit candles rested beneath an image of a dove. The young acolyte lit the oil lamp with a flint striker before closing the cell door. "We shall not be overheard now," began the boy in conspiratorial tones. "You wanted to know about the history of the island?"

"Indeed," replied Gidran.

"I believe there was a great castle here. It was in disuse for many centuries and eventually fell into ruin. Sometime much later, the abbey was built upon its foundation. I have discovered a way to go underground, where you can still see parts of the old stronghold. If you wish to know who the original occupants of this place were, I would suggest you visit these vaults."

When the boy mentioned the underground, the uneasy sensation Gidran had felt earlier returned but was supplanted by eagerness. "Can you take me to this area?" Gidran waited as the boy hesitated, but then he added, "This is strictly for my edification. Father Monbatten need not know. If I am discovered, I shall take full responsibility."

As he thought over the question, Tryam picked at blisters on the palms of his hands. Finally: "I shall, but I can't now. I can show you after the evening prayers."

"Thank you, young man. I look forward to tonight."

Chapter 7
Darkness and Light in the Vaults

Gidran prepared himself for his daily devotions to Terminus. He locked the door to his cell before pulling from a pocket in his brown robes the ivory statuette of a winged scorpion, only one of many forms the Dark God took. He knelt before the statuette and began his meditations. He invoked his God's name, then chanted verses from the Words of Terminus while letting his mind ponder today's events.

The architecture alone had convinced the shaman that the abbey rested on the remains of the fortress of Theragaard, the paladin who had hunted and killed the last rogue archmagus during the War of the Broken Spire. However, without securing definitive proof, he could not return to Dementhus.

After meditation, Gidran rested. He woke to the sound of the church bells ringing for the noontime meal. He had overslept the call to the midmorning prayer and had missed the opportunity to explore the abbey while the monks were preoccupied in the church.

Feeling the pangs of hunger, he exited his cell and walked back to the dining hall. Once again, he ate in silence with the monks. After the meal, he avoided further philosophical arguments and asked Father Monbatten for a chance to tour the abbey's library. The abbot agreed and let Brother Emil show him to the modest room. Gidran was disappointed, but not surprised, that none of the works he searched through made any mention of the history of the abbey or of the town of Arkos.

When it was time for the monks' liturgical study period, Gidran was irked to discover that Monbatten had arranged a two-hour recitation for

THE TOMB OF THERAGAARD

his benefit. Monbatten and his loyal followers gathered in the cramped church and sat patiently in the pews while the abbot recited passages from the Book of Saint Paxia.

Gidran listened to the lecture with curiosity, amused by the philosophy Monbatten espoused. It was a philosophy for the meek. He regarded these monks as lambs who would willingly submit themselves to slaughter, a fate Gidran and his fellow Terminus clerics were more than ready to help set in motion.

After the lecture, Gidran approached Monbatten to gauge the abbot's attitude toward him. "Now that I have heard the teachings of Saint Paxia, please forgive my comments from this morning. A lack of education and the stress from my travels unnerved me, and I should not have brought up this matter."

Monbatten smiled, eagerly accepting what appeared to be a new follower. "You are forgiven, Brother Gidran. There are no perfect human beings. All that matters now is that you understand Aten's will. In fact, to help your studies further, take this copy of the Word of Saint Paxia."

"Thank you, Father Monbatten. I shall read this on my journeys." Gidran placed the book inside his robes, hoping to get rid of the tome as soon as possible. "Have you had the time to ready my supplies? I do not mean to rush, and I wish to stay longer, but I do not know the whims of my leader, who could summon me at any time."

"Brother Emil has anticipated your needs and has collected all the supplies that we could spare. They await you at the dock. Be our guest for as long as you need to be, and take that time to meditate on Saint Paxia." Monbatten turned to the church's exit. "Tryam!" he shouted "Tryam, come here at once!"

After a few moments, the youth poked his head inside the church, then proceeded cautiously toward the altar, where he saw Monbatten waiting. "How may I be of service, Father?"

"Take Gidran down to the dock. His supplies are waiting there. I give you permission to take the skiff to his vessel."

"Yes, Father," the boy replied enthusiastically.

Gidran nodded to Monbatten. "Your hospitality to a fellow brother of Aten will not be forgotten." To the boy he said, "Lead on."

Tryam led the way out of the church and then down through the ruins. At the dock, the old man Emil had already loaded a flat-bottomed skiff

47

with a dozen cloth bags. Gidran pretended to inspect the supplies; then he nodded his approval and thanked Emil for the salves, bandages, holy water, and medicines.

Once the three were on the skiff, Tryam took the lone set of oars and rowed toward the Arkos harbor. The magical fog was still thick, and it was Gidran who had to guide Tryam to the dock where the galley was moored.

Once they neared the vessel, Gidran ordered Tryam to stop. "We don't want to get too close to the ship until the crew knows who approaches." Gidran shouted up to the railing. "Abbaster, I have returned from the abbey with supplies."

A plank lowered from the port side of the vessel and onto the pier.

"It is safe," ordered Gidran. "Get us closer."

The young acolyte complied and skillfully eased the skiff into position at the end of the pier, near the bigger ship's stern. As he did so, a swarthy, battle-scarred face appeared over the ship's railing.

"I thought those monks had thrown you to the dogs," exclaimed the giant Abbaster.

The looks of shock from Emil and Tryam at Abbaster's appearance amused Gidran. "Fear not. Look past his scars and hulking size. Abbaster is an ally of mine." Gidran disembarked from the skiff. "Tryam, help bring the supplies aboard, but don't venture too far past the railings, or you risk getting infected. I must discuss the mission with Abbaster in private."

Gidran walked up the plank and shook hands with Abbaster. He whispered in the big man's ear. "We have things to discuss."

Abbaster nodded his head, and the two left Tryam to offload the skiff. Once belowdecks, Gidran gave an update: "My investigation of the abbey is proceeding well, but I need more time to complete my objectives there. Have you heard from Dementhus?"

"He has not returned."

"Excellent. That means I have time to explore the ruins. I sense something important on the island. If Dementhus should return, tell him I believe this is the fortress of Theragaard and that I now seek to destroy his tomb."

"I shall comply, but do not overstay your time there. Dementhus is a man of quick action and temper."

The brute need not have reminded Gidran of Dementhus's temperament. "I have no doubt he would abandon me without a second thought. However, what I am doing is vital to our mission."

THE TOMB OF THERAGAARD

Wary of what might lurk in the ruins beneath the abbey, Gidran excused himself from Abbaster's presence, went to his cabin, and exchanged the Book of Saint Paxia in his robes for a mace. He emerged back on deck and was pleased to see that Tryam had placed the supplies in a stack near the forward hatch.

"I have experience in treating the sick. Are you sure you do not need my services here?" offered Tryam. "Are the crew belowdecks? May I help?"

Gidran positioned himself to block the stairway down. "No, that is unnecessary, but I thank you. The crew is over the most dangerous phase of the illness, but they are still contagious. I would not endanger you by exposing you to their sickness." He ushered Tryam to the railings. "As I expected, my wizard companion's business with the town mage is not finished. I shall be able to spend more time at the abbey."

On the return trip, Emil questioned Gidran about Abbaster. "He has the look of a warrior, a hard man," he stated. "I have seen his like before in my time. I would keep a watchful eye upon him."

"I do, Brother. He has seen many battles, but he is loyal. He saved my life once, and I returned the favor by saving his soul."

Emil's scowl did not slacken.

At the island, Gidran thanked Emil for his concern and prevented further questions by sending the old monk back to tell Monbatten that the supplies had been safely offloaded, thereby affording the shaman the opportunity to speak with Tryam alone. From above, the church bells rang for the evening meditation period as the autumn sky darkened.

"Are you now free to show me the underground?" Gidran prodded.

The youth glanced at the shadows. "I believe so." Tryam rubbed his callused hands before continuing. "We can't afford to be spotted by anyone."

After securing the boat, Tryam led the way up the winding path toward the top of the island. Once the abbey was in sight, he led Gidran off the path, along the side of the church and to a cemetery. In the growing darkness, the two walked past the graves with slow and measured steps.

Buttressing the cemetery was a moss-covered stone wall with a bronze gate. Opening the gate slowly to reduce the noise, Tryam led Gidran a few feet farther to a series of squat, interconnected brick buildings. It was the nearest building that the youth approached. He strained to push open its warped wooden door, and when it yielded, Gidran stepped forward to peer inside the building.

Broken chairs, cracked pottery, and stacks of dust-covered wood cluttered the small square room. Doors led to rooms to the left and right, and straight ahead were stairs leading downward.

"The passage to the vaults is just beyond," said Tryam. "Wait here while I grab a torch. I left one nearby."

Tryam disappeared into the room on the left and emerged with a lit torch. The light it cast sputtered but was bright enough for Gidran to see the well-worn stone steps leading down. The young acolyte led the way down, holding his torch high. In the cellar, racks with dusty wine bottles lined the walls, while large casks sat on the floor.

"See that crate in the far corner? It conceals the way into the vault. I doubt that any monks have the strength to move it like I can," boasted the youth. He looked back at Gidran, his face now showing concern. "Are you sure you want to do this? The paths are dangerous. There are many things to trip over and many holes to avoid."

"I am most sure. Please, indulge my curiosity, and show me the way."

Tryam shifted his large form into position and pushed on the wood crate. He appeared to be struggling, and the shaman was growing impatient.

"Let me help," offered Gidran.

With Gidran's aid, the crate slid easily away, revealing a two-foot-wide jagged crack in the cellar's stone floor. Tryam poked the torch through the hole, revealing a room below, choked with large rocks. "I shall go through first," he offered.

Tryam lowered his legs, then squeezed his broad-shouldered body through the crack. Gidran followed the youth's lead and was greeted with his smile. "This is it," said Tryam. "This is the underground. I've spent a lot of time down here, but I don't think even I have seen it all."

"It might be wise if I explore the vaults on my own," stated Gidran. He did not want to waste time having to kill the lad and risk raising alarm unnecessarily. "It is getting late."

The youth first looked disappointed, but then his expression changed to alarm. "I nearly forgot! I am supposed to meet friends at this time for some late-night training. I'm hoping to become a warrior." When the youth saw Gidran's shocked reaction, he pleaded, "Please don't tell the abbot. Father Monbatten does not know!"

"You can be assured I shall not tell Father Monbatten. It would be equally wise of you not to mention to him my interest in the vaults."

THE TOMB OF THERAGAARD

Gidran tapped the youth on the shoulder. "You have been of great help. I am sure you will make a fine warrior one day. If that is what God wishes."

"Shall we not see each other again?"

"The supplies have been delivered, and I expect our expeditionary leader to be ready to leave on the morrow."

"In that case, I wish you success on your mission and will pray for the safety of you and your companions." Tryam handed the torch to Gidran, then used a sturdy but battered chair to climb back up into the wine cellar. Before leaving, the young acolyte stretched his arm back into the hole to shake Gidran's hand. "I am glad for your visit. Be safe."

"I shall. Go in peace."

✠ ✠ ✠

Holding the torch out to illuminate the chamber, Gidran surveyed his immediate surroundings. He had explored many ruins in the past, but mostly those preserved under shifting sands. This was different. These ruins had been buried by design. Above, he surmised, the main features of Theragaard's castle had been demolished and the remains thrown over the cliff or used to build the church and the cloister. Looking at the enormous blocks of granite that comprised the walls and floor of the underground, he understood why the vaults could not be destroyed and instead had to be buried.

Ahead was a dusty passage that sloped downward into darkness. With no other choice, Gidran proceeded forward, counting his footsteps as he built a map in his mind while examining the floor, ceiling, and walls for any markings. The workmanship of the underground was consistent with the quality of the ruins he had observed near the victory arch.

After thirty paces, the corridor split three ways. Debris blocked the west passage, broken furniture and other assorted refuse cluttered the north passage, and the east passage showed signs of recent use, with footprints trailing into the darkness ahead. *The youth's?*

As he considered which way to proceed, Gidran felt upon his flesh a rush of warm, moist air coming from the dark depths of the eastern passage. Intrigued, he stepped forward and proceeded down the damp hallway.

The corridor widened enough to enable two men to walk abreast a short distance down its length. When the corridor opened into an oval-shaped room thirty feet in diameter, a faint odor of mildew filled the shaman's nostrils.

In the center of the chamber was an empty pool. Covering its bottom was an extravagant mosaic depicting dolphins swimming through the crests of frothy white waves. Bending down, Gidran noticed the floor was warm to the touch. He held his torch up toward the room's domed ceiling. Painted on the tiles was a feast of fruits and vegetables.

The shaman was familiar with the layout of baths from ancient Antium and believed this area to likely have the same layout. The chambers were designed to take bathers from rooms of extreme warmth to a soothing cool.

Gidran followed the passageway to the next room. In this chamber, large sections of ceiling stone had crashed to the floor. Gidran's foot plunged through a broken tile, and his ankle wedged between two jagged rocks. After he extracted his bruised foot, he saw proof of the volcanic heating system. Rubble blocked further progress to the next chamber in the bathing complex. As he thought about the time he had already wasted, the shaman cursed.

This underground area is too vast for me to go searching about blindly. I need to beseech Terminus for guidance.

Gidran returned to the oval pool room, set his torch aside, and fell to his knees. He removed from his robes a scroll of the Words of Terminus and prostrated himself before it. He recited the Prayer of Atonement, repeating the prayer each time with increased fervor. He did so until the echoing words nearly deafened him.

He had grown hoarse when the will of Terminus touched his soul and imbued his body with the strength of his God. He had felt this closeness only two times before and cherished it more than anything else on Medias.

Gidran rushed to his feet, retrieved the torch, and ran back to the three-way intersection. He felt a compulsion to take the north corridor. Using the preternatural strength Terminus had just granted him, he pushed aside the debris blocking the passageway. He passed abandoned rooms and multiple intersections with dark corridors that spread in dozens of ways, until he stopped at a collapsed stairway blocked by a thick mass of stone and hardened mud.

The shaman stuck his torch in the ground and tunneled through the dirt with his bare hands. As he continued to do the work of Terminus, his fingernails bled, his arms felt as if weighted by lead, and his body became

THE TOMB OF THERAGAARD

soaked in sweat. When the hole was large enough to accommodate his bulk, he stopped. He thrust the torch through the gap, wedged himself head first into the narrow opening, and hurried down the steps.

Beyond was another, deeper, level of the underground. The air here was cool and had a different smell about it. Gidran surveyed his new surroundings with his torch, and the light touched the recesses of the chamber. Lining both sides of the wall were alcoves, and inside the alcoves were carved tombs. Terminus had guided him swiftly to the fortress's buried crypts.

The lid on the first grave he passed was in the shape of an armored man, arms folded across his chest, his sword at his side. At the base of the tomb was an epitaph. Gidran was learned in the ancient writing of the Empire of Antium, and he read the words aloud: "'Here lies Dolus Equilius, knight of the Empire, paladin and protector of the Faith of Aten, and hero on the Plains of Glacia.'"

Gidran's body flushed with excitement at this discovery. The shaman proceeded through the gallery of tombs to the end. The date on each grave was of the time of Theragaard; however, the great paladin's tomb itself was absent.

The hallway of crypts terminated at marble steps going deeper underground. Still sensing Terminus and His guiding hand, Gidran proceeded down. The blue and white marble steps led to a rotunda formed with ten-foot-high columns. White lintels connected the columns and featured painted depictions of armored men in combat. Unlit torches in bronze sconces were affixed to the three exits that led out of the room. The east and west passages led to dark corridors, while the path ahead led to steps deeper underground.

Gidran pondered the three exits but felt no guidance about which way to go. He decided to finish exploring this level before going deeper into the crypt vault. He chose the easterly passage first, and after a short walk, he was led into a forty-by-twenty-foot-wide underground church.

Inside, polished wood pews faced a simple stone altar. Iconography associated with various saints of Aten adorned the walls, floor, and ceiling. He could sense Aten here, and it made him uneasy.

Shaking the unnerving feeling, the shaman stepped up to the altar, where he found a Book of Aten opened to a psalm for the dead, a wooden cross, and a silver chalice that still showed the fingerprints of the last priest to hold it. The sight of these objects sickened Gidran. He picked up the cross, threw it to the floor, and crushed it with the heel of his boot. He then took the torch to the frail ancient holy book and watched it burn. Nevertheless, his feeling of unease intensified.

Gidran quickly exited the church, backtracked to the rotunda, and proceeded down the western passage. This corridor led to a diamond-shaped room perhaps fifteen feet in diameter. Covering nearly every inch of the room's walls were images depicting the work of Aten's followers, such as priests aiding the crippled and feeding the hungry. Gidran extracted his mace. With the torch in one hand, the weapon in the other, he smashed the images with righteous fury.

Having satisfied his anger, the shaman returned to the rotunda, where his final choice awaited. Before taking the steps, he took a deep breath. There was something in that gloom. He was sure of it. Tightening his grip on the mace, he walked down the stairs.

The steps descended twenty feet before ending in a ten-foot-wide corridor. In the distance, the torchlight caught the outline of an open archway. On either side of the arch were two statues. The statues depicted winged female Aemon warriors, swords in their hands pointing skyward, shields across their chests, their heads bowed.

Despite his having explored many underground ruins, the weight of the rock above his head felt oppressive, and he momentarily had to fight to regain his breath. As he proceeded forward again and passed by the watchful eyes of the stone angels, he prayed to Terminus.

Beyond, in the new chamber, a shaft of pale light from an unknown source illuminated a statue of a warrior on bended knee, resting on a pedestal. Behind the pedestal was a stone mausoleum.

Gidran approached the tomb, his heart beating in his ears as loud as a war drum. His unease increased with each step. By the time he was within arm's length of the warrior statue, his legs tingled with numbness. Ignoring these ill effects, the shaman inspected the statue.

The warrior depicted in stone had a full bearded face and a noble bearing. His eyes were closed as if in prayer. A sword was before him, both hands resting on its pommel. The crest he bore on his torso was that of a crowned lion. A nameplate was at the base of the statue. Upon reading it, Gidran fell to his knees and thanked his God. *Blessed be Terminus! You have guided me to Theragaard's tomb!*

THE TOMB OF THERAGAARD

Dementhus had ordered him to defile the warrior's grave. Men blessed by Aten in life could become powerful allies in death. If Gidran could destroy Theragaard's tomb, no one could venerate the warrior and thus benefit from the warrior's blessings. He stepped past the statue and strode to the tomb. A door locked by a silver chain prevented entry. He attempted to bash the chain with his mace, but to no avail. Gidran replaced his mace with his dagger and hacked at the chain, but again with no effect. He stabbed at the door, but he could make no mark on the black wood.

Gidran kicked at the door and spat curses at the dead warrior inside. "I *will show* you the power of a true God!"

Laying his torch at his feet and placing his dagger back in his belt, he grabbed from his deep pockets the Words of Terminus, which he placed before the door to the tomb. Gidran prostrated himself and spoke to his God: "O mighty Terminus, God of All Things, strike this door open, and let me punish this blaspheming infidel!"

The shaman waited for a response from his God with the patience of his people. A vision of another tomb entered his mind.

Gidran gathered the Dark Scripture, grabbed his torch, and fled from the room. He raced by the guardian Aemon warriors, up the stairs, through the rotunda, and back to the gallery of tombs. He searched for the sarcophagus he had just seen in his vision. He found it in one of the small arched alcoves near the entrance. He smashed open the lid with his mace, and with God-granted strength, he slid the heavy marble to the floor. Casting light into the coffin revealed a slumbering skeletal knight with an axe laid across his chest. The axe glowed blue.

Gidran spat on the dead man and grabbed the incredibly well crafted axe in his hands. The shaman sensed the power of magic flowing from the weapon. He rushed back to the tomb of Theragaard and once again stood before the locked door. "Prepare yourself for the wrath of Terminus!"

Dropping the torch, Gidran hefted the axe high overhead. He swung the ancient weapon at the silver chain with the ferociousness of a native Berserker. As the blade struck, magical energy flowed from the axe, causing frost to form. The blessings of Aten at first prevented the chain from breaking, but the axe's magic began taking effect: The frost was causing the blessed metal to become brittle. The second blow cut deep into the silver chain. With the third swing, the chain blew apart.

Gidran tied the axe to his waist and pushed open the tomb's door. When he poked his torch inside, the light showed a humble-looking, unadorned stone casket. He took a step forward and readied a prayer that would send the man's soul to oblivion, when he heard a humming noise coming from within the tomb.

The sound grew in intensity and became physically discomforting. Trying to block the noise, the shaman covered his ears, but his skull still throbbed in pain. He made to grab the lid of the casket, but a powerful gust of wind blew out his torch and threw him to the ground. In the darkness, he struggled to his knees. He cried out to Terminus, but he could not detect his God. A blow to his head knocked him backward, and warm blood ran down his face.

Gidran reached for the axe tied to his waist but could not find it. He crawled out of the tomb on his knees as the fierce wind continued to buffet him. The light no longer shone on the warrior on bended knee.

In total darkness, Gidran struggled for each step until he escaped the chamber. The terrible presence of Aten faded, and when he crossed the threshold, the wind ceased.

Breathing heavily, the shaman took time to catch his wits. *Dementhus was right. Theragaard is here, and his spirit is strong.* He prayed to Terminus. *I have not survived the wastes of Lux nor the lash of Bafomeht to be turned away by the ghost of a weakling infidel knight!*

After the brief rest, he stumbled his way back to the stairs and into the rotunda. He felt along the walls, searching for a torch from one of the sconces he had seen earlier. He found one and lit it with a piece of flint he had in one of his pouches. Gidran fell to his knees and called upon the powers of his God to endow him with the strength he needed. Once again, he was rewarded for his faith. He wept in thanks.

With the axe having disappeared, he hefted his mace in his right hand. The shaman took cautious strides down the marble stairs that led back to the tomb. Once again, he laid his eyes upon the twin Aemon statues that stood on either side of the entranceway. Their pupil-less eyes stared back at him on their placid faces. He hesitated. After a moment of concern, he took another step forward, but as he did, the Aemons reacted. Each statue lowered their stone swords, forming a barrier across the portal.

Gidran took another step.

The guardians dropped from their platforms, leveling their stone swords at his head. Unprepared for such a threat, the shaman backed up the stairs and into the rotunda. The guardians followed and did so with incredible speed.

Gidran braced for their attack. He could not flee. Still under the touch of Terminus, he would make his stand among the columns of the rotunda.

The two guardians swung their swords. Gidran dodged both strikes, then swung back. His mace struck one of the guardian's shield solidly. As the mace bounced off with a loud crack, removing only a small fragment of stone, the shaman's arm went numb in response.

The undamaged Aemon statue stepped in front of its companion and thrust its sword arm at the shaman's face. Gidran sidestepped the attack, and with the strength of Terminus behind his stroke, he landed his mace firmly on the outstretched stone arm. The arm cracked at the elbow. The shaman quickly followed with a stroke to the damaged area, and the forearm and the stone sword it held crashed to the floor.

The maneuver cost Gidran, however. The other guardian, attacking from the shaman's blind side, cut at his legs. He was able to sidestep the stroke with only a slight wound to his right thigh.

Gidran turned his back to the weaponless guardian and faced his other attacker. The two traded blows, with neither gaining an advantage. *The thing means to tire me and then go for the kill!*

His situation grew more dire when he saw a flash of blinding blue light and the sword arm reattach to the injured guardian.

With the two guardians attacking him, Gidran fought to hold them off. When his defenses finally slipped, a sword point pierced his left leg, causing blood to gush profusely. Out of breath, faint from blood loss, and with his muscles weakening, Gidran stumbled back behind a column and called upon Terminus again.

"God, I beseech You with my last breath, aid me so I may continue to serve You!"

The loyal shaman saw the power of Terminus appear before him in the form of a glimmering bubble of energy. The ground beneath him quivered, and what started as a minor trembling soon threatened to rattle the teeth out of his jaw. Then, in an instant, the bubble burst, and a violent upheaval of marble and stone knocked both the guardians and himself to the ground.

Gidran, now deaf and on hands and knees, crawled between the swaying columns and headed toward the steps leading out of the rotunda chamber.

The shaking continued to intensify.

Risking a look back, Gidran watched the lintel above the guardians collapse and the columns supporting it topple. The shaman picked himself up and ran up the steps. He did not stop running until he was out of the underground.

Once in the quiet wine cellar, Gidran applied makeshift bandages to his wounds. He then shoved the crate back over the crack in the floor and made his way back to his cell. There he examined his injuries more thoroughly. The new scars he carried were all the evidence he needed to show Dementhus that Theragaard's presence was still on this island and that it would take a great power to destroy his tomb.

Chapter 8
Point of Departure

Dementhus quickly studied the complex symbols, words, voice inflections, and hand gestures of the entry spell to Antigenesus's fortress. Though Myramar was only a red wizard, the Albus mage did not want there to be any chance the old man would discover the real purpose for his studies. Not yet anyway.

He gathered up the pages of Antigenesus's writing and returned them between the sheets of tower observations. He then placed the pages back inside the hidden compartment in the floor, covering up any trace of his discovery. He then exited the magic library.

Descending the stairs to the first floor, Dementhus found Myramar sitting in a cushioned chair, examining in the light of the fireplace the gift he had been given the night before. A glance at the water clock on the table beside the old wizard indicated it was early morning. Dementhus was quite pleased to see Myramar already so enthralled by the amulet. He coughed to get the tower mage's attention.

"I fear you were correct about the ancient records. I was not able to find any useful information. But I must thank you for your hospitality. In any event, I have lingered in Arkos too long. With each new day, the rogue wizard gets farther away." Changing the topic to avoid questions about his research, Dementhus said, "I see you are as intrigued by the amulet's mystery as I was. I hope you have more luck with your studies of the bauble than I had in mine. I am certain you are up to the task."

Myramar reluctantly lifted his gaze from the glowing jewel. "That is unfortunate with regards to your research. But if I hear of reports of a Blue wizard traveling in these parts, or anything unusual, I shall send word to you immediately. As far as the answer to this riddle," the old man patted the amulet as if it were a small pet, "I shall write to the Council as soon as I have my results."

The old man struggled to get out of his chair. Exhausted from the effort, he leaned on the chair for support before shouting to the kitchen. "Telvar, come here!"

After a loud crash followed by a curse, Dementhus saw the haggard young apprentice appear in the doorway. He was covered in flour. "Yes, master. What do you want? Breakfast is almost ready."

"Please show our visitor to the door."

Looking past the flour, Dementhus read the young man's face and was reminded of his former apprentice. *The amulet will take care of Myramar, but what of this youth? Will he try to stop his master once the old man begins to do Terminus's bidding? Or can I persuade this ambitious young man to join my cause?*

As the apprentice walked him to the door, Dementhus decided to give the young man some advice. "I can understand your wish to learn magic, but you first must learn to follow your master's commands. Whatever Myramar asks of you, do it. Whatever he does, support him. The rewards you seek will come in time."

The young wizard eagerly bowed his head. "Of course, Master Dementhus. I shall make every effort to please Myramar."

"Good. Perhaps we shall meet again, when my business allows it."

Telvar bowed lower. "I hope that is the case."

When the young wizard opened the door, Dementhus stepped into the light of dawn and was overwhelmed by the smell of the variety of plants from the old wizard's lush grove. He nodded his head curtly to the apprentice and proceeded out of the grounds with his thoughts now singularly set on the entry spell to be mastered.

When he arrived at his ship, the brute Abbaster was at the railings and informed him that Gidran was still investigating the origins of the abbey. Dementhus told him to delay departure and then left additional instructions not to be disturbed.

Inside his cabin, the Necromancer rested his aching extremities, but only for a moment. Once he was able, he took another swig of his healing elixir and then began the exacting process of copying the entry spell to parchment. The incantation was complex. A misplaced syllable, an incorrect gesture, or the wrong word could cause death to the caster.

THE TOMB OF THERAGAARD

Sweat beaded on his bald pate, and his hands cramped as he converted the images in his mind to his leather-bound spell book. He had to work fast, for fear of losing the details.

When he was done, he dropped the serpent-toothed stylus and collapsed in his chair. In the light of the oil lamp, he examined his work. It looked right, and it felt right; however, he would know if he had copied the spell correctly only when it came time to use it.

Done with the immediate task, he emptied his mind of the spell and replayed the visions from Terminus. He was now certain that the ancient Golem he was tasked to find would be under his control soon. Many Golems had been created, but this one was unique. He doubted if even Bafomeht understood what it was he sought.

Dementhus was preparing to make arrangements to get the galley underway when the door to his cabin burst open. He was about to incinerate the intruder before he saw that it was Gidran. The fool of a shaman, his robes torn, his hair disheveled, had a wide-eyed look about him. "What in the Abyss happened to you?" questioned the Necromancer.

"I found what it was you had me seek! Not only is the abbey the site of Theragaard's ancient fortress, it is also the location of his tomb!" Gidran pointed to the multiple bloodstains on his robes. "But his spirit is strong! Two Aemon guardians attacked me. We must return to his tomb and destroy it now!"

"It shall be done, but only after we have recovered the artifact Bafomeht sent us to recover. With the Golem, we can obliterate the town and crush the abbey into dust." Dementhus closed his spell book and walked to the cabin door. "That is, unless you believe the monks in the abbey could pose a threat to us."

The Eastern cleric unleashed a deep-bellied laugh. "That is the best part. The abbot is a wormy pacifist, and his order is one that eschews violence of any kind, even at the cost of their own lives. When it is time, they will fall to us like swooning maidens. None suspected who I was or what I was after."

Dementhus shared his own good news with the shaman. "My mission at the mage tower went better than expected. Though we still have to find where the Golem resides, I have no doubt it is near the twin-peaked mountain of my vision. And deep inside that mountain is the location of the fortress where the Golem was birthed. I now possess the key to this fortress, as a spell to disarm any defenses placed over Antigenesus's lair. It is now only a matter of time before the Golem is in our possession and under our control. Praise be to Terminus!"

"Praise be to Terminus!" repeated Gidran.

Chapter 9
The Fire Inside

Tryam rushed from the kitchen, placing the last plate on the table just as the bell tower clanged to signal the start of the evening meal. Cordon, the abbey cook, smiled appreciatively before joining the elders at the main table. It was only after all the other monks were seated that the youth himself sat before his own plate, head bowed.

While the rest of his brothers were undoubtedly contemplating the words of Saint Paxia, the young acolyte was contemplating the choices he would soon have to make. He was also nursing numerous cuts and bruises from his clandestine activities.

The training sessions with Wulfric and Kara had been going on for weeks. Not only had he improved his skill with the sword and bow, the training had the unexpected benefit of raising his morale. Each day now had a purpose and was filled with promise. He completed his chores with more alacrity and had asked more questions in scripture studies than he had during the previous eight years combined. Monbatten had even praised him for his newfound enthusiasm. *If he only knew the truth!*

After the evening meal, Tryam cleared away the dirty dishes in record time, his last chore before he was expected to enter private meditation. Cordon complimented the youth for his speed, but Tryam sensed that the chef was suspicious as to why he was so eager to return to his cell. Tryam accepted the compliment and excused himself. When he left the kitchen, he headed in the direction of his room before surreptitiously taking a side passage out of the abbey to the abandoned graveyard among the ruins.

From a broken tomb, Tryam retrieved a batch of torches, his practice sword, a dagger, and one of Kara's old longbows. He had grown so casual in this routine he failed to notice before it was too late a glowing light coming down from the abbey. When a voice in the shadows spoke to him, his legs froze in fear.

"Aha! I've finally caught you!"

Tryam prepared to run and was about to do so when he recognized the gravelly voice belonging to Emil. The young acolyte believed that Emil, even though in his late seventies, had the sharpest mind of the monks and was the only one among the order to treat him as a friend. "Brother Emil, I am glad it is you. I thought it was Cordon or even worse, Father Monbatten."

"I've been trying to speak to you after the evening meal for weeks, but you always ran away faster than my old legs could catch. And when I tried to visit you in your cell, you would never answer my knock. Are you doing something Father Monbatten would not approve of?" The old man shivered. "It is bleak and cold outside. Why are you wandering about this old cemetery?" Emil stepped forward and waved his lantern in front of Tryam. "And what are you hiding behind your back?"

Tryam hated deceiving the kindly old monk. "Hiding? Just tools of a trade I may take up if I decide not to join the order."

Concern crinkled the old man's forehead. "Tools, eh? Perhaps not for a trade wholly to the abbot's liking?" He put his free hand on Tryam's shoulder. "It is best not to defy him openly. Father Monbatten is a decent man, who truly wants what is best for you. Has he not provided food, shelter, and an education?" Emil stepped closer and made to grab Tryam's hand. "Come with me. Let's go back to the rectory, so we can discuss your future. That is why I have been seeking you out: I know your decision to stay or leave is coming shortly."

Tryam gently removed Emil's wrinkled hand and took a step backward. "I appreciate what the abbot has done for me, but I don't know if it is in Aten's plan for me to spend the rest of my life here. There is so much I want to see, so much I want to do."

"If it is Aten's will that you leave this place, He will make His will known. In the meantime, it would not be wise to disobey the rules laid out by the abbot." Emil's thin body shivered harder. "I'm freezing, and at my age, I fear I shall never thaw back out. Let us discuss this before a warm vent."

The old monk stepped closer and again reached out his hand to escort Tryam back to the church. Before he could do so, however, a voice from the darkness barked, "Back away, old man! I shall handle this miscreant!"

Both startled monk and acolyte whirled toward the voice.

Before them was a short, slight figure wearing a visored helm and a dented breastplate. The warrior pointed a sword in their direction. Tryam instantly recognized the newcomer as Kara; her red arrows could be seen protruding out of a quiver on her back, and her long golden hair flowed out from under her helmet.

"I said, back away, monk!" Kara was trying to make her voice as deep as possible, but it only made her sound ridiculous. "I am a knight of Engoth." She pointed her sword menacingly at Tryam. "I was following this fool. He should be in his cell saying his prayers, not wandering around out here." She inclined her head at Emil. "You can go back to the church, go to sleep, forget what you saw, and speak to no one. I shall take this menace back to Father Meanbatten."

Emil lacked the sight and hearing of his youth, but Tryam doubted that Kara's disguise would fool anyone unless they had lost the entirety of their mental faculties. The monk confirmed Tryam's doubt. "Kara, is that you? What on Medias are you wearing?"

Kara let out a forced laugh. "I know not of this 'Kara' you are speaking of, old fool." She stepped up to Emil and waved the sword in his face. "Now step away, or I may be forced to use this."

Tryam had to put a stop to this. "Kara, I—" he began, but she silenced him with a hard kick to his shin.

Realizing it might be safer to play along, Tryam started with a different tack. "Brave knight, let me reason with Brother Emil. There is no call for bloodshed."

"Yes, sir knight," replied Emil, playing along. "No need for the sword. Let me speak to the boy in private for just a moment. Is this acceptable?"

Kara lowered her sword arm and paused as if weighing her options. "Yes, this is acceptable," she responded in her regular voice before catching herself. "I mean, this is acceptable. Just be quick about it. I shall stand aside. If you make any sudden moves, however, I may be forced to get violent." She stabbed the air before retreating out of the light of the lantern.

Emil bowed to the pretend knight. "Oh, thank you, kind sir." To Tryam he said, "Now, before Kara takes this too far, please tell me what you are doing here. I shall play along with this amusing theater, but only if I am assured you are not doing anything that would bring dishonor to the order or harm to yourself."

The monk's pleading face forced Tryam to reveal the truth. He could not lie. "I have been training to compete in the upcoming tournament. I do so not to dishonor our order; I do so because I feel it is the right thing to do."

Emil scowled.

"Kara and Wulfric have been helping me," Tryam continued. "I can take care of myself. I am not the small boy I was when I arrived at the abbey."

Emil sighed. "To be young again and have a future full of possibilities! Do you know how you can tell when one is old? It is when have you more memories of the past than dreams of the future." The monk patted Tryam on the back. "If this is something you want to do, then you have my blessing. But be warned: If Father Monbatten finds out about this, he will likely do anything he can to discourage you, including locking you in your cell."

Emil's words caused Tryam to pause. There was a healthy chance he would not win the tournament, and if he didn't win, he could end up sweeping the abbey's floors for the next fifty years. "Thank you, Brother Emil, I know what is at stake and the cost of failure."

"May Aten watch over you wherever your life takes you." Turning toward the faux knight, Emil said, "This miscreant is all yours. Please make sure you punish him severely!"

Kara saluted Emil with a flourish of her sword. She then waited until the old monk disappeared in the darkness before lifting the helmet's visor and unveiling her disguise. "I fooled him!" Kara said, recovering her breath and resuming her natural voice. "But you almost blew my cover!"

It was always better to agree with Kara. "Sorry about that. It was lucky you arrived when you did. If you hadn't, Monbatten would have had me in shackles by now."

"You would be lost without me," agreed Kara. The Berserker girl took practice swipes with her sword. "Are you ready for your final test? Wulfric plans on challenging you tonight like never before."

"I think so," answered Tryam cautiously.

"Great. I hope to see some serious fighting tonight—maybe even blood!" Kara smiled wickedly. "Let me set up the arena!"

To simulate what single combat in the tournament might be like, it had been their custom to form a circle with torches and fight within their light.

"Where is Wulfric?" Tryam asked, realizing for the first time the two had not arrived together.

Kara continued arranging the torches while answering. "Wulf was trading pelts with the guards at the north gate. The soldiers can't get enough of the warm cloaks we Berserkers can provide. But wait until you see what he's traded them for. It has taken him weeks to arrange this deal!"

Tryam could not even guess what Wulfric might be up to. It was not long before Kara shouted, "Here he comes!" and pointed toward a lumbering figure heading up from the dark ruins.

When Wulfric entered the circle of torches, the flickering light gave the youth an appearance more savage than usual. The young barbarian clasped forearms with Tryam in the way of the Berserkers, and the two exchanged greetings. Afterward, Wulfric dropped a bag he had slung over his shoulder at Tryam's feet. "Open it," he commanded with a wolfish grin.

Tryam bent down and undid the rope. What he saw took him aback. Inside was a set of armor that matched Kara's disguise, along with a shield and sword.

"Those are for you," informed Kara, who had been covering her mouth to avoid spilling the secret too early.

Tryam fumbled for words. "I don't know what to say. Or how to repay you."

Kara stepped in between the two young men. "You can repay us by winning the tournament!" She picked up the armor. "Let me show you how to put this on. I'm an expert now."

After listening to Kara's instructions, Tryam put the armor on. Once wearing the breastplate, he picked up the shield and placed it in his left hand. Kara gave him her approval. "Now you look like a proper knight. Like me," said Kara, laughing. "Hey, maybe we can sneak into the keep and see if we can fool the commander."

"I'm not ready for that just yet," said Tryam, unsure if she was serious or not.

"Let him get comfortable before you get him killed," scolded Wulfric.

Tryam took some awkward steps in the heavy armor. Kara then placed the helmet over his head. He felt a moment of pain, because the padding had long since rotted away and the metal inside rubbed against his head. Tryam fumbled to make the helmet fit more comfortably. "It's hard to see."

"Raise the visor, silly!" Kara said as she completed his attire by placing the new sword in his hands.

THE TOMB OF THERAGAARD

When Tryam lifted the visor, he saw a grinning Wulfric. "Let's put this brave knight to the test! Are you ready?" the Berserker asked.

"Yes," replied Tryam, even though he was not yet comfortable wearing the armor.

Wulfric stood in the center of the torches and began his instruction. "The more you walk around, the more at ease you will feel in that heavy armor. And now that you have a shield, let me show you a way you can use it as a weapon. I shall lunge at you, and instead of dodging as we have done in the past, I want you to step toward me and stick your shield into my chest."

"You wear no armor. Are you sure you want to try this?" Tryam was afraid his inexperience could end up hurting his friend.

"Yes. I am no thin-chested monk! It would take the charge of a mammoth to injure me," the Berserker boasted before launching his attack.

Tryam lowered his shoulder, stepped forward, and pushed his shield into the barrel chest of the Berserker. The collision left Tryam on his backside and Wulfric looming over him with a disapproving glare.

Wulfric was in no mood for failure this night and swatted his sword against Tryam's helmet. The ringing in his ears almost unbalanced him as the young acolyte scrambled to his feet.

The Berserker snapped: "Do you think I am an old monk to be treated with caution? Charge me as if your life were in the balance!"

Again, Wulfric stalked him, the cold causing the hulking warrior's breath to frost in the air like the smoke from a dragon's nostrils. A flash of muscle was Tryam's only warning of Wulfric's attack. This time, using the full force of his body, Tryam shoved the shield into the exposed chest of his opponent. The force knocked the Berserker onto his backside. Kara let out a cheer of approval.

"Ha! That's more like it!" she shouted, beaming. "You looked more like a knight than a monk that time."

Tryam was shocked and, for a moment, worried for Wulfric's safety. The stunned warrior let out a hearty laugh and brushed aside Tryam's offer of a helping hand. "Now that," he declared, "was what I wanted to see!"

Wulfric rose to his feet, still laughing, more so when he looked at Tryam's wide-eyed expression. "I wanted to show you this maneuver because of your inexperience with the sword. During the tournament you may get disarmed, and it might become useful. Only those with our size would even attempt it. Let's try this again."

The two youths practiced the maneuver over and over until Tryam was able to execute it reliably. When the young acolyte was battered and dripping with sweat, Wulfric ordered them to stop. Tryam never failed to be impressed by Wulfric's stamina.

After only a few moments of rest, the big Berserker brushed the dirt from his tunic and took a fighting stance in the center of the ring of torches. "Now that we are both warmed up, let's find out how much you have learned about combat with the blade. You may look the part of a knight, but now is the time to prove it."

"I hope you are ready for the fight of your life," answered an emboldened Tryam.

The blade, breastplate, helmet, and shield, combined with the weeks of training, gave Tryam a measure of confidence he'd lacked at the start of this endeavor. As he stood before a true warrior in his friend Wulfric, he did not feel awkward or out of place. *A short time ago, I was a simple acolyte, the lowest member of an order of pacifistic monks. Now here I am, clad in armor, challenging a member of Clan Ulf!*

The battle began with Tryam thrusting at his opponent. Wulfric, unencumbered by heavy armor, dodged aside but just barely. The Berserker countered, and Tryam skillfully blocked his opponent's blade with his shield. Wulfric followed up with another quick strike, which Tryam deflected by allowing the breastplate to absorb the blow. The two traded moves and counters with no one gaining an advantage. Sweat burned Tryam's eyes, but even with this obstacle, he did not give up any ground.

Eventually, Wulfric's superior speed, stamina, and swordsmanship began to dominate the contest. A hard strike from Wulfric's blade crashed against Tryam's breastplate, staggering the acolyte and further denting the armor. It was the combat's first significant blow, and it had Tryam rattled.

"Come on," taunted Wulfric, "I thought you Engothians were made of sterner stuff. You cower like a child before a thunderstorm! Do you want to live in that gloomy monastery all your life?"

Images of a lifetime under Monbatten's stern gaze flashed before Tryam's eyes. He answered Wulfric's challenge with strike after strike from his sword, each blow faster and with more power than the one before. Wulfric dodged the attacks skillfully.

Tryam was near exhaustion, and one of his attacks missed completely, striking a nearby headstone and fracturing it. Wulfric howled with laughter.

An anger grew from a dark place in Tryam's soul, and the skin on his chest burned as if on fire. The anger took over his will, and he grew mad with fury. With a sudden burst of strength and speed, he knocked the Berserker to the ground with a sideways swipe of his sword. Tryam furiously threw off his helmet and raised his sword to attack the defenseless Berserker.

The small fraction of Tryam's mind that was still his own enabled him to glimpse movement from the corner of his eye just as he was about to strike at the supine Berserker's body. A flash of blond hair and a glint of hardened steel was all he could make out before he felt a hard blow to the back of his head.

The world darkened, and his limbs were suddenly very heavy.

I stand upon a ridge, surrounded by men in black armor. The warriors at my side hold spears bearing a black flag with a red scorpion crest. Below, the enemy waits in their gleaming silver, the hated cross of Aten on their standards. I wave my great broadsword above my head and shout the command to charge.

Fire flares from the hands of wizards, and the smell of death fuels my hatred for the enemy. I know I might fall this day, but the will of Terminus must be served. I wade through the mass of bodies, using my broadsword as a scythe to slice through flesh and bone, to reach my counterpart on the enemy's side. Blood falls as rain, growing corpses on the desert sands, until I stand before the leader of the paladins. A flash of sun on blade signals impending death. With a mighty stroke, I remove the man's head, his lifeless body falling before me. I gaze down at the dead knight and see my reflection in the silver armor. I see my face, but it is scarred, with a long, gray-speckled beard. I should be shocked, but I am not. Before I can kill again, my chest begins to burn as if on fire. I fall to my knees ...

"It burns, it burns!" Tryam clutched his chest and screamed in agony. He tried to get up, but two figures held him down. "Get this armor off of me!"

The smaller figure slapped him, and his mind cleared. He blinked his eyes open, and the figures came into focus. It was Wulfric and Kara. "My chest burns. Help me take off the armor."

He was quickly stripped of the breastplate. Kara opened his white robes to look for an injury. She gasped while Wulfric spat upon the ground and uttered a Berserker curse to ward off evil. Tryam looked down at his chest and saw a bright red scar in the shape of the cross of Aten. It looked newly branded.

Tryam ran his fingers carefully over the scar. "What happened?"

"You went mad from bloodlust," Kara answered. "That happens in combat. Before you went too far, I had to knock you in the head!" She pointed to his chest. "But I don't know how you could've been burned. Could the breastplate be cursed?" She glared at the armor with suspicion.

Wulfric picked up the breastplate and inspected it with narrow eyes. "If it is, I shall brain that guard who traded it to me!" Wulfric threw down the armor and turned to Tryam. "What do you remember?"

"I remember getting worn down. You challenged me, and I wanted to respond. I sensed anger growing in me, a frustration, but it was almost as if it weren't part of me. It is hard to explain. After I knocked you down, all I could feel was the desire to destroy my enemy. After Kara hit me in the head, instead of falling senseless, I was transported to another battle far away."

"What do you mean, 'another battle'?" asked Kara. "Maybe I hit you too hard."

"It is difficult to explain. I was on a battlefield, and I was a butcher without mercy. For just the briefest of moments, I saw my reflection. I looked much like myself, but older. I do not understand. Then there was the burning sensation on my chest, both in the dream and here."

"I do not know what to make of your dream, Tryam, but I would not worry about it." said Wulfric. "Kara's blow was well laid."

"What about the scar?" asked Tryam.

"Take it as a sign of approval from Aten if you like. It is in the shape of His cross. And does not the cross represent the rays from the gleaming sun? One thing's for certain," joked Wulfric, rubbing his aching backside. "I think you are ready for the tournament."

Kara, trying to be cheerful, added, "What a way to end your training!" His friends helped him to his feet.

"I'm glad you are not hurt. I am sorry. I wish I had not lost control."

"Think nothing of it," consoled Wulfric. "I have had the same rage."

"I also wish we had more time together," lamented Tryam, "but I know you have to leave."

"Yes, I must return to my father's side. As jarl of our clan, he expects me to become our clan's greatest warrior," Wulfric said with pride. "I also have a trial of my own, a test of manhood that all male youths must undergo. We call it the Trial of Blood."

"The Trial of Blood?" gulped Tryam. The name alone caused the young acolyte to shiver. "That sounds more daunting than what awaits me at the tournament. What must you do?"

"I must climb our sacred mountain called Crag and return with the pelt of the white bear. If a youth does not return with the pelt, he is exiled. Being the jarl's son, I must succeed or die in the attempt."

Kara squeezed up beside Wulfric and put her arm around his shoulder. "Not only will Wulfric return a warrior, but he will become the greatest jarl of all the Berserker clans!" promised Kara. "He will be the first to unite us all."

"I know he will," agreed Tryam.

The torches burned low, and dawn threatened to arrive. "Thank you both for all you have done for me," said the young acolyte. "My fate is now in my own hands. I shall spend the remaining time preparing on my own."

He clasped Wulfric's forearm and then received a big hug from Kara.

"When we see each other again, we shall greet each other not only as friends but as fellow warriors," said Wulfric, grinning. "A knight of Engoth and a warrior of the Ulf clan."

Kara laughed and tugged on Wulfric's arm. "Ha! As for me," she crowed, "I already am a warrior!"

Chapter 10

Refusal of the Call

With Kara's laughter fading from his ears, Tryam watched his friends descend into the ruins until they were swallowed by the dark. Alone, save for the dead, he let his thoughts return to the inexplicable rage that had taken control of his mind and body. *Wulfric's insults did not trigger my anger. Was this, perhaps, a warning from Saint Paxia on the perils of violence? And what of the vision?*

He touched the scar on his chest. Time had diminished the pain, along with the streaks that had formed the outline of the cross. *How had this mark formed?*

When the rage occurred, he had become stronger—strong enough to knock Wulfric on his back. *How was this so? If I could only speak to the abbot without fear of his wrath.*

Before retiring to bed, Tryam needed to gather his thoughts. He placed the torches and new equipment into the cracked tomb, then wandered up toward the church. Instead of heading inside, however, he walked along the perimeter of the old wall. When he passed near the storage rooms, the foreign monk Gidran entered his mind. The strange monk had left in great haste some weeks before, without having told Tryam what, if anything, he had discovered in the vaults.

Gidran was still a topic of interest among the insular monks. The way the foreigner had carried himself, the way he had challenged Monbatten, the rumor of plague, and a mission for the Wizard Council—nothing like this had disrupted the monks' lives before. The mystery intrigued Tryam.

The young acolyte passed through the abbey's new cemetery to the moss-covered stone wall that bordered the supply houses. *If I could retrace* his steps, I could see where it was he ventured. He pushed open the bronze gate that led to the brick buildings and made his way to the one that concealed the entrance to the underground. He pushed open its warped door, then stepped inside. Before heading down into the cellar, Tryam retrieved a torch from a side room and lit it with flint.

At first glance, the cellar appeared as it always had, but when Tryam looked at the crate that covered the way to the underground, he discovered it was slightly askew and the opening to the vaults was exposed. Tryam shoved the heavy box completely aside, then peered into the dark. A splash of blood covered the rubble below, and a trail of blood disappeared down the corridor. *Brother Gidran must have injured himself! Perhaps that is why he left in such haste?*

Tryam dropped into the hole, holding his torch aloft, curiosity driving him to follow the blood. The acolyte was familiar with most of the passages in the vaults, but where the blood drops led was to a passage he had always considered impassable. Now, however, he saw that a hole had been bored through the blockage.

Staring at the size of the pile of material removed to make the opening, Tryam wondered how Gidran could have cleared away that much dirt and heavy stone. *Something important must have fueled the strange monk.*

Youthful curiosity overrode better judgment, so he pressed onward. Once through the opening, he examined the area beyond with his torch. *Look at the enormity of this passage! I thought I had seen most of the underground, but I have seen but a small part.*

Archways lined both sides of the long corridor ahead. The blood trail never veered, however, going straight into the darkness. Curiosity getting the better of him again, he ignored the trail for a moment to examine a random room to his right. When he pushed its door, the wood crumbled in his hand. Inside, torchlight revealed a room covered in cobwebs, with broken chairs, smashed crates, and shattered pottery littering the floor. Everything smelled musty.

Hoping to find a relic from the time of the Ancients, Tryam scanned the debris with his torch held low. He uncovered two small coins, each with the face of a different bearded king, but Tryam had no use for coins in the abbey.

Tryam abandoned his side exploration and resumed his original search for Gidran's path. The monk's blood trail never wavered, even when multiple intersections and side passages became available.

The underground was so vast and the hour so late that Tryam pondered if it were wise to continue his exploration, but he could not restrain his curiosity. When the trail led to a collapsed stairwell, the young acolyte thought he had reached an impasse, but once again, Gidran had taken great pains to remove the obstructions in his way. Tryam squeezed his large frame through and under slabs of marble and emerged at yet another, deeper level of the vaults.

On this new floor, the stone used to construct the walls changed from granite to marble. And instead of archways leading off into different tunnels, alcoves lined the passage. Tryam walked up to the first alcove with trepidation. Once the torchlight erased the shadows, he saw the lid of a tomb with a solemn face staring up. He went from crypt to crypt, stopping at one that had been defiled, the skeletal remains exposed. *Was Gidran here to loot an artifact? No, that can't be possible.* Tryam said a prayer over the dead man's scattered remains.

After he'd spoken the last words of the prayer, the young acolyte's ears picked up what sounded like wind blowing through the leaves of a tree. The sound emanated from the far end of the hallway, a place still shrouded in thick black nothingness.

Tryam held up his torch, but the light could not penetrate the ominous black. He moved forward, but it was not curiosity that drew him in; it was a compulsion.

With tentative steps, he proceeded along the trail of blood past the gallery of tombs. The corridor ended at stairs with blue and white marble steps that led deeper underground. The compulsion urged him ahead.

He walked down the steps, which terminated at a subterranean rotunda. Ruined marble columns and smashed lintels leaned against one another on a floor that looked to have been buckled by an earthquake. Despite the damage, the elegant grandeur of the room remained.

Tryam gasped, however, when he saw the blood trail end in a pool of gore in the center of the room. *How could Gidran have survived such a grievous injury? Had he been struck by a fallen column?*

Despite his having worked in the abbey's sick ward, the sight of the thick black blood made Tryam sick to his stomach. The young acolyte turned away and stopped to listen for the unnatural wind over the drumming of his own beating heart. The sound had changed. It now seemed more like whispers in the sleeping ear of a dreamer. Tryam was thankful for the courage he took from his faith in Aten, but he wished he had his sword.

Of the three exits, it was the north passage that led down deep steps from which the whispers eerily sang. Tryam abandoned reason and descended into the gloom.

In the corridor at the end of the stairs, the air was fresh but the darkness oppressive. Tryam took lurching steps forward. Ahead, he could see the outline of two figures. His body stiffened until he noticed the figures were too still to be alive. He led with his torch and moved closer until the light was bright enough on the shadowy forms to show them in greater detail. The light showed statues of twin sword-wielding, winged Aemons in a protective stance. *Angels protecting what?*

Blood stained one sword. *Is this where Gidran injured himself? But no blood is on the floor.* The young acolyte could make no sense of what he had discovered.

Curious, Tryam examined the stone angels closer. From his studies he recognized them as the Aemons Judithia and Minova, known as the guardians of the honored dead. *Whose tomb must lie ahead?*

The torch in his hand flickered as if touched by a gust of wind, and the unnerving whispers become more forceful, like pleas from a chorus of tortured voices. Tryam's breath came in quick gulps, his lungs burned. He wanted to flee but could not move his legs. He was forced to listen to the words, words he understood came from the dead.

"... come ... our promised one ... let us show you ... the enemy has awakened ... the enemy has returned ... Theragaard ... Theragaard ... must live again ... help us ... help ..."

Tryam covered his ears, but the heart-wrenching voices persisted. A madness gripped the young acolyte. The voices were too many, Tryam's will too weak. He had to flee from the underground.

In a blind panic, Tryam banged into walls and occasionally tripped, until he made his way, bloody, bruised, and exhausted, to the wine cellar. There he moved the crate back over the hole and extinguished his torch.

The voices were gone, but now he felt shame for his fearful reaction: *I have turned my back on souls in desperate need.*

Chapter 11
Revelations

A new sun was already low in the sky when Tryam emerged back in the open air. Despite his misgivings, he had to tell Father Monbatten what he had experienced, what he had discovered. He was prepared to face the consequences of his actions. As he hurried his way back to the cloister, he removed as much dirt as he could from his hair and robes.

When he arrived outside the abbot's cell, he heard the sound of two voices arguing. Tryam paused before entering, not wanting to interrupt but also curious to overhear what was being said. The first voice he recognized was that of Monbatten's.

"Manning the ward tower is the only obligation the Order of Saint Paxia owes to the defense of Arkos. I would not even allow that if it were not part of the arrangement that allowed the order to settle in Arkos. Your talk of a threat from a Daemon is absurd!"

The second voice, equally adamant, responded: "How can you dismiss the threat so casually? I have just returned from a confrontation with a Daemon in the mines right outside of Arkos! It did not sink back into the Abyss easily; it was powerful and hungry. Darkness is spreading across the world, whether you want to see it or not. The Church must be prepared to push back, especially in remote places such as Arkos."

"I agree with you on one point. A darkness is spreading across the world, but a darkness cast from the shadows of mortal men, not by the Dark God and his minions. When violence governs hearts and minds, then darkness extinguishes goodness. The only solution to these ills is listening to the Word of Aten, not seeking out dark spirits to fight!"

THE TOMB OF THERAGAARD

"I am afraid, Father Monbatten, that the hearts of men are being inflamed by the Dark God himself and not by some vague lust for violence. I have read the reports from my compatriots in Outremer. They speak of the rise of a new Prophet, one who has ventured to the ruined city of Antium and communed with Terminus. A Prophet who is spreading the Dark Words across the Eastern lands with the quickness and lethality of an insidious plague. The black obelisk temples of the Dark God now rise far beyond the dominion of small sects hiding in far desert sands. The creatures of the Abyss can sense this growing malevolent force, and they want to be a part of it. They want to resume the Abyssal War."

Monbatten grunted, and the room became quiet for many moments. After a deep breath and a silent prayer to Aten, Tryam stepped in front of the open threshold. Two grim faces turned his way.

He now recognized the second speaker as that of Kayen, a dark-haired and bearded monk in his late forties. The man was a missionary. He was not a member of the Order of Saint Paxia but a member of the Order of the Imacolata, which specialized in spiritual matters relating to creatures from the Abyss. The man rarely stayed on the abbey grounds, and he kept mostly to himself when he did stay. Monbatten treated him as an outsider. Tryam always wondered why the abbot permitted Brother Kayen to stay in the abbey at all.

"What do you want, boy?" barked Monbatten.

The abbot looked flustered, his face red as he fidgeted in his high-backed oaken chair behind his cluttered desk. Kayen appeared calm. The missionary was seated across from the abbot, his arms crossed contemplatively, with a large hooked shepherd staff, similar to the abbot's, across his legs. Kayen's brown robes were covered in dust, and he was drenched in sweat as if he had endured some hardship recently.

"I beg forgiveness for the interruption, but I have something important to say," announced Tryam, doing his best to ignore the abbot's narrow eyes under beetling brows. "I may have heard the voices of the dead in the crypts below the abbey."

"The crypts?" snapped the abbot. "What were you doing down there? That place is dangerous and was sealed off long ago! How did you find a way inside?"

Tryam felt his face flush at the barrage of questions. "I discovered a way into the crypts by accident when I had to retrieve a bottle of wine for Brother Cordon. Tonight, I went into the vaults to clear my head." He waited for a reaction from the abbot, but none was forthcoming. "Did you hear what I said? I heard spirits!"

"Yes, I heard what you said, and it is utter nonsense," blasted Monbatten, dismissively waving his hand. "There are no spirits in the crypts, only ruins from a time long ago and the resting place of men now long forgotten."

Kayen rose from his chair, then looked over the disheveled acolyte. "Give the young man a moment to speak!" he admonished Monbatten. Then he turned again to Tryam. "Take a deep breath, and tell us what happened."

Tryam swallowed hard, then responded. "I need to go back a few weeks, when a visiting monk from Tiranople named Gidran and Father Monbatten had a confrontation during the morning meal. After everyone else had left, Gidran came to me and asked to speak in private. I agreed. When we talked, he disclosed that he wanted to know more about the history of the island." Tryam wiped sweat from his brow. "It was then that I told Brother Gidran I had discovered ruins beneath the church that might answer his questions. I took him to the entrance of the vault, where he took it upon himself to explore on his own. Unfortunately, he left before I could ask what he might have discovered." He cast his eyes downward. "This past night, I could not sleep ..." Tryam hesitated to tell the rest of his story, unsure why he was leaving out his nightly training sessions, the rage that had overwhelmed him, and the scar that had formed on his chest.

Perhaps sensing his unease, Brother Kayen guided the youth to the chair he had just vacated. "Do not be troubled, son. Please, continue and leave out no details."

Tryam sat down and continued his tale. "After a troubling nightmare, I went for a walk. When I passed by the wine cellar, I was reminded of Gidran. Curious to see where Gidran had explored, I returned to the crack in the cellar that leads to the underground. On the ground I saw droplets of blood. Curiosity overcame caution, and I traced the blood to a level deep underground with ancient tombs. I think no one besides Brother Gidran had been to these crypts for a long time." He swallowed hard. "I followed the blood trail until I reached a large rotunda with shattered columns. On the ground was a large pool of blood. It was here I heard a whispering. I followed the sound down a dark corridor, at the end of which were twin statues of Judithia and Minova." He moved to the edge of his chair. "There

THE TOMB OF THERAGAARD

the whispers became clearer. It was a chorus of desperate men pleading for help. I was too frightened to make sense of it and fled. If they were not from the dead, could I have heard the words of a Daemon?"

The room went silent. Tryam looked up at Monbatten, who now paced, the gold robes of office twisting about him. Kayen, on the other hand, calmly stroked his short brown beard.

The missionary spoke first. "The voices you heard were not from a Daemon. If they had been, you would not be with us right now. But it is possible those voices may have originated from the spirit realm." Kayen hesitated and then concluded alarmingly: "It only makes sense, given who you are."

The words hit Tryam like an unexpected slap to the face. "Given who I am?"

Monbatten exploded and turned his ire at Kayen. "Here, in one night you speak of fighting Daemons, and now you scare one of my order into thinking they have been conversing with the dead!" Monbatten walked up to Tryam and pulled him bodily from the chair. The abbot looked into Tryam's eyes as if trying to peer into his soul. "Perhaps it is time for you to know your past, so you can understand the true nature and power of evil."

"My past?" Tryam recalled the nightmarish vision of the bloody battlefield and his role in it. His head spun, and he feared that this vision was more than the result of a blow to the head. "What of my past? I was told that my history was unknown to you. That I came here as a child, in a fevered state, and without knowledge of my origin."

The abbot sat back down behind the desk and folded his arms across his chest. "Perhaps Brother Kayen should be the one to answer the young man's questions."

This time it was the missionary who looked uncomfortable as he ran his fingers through his hair. "When it was decided that you should be brought to this monastery, we thought it best to keep certain knowledge from you," confessed Kayen. "Even now it would it would be unwise to divulge too much."

"We?" asked Tryam perplexed. "You played a part in my coming here?" He had always felt the missionary took particular steps to avoid interacting with him whenever he was staying at the abbey, even though he had heard from others that Kayen had inquired about him frequently. "Is that why you are here, the only monk among us not a member of the Order of Saint Paxia? Are you here to watch over me?"

"In part, yes. I played a role in the decision to bring you to the abbey, but ever since, Father Monbatten has requested that I keep a respectable distance. I served as your father's priest, and he was a great friend and a greater man. The fate that took the lives of your family also robbed you of your memory. That was not our doing. It was my decision to bring you far from those who might try to hurt you, and with Father Monbatten's blessing, it was decided that Arkos would be the best place to raise you."

"Your family," Monbatten added, "were victims of a great evil, for a cause that has brought only more violence and death to this day."

"Am I in danger?" asked Tryam.

Kayen chuckled. "Be at ease. You are in no danger. Not today, at least. In any event, I have been watching over you, and I am prepared to take any measures necessary to prevent you from coming to harm. I am a member of the Order of the Imacolata, which is dedicated to the study of creatures from the Abyss." Kayen drew forth from his robes a large metal cross of Aten and placed it into Tryam's hands. "This is no ordinary cross. Notice the words inscribed along the edges of the cross? Can you read them?"

"Of course not," scoffed Monbatten. "He's only an initiate. He could not know the language of ancient Antium."

"I can read them," admitted Tryam. When Monbatten gasped, he offered, "Perhaps I learned the language as a child? I have always been able to read the old scrolls in the library."

"Read them aloud and show us," prodded Kayen.

The engraved letters were small, but Tryam could read the words thanks to the expert craftsmanship used to create them. He quoted the text: "'Defending the faithful, from threats mortal and Abyssal, from within and without.'"

"Nicely done." Kayen retrieved the cross and placed it back under his robes. "I believe it is important for us to investigate what Tryam may have discovered in the crypts. Closing our eyes to evil does not make it go away. This visiting monk risked his life to venture into the crypts. We should see for ourselves what he was after."

The abbot glared at Kayen. "I cannot ban you from this abbey, Brother Kayen, but I can restrict your access. No one is allowed in the vaults. The Church has placed me in charge of Tryam until he has come of age. I don't want you speaking of things he is not ready to know. Do you understand?"

"Understood," the missionary answered.

"Good. Now leave us," ordered the abbot.

"I believe you are making a grave mistake by not discussing this further," responded Kayen as he made his way to the door. "Soon, Tryam will be old enough to make his own decisions. I shall be ready when he is."

The abbot scowled after Kayen departed. "That man is irresponsible. Do not listen to his reckless words. Those crypts were buried to enable the spirits there to rest, and rest they do." He slammed his fist on the desk. "That serpent-tongued Gidran was likely here to rob one of the tombs for use on his foolish quest. He may have triggered a trap left behind by the Ancients. I wondered why he left in such haste. I should never have welcomed that foreigner inside our home." He fixed his eyes on Tryam. "Forget what you heard, and do not dwell on your past. Pray for your future."

The church bells signaled the breakfast hour.

The abbot stood up from his desk and walked Tryam to the doorway. "It is mealtime. You should hurry to aid Brother Cordon. This is the place you are meant to be and where you can have a rich spiritual life."

Almost numb, Tryam nodded his head. He had hoped that he would find out what had happened in the vaults, but now his thoughts had turned to the fate of his parents. Hearing that they had been victims of violence and great evil was almost too much to bear.

He made his way to the dining hall, but he was not hungry.

Chapter 12
Tryam's Unanswered Questions

The day passed interminably slow, all of Tryam's newfound enthusiasm sapped by the recent events. At night, a torrent of emotions hindered the young acolyte's sleep. With the dawn, he opened the worn wooden shutters of his dreary cell and watched the sunrise, its powerful rays effortlessly erasing the shadows that clung to the abbey grounds. Outside his second-story room, the world started anew.

With the new day came a new perspective. Tryam would defy Monbatten, confront Brother Kayen about the circumstances of his arrival at the abbey, and ask about the tragic events that had led to his becoming an orphan. As if his thoughts were guided by Aten's hand, he spotted the man he was thinking about exiting the church grounds. He was too far away to hail, but that it was a sign from Aten he had no doubt.

Tryam dressed in a hurry and raced out of his cell and down the deserted corridor. He took the narrow stone stairway that led out of the cloister two steps at a time. He caught up to the missionary near the bell tower. Kayen was dressed and packed for travel, with a full backpack along with a brown traveling cloak about his shoulders. He walked with his shepherd's staff. "Excuse me, Brother Kayen, can you stop a moment?"

The missionary turned around and leaned on his staff. "I don't think Father Monbatten would approve of us talking."

"I have a lot of questions, and—"

Kayen raised his hand. "I know you do. But now is not a good time. I thought it best to put distance between Father Monbatten and myself.

I am headed to Clan Ulf, where, I believe, you know two Berserkers. Ones who have been … let's say … visiting you late at night? Isn't that so?"

"Uh, yes, my friends Wulfric and Kara. How do you know them?"

"Besides keeping a watchful eye on you, I travel the lands outside of Arkos as part of my duty for my order, making sure the creatures of the Abyss do not threaten us. I also spread the Word of Aten to the natives, so they may be lightbringers in the darkness. Spreading the Word of Aten is the first line of defense against the Abyss. Your father believed that."

"I have many questions," implored Tryam, "and I beg you for answers."

"That knowledge might put you in personal danger. I promise you, when the time is right, I shall be free to tell you the whole truth."

"Then I must have patience," sighed Tryam. "If the past is forbidden, may I ask about the present? I neglected to tell Father Monbatten about the incident that preceded my entering the underground."

Kayen laughed. "'Neglected,' you say? Please, go on."

"While I was training with Wulfric, I lost my temper and went into a blind rage. Kara stopped my rage by hitting me over the head and knocking me out cold. While I was unconscious, I dreamt of a battle where I was on the side of darkness. When I saw my reflection, it was not myself, but it was somehow familiar. I fear Aten was warning me not to take up the sword. I do not want to suffer from the same fate as that of my family."

The missionary's eyes gazed beyond Tryam as if viewing something from the past. He stroked the cross through his robes, then responded in a calm but stern voice. "God lets everyone choose their own fate, for good or for ill. If, in your heart, you believe that joining the Engothian knights is what you are meant to do, then pursue it. A dream needs not foreshadow your fate."

The church bells rang, calling for the morning prayers. "You had best get back to the abbey before Father Monbatten finds you here talking to me," Kayen continued. "We can discuss this more when I return." He placed a hand on Tryam's shoulder. "Don't brood upon the past, and don't fear the future. Let the will of Aten guide you."

"I shall try," said Tryam. "Farewell and safe travels."

"Good luck," said Kayen, winking.

As Tryam's eyes followed Kayen's descent down to the dock, unanswered questions lingered in his head. Alone, he was without direction. He regretted not having the courage to tell the missionary about the burning scar that had appeared on his chest, but he feared to learn what its cause might be.

Tryam decided to focus on this day and this day alone. He would start by asking for guidance during the morning prayer. Then tonight, sword practice against the shadows.

Chapter 13
Telvar's Test of Fire

Learning patience was far more difficult for Telvar than learning magic, but being an unpaid servant in a mage tower was far more acceptable than returning to his parents' mercantile store in Secundus. He would endure any hardship in his quest for magic.

Myramar had been so obsessed with finding the secret of Dementhus's bauble that in the weeks since the Albus mage had departed, the old wizard had rarely ventured out of the laboratory in the tower's underground, leaving Telvar in relative peace. This freedom allowed for experimenting in the alchemy laboratory on the tower's third floor, where Telvar could practice the art of combining reagents with magic to endow them with unique properties. Though making potions had its own rewards, it was not enough. He still had yet to receive permission to access the tower's magic library, and without this access, Telvar would be unable to learn new spells. He was only a first-level Rutilus mage, the lowest level of the lowest rank, and unless he could expand his repertoire of magic, he did not foresee his status changing.

Telvar could not fault the old man's obsession with the bauble; a magical riddle is too irresistible for any wizard to ignore. If Telvar wanted to prove his competence in magic, he needed to convince Myramar that he could aid with this mystery. He might even solve it quicker than the plodding old wizard. In fact, he was sure he could.

Telvar knocked on the magic library's red door and waited only a single heartbeat before barging in to prevent Myramar from yelling at him to go away. The old man was balancing on the topmost step of a ladder, examining a book. He showed no sign of discomfort. *Either the old man* was lying about his physical limitations, or this mystery has made him forget his ailments! In fact, I can't even remember the last time he asked me to brew that noxious healing tonic of his.

"How goes your research?" asked Telvar. "Well, I hope. Have you thought to consult *Hector's Artifacts and Arcana*? It's the most extensive volume on magical items from before the fall of Antium."

The wizard lowered the book he was holding just enough so that Telvar could see his green eyes appearing over the top. "Don't be a fool. Of course, I did. That was the first codex I consulted."

"Should you be up on that ladder?"

"Your concern for my health is unwarranted. In fact, I have not been this energized in years. Now begone before your interruption causes me to get angry."

Telvar pressed on. "Have you made any progress regarding the artifact? Perhaps if you share with me what you have discovered, I could help." The amulet now dangled from Myramar's neck. *Has it grown brighter?*

"Progress, yes, in a manner of speaking. I've been able to determine what it is not."

"If the jewel is an elemental artifact of fire, I could do experiments on it. Maybe offer a different perspective."

"So, you fancy yourself an expert on the fire element?" Pettiness and contempt, emotions Telvar had not before seen from Myramar, dripped from the old man's mouth. "Let's test you, then! Perhaps if I show you how much you still need to learn, you will stop pestering me."

This had not gone the way Telvar had hoped, but the implacable young mage feared no test of his skills. "I am ready to prove myself worthy, master!"

"Is that so? We shall see." The old man climbed down the ladder and slammed the book he held onto a table. "We shall see how much control you have. Follow me."

The orange-robed mage exited the library through the antechamber and took the steps that ran along the side wall of the tower to the third floor. So fast did his master move, Telvar had a hard time keeping up.

At the third-floor landing, Myramar led Telvar into one of the laboratories. He shut the door behind them with a loud thud. The young apprentice fought back against the irrational fear he was being led into a trap.

THE TOMB OF THERAGAARD

Noonday light spilled inside the room from the lone window along the curved outer wall. Dead leaves and other windblown debris on the floor led Telvar to conclude that Myramar had not used this particular laboratory in a long time. Black ceramic tiles covered the walls. The floor was a black marble. The room's only furnishings were a metal cabinet and a large stone table. The room reminded Telvar of the laboratories at the Veneficturis in Secundus, where spells could be tested.

Myramar opened the cabinet and removed a hefty black candle. The wizard then placed the candle in the center of the stone table. "You burned down a laboratory before. Let us see how well you can control fire now." After taking a step back, Myramar looked into Telvar's eyes and ordered, "Ignite the wick."

"As you command," replied Telvar.

The young mage spoke the words to open a connection to the astral plane, and a link between him and the world of magic was established. When he felt the connection was stable, he focused on the symbol of the fire element and reached for it with his mind while his physical hand made a corresponding gesture.

The power of his mind forced the fire element to the material plane, and when Telvar opened his hand, a small flame was in his palm. He walked over to the table and dropped the flame onto the candle's wick.

"Very good," said Myramar. The tower wizard folded his arms over his long white beard and took another step away from the table. "Now gradually increase the flame's intensity."

"As you wish."

Telvar concentrated on his mental connection to the astral plane and brought forth into his mind's eye more of the fire element. Gesturing with his hands, he moved the additional fire element to the material plane, then channeled the element to the candle. He watched with satisfaction as the flame increased in strength, stopping only after Myramar held up his hand.

"I need to see a real fire. Something worthy of a pyromancer! Channel enough fire to melt the entire candle."

Telvar hid a smile. He had been waiting for an opportunity to prove his quality. He allowed still more fire element from the astral plane to flow into the material world and directed it toward the candle. Flames overflowed the melted wax and danced upon the stone table, scorching its surface. The heat was that of a kiln. The candle was quickly consumed.

Myramar seemed pleased, as a smile spread across his wrinkled face. "Now extinguish the fire."

Telvar nodded.

The young wizard reversed the flow of energy. He watched for a corresponding decrease in the intensity of the flames, but the fire did not wane. Puzzled, he repeated the command. This time, instead of decreasing, the flames intensified.

Telvar was sure he could break the connection to the astral plane to extinguish the flames in an instant, but he did not want to give Myramar the satisfaction in watching him fail to control his magic. He tried again to reverse the flow from the astral plane, but the flames grew to encompass the entire table and spread onto the floor.

Alarmed at this inexplicable phenomenon, Telvar decided he had no other choice but to admit defeat. "Stand back, master! I shall terminate the flow!" He had to shout to be heard over the increasing roar of the fire while the heat forced him back toward the room's only window.

Telvar spoke the command to end his link to the astral plane, and the connection between his mind and the realm of magic broke. This should have caused the fire to die, because there should be no magical energy nor any physical material to fuel it, but the apprentice was stunned to see that was not the case.

"What have you done, boy?" Myramar was trapped between the table and the cabinet by the growing firestorm. "Break off your connection!"

Telvar searched for any residual connection to that other realm. *Nothing! What is going on?*

The young mage tried to establish a new connection. He remained calm and spoke the words of command. He peered into the astral plane, scanning for any sign of a lingering connection leaking into the material world, but something blocked him from doing so. When he tried to see what it was, his body shuddered as he made contact with another entity—one not human. *A creature in the astral plane? Impossible!*

The flames had now spread to encompass the floor surrounding the table, and they threatened both mages. Telvar backed away from the fire until his body pressed against the window. As the flames threatened to engulf him, he feared that he might have to jump. Telvar shouted to Myramar, "I can't stop the fire. Please, master, do something!"

Flames blocked Myramar from Telvar's line of sight, and he was not sure the old wizard had heard his plea. *I will not die without trying another spell.*

THE TOMB OF THERAGAARD

Telvar closed his eyes and concentrated on his connection to the astral plane with the thought of summoning water, but when he tried to enter the plane, he could not focus his mind to make the link. He felt his hair singe. He opened his eyes, but whether it was madness or a trick of the flames, Telvar saw a bestial face in the fire.

The flames scorched Telvar's robes. He leaned far out the window to get away from the intense heat. The ground was thirty feet below, and if he were to jump, he was not sure he would survive the fall. Before he put a foot on the window's ledge, out of the corner of his eye he saw Myramar approaching. In his hand the wizard had a staff with a blue crystal tip. Telvar watched as a cone of frost issued from the jewel.

Flames and frost battled in a cloud of smoke and steam. Gradually, the old wizard made his way close enough that Telvar could grab hold of the man's arm. Together, they walked toward the exit, their backs against the wall as the old mage hurled a continual flow of ice into the conflagration. Once they reached the door, Myramar pushed Telvar out of the room. "Stay back," he ordered.

From the doorway, Telvar watched as the tip of Myramar's rod glowed with a brightness equal to that of the fire, and the cone of frost doubled in diameter and intensity. The fire retreated as frost coated the floor, ceiling, and eventually the table itself. Telvar did not see the bestial face again.

When the immediate danger was over, Telvar fell to his knees. His brain searched for answers. *This test was a disaster, but it was not a repeat of what happened at the Veneficturis in Secundus. That was due to my inexperience; this was something far different.*

As he lifted Telvar to his feet, sweat poured down the old wizard's face. Myramar revealed no emotion as he spoke. "You have failed, once again, to prove you can control your magic. If you think I shall allow you to help me research this amulet," the tower mage clutched the glowing jewel that hung from his neck, "you are the biggest fool in all of Medias. Now clean up this mess. I must lock the library from now on, for I fear what you would destroy next if you tried to learn more magic. You are a menace."

For once, Telvar was left without words. He thought of telling the old mage what he had seen, but for the first time since arriving at the tower, he felt he could not trust his master. Telvar was certain that something, *or someone*, had interfered with his test.

Chapter 14
The New Beginning

The galley creaked and moaned as its metal-plated hull strained against the ice on the narrow stream. Undead hands manned the oars, enabling the ocean-going vessel to push through the shallow waterway that the boat had never been designed to navigate.

An expanse of land spread out before Dementhus. *So vast, so barren.* The freezing winds from the mountains signaled that autumn had arrived in full. *Where does Antigenesus's fortress lie? Where is his ultimate weapon?* The sound of footsteps interrupted his thoughts.

"We have a problem. Another breach has formed. Water is pouring in."

Dementhus acknowledged Abbaster's report. "Show me."

This was not the first time the galley demanded attention. Dementhus had used several spells to mend broken timbers and snapped oars. When he inspected the damage in the forward compartment, however, he knew that their time on the vessel was coming to an end. His hands and feet throbbing in pain, he gave Abbaster his assessment. "The ship has served its purpose. I could patch this breach, but the ship's keel is split, and the keel plating is coming loose." He pointed to a giant crack that extended from the ruptured hull to the great beam that ran along the center of the ship. "We shall have to abandon ship. Steer us to the bank."

"What about the crew?" The swarthy brute jerked his thumb toward the oar room.

Dementhus shook his head. "They are no longer of use to us. They shall remain on board."

The warrior shrugged his shoulders before heading in the direction of the wheelhouse.

The Necromancer clenched his fists to get sensation back into his fingers, then returned to his stateroom, each step bringing shooting pain throughout the length of his spine. He retrieved a vial of his noxious tonic from his trunk, pulled out the stopper, and quaffed the entire potion in one gulp.

The effects were immediate. He felt the vigor of youth again. With his new energy, he emptied the chest of every vital potion, reagent, map, and book and placed them in a large leather backpack he then slung over his back. A few minutes later, the ship rubbed along the river bottom.

Dementhus exited his stateroom and walked to Gidran's cabin to discuss with the shaman the next phase of their journey. He knocked on the door and entered. He found Gidran bare to the waist, prostrate before an obsidian scorpion idol. Upon seeing the wizard, the shaman stood up and covered himself in his brown robes.

"The ship is finished," informed Dementhus. "We proceed on foot. Pack only what you need."

As if emerging from a fevered dream, Gidran shook his head as if to clear it. His eyes had the glimmer of madness to them when he spoke. "We are getting closer! I can sense the machinations of Terminus! Praise be to Bafomeht for guiding us here!"

Gidran promptly packed his sacred relics and followed Dementhus up on deck. Abbaster had beached the ship on the southern bank of an uncharted river that had its source high up in the Corona Mountains, and the vessel now listed considerably. The big warrior lowered a plank, and the three men abandoned ship. The undead crew would eventually freeze and make for a horrifying discovery to some unlucky native.

With the grounded galley as a backdrop, Dementhus addressed the two agents of Bafomeht. "We are now committed to this mission, for we have no ship to flee back to Lux. We have nothing save what gifts Terminus has blessed us with and what meager supplies we carry on our backs. We shall either find what we are after or die in the effort."

Abbaster raised his scimitars in salute, while Gidran shouted praises to Terminus. Dementhus basked in the euphoria of the moment, but his eyes were already trying to distinguish the twin-peaked mountain from the hundreds of peaks that crowded the eastern horizon.

Days of brutal hiking followed, as Dementhus led the party ever onward into the rugged expanse. The rigors of the journey exacted a toll on their bodies, but Dementhus, whose life hinged on the success of this mission, drove them on relentlessly. As the Necromancer's supply of healing elixir diminished, he passed the weight of his backpack to Abbaster. He even allowed Gidran to pray for his health. Dementhus himself understood that his body was failing and doing so quickly.

As the days stretched to weeks, the three seekers formed a routine: Abbaster hunted for food, Gidran sought guidance from Terminus, and Dementhus used his magic to provide warmth and shelter. When the lower foothills proved devoid of clues, and with no other choice available to them, the Necromancer led his companions farther east, into the teeth of the arctic wilds, always climbing higher.

The arctic wind shredded Dementhus's cloak, freezing him to his core, and each step on the unforgiving tundra threatened to shatter his bones. But none of these physical hardships could extinguish the fanatical desires that burned in his mind. The Prismatic Tower, the Golem, the magic—they existed in his visions; now he had to find them in the material world. *Terminus, do not forsake me!*

It was Abbaster's keen eyes that first spotted the hunter. The warrior signaled the party to halt. At first, Dementhus could not see the movement, then he traced the path from Abbaster's finger to a distant figure on the horizon.

"At last, a sign of human inhabitation. We must have ventured into the realm of the local barbarians," observed Dementhus, reinvigorated with the discovery. "The natives who live on this side of the Corona Mountains are called Berserkers. They are the cousins to the Reavers, who plunder trading vessels from the Western Kingdoms. These Berserkers are tied to the land and live in small villages organized by clan. They are a primitive and fierce warrior society and live a short and violent existence." Dementhus pointed to the figure on the horizon. "If we capture this lone hunter, we could—with sufficient *persuasion*—be one step closer to finding what we seek and to leaving this unrelenting waste that threatens to take our bones."

It did not take long for Abbaster to gather Dementhus's meaning. "I shall be back," the brute said, his hands gripping the hilts of his twin scimitars.

Gidran and Dementhus followed Abbaster at a distance. The sun was low on the horizon, and the flat land gave no cover. The Berserker hunter, however, showed no sign he was aware of the brute's approach. He moved slowly, as one does when stalking prey, and he held a spear ready to strike.

THE TOMB OF THERAGAARD

A walrus, five times the bulk of a man, burst through the ice near the Berserker. The wailing of the massive beast echoed across the snow-covered plain as it attacked. Dementhus watched the brave hunter stand his ground, using his spear to keep the beast at bay.

The Berserker did not remain passive, however. He stabbed repeatedly at the walrus. Deadly tusks blocked the weapon, and a gaping mouth snapped in response. Each prick by the spear, though, enraged the walrus, enabling the Berserker to lure the beast away from the dangerously thin ice from which it had emerged.

The deadly duel raged on, but it was clear that the Berserker was getting the upper hand. The walrus was bleeding from a dozen small wounds. It grew lethargic, its attacks less ferocious. The Berserker ceased his probing attacks and cast his spear with a mighty throw. The metal-headed weapon lodged deep into the walrus's flank. The Berserker then drew a blade from his waist and held it before him. The beast made a desperate lunge. The Berserker anticipated this response and sidestepped a tusk intended for his torso, but he stayed close enough to thrust his blade through the back of the beast's thick skull. It was a quick and efficient hunt.

Abbaster wasted no time appreciating the kill. He descended on the Berserker hunter like a snake its prey. The Berserker's keen senses gave him the briefest of warnings, and he turned his head in time to see Abbaster's charge. He tried to extract his sword from the slain beast's skull, but the blade was lodged too deep and could not be freed. Abbaster struck at the Berserker with his twin scimitars, one blade directed at the hunter's chest, the other, his stomach. The Berserker made a desperate block of Abbaster's upper thrust with his forearm, but the second blade struck deep into his stomach. Blood erupted from the wound, staining the Berserker's white pelt cloak a dark crimson. He fell to the ground.

Dementhus hurried to the battle. Abbaster stepped aside, leaving one of his scimitars lodged in the fallen man's abdomen. The Necromancer addressed his companions before they took actions on their own. "Before he passes from this realm, I must speak to him." The wizard then cast a spell. Manacles of ice formed around the Berserker's wrists and ankles.

Abbaster grinned. "If he needs encouragement to speak, I know many methods of torture."

"That will not be necessary." Dementhus looked down at the trapped native. He was impressed that the impaled blade did not cause the Berserker to scream out in agony. The man's face was bearded, his blond hair matted with blood, but his eyes showed strength as they met his captor's with a defiant stare.

Dementhus addressed the man: "You are an excellent hunter. That was quite a feat, killing that creature by yourself. I am sorry to say, you will not be able to enjoy the meat from your kill, but I can promise you it will not go to waste."

"Go back to the Abyss," spat the man through blood-frothed lips. "I care not what you do with the meat, but I can promise you something as well. If my hands were unshackled, I would split your skull and cast your meat to the wolves."

Dementhus let out a hearty laugh, his first in a long time, and leaned on the scimitar, pushing it deeper into the Berserker's innards. This time the man cried out in pain. "I'm sure you would try. But before I send you to your ancestors, I have a few questions."

Spasms caused the Berserker to writhe in agony. He responded between gasps for air. "I shall use my last breaths to curse you."

"If that is what you wish, then so be it." Dementhus pulled the scimitar from the man's abdomen and thrust it into his heart.

"What have you done?" cried Gidran. "Have you gone mad? We needed answers from him."

"Gidran," chided Dementhus, "have you no faith?"

Blood oozed from the chest wound, and the Berserker ceased struggling against his restraints. His mouth opened, and he beckoned Dementhus closer with a manacled hand. The wizard kneeled to hear the man's last words.

"This is a cruel land, and you shall never leave it." The dying man punctuated his words with a smile through bloody teeth. Moments later, he was dead.

"We shall see, my friend."

Dementhus returned the bloody scimitar to Abbaster. "Be ready," he advised the brute.

He then removed from his robes his magical gem-tipped rod and pointed it at the Berserker's head. He closed his eyes and spoke in the language of magic. With a word, a green beam of energy shot out from the rod and enveloped the body, which twitched like a man beset by an attack of palsy. Blood leaked from the dead Berserker's eyes, mouth, and ears, as the corpse contorted and thrashed so violently that the manacles that had bound the man's limbs shattered into sparkling ice shards.

The wizard kept the beam focused on the Berserker, even as the demands of the magic forced him to his knees. He was out of breath, and his hands burned as if awash in fire, but he continued to pour the necrotic energy into the Berserker's twitching body. Dementhus ended the spell only after he was sure of his magic.

"Abbaster," commanded the drained Necromancer, "help me to my feet."

A large, rough hand lifted the wizard. Once on his feet, Dementhus brushed the brute's arm aside. The Berserker's skin had turned an unnatural shade of gray, his eyes were open but unfocused. Satisfied, Dementhus removed the velvet glove from his right hand. He then placed his bare palm on the undead's forehead. He closed his eyes and spoke another phrase in the language of magic. *The corpse is now bound to me.*

Dementhus climbed to his feet and spoke to the newly born man. "From which clan do you hail from?"

"Ragnar," moaned the undead, the voice a faint shadow of its former strength.

"Where is your village?"

A bloated tongue licked bloody lips as the sepulchral voice answered. "Past the frozen river, to the east, in the deep valley of the Coronas, beneath a mountain crowned with two peaks."

At the revelation, Abbaster gasped, and Gidran fell to his knees, uttering words of praise to Terminus.

"Quickly, Abbaster," ordered the wizard. "Fetch my backpack."

The desert warrior unslung the backpack and dropped it at Dementhus's feet. The wizard opened the bag and pulled out two vials. One he downed now, the second he pocketed in his robes. With both hands now free of pain, he grasped the undead Berserker's skull.

Energy erupted from his fingertips as Dementhus forced his mind into the rapidly decaying brain of the undead. He struggled to resurrect the barbarian's quickly fading memories. He saw the barbarian hunter's last moments as if through a fog: the struggle with the walrus and the unexpected attack by Abbaster. Probing further back, he saw the journey the man had taken from his village. Earlier still, he saw the man emerging from a small hut that was shaded by a mountain. When the barbarian had turned to leave his village, the mountain that shadowed the valley came into full view: It was the twin-peaked mountain of Dementhus's vision.

Exhausted but filled with euphoria, the Necromancer released his grasp.

Eager ears awaited to hear what he had seen. Before speaking to his cohorts, Dementhus gathered his thoughts. "Our prayers to Terminus have been answered. We have found the mountain, for I have seen it!"

Gidran again fell to his knees and praised the Dark God, while Abbaster, with a satisfied grin spread across his face, hacked the animated corpse into pieces after Dementhus ordered the man to be sent to the Abyss.

When Abbaster grew frustrated that the severed body parts still wriggled on the gore-smeared ground, Dementhus laughed. "Only fire can kill the undead." The Necromancer spoke words of magic, and fire danced on Abbaster's blades. "Take this fire to the corpse. Tonight we shall feast on the flesh of the walrus. Eat heartily, for tomorrow we follow the river deep into the Coronas and to our destiny."

After the feast, Dementhus downed another potion and then fell into a deep sleep. For the first time in many nights, the pain in his extremities did not cause him discomfort. The visions granted to him by Bafomeht played in his slumbering mind along with new insight into what awaited. He imagined himself before the twin-peaked mountain, understanding that within its depths was the fortress of Antigenesus. He then saw himself inside the mountain, digging through crumbling tunnels in search of glittering artifacts. As he stumbled through the ruins, he emerged inside the dark confines of an ancient laboratory, the birthplace of the mighty Golem—the ancient archmagus's attempt to create life. More than an unstoppable weapon was to be found in the fortress. Perhaps buried in the darkness was a path to immortality.

When the sky showed a sliver of red above the mountains along the eastern horizon, they awoke.

"I feel this will be the last night we sleep on the frozen ground," shared Dementhus. "Soon we shall enter the dominion of these Ragnar clan barbarians, where we shall ingratiate ourselves with their leaders. We need their help to do what it is we must do. They are a warrior people and dislike outsiders, but they do respect power. Of this Berserker hunter, we shall not speak again."

The wizard sat by the smoldering embers and read from his spell book. He turned the book to the pages where he had fastidiously copied the spell he had discovered in Myramar's tower. The Necromancer closed the spell book, confident he had mastered the complex spell.

After breakfast, Dementhus prepared his two companions for what was to come.

"Gidran, keep your spirit attuned to Terminus and beseech Him for guidance. Seek His minions, who lie in deep crevasses between the roots of these mountains. We may be in need of their assistance."

Gidran nodded his head, and his stringy hair obscured his face. "My ear is filling with the whispered words of the Daemons in this area. In time, I should be able to hear them more clearly."

Dementhus detected a change in Gidran's demeanor since their encounter with the Berserker hunter. *Is it possible the shaman's doubts about me have evaporated?*

The Necromancer then addressed Abbaster. "Keep your keen eyes open for any sign of the natives who make this forsaken land their home. Your blades will have a part to play in Terminus's quest."

"Yes, Master Dementhus," assured the brute. "You need not worry."

Guided by the memories stolen from the dead barbarian hunter, the party followed the frozen river deep into the mountains. The sky was cobalt blue, and the sun was directly overhead when the group stopped to rest. Dementhus studied his spell book as Abbaster scouted ahead.

The brute returned with a grim face. "I heard something," he warned, his twin scimitars in his hands. "A sound coming from the north, over that ridge."

Dementhus strained to listen, but he could not hear a thing. He signaled Abbaster to lead the way forward. The brute obliged and hiked up the rocky incline above the river valley. Not long after, Dementhus heard the noise Abbaster had reported. It was the sound of a crowd of cheering men echoing off the sides of the mountains.

When they reached the lip of the ridge, they looked down the other side. The sight that Dementhus beheld both shocked and excited him. He blinked to make sure the harsh sunlight was not deceiving him. Across the valley was a massive amphitheater, the seating carved into the base of a mountain. The mountain itself stretched far into the sky, and when the wind blew the misty clouds aside, it revealed a snow-covered, twin-peaked cap. The Necromancer's legs gave out, exhaustion overwhelming his ailing body.

He closed his eyes, then reopened them. He stood with the aid of his staff. He looked down into the valley. On closer inspection, he spied rows upon rows of animal-skin-clad Berserkers of the Ragnar clan roaring from the icy seats of the amphitheater. Before the Ragnar, on a bloodstained stage, two men engaged in mortal combat around a peculiar-shaped altar. The crowd cheered at each thrust of a broadsword and stamped their feet at the sight of freshly spilt blood.

The men of Terminus watched with fascination as the combatants hacked at each other with the ferocity seen only in primitive men. Eventually, one weakened, and the other pressed his attack. The victor ended the combat with an explosion of violence, which saw his opponent's vitals ripped from his body and exposed to the air. The crowd roared in bloody appreciation.

Dementhus grabbed hold of Abbaster's broad shoulders and spun the warrior around. "This is not the end of our journey. It is a new beginning. I do not know what role these Ragnar will play in our future, but I know we need them to aid in our cause. For you, brave warrior born and bred in the sands of Lux, I have a special task."

Chapter 15
The Gigantic Hand

As he listened to Dementhus's plan, Abbaster sharpened his blades. If he had not witnessed the power of the Necromancer, he would have thought the man mad as he explained his audacious scheme.

With a gleaming scimitar in each hand, Abbaster did not waste time contemplating the risks of what he was asked to do, nor did he calculate the odds of its success. The head-shaved warrior raced down the snow-covered slope toward the open-air amphitheater, running as fast as his legs could take him.

Upon his approach, some Ragnar stood from their seats and made for the intruder, but not in time to stop him. When he reached the bloody dais unmolested, he turned to face the crowd, raising his weapons over his head. "I challenge your champion! I challenge your champion!"

The crowd reacted predictably, throwing all manner of insults and objects in Abbaster's direction. Abbaster howled in laughter as he basked in the hate from the crowd. One man made to challenge him, then another, and soon a wave of Ragnar, murder in their eyes, flowed down the ice-carved steps toward the dais. He was only moments away from drowning in a sea of swords, axes, and spears. Abbaster had no fear. *Terminus will protect me.*

Before the first blow was struck, a figure parted the crowd. The man's long hair and beard were gray, but his body was well muscled. He had the bearing of a king in any culture. "Silence!" he called out. "If this outsider wants to have his blood spilled before our God, then so be it! Halldor, you are the champion. Give this man the death he wishes."

Halldor, the man Abbaster had seen win the duel just moments earlier, cleaned the gore from his broadsword and grinned. "It will be my pleasure to crush this foreigner's skull."

"And it will be my pleasure," returned Abbaster, "to see what you barbarians look like on the inside."

The Ragnar king ordered his people back to their seats, then stepped between the two combatants and pushed them apart. "Go to opposite ends of the dais." To Abbaster he explained, "When I strike the altar with my broadsword, the combat begins. This is a fight to the death. There are no other rules."

Abbaster and Halldor exchanged threatening glances before moving apart. The king then struck the altar, a monstrous black metallic hand fashioned to appear as if reaching up from the ice. The resulting clang echoed up and out over the amphitheater. As the fight began, the crowd erupted in bloodthirsty howls.

Abbaster sized up the champion: Halldor was his equal in height, but where Abbaster was broad in shoulders and chest, the Ragnar was more thickly thewed in arms and legs. Abbaster would have to respect his opponent's brute power. In his own favor, he doubted the Ragnar had encountered a fighter trained in Eastern sword-fighting techniques.

When the echo of the struck altar faded into the sound of the crowd's howls, the two combatants circled each other, the Ragnar champion with a crude broadsword, Abbaster with twin scimitars. The impatient crowd raged and jeered for the combatants to engage.

Abbaster laughed with each new insult hurled his way; the champion lost his patience, however, perhaps embarrassed that it seemed he feared to make the first move. Halldor rushed Abbaster and attacked with a strike straight to the head. Abbaster blocked the swing with his two scimitars, trapping the heavy broadsword between the blades. The Ragnar swore in anger, and only with his barbarian strength was he able to rip his own blade free.

More insults and threats rained down from the furious crowd at Halldor over his failed attack. Ragnar rage took hold of the champion as he pulled back his broadsword and took aim at Abbaster's head again, this time with a deceptively quick sidearm slash. Abbaster deftly ducked the strike and slashed the Ragnar's overextended leg. Blood trickled out of the wound, along with curses from the champion's mouth.

The fight then began in earnest. While the Ragnar raged and went for killing blows, Abbaster, using his dual wielding skill to great advantage, preferred to bleed the man with slashes.

THE TOMB OF THERAGAARD

Abbaster feigned with one scimitar to engage the Ragnar's broadsword, while with the other he slashed his opponent's forehead, causing blood to flow over the champion's eyes. Halldor was tiring. He had already battled one man to the death, and the multiple slashes to his flesh had drained his body of blood and vigor. Abbaster sensed that it was time to finish his opponent. He took a glance at the hostile crowd and the rows of angry Ragnar who stretched far up the side of the frost-shrouded twin-peaked mountain.

"You want blood? You shall have it!" shouted Abbaster as he played to the crowd. He was now the aggressor. He savaged the barbarian with lightning-strike slashes. Chunks of flesh and bursts of blood shredded off the barbarian.

The proud champion would not give up his ground.

"Do you yield?" teased Abbaster.

"I shall never yield. Not to the likes of you!"

The champion leapt at Abbaster, who stepped back and let the man fall to his knees. Abbaster roared to the heavens and, swinging his twin blades in unison, scissored the Ragnar's head clean off. The body fell forward as blood fountained from the champion's ruined neck.

"A gift for your god!" mocked Abbaster as he grabbed the head and placed it upon the blood-stained altar.

The crowd, which had been frothing with rage, now looked down upon Abbaster in stunned silence. The brute's only fear was that he had killed his opponent too quickly.

Abbaster took his eyes off the crowd to quickly glance toward the slope. During the combat, his two companions had made their way near the edge of the bloody stage but had made no attempt to reveal themselves. Before Abbaster could decide what to do next, the warrior king stepped up to the altar and shouted to the masses.

"For the first time, an outsider has defeated our champion. As is my right as head of this clan, I challenge this foreigner myself!"

This was not part of Dementhus's plan.

"You would challenge me?" stalled Abbaster as he contemplated what would happen if he had to kill the Ragnar chief. "Surely, there is another with fewer gray hairs and sharper steel to return my challenge."

"Outsider, I am Ivor, the jarl of the Ragnar. I have slain many challengers and plan to slay many more before the Mountain God takes me. Who are you to defy me?"

"I shall not defy you, Jarl. I accept your challenge. But know who I am. I am Abbaster, from the far deserts of Lux. I have traveled the ends of Medias to find this land, guided by my leader Dementhus, and following the will of our God. We were led here to help your people."

The jarl laughed, and the mirthless sound echoed to the ends of the amphitheater. "No desert man nor desert god can help us. Enough of this banter."

The Ragnar king drew his broadsword.

✠ ✠ ✠

Dementhus had watched Abbaster's duel with Halldor with satisfaction. The brute had bested the Ragnar champion and had done so in a manner that had to have impressed the primitives. The barbarians of the north respected power and those who wielded it. However, he could not allow Abbaster to kill their leader. Their respect for power had limitations.

From his position at the edge of the dais, and over the noise of the crowd, he shouted to Abbaster in the mother tongue of Lux, "Do not kill the jarl! Fight him, but do so honorably. I need to inspect the altar."

The crowd of bloodthirsty Ragnar in the amphitheater were standing; most had weapons drawn, and many now pointed accusatory fingers at Dementhus. It was obvious the crowd did not want a foreigner interfering in the duel to the death, but the Necromancer felt that as long as he kept his distance from the combatants, he would be safe.

Abbaster deftly circled behind the jarl, luring his opponent away from the altar. Ivor wielded a two-handed sword, his only armor thick bear-pelt hides. With a sudden move forward, the jarl closed the distance and got inside Abbaster's guard, knocking a scimitar from his hand and launching a near-fatal strike at his exposed head.

Though Dementhus was shocked by Abbaster's initial failure, his faith in the brute was soon restored when he saw the swarthy man twist away, kick the jarl in the chest, and substitute a long dagger for the missing scimitar. Both men stepped back and circled again, Abbaster leading Ivor to the front of the bloody stage.

With the crowd's attention back on the combat, Dementhus stepped up to the stage and advanced toward the altar, which held the severed head of the former champion. The light of the sun did not reflect off its black metallic surface but rather was absorbed into it. The altar's shape, that of a grasping hand, was precisely carved, as if by a master artisan—with the lines of the palm, and even the fingerprints, clearly visible. Dementhus was certain that no primitives could have been involved in its creation. He did not need to cast a spell to determine if the altar was magical, for he could feel ripples of energy flowing out of the black object.

Dementhus paused and nearly stumbled. He was brought back to his time with Bafomeht and the vision he had had of the behemoth metal hand reaching out from the ice. He was incredulous at what he was seeing and needed to voice his discovery. "Gidran, take a look at the altar! This is what we have been seeking! This is the hand of the Golem!"

Gidran, who had sought to keep hidden by crouching behind the bloodstained stage, peered above the lip of the dais. Tears formed in the shaman's eyes as the black metal hand filled his pupils. Overwhelmed by the fulfilment of Bafomeht's quest, Gidran fell to his knees. "Praise be to Terminus. Praise be to Bafomeht! Praise be to Dementhus!"

The butt end of a hurled dagger glanced off Dementhus's bald pate, and the Necromancer was rudely brought back to his present, precarious situation. He looked up to see a mass of armed Ragnar approaching, some hurling various objects, murderous intentions clear on their faces.

"Wait!" he implored as he approached the crowd.

Gidran, who was now closest to the horde, was thrown to the ground as a dozen hands grabbed him.

"We are here as messengers from your Mountain God!" pleaded Dementhus, but the axes and swords only came closer. "Let me prove what I say!" he insisted as the horde's angry eyes were turned to him.

The Necromancer pulled out his rod and pointed it at the altar. With a single command, a beam of red light shot from the gem and into the gigantic grasping hand. The ground rumbled and shook. When the altar glowed crimson, cries of fear and superstitious awe replaced those of anger. Gidran scrambled to Dementhus's side.

The two combatants, Abbaster and the jarl, however, had kept up the furious pace of their combat. Dementhus stopped the flow of energy into the altar and yelled to the two men fighting. "Jarl, end your battle! We are not your enemies! We have come as messengers from the Mountain God!"

Abbaster sheathed his weapons. "What my companion says is true. I challenged your champion to show you I was a skilled warrior willing to risk my life in honorable combat. Take a look at the altar! See for yourself. Or now skewer me, who am unarmed, on your broadsword. It is up to you."

Abbaster's words and deeds impressed Dementhus, who had thought the brute incapable of such a pragmatic solution. It must have been the same for the barbarian king, who now slowly backed away and lowered his weapon. The jarl then glanced warily at the altar.

The ground stopped shaking when Dementhus lowered his rod. The crowd went silent. "Listen to what I have to say." The Necromancer's voice echoed throughout the now eerily still amphitheater as he spoke with the flourish of an actor on a stage. "Trust what you have just seen. I have traveled very far to reach this land. The Mountain God sent me here to bring the Ragnar clan great power!"

The sound of the jarl's heavy-booted steps likewise echoed up the amphitheater as the Ragnar king drew closer to the altar and Dementhus. His face was impassive when he spoke for the Ragnar clan. "We may be a warrior race, but we do not succumb so easily to a sorcerer's trickery. A bright light and a shaking of the ground will win no battles. *How* are you going to bring us power? You had better offer greater proof and do it quickly." The jarl pointed his broadsword in the wizard's direction.

"I can prove I am no trickster, for I can unleash the power of the Mountain God. Power that has been trapped for centuries!"

To summon more energy, Dementhus focused his mind to the astral plane. When he looked to the altar from his perspective of the realm of magic, he was almost blinded by the energy the exposed hand exuded. It was unclear how the ancient artifact worked, but he had enough of an idea to make an impressive demonstration. Pointing at the hand, Dementhus commanded, "Destroy!" As he did so, he subtly applied magic to the artificial nerves he could see with his magic sight. In response, the hand flexed and crushed the severed head of Halldor, which Abbaster had placed in its grasp.

The crowd ended their awe-induced silence with roars of delight at the violent display.

"Now behold what has long been hidden from you. Here resides the God of the Mountain!"

Using his remaining strength, Dementhus stabbed the ground with his rod, releasing the last bit of magic it stored.

THE TOMB OF THERAGAARD

From the frozen ground below, a black form outlined in red took shape: the form of a fifty-foot warrior, in the style of the Ancients, one arm by its side, the other reaching through the ice.

The crowd of Ragnar froze in wonder at what Dementhus had revealed. Even the jarl, Dementhus observed, took a physical step back.

The Necromancer feigned reverence to this God, hiding his true thoughts. *The Ragnar will soon be mine to command.*

Chapter 16

A Blow to Tryam's Plans

Since coming to the abbey as a child, Tryam had run many errands to the keep in Arkos. Even so, he now looked at the fortress with new eyes, as he walked under its rear gate, carrying a message from Father Monbatten to the knights' commander, Lord Dunford.

As he gazed upon the two flanking towers and the knights standing guard, he pictured himself up there, as one of them, keeping vigilant eyes toward the rough waters of the harbor and the world beyond.

After flashing Father Monbatten's seal to the watchman, Tryam was waved through the gate. The acolyte passed the stables, the smithy, and through another gate, which led to the inner courtyard. He watched with envy a company of knights on horseback as they galloped past, likely on their way to patrol the foothills of the Coronas.

Tryam proceeded to the grass-covered grounds of the inner bailey. In other visits to the keep, he had seen knights gathered on the proving grounds as they drilled and sparred. He had looked upon them with novice eyes. Now when he spotted two men dueling, he recognized the moves and countermoves being employed.

Perhaps Father Monbatten's letter can wait a little while longer.

Tryam tucked the missive into a deep pocket and walked over to a cordoned-off area, where the two knights dueled with blunted wooden swords. A handful of other knights sat on low benches just outside the area, cajoling their fellow brothers-in-arms as they awaited their turn to spar.

THE TOMB OF THERAGAARD

In the arena, the dueling knights ignored the taunts, and their wooden swords slapped against thick leather jerkins. The combatants did not seem to take the sparring too seriously, as fits of laughter and exchanges of insults frequently interrupted the fight. Tryam was so intrigued by the fighting, however, he did not notice that he was shadowing the moves the fighters were using until one of the knights on the bench called attention to him.

A mocking voice erupted: "Hey look, we have a fighting monk here. All he is missing is a suit of armor."

The others laughed.

Tryam's face flushed. He waited until the laughter stopped before speaking, and when he did, he surprised even himself: "I am entering the tournament to become a knight," he admitted, "and I was observing how you spar. I am not impressed."

The mocking knight, a young man in his twenties with bright red hair, got up from the bench, spat upon the ground, and bounded toward him. Closing within a few inches, the knight poked Tryam in the chest. "Not impressed, are you? Want to have a go with me when the lads are finished? Pick up a sword, or do you have to run home to empty the abbot's chamber pot?"

The other knights gathered to restrain the hotheaded young man. A weasel-faced youth spoke up from the crowd: "Roderick, take it easy on him. Who knows what Dunford will do to you for beating the tar out of a monk?"

One of the other knights chimed in with more caution. "If you break one of his bones, Lord Dunford will make you beg for forgiveness from their abbot personally! That man is meaner than the ugliest Berserker."

"Bah," chimed in a third. "There will be no combat. Monks of Saint Paxia are all daft. Don't you listen to their sermons when they speak in our chapel? They make me sick! They wouldn't lift a gauntlet to save a maiden's virtue."

Their mockery and lack of discipline stunned Tryam. He swallowed his disgust, turned his back to the knight, and removed his outer white robe, revealing his well-muscled chest. When he turned back, there was a look of astonishment upon the other knights' faces. Wulfric's training had transformed him from a bookish acolyte to a powerful young man.

As the sneer on Roderick's face was replaced by an open-mouthed gape, Tryam couldn't resist a smile. To the crowd, the young acolyte said, "I accept the challenge."

107

The gathered knights erupted in spontaneous cheering. One of them ordered the sparring knights to yield the training grounds to Roderick and Tryam. The weary fighters eagerly obliged, and one of them even graciously offered his leather jerkin to Tryam, while the other helped the young acolyte put it on.

Roderick, already in his sparring attire, waited inside the enclosure and smirked when Tryam entered to stand before him. The young acolyte recalled Wulfric's advice and sized up his opponent as best he could. The red-haired knight was shorter but still more than six feet tall, and slim. Tryam was confident he was stronger than the knight, but his opponent was likely more skilled with the blade. The most important thing he observed was the overconfident and dismissive attitude the knight displayed toward him. He did not regard Tryam as a threat.

Roderick snarled, then snatched a rawhide-covered shield and one of the wooden swords from a rack near the bailey's wall. Tryam did likewise and struck a fighting stance a few feet away.

"What are the rules?" inquired Tryam. "I have sparred only with a friend, never with a true knight."

"Try not to get yourself killed," joked Roderick.

The knights on the bench laughed at the lame retort before one of them called for silence and explained the rules in more detail. "My name is Jarrard, and I am the sergeant in charge of these men. The rules are simple: Both combatants must remain within the enclosure. If you are knocked out of the arena, you are disqualified. No kicking, biting, or other barroom tactics. Combat continues until either one of the two combatants yields or surrenders what would have been a killing blow if a real blade had been used. If no kill shots occur after a quarter of an hour, I shall judge the winner based on the number and the quality of blows landed. Combat will begin on my mark."

With his body overwhelmed by excitement, Tryam nodded but wasn't sure he heard everything the older knight had said. He knew, however, that he would never yield to the smirking youth. When the sergeant gave the command to start, Tryam nearly dropped his sword because of his overeagerness. Luckily, Roderick did not rush to attack as Tryam had expected. Tryam wanted to test his assumption that Roderick was skilled with the blade, so he took a quick poke at the redheaded youth's torso. Roderick slipped away adroitly and countered with a thrust to Tryam's ribs.

The blow landed solidly but lacked strength behind it. It did, however, draw delight from the seated knights.

After the initial melee, Tryam took on a more defensive posture, keeping his shield tucked to his chest, and waited for Roderick to make his move. Roderick used his speed to land numerous light blows to Tryam's shoulders and legs. The crowd laughed at Tryam, taunting him with derogatory comments.

"Do you yield yet?" mocked Roderick.

Tryam responded with a quick slash, this time aiming for his opponent's legs. But once again, the young knight sidestepped the wooden sword and replied with a vicious swing aimed at Tryam's head. A raised shield saved Tryam from what could have been a knockout blow. *Patience. I need to be patient!*

Roderick's overconfidence manifested itself in his next assault. The knight's blows were all broad, exaggerated strikes aimed at Tryam's head. In the process, Roderick was neglecting his defenses and, to impress his companions, passing up safer strategies.

Tryam saw his opening.

When Roderick lined up his next overhead swing, Tryam saw the move coming and was able to duck beneath the blow. Roderick lazily tried to recover from the miss and carelessly held his shield low and down at his side. The acolyte took a deep breath, reared his wooden sword back, and then, with all his strength, aimed a blow for the young knight's head. Roderick turned in time to see the sword and lifted his shield to block, but he was too slow.

The strike, carrying the full force of Tryam's considerable strength, caught the top of the knight's shield, smashed through the rawhide and oak, and with a solid thud, struck the side of Roderick's head. The shield's exploding remains flew high into the air as the young knight fell to the ground with the grace of a collapsing tower.

All taunts from the knights ceased. Jarrard rushed into the sparring grounds and interposed himself between Tryam and the fallen knight. The sergeant, who looked shaken, inspected the still body of Roderick and quickly declared the obvious: "Combat has ended."

Tryam looked at his sword and then down on the destruction he had caused. He took no joy in what he had done.

The other knights rushed inside the enclosure and formed a circle around Roderick. Tryam felt his body going numb. "I did not mean to injure him so. Please stand aside, and let me help him. We are taught the ways of healing in the abbey."

The young acolyte grabbed a flask of water from one knight, knelt before Roderick, and examined the head wound. There was a large bump and a significant flow of blood oozing down the knight's face.

Tryam poured water on the wound and pressed a makeshift bandage against it. The acolyte then said a prayer of healing to Aten. Whether it was the prayer or his bandage, the blood flow slowed.

Roderick's eyes fluttered open.

"Such vicious blows are reserved for the enemy, not for your sparring partner," scolded Jarrard as he helped Roderick to his wobbly legs. "It is fortunate Rod has a hard head."

Before Tryam could apologize and explain his actions—or mention that Roderick had likewise taken powerful swings at Tryam's head—a booming voice stopped everyone where they stood.

"What's happening here?"

Tryam recognized the voice and the barrel chest from which it bellowed as belonging to the commander of Arkos, Lord Dunford. His expression was hard to see, his face half hidden beneath a thick blond and reddish beard, but it was obvious the man was angry.

The commander stepped onto the proving grounds, and the knights fell into formation, except for Roderick, who slumped down back into the mud.

Dressed in golden armor with a fur-lined velvet cloak about his shoulders, the commander shook his head as he looked upon the prone Roderick. "Why is one of my knights wallowing in the mud?"

When silence followed his question, the commander's face contorted in exasperation. "Jarrard! You are in charge of these men! I see a barely conscious knight and a boy, a monk, wearing a leather jerkin, with a practice sword by his feet."

Jarrard stepped forward and saluted. "Commander, sir. I can explain. Roderick and the monk ... uh ... they were sparring, you see. The monk was the winner."

"I can see that!" blasted Dunford. The commander's eyes fell to Tryam and locked on him as a hunter does its prey. "Assaulting a knight of the realm is against the law."

"I know, sir, but it was an accident! I was here to deliver you a message from Father Monbatten." Tryam removed the crinkled parchment from his pocket as proof. "I was headed to the great hall when I saw two of your warriors sparring. I was curious to watch them. Roderick saw how interested I was in the combat and challenged me to spar."

Lord Dunford snatched the missive from his hand. "Whoever taught you to spar must not have told you to save the real blows for combat." Dunford folded the letter and tucked it into his belt. He then pointed to the prone form of Roderick. "Jarrard, get him out of my sight and to the infirmary."

Jarrard saluted. "Yes, sir!"

"You are all dismissed," growled Dunford.

Jarrard lifted Roderick to his feet, and the knights fell into line and headed back to the barracks.

Tryam started for the exit.

"Not you, son. I am taking you to jail. An example must be made of those who cause harm to one of my knights." Dunford locked eyes with Tryam. "I find it hard to believe you did so in a fair and upright manner."

Tryam stuttered, "It was a fair but hard blow. I meant no harm. Please let me go back to the abbey!"

With a wave of his hand, Dunford silenced the young acolyte and grabbed him by the back of the neck. As the commander led him toward the dungeon, Tryam's head spun. *I shall never get free in time for the tournament, and I can't even imagine what Father Monbatten will do when he finds out.*

Tryam prayed as the wide-open future he dreamt of collapsed into a small, dark cell.

✣ ✣ ✣

A plain wooden bench, a foul-smelling bucket, and the occasional curious rat were the only other things inside the cold, windowless cell. Three walls were solid stone, and the cell door was made from thick iron bars. Based on the schedule of meals, Tryam had calculated he had spent two and a half days in prison, which meant that the tournament would be in just three days. His body ached, and his spirits were low. Other than brief interactions with gruff-looking jailers, he had plenty of time to be alone with his thoughts. He paced the small room. *Is this a sign from Aten that I should not enter the tournament, or is it only an obstacle I need to overcome as a test of my resolve?*

It was after his evening meal of stale bread and watery stew that he heard multiple people descending the dungeon's steps. From the gloom, he heard a voice just outside the range of the jailer's torchlight. "So, there you are."

It was Father Monbatten.

Tryam rose to his feet and walked up to the iron bars. Father Monbatten's face was already scowling. "Yes, Father. I can explain what happened!"

"I already talked to Lord Dunford. He told me what happened. I don't have time for your excuses. The commander wanted you to stay here for a month, but I don't see you learning anything by lingering near sword-wielding brigands. Guard, please, release him."

The jailer unlocked the door, and Tryam rushed out of the cell and grasped the abbot's hands in gratitude.

Under the glare of the torchlight, the abbot looked him over and shook his head. "If you think your punishment is over, you are wrong. Once we return to the abbey, you will spend the next two months locked in your cell, copying the words of Saint Paxia."

"Can't we postpone this punishment?"

"No! And do you think me a fool? You will not participate in that spectacle of violence. It is out of the question!"

Tryam felt all hope leave his body.

He had no defense for his actions, and like a beaten-down dog, he followed Monbatten out of the gloomy dungeon into the gloomier world.

Chapter 17
An Unwelcome Discovery

Myramar's increasingly hostile and erratic behavior overshadowed the mystery of the creature Telvar had encountered in the astral plane. After the disastrous fire test, the apprentice observed the tower mage going days without sleep, eating rarely and always alone, and spending the majority of his time in the subterranean laboratory of the tower, an area Myramar had claimed upon Telvar's arrival as having been unused for years. Telvar could not fathom the reason for such puzzling behavior and concluded that, at the moment, Myramar was not fit to be his master.

Perhaps if age has robbed him of his senses, I should challenge him for control of the tower! I have far more skill than any novice Rutilus wizard and can learn faster on my own than I can with his crooked nose perched over my shoulder. At the very least, I need access to his research materials in the magic library.

Telvar decided it was time to act and headed down the steps to the underground laboratory. The passageway was dark. For unknown reasons, Myramar had removed the torches, and only an eerie green light, leaking out from under the laboratory door, gave off any illumination. The young wizard approached the door with some trepidation, and the noise of his leather boots scuffing on the stone floor sounded as loud as thunder in his ears.

Noxious fumes seeped from under the door. He sniffed deeply and recognized some of the odors as sulfur and wormwood, but he could not identify some of the more exotic scents. The young wizard pressed his ear to the door and heard Myramar's booted feet as they paced about the room. Satisfied the old wizard was preoccupied, Telvar returned upstairs and continued up to the second floor and to the red door of the tower's magic library.

In his growing paranoia, Myramar had now kept the magic library locked at all times. Telvar examined the door and its lock for any hint as to the magic used. The door was of stout oak, overlaid with a red copper alloy commonly used by wizards because of its ability to be magically imbued. There was neither a handle nor a keyhole. Instead, the door was covered with runes etched into the copper. The runes either determined the method of entry or would activate a trap if triggered.

Observant to all things related to magic, Telvar had spied Myramar, on multiple occasions, unlocking the door. There were two elements to the spell: a spoken phrase and a hand gesture. The phrase he was sure of: *Sit pruína liquefaciet.* That was easy to catch. He had not been able to see the hand gesture, however, because Myramar always faced the door. Short of asking the old wizard, there was only one way to know the gesture: Connect to the astral plane and see if he could decipher the runes. If it was too complex, he would have no chance, but he was confident he could outwit Myramar.

Telvar hesitated before he connected to the astral plane. *What if I see the creature again?* He refused to believe that what he saw was a product of his imagination, but he was still not sure what it was. *Had it been an illusion cast by Myramar? It must have been.* His confidence trumped caution, and he prepared himself to enter the astral plane once more.

The young wizard held his gem-tipped metal staff in his right hand. If needed, he could draw magic from the staff directly into his body. He closed his mind to the material plane and focused his entire being to that strange, energy-filled void left by Aten when He'd created the universe. After a flash of uncertainty, Telvar found the connection. The thrill of the magic emboldened him, and he held onto the connection. When he looked about the astral plane, there was naught but the endless sea of magic.

Sighing at his foolishness for worrying so much about that creature he'd seen in the fire, Telvar focused on the magical links from the astral plane to the door. When he opened his eyes on the material plane and examined the result, an energy signature revealed the location and design of the lock. As he examined the lock more closely and determined that it was protected by a lethal fire spell, he was alarmed. *The old mage is more ruthless than I thought.*

THE TOMB OF THERAGAARD

To boost the clarity of the runes, Telvar discharged energy from his staff into the lock spell. He was now comfortable enough to break down the spell and see its components. The trap trigger, the phrase, and the hand gesture all revealed themselves to him as formulas written in magic. He did the mental calculations to solve the runes' complex formulas and was satisfied that he had done so correctly. He terminated the connection.

The young wizard stood back and cleared his mind of all thoughts but the spell. If he wanted to unlock the door, he would have to put the distinct pieces of the lock spell together flawlessly.

"Myramar, prepare for your new challenger," boasted Telvar. He began with the magic phrase, *"Sit pruína liquefaciet."*

An area in the center of the door glowed an ominous deep-red color.

Telvar calmly imitated the hand gesture he had deciphered from the formulas, and the glowing stopped. *Take that, master!*

Sweat poured down the young wizard's face. *I said the phrase and did the gesture. Now to see if the door is unlocked.* Telvar pushed on the door with his staff, and it opened inward. Crossing the library's threshold, he let out a sigh of relief. *Another milestone passed.*

As he surveyed the stacks of books, another thought quickly overwhelmed him: *Where do I begin?*

Myramar had set up a small alcove with bookshelves to hold his personal collection of scrolls and a desk where he could read and study them. Before Telvar looked for a spell to study, he glanced at the parchments left behind on his master's desk. It was the old wizard's research into the strange gem that the Albus wizard had gifted him. Telvar eagerly read over Myramar's notes. The old wizard's summaries detailed a variety of tests he had used to determine the gem's properties.

Myramar had started by focusing beams of varying intensity through the gem to see how the light was refracted. Shockingly, he reported, the gem absorbed the light. His notes left no answer as to the cause.

Myramar had also tested the density of the gem by weighing it and then by measuring the volume of water it displaced in a beaker. The gem proved to be higher in density than any naturally occurring gemstone, even denser than lead. He wrote that it was almost as if something invisible were trapped inside the gem, augmenting its weight.

The final test had involved heating and cooling the jewel. Despite his having placed the bauble under an open flame worthy of that of

115

a blacksmith's kiln, when Myramar had removed it, he reported that the gem was unchanged. The same result happened when he had tried to freeze the gem with a spell known to be cold enough to shatter diamonds. The amulet appeared to be resistant to any form of energy input.

No physical or magical tests Myramar had performed changed the amulet's form. His startling conclusion was that the gem was something he called an *Anima Crystallum*.

Telvar searched his personal knowledge for the term but could not come up with anything. He sought out a book in the library that contained a list of obscure magical items, and his heart pounded when he read the definition: An Anima Crystallum was an artificial crystal, forged by great magic, used to trap a being from another plane of existence. A wizard of old might summon a creature from another realm, another world, and then entrap the creature inside such a gem. The wizard would then draw upon the trapped being's otherworldly power for his own use. Unfortunately, the transfer went both ways. If the wizard was too weak, he would unknowingly surrender his own essence into the being trapped in the gemstone.

If this were such a crystal, Myramar could be at the mercy of whatever creature was trapped inside the Anima Crystallum! A coldness came over Telvar, as he realized that he would neither be studying spells nor challenging for control of the tower anytime soon.

Chapter 18
The Last Normal Morning

Tryam brooded on his fate as he copied the psalms of Saint Paxia. He could now recite the scripture as if he had written the words himself. Despite the pacifistic teachings espoused by the former warrior who had found another path, all the young acolyte could think about was the tournament that was set to begin in a couple of hours. Today would be the longest day of his confinement. After many hours, his hand cramped, ultimately forcing him to put the stylus down and rest ever so briefly.

It would be just my luck for Father Monbatten to come in and see me resting!

After massaging the pain from his hand, he once again put ink to parchment, and he started on another copy of the scripture. When he was nearly done with the first line, a gentle tapping on the wooden shutter of his second-story cell caused him to pause. *What in the Abyss?*

Tryam returned his stylus back to the inkwell, and he stared curiously at the shuttered window. The tapping sounded again, very softly. He reasoned it had to be a bird. *But haven't most birds gone to their winter homes?*

The third time he heard the tapping, he was less sure what it could be, because it now sounded more insistent and suspiciously like someone knocking. As Tryam thought back to what had happened down in the vault, his heart pounded. He fought against his emotions. *Never again shall I run in panic!*

The young acolyte straightened his back and clenched his jaw. He rose from his chair, and with no thought to his fears, he rushed to the window and flung open the shutters.

A scream filled Tryam's ears, and a blur of golden hair flashed before his eyes. Tryam reflexively grabbed the falling object. He ended up halfway out the window, struggling to keep his balance with a squirming weight in his hands. It took a moment to realize he held Kara's wrist. "Kara!" he said incredulously.

Below the window dangled Kara, looking up at him with her blue eyes sparkling in the predawn light. "And I thought *I* wasn't a morning person. Who throws their shutters open like that? Help me up!"

"Sorry, it was an accident. Hold on!" Tryam pulled Kara up and through the narrow window. Exhausted more from fright than from exertion, Tryam collapsed on his bed. "What were you thinking? Why didn't you say something instead of knocking?"

"I wasn't sure if you were awake or not."

Tryam was not sure he understood her logic, but he did not dispute her. He rose from the bed and looked out the window at the abbey grounds below. No one appeared to have noticed the ruckus. "How did you get up here anyway? The window is almost twenty feet off the ground!"

"It was easy. I climbed up the drainpipe and then jumped over to the window ledge. I didn't want any of those gloomy monks seeing me; otherwise, I would have used the front door." She smiled and pointed to the window. "It's not that hard, really. Want me to do it again? I shall show you!"

Kara started for the window. Tryam raced over to block her. "No! That's okay. I believe you. I don't need any more excitement today." He stared at her quizzically. "What are you doing here?"

Kara raised her eyebrows, and her mouth gaped open. "I can't believe you forgot. Today is the tournament! Wulfric wanted to be here, but his father forced him to stay back in the village. I'm here to cheer you on, stupid."

"But you don't understand what happened," said Tryam shamefully, turning away from Kara. "I cannot go."

Kara kicked him in the shins. "Stop your joking. That isn't funny!"

Tryam turned back to face Kara. "I am being serious! I was caught sparring with a knight at the keep and put in the dungeon. Father Monbatten freed me on the condition I stay in my cell."

Laughter erupted from the girl. "When I came into Arkos yesterday, everyone was talking about that in the tavern. You didn't just spar with the knight, you kicked his butt! Everyone wanted to know who the fighting monk of Saint Paxia was. I knew it had to be you, so I told everyone there you were entering the tournament!" She punched Tryam in the shoulder. "Enough talk, we have to hurry!"

Kara pointed to the window, then seized Tryam's arm and dragged him toward it. "Trust me, it's a lot easier climbing down. I shall go first."

Shrugging off her grip, Tryam stepped back. "No, Kara, I can't. I really can't."

"Why not? Are you afraid of heights? Trust me, sneaking out the front would be harder. Monks are morning people. I was almost spotted five times getting here."

"That's not it, Kara." He could not look the Berserker girl in the eyes. "I can't disobey Father Monbatten."

"It seems like you were rather good at disobeying him before. Remember the training we did at night?" She pulled on his arm. "Come on, let's go! You can't get into any worse trouble. Right? We can sneak out and be back before anyone knows you are missing!"

"I suppose you are right. I couldn't get into more trouble." Tryam paused. "Could I?"

Kara looked around the tiny cell and the copies of scripture Tryam had written. "Nope. This room is more boring than any dungeon I've ever heard of."

Tryam agreed with Kara's logic this time, and the realization frightened him. "Okay, you are right. But if I lose, I may have to sweep every square inch of the abbey's floors for the next hundred years."

"You won't lose," assured Kara. She started for the window when the sound of the church bells echoed in the courtyard below. "Are those the bells for morning prayers?"

"Yes, they are."

"That means we have to hurry!"

"Perhaps we are already too late," fretted Tryam. "We might be stopped by a monk on his way to church."

"Nonsense! Watch what I do. Then follow me."

Kara hopped onto the window ledge, leaned as far out as she could, then jumped for a clay drainpipe that ran down the side of the building. She clung to it with the grace of a snow ape. "See, it's easy!" she said, smiling.

"I'm sure," gulped Tryam as he compared the size of his body to that of Kara's and considered the narrowness of the ledge and the sturdiness of the pipe.

"Time is passing," reminded Kara.

The young acolyte steadied his legs before he moved to the window ledge. He was a lot bigger than Kara and a lot less nimble. He watched as Kara shimmied down the pipe, using her legs to control her descent. She landed safely on the ground, then called up words of encouragement.

Tryam grunted as he barely squeezed his shoulders through the narrow window. He turned his body sideways and looked for the drainpipe. It was a good eight feet away. He then looked down at Kara. As if she believed Tryam had forgotten the next step, she used her body to mimic a person jumping. Her face had an unconcerned look on it, and she grinned as if she witnessed this type of thing every day.

Tryam considered the jump. If he missed the pipe, his career as a warrior would be over before it began. The young acolyte closed his eyes and concentrated, visualizing what he had to do. He opened his eyes, took a deep breath, then jumped from a crouching position. As he stretched out, his hands reached for and seized the narrow pipe. As his body collided with the pipe and the building, he grunted, and he swung wildly back and forth. To stabilize himself, he had to use his legs and hold himself close to the wall.

"Now use your arms and legs to slide down," shouted Kara.

Sighing, relieved that the worst part was over, Tryam imitated Kara's method for a gradual descent.

Kara's gasp and the sound of the drainpipe cracking happened almost simultaneously. Tryam knew something was horribly wrong but could do nothing to stop it. He felt himself grow weightless as his view changed from the white wall of the rectory to the gray of the clouds overhead. His ride was over quickly, and he landed flat on his back, covered in the shattered remains of the ancient drainage system. He did not move.

"Don't just lie there! Get going!" Kara dragged Tryam to his feet so quickly the young acolyte did not even have time to check if any of his bones were broken.

After taking a moment to gain his breath, Tryam took in the destruction he had caused. "The pipe!"

The young acolyte rushed to the side of the building and attempted to stick the broken pipe back against the wall. Dirty water from the gutter above now gushed down from the top of the building and was already pooling on the ground.

"Don't worry, no one will notice." Kara grabbed Tryam's arm and started pulling him away. "We have to move!"

The sky was brightening with dawn, but the thick blanket of gray clouds were foreshadowing rain. Kara led the way out of the church grounds and down through the ruins toward the secret subterranean tunnel that connected the abbey to the Arkos harbor.

It had been a while since Tryam had used the secret path to the mainland, but he recognized the entrance hidden inside a ruined building that leaned against a section of the wall girding the lower level of the island. Kara slid open the concealed door, revealing steps leading down. A pungent smell caused by mold and stagnant water escaped from the gloom.

"Somebody really needs to clean this tunnel," complained Kara as she started down the muck-covered steps.

Once inside, Tryam slid the door back into place.

The tunnel was darker than a starless night. There were no side passages or pits to avoid, but it was still possible to slip or trip on the slick flooring. Kara wasted no time and raced ahead, carefree. Tryam heard the sound of her rapid footsteps fading into the distance. He gave chase. After five hundred yards, he collided into Kara, who had been waiting for him in the dark to catch up.

"We are near the exit," she whispered. "Let me look outside and see if it's clear."

Tryam heard Kara walk ahead and then the sound of stone scraping against stone. Dim light seeped down from the exit, which was a cleverly designed sliding door that matched the colors and shape of the rocky shore where the tunnel emerged.

"All clear!" confirmed Kara after a quick scan.

Tryam followed Kara out of the tunnel and emerged into the light. They stood on the boulder-choked shore that buttressed the south wall of the keep. Kara swept the area with her eyes, looking for knights atop the wall or people moving about the harbor. "We can head for the harbor gate. No one is about!"

Kara led Tryam, the two of them clinging tight to the keep's wall. Once they rounded the corner, they were on the shore of the harbor, where they mixed into the crowd of early-morning fishmongers and dock workers.

They then casually walked through the unguarded harbor gate and into the town proper.

At this hour, there was usually little activity on the streets of Arkos, save for weary miners coming back from long shifts and the small crew of the town's sanitation guild. However, today was no ordinary day, for everyone was excited about the tournament. White smoke puffed into the air from almost every abode they passed, as the townsfolk ate their breakfast early. The smell of smoke from cooking fires filled Tryam's nostrils and made his stomach growl.

They continued at a brisk pace and made their way through the narrow and winding streets, past the imposing mage tower, past the blacksmith's, and finally to the north gate. The portcullis was open, but guards, leaning on poleaxes, blocked their way.

"What's your business?" grumbled a sleepy knight as he and his companion made a halfhearted threat with their weapons.

"Out of our way," barked Kara as she attempted to burst between the two knights. "The fighting monk is here to win the tournament!"

When the two guards erupted in laughter, Tryam's face went flush. Kara's face also turned red, but for a different reason. When the guards did not part their weapons, she balled up her fists.

"Oh, she's mad," mocked one. "I fear she may bite me."

Kara made a move for her quiver, but Tryam put a hand on her shoulder and whispered in her ear. "I don't want to get in a fight on my way to a fight."

Kara growled.

Tryam gently pushed Kara aside. "Sorry, sir knights. Please let us pass. The tournament is about to start, and I do not want to be late."

The guards' collective mirth quickly dissipated when they saw the very tall young acolyte's serious face.

The elder guard was the first to lower his poleaxe. "You are a big'un. We was just joshing. Good luck, son."

The second guard then stepped away. "You *must* be the fighting monk. You sure did lay a whoopin' on ole Roderick."

"It was an accident," began Tryam in explanation before Kara dragged him through the gate.

A horse trail led north to a field. The field was where the knights usually practiced cavalry maneuvers, but preparations for the tournament

THE TOMB OF THERAGAARD

had transformed the area. Now large canvas tents, a fenced-in enclosure, and a viewing gallery had been installed for the participants and spectators. The setup was quite the spectacle, and Tryam felt a tad intimidated at the thought of being watched by so many people.

"Look at that!" exclaimed Kara. "You Engothians know how to put on a show."

Tryam watched a mob of young men head into a green tent, beside which was a sign that read *Register Here*. Kara walked with him to the tent, and when he hesitated before stepping through the flap, she gave him an encouraging kick to his backside.

The air inside was warm from the body heat of all the potential recruits. A quick headcount showed about thirty-five participants. Some had smiles, some looked nervous, a few looked deadly serious.

An Engothian knight, his features hardened by years of service and decorated with scars along the right side of his face, entered the tent from another flap and mounted a crate beside the registration table. When the old man cleared his throat, the assembled young men fell into silence.

"Welcome to the Engothian Knights' Tournament. My name is Captain Kreegar. Today is a great day for the residents of Arkos, for they will witness three trials of combat, by the end of which we shall, hopefully, find one worthy candidate to join our ranks. The wars on the continent are never ceasing, and King Athelrad needs more men. Do you think you have the courage, the dedication, and the skills necessary to join the armies of our king?"

As the gathered young men stayed silent, a frown wrinkled the veteran knight's forehead. Kreegar shook his head in obvious disgust. "I shall ask again: Do any you think you have the courage, the dedication, and the skills necessary to join the armies of our king?"

This time the knight aspirants responded with an enthusiastic "Yay!"—Tryam included. Kreegar nodded his head approvingly.

Before the captain descended from the crate, he pointed to a table. "Make sure you sign in with your name and your next of kin. The first test will commence in mere moments."

"What is the first test?" asked a bold, brawny youth.

"It will be a test of your skill with the longbow," replied the irritated Kreegar. "Now, no more questions until you register."

Kara punched Tryam in the shoulder and smiled at the mention of the longbow. She then frowned when she saw the crowd surging toward the registration table. "I'd better go. I shall watch from the stands and cheer you on. Don't forget what I taught you. Stay focused. Show these boys who the fighting monk really is!"

"I shall, and thank you for your encouragement and the training."

"Don't be afraid to break bones out there! It may be necessary. Do not let up. Ever!"

Two knights pushed through the crowd of entrants and headed toward Kara. Tryam heard other aspirants around him mentioning that girls were not allowed in the tournament. The Berserker girl hugged him briefly and smirked while she said, "I am more warrior than any one of them anyway!"

Tryam agreed and watched Kara turn and head for the exit before the knights could get hold of her. He then shouldered his way to the registration table. Tryam signed his name in bold clear letters, making sure the knights would have no trouble reading it. For his next of kin, he had no choice but to put Father Monbatten. After Tryam signed the parchment, an old knight with a gray beard smiled at him and wished him luck.

Tryam prayed he was making the right decision. *If it is Aten's will, I shall triumph.*

Chapter 19
The Tournament

A gloomy sky unleashed large droplets of cold rain on the gathered potential recruits. Tryam was disappointed, because he had envisioned the day of the tournament as having a cloudless cobalt blue sky with a golden sun shining down on contestants in gleaming armor. *I suppose it was just not meant to be.*

Saint Lucian had had such a day when his journey into knighthood began. Of all the works in the library, it was the life story of Lucian that Tryam enjoyed reading the most. The saint had led the life of a simple farmer, but that had changed after one heroic act. On a trip to town to sell his goods at market, the rugged youth had seen a royal maiden surrounded by a group of sellswords who had been hired to capture or assassinate her. He leapt from a crowd of frightened onlookers to protect her. Historians recorded how the clouds had parted and the sun had basked Lucian in holy light when he faced down the men. Without ever having taken up the sword before, Lucian beat back the veteran warriors, one after another.

Tryam laughed at how absurd he had been to compare himself in any fashion to a legendary saint. He then thought of Kara's parting words and stopped daydreaming to focus on the present.

Along the northern perimeter of the enclosure, Tryam noticed five archery targets with painted rings around a bullseye. The distance from the shooters to the targets looked like it would be fifty yards. *They ought to be easier to hit than an urn in a cemetery at night!*

A commotion from the stands had drawn everyone's attention. Tryam was alarmed to see Kara's golden hair bobbing its way through the crowd to a front-row seat while curses and stern looks radiated from the normally mild-mannered townsfolk. Kara screamed his name to get his attention. She stopped only when Tryam waved back at her. Glares from the knights and his fellow competitors caused the young acolyte to blush as red as a polished apple.

I have one leg up on Saint Lucian: He had no Kara on his side.

"Listen up!" blared a shrill voice, focusing the knight aspirants' attention away from Kara. "I shall tell the rules only once, and failure to follow these rules will cause your immediate elimination! Is that understood?"

I know that voice!

When he scrutinized the face of the knight who now addressed the cold, wet potential recruits, Tryam winced. It was Roderick. The evidence of their combat was still fresh: He sported a bandage around his head, and he had two black eyes.

"You will have three shots at the target. A bullseye is worth fifty points, the next ring is worth twenty, and the outer ring is worth ten. The top sixteen scorers will pass on to the next challenge." He scanned the recruits with contempt in his eyes. "Now, quickly, divide yourselves in front of each target."

Tryam avoided Roderick's gaze by slipping to the back of the line of shooters, behind the second target. The young acolyte also recognized the knight assisting Roderick. It was Jarrard, and he was handing out the longbows to the first knight aspirants in line. Tryam suspected that working the tournament was punishment for the sparring incident.

After the first five aspirants took possession of their longbows, it was Roderick's duty to hand each shooter an arrow. The red-haired knight spoke barely loud enough to be heard: "When I lower my arm, take your pitiful shots."

The first wave of aspirants got in position and notched their arrows, some with more efficiency than others. Roderick stationed himself a reasonably safe distance away from the targets, raised his arm, waited a moment, then swiftly lowered it. The twang of five bow shots filled the air. Three arrows hit their targets, none a bullseye, while two missed entirely.

"Pathetic," sneered Roderick.

The group was allowed two more rounds, and the resulting shots were no better. As each successive group struggled to find their target, the knight's belittling continued. The wind, the cold, and the rain—none of that was a valid excuse, Roderick again and again contemptuously pronounced.

While the red-haired knight disparaged, Tryam's confidence grew. When it came time for the last group of five, Tryam was sure he could compete for the top spot. His only fear was that of a confrontation with Roderick.

Here he comes.

The wiry knight stepped in front of Tryam. If Roderick had remembered him, he gave no indication. The young knight gave him an arrow. Tryam accepted it and nodded thanks, but the sour knight moved to the next shooter without acknowledging him. Relieved that the knight seemed to hold no grudge, Tryam notched his arrow.

Roderick moved back into position. When he gave the signal to shoot, five more arrows flew into the air.

Tryam felt the arrow release, and he tracked it as it flew to the target. The arrow was shot without incident but inexplicably veered off course after thirty yards. The miss left Tryam stunned. He scored zero points.

The young acolyte had little time to recover before Roderick passed out the arrows for the second round. *Had I not adjusted for the wind?*

Tryam notched the arrow, cleared his mind with a whispered prayer to Aten, and then fired when the signal was given.

The arrow took the same wayward trajectory as the first shot.

Another miss? Something is not right.

The crowd had cheered and jeered with each round. Tryam looked for Kara's reaction. He saw her leaving the stands, knocking over people in her haste. Tryam was ashamed. He had embarrassed her so badly she could not even stand to watch him.

Almost as if Aten too had forsaken him, the wind gusted, and the rain poured. Tryam checked the scores posted near the stands. If he wanted to continue, he would have to score a bullseye. He shivered as some of the targets, knocked down by the wind, had to be repositioned; he was thankful for the small delay.

Shouts from behind snapped Tryam out of his shock.

"We don't take girls! Get her out of here now!"

The voice was that of the gruff knight Kreegar.

When Tryam saw a bright shock of yellow hair and Captain Kreegar being knocked onto his backside, he knew it had to be Kara. A crowd surrounded the Berserker girl. Tryam pushed through the bewildered knight aspirants to come to her aid. *Tournament be damned! I shall not allow them to manhandle her!*

When Kara was within arm's length, she thrust herself toward Tryam. She hugged him around the neck, causing the women in the crowd to cry in delight at the perceived show of true love. Kara had other thoughts, though. She spoke into his ear: "That bastard of a knight is tricking you! Right before he hands you the arrow, he damages the fletching."

In her hand was an arrow. She slipped it down the back of his robes. Kara played to the crowd in order to give Tryam time to secure the arrow in his sleeve. She planted a big kiss on his lips and then shouted, "This is the fighting monk of Saint Paxia, and he is my one true love!" Kara's words got the crowd on her side and against the knights trying to remove her. Tryam's face turned a deep red once again.

Jarrard waded into the melee and tried to return order to the tournament. The knight helped Captain Kreegar back to his feet and then shoved the aspirants away from the couple. "Get back in line, or you will be disqualified!"

"Kara," whispered Tryam. "Thank you."

"Just get a bullseye!" demanded Kara, kissing him on the cheek before Jarrard and another knight lifted her into the air and out of the enclosure. The crowd booed heartily as order was slowly restored.

Tryam held Kara's arrow to his side so no one would see it. This time when Roderick handed him his arrow, the knight scowled at him with utter contempt. After Roderick moved to the next potential recruit, Tryam inspected the fletching. Kara was correct: His arrows were being tampered with.

The young acolyte dropped the ruined arrow and buried it in the muddy ground with his boot. He then surreptitiously notched the arrow Kara had given him. He prayed to Aten that no one would notice that the arrow's shaft was now crimson.

Tryam cleared his thoughts and whispered another prayer to Aten. Roderick stood off to the side, and without delay, he gave the signal to shoot. The arrow flew from Tryam's bow and with it his hope for the future. When it landed, the crowd erupted in applause.

Bullseye!

Tryam wanted to shout his excitement but thought better of it; instead, he went to the other knight aspirants, most of whom had disappointed looks on their faces, and shook their hands. Kara would've been proud of him, if she had been able to see it.

THE TOMB OF THERAGAARD

Kreegar, Jarrard, and Roderick gathered to confer at the slate board. Kreegar looked over the scores as Roderick stood by him, pointing first at Tryam and then at the red arrow still embedded in the target. The captain shook his head and waved Roderick away; then he walked to the potential recruits, who had gathered in the center of the archery range. Kreegar read the names aloud of those who would move on. When Tryam's name was called, it was met with resounding cheers from the crowd, and chants for the "fighting monk" started.

Some of the losing aspirants shrugged their shoulders, others seethed with envy and stormed from the enclosure. The magnanimous ones congratulated the winners.

Tryam did another headcount. Sixteen potential recruits remained.

The old captain approached those moving on to the next round and expressed his disappointment. "No one distinguished himself in the first round. If this continues, the tournament may conclude with no victor." He rubbed the back of his neck. "Rest while you can, for the next challenge is much more demanding. It is a test of strength, endurance, and teamwork."

The knights working the tournament disappeared under the protection and warmth of the tents, leaving the freezing knight aspirants to speculate as to the next test. Some thought it would be a tug of war, others thought a mock battle with two opposing armies. Tryam did not waste time speculating and instead looked for Roderick. Not spotting the knight, he sought Kara, but she had not returned to the stands. He hoped she was all right.

After a time, a group of four knights emerged from the tent. They removed the archery targets, then dragged two circular tarps—one red, the other blue—to opposite ends of the enclosure. When Kreegar finally appeared, he held a cinched leather bag. The tournament hopefuls ended their speculation and gathered around the captain as he addressed them. His mood had not changed, and he scowled at the shivering hopefuls.

"Each of you will reach inside this bag and draw a stone," instructed Kreegar. "If you draw a red stone, stand on the red tarp. If you draw a blue stone, stand on the blue tarp. Do you slackwits understand?"

Eager hands threatened to rip the bag from Kreegar. Tryam patiently waited his turn. When he reached into the bag, his fingers found the smooth stones indistinguishable from one another. He was hoping for a red stone, since that team had already gathered some of the stronger aspirants.

He knew one of them, Maxius, the bull-sized son of the town's blacksmith. When he pulled a blue stone, however, he accepted his fate and walked to the blue tarp, where a friendly but unfamiliar face greeted him.

"Hey, I saw what that knight did to your fletching! I tried to alert you, but I was too far away to get your attention. You must be the monk who knocked him senseless!" The youth offered Tryam his hand. "My name is Gavin."

"Hello, my name is Tryam, and I am not a monk, actually. I am an initiate at the Abbey of Saint Paxia." He shook Gavin's hand, then frowned and shrugged his shoulders. "What happened with Roderick was more of an accident. I had no intention of hurting him. I guess he holds grudges."

Gavin's eyebrows raised. "It would appear so. I hope he doesn't get the chance to interfere this round."

Shouts of excitement exploded from the crowd, and the two stopped their conversation to see why. At the western side of the enclosure, knights moved to a gate that opened to the misty plains beyond. A hulking beast emerged from the fog.

"A mammoth!" cried the observers.

A knight holding thick leather reins led the tusked monster into the arena. Each step of its tree-trunk-sized legs caused the ground to tremble. When the beast was prodded, it reared on its back legs and unleashed a deafening trumpet with its trunk.

"Wh-what are we supposed to do with that?" stuttered Gavin.

The handler positioned the mammoth in the center of the arena and handed the beast's reins over to Kreegar.

The captain had to shout over the excitement of the crowd to instruct the potential recruits. "One of the most feared weapons in the Engothian armies is our division of great-tusked mammoths. These beasts are captured from the rugged plains of the north and then brought to Secundus to be trained for combat. As you can see, this beast has yet to be tamed by man. Your goal is to be the first team to get this mighty creature on your own colored tarp. You must work together, or you will lose together. Beware! This creature can kill with its feet, its tusks, or its trunk!" He paused and let the silence give gravity to his words of caution. "When I give the signal, the contest will begin."

Gavin paced along the edges of the blue tarp. He then pointed at the red team, at the other side of the enclosure. "I don't think the two teams are evenly matched. The red team has a significant size advantage over us."

Tryam agreed with the conclusion but hoped teamwork would be more important. "This contest will not be won by brawn alone. Look at the size of the mammoth. You would need fifty men to move it. From everything I've read about warfare, it isn't always the larger army that wins. We must use our wits." He pointed to the red team. "What I fear is how much more organized they appear to be. Take a look."

The red team had already formed into a group around Maxius, who was instructing each youth on what to do.

The blue team members looked at one another, waiting for someone to speak. When no one did, Tryam stepped forward. "We need to get organized, or we shall lose. Introduce yourselves, and say what you might have to offer for this challenge."

The blue team members stated their names and then described their background and skills. Some even offered ideas on how best to tame the beast, but before they could agree on a plan, time ran out.

We shall have to organize on the run.

Kreegar dropped the reins of the mammoth and slowly backed away from the beast. The mammoth remained agitated but stayed in the center of the enclosure. As the two teams stood poised on their respective tarps, the crowd rose to their feet in anticipation. With a dramatic flair, Kreegar signaled the start of the competition by thrusting his arm toward the mammoth and shouting to the teams, "Tame the beast, lads!"

The sixteen knight aspirants bolted from their starting points and headed for the beast. A tangle of arms fought for possession of the reins as teeth were chipped, curses shouted, and bodies bruised when the teams collided in the center of the enclosure. Tryam was able to knock one member of the red team off the strap, but another red team member stepped in. *This is chaos!* The young acolyte realized he was soon among the few members of the blue team even in position to fight for control of the leather strap.

The mammoth reared up on its back legs and trumpeted its annoyance at the small creatures fighting at its feet. Tryam saw an aspirant get bashed against the side of one of the ivory tusks and fall limp to the ground. He looked down on the unconscious face and saw it was one of his team members, an aspirant named Skracks. The young acolyte rushed to the fallen youth and dragged him to safety before the beast could trample him.

Out of the action, Tryam watched helplessly as Maxius led the red team. With the reins firmly in their possession, they moved as a unit to the head of the creature. The red team then formed a protective circle around Maxius, who now held the great leash by himself.

Gavin rallied the blue team into a wedge and led them rushing into the red team's ranks. However, the larger red team members stood their ground; they kicked, punched, and threw the smaller blue team members into the mud and out of their way.

With each step the mammoth took toward the red tarp, Tryam's dream of becoming a knight receded further away. Before he stepped back into the fight, Tryam prayed to Aten, and a new idea came to his head. *No book I have read gives me any insight, but I do have other resources. My friends from the north, Kara and Wulfric! They often talk about the great beasts they have encountered.* Tryam recalled a story Wulfric told about how his father had turned away such a beast when they were out hunting.

Tryam left Skracks in the care of a knight, who removed the unconscious competitor from the enclosure. The young acolyte then ran back to join his team, shouting. "Here! Form on me. I have an idea!"

The remaining members of the mud-covered blue team withdrew from the mammoth and huddled near Tryam. They looked glum and listless.

The blue team's withdrawal had not gone unnoticed. "Look, we go unopposed!" exclaimed Maxius as he tugged on the reins of the mammoth with extra vigor. "Pull! Pull! The cowards flee in panic!"

The blue team heard the taunt from Maxius. Krell, the smallest blue team member, looked back nervously. "They are almost halfway to their tarp. We have to stop them! This is no time to gab."

Tryam pulled the youth roughly back into the huddle. "We have to work together! Please hear my counsel. I have a plan."

The blue members listened with cocked ears while Tryam quickly described what he intended. Once he finished, the group rose as one, enthusiastic faces having replaced their glum ones. Tryam ordered two members, Arion and Claes, to flank the sides of the beast while he lead the rest of his team to the rear of the animal.

"Stage one!" ordered Tryam as soon as the blue team members were in position.

In response, Arion and Claes picked up clumps of mud. With accuracy and speed, the two skilled marksmen threw mud balls at the mammoth's ears. Whenever the beast would turn its head, a mud ball exploded into its exposed ear canal. As Tryam hoped would happen, the beast grew more agitated. When it had had enough, it reared up on its back legs and dragged Maxius to the ground, halting all forward progress.

Arion and Claes, emboldened by their success, increased the pace of their attacks. The animal's flailing tusks and stomping feet forced the red team to scatter. The crowd of spectators applauded the unusual tactic and started rooting for the blue team and their leader, the fighting monk.

Even though the leash was free, Tryam reminded his team not to seize it. During their brief planning session, he had told them that in combat, a strap was never used to lead such a beast. The animal was controlled from above by a rider. With the red team in disarray and now scrambling to stop the two mud throwers, Tryam called out, "Stage two!"

In response, the blue team formed a human pyramid at the rear of the nearly twenty-foot-tall creature. Before Tryam could do his part, he had to wait for the right moment. It came when Claes scored another direct hit to the beast's ear. The mammoth reacted to the hit by trumpeting a deafening roar and coming to a complete stop. Praying to Aten, the young acolyte took a running start and jumped onto the backs of the other blue team members. Krell, the slightest of the team and at the apex of the pyramid, stood up and flung him the final few feet. Tryam landed in the middle of the creature's back.

The beast responded to the unwelcome rider by shaking its head and rearing up and stamping its feet. Tryam was thrashed about, and he slid down the creature's back and almost off entirely. He stayed on the beast only by holding onto its hairy tail.

The crowd reacted to this bold move by leaping to their feet.

Tryam used the tail like a rope and climbed farther up the beast's back. He then grabbed tufts of its thick fur and crawled toward the mammoth's neck. The pungent odor from the beast was a jolt to his senses, and for the first time, he was aware of just what an incredibly ridiculous and dangerous situation he now found himself in. *Kara would be proud of me.*

Once he felt somewhat secure, Tryam sat up and straddled his legs around the creature's muscular neck. He noticed that the red team had knocked down the two mud throwers and had regained control of the strap. The mammoth was only a few yards away from the red team's tarp. He watched as Gavin tried to secure the leash from Maxius, but the blacksmith's son held on like a drowning man to a piece of driftwood. The red team then added their strength to Maxius's and pulled on the strap in unison. Underneath him, Tryam felt the mammoth rock back and forth as the beast swung its tusks to break free from the pull of the leash. Tryam was inspired by the mammoth's desperate actions. *I can help you get free from those pesky creatures!*

Tryam found the knot that secured the leash around the mammoth's neck and used his hands and teeth to loosen it. He was almost thrown from the beast in the process, but the knot came free and the harness fell away. The resulting slack in the rope caused the red team to fall down into the mud in one big pile. They had been only a few feet shy of their goal.

The blacksmith's son reached for the beast's trunk, but a powerful swipe of a tusk knocked him hard into the mud. Tryam feared that in its rage, the mammoth might trample both teams. He focused his thoughts on his situation and said a quick prayer to Aten. Having no experience with riding a mammoth, Tryam hoped the third part of his plan would work: He would try to control the mammoth by mimicking what he had learned from riding a horse.

With no reins to hold on to, Tryam grabbed hold of the beast's ears. He yanked hard on the right ear again and again until the beast responded. Much to his amazement and delight, the mammoth slowly turned its massive body away from the red team's tarp.

Thanks be to Aten!

Tryam kicked his heels into the side of the beast's neck, and the mammoth reacted much like a horse by lumbering forward.

"Go! Go!" cheered on Gavin.

The red team stepped over the blue team as Maxius ordered his teammates to surround the mammoth. Tryam was not sure what Maxius intended to do until he saw them attempting to replicate Claes and Arion's mud-ball-throwing technique. However, more mud landed on Tryam than in the beast's ears.

Maxius was forced to change tactics. The red team once again used their superior strength to overpower the blue team as they rushed to the front of the mammoth. Tryam was alarmed to see them forming a human barrier to stop its progress. Instead of slowing, though, the creature, unafraid of the threat, charged, blasting its trunk as it crashed ahead. The beast lumbered through their ranks. To Tryam's relief, none of the knight aspirants had been trampled.

By the time the mammoth reached the halfway point, the red team was desperate and disorganized. With his eyes the only thing not covered in mud, Maxius glared up at Tryam and threatened, "I shall drag you down from there myself!"

It took Maxius time to reorganize his team. Their next strategy involved them trying to get close enough to the mammoth to throw Maxius up onto the creature's back. The first attempt came up short, and Maxius landed face down in the mud. Their second attempt was more successful, and the red team leader grabbed two handfuls of the mammoth's fur. A sharp tug of the mammoth's ear, however, was all Tryam needed in order to throw Maxius clear.

In an act of sheer desperation, a red team member stood in front of the beast and tried to grasp the mammoth's trunk. The mammoth responded by lifting the large youth over its head and throwing him outside the arena's enclosure. The crowd gasped.

Tryam was now within feet of his goal. He could hear his team members joining in with the crowd and chanting, "Hail to the fighting monk!"

Not wanting to risk any further injuries to the red team, Tryam kicked the mammoth's neck, urging it forward. Moments later, the beast stepped onto the blue tarp. The townsfolk erupted in applause.

"The winner is the blue team!" announced Kreegar, storming into the enclosure.

The members of the blue team gathered together in celebration. Tryam could hardly believe that the audacious plan had worked and wanted to join his teammates, but when he went to dismount, he lost control of the mammoth. He pulled back on the ears to stop the creature but ended up having the beast stand on its hind legs. The creature then dipped its head, throwing Tryam forward and off. Possibly in anger at being manipulated by the small creature on its back, the mammoth swung its tusks at Tryam. One tusk caught the young acolyte in the hip, piercing deep into his flesh. Tryam rolled away to avoid getting trampled. When he was clear, he put his hand on his hip and felt warm blood soaking his robes. Four handlers then came rushing inside the enclosure and secured the mammoth in a new harness. The knights used blunted spears to coerce the creature away and out of the arena.

Gavin came over and helped Tryam to his feet. "You were almost trampled. Are you all right?"

"I'm fine," lied Tryam, short of breath.

"I can't believe you just rode a mammoth!"

"Neither can I," replied Tryam weakly as the pain in his hip throbbed with each beat of his heart.

135

The rest of the blue team gathered around. He hoped no one had seen his injury, and none reacted as if he had. As Wulfric had often warned, an injury is a weakness that opponents could exploit in combat. Trying his best not to grimace, Tryam addressed his teammates. "Well done. Just as Saint Lucian and his men used their wits to overcome the superior forces of the Abyss at Abbadon, so did we." The blue team cheered, and even if they did not understand his reference, smiles spread like a contagion from one potential recruit to the next.

While they celebrated, knights escorted the broken and bruised red team out of the enclosure. "It is unfortunate," lamented Gavin, "that we have to compete against one another in the next round."

The blue team members all agreed.

The pain forced Tryam to part company with the others. He had to tend to his wound. "If you'll forgive me, I need a few minutes to give thanks to God."

"We would expect nothing less from the fighting monk," joked Krell.

The injured acolyte excused himself from the other competitors and hid inside an unoccupied privy tent to examine his wound. His mud-caked robes hid any outward sign of INJURY, but he could feel the warm blood flowing down his leg. He parted the rent in the robes' fabric. It was a deep cut, but it was not severe enough to stop him from continuing. Tryam stripped off a portion of his robes and tied it around his hip to stanch the flow of blood. He gave thanks to Aten. When he returned to stand with his teammates, they were discussing the health of another member.

"He wasn't moving," stated Claes. "That's for sure."

"I saw him get knocked out," added Vrooman, the quietest of the blue team members. "Blood was coming from his nose."

"If Skracks can't continue, who will take his place?" asked Gavin.

"He is my friend and a skilled warrior. His loss will make my win that much easier," boasted Braxis, the portly knight aspirant who had formed the base of the blue team's human pyramid.

As the realities of the danger to come entered his mind, Tryam whispered a prayer for Skracks's health.

The arena was being prepared, and speculation again spread among the final aspirants as to the last combat trial. All agreed it would be duels with the sword.

The crowd, suffering from the drenching rain as much as were the participants, grew irritated with the delay. They amused themselves with taunts directed at the remaining aspirants while the women swooned over Tryam. The young acolyte felt his face grow hot in embarrassment. Kara was still nowhere to be seen.

Arion poked Tryam in the chest. "If you don't win, at least you have a lot of other opportunities. If you know what I mean!"

"He's with that Berserker girl!" pointed out Krell. "He would be crazy to leave her."

Before Tryam could protest, Kreegar emerged from the registration tent. The crowd ceased their taunts and erupted in applause that the delay was over.

With a wave as the potential recruits gathered around him, the old knight acknowledged the townsfolk. He had to shout over the rambunctious crowd to be heard. "Unfortunately, during the last round, one of your team members was seriously injured and cannot continue. Since we need even numbers for the final stage of the tournament, the Round of Swords, it is decided that Maxius from the red team will take his place. Maxius showed courage and leadership and should be duly rewarded."

The crowd showed their approval of Kreegar's decision by welcoming the brawny black-haired youth back to the enclosure with shouts of encouragement and applause of appreciation. The blue team members, however, exchanged glances that revealed they were not as pleased with the news.

As workers hammered stakes in the mud to create a sparring ring near the stands, the eight contenders were herded to the center of the enclosure. Workers also placed a table with assorted weapons and armor near where the contenders waited.

Seeing the ring and the weapons, the potential recruits traded barbs and challenges with one another. Tryam kept quiet and tried not to move his hip.

When Kreegar stood before them, all conversations stopped. The old knight walked down the line of youths and looked each one in the eye as he passed. When he was done, he crossed his arms over his armored chest. His face became as hard as a statue's. "The preferred weapon of the Engothian knight is the sword. Poets and bards praise the lance and romanticize the joust, but the sword wins wars and keeps you alive. We don't expect any of you to have perfect blade work, but you must show some natural ability. The Round of Swords tests this instinct. Each knight aspirant will be given a helmet, greaves, a breastplate, a shield, and a sword. This is not a contest to the death, but we shall be using steel." He again walked down the line of youths. "Aspirants may not seriously injure each other. However, accidents do take place, as you have seen with young Skracks. Each contest will end when one fighter yields or opens himself up to what could have been a killing blow." He rocked back on his heels. "Questions?"

The captain again stared into the eyes of the would-be knights. "No? Good! Find armor that fits, and a sword to your liking. A random drawing will decide the matchups."

As the other aspirants headed to the table to get their equipment, Tryam took the time to inspect the sparring arena. Inside the circle, the mammoth had torn the grass into mud, and now the heavy rain caused deep pools of water to form. Maneuverability in these conditions would be treacherous.

"Good luck, but not too much," joked Gavin as he and Tryam again shook hands. "Let's hope we don't meet until the last round!"

"Yes," replied Tryam sincerely.

Some of the contenders used their own equipment, but most chose at least one item from the table. Tryam, devoid of any equipment of his own, was relieved that he had a nice selection of well-crafted items from which to choose. When he was done, he examined the items: The sword felt well balanced, the breastplate light, the shield sturdy with firm leather straps, the greaves well oiled, and the conical-shaped helmet protected his head yet did not block his vision.

When everyone was finished with their selections, the contenders formed a circle, with Kreegar at the center. Jarrard gave the gray-haired captain an upturned helmet. Inside, on slips of soggy parchment, were written the names of the final eight recruits.

"I shall draw names until we have four pairings," explained Kreegar. "The combatants will fight in the order they are drawn,"

Tryam did not want to fight Gavin or Maxius first.

Kreegar announced the pairings with the gravity of marching orders. Gavin would fight Braxis in the first match. Tryam had the second match against the much smaller Krell. Maxius and Vrooman would fight third, and the mud-throwing team of Arion and Claes fourth.

THE TOMB OF THERAGAARD

Tryam considered himself fortunate with his draw. Fighting second meant that the young acolyte could take his time sizing up his opponent and drawing up a strategy. When he looked for Krell, the slender youth was still struggling to get his breastplate strapped on. Tryam remembered his own struggles and approached. "May I help you?"

Krell looked surprised and suspicious at the offer. When Tryam smiled, Krell smiled back. "You really are a monk. Thank you. But don't think this means I shall go easy on you."

"I know it won't. I have seen your fighting spirit."

Tryam helped strap on his armor and even showed Krell how the equipment would impact his movements. The other contestants had surprised looks on their faces, but Tryam thought he caught a nod of approval from Kreegar.

When the potential recruits were ready, the captain called for Gavin and his opponent to stand before each other in the center of the impromptu ring. Gavin saluted Braxis with his sword, while Braxis replied with a boast about how easy his victory would be.

The two participants stood ten feet apart, swords at the ready. Kreegar stepped away and stood outside the ring with the other knight aspirants. When the grizzled knight gave the command, the two youths roared, swords raised, and rushed at each other.

Braxis opened the combat with a broad sweep of his sword in a fashion usually reserved for actors depicting a melee on stage. So outlandish was the maneuver, it evoked laughter from the crowd. When Gavin deflected the stroke with ease, fear formed on Braxis's face. Gavin had showed an expertise with the blade that surprised Tryam. Despite the muddy conditions, his footwork was sure and his strikes well planned. Gavin quickly overwhelmed his opponent, who threw down his sword and fell to his knees after a series of bone-jarring strikes to his head and torso.

Kreegar stepped in and announced Gavin the victor. The crowd was displeased by the actions of the foolish loser and pelted him with insults and the occasional piece of rotten fruit.

After Braxis was led away, Tryam walked over to Gavin, keeping a smile on his face despite the shooting pain in his hip. "That was amazing! He had no defense against your attacks! He was smart to quit when he did."

"Yes, it was hardly fair," said Gavin, smiling and shaking his head. "I don't think Braxis has ever wielded a sword against a real opponent before. Good luck on your match."

"I just hope to perform well enough not to be pelted by garbage," quipped Tryam.

Tryam had little time to prepare. The young acolyte's hip throbbed, rain soaked him to the bone, he was cold and bloody, but he was more excited than he had ever been in his entire life. He channeled Wulfric and again attempted to size up his opponent. Krell was smaller and nimbler, and unlike Braxis, he held his sword with a practiced ease. *I need to use my size advantage.*

Tryam stepped into the enclosure with a prayer to Aten on his lips and felt a calming force come over his body. When Kreegar barked the command for combat to begin, Krell rushed to meet Tryam and went on the offensive.

The smaller youth thrust, pivoted, and danced his way around the slower acolyte in a display that Tryam believed was meant to intimidate or tire him. It worked to some extent, as Tryam struggled to keep up and could only parry the assaults. Krell smiled confidently. *He must think I have no experience sparring with an opponent! Maybe I could use that to my advantage.*

Tryam let his shield and sword hang low to lure Krell into riskier attacks. The crowd noise rose as they saw Tryam seeming to falter, and many of the women in the crowd gave the fighting monk words of encouragement.

An unexpected jolt of pain in his hip caused Tryam to fall to one knee. The smile on Krell's face widened. The aggressive aspirant held his sword high and was ready to strike at Tryam's helm, but the move left his midsection open to attack. Tryam held his breath, pressed his shield tightly to his body, then lunged, shield first, at Krell's stomach.

Krell was not expecting the maneuver. The impact of the shield, with Tryam's full weight behind it, sent Krell flying backward. Krell's sword dropped into the mud, and his shield sailed ten feet off to the side, nearly into the crowd. If not for his breastplate, the smaller youth would have suffered several broken ribs.

The crowd, as one, rose to their feet. Tryam stood over the crumpled knight aspirant in disbelief. Krell was nearly unconscious, his eyes unfocused. Tryam pointed his sword at Krell's neck, signaling that he could have scored a killing shot. Kreegar quickly rushed in, stood over the fallen Krell, and announced to the crowd. "We have a winner. Tryam!"

Tryam could hardly believe what had happened. He had used Wulfric's shield maneuver, and it had worked. The young acolyte walked over to Krell and lent a hand to his woozy opponent.

THE TOMB OF THERAGAARD

As Tryam pulled him to his feet, Krell smirked. "That was a pretty sneaky trick for a monk, but it was my fault for being so aggressive."

The two combatants shook hands. "I had no other choice. You were too fast!"

The crowd saluted their sportsmanship as the vanquished aspirant was escorted out of the arena. This time it was Gavin who walked over to him and shook his hand. "Nice move, I thought you were done for, for sure."

"It was a tough battle. I could not keep up with his attacks, so I had to make him feel overconfident."

"I shan't make that mistake." Gavin laughed and winked.

Two matches remained in the first round. The first of these matches saw Vrooman, the inscrutable brewer's son, challenging Maxius, the aggressive blacksmith's son. The contest was over quickly, as the stronger Maxius overwhelmed his unskilled opponent. Maxius seriously injured Vrooman when his powerful sword strike connected to the side of Vrooman's helmet. Gavin and Tryam exchanged knowing looks after the match; neither one wanted to fight Maxius.

The last contest paired two equally unskilled but aggressive warriors: Arion the huntsman and Claes the farmer, the mud-throwing duo. The two aspirants stood toe to toe, striking each other about the head. Neither parried, and neither backed down. The crowd loved the absurdity of the match and taunted the pair for their lack of any known fighting technique. When Claes's helmet slipped off his head, Kreegar stepped in to stop the contest. Arion raised his sword in victory and bowed to the crowd, oblivious of their mockery. Claes claimed he had not been given a fair opportunity to continue and had to be taken away by force.

The four remaining contestants stood together to await the pairings for the second round. After another conference among the knights, Roderick still not among them, Kreegar again drew names from the upturned helm. Tryam's name was announced first.

The young acolyte did not want to face his new friend, Gavin, and was wary of facing Maxius. When Kreegar announced Maxius as his opponent, Tryam reminded himself of one of Aten tenets: The loftiest of goals can be achieved only with the completion of the most arduous of labors.

With only a brief chance to wish Gavin good luck in his match with Arion, Tryam rushed to the center of the ring. Maxius stood before him with a broad smile on his square face. The blacksmith's son's strength was easy to see: His hands were large, his thews unmatched among the competitors. *His lack of height could be a disadvantage. He has stubby legs and short arms.* A strategy formed in Tryam's head.

The rain picked up as the crowd, now standing, shouted encouraging words to the fighting monk. Kreegar barked the order for the match to begin. Maxius rushed at Tryam, no doubt hoping to keep him in close quarters. Tryam appreciated the strength behind Maxius's swing and braced himself for the first blow by raising his shield. Maxius positioned himself to strike with an overhead attack; however, at the last possible second, Maxius changed the angle of his blow, rendering Tryam's shield useless. The young acolyte pivoted away from the strike, a simple-enough maneuver but not for one with a wounded hip. Instead of recovering his balance, Tryam fell to one knee. It took all his strength and will to overcome the pain and get back to his feet.

Maxius wasted no time and took advantage of Tryam's slow recovery; he launched another strike, this time at the young acolyte's midsection. Tryam saw the swing coming and, planting his legs as firmly as he could in the muddy ground, raised his shield in defense. The strike hit the center of his shield, forcing his arm back against his chest. As the energy of the attack traveled down his body, Tryam's bones shook, and his teeth rattled.

Like a blacksmith before an anvil, Maxius pounded blow after blow on Tryam's shield. While Tryam absorbed the physical pain, his mind raced, attempting to figure out a counter. He realized that Maxius's attacks reminded him of his own first attempts at combat with Wulfric: There was no thought or strategy in their placement. Wulfric had demonstrated that attacks with little chance of being successful wear down the attacker faster than they do the defender.

Tryam could hear his monicker being chanted by the crowd and fed off their energy. The young acolyte let out a roar to alert the crowd that he heard them. Maxius paused, shocked at the sudden outburst. Tryam, feeling better than he had at the start of the match, easily countered the next attack. The strike hit his shield, but instead of feeling a jolt across his body, he held his arm in place. Maxius was panting now, sweat pouring down his face. Tryam stepped back, then thrust his sword at his opponent's helm. Maxius deflected the blow but could not counterattack, since Tryam was out of reach.

Strategies were becoming realities. Tryam took a step toward Maxius and struck with a stabbing motion. Maxius swung wildly at Tryam in return, but his stroke was at least eight inches too short to reach. Each time the blacksmith's son went to counter, Tryam was already out of range. Maxius couldn't keep up with Tryam's speed, and although none of the acolyte's attacks were overwhelming, they inflicted deep bruises and drained strength.

Perhaps as a reminder from Aten not to be overconfident, Tryam fell to his knees when stepping back to avoid a strike—his injured hip the culprit. Maxius took advantage of the fall and charged Tryam with shield raised, hoping to bowl him over. The young acolyte called on all his strength, raised his shield, and braced himself for the collision. A resounding thud was heard throughout the field, both shields splintering in their owner's hands, and causing both potential recruits to fall face first into the mud.

The crowd gasped in shock at the brutal stratagem of Maxius and the resulting impact. Tryam, his ears ringing and with stars in his eyes, was the first to recover. He pulled his sword out of the mud and, using it like an elderly man does a cane, rose to his feet. The crowd cheered, urging Tryam to take advantage of his prone foe. But before he could, Maxius rose to his feet, and combat began anew. The crowd cheered their approval.

Maxius stood on wobbly legs. The beleaguered youth searched for his sword in the muck and found it nearby, but he could barely heft it. Tryam worried that Maxius, without his shield and in such a weakened condition, could not adequately defend himself. However, the resolute leader of the red team would not give up and staggered toward Tryam for another attack. The effort nearly cost him his balance, as Tryam deflected the slow and misguided swing. Tryam's counterattack landed a hit on Maxius's greaves, knocking the sword from his hand.

With Maxius unable to defend himself, the fight was over. Kreegar rushed in between the two weary warriors and halted the contest, declaring, "Stop and separate! We have a winner: Tryam!"

The crowd's chant of "Fighting monk! Fighting monk!" roared into the dreary sky. Tryam, too weary to celebrate, respectfully bowed his head to Maxius and then to the crowd. He limped his way over to the fence and sat down to watch the next contest. His hip was on fire, and his heart pounded in his ears, but he had never felt so proud. He wished only that he had someone with whom to share the joy he felt.

After a surprising offer of water from a knight in attendance, Tryam drank up and watched the last match before the final round. As expected, Gavin made short work of Arion. He demonstrated his skill with the sword by displaying an array of clever moves, and he demonstrated his honor by treating his inferior foe with respect.

The knights removed the defeated Arion with little fanfare, and the remaining two knight aspirants were given only a brief time to recover.

Kreegar stood before the boisterous crowd, and with the authority of his voice, he brought them to silence. "Ladies and gentlemen, standing before you are two most worthy knight aspirants. The realm would be well served with either of them among our numbers, but, alas, only one will have that honor. Roderick, bring the fighting monk a new shield, and let the contest begin!"

At the end of Kreegar's announcement, the crowd returned to cheering, chanting, and laying wagers on who they thought would win. Roderick, reluctant to obey Kreegar's command, trudged sulking to the supply tent to find a new shield. This brief pause before the final match gave the two warriors a moment to speak.

Gavin, whose bright smile contrasted with the gloomy day, spoke first. "We made it to the end. I am glad it is you I am facing. You and I have two things in common: We both are true competitors, and we both share a respect for Aten. Whoever wins this challenge will be a worthy knight."

"Perhaps faith has guided us to this moment. May Aten inspire you to do your best."

The two shook hands and then were ordered to separate.

Before the combat began, Tryam strained to see the abbey out in the Arkos harbor. He wondered if his absence had been noticed and if he would ever step foot inside the gloomy walls again. Roderick interrupted his musings when he presented him with a new shield. Tryam took the shield and checked the soundness of the wood, the quality of the leather straps, and even the nails holding the shield together. All was as it should be. Had he won over the sullen young knight through his success in the tournament so far? *Probably not.*

Tryam took one last look for Kara but could not find her in the stands. *Where is she? They had better not have hurt her!*

Kreegar returned and motioned the two warriors to stand together in the center of the combat area. In a voice only the two could hear, he said, "Good luck, lads. Remember, this is not a contest to the death, but that doesn't mean it should be an easy victory for either of you. I shall not step in to stop the fight until we have a clear victor."

THE TOMB OF THERAGAARD

Both aspirants nodded that they understood. Kreegar backed away, then gave the sign for combat to begin.

The two youths did not rush to battle but instead circled each other like predators stalking their prey. Tryam had scouted Gavin when watching his previous matches and was content to start more cautiously. His fellow traveler in Aten was physically fit but lacked his raw power and long reach. However, Gavin was clearly more experienced in the art of swordplay. The young acolyte knew he would have to keep all of Wulfric's lessons in mind to avoid being outwitted.

The fickle crowd grew impatient and whistled at the combatants.

"Let's give the audience something to cheer for," encouraged Gavin.

Tryam grinned. "Okay, let's go!"

The two youths let out a shout and charged each other. Tryam took a swing at Gavin; Gavin took a strike at Tryam. They traded blows, and they hammered and smashed each other's shields repeatedly, neither gaining an advantage. The sound of metal on metal echoed across the arena and out into the plains.

With each blow, the cheers from the crowd grew louder and louder. The makeshift stands threatened to come apart from the pounding of the crowd's feet.

The two knight aspirants sloshed through the mud, parrying and dodging, giving and taking blows. Even the veteran Engothian knights who had sought shelter from the rain inside the tents now emerged and started giving approving comments.

The exchange of blows continued as the rain fell heavier. Each time Tryam lifted his foot from the deep muck, his hip throbbed in agony. The young acolyte was certain the wound had reopened.

The muddy conditions forced Tryam and Gavin to close, while the pain and blood loss was getting too much for Tryam to bear.

The two brushed shields and locked swords. This was the opportunity for Tryam to use his superior strength. The young acolyte dropped his shield and reached out with his left hand to grab Gavin's sword wrist. As Tryam attempted to rip the weapon free, Gavin struggled to maintain his grasp on his sword.

As the two struggled, Tryam felt his hip weaken and blood flow down his leg. He could not, would not, let his dream of becoming a knight come to naught. Rage born from some hidden source buried deep inside Tryam's

145

past came rushing to the surface. And as it had with Wulfric, his chest burned. Tryam's breathing came easier as he planted his legs in the mud and forced Gavin to his knees. The rage-filled acolyte wrested the sword from Gavin's grip and then forced the overwhelmed aspirant flat on his back in the deep mud. As a madness filled his brain with red thoughts, Tryam dropped his own sword and made to wrap his hands around Gavin's throat.

Stop. This is not the way.

The calming words drifted into Tryam's head as if carried on an autumn breeze. His rage ebbed, his chest cooled. "Okay, all right," Tryam responded in a haze, but to whom he spoke to was uncertain.

The hesitation cost Tryam. Gavin sat up and grabbed him in a bear hug. The fresher aspirant then twisted out from the mud, flipping Tryam on his back. The maneuver sent a bolt a pain from his hip into his head. Tryam nearly lost consciousness. He watched Gavin stretch for one of the loose swords. Feebly, Tryam attempted to grab hold of Gavin's arm. The pain was too much. His body gave out. Gavin grabbed the sword and pointed it at Tryam's unprotected neck.

Kreegar rushed in and signaled for the fight to stop.

Tryam was too weak to stand, but he did not care. He may have lost the tournament, but he had fought against the rage inside of him and had won. As he slipped into unconsciousness, he sensed the warm embrace of Aten.

Chapter 20
Tryam at the Crossroads

Tryam's injuries would heal in a matter of weeks, and his acceptance of Aten's will would come in time. At least, that is what Emil assured him would happen when he first awoke in the infirmary with the devastating realization that he had lost the tournament and that his dream of become a knight was over.

Tryam had vivid memories of what had happened at the tournament, but he had to rely on Emil to relay to him the events afterward. The kind monk informed him that it was Kara who had brought him back to the abbey. She had told Father Monbatten that Tryam's injured hip was a result of his leaping in front of a sword, intended for her, from a drunk rogue in town. No one believed her, but she'd been so insistent that the monks let the matter drop and treated his wound without further questioning. Emil said Kara's quick action had saved his life.

Tryam wished he could have spoken to Kara, but Emil informed him that, after spending many days at his bedside, she'd had to return north.

A month of healing and prayer had passed since then, and in that time, Tryam had come to a decision. He rose from his sickbed and made his way to Father Monbatten's isolated cell in the depths of the rectory. After a moment of hesitation, he knocked on the dark door.

"Enter," growled Monbatten from within.

Tryam stepped into the room. Monbatten was at his desk, hunched over a scroll. Tryam stepped closer, and his large frame cast a shadow, hindering the abbot's ability to read. Monbatten lifted his head.

"Ah, Tryam," greeted the abbot dryly, leaning back in his chair. "It is good to see you up. Have you come to return to your duties? There are quite a few heavy boxes and barrels that need to be moved. No doubt the 'fighting monk of Saint Paxia' could manage such a task."

Tryam ignored the reference to the tournament and responded in a calm, level voice. "Thanks to Aten and my fellow brothers, I am well and ready to help in any way I can, though that is not the primary purpose for my visit."

Monbatten steepled his fingers under his chin, his full attention now on Tryam. "Well then, what is so important that you need to disturb my studies?"

Tryam stepped in front of the abbot's desk, straightened his spine, and cleared his throat. "Father, I have decided to dedicate my life to Aten and the teachings of Saint Paxia. Upon my eighteenth birthday, I shall take the oath."

A broad grin split the older man's face and erased the lines caused from years' worth of scowling. "Excellent, my son. Aten's will has prevailed." He placed his hands flat on his desk. "Still, we cannot ignore your actions. The 'fighting monk' is now infamously mentioned in the annals of the town of Arkos. Our reputation for pacifism took a harsh blow with your antics."

"That was not my intention. How shall I make amends for this indiscretion?"

The abbot pushed away from his desk and walked over to Tryam, placing his arm around his shoulders. "Your body has recovered, and now your soul must heal. Manual labor can help cleanse the mind of unhealthy thoughts. Beginning tomorrow, I want you to resume your regular chores." He hardened his face, the pleasantness from moments ago now gone. "In addition, I want you to work at the library. While you were recovering, we received a shipment of scrolls from our brothers on the continent. I want you to catalog the many new tomes. You will be very busy."

"Yes, Father, I shall do as you wish."

✠ ✠ ✠

It was while taking a break from cataloging to read one of his favorite works, *The Other Side of the Horizon: The History and Legend of Saint Lucian*, that Tryam saw Father Monbatten enter the scriptorium. The young acolyte grimaced. *I have been working hard to catalog and organize the new scrolls, and the first time Father Monbatten comes to inspect my progress, he catches me with my head in a book.*

When he saw the title of the work that Tryam was holding, the abbot frowned. "What's that you have there?" he snapped. "Give me that."

Tryam reluctantly handed over the leather-bound book. "I was about to put it away." *Eventually.*

"Nonsense, you were reading it." Monbatten read the title aloud. "I don't know where you gained the ability to comprehend ancient languages, but I don't want you reading books like this again. I remind you: Your troubles with the order stemmed from your fantasies about becoming a warrior. You have forsworn such a life and have promised to dedicate yourself to the teachings of Saint Paxia. This book glorifies the deeds of warriors from a lost age, an age we should not look to for guidance but learn from their mistakes."

Tryam countered: "Saint Lucian was a very pious man who devoted his life to Aten. I just read an incident that struck me as being oddly familiar. As a youth, Lucian discovered that he could contact the spirit world. Under the vaults and in the tournament, I thought I heard voices. Do you—?"

Monbatten shook his head. "Under the vaults, you were frightened out of your wits and do not know what you heard! If you heard any voices at the tournament, it was likely due to lightheadedness." He pointed at Tryam. "Don't speak of this again. Trust my wisdom."

"It is hard for me to gain wisdom, having never left the confines of this small community in the middle of a vast wasteland."

"A hermit can gain wisdom living alone in a cave." Monbatten appeared amused, and a smile cracked his face. "But I understand what it is to be young. In fact, that is why I came here. Brother Emil, who is no youth, is leaving for a mission to one of the Berserker villages. He is delivering supplies to Brother Kayen. I think this task is something for which you, as the strongest among us, are particularly qualified."

"Supplies?" asked Tryam, genuinely confused. "For Brother Kayen?"

"Yes, our wayward Brother Kayen thinks he can convert these violent brutes to Aten. I have my doubts, but despite our differences, I do admire his tenacity and devotion. I would normally not have allowed you contact with that man again, but now that you have committed yourself to join our order, I cannot see the harm. It will do you good to experience a sample of what the world can be like beyond these walls. You will never again take for granted the comfort you have here."

For a moment, Tryam doubted his ears at Monbatten's offer. *Why is he giving me another chance to talk with Brother Kayen?* "I would welcome the opportunity," he said.

"Good. You should pack immediately, since you will be leaving in the morning." Monbatten placed the Saint Lucian book back in Tryam's hand. "Put this book back where it belongs, well out of your thoughts!"

"Thank you for this opportunity," said Tryam humbly.

"You may not be thanking me when you are facing the freezing bites of the arctic wind, which roars down from the mountains. Or when you have nothing but rocks to sleep on as you cower under a flimsy blanket and the howls of hungry ice wolves draw nearer." He gave Tryam one last stern look. "This is no easy undertaking."

"I understand, Father," acknowledged Tryam, though he had no idea what to expect on the trip. With his head awhirl, he was halfway back to his cell when he realized he still held the Saint Lucian book in his hand.

Chapter 21
Telvar at the Crossroads

Sweat poured down Telvar's brow, and his heart thudded against his rib cage, but his hands remained steady as he prepared for the spell he was about to cast.

It was the first spell the young mage had created on his own, and he was confident of its success; however, it was the circumstance for which he was about to cast the spell that made him wary.

He recalled how he had gotten to this point.

Myramar had now stopped communicating with him altogether and spent most of his days and nights in his basement laboratory. Telvar worried that whatever was inside the Anima Crystallum had enthralled the tower mage. *What dark magic is happening in the bowels of this tower?*

Telvar needed to find out.

The young wizard had rummaged through the spell books in Myramar's personal collection. Most of the spells used symbols and phraseology he was not familiar with and required more time than he had to decipher. Myramar, like himself, specialized in elemental magic—the magic used to manipulate fire, water, air, and earth. With that in mind, Telvar concentrated his research to books that dealt in elemental magic. He found a book called *Equam Manipular*. Once he perused the text, he was sure it was exactly what he needed.

One section of the book explained the concept of the transmutation of matter and how a wizard could use magical energy to manipulate the properties of an element. Telvar was using a spyglass to read the small, detailed writing when the idea for a spell struck him. If he could alter a small section of the wood of the door to the underground laboratory to become transparent like his spyglass, he could safely observe Myramar without having to risk his presence being detected.

He considered the practical application of the spell and determined that transmuting the door was beyond his power. The door was wood, and changing plant or animal life required a set of magical skills he lacked. He considered peering through the walls of the laboratory, but they were three feet thick and required more power than he had at his disposal. He settled on a third choice, the laboratory's thinner ceiling.

From what Telvar could determine, the stone separating the basement laboratory from the first floor was only a foot thick. The ceiling choice had the added benefit of putting him in a safer location when casting the spell: the kitchen. The basement laboratory was directly below the kitchen, a location that Myramar had not entered in weeks, if not months.

Once he'd decided on a strategy, Telvar turned his thoughts toward creating the spell. Since the magic he required would transmute granite to glass, he first took a sample of the floor by scraping stone from beneath a rug and performing a series of experiments to determine its properties relative to a sample of glass he took from his spyglass. After recording his findings, he translated that knowledge into a set of magical symbols and words needed for the transmutation process.

The spell also required the use of a reagent to act as a bridge between the granite and the glass. After some experimentation, Telvar determined that obsidian was the proper intermediary between the two elements. Obsidian was a stone, but it had light-reflecting properties. Not a perfect match, but the best choice available, since Myramar had taken many reagents from the reagent room to his laboratory.

Finally, he had to determine how much magical energy he would require to perform the spell. The amount of energy needed was a function of how much material he was transmuting and the efficiency of the bridge. If he could not safely manipulate the energy, the spell would fail. He calculated the power required to combine one small sample of glass with a small sample of granite. To make a rough estimate, he multiplied that sample value by the amount of stone and glass he would need for the actual attempt.

THE TOMB OF THERAGAARD

Telvar smiled in satisfaction with the research that had led him to where he was right then. The sweat on his brow he blamed on his proximity to the kitchen's stove and his pounding heart on his heightened alertness. Since it would be almost impossible to replace the obsidian reagent, the young wizard would have only one chance to cast the spell. He poured the crushed obsidian on the area of the stone floor that he wanted to transmute, roughly six inches in diameter; then he placed a thin layer of glass on top of the reagent. He calmed his mind and, in the arcane language of magic, uttered the commands to begin the transmutation process.

With a rush of excitement and a tinge of anxiety, Telvar sensed the power of magic from the astral plane coursing through his body. It was this feeling of being in control, of harnessing a power greater than himself, that had made him suffer through the years of ridicule at the hands of the other students, the teachers, and even his family.

The anxiety fled his mind and was replaced with the confidence and power of one who wields magic. Telvar continued to funnel power from the astral plane into himself, and then, when he was certain he had enough magic, he channeled it into the obsidian reagent.

The determined young wizard watched with eager eyes as the obsidian absorbed his magic and transferred the energy to the glass and ultimately to the granite floor beneath. Telvar continued to channel energy until the glass and obsidian melted into a steaming black puddle.

"*Elementium, septimorious, el motivium,*" chanted Telvar while he manipulated his hands over the mixture.

The transformation of the mixture began. However, after a few minutes, the apprentice wizard realized the process was taking far too long. At the current rate, he would surely run out of magic before it was complete.

Telvar reached for his staff and absorbed the energy stored in its gem. With the staff depleted, the young wizard put it aside and then channeled more energy through his hands and into the obsidian mixture. With the added energy, the transformation would be complete in a matter of minutes, but his reserves of magic were gone, and the muscles in his body ached and trembled. All the exhausted wizard could do now was wait while the magic did its job.

Once the molten pool cooled, Telvar bent down to determine if his spell had worked.

A small section of the sleet-gray stone floor was now transparent, and Telvar could clearly see into the room below. *Yes! My first successful experimentation. I had no doubts.*

The area affected was smaller than he had anticipated, only four inches in diameter, but he was quite satisfied nonetheless. Telvar smiled smugly over the transmuted stone. *I doubt any of my classmates could have done this!*

So pleased was he with the result of the spell that the excited young mage nearly forgot the grim purpose of his efforts. Now he pressed his eyes close to the floor and, with a bit of trepidation, peered into the room below. Through the murky glass, he saw the unmistakable form of his master.

Myramar was stripped to the waist, his skin unusually gaunt, and the ever-present amulet around his neck glowed a deep crimson. In the center of the room was a table, which held braziers that burned green and yellow flames. His master was leaning over something on the table, but Telvar could not make out what it was. The old wizard gripped a bloody dagger.

Telvar watched the spectacle with great interest, but he could not tell what magics were being used. The scene reminded him more of the trappings of a religious ceremony than of magical experimentation.

Myramar finally moved away from the table, allowing Telvar his first glimpse of what rested upon it. As his brain strained to verify what he was seeing with his eyes, the young mage's blood chilled. On the table was a corpse, bloated and disfigured.

Myramar returned to the table, the edge of the bloody dagger now glowing with a slight greenish tint. The tower mage poked the corpse with the blade's tip. As the blade pierced the flesh, what appeared to be a spark of energy leapt from the metal into the rotting tissue. The corpse responded to the stimulus, and its fleshy torso writhed upon the table.

The transmuted glass grew hazy. Telvar strained to make out more details before the spell failed. The last image the apprentice saw was the corpse rising from the table as if alive again.

Shaking, Telvar climbed to his unsteady feet and gripped the kitchen table to keep from toppling. Once relaxed, he sat on a nearby chair.

Myramar is practicing the dark art of necromancy! The practice of such magic is forbidden by the Wizard Council! Where did he learn such magic?

Telvar cleaned up the mess caused by the spell and returned to his room as more questions filled his head. His mentorship was irrevocably destroyed, and he now wondered if his own life was at risk.

Chapter 22
Dementhus at the Crossroads

Dementhus was pleased.

In the distance, down in the valley of the Ragnar, the Necromancer could see a dozen forges filling the blue sky with thick black smoke. The forges, fueled by his magic, created arms and armor for the Ragnar warriors from the coronium ore mined from the very twin-peaked mountain he had long sought. The lighter, sharper, and stronger weapons and armor would give the men of Clan Ragnar a significant edge over their adversaries.

Directly before him was the Golem, an ancient weapon of enormous potency, about to be exhumed for the first time in half a millennium. His visions from the Prophet Bafomeht were coming true, and his faith in the Great God Terminus had rewarded him.

The timbers groaned as the bare-chested, well-muscled Ragnar operated the pulleys deployed to lift the black metal warrior from its icy tomb. It had taken a week for Dementhus to design a mechanical framework powerful enough to lever the heavy artifact out of the ice. It had taken even longer for the members of the Ragnar clan to clear the rock-hard layers of frozen ground around the trapped artifact. Dementhus dared not risk using anything but simple magic around the Golem, for fear he might rouse it from its slumber prematurely.

The grunts of the workers and the sound of the creaking wood intensified as the Golem was, at last, eased into an upright position. Overseeing the operation was Abbaster, who commanded the men to hoist the Golem from the pit. When a cement-like mixture of ice and soil had ensnared the magical warrior's metal feet and needed to be cleared, he ordered two Ragnar men into the pit to clear the obstruction.

Superstitious from birth, the two workers, afraid to risk angering their Mountain God, refused Abbaster's command. Without hesitation, Abbaster grabbed a massive iron pickaxe and jumped into the pit himself. With his great strength, he methodically smashed the last bits of ice from around the artifact's legs.

Rising from the pit by way of a rope ladder, Abbaster threw his pickaxe at the feet of the two men who had refused his command. The brute laughed in their faces and addressed the crowd of Ragnar who had come down from the village to see the Golem, their God, hoisted free from its tomb.

"We must work together to free the Mountain God!" exclaimed Abbaster. "The old ways, where fear and superstition held you from your destiny, must end. Under the leadership of your jarl and your new ally, Dementhus, nothing is out of your grasp, and no foe can stand before the Mountain God!"

Dementhus observed Abbaster's performance on the stage of the amphitheater. The warrior from Lux had taken to his role as an emissary from the Mountain God with aplomb.

Abbaster once again ordered the God to be lifted from the pit. When the workers now pulled on the ropes, the Golem was extracted without incident. The giant black metal warrior was placed upright on the dais, one arm by its side, the other arm, which had been used by the Ragnar as an altar, stretched out before it as if bracing for a fall.

Murmurs spread throughout the workers, then up into the icy seats of the amphitheater to the Ragnar gathered there. When Ivor and his son, Crayvor, made their way down the steps of the amphitheater and stood before the Golem, the crowd hushed.

When the pair saluted the nearly fifty-foot-high black metal warrior, the Ragnar cheered, unleashing a flood of violent calls for the death of their enemies, all in the name of the God of the Mountain. Dementhus was not surprised at the bloodlust the artifact inspired. It was a powerful piece of magic. The Ragnar would die for their God—but, more importantly, they would also kill.

The Necromancer also looked upon the artifact with awe, albeit through the prism of magic. He was somewhat overwhelmed by what was before him. The Golem was styled to appear like an ancient warrior clad in loincloth with a plumed helmet. Its blank face stared into oblivion. The detail was unlike any statue he had ever seen, the black skin so lifelike that Dementhus would not have been surprised to see it bleed if pricked or sweat if warmed. Carved into its skin, at seemingly random places, were crimson runes whose purpose Dementhus would have to divine.

The wizard held no reverence nor felt any superstition when regarding the Golem, but he respected powerful magic when in its presence. This magic was far above the primitive magics that were practiced in these days. When he stared into the blank eyes of the artifact, he felt the creature staring back at him. *To be its true master, I need to find the entrance to Antigenesus's fortress and the lab in which this creature was birthed.*

The word of the Mountain God's freedom had spread to the village, and soon the entirety of Clan Ragnar had traveled the short distance up from the valley to see the God for themselves. Most of those who came lingered in the shadows or stayed in their seats in the amphitheater, perhaps fearful that the God of the Mountain would find them unworthy.

When nearly the entire village was in attendance, Dementhus illuminated the gem atop his staff and drew the crowd's attention away from their God. The wizard stood flanked by Ivor and his son and spoke in a deep, commanding tone.

"Those of you in the shadows come forward," beckoned the wizard. "You have nothing to fear. Please, gather around the God of the Mountain. It is okay. Come, come!"

Hesitant at first, then one by one, man, woman, and child, they fought against their primitive fears and made their way with cautious steps to the Golem like uncertain pilgrims to an ancient shrine. Dementhus pondered, *Had the Ragnar developed a true spiritual connection to the magical being?* Possibilities raced through the wizard's head.

Once the Ragnar had gathered in the Golem's shadow, Dementhus nodded to the jarl. Ivor, the imposing leader of the Ragnar, waded into the midst of the massed villagers.

"My Ragnar brothers and sisters," began Ivor. "Freeing the God of the Mountain from His prison was but the first step. As explained by the foreigners, this metal form you see is but an avatar through which He walks upon Medias. Right now, He slumbers, for He needs sustenance to thrive. The Mountain God craves the souls and blood of our enemies and yearns for the taste of their flesh, and I mean to feed Him! We shall satiate that hunger now with a small morsel." He turned to look behind him. "Gidran, bring forth the prisoner!"

From out of the shadows came Gidran and the prisoner: a bloodied and beaten Berserker, an enemy barbarian, with chains about his wrists and ankles. The prisoner stopped his struggles when his gaze fell upon the Golem. Gidran paraded him through the crowd before presenting him to Ivor and forcing him to his knees.

Ivor looked down upon the prisoner's battered face and shook his great bearded head in disgust. "This man is an enemy, a thief from Clan Gnoll. He was found in our lands, hunting on our grounds, taking food from our very mouths. He was so brazen he thought us too weak to defend our own territory. Is he right?"

The crowd responded as Dementhus hoped, with indignant fury. Ivor had to physically push the crowd back to stop them from surging toward the prisoner. Man, woman, and child alike gestured menacingly with axes, broadswords, and balled fists.

The prisoner, sensing the crowd's rage, struggled to his feet and with the last of his strength said, "These lands belong to all the Berserkers!"

The doomed Berserker's outburst was met with a punch to the head from Ivor. The prisoner fell to his knees again.

Ivor silenced the crowd with a glare. "In other times, when we had not the will to fight, we would have returned him for wergild. But not today. His life will serve a higher purpose. His blood is to be the first fed to our ravenous God. Stand back! Stand back!"

The crowd, heeding the jarl's command, cleared away from the giant metal warrior. Gidran, after a nod from Dementhus, went on bended knee before the artifact. Words in the Dark Tongue of Terminus slithered out from Gidran's lips.

When Gidran's incantations reached their apex in volume, Ivor drew his two-handed broadsword. With one swift stroke, the jarl severed the head of the prisoner. Blood erupted from the prisoner's neck and pooled about the Golem's feet. Ivor picked up the head by its long blond hair and displayed it before the bloodthirsty Ragnar. The jarl then turned to the Golem and scaled one of its massive legs. Once he was level with the Golem's waist, Ivor placed the head in its grasping hand. The jarl leapt down from the Golem.

"Watch as the Mountain God feeds!" implored the jarl.

Gidran ceased his chanting. Now clad in the bearskin and animal furs of the natives, the shaman prostrated himself before the Golem and kissed the bloody ground it stood upon. With all eyes focused on the Golem, Gidran prayed in the language of the Dark God from a scroll he pulled from one of his pockets. As he did so, the severed head, resting in the outstretched hand of the Golem, decayed: the flesh peeling back, the hair withering like dried grass.

"He feeds!" shouted a warrior near the Golem.

"It's true," added an old woman. "The Mountain God sucks the flesh as a newborn on a teat!"

A hush fell over the Ragnar after these initial outbursts.

Dementhus scanned the crowd and saw the collective wide-eyed, slack-jawed reaction of the Ragnar to his simple trick. It was enough proof to Dementhus that Gidran's prayer had inflamed a religious fervor in the superstitious brutes. With a nod of his head, the Necromancer encouraged the shaman to continue.

Gidran pocketed his scroll, then waded into the crowd and returned each tentative gaze with a confident smile and firm forearm grasp. After he had greeted most of the clan, he returned to the front of the group and spoke. "Brothers and sisters, soon you will feed the God of the Mountain with the blood of your enemies. But its thirst is severe. You must wage war upon your enemies until they are united under the rule of Ivor!"

The crowd roared in agreement with their new cleric.

Ivor laid a hand on Gidran's shoulder as one would a dear friend and added, "Go now, my clan, and perform those duties you have been tasked with! For with every blade forged, and for every axe sharpened, we are closer to achieving our destiny."

The euphoric crowd dispersed, off to their various duties with renewed vigor. All save the Ragnar jarl. "What is the matter, friend Ivor?" asked Dementhus.

The jarl stood transfixed. He spoke to Dementhus, but he stared at the Golem, which towered above them all. "If we are to unite all the clans of the Berserker tribe, I need to know when the God of the Mountain will be ready to lead us. Our army is too small for such a great task."

"We are preparing for the God's return, but He will not do so until the Ragnar clan is ready to receive him. There is much preparation and bloodletting we must do before the God shall rise. But when He does, the ground will tremble and men will die. The weapons and the armor we have forged will ensure that the first of our enemies will fall to us like overfed cattle before an eager young hunter."

The jarl was a simple man, but he was no fool. Dementhus could speak the man's language: that of power. So, he continued: "Not since the fall of Antium has an army wielded such steel. A steel that can slice through metal, flesh, and stone. No Berserker clan can stop you if your men are properly commanded."

The jarl turned from the Golem to Dementhus and smiled, a bloodthirsty look in his eyes. "I can hardly wait to test the new weapons in battle."

Dementhus bowed to the jarl. "Ivor, your people have humbled me. Soon the Ragnar will overflow with the spoils of war and expand their dominion until it stretches from the mountains, to Arkos, the oceans, and beyond."

Chapter 23

Departure

Tryam thrashed about in bed, his dreams corrupted by images of wars he knew not when and battles he knew not where. A sense of foreboding weighed on his soul. Covered with sweat, he abandoned sleep and staggered out of bed.

Adding to his anxious state was that the expedition was heading to Clan Ulf. What would he say to Wulfric about his loss at the tournament? What would Wulfric's reaction be?

With sleep no longer possible, Tryam used the time to pack up his breastplate, sword, and shield. He placed Wulfric's gifts in the bottom of a trunk and covered them with a blanket. Handling the items again stirred in him feelings of regret. He hoped his friends would accept them back with the same goodwill in which they had been given.

Also running through his mind was another encounter he was anticipating, an encounter with Brother Kayen. The missionary held secrets to his past. Perhaps now that fate had firmly set the young acolyte on the path to monkhood, Kayen would reveal more to him.

The hour was just before dawn. Tryam went to his desk and lit a candle. From his drawer, he pulled out the book he had yet to reshelve, *The Other Side of the Horizon: The History and Legend of Saint Lucian*, and read a passage from the ancient text:

> The knights' spirits were low, and their hearts heavy after their defeat at Dragon's Ridge. Prince Dolobreth had fallen, and the armies of the enemy roamed unopposed across the plains of Dorica. It was Lucian alone who raised the banner

high over the ruins of Harmona, and he alone who held off the waves of attackers, until the knights, inspired by his example, rallied to his side. It was Lucian's blade that gleamed the brightest when a new day dawned. One man had made a stand, and one man had made a difference …

Tryam lifted his eyes from the passage and felt a renewed sense of purpose. Tales of Saint Lucian's humility, sacrifice, and valor served as inspiration. Though the young acolyte might never take up the sword, when the time came, nothing would deter him from doing the will of Aten.

Engrossed in his book, Tryam nearly fell out of his chair when the bell for the morning prayers rang. Rushing to his small wardrobe, he grabbed three pairs of his thick gray traveling robes, all of his heavy woolen undergarments, a fur-lined hat, and a pair of hardy gloves. He stuffed everything, without folding, in his large backpack. (Of his precious book, he gently hid it under his bed.) He hooked the pack over his shoulders, then hefted the armor-filled trunk in his arms before rushing from his cell and out of the rectory—leaving his anxieties behind, he hoped.

The morning air was brisk, the sky clear. He dashed through the archway in the ancient wall that surrounded the church grounds and down the winding road to the ruins below. Upon arriving at the dock, he counted four monks: Samuel, Frey, Cordon, and Emil, all waiting patiently by the supplies they were to take to Clan Ulf.

Sam, with graying hair and a black beard, was second oldest of the group after Emil. He was a confidant of Father Monbatten, always in a foul mood, who would never back down from an argument. Tryam assumed he was the abbot's eyes and ears on this mission.

Tryam was relieved to see Cordon. The beleaguered burly chef was likely going on the mission to get a break from the busy kitchen. *At least we shall not suffer from ill cooking.* With a sly smile, the young acolyte wondered who would take over the cooking and cleaning duties now that both he and Cordon were away.

Last was Frey, who was nearest in age to Tryam but with whom he was never close. The black-haired youth had never once challenged Father Monbatten or the teachings of Saint Paxia, challenges Tryam did almost daily. Tryam was envious that Frey was a true believer.

THE TOMB OF THERAGAARD

The trunk was awkward to carry, and with sweat beading on his brow, Tryam dropped it next to the other supplies.

Brother Emil beckoned the youth to his side. "I am glad you finally arrived," he chided. "I was going to send Father Monbatten to drag you from your bed!"

"I could not sleep, and I lost track of time," explained Tryam. "But I was heartened, though a bit perplexed, when Father Monbatten said you were leading the expedition. I never knew you to leave the walls of the abbey before."

"I was inspired by your misadventures," quipped Emil. "But you are right, my boy. This is the first time I have left Arkos in over a decade. I am doing it for Brother Kayen. He was a former associate of mine, a long time ago, and in another order. In fact, it was I who made Kayen aware of the Order of Saint Paxia and the reason why he brought you here." Emil whispered into his ear. "I also have important spiritual matters I would like to discuss with Brother Kayen—topics Father Monbatten would find troubling."

Tryam had not expected this intrigue, but out of respect for Emil, he did not press the old monk with questions.

A cold breeze blew off the choppy water and sent a shiver down Tryam's spine. "It is getting cold already. I hope we can make it to Clan Ulf and back before the first serious snowfall."

"If we make haste, we should be home before the start of winter." Then Emil paused. "But in this land, storms can come during any season," he noted with some concern. "The daylight hours are already so short."

Daemons were said to leave their lairs when the sun went down, so the thought of trekking through the unfamiliar north in complete darkness was unappealing to Tryam. The expedition would be far from the protective light of Aten shining from the ward tower in Arkos.

A familiar voice disrupted Tryam's grim thoughts.

"Morning, Brothers."

The voice was that of Father Monbatten. As he stood with one hand on his shepherd's staff and the other on his hip, the abbot eyed the monks critically. "By Aten's blessing, I see we are all hale and accounted for. However, before you depart on this noble mission to spread the word of Saint Paxia and the light of Aten to our savage neighbors, I wish to impart blessings and some words of advice. I advise you to listen carefully."

Monbatten's eyes locked with Tryam's briefly before turning to the others. "Sam, I expect you to provide guidance to our younger members and wisdom to Brother Emil as he leads the others into the unforgiving north. Be not afraid to give counsel nor to take it. Cordon, we shall miss your services at the abbey, but I expect you to ensure the health and safety of the others on this trip. Tryam and Frey, I expect you, as representatives of the youth of the order, to be an example of the best of us to these Berserkers. They should see how you benefit from Aten, see how you live by the words of Saint Paxia, and want to be touched in the same way. Together, you should all follow the sage leadership of Brother Emil. Though he has not been to the Berserker lands before, he had extensive experience leading missions to dangerous places before joining our order." He tapped his staff on the ground. "Now gather around, so I may lead a prayer for a successful mission and a safe return."

Somber and respectful, the monks took to their knees before their spiritual leader. Once all focus was upon him, Monbatten recited the Prayer of the Traveler, a hymn for the safe return of those on a dangerous journey. When the prayer was finished, the abbot called for a moment of silence before continuing, in remembrance for those souls lost on prior missions.

"Now that we have assured ourselves of Aten's protection," Monbatten continued, "let's not forget the protection bestowed upon us through the gift of common sense. The Berserkers are brutes of questionable intelligence. They do not think like we do, nor do they believe what we believe. Be careful not to provoke them, for they are short-tempered and armed at all times, a most dangerous combination. Theirs is a warrior culture. Changing their culture and bringing them to the light of Aten is our primary mission. Rely upon the teachings of Saint Paxia for all dealings, and you will be safe."

The monks rose to their feet.

Emil bowed deeply to the abbot. "Truly wise words, Father. We shall take them to heart."

A small skiff appeared and began to make its way through the rough waters to the dock. Monbatten made a point to alert the others. "I see your boat has arrived. Once at Arkos, you will meet up with your escorts. Lord Dunford has generously offered two of his knights to protect your mission. Be polite and let them guide you safely to your destination, but do not let them influence you with their warrior ways."

THE TOMB OF THERAGAARD

The second call for morning prayers rang down from high atop the island, interrupting the abbot. "I must get back to church. May Aten be with you all!"

The monks responded in unison: "May Aten be with you!"

While the others headed for the skiff, Tryam caught Father Monbatten's attention just as the abbot was turning away. "I hope to represent the church well and make my brothers proud."

"You will, if you do as I said," answered the abbot. He patted Tryam on the shoulder, turned, and headed back to the abbey. Tryam could not help but think that the abbot was rooting for an especially cold and rough trip.

After the Engothian sailors tied the skiff to the dock, Tryam and Frey loaded the supplies. When they were finished, the monks cautiously stepped into the overburdened vessel. The young acolyte waited until everyone was on board before he wedged his large body in the back. After the boat pulled away from the harbor, Tryam felt compelled to take one last look at the abbey high above. He felt an intense melancholy overwhelm him. *Shall I be the same person when I return?*

A light mist hovered over the foamy waters as the three-man crew, their armor painted blue with a depiction of an anchor on their breastplates, rowed the small craft toward the mainland. From his spot in the back, Tryam grew concerned at seeing how low the boat sat in the water. When the water washed over the sides, Tryam frantically searched through the stores and grabbed a cast-iron pot to bail.

"Hey," piped up Cordon. "I shall be needing that pot back if you expect me to cook us anything. There will be no welcoming taverns where we are going."

The mariners laughed at Tryam's concern for the safety of the boat. His fear was allayed only after the mariners eased the boat alongside one of the long stone piers in the Arkos harbor. Tryam meditated briefly. *I have already panicked on the trip, and we have not yet left the harbor!*

Dozens of ships of various sizes and designs filled the small port. Tryam spotted a sleek caravel unloading supplies, a banner depicting a golden lion on a blue field high over its crow's nest. Tryam recognized the sigil as that of Engoth. Along the largest pier, Tryam's eyes were drawn to a giant ore freighter. These freighters were the most important ships to the economy of Arkos, since they transported coronium ore back to the continent, where people coveted the rare metal.

The harbor would soon freeze over, so dock workers were rushing about like windblown snowflakes to get the last of the boats on their way. Dirt-covered miners brought in wagons filled with coronium nuggets and stored them in large warehouses near the docks. Containers of ore were then taken from the warehouses and lifted into the ships with nets, using an intricate pulley system. When fully burdened, the freighter would sit a good twenty feet lower in the water. Tryam had been told that only the most capable of captains were given command of such ships, since they were very hard to handle in the open seas.

Tryam was disappointed that he could not see any military vessels, usually the most brightly painted and impressive to look at.

The seamen secured the skiff with a thick line of rope to a nearby mooring. Tryam was the first of the party to exit the boat, and he extended his hand to each of the monks as they disembarked.

Two four-wheeled wagons, each pulled by two draft horses, waited far down the pier. The leader of the mariners turned to Tryam and said, "You can load your supplies on the wagons. Your warrior escorts will arrive soon. Best wishes on your journey!"

The older monks stood aside as Tryam and Frey divided the crates by weight. The lighter crates contained parchment, ink, candles, and blankets, while the heavier crates contained lanterns, oil, food, plates, and cups, along with leather-bound copies of the Word of Aten and Saint Paxia's teachings. They loaded one wagon with the heavier supplies, leaving the other wagon less burdened to transport themselves.

"Where are our escorts?" asked Frey, wiping sweat from his brow. "We can't drive the wagons ourselves, can we?"

"Actually, we could if we had to," boasted Cordon. "In my youth, I used to transport goods between Secundus and Balafax."

"That may be true, Brother Cordon," said Sam with a scowl, "but who will protect us from the Berserkers? I trust the teachings of Saint Paxia, but I would not want to put ourselves at the mercy of barbarians."

While the monks waited for their escorts to arrive, dawn turned to midmorning. Emil's face frowned. The frustrated leader paced back and forth between the two wagons, his fists shaking in a way Tryam had not seen before. "Unacceptable! We have to be going! If we don't leave soon, we shall not reach the cover of forest by nightfall!"

Tryam wanted to help but didn't want to usurp Emil's authority, so instead of acting on his idea, he suggested it to Emil first. "Brother Emil, do you think it would be wise if Frey were to check with the knights at the keep and see if something is amiss?"

The flustered monk scowled, then stopped his pacing as he thought on what Tryam had said. "You may be right. Something may have come up." He turned to the other youth. "Brother Frey, see what you can find out. Tell them the urgency of our mission."

When Frey returned a half hour later, he had two knights in tow. The first was a youth dressed head to toe in worn chainmail with a plain metal helmet. When Tryam glimpsed the young knight's face, he realized, to his delight, it was Gavin. He tried to see who the second knight was, but that one wore a cloak closed tightly over his head as if trying to keep the sun out of his eyes. The second man also walked on unsteady legs.

Tryam rushed down the dock to greet Gavin. "I can't believe it's you! They have you working already?" He was impressed with Gavin's transformation. "Look at your armor. You look like a proper knight."

Gavin nodded, his face strangely glum. "It is only common chainmail given to all the new recruits. I swear this suit must be older than Arkos." He lowered his eyes for a moment. "I regret I never had time to see you in the infirmary, but it gladdens my heart to see you whole." Gavin glanced back to the other knight. "Do your lessons at the abbey include forgiveness? You will not like the one Lord Dunford put in command of this mission."

After Gavin made the remark, the other knight, in a slurred voice, hollered from the top of the lead wagon. "Get over here, squire. We have no time to waste talking to these monks. They are just cargo."

From his perch, the knight's blurry-eyed gaze fell on Tryam. The man froze for a minute, but then a wry grin appeared on his face. The man took a pull from a flask and then said, "It appears some of us will be in for an interesting journey."

Tryam recognized the knight. It was Roderick. The young acolyte closed his eyes and made the sign of Aten, praying for patience and forgiveness. *Why is he here to torment me again?* Tryam whispered to Gavin. "Is this a cruel joke by Lord Dunford? Of all the knights in the world, why did it have to be him?"

Gavin shrugged his shoulders and could offer no explanation.

"Let's move," slurred Roderick as he slumped into the seat of the lead wagon. "Or else before we reach where we are going, half of you may die of old age!"

The monks exchanged worried glances.

"This is outrageous," grumbled Sam, keeping his voice low. "It is not even noon, and this man is already in his cups."

"Our lives are not safe," exclaimed Cordon. "I am too old to put up with such foolishness."

"Stop chattering like milkmaids!" shouted Roderick. "We are late enough!"

"Just a moment," Emil responded in a calm tone. "Let me make introductions. I am Brother Emil, and these are my brothers Sam, Frey, Cordon, and Tryam."

Roderick pointed to all the monks but Tryam. "You four shall ride in the rear wagon."

"A wise suggestion, sir knight, but what about Tryam?" questioned Emil. "I think we could make room for him in yours." Emil shifted a crate so it nestled more snuggly with the others, allowing a generous space where a rider could sit comfortably. "See? Right here will do."

Roderick laughed as if the monk had told a great joke. "We are going into rugged terrain, we must keep the animals fresh, we can't overburden the wagons. The 'fighting monk of Saint Paxia' must walk. If he is too injured from his pathetic attempt to win the tournament, he should stay behind."

Cordon smiled and approached Roderick. "Sir, I have driven wagons for many years. I can see the front wagon has room and weight to spare for Tryam. Surely, it is better for us all to ride?"

Roderick's face matched the red of his hair. "Brother Cordon, my name is Roderick, and I am in charge. Gavin is my second in command. Tryam shall walk. I shall hear no more of it." Spit flew from his lips with each word. "Gavin, take the reins of the rear wagon. Now!"

"Yes, sir," replied Gavin meekly.

Emil's scowl discouraged the other monks from protesting.

"I shall be fine," assured Tryam as the rest of the monks took their spots in the back of Gavin's wagon.

Roderick took the lead and guided the wagons past the wharf and through the large iron gate that sealed the harbor from the rest of the town. He scowled whenever Emil asked about the route they would take and responded only with a gruff "North." Tryam was somewhat relieved that Roderick, despite his inebriated state, could maneuver his wagon through the town's narrow streets.

THE TOMB OF THERAGAARD

The young acolyte had no trouble keeping up with the others and enjoyed taking in the fresh air and watching the townspeople he passed by. It was late afternoon, and the streets of Arkos were alive with commerce. Before storefronts goods were eagerly bartered over as merchants waged verbal battles with the always-wanting public, while craftsmen practiced their arts in the open air before curious onlookers. Outside taverns, under awnings, sat miners easing their pain from a hard night's labor, speaking loudly, ubiquitous frothy beers in their hands.

As the party made their way to the center of town, Tryam looked beyond the wall that surrounded the mage tower to the lush grove within. Tryam found it remarkable that the different varieties of trees and plants could survive the harsh winters. Whenever he had the chance to view the garden, it had always looked as if in full bloom. Tryam believed that magic was a part of Aten's creation and, when used in concert with His will, was a good thing. The abbot thought differently, however, and despised the town mage's presence in Arkos and likely the practice of magic anywhere on Medias.

Farther north, the young acolyte spotted the ward tower with its brilliant blue crystal. He said a prayer of thanks to those living inside, who were dedicated to keeping the Daemons at bay.

Past the ward tower and blacksmith shop, Roderick steered the procession toward their destination, the north gate. When they reached the shadows of the imposing wall, Roderick waved matter-of-factly to two knights who leaned lazily against the battlements atop a walkway that linked the two flanking gatehouses. Tryam sensed that the guards were bored with their duty, a complacency no doubt brought about because there had been little trouble from the Berserkers in years.

One knight eventually acknowledged Roderick and waved the party through the open gateway, asking no questions.

As he left the town for the first time since the tournament, Tryam felt a moment of hesitation. *Am I prepared for what might happen?*

When the wagons passed the tournament grounds, now reverted back to a parade ground for the cavalry, Tryam's hesitation melted away. He was with his brothers and was on the path that Aten has chosen.

Chapter 24
Beyond the Threshold

Tryam absorbed the surrounding vistas with hungry eyes. As he watched the sun dance off the distant Corona Mountains, he no longer fretted about Roderick's presence. The ill-mannered knight was insignificant in Aten's grand scheme.

Every step the young acolyte took filled his eyes with a view he had never seen before. He may have once trod those paths before coming to the abbey, but that did not matter, because now each step was part of a new journey, and he found himself awed by nature's spectacle.

The monks were forced to take a detour to the coronium mine complex, where Roderick maintained they had to pick up much-needed provisions. Emil was perplexed with the detour and explained that the monks had been very thorough, but Roderick refused to listen and insisted on the delay.

After having heard so much about it, Tryam was curious to see the coronium operation. The warehouses and associated buildings were protected by a palisade with guard towers. A small ballista was even in evidence. Leading into the fort was a network of roads that disappeared deep into the mountains. Tryam guessed that over two hundred people lived permanently at the mine—most, even now, deep underground. The workers he did see carried shovels, pickaxes, and heavy hammers. Piles of tailings were scattered about, along with carts filled with ore or overburden. Tryam was left with the impression that mining was hard and dangerous work.

When Roderick returned to the group, the monks shook their heads in disapproval when they realized the provisions he'd said were necessary consisted solely of a barrel of wine.

THE TOMB OF THERAGAARD

The party turned northward, once again heading toward their destination. The road faded into the surroundings, and not long after, it disappeared altogether. Not many travelers took the path they now trod.

Roderick continued guiding the rugged wagons over the uneven terrain into the lowland plains (the primary chain of Coronas still far to the north and east), where tall, hardy grasses still showed green despite the early frost. Before they could reach the safety of the forest that stood tantalizingly close, the sun set. Roderick called the party to a halt, and they set up camp under the dark blue sky.

Cordon was about to start a fire when Rodrick slapped the flint from his hands. "It is too late for that. The fire would draw dangers to us. Berserkers roam these lands, as do all kinds of natural and unnatural beasts."

As a result, the party ate dried fruit and salt pork, doing so in darkness. After the hastily prepared meal, Roderick ordered Gavin to take the first watch, and he went to the back of his wagon to get another drink. With no fire, the monks bundled themselves with woolen blankets to keep out the bitter night air. Exhausted, Tryam fell asleep even before the evening prayers were complete.

Tryam awoke just before dawn and discovered Gavin still seated in his wagon, while a snoring Roderick was passed out drunk on the ground. The young acolyte crept over the snoring knight to stand by Gavin, making sure not to awaken any of the others.

"Did you spend the entire night on watch?"

Gavin nodded, then stood up and stretched his legs. "I'm afraid so. My commander was more *exhausted* than he realized."

"Yes, it looks that way," said Tryam. "I'm afraid his *exhaustion* might become a nightly problem. Next time, let me share watches with you."

"Thanks. However, Roderick might object. I am certain he is not overly fond of you."

Tryam laughed. "Probably true."

The two conversed for a time before the rising sun brightened the sky to the east. Tryam smelled something familiar and turned his attention back to camp, where Cordon was tending to a small fire.

"Is that your chicken and potato soup?"

Cordon stepped back from the fire, where a large copper pot was suspended over low flames. "That's right, lad. A bit of home to soothe the spirit."

The smell of food must have made its way over to Roderick, because Tryam saw the well-rested knight finally stir. Roderick's beady eyes spotted the fire, and he was quick to make his way toward it. "Ah, I see you have prepared my breakfast. Step aside," he commanded.

After snatching a bowl from the hands of Frey, who had just finished a prayer to Saint Paxia, Roderick, ignoring Sam's concerns about rationing, ladled himself a double portion of soup. When Roderick was finished, he belched loudly. "Finish up quickly!" he barked. "We can't linger here all day!"

Emil, who had witnessed the entire scene from a few feet away, had to restrain Sam from starting in with the knight. Tryam wished that Emil would have let the old man go, since *no one* could withstand Samuel's withering verbal assaults. *If Roderick's behavior continues unchecked, something bad is bound to come of it.*

By the time the party began their second day of travel, clouds had thickened, and a gentle rain fell. A mist shrouded the forest, which had been just out of reach the day before.

When they reached the woods, Roderick and Gavin struggled to get the wagons past the younger trees that grew close to the forest edge. Roderick tasked Tryam with cutting branches and pushing the wagons over exposed roots and fallen logs.

Hours passed as the party made their way methodically through the ancient forest. Brief glimpses of the Corona Mountains helped guide Roderick north, but large trees blocked most of the meager light the sun offered. In the misty gloom, Tryam felt the unseen eyes of predators upon him. *Wolves? Bears?* He could not imagine how Kara braved a forest like this by herself, and he was glad they had not spent the night inside its confines, despite the cover it offered.

It took until evening to break through the suffocating forest, and when they did so, Roderick informed the group they had traveled beyond the range of the Engothians' dominion. Before them now stood the inhospitable rocky highlands the Berserkers called home.

Rolling hills replaced grassland and trees. The weariness of travel did not diminish Tryam's wonder at the world, but when he heard a cry of some great beast in the distance, a shiver went down his spine. This land, from the vegetation and animals, to the hills and valleys, was dramatically different from home, despite the relatively short distance they had traveled.

THE TOMB OF THERAGAARD

When it was dusk, the clouds parted, and the weak rays of light fell upon the Coronas, glistening off their snow-capped peaks. Tryam looked to the mountains and wondered what secrets the stone giants held.

Around midnight, Roderick signaled the party to stop and led the wagons behind a moss-covered boulder that a receding glacier had deposited aeons before. Roderick allowed a campfire, saying the cover of the boulder would shield them from prying eyes. After taking two helpings at supper, the red-haired knight drained his flask before passing out, with no concern for setting a watch. Gavin volunteered to do so, while Emil led the monks in prayer, calling on Aten for protection.

Tryam slept little, despite his exhaustion; he was too excited, anxious to see what the next day would bring.

✠ ✠ ✠

"The immediate cost of violence is clear," lectured Emil on the evening of the third day. The venerable monk sat atop a crate in Gavin's wagon, engaging the others as if they were back home during liturgical study period. "You see it with blood and broken bodies, and you smell it in the smoke of burning cities. The benefits of violence are dubious. How many times has a war ended only for another to begin anew with different players on the same stage? These are the lessons we should impart to the Berserkers."

"But what about the immediate problems with pacifism?" asked Tryam, his long strides keeping up with the wagon. "When brigands attack a city, do the people not have a right to defend themselves? When a traveler is waylaid by a highwayman, should he just accept his fate?"

"You must look to why those brigands are attacking or the highwayman is robbing," answered Emil, "and consider what violence had first been committed upon them that had led them down this path of evil. The cycle of violence must be broken, and it is up to us, as disciples of Saint Paxia, to do so."

"So, we should be the first to lay down our arms," Tryam asked dubiously, "and others will respond in kind?"

"Absolutely," answered Frey. The black-haired youth was at his most talkative when defending the order. "Is that not what happened to Saint Paxia when he laid down his arms? Peace, not swords, greeted him and his followers."

Tryam was about to respond when a light flashed from a clump of pines parallel to their path. "Did anybody else just see that?"

The monks turned to see where Tryam pointed, but no further flashes were seen.

"My eyes are not those of an eagle," said Emil. "I can't see anything past my nose. What was it?"

"A flash of light, as if something metallic caught the rays of the setting sun."

"Let's not distract ourselves with flashes of light," scoffed Sam. "Our escorts would have said something if there were anything to see."

Emil resumed his lecture, but after they had traveled another mile, Tryam spotted the flash again, this time closer to their position. Tryam excused himself and ran to the head of the wagon, where Gavin was fighting the urge to sleep.

"I think I spotted something. Twice now, I saw a flash as if sun glinted off steel. Do you think someone could be following us?" He pointed. "It was from over there."

Gavin roused himself and peered into the woods. "I suppose it's possible. You could hide an army in those trees. But why would anyone want to follow five monks with two knight escorts? We have no valuables."

"True, but they don't know that. Should you alert Roderick just in case? I would speak to him, but he is so bullheaded, he would ignore me out of spite."

Gavin nodded and spurred his wagon ahead until he was alongside Roderick. They were too far away for Tryam to overhear what was being said; however, it was obvious from Roderick's body language that the hungover knight did not give Gavin's warning much credence and that he waved the new recruit back to the rear.

"He told me that any threat to us was preposterous," confirmed Gavin, who looked as angry as Tryam had ever seen him. "He treats this mission like a furlough rather than an expedition." The young knight jerked his thumb back to the monks riding in back. "It will up to us to keep them safe. We must be vigilant."

Tryam frowned and nodded his head.

Shortly after nightfall, Roderick called the expedition to a halt just as they reached the cover of pines. It was the coldest night so far, and the red-haired knight called for a great fire to be made. Since it was too dark to

THE TOMB OF THERAGAARD

look for kindling, the monks used wood they had stockpiled in Roderick's wagon. Cordon cooked a stew from game that Gavin had caught the previous night, while Roderick excused himself to check the surroundings. When the knight disappeared, however, Tryam noticed that he had left his sword behind. When he returned, Roderick looked unsteady on his feet.

After prodding from Frey, Emil held court around the campfire and lectured once more on theology. Roderick sat down beside the monks, his expression one of irritation.

"In days past, it was common for monks to be advisors and close allies to kings," Emil was saying. "The imperators of Antium always traveled with a cleric, who advised on martial and spiritual concerns. Today, as you know, the petty lords we call kings rarely seek counsel from the Church of Aten. The clergy who do advise them only pray for the army's success, the will of Aten being secondary to the desires of the lords of the realm."

"When our order gains more prominence in the Church," vowed Frey, "we shall offer wiser counsel."

The curmudgeon Sam concurred with young Frey's sentiment. "Our time will come, of that I have no doubt. I would not be surprised if our very own abbot became one such advisor. Perhaps, Roderick, even an advisor to your own king."

A belly laugh erupted from the knight. "King Athelrad is a warrior king and would laugh in your abbot's face." He chortled to himself, then threw up his hands when none of the monks responded. "Enough of this. I can't stomach this talk. I need to start my watch."

Roderick grabbed another helping of stew before disappearing into the dark.

Gavin, his face turning red, said sheepishly, "I apologize for Roderick's rude behavior, but everything I've seen in my short time with the knights confirms what he said. No one would listen to your abbot. At least, not at first."

Emil leaned over to pat the young knight on the shoulder. "Mayhap there is some truth in what Roderick said, but no one can know the will of Aten. Keep an open mind to our teachings. I hope that the next generation of warriors will see a greater role for Saint Paxia in their lives."

"I was raised with a strong belief in Aten," offered Gavin, "and I shall always lend my ear to a monk,"

"That's good, my young man," said Emil, smiling, before taking another spoonful of stew. "That reminds me, I hope Tryam doesn't mind me asking, but could you tell us about the tournament? It was quite a scandal back at the abbey, but from all the tales we've heard, it's hard to tell fact from fiction. We are lucky to have the two finalists with us this night."

"I don't mind," assured Tryam as Gavin hesitated to answer. "My wounds have healed, both physical and spiritual."

Sam, his face wrinkled in a frown, spoke up. "The tournament is anathema to what we believe! We don't need more knights in Arkos." His expression grew more severe. "Gavin is a fine youth, but his talents are being wasted. Where he could be bending his back in honest labor, he instead will be ordered to protect Lord Dunford's coronium." He balled his fists. "Lord Dunford, bah! I have never met any man more obsessed with material things. It seems as if the mines are his singular focus."

Sam's outburst caused the others to argue among themselves until Emil raised his hands to quiet them. "Lord Dunford is a good man, but I agree his priorities are askew." He cleared his throat. "Now, Gavin, please tell us about the tournament."

The young knight cleared his own throat and placed his stew down near the fire. "There were three parts of the competition. The first one tested your ability with a bow. My father, before becoming a miner here in Arkos, was an avid hunter who could fell a hawk at great distance. He taught me well, and I finished second overall. The only interesting part of the first trial was Tryam. A Berserker girl came onto the field and planted a big kiss on him. It caused quite a commotion."

"Kissed?" questioned Frey, mouth agape. "Berserker girl?"

"The girl is Kara, but she is just a friend!" assured Tryam, more harshly than he intended. "She alerted me to the fact that Roderick, still sore after the sparring incident, had been tampering with my arrows. She caused the distraction so she could slip me a true arrow."

"Sparring with a knight? Participating in a blood sport? Cavorting with Berserker women? Tryam, your failings seem to be unending," groused Sam, shaking his head. "Is she why you are on this trip? Our order requires celibacy of its members. I shall make sure the two of you are kept separated!"

"Enough, Brother Sam," scolded Emil. "Tryam has pledged his loyalty to the order and should be forgiven the sins of youth." He looked at Gavin and gave an encouraging nod. "Gavin, tell us what happened in part two."

The newly minted squire coughed to clear his throat in the awkward silence that followed. "Yes, well, the next round was a test of teamwork. The

THE TOMB OF THERAGAARD

archery targets were removed, and a mammoth was brought into the arena. We were divided into two teams and were tasked to herd the colossal beast to our respective tarp. Maxius, the blacksmith's son, almost led his team to victory, but we wisely followed Tryam's plan to use the beast's strength against it. He commanded us to rile the mammoth up by throwing mud at it, causing it to thrash the other team aside. Then, instead of trying to pull the beast's harness, Tryam jumped upon its back and rode the beast to victory. Can you can believe it?!"

Sam clucked his tongue. "Had Tryam shown wisdom, he would not have entered the tournament. He had no chance to win. It was not in Aten's will. He nearly died!"

The monks erupted in crosstalk, some defending Sam, some arguing against him. It was Cordon who brought the commotion to an end. "Let's get to the final test," he begged, "before the stew gets cold."

Gavin hurried to the end. "The final test was duels with the sword. My father had prepared me well for this part, and the first rounds were easy. It came down to Tryam and me. Although we were both skilled, the real difference was Tryam's injury. Without his sacrifice in the test with the mammoth, he would have been the winner. In fact, Tryam had me defeated, down on the ground, both our swords abandoned, and with his hands about my neck. He could have killed me, assuming the knights would not have interfered, but he saw my helplessness and abandoned his grip. His injury finally overwhelmed him, he passed out, and I was declared the winner."

Dark memories came rushing to Tryam's mind like a fast-approaching storm. "I appreciate your humility, Gavin. But injury or no, I lost control of myself at the end of the match, and that caused me to fail. I only hope you can forgive me for my behavior. You fought bravely and honorably. I agree with Brother Samuel and now understand that my destiny lies with serving Aten."

"And the world will be better for it," asserted Emil. "Be glad that your revelation ended with friendship, for not all revelations are so rewarding."

"What do you mean?" asked Tryam with genuine concern.

"Yes, tell the younger ones why you joined the order," prodded Sam, crossing his arms around his chest.

The old man stared into the fire. "When I first chose the clergy, I joined the Order of the Imacolata, an order that actively confronts agents of the Dark God. I learned much about sacrifice and faith, but on one of our missions, I witnessed something so dark, so fiendish, that the horror of the event haunts me to this day. I had to leave the Imacolata to find peace in my heart, and I joined the Order of Saint Paxia. Still, late at night, visions of what I had seen haunt me. No, do not ask what of, for I shall not say." Emil wrapped his arms around his body.

"The fire is getting low," observed Sam, breaking the tension. "Tryam, fetch us some more wood."

"Yes, sir. At once." As Tryam stood, he could only wonder what Emil had seen that had disturbed him so. The young acolyte shook off the gloomy thoughts, left the campfire, and walked to Roderick's wagon to see if there was any firewood left there. Roderick was nowhere to be seen, and to Tryam's disappointment, the supply of kindling there was exhausted. He would have to venture into the woods to find more.

It did not take long before Tryam was out of sight of the camp and was wishing he had had the foresight to have taken a torch. After a while, his eyes adjusted to the darkness, and to his fortune, a luminous quarter moon shone through the departing clouds above the pines.

Venturing farther into the woods than he had planned, Tryam stumbled on a tree that had fallen during a storm. Not having a hatchet, the young acolyte used his muscles to break up the branches. After a while, Tryam had collected enough kindling to sustain the fire for the rest of the night, so he headed back.

Before he reached camp, however, his ears caught unfamiliar voices. Though he was too far away to make out what they were saying, he could tell from their tone that something was amiss. He placed the firewood at his feet and crept toward the encampment, using trees to hide his approach. The strangers spoke again, and this time Tryam could determine their accents: that of the northern Berserkers.

Tryam inched closer until he could duck underneath Roderick's wagon and peer behind a muddy wheel into camp. There he spotted two brawny Berserkers standing casually beside the fire. Roderick was quivering before them, with his arms bound behind his back. The Berserkers wore bearskin cloaks, under which they wore greenish black armor, and they held axes whose metal heads had a greenish tint. Cruel smiles played on their tattooed faces. Tryam cocked his ear to listen.

"It looks like we got ourselves a party of monks," the Berserker with a scar across his forehead said. He poked Roderick in the chest. "One of you is missing. Where is he?"

Roderick remained silent.

The scarred Berserker threw the Engothian knight face first to the ground and kicked him in the head.

Roderick rolled over and spat dirt. "I suggest you stop whatever you are planning on doing. There is a company of my brother knights only a few days' journey from here. They will not rest in bringing justice if any of us are harmed. They do not fear you barbarians and could easily destroy you!"

The two Berserkers laughed in unison before the scarred Berserker kicked Roderick in the groin. "You speak rather boldly for one who did not put up a fight."

"We don't want a fight," interjected a gravelly voice.

It was Emil. The old monk sat beside Gavin, Cordon, Sam, and Frey, near the edge of the fire.

Tryam prayed as Emil calmly rose to his feet and extended his empty hands to the two Berserkers. "We are members of the Order of Saint Paxia from the abbey in Arkos. Our order is dedicated to peace and coexistence among all people. We are on this expedition to bring supplies, goodwill, and the Word of Aten to your brethren. We carry nothing else of value. Stay and join us, and listen to the teachings of Saint Paxia, or let us go on our way unmolested."

Tryam's heart pounded as he fretted about what he should do. According to the teachings of Saint Paxia, he should join his brethren in trying to convince the Berserkers to settle this with friendship. According to logic, he should escape and notify the nearest band of Engothian warriors. He knew in his heart, however, that neither option would rescue his friends, for these Berserkers would not listen to reason, and they were now days away from the protection of other knights. He looked to the back of the wagon and to the trunk that contained his sword. He bowed his head and prayed to Aten for guidance as he listened to the Berserkers respond to Emil's plea.

"Graybeard, we have our own mission. Now sit down before you make me lose my temper." This came from the second Berserker, who had on his face a tattoo of a grasping fist inked in blue.

When Emil hesitated, the man shoved him down. He then pointed to Gavin. "I want you to tie everyone's hands behind their backs, except for the graybeard's."

"Do as they say," instructed Emil in a commanding tone, even as he struggled to sit back up. "Do not resist."

Tryam couldn't wait for a sign from Aten. He crawled out from under Roderick's wagon and reached over the side to gain access to the trunk. The sword was quickly in his hand, and he returned to his hiding spot.

Back at the fire, Gavin had tied Cordon, Samuel, and Frey's hands behind their backs. The two Berserkers conferred with each other in low voices Tryam could not overhear. The young acolyte gripped his sword in the manner Wulfric had taught him. It was time to act.

Tryam crawled out from behind the wheel. Different attack scenarios were playing in his head when light from the campfire reflected off the blade in his hand and caught Emil's attention. The old monk looked Tryam's way and shook his head.

"Our other member has returned," announced Emil to their captors. "Come, Tryam, lay your weapon aside. Reason will serve us better."

Dumbfounded by Emil's words, Tryam froze. He had missed his opportunity to strike at the intruders and take them unawares.

Emil repeated his command for Tryam to lay down his sword.

The two Berserkers turned to where Emil was directing his voice. The scarred one shouted: "Come out! Come here right now!"

After more imploring from Brother Emil, Tryam stood up and dropped the sword at his feet, praying that the old monk knew what he was doing. The nervous acolyte stepped over his sword and made for the campfire with short, deliberate steps, his empty hands palms up. "I'm here. I shall not resist."

The scarred man smirked once he saw Tryam enter the light of the campfire. "Now, this is more like it. You are no feeble monk. You," he barked, pointing to Gavin, "tie up our would-be hero."

As his hands were being bound, Tryam whispered to Emil, "Are you sure I did the right thing?"

Emil nodded, his face a mask of calmness. "I am. If we don't show aggression, neither will they."

It took no wizardry for Tryam to read Gavin's thoughts, his facial expressions acutely showed both fear and shame as he secured the leather strap around Tryam's wrists. The scarred brute threw Tryam to the ground, where he landed between Frey, who was shaking uncontrollably, and Roderick, whose eyes stared up at the Berserkers with seething rage.

The scarred Berserker offered Emil a leather strap and pointed to Gavin. "Now you, old man. Tie up this young warrior."

THE TOMB OF THERAGAARD

Emil refused to take the strap and instead challenged the barbarian. "I cannot do this unless you inform us of your intentions."

"Our intentions?" the Berserker said, laughing. "I am not so sure you really want to know, but I shall tell you, since you asked. Our God thirsts for blood, and our leader asks for strong prisoners." Then he scratched his head, winked at his companion, and laughed even louder. "Now that I think about it, we do not need an old fool like you."

In a move too quick for Tryam to react to, the scarred Berserker pulled back his axe and swung it toward Emil. The young acolyte watched helplessly as the axe sank deep into Emil's neck with a sickening thwack. Before his frail body hit the ground, the leader of the monks' expedition was dead.

Adrenaline flushed into Tryam's body, and he struggled against his bonds. Beside him, Roderick likewise twisted his body in a futile, rage-filled struggle. Of the monks, only Frey cried out, while Cordon and Sam sat in shocked silence. Gavin, the only one free to react, did so.

The unarmed recruit knocked into the scarred Berserker with his shoulder while making a play for his axe. He was not quick enough, though, and the two struggled briefly before the larger Berserker threw Gavin outside the light of the fire and toward the wagons.

"Gavin, grab my sword!" shouted Tryam. "It's behind you!"

The scarred Berserker turned around and kicked the young acolyte in the stomach, forcing the air from his lungs. The warning, though, had paid off, and Tryam's sword was in Gavin's hands already. The recruit stood before Emil's killer, waving the blade provocatively.

The scarred Berserker taunted Gavin. "C'mon, boy. You want to fight? Then let's fight!"

With that, he rushed Gavin, and the two traded blows, axe clashing against sword.

Desperate to help the young squire, Tryam, his hands still bound behind his back, tried pulling his arms apart until his bones nearly snapped, but no matter how hard he strained, he could not free himself. He took a breath and let his faith guide him. Instead of trying to snap the leather strap, he stretched and twisted until he pulled his arms underneath his legs. He continued to contort until he managed to get his hands in front instead of behind him.

The tattooed Berserker was intent on watching his companion fight and had his back to the bound men. Tryam rose to his full height and came up behind the distracted barbarian. With the speed of a pouncing wolf, he wrapped the strap around the young man's neck.

"That's it! Choke him! Don't let him go!"

Tryam heard Roderick's plea in the background, but soon thereafter, all other sights and sounds faded away. The young acolyte let hate flow into his soul like a river of lava. The scar on his chest burned in agony. He used his superior position, height, and weight to bend back the brute. The leather strap dug deep into the soft flesh, and blood poured down the Berserker's neck as the man's hands blindly tried to grasp Tryam. The young acolyte loosened his grip only when the Berserker's thrashing ceased. The lifeless body fell to the ground.

Flush with fury, Tryam blocked out the feeling of warm blood on his hands and the sight of the purple, contorted face at his feet. With the dead man's axe, he cut the leather strap that had bound his hands. He then entered the melee between Gavin and the scarred Berserker, ready to deal out murderous blows.

Gavin was bleeding from a thigh wound and was staggering from repeated blows. The chainmail he wore was not protecting him from the Berserker's weapon. With the scarred brute's next attack, Tryam saw the green metal axe slice through Tryam's old sword, rendering his friend defenseless. Gavin fell to his knees, awaiting certain death.

Rage blinded Tryam as he swung his axe at the Berserker's back.

The sharp-edged weapon swished through the air, then sliced deep into the Berserker's shoulder. The barbarian dropped his weapon and roared in agony. The look of disbelief on the brute's face when he turned to look at Tryam was one of complete shock. Tryam swung his axe again, and the edge bit deep into the Berserker's green breastplate. Blood squirted freely from both wounds.

"I shall not beg for mercy," the doomed man said.

Tryam heard the words and did not let up. Urged on by Roderick, Tryam connected his axe to the side of the Berserker's neck. Blood splashed high into the air. The man fell backward, his limbs loose about him, as his life emptied onto the pine needles of the forest floor.

Tryam, breathing heavily, looked down at the dying man. A bloody foam was coming out of the Berserker's mouth. The scarred warrior beckoned Tryam to come closer.

Tryam bent down and placed his ear near the helpless Berserker's mouth, uncertain as to what the dying man wanted to say, and he listened.

"I greet my ancestors now, but be aware that more of us are coming. Many more! The God of the Mountain has awakened!"

The light that burns in all men's eyes left those of the Berserker's.

Rushing into Tryam's consciousness was all that he had just seen and done and had blocked. Tryam stood up, dropped the axe, and looked about the grisly battle scene with an expression as blank as an unused roll of parchment.

Gavin guided his numb body back to the campfire. After the young squire had unbound all of his companions, he turned to Tryam. "What did he say to you?"

"Yes," added Roderick, who had sobered quickly, "what did that vile barbarian whisper in your ear?"

The question helped Tryam focus on the present. "He said more are coming."

Roderick ran his fingers through his sweat-soaked hair. "If that is true, we must return to Arkos at once and inform Lord Dunford. We are not safe out here."

No one disagreed.

Emil's body was already cool when Tryam closed his old friend and mentor's eyes. Frey, Sam, and Cordon gathered beside him, and they said a prayer over their fallen companion.

"He died for his principles and for his faith," said Samuel.

"He now sleeps the sleep of the saved," added Cordon.

Their words left Tryam shattered. Emil was dead, and the young acolyte might have been able to save him had he not frozen when he should have acted. Regret and sorrow cooled the rage in his soul.

The expedition packed the wagons in silence and in great haste, placing Emil in a thick blanket and adding his weight alongside the crates as if he were just another piece of cargo. By the time the red sky of dawn appeared, they were already headed south.

Chapter 25

Puzzle Pieces

Myramar's odd behavior began after the unexpected visit from the Albus mage. Of that fact, Telvar was sure. Of anything else, he was uncertain.

After he had observed Myramar's macabre doings in the basement laboratory, Telvar made every effort to keep the tower mage unaware of any concern he harbored. If there was a spirit inside the amulet and it was exerting its will over Myramar, it would not be wise to provoke it. They had multiple interactions after he had spied upon his mentor, but Telvar made sure not to show his suspicions. To avoid antagonizing Myramar, the young wizard never pressed his mentor on when he would resume his apprenticeship.

The old man rarely slept or ate but somehow maintained his newfound vigor and even hosted Lord Dunford without causing alarm from the irritable commander. Despite his precautions, though, Telvar knew it would be only a matter of time before Myramar turned against him.

Should I alert the Wizard Council? Telvar laughed at the notion of a first-level Rutilus mage barging into the Veneficturis with a story of a mad tower mage.

Telvar focused on what he needed to find out on his own. *What was Dementhus's role in this? Why would Dementhus travel to this insignificant outpost?*

Dementhus was himself a member of the Wizard Council. News of necromancy being spread by a member in good standing would shake the foundations of the wizard hierarchy. *But why pass along the secrets of necromancy to ancient Myramar? Wouldn't I have been a better choice? I am young and ambitious, Myramar is at the end of his career. There must be something I am missing.*

The water clock in Telvar's room indicated it was midnight. Done with his chores, Telvar proceeded directly to the magic library down the curved hallway. The young mage walked between the stacks of scrolls, parchments, and leather-bound tomes, searching for clues. He found it hard to believe that an Albus mage would need to consult the magic library of a small outpost when he had access to the great libraries in Secundus.

The young mage searched for the journals of the previous tower wizards. When he found them, he realized they had been examined recently; they were clear of dust and out of order. Telvar took the journals off the shelf, placed them on a nearby writing desk, and perused them.

The texts contained the typical records: accounts of research activities, performance of the tower lens, and missives written to fellow wizards. The only curious thing Telvar noted was that the tower records of the first mages were missing. An explanation came in one dry entry from a later wizard named Korddainer, who noted that he had destroyed the early journals at the behest of a new sect of monks who had arrived in Arkos from Engoth.

Telvar fumed at the shortsighted wizard Korddainer and dropped the journals on the desk. He was at a dead end.

Telvar slumped in the chair and rubbed his eyes. *What if Korddainer had hidden the records rather than destroyed them?* He sighed, then scrunched his face. *Dementhus would not have given up, and I won't either. An Albus wizard could cast a spell to find the last breath of a butterfly!*

After taking a moment to think, Telvar got on his hands and knees and looked for footsteps in the dust on the floor. He found three distinct sets of prints. He recognized his own and determined Myramar's by their size, leaving the third prints to be the Albus wizard Dementhus's.

As he moved along the floor, he detected something else mixed in the dust, a peculiar metallic powder. Telvar took a pinch of the strange gritty dirt and examined it with a practiced eye. When he detected magic in the tiny particles, he felt his spine tingle. *Dementhus was seeking something hidden …*

He focused on finding more of the particles.

After crawling along the entire library floor, Telvar located the area that held the highest concentration of the magical dust, an area on the floor opposite the red door.

He examined the area but detected nothing unusual. If a spell had been placed on the marble, it had to be powerful magic to remain hidden.

Telvar sighed. He would need to risk casting another spell.

The young wizard summoned magic and made a gesture with his hand. A small beam of light shot from his fingertips, and he directed the rays to the floor. When he looked again, he saw that his light spell had revealed the runes and symbols for an illusion spell carved into the stone. Unfortunately, the intricate nature of the spell was far beyond his current abilities to counter.

Undaunted, Telvar considered alternative possibilities; however, only one idea seemed practical. Thinking back to his alchemy lessons, he understood that even marble would melt if sufficiently heated. He could use the alchemy laboratory in the tower to make a powerful fuel. The idea came with drawbacks. The spell risked damaging what was hidden, and it would be hard to hide the damage from Myramar. Nevertheless, Telvar exited the library and proceeded to the alchemy lab on the third floor.

Although Myramar had moved many of his supplies to his underground laboratory, he still kept a wide variety of reagents in the alchemy lab. Most of the organic materials were provided from the tower's grove, but the inorganic material had to be shipped in from the continent, and their supply was limited. The young wizard found the proper proportions of dung, sulfur, and a rare mineral known as arganta, and using a pestle, he mixed the concoction quickly but carefully inside a crucible. He then poured the mixture into a yellow gourd and rushed back to the library—but not before retrieving his staff from his chambers.

The young wizard made sure the library door was locked before he proceeded. Telvar sighed when he realized he had forgotten to mark the spot and had to retrace his steps. After a dozen curses, he found the concentrated magical dust and poured the mixture from the gourd into a small pile. He grabbed his staff and focused on a spell to conjure the fire element. Seeing the element in his mind, he summoned it to his hand. He then dropped the magical fire onto the ground and watched as the mixture burned.

Haste, at this stage, was unwise. Telvar regulated the flames with his mind, a skill he had failed to demonstrate during Myramar's fraudulent test. But this time, there was no sign of the creature, either.

The pungent odors of the burning fuel floated up a chimney linked to the flues from the floors below, and when the fire reached the necessary temperature, the marble began to melt. However, the heating process had taken longer than Telvar had calculated, and little of the fuel remained. After a few more minutes, the fuel was spent.

Telvar waited for the marble to cool, keeping his ears open for signs of Myramar's footsteps. When it was cool enough to touch, the young wizard scraped away the burnt remnants and inspected the damage to the floor. He had created a two-inch-wide hole. Looking through the hole confirmed his suspicions: There was a hidden compartment below.

The nervous wizard reached inside with his right hand. His fingertips made contact with a piece of parchment. He pinched the parchment and pulled it up through the small opening. The parchment was ancient and split in his hand, revealing another page between the crumbling halves. Inscribed on the hidden page was writing done by a deft hand, with many complex glyphs, diagrams, and runes. Each parchment he retrieved from the hole was like that: It split, revealing a secret page between the halves.

This is what the Albus mage was after!

Telvar collected all the pages he could, moved a shelf to cover the hole in the floor, and headed back to his own room.

By the flickering light of his lamp, Telvar examined the pages he had discovered. It was dawn by the time he understood what it was he held in his now-quivering hands. Over and over he questioned his logic, but he could not contradict the conclusion he had made. The parchments he held contained a spell to unlock the entrance to a wizard's tower. *But not any tower! The tower of one of the greatest archmagi to have ever lived: Antigenesus!*

Telvar went over the facts in his mind and came to a conclusion. *Dementhus must be on a quest to find Antigenesus's old laboratory. But such an undertaking would not be sanctioned by the Wizard Council. They would require a team of wizards to enter such a dangerous place. Dementhus must have his own agenda, one the Wizard Council is surely not aware of!*

Chapter 26
Interrogation

The white walls of Arkos had never looked so welcoming to Tryam's eyes. No one in the devastated party had spoken since the attack five days before, making the sound of the voices of the guards along the sentry walk momentarily startling. Tryam's feet were weary and his heart heavy when the expedition passed, once more, through the north gate.

Tryam's thoughts remained on Emil and the Berserker lives he had taken. He had never experienced death this personally before. Even after five days of prayer and contemplation, he had not come to peace with what he had seen and what he had done.

Roderick led the wagons through the narrow streets toward the keep. Townsfolk greeted the party's grim expressions with concern, some making the sign of Aten when they saw the wrapped body of Emil in the back of the lead wagon.

The knights on guard at the keep's main gate waved Roderick through without a word. Roderick acknowledged his brother warriors and guided the wagons to the front of the inner fortress, the location of the knights' headquarters. The red-haired knight had not had a drop to drink since the attack.

Roderick ordered the monks to follow him inside the inner keep to meet with Lord Dunford. As the fortified double doors of the knights' headquarters opened before them, Tryam did not welcome what was about to come.

Inside, ornate candelabras lit the great hall and illuminated statues depicting various heroes from Engoth's past. A large portrait of Lord Dunford, in his most regal pose, dominated the north wall straight ahead.

THE TOMB OF THERAGAARD

Several rooms, including an armory, led off from the main chamber. Roderick ordered the group to a side room, where a fireplace roared and a large round table stood empty. The knight excused himself and took Gavin with him, leaving the monks to talk among themselves.

"I don't like leaving Emil unattended," grumbled Cordon. "Our brother must be buried at once! This delay is intolerable."

"This is the way with knights," assured Sam. "They need to write reports and record everything that happened before they can decide what to do. Emil's spirit already rests with Aten, be assured of that."

After an interminable wait, the young acolyte's anxiety increased when he saw the bearded Lord Dunford along with the golden-robed Abbot Monbatten enter the room. From the somber looks on their faces, it was clear that Roderick must have already given them a summary of the events.

"Everyone, please sit," ordered Dunford.

The burly commander remained standing as he waited for the monks to be seated. After a long pause, during which Dunford stroked his beard, he finally spoke, addressing Monbatten, who had taken the seat right next to Tryam.

"First, as the representative here for His Majesty, King Athelrad, I express my regrets at the loss of one of your order and for our inability to protect the mission. I did not know Emil well, but I knew his reputation as a man of the highest quality."

"Thank you, Lord Dunford," replied the abbot, who humbly nodded his head.

"Any loss of life is unacceptable," continued Dunford. "We shall not and cannot let this event pass without justice being served. However, to decide on a course of action, I need to know precisely what happened."

Dunford walked behind Roderick, who squirmed uncomfortably in his chair. "Roderick tells me the company was ambushed by two Berserkers while you were making camp. Is this correct?"

The four monks agreed.

"He also told me he was on watch when the Berserkers entered camp, but they had approached from a hidden path in the unfamiliar woods. He stated that he struggled with them but was overpowered and then subdued."

The monks exchanged glances but did not question the account. Tryam doubted this was true. Roderick had been in no condition to put up a fight that night. *He had been "subdued" before the Berserkers even arrived.*

Dunford turned his gaze to Tryam, who was taken aback by the commander's intense stare. "You were out collecting firewood when the Berserkers first came. What did you see?"

Tryam wondered if he would have the courage to relate the story; however, when he started, the words flowed fast like water through a crack in a dam. "As I returned to camp, I could make out unfamiliar voices, so I proceeded with caution. When I got closer, I realized that two Berserkers were threatening our group, and the brutes had Roderick restrained. I hid behind the wagon and watched as they tied everyone up. From the wagon I retrieved a sword I had intended to return to my friends at Clan Ulf. I did not believe I could either reason with them or get help in time, so I hoped to catch them unaware and turn them away, with Gavin's and Roderick's help. Before I could spring my plan, though, Brother Emil spotted me. He called out, urging me to reveal myself and by so doing alerted the Berserkers to my presence. I had no choice but to do as Brother Emil commanded."

"Then what happened?" pressed Dunford.

Tryam took a deep breath and continued. "I dropped my sword and walked into camp. The Berserkers had me tied up alongside the others, but Brother Emil demanded that they state their intentions before he would agree to bind Gavin. They laughed and then struck Brother Emil down without mercy! I acted instinctively and got the leather strap that bound my hands over the neck of one of the Berserkers while Gavin engaged the other. We managed to kill both of them."

Before he could continue, Monbatten stood up and pointed a gnarled finger at Tryam. "Your actions may have provoked those brutes! You had no right to even touch a sword, let alone ponder using one to kill another being. You have brought shame to us all."

The yellow-haired commander raised his arms to calm the old monk. "Abbot Monbatten, Tryam complied with Emil's order and dropped the weapon. Had he not acted after the monk's death, perhaps we would now mourn the deaths of five members of Saint Paxia and not one." He inclined his head and turned to Gavin. "How did you see it, Gavin? Should we not praise the young monk's actions?"

Clearing his throat, the young knight answered. "I agree. Tryam saved us all. He acted with violence only after the Berserkers savagely and without warning killed Brother Emil. He acted out of necessity, not vengeance."

Tryam felt his blood run cold at the word *vengeance*, and the contorted faces of the men he had killed returned to his mind. *It was vengeance that had ignited my fury and thrust me into action. Saint Paxia, forgive me.*

With a disapproving frown on his face, the abbot returned to his seat. He took a deep breath. "Tryam is not yet a full member of Saint Paxia, so I cannot punish him for violating our tenets. Nevertheless, no act of violence, however you may justify it, is praiseworthy."

"Then I believe this tragic story is at a sad end," concluded Lord Dunford. "The Berserkers were meted out the proper justice, and there is naught else we need to do." He turned toward the exit. "Father Monbatten, may you and your brothers go in peace!"

No one moved from the table. All were shocked at the commander's quick dismissal. Tryam was the first to protest. "I must tell you something very important, Lord Commander," begged the young acolyte. "Please hear my words!"

Dunford stopped where he stood. "You have more to say on this matter?"

"Yes, I do. Before the last Berserker died, he whispered something in my ear."

"Go ahead," said Dunford as he crossed his arms over his barrel chest.

"When the last Berserker lay dying, he beckoned me closer. With a smile on his bloody lips, he whispered into my ear. He said, 'I greet my ancestors now, but be aware that more of us are coming. Many more. The God of the Mountain has awakened.'"

Tryam looked for any reaction from Dunford, but he saw none. He added for emphasis: "I am afraid the attack on our party only portends to a greater attack on Arkos itself."

For the first time in the meeting, Roderick spoke up: "In fairness, Lord Commander, only Tryam heard these words."

Gavin rose from his seat and added: "I did not hear the words, but I know the man whispered something. Roderick believed Tryam at the time, for he ordered us back immediately."

"We had to return!" countered Roderick. "Emil was dead!"

Dunford paused as if considering the evidence, but he seemed more irritated than concerned. "I think the man was trying to spook you, nothing more. Attacks like this are rare, but they have happened in the past."

Tryam rose from his chair, clenching his fists. "So, you plan on doing nothing?"

Dunford chuckled dismissively. "The two brutes are dead. I have no intentions of sending out a war party into the teeth of the Corona Mountains to look for trouble. It would be like throwing stones into a bear cave. I do not wish to make war." He stared at the abbot. "I am sure Father Monbatten would agree with me on that."

"Absolutely," said Monbatten. "It was a tragic event, and we mourn Brother Emil's death, but making war upon the Berserkers would not bring him back."

Dunford's gaze swept over the assembled men. "This matter is now closed. We shall remain vigilant, but no further action is required."

The group divided in two; Roderick and Gavin followed the commander out of the room, while the monks huddled behind the abbot. When they exited the inner keep, Tryam was expecting harsh words from Monbatten, but they did not come. Instead, the abbot reminded the group of the grim task ahead of them: the funeral for Brother Emil. They would ferry their brother to the abbey and begin preparations for his interment. It had been a long time since the graveyard had welcomed a monk.

Chapter 27
Endless Vistas

Wulfric breathed in the mountain air that chilled the land of his ancestors. The sky was vast and the horizon limitless, but even still, as he walked the familiar trails of his village, he longed to turn back and travel the innumerable unexplored valleys that always seemed to lie just past sunset.

It was not just the familiar that caused him unease. The tension between him and his father remained. Since the death of his mother from a wasting disease years before, his father had urged him to stay by his side, as the son of a jarl should. Instead, Wulfric wandered to Arkos, to other places.

Although it was his father he now sought, it was on a different and more contentious matter he needed to discuss: He was to inform his father, Alric, that he intended to make Kara his mate. Though she had been adopted into the Ulf after her family had been killed in a dispute between clans, Kara had never been fully accepted by Wulfric's father. The main reason was that Kara shared a similar wanderlust.

Wulfric headed for the centrally located longhouse in the small village of huts that was Clan Ulf. Without hesitating, he parted the wolf pelt covering the door and entered the large wooden structure covered in thick hides. With purpose he strode down the narrow corridor that led to the jarl's private chamber. When his eyes adjusted to the darkness inside, he could see that his father was already in council with another man. When neither took notice of his presence, Wulfric interrupted.

"Father, may we have words?"

Alric looked up with blue eyes that matched his son's. "Sit and join us. I am listening to troubling words from our visiting friend."

Wulfric recognized the man seated across the table: Kayen, a missionary from Arkos who made regular visits to the Ulf. The monk was the bravest Engothian Wulfric had ever met, for he feared neither the terrain nor Wulfric's fellow Berserkers. To see him before his father with concern on his face was troubling. Wulfric took a seat on the bench beside his father as the missionary spoke.

"As I was telling your father, these are disconcerting times. Wars from the disputed lands in Outremer have spread like a fire into the Western Kingdoms. I fear nowhere on Medias is safe from this growing wave of destruction, not even your home here at the crown of the world."

The missionary paused to stroke his thick brown beard and to take a sip of warm water. He closed his hand around the shaft of his crooked shepherd staff, his constant companion, then resumed his thoughts. "As a member of the Order of the Imacolata, I was trained to recognize the signs of malevolent forces. These past few months, I have sensed the growing presence of dark magic not seen in these parts since the time of the Ancients. But it is not only dark magic. Daemons have been growing both in strength and number, as if a gate to the Abyss has opened nearby. I have, in fact, encountered a hellspawn in the mines near Arkos and could barely fight it off."

All sat in silence while contemplating what Kayen had said. Wulfric found the missionary's words difficult to believe. Out of respect for Kayen, he kept quiet, however. It was his father who broke the silence.

"We have long been friends, Kayen. Rumors of dark magic and Daemons are disturbing, but I have yet to see any evidence of trouble this far north."

"I might have," stated the missionary. "I was expecting brothers from the abbey here a week ago. They have yet to arrive. I have prayed on the matter and decided I must leave Clan Ulf prematurely to seek them out. I am concerned that these dark forces tie into their reason for being late."

Wulfric jumped up from the bench. "Father, let me form a hunting party. I shall search for them at once. I know the way to Arkos better than anyone in our clan."

His father grabbed him by the wrist and forced him back down. "No, you will not," said Alric sternly. "You have other obligations. It is time you end your wanderings, take up the axe, and become a full member of this clan. You must undergo the Trial of Blood!"

Wulfric clenched and unclenched his fists. "My blood is as ready as my axe. But what about the missing men? I could help Kayen find them!"

The jarl stood, his large battle-axe hanging loosely on his belt loop. "Once you have passed the Trial, then you can be trusted with such a task."

Wulfric relaxed his hands. His father was right, and he knew it. He had put off the Trial for far too long. He had set his mind to undergo the ordeal after helping Tryam prepare for the tournament, but his wanderings had led him astray again. He would undergo the Trial and prove that his wanderings had not weakened but rather had strengthened him. "As you wish, Father. I shall leave on the morrow."

Making ready to leave, Kayen stood. He grasped Wulfric's forearm. "You are wise to do as your father asks. Aten shall protect you during your Trial. And do not fret about my lost sheep; I have ways of tracking people. If dark forces are involved, perhaps it is better I deal with them alone. If they arrive while I am gone, Alric, I ask you to tell them to stay here until I return."

"I shall," promised Alric. "And I shall alert our hunters to look south for your men."

Wulfric followed as his father escorted the missionary down the longhouse corridor. They paused at the exit, and the jarl turned to Kayen. "May any dark forces you encounter flee from your presence!"

Kayen nodded respectfully and exited the building, his trail leading south.

Alric put his hand on Wulfric's shoulder, and the two men locked eyes. "My son, the Trial of Blood has taken the lives of youths stronger and more skilled in the hunt than even you." Alric thumped Wulfric's barrel chest. "This, and only this, the warrior's heart, is what you must rely upon. You are my only son and the last of our line. You carry with you the honor of our ancestors." He squeezed Wulfric's shoulder. "Are you truly prepared?"

Wulfric focused on his father's battle scars and deep lines and for the first time thought about his father's mortality. "Yes, I am ready. I shall make you proud and will honor the memory of my mother."

Anger flashed in his father's eyes. "It is not just our family your actions must bring honor to, it is our entire clan! Remember always, it is Clan Ulf that you serve, not your own interests or even mine."

The force of his father's words had an emotional impact on Wulfric. The youth beat his chest with his fists. "Father, I vow to you, when I return from Crag, I shall return a warrior!"

Alric placed his meaty hand upon Wulfric's shoulder. "Go then. Rest tonight, knowing that our ancestors will be with you."

"Yes, Father. I spend my last night as a reckless youth. I shall leave at dawn only to return a man."

The young Ulf exited the longhouse but not before turning to see his father retreat into its shadows. *I shall make him proud.*

Outside, the sky was getting dark. Wulfric headed not toward his own hut but instead to Kara's. He would tell her about the Trial of Blood.

Kara! I had forgotten to tell Father about Kara! Wulfric cursed to the sky. *Perhaps it is better I do so when I return from the Trial. Once I'm a warrior, he cannot deny me.*

Kara lived outside Clan Ulf, in a hut nestled in the forest that lay at the foot of the hill where the village stood. He had not planned on telling Kara his intentions to be her mate until he had first informed his father, but he would have to do so now. The Trial frightened her in a way that did not frighten him. Perhaps if she knew they were to be bonded, she would draw comfort, knowing that he had her love to draw strength from. *At least, that is what the poets say about women.* Wulfric was not sure many poets knew of a female like Kara.

Wulfric exited through the palisade gate, turned south, then east straight down to the dark edges of the Milfaar Forest. These dense woods buttressed the Corona Mountain Range for many a mile and provided a bountiful place to hunt. Kara's hut stood only a few dozen yards inside, under the low-hanging branches of a giant oak.

Before he got too close, Wulfric announced his presence. Kara has been known to shoot arrows at unexpected visitors, especially at this late hour. "Kara, it's me, Wulfric!"

He listened for any sounds from inside the hut but heard nothing.

Perhaps she slumbers? The young Ulf strode up to the wooden hut and knocked on the closed shutter of the dwelling's only window. After a moment, he rapped again, this time harder. He did not hear her stir. Wulfric moved to the hut's entrance and parted the wolf hide pelt. It took only a glance inside the small hut to see she was not there.

Disappointed, Wulfric stepped back and looked deeper into the woods. Kara often hunted small game at twilight hours to hone her archery skills. He knelt down and looked for any fresh prints in the area around her hut. He recognized her small footprints and saw they headed toward the heart of the forest.

THE TOMB OF THERAGAARD

The shadows were growing long, since the sun was about to set. If he did not find her soon, it would be almost impossible to track her. He followed her footprints until they disappeared into the dark. He then looked for broken branches or signs of recently disturbed foliage. He followed a trail of disturbed fallen leaves for a couple of miles before he realized he now stood where he had been earlier. He was being led in circles. He decided to pause and rest with his back against a tree. He would not give Kara the pleasure of making a fool of him.

From his comfortable resting spot, Wulfric shouted to the trees. "I can't see you, but I know you are out there, Kara. I am done running in circles."

The only audible response was from the creaking of trees.

"A man's first duty is to his woman, but when that is thwarted, he turns to his second duty, his stomach. Come forth, or I shall return to the village and have my sup."

An owl hooted in the distance, and a squirrel scurried up a tree—but not a sound from Kara.

"All right, I go back alone."

Wulfric started to step away from the tree when a red arrow thudded an inch below his manhood. He jumped away as if set on fire. He cursed himself for being surprised.

"That was too close, Kara!"

Wulfric inspected the arrow. From the angle it had hit the trunk, he guessed she was perched about twenty feet up in one of the trees to the east. He ripped her precious red arrow from the tree.

"If you want this back, you better show yourself."

This time the answer was immediate. "I have plenty more!"

Wulfric heard Kara's voice, but it was from ground level and to the north, not from high in the trees off to the east. He broke into a headlong run, but an arrow stopped him in his tracks. She was back in the trees again.

"I have something important to say," said Wulfric, attempting a different tactic.

A laugh came from his right, and Wulfric felt the hairs on the back of his neck stand in anticipation of another arrow coming his way. The frustrated Ulf leapt to the lowest branch of the nearest tree. He dropped Kara's arrow and started to climb.

Halfway up the eighty-foot pine, he paused to look for the exasperating girl but saw nothing. He climbed to a higher branch and shifted his position. Poised like a hawk, Wulfric looked for Kara through the branches and trunks of nearby trees. He knew Kara was an expert climber, and likely as fast as he. There was no movement save branches swaying naturally in the now-nighttime's gentle breeze.

"Let's talk up here."

Kara's voice came from a tree to Wulfric's left, an oak. He turned in time to make out her lithe body before it disappeared up through a network of branches.

I've got you now!

The young Ulf braced himself against the trunk, then jumped for Kara's tree. His leap was awkward, and he bounced off the limb he had intended to grab. Wulfric reached for another branch, but his hands found only air. The big Ulf began an unplanned descent down the tree, the sound of Kara's laughter somehow finding its way to his ears.

He continued to fall, his weighty body snapping tree limbs on the way down, until he was finally able to snag a branch slightly thicker than his wrist.

"That was the funniest thing I have seen in my entire life!" teased Kara from above.

With his face full of scratches, Wulfric breathed heavily in relief, but his respite was short-lived; the limb he held was snapping under his weight. Wulfric wrapped his legs around the trunk and held on like a drowning sailor to a piece of driftwood. Sweat poured down his face, and his muscles twitched in exhaustion. When he felt twigs rain down on his head, Wulfric feared the whole tree was falling—until he heard Kara chiding from above: "It must not be that important if you're dawdling so."

Wulfric squashed the curse he wanted to utter, cleared the twigs from his head, and inched his way up the tree, using the branches as wobbly steps. Resting briefly, he arched his back and looked higher up into the tree in search of Kara. He could see her climbing toward the very top. *Thank Aten there is no place higher she can climb!* He continued his ascent.

"You have to see this!" Kara said, her voice now very close.

Wulfric stepped gingerly on the topmost branch and steadied himself with his bloodied hands. At last he found Kara. She had managed to find the tallest oak in the entire forest, and she sat upon the tree's oddly twisted crown as one would a stool. He squeezed beside her and looked out at the view. Around them was the forest, while above, an umbrella of twilight stars glistened in the dark blue sky.

"Isn't it wondrous and so vast?" Kara asked, looking heavenward.

"I guess so," grumbled Wulfric, not seeing her point as he tried to ignore the pain of the scratches.

"How big do you think the world is?"

Wulfric looked to the purple mountain peaks to the east, the vast expanse of snow-covered plains to the west, and then up at the sea of stars. "Big enough so that it would take more than a thousand lifetimes to see it all, yet small enough that I was able to find the most beautiful creature in it."

Kara grabbed his head and planted a kiss on his shocked face. Her warm lips melted the chill of night away. After a few moments, she released her hold and looked back at the heavens. "I want to see it all!" she demanded.

"You will. Nothing can stop you."

"Will you go with me?"

"Of course! I shall be with you always."

Kara turned away from the sky and looked at Wulfric. "What do you mean?"

"Just what I said."

"Say it again."

Wulfric grabbed Kara's shoulders. "I shall be with you always, and you will never again leave my side. I intend to bring you into Clan Ulf as my bondmate."

Kara screamed and hugged him in one flash of energy. When the moment passed, she pushed him back, and her head tilted to one side. "Do you mean it?"

"Of course, I mean it, and I can prove it." From his tunic Wulfric brought forth a necklace. Strung through the leather thong was a whalebone, on which was carved a series of intricate patterns. "My father crafted this after he harpooned the great beast. He presented it to his bondmate, my mother. She treasured it and never removed it from her neck while she lived."

"May I wear it?"

"Of course." He put the necklace around her slender neck.

Kara felt the necklace with her fingers and smiled. "I wish I had met your mother." Her face turned serious. "But when are we to be bonded?"

"Soon, but there is something I must do first. I have to undergo the Trial of Blood. I intend to leave in the morning. That is why I sought you out. I wanted to speak to you before I left."

"Tomorrow? Why so soon?"

"It is important for my father and the clan. He is right. I have waited too long."

"But you could die!"

Wulfric looked toward the sky again and paused. "If Aten wills it, then yes. But I am strong and skilled. I shall not surrender to death easily." Wulfric erupted in laughter at Kara's sad face. "I shall not die today at least! I have the strength of your love to aid me!"

The words appeared to relax Kara, and her facial expression lightened. "You will return. I know that. But let's stay here a little longer."

Wulfric could not argue as he brought her closer.

Chapter 28
Remorse and Return

Kayen recognized the gully ahead and made for it. He knew the land between the northern barbarians and Arkos as well as any place on Medias. *For ten years, I have walked these paths, and it has just occurred to me how much this place has become my home.*

A freezing mist hung over the water-worn ravine. Winter was coming fast.

It was at the onset of winter, when the Frostfoam Sea would freeze, endless nights would begin, and warmth would be hard to come by, that he missed the small river town of Embredge, the place of his birth. There he had grown up the son of a farmer and had a family of his own. There he had lived in comfort and peace, for a time.

For whatever reason distant memories drift into one's mind, Kayen thought about a journey home to Embredge he had taken nearly twenty years earlier. Perhaps because it was on a similarly chilly morning or maybe because of the dread he felt over the missing expedition. Either way, he could not stop his mind from bringing the memory forward.

I was headed home with my wagon empty and my purse full. I would surprise my wife with a broach, and I carried three painted dolls, one for each of my children, purchased from silver earned from the sale of my crops. I can still see clearly the strange sight of the rough-looking knights, wearing helmets with long, beaklike noses, who stopped me on the road. The town had been cordoned off. They said a stranger had wandered into town, bringing the plague with him.

Kayen shivered more from the memories than from the cold.

I grappled with the knights to let me pass, but their gauntleted hands and long poleaxes held me at bay. I had to wait as the knights, house by house, cleared the dead. I refused to believe my family was among them.

Men on draft horses led cartloads of corpses to the giant pit that had been excavated outside town. I strained to see the victims as they were cruelly dumped into the forsaken hole, but their faces were so covered with sores and filth that each corpse was indistinguishable from the next.

The smells and the eerie quiet that "welcomed" me when I was finally allowed to pass was something no man could ever prepare for. As I stumbled through its lonely streets, the town was a crude memory of itself. I clung to the hope that my family had stayed hidden, waiting for me to come home to tell them everything was safe, but it was not meant to be.

The smoke from the pit blanketed the town as if it were midnight. I found my small farmhouse and shouted my wife's name, Muriel, and then my children's names, Kalla, Dorn, and little Amelia—but no answer would ever come. My family was dead, along with most everyone I had ever known. At that moment of anguish, I wished I had been among them.

I almost ended my life soon after, but a monk of Aten, giving blessings to the dead, showed me where my life could lead if I did not give in to sorrow. I listened to the monk and watched as he comforted the bereaved. I dedicated my life to the Church that day and joined the clergy. Aten showed me the courage I had always possessed but had not known I had.

As a member of the Order of the Imacolata, I traveled to places I'd never dreamt of having the courage to visit, including places much deadlier and foreboding than the Corona Mountains. I do not fear the Berserkers. Warlike, to be sure, but what they lack in gentleness and sophistication they make up in honesty and valor.

Kayen's thoughts turned to more recent days, back to his discussion with Alric about the growing darkness. If some dark force had attacked the party, Emil would have known what to do. He had faith in his former brother of the Imacolata, but the older monk's adherence to the tenets of his new order may have changed how he would handle such a difficult situation. Whatever had befallen the party, it must have been dire. He had to pray more on the matter, to get a clearer sense of what was happening in these wild lands.

Days passed, with no sign of the expedition. The weather had been gray and cold but free of storms. Kayen moved swiftly across the soon-to-be-frozen plains. After a time, he found traces of two wagons heading north and followed them back to a forest of pines. Soon afterward, he spotted two frozen corpses beside an abandoned campfire. When he bent

THE TOMB OF THERAGAARD

down to inspect the bodies, he discovered, to his relief, that they did not belong to any of his brothers; they were in fact Berserkers from a clan much farther north. From the many footprints at the site he determined that Emil's expedition had been there.

Did the escort knights kill these men and then force the expedition to return home? That seemed the most logical explanation; however, he was unsure why two Berserkers from a clan far north of here would waylay an armed host from Arkos. The more he thought about it, the less sense he could make of it.

During the next few days, as he hurried home, he ate little, slept less, and prayed more.

As he neared Arkos, he quickened his pace even further. When he approached the north gate, the guards on the ramparts spotted him and called out. "Brother Kayen, what wind blows your sails so quickly toward town? The weather getting a bit too cold for you?"

"I have urgent business with Abbot Monbatten that I must address." He was in no mood for idle chatter.

"Business with that old crow? You have our sympathies!" said the guards, laughing, as Kayen rushed through the open gate.

Once inside the walled town, he thought about consulting with Lord Dunford before heading to the island. The commander had been quick to ask for his help in banishing the Daemon encountered in the mines, but afterward he'd shown little gratitude. *No, there is little point in visiting Dunford.*

The morning mist shrouded the abbey complex in gloom. The buildings were slick with moisture, and the ground had turned to mud. Kayen prayed inside the church before seeking the abbot. The curt responses from his fellow monks to enquiries about Monbatten's whereabouts were troubling. He found Monbatten in his chambers, a solemn look on the dour man's aged face.

"Brother Emil is dead."

The grave words from Monbatten, spoken so plainly, shook Kayen. "I saw evidence of a battle. Was it from a Berserker attack?"

"Yes."

Kayen slumped into the seat opposite the abbot and rubbed his beard nervously. "Everyone else is okay?"

"Yes, everyone else survived."

"What happened?"

"Roaming warriors stumbled upon the party at night. One of the Engothian warriors was drunk, the other inexperienced, but it was the monks, who did not stay true to Saint Paxia's teachings, who caused this disaster. Most troubling was that Tryam had a hand in killing both of the Berserkers."

"Tryam?" gasped Kayen.

The abbot nodded.

As Monbatten filled him in on the rest of the details, one thought kept coming to Kayen's mind. "Tryam was on this expedition? I am surprised you let him go."

The abbot steepled his fingers. "I don't suppose you knew of his intention to join the Engothian knights? Tryam entered their tournament and nearly died as a result! He failed and afterward pledged to become a brother of Saint Paxia upon his eighteenth birthday. I wanted to make sure he kept true to his word." He scowled. "The world is a harsh, violent, and uncaring place. Especially, the dark corners where the light of Aten has not yet reached. I thought by showing the cruelty outside these walls, Tryam would see how fortunate it is to be able to live and learn under my protection." He slowly shook his head. "However, what happened out there was an incident graver than I had anticipated. I'd merely wanted him to feel tired, hungry, and cold."

"You could not have foreseen such an attack," acknowledged Kayen. "How is Tryam dealing with his having taken two lives?"

"Very hard. He has been brooding since his return. He is not one to express his emotions, but I know he blames himself for Emil's death. This was the most important lesson he has ever learned: There is no glory to be found in battle."

"Despite what has happened, I still intend to bring Clan Ulf copies of the Book of Aten. I have already converted several youths and have the ear of their jarl. We cannot let the light of Aten be snuffed out by a pair of outlaw Berserkers." He leaned forward in his chair. "I know you doubt they can change their ways, but this struggle is a test of our faith. Only light can end darkness."

Monbatten arched his gray eyebrows. "Actually, I agree. You have convinced me that converting these barbarians is the only way to get them to change their violent instincts. If we do nothing, their attacks may come closer to home. Aten's light must spread. This incident proves we must do more."

Kayen did not let the shock of Monbatten's words show on his face. "I would like to take Tryam with me. Just the two of us, with minimal supplies. If he does not go back out, he may never have the courage to uphold the tenets of Saint Paxia."

Monbatten frowned, then rose from behind his desk. "Do you really think it wise? Another attack could bring forth his lost memories. He might turn into what his father became."

Kayen took a deep breath and slowly rose to his feet. "With all due respect, I insist that his father was a great man, and the world would be a better place with more men like him."

"We have been arguing about this for ten years. Let us not continue for ten more. If you can convince Tryam to go, then I shall allow it. Perhaps he will be the one to spread Saint Paxia's teachings to these savages. He does possess a drive that the meeker members of the order do not. If he declines your offer, though, I want you to promise to leave him be. He is soon to be a grown man and will not need you watching over him."

Surprised by the abbot's response, Kayen was at a loss for words. He bowed respectfully to Monbatten, deciding against pressing his luck with further negotiations. "Thank you, Father. If I can't convince him to take this mission, I shall not pursue the matter further."

"Go in peace then, Brother," said the abbot.

Kayen proceeded toward Tryam's cell, passing stony-faced monks as he took the steps to the second floor. He would not give up on Tryam. The youth had the potential to do great good for the world, and the world was in desperate need of good men.

✠ ✠ ✠

Lucian stood over the broken bodies of the enemy, their cruel faces showing more darkly in death. After the rush of battle had passed, the men looked upon their bloodstained hands in horror. Lucian declared, "Men, neither feel shame in your deeds, nor boast pridefully of them. Our actions brought us no dishonor, so do not dishonor yourselves now in grief. Though we may feel the weight of shadows, our actions were just, and the light of Aten has been preserved."

Tryam put down the book and walked to his window. He looked out at the cloister, then across the harbor toward the town of Arkos. He listened to the sounds of the outside world: seagulls in the air, the water breaking against the island's rocky edge. Life was thriving out there, but so was death. Beauty but also horror.

A knock on his door interrupted his ruminations. Tryam rushed to hide the book beneath the coverings of his bed.

"Enter," spoke Tryam.

The acolyte was shocked to see the warm smile and bearded face of the missionary Kayen, and by the look of his muddy cloak, it was apparent that he must have just arrived. The order had no way of informing Kayen of the disastrous expedition to his mission. Tryam dreaded telling Brother Kayen why the party had never arrived.

"I hope I am not interrupting," asked Kayen as he entered the small room.

"No, not at all. I am still contemplating the events of these past few weeks," answered Tryam. "There is much I would like to talk to you about, but I do not know where to begin."

"Let me help you then," interrupted Kayen. "Father Monbatten's own lips told me the horrific details of what happened. I hope you do not blame yourself for what has occurred. We all mourn the loss of Brother Emil, for he was a good man and a friend to all. The world is not as bright a place without him."

Tryam paced back and forth. "How can I not blame myself for what happened? If I had only acted sooner, perhaps Brother Emil could have been saved."

Kayen struck the floor with his shepherd's staff. "Sit down. I shall tell you why you should not blame yourself."

Tryam sat on the edge of his bed. He was prepared to listen, but his heart remained heavy.

"The blame for Brother Emil's death lies solely on the Berserkers. Whether you could have done something different is irrelevant."

Tryam understood what Kayen was saying, but he remained unmoved. He wanted to block out what happened, but he was not ready to do so.

"But I failed to act when I could have. Is not failing to act to prevent a death as great a sin as directly taking someone's life?"

"It is true that we all have a duty to preserve life, to act when we can. But this case is not so simple. Before being spotted by Emil, you were confronted by two armed Berserkers—predators since birth. Most would say confronting them in open combat, with as little experience as you have, would be suicide. Aten forbids suicide. Further, such an opportunity was denied you, since Emil spotted you and ordered you to lay down your arms. He was in charge of the mission, and you had a duty to obey him."

"But I still took the life of another! Those two men will never know the light of Aten. I have condemned them to the Abyss. This is a burden I can never forget."

"Nor should you. But you also helped save the lives of everyone else." The missionary walked to Tryam's window. "Out there a darkness is spreading. The world needs people to take a stand, to bring light into the darkness. Let us, in a small way, bring light back into the world. I am going back to Clan Ulf, and I want you to come with me."

Tryam leapt from the bed. "Out of the question! What if we are attacked again? I have none of the qualities a person needs to possess in order to stand up to the darkness!"

Kayen stared into Tryam's eyes. "I believe you do. When you realized the danger to your fellow brothers of Aten, what was your first reaction? It was to save them, heedless of the danger to yourself. You are a man of action and of self-sacrifice." Kayen walked over to Tryam's bed and lifted the pillow to reveal the book he had hidden. "I see you know of the paladins. I am aware that you have pledged to join the order on your next birthday, but I think you have the qualities to be a paladin like Saint Lucian. Did you know that the order of paladins still exists? Their numbers are dwindling, sadly." Kayen picked up the book and thumbed through the pages. "If you doubt me, think back to what happened at the crypts. Not everyone has the ability to hear spirits. It is a gift. A gift worthy of a paladin."

"Lucian is a saint. I am not a saint."

Kayen laughed. "No, of course not, but even saints started out as ordinary men. The difference is that they dedicated their lives to Aten in ways others lack the will to do." He shook his head. "In any case, you don't want to be a saint quite yet. One of the requisites is that you die first, often very painfully!"

The missionary continued to chuckle as he placed his arm around Tryam's shoulder. "Come with me. I shall tell you more of the paladins on our trip, and I shall help you explore your gift of spirit sight."

"Will Father Monbatten allow it?"

"I already have his blessing for the trip, and for you accompanying me. He did not limit what I could teach. He knows the value of the work I do. I have made the trip dozens of times. Do not fear, I shall be more vigilant than your escorts were." He looked into Tryam's eyes. "What do you say? Will you come along?"

Thoughts of the future clouded Tryam's feelings on the present. The journey with Kayen would enable him to ask more about his family and their fate. Also, at Kayen's mention of the paladins, Tryam felt something stir in his soul. He took a deep breath. "I *will* go."

A grin spread upon Kayen's bearded face. "Good! We leave tomorrow after breakfast. Pack your clothes. We shall not need a wagon; it will be just the two of us and a few copies of the Book of Aten and the Words of Saint Paxia." His grin turned into a big smile. "Meet me at the main gate when the morning recitation bells ring. I have to inform Father Monbatten and then pay my respects to Brother Emil."

Kayen returned the book on Saint Lucian to Tryam. "Don't be surprised if by journey's end, you reconsider your decision to join the order. See you on the morrow."

Tryam walked over to the chest that contained his training equipment and opened it. The youth placed the book about Saint Lucian alongside his dented breastplate. His eyes then traveled toward a copy of the teachings of Saint Paxia on his bookshelf. *Which will be my fate? I pray that I have the wisdom to see the path Aten has set for me.*

The discussion with Brother Kayen left him with a renewed sense of excitement. The pain over what had transpired receded. Now he was traveling toward an exciting and uncharted future.

Chapter 29
The Trial of Blood

Few things were more sacred to the Berserkers of Clan Ulf than the squat mountain they called the Crag. Legend had it that their race had been birthed on the mountain's rocky summit, and it was there that young men of the clan ventured to undergo the Trial of Blood.

Before being accepted as a true warrior, each male youth was expected to climb the unforgiving peak and return only when he had slain a frostwolf, a giant caribou, or—in an extreme case—one of the great white bears that lived in deep caves. Only when he brought home proof of his kill could he return to the clan and claim his spot alongside the warriors. Of all the trophies, it was the white bear Wulfric sought. The clan would expect nothing less from the son of a jarl.

Armed with his axe, his sword, his dagger, and his instincts, Wulfric journeyed toward the grim peak, with all thoughts of Kara and his father left behind as he focused on the perils ahead. He used all of his senses to search for dangers that could lurk from behind any rock, tree, or shadow.

When he arrived at the base of Crag, the bright sun rose over its uneven white peak, an inspiring sign to mark the beginning of his ordeal. And as he began his ascent, he experienced no fear, only impatience that he still had yet many feet to climb.

The pine forests that ringed the lower portion of the mountain offered a wide variety of game, both large and small, many potentially deadly but none worthy of bringing back to the village.

As he progressed up the mountain, winds blowing from the west carried with them dark clouds filled with snow, occluding the bright sun behind a thick gray blanket and blocking the scant heat it had provided.

The trees offered protection from the winds but not from the bitterly cold air. He listened for sounds of movement, sniffed the air for the scent of any predators, and sought with his eyes signs of broken twigs and disturbed vegetation.

Wulfric ranged through the pines, looking for prey. He found evidence of recent bear activity in the form of a warm pile of manure. Disappointingly, the dung pile was too small to be from the white bear. Wulfric was not surprised, for only brown and black bears were common at this level of the mountain. The white bear, king of the mountain, dwelt above the tree line.

Wulfric scanned the mountain for a path to the summit. He considered himself fortunate when he found a stream that flowed from an unseen source high above and meandered down through the trees. The young Ulf followed the creek upstream. However, as if Aten were sending him a warning to keep his senses alert, on the stream's icy bank he stumbled upon human remains. Wulfric bent down and examined the weathered bones in the dim light. Teeth marks revealed that an animal had eaten the flesh. The young Ulf thought it was the bones of Gord, the youth who had been sent on the Trial of Blood six months earlier but had never returned. Wulfric did his best to cover the remains before resuming his trip higher up, to where the white bears awaited.

After three days of arduous climbing, Wulfric could no longer see the stream; it had disappeared under a sheet of ice. He had to find another path. He scrambled up and over a piece of jutting rock that even the most experienced mountaineers would have avoided. It was on this rock's topside that he found a goat trail, which he followed until it too faded into the surroundings—but not before it had led him above the tree line. He rested and looked out to the west. A reddish glow from the day's dying sun now filtered through storm clouds. He would have to hurry if he was to find the white bear before darkness took hold.

Axe in hand, he steadfastly continued his climb up the trackless mountain, always mindful of his surroundings. Once he reached the base of the summit, the smell of a carcass filled his nostrils. The reek of fresh death caused the hair on his neck to stand on end.

Wulfric followed the scent higher up the slope, mindful of the fact he was now in the domain of the white bear. Though the beast's hindsight was limited, its sense of smell rivaled that of the wolf. After he rounded

THE TOMB OF THERAGAARD

a boulder, he found the source of the scent: the carcass of a mountain goat, its body brutally savaged. Around the body were bloody bear prints matching that of the white.

Wulfric stayed low against the boulder and scanned for signs of the goat's killer. As he did so, he realized the remains lay in a depression and that there was only one means of egress should the bear return. *It's unwise to linger in this spot too long.*

Patiently, the young Ulf crouched in silence and scanned about for any sign of danger. When he deemed it safe to proceed, he walked to the gory remains. Why the white bear had not devoured the beast or dragged it back to its den mystified Wulfric. *It's almost as if this particular meal had been interrupted.*

The wind picked up and made a mournful howling as it blew through the crevices of Crag's summit. In the red light of the setting sun, Wulfric examined the bear prints. By the depth and breadth of the impressions in the hard ground, he judged the white bear was over fifteen feet tall and weighed as much as twenty grown men. The village would sing songs of his triumph should he bring back such a pelt.

The wind continued to howl and the temperature to drop. Wulfric tracked the bear prints and climbed over the rocks that curved around the side of the depression. The sheer mountain face was now only a few dozen yards away. Falling snow whipped around in the fading light, but with his hawk-like eyes, Wulfric could make out tracks leading to a cave entrance along the side of the mountain.

That is where the white bear awaits!

Chapter 30

The Sacrifice of Blood

The Mountain God rested on a bed of freshly cut logs, under a tent placed over the slumbering deity to keep prying eyes away. Strapped to the God's metal chest was a sacrifice. Abbaster stood above the dead man, using a curved dagger to slice strips of flesh from his torso. Gidran lay prostrate before the metal gargantuan and observed the brute practicing his macabre art.

The shaman was sure that the Golem, in the years since it had been separated from the archmagus's control, had gained a life force of its own. In the language of the Dark God, Gidran intoned prayer after prayer for Terminus to grant him the ability to commune with the nascent consciousness that stirred inside the enigmatic metal mind. Sweat poured down Gidran's face, his voice nearly gone, his muscles trembling, as he begged for an answer to his prayers. However, nothing was forthcoming, and his weary body succumbed to exhaustion.

Gidran slowly rose to his feet and watched with fascination as the black metal absorbed the blood spilled after each slash from Abbaster's dagger. The shaman had seen nothing like it in all his travels, and the implications of the power behind the Golem's creation frightened him. *Is any wizard alive truly powerful enough to control such an abomination? Is Dementhus? His magic has so far failed to reanimate the Golem, and he pressures me to bring the artifact back to life!*

The canvas parted, and the Necromancer entered as if he knew Gidran had started to doubt him again. He had a furrowed brow, and his velvet-gloved hands clenched and unclenched.

"I heard your prayers stop. Have you had any success in contacting the Golem?"

THE TOMB OF THERAGAARD

"None. I stopped only because I became too weary," admitted Gidran. "I need more time."

Dementhus walked beside the immobile giant, then uttered words in the language of magic. His eyes turned black, and he looked down on the Golem, paying particular attention to the strange tattoos that covered parts of its body.

When his eyes turned back to normal, the wizard pointed to the stack of corpses at the back of the tent. "Abbaster has sacrificed many so far, all to no avail. How much more time do you need? Time is our adversary."

A coughing spasm terminated Dementhus's queries. Gidran was aware of the wizard's failing health. The man's shuffling grew more pronounced each day, and a chance glimpse of his uncovered hand showed flesh resembling that of a withered corpse. He wondered if the wizard would live long enough to enjoy the destructive force the Golem would unleash. "I am working as quickly as I can, but as you know, strong magic is involved."

"I am aware of that," snapped Dementhus. "Bafomeht sent you to aid in the Golem's recovery. Have you heard from Terminus? Has He granted any visions, imparted any information, shown us a direction we should go? We could spend weeks, months, looking for the entrance to Antigenesus's fortress."

Gidran politely bowed to the wizard. "No. I have learned only that we have yet to prove our devotion to Him."

The wizard turned his gaze to the bloody corpse strapped to the Golem. "We have more prisoners. Enough for a dozen more sacrifices. Will that suffice?"

Gidran paused a moment and tried to divine the will of Terminus. As the answer came to him, he nodded his head in understanding. "Sacrificing more of the Berserkers will not be sufficient. Terminus requires us to *show* our devotion."

Dementhus narrowed his black eyes. "Show our devotion? How?"

"By giving of our own flesh." Gidran stripped himself to the waist and mounted the Golem's broad chest, shoving Abbaster and the corpse aside. He fell to his knees and drew a straight-edged dagger from an ivory sheath strapped to his thigh. The shaman stretched out his arms and began a prayer. After each recitation he increased the volume of his voice, and after each verse he slashed at his chest with the dagger, painting his body in crimson.

The Golem's metal flesh absorbed the blood dripping from the shaman's wounds with an audible hiss. Gidran ignored the bewildered Necromancer's warnings to stop, and he continued to slash at his body until he was so weakened from the loss of blood that the dagger fell from his hands.

Unable to stand, Gidran fell forward, his bloody chest falling against the Golem's cold metal. With direct contact, the black skin drank his blood more thirstily, making his body burn as if aflame. The shaman fought against the urge to preserve his own life and pressed more closely to the Golem. Then, on the edge of losing consciousness, he felt a throbbing in the Golem's chest that matched the beating of his own heart. Through the agony, he prayed to Terminus for more strength, even as his mind merged with that of the Golem.

His consciousness left the material world, and the pain of his injuries receded as Gidran floated over his physical form. He called out to Bafomeht in the void of nothingness, and though he could not sense the Dark God's presence, he did sense a presence. The shaman was afraid. *Where am I? Who am I?*

Visions of wonders and of horrors, of men and women and their acts of bravery and cowardice, flooded into Gidran's captured soul. He felt Himself rising from a table, towering over *His* master, the Creator He knew as Antigenesus. He then saw a battlefield where Antigenesus's army marched against the forces of the imperator. He stomped men in armor as a man can stomp insects, His sword chopping off the crowns of towers, His hands squeezing the life out of a dozen warriors said to be heroes. Then the forces of Aten came, and He retreated to the land of His birth. Scenes of war, blood, and death filled His eyes. A bright light flashed, and a great noise shook the ground, causing Him to plummet down the side of a mountain. Far and fast He fell, until He crashed to the ground, unable to move, His link with His Creator broken seemingly forever.

Then nothing but darkness and quiet for ages.

Time became fluid, and Gidran was adrift.

The shaman felt hands about his shoulders and the cold floor slap against his bare back. He fought to open his eyes and found the Necromancer hovering over his supine form like a ghoul and shouting. It took a moment for Gidran to comprehend the meaning of the wizard's words: "What did you see? Speak, you fool, before the memories flee!"

THE TOMB OF THERAGAARD

Fumbling for the words, Gidran listed the visions that had floated through his mind. "I saw great battles and images that the Golem's eyes saw centuries ago."

"What about Antigenesus? Where is the entrance to the fortress?"

The bald wizard slapped him hard in the face. Gidran was conscious enough now to see Dementhus's withered hands uncovered by the velvet gloves.

"I saw the table from which I—or, rather, the Golem—was created." Gidran, fully alert now and alive with awe, rushed to his feet and grabbed Dementhus about the shoulders, shaking him. "I saw the archmagus! We retreated to the twin-peaked mountain after a great battle. I know where the entrance to the fortress lies!"

As the wizard extracted himself from Gidran's grasp, a menacing grin appeared on his face. "Commit the location to memory. We shall organize a search party, and you will lead it. Clean yourself up and get ready." He waved his staff in the air. "Abbaster, see to the Ragnar warriors and prepare them!"

Alone now, Gidran walked up to the black metal marvel and placed his hand on the warrior's stomach. *Dementhus does not know your true power!*

Gidran went about dressing his wounds, taking only long enough to stanch the flow of blood. The shaman then donned the bear-skin clothing the natives had presented him with and gathered his meager supplies.

He left the tent for the first time in three weeks and rushed to be by Dementhus's side. As the two made their way to the new palisade gate, Gidran was taken aback by how much the preparations for war had drastically altered the villages' appearance; he now saw expanded barracks, the construction of siege weapons, and the Necromancer's forges that blanketed the town under a perpetual pall of thick black smoke.

The two foreigners made their way to the jarl's longhouse. The structure, the largest of any of the dwellings, was covered with leather hides stretched over the bones of a great whale. Giant walrus tusks were on either side of the tent's entrance, giving the appearance they were entering the mouth of a giant beast.

Covered braziers lit the great hall inside. Side rooms, separated by canvas walls, lined the rounded structure, while at the far end was a throne made from the bones of the conquered dead. The jarl rushed up and greeted Dementhus with an enthusiastic bear hug. With Gidran, Ivor kept a respectful distance, which the shaman suspected was because he worked so closely with the God of the Mountain.

"What brings you here in such a hurry and at a late hour?" questioned the Ragnar king.

"I have great news," proclaimed Dementhus. "Gidran has heard the voice of the Mountain God!"

Ivor's bearded face cracked a smile as wide as that of a canyon. "What has the God of the Mountain said? You must tell me at once!"

The hall turned quiet as the wizard spoke. "Gidran was granted visions witnessed through the God's very own eyes. He was shown the location of an ancient fortress. It was here where the God's metallic avatar was birthed and where it must be returned before it can lead our army to victory! We are close to ultimate power!"

The word *power* set fire to the jarl's eyes. "Ultimate power? I shall be not only lord of this tribe but soon king of all the lands within sight of the Corona Mountains and beyond." He beckoned the wizard. "Come, sit with me. Feast while we set about making our war plans."

The jarl led the group to a room where sat a table on which an assortment of cooked meats awaited. Two female Ragnar, clothed to reveal their full bosoms, stood poised to attend. Ivor's son, Crayvor, already seated, now jumped to attention as his father and his guests entered.

The jarl clenched a tankard of ale from the table and downed the contents in one swig. "Take a seat and eat. This may be the last time we lavish in the warmth of the hearth."

Crayvor looked confused. "What has happened, Father?"

Ivor looked at his son with joy. "The God of the Mountain has spoken! He has given us the location of the entrance to the fortress where the God Himself was birthed! It is there we must go!"

Crayvor's smile mirrored his father's. "I shall assemble a war party immediately. I have feasted enough!"

The jarl laughed. "Do so, my son."

"Wait, young Crayvor," interrupted Dementhus. "We need only a small party, maybe a dozen men. Men who can move with haste but also with caution and stealth. Gidran will be your guide." He lowered his voice. "Beware, the fortress hides the laboratory of a great wizard. You should be prepared for many dangers, both magical and natural. Speak to no one else on the purpose of our trip, for we do not want to attract unwanted attention."

The youth nodded, then headed from the room.

Gidran's thoughts turned back to his encounter with the Golem. The violent imagery he had seen had ruined his appetite. He watched in silence as Dementhus and Ivor ripped into the meat with their teeth. *Death and destruction are coming. I wonder how many of us around the table and in this village will be alive to see its ultimate conclusion.*

Chapter 31

The Cave in the Mountain

Wulfric gripped the handle of the battle-axe with both hands as his body tensed to strike with lightning speed. Wind-whipped snow obscured the cave entrance, and the sun, low and at his back, cast long shadows before him.

He advanced with the patience and silence of a snow leopard stalking its prey. From tales told around campfires by seasoned warriors, Wulfric understood that his only chance against the white bear was to surprise the beast. However, he had never known of a warrior attempting to hunt the creature inside its own lair. Yet he advanced.

The intense smell of rotting flesh and offal filled Wulfric's nostrils. He pressed his body against the side of the entrance. When his eyes adjusted to the darkness inside, he took a cautious step forward.

As he stepped farther inside, he listened for any sign of the beast: claws against the rocky cave, a low growl, or even the sounds of the heavy breathing of the great bear in sleep. All he heard, however, was the sound of water dripping from stalactites.

Was the beast not here?

The small, jagged cave mouth belied how truly large the cave was and how far it plunged into the heart of Crag's summit. Wulfric bent to his knees and examined the floor. He found a copious amount of white fur, along with prints the same size and shape as he had seen earlier.

This is the beast's lair.

THE TOMB OF THERAGAARD

The mournful howl of the wind lessened, the deeper he went inside the cave, but the sound of blood pounding in his ears did not.

To make headway stealthily was difficult, for the uneven ground was cluttered by the discarded bones of deer, goat, wolf, and human. The sound of a scattered bone seemed to echo to infinity with each misstep the young Ulf took. He progressed past the light of the cave entrance until he was at the edge of utter darkness. It was then when he saw the unmistakable form of the white bear a dozen feet away. The beast was slumbering, sated after its recent meal.

Honor prevented the killing of a sleeping foe, but he would not give up his advantage of surprise entirely. The Ulf filled his lungs with air and unleashed a battle cry loud enough to shake the mountain itself. He charged forward, axe on his shoulder ready to strike, but he stopped short when he saw no reaction to his deafening roar.

He stood over the prone giant.

The white bear has been slain! Butchered in its own den!

In disbelief, Wulfric nearly let the axe fall from his hands.

What could kill one of the kings of the mountain?

He bent over the corpse and stared at the wounds with mystified eyes. The flesh was torn from the creature's abdomen, the head bitten clean off.

Wulfric examined the bloody area as one would the scene of a murder. He found a second set of prints, larger than those of the bear. By their distinct shape, the young Ulf could tell they were from a wolf—and a monstrous one at that. The bear had put up a mighty struggle against this other creature. Grayish fur, covered in sickly, sweet-smelling blood, he found tangled in the bear's claws. Most alarming of all was a tooth, longer than a man's forearm, found lodged inside the white bear's rib cage.

Pausing a moment to gather his wits, Wulfric recalled stories from his youth told by the graybeards—stories of wolves born in the Abyss. Wolves known as the Hounds of Fenrir.

Chapter 32
The War Machine

My former colleagues on the Wizard Council would think me mad if they spied upon me now.

In front of the Golem was a long metal table upon which lay a staff, a silver dagger, and various other magical instruments that Dementhus had assembled for this unique investigation into an artifact long thought lost to history.

Over in a corner of the gargantuan tent was a fully stocked alchemy cabinet, replete with bubbling potions, beakers, and flame-heated cauldrons spewing forth noxious fumes. Behind the Golem, painted on a large rectangular canvas, was a pentagram, now torn and burnt from attempts at reanimation of the Ragnar's Mountain God.

So far, the Necromancer had not been able to replicate Gidran's success.

I shall be damned before I strip my flesh to the bone to commune with the Golem! Terminus has another role for me to play.

Frustrated, Dementhus paced the perimeter of the black metal warrior as it lay unmoving on its bed of logs. The Golem was not ready to lead the swelling and eager Ragnar forces into battle, and it appeared it would not be ready for quite some time.

The oddly beautiful red runes carved into the Golem's flesh intrigued the wizard. They were not written in any magical language he was familiar with. *What part did they play in its creation and its operation?*

The Golem was alive, after a fashion; Gidran had proven that. Its consciousness slumbered. He had to wake it, but he could not do so inside a tent in the valley of the Ragnar with such limited resources. Only in Antigenesus's laboratory, where it was created, could the Golem be revived.

THE TOMB OF THERAGAARD

When the tent flap parted, Dementhus knew who it would be. Ivor stepped inside after being beckoned, keeping his broad-shouldered body clear of the Golem.

Dementhus bowed deeply to the superstitious king. He would show deference to the man until he was no longer useful. "Greetings, friend. Have you come to bring word from the expedition?"

The jarl had the look of a man bearing ill tidings. His eyes shifted between the black metal warrior and the red-robed wizard. Ivor shook his gray head as he delivered his answer: "They have yet to return, but it is not the expedition I came here to jaw about."

Dementhus gave the jarl his complete attention. "Speak your mind."

"I can no longer hold the leash to the army we have built. If we do not let the warriors quench their thirst for blood, they might start fighting among themselves."

"Is that the only matter that weighs on your mind?" inquired Dementhus, suspecting Ivor was concerned about something more important.

"The God of the Mountain still slumbers," answered Ivor. "We need Him to lead us against our enemies!"

"He will slumber until we prove to be worthy of being His warriors on Medias," explained Dementhus. "Tell me, Ivor, have not your numbers swelled since just the word of His recovery spread to neighboring clans?"

"Yes," admitted Ivor.

"Then, if your men thirst for blood, give it to them! Let them take up the arms and armor I have forged. Let them bear the mark of the Mountain God on their banners as they slay in His name. Slay enough so that the cries of the dead ring in His slumbering ears!"

"That I shall," growled Ivor, whose eyes glowed eerily.

Dementhus rubbed his aching hands together and beamed a smile. "Whose blood shall the Ragnar spill first?"

When the Jarl spoke, he did so with no emotion. "Clan Ulf. Their jarl, Alric, killed my firstborn. I have waited a long time to avenge him."

Dementhus laughed. "You will! You will!"

"Will you be joining us?" asked Ivor. "Your magic could be of aid to us."

"I must wait here for the return of Crayvor and his scouting party. It is of utmost importance I stay with the Mountain God until He is taken to the place of His creation. When I do return to the Ragnar, though, I expect to be welcomed by a victorious army led by a less-glum jarl."

Chapter 33
The Hound of Fenrir

As Wulfric followed the Hound's prints away from the white bear's corpse, a fetid stench reached his nostrils. The odor smelled of decaying flesh and burning fur. The young Ulf's instincts told him the powerful reek also carried with it the smell of the Abyss.

It was too late to turn back, Wulfric understood. According to the tales spoken by the elders, the Hounds of Fenrir had heightened senses and were as intelligent as man. If it was a Fenrir beast he tracked, it most likely had already sensed his presence.

The Hounds of Fenrir were the offspring of the great Daemon Fenrir. It was said these Hounds crippled their prey before devouring them, taking additional nourishment from the torment inflicted. Wulfric was morbidly curious to discover if the tales were true.

He remembered his grandfather telling him tales of the attacks on Clan Ulf by the Hounds of Fenrir. The Abyss-spawned creatures had appeared after a violent lightning storm struck the top of Crag. The horrifying creatures stalked and fed on anyone who was unfortunate enough to be caught outside the palisades. Despite numerous hunting parties, none of the Hounds had ever been killed. It was only when a similar storm struck the mountain a month later that the Hounds had disappeared.

Had one remained?

The darkness ahead began to turn gray. When Wulfric turned a corner, light spilled inside the tunnel, revealing the outside world, framed through a jagged opening a dozen yards ahead. He could tell it was night, since gloomy moonlight painted the cave walls the color of bone. He summoned all his innate Berserker courage and proceeded

THE TOMB OF THERAGAARD

toward the exit, axe in hand, hugging the left side of the cave to stay in the shadows that remained.

At the irregularly shaped mouth were fresh prints, which appeared to vanish only a dozen steps past the entrance. Puzzled, Wulfric did not know what to think. He took one step outside the cave. The landscape ahead was flat, leading to a drop-off that undoubtedly led to a very sheer cliff. There was no place to hide.

Had the creature jumped off the mountain?

Before he took another step, he felt a crushing weight on his back. Wulfric fell hard onto the ground, his axe flying from his hand and sailing off the side of the mountain. Cursing his own carelessness, the quick Ulf warrior slid out from under whatever had fallen onto his back. When he whipped around, there stood a Hound of Fenrir, exactly as the elders had described. The Abyssal wolf had lain in wait on a ledge above the cave mouth.

Wulfric rose to his feet and unsheathed his dagger. The young warrior's terrified eyes struggled to take in the unholy creature in its entirety. Standing a head taller than he, the hellspawned wolf wore a thick coat of white and gray fur. The monster had the body of a wolf, a slobbering mouth, and a barbed tail that swished menacingly from its rear. Conspicuously absent from its row of razor-like teeth was an incisor, the huge tooth it had left behind inside the white bear's rib cage. The intelligence behind its red eyes was obvious and malevolent.

Blood pumped vigorously through the Ulf's body, his thews tensed. His will to live overrode paralyzing fear, and he rushed the creature, screaming a battle cry. The Hound leapt aside but not before Wulfric's dagger slashed one of its hind legs. Sweet-smelling blood stained the blade. Wulfric was pleased that its hide, at least, was like that of mortal flesh.

Instead of leaping to the attack, the Hound stepped back. The two stood facing each other again. Not a hint of fear was in the demon wolf's eyes.

It mocks me!

Infuriated, the Ulf cried a challenge. "Come, hellspawn! Fight me!"

When black lips around its slobbering mouth formed words to answer his challenge, Wulfric froze in disbelief and horror.

"You challenge me? I spared you only to look upon the face of the foolish human who dared to enter my domain. I am not disappointed. Your bravery is exceeded only by your stupidity. Why are you here?"

"I am here for your pelt, devil!" spat Wulfric.

The Abyssal wolf laughed as it pawed the ground before it with its razor-like claws. "Foolish and a braggart! I would like to see you try."

"And you shall!" vowed Wulfric. The young warrior threw his dagger.

The blade sailed through the air and clipped the wolf's ear. The Hound of Fenrir growled in annoyance, then leapt over the Ulf and down below the edge of the plateau.

It dares me to follow!

Below the shelf-like ledge was not a sheer cliff but instead a maze of rocks, snowdrifts, and crevasses. Wulfric did not see the Hound, but he could follow its prints easily enough. He lowered himself down the six-foot drop and gave chase. He scrambled up a boulder, where he spied a barbed tail swishing around a corner nearby. He jumped from the stone to give chase, his sword now in his hand.

The Ulf's legs churned, and his feet pounded on the ice-coated ground. He caught up to the beast and took aim at its hindquarters. As the blade arched toward its target, the Hound bolted around a corner, and Wulfric instead struck stone. The enraged Ulf rounded the rock and, at the last second, dug his feet into the ground to avoid falling down a deep chasm that would have spelled certain doom.

It is cunning. That trap was deliberate!

As he looked for the beast in the dark passage past the crevasse that had almost been his tomb, a claw from behind tore into his shoulder. Wulfric let out a cry of anguish. The warrior leapt over the chasm to get away from the Hound, then braced for another attack; however, it did not come. The Daemon was lost to him again.

He looked, listened, and smelled for signs of the beast. He did not have to wait long. The sound of claws on stone came from behind, and Wulfric again gave chase, this time more wary of the Hound's tricks. Right, then left, then right, he turned down the icy corridors of rock. When the sounds of the beast's movements stopped, so did he. Ahead was a cul-de-sac, the Hound apparently trapped within. Sword point leading, the Ulf headed down the gloomy passage.

"You can't run forever," he taunted.

The beast turned to face Wulfric, baleful eyes staring hungrily into the dark. When its mouth yawned open, a whiff of sulfur hit Wulfric in the face, causing his eyes to water. When flames erupted from the Hound's open throat, the Ulf instinctively covered his face with his forearm.

THE TOMB OF THERAGAARD

Fire! The hellspawn breathes fire!

The flames licked his arm, burning away the tough leather sleeve and singeing his flesh underneath. His face was spared, but the pain was intense, and he cried out in agony.

The Hound was on the move again and leapt over Wulfric, slamming its barbed tail into his chest as it did. He was knocked to the ground.

It enjoys my torment. I must turn the tide of battle quickly. Guile is needed where brute force is failing me.

Bounding atop a boulder, Wulfric risked a quick glance at his surroundings. In the distance he could see a flat area free of large rocks and cul-de-sacs, one giving him room to maneuver and to see in all directions. He did not seek the beast but instead jumped down and pumped his legs as fast as he could. The move must have surprised the Hound, for Wulfric enjoyed a good ten-second head start before he could hear the sound of claws on ice in pursuit.

As he entered the open ground, he turned to face the beast. Here would be his last stand. He held his sword in both hands as he prepared for the Hound of Fenrir's assault. His breathing slowed, and his mind focused to a single thought, that of finding one weak spot on the huge wolf's body to attack. However, he never got that opportunity.

The sound of ice cracking was the Ulf's only warning that the ground he'd thought was solid was merely a thin ice sheet formed over a fissure in the mountain. He fell more than a dozen feet before landing flat on his back, his head bouncing off the ground.

Everything turned black.

When consciousness returned, Wulfric discovered snow had collected on his face, his head spun, and his entire body ached. But all things considered, he thought himself fortunate.

He risked opening his eyes a crack and discovered that providence had left his sword in reach of his right hand. However, above him was the Hound of Fenrir, pacing around the fissure's perimeter, its foul slobber occasionally dripping down into the pit.

Wulfric lay still and kept his breathing slow and shallow. From the slits of his eyes, he watched the Hound pace and sniff the air. *Perhaps it thinks me dead and no longer a source for torment and nourishment?*

After a long period of anxious moments, the beast casually jumped down to Wulfric's level.

Panic was foreign to Berserkers, but the reek of the Abyss tested Wulfric's resistance to his instinct to flee. The Hound of Fenrir walked around the Ulf's supine body, nudging his legs with its drooling muzzle, slobbering on his chest, and even using a paw to claw at his head. All that time, Wulfric moved nary a muscle.

The Hound reared back its thick neck and unleashed a deafening howl toward the dark sky overhead. The Fenrir beast then spoke: "Foolish man. You wanted my pelt? Have my teeth!"

Through slitted eyes, Wulfric watched the monster crack open its menacing jaw. The odor of sulfur and death poured from the beast's gaping mouth, and slaver dripped down from between its teeth. The supine warrior reached with his right hand to grab the pommel of his sword. When the muscles on the Hound's neck rippled, Wulfric twisted his body from under the creature and struck.

The sword slashed into the Hound's flank, slicing off a chunk of rank flesh. Wulfric used his momentum to leap onto the creature's neck in a single, fluid move. Like a rider on a bucking horse, he wrapped his legs around the beast's withers while he used his left hand to grab hold of its furry neck.

As it whipped its head back and forth to free itself from its unwanted burden, the Hound snapped its jaws into empty air. Unable to bite into Wulfric's body, it used its barbed tail to whip the Ulf's back, cutting into his flesh.

Wulfric ignored the pain and bashed the Abyssal wolf's thick skull with the pommel of his sword. The skull cracked. In fury, the beast jumped out of the pit and rolled on its side. Wulfric lost his grip on his sword, but he remained on the creature's back.

"I shall feast on your flesh!" snarled the Hound of Fenrir. "You shall beg for death before this day is over. Then I shall hunt down your kin!"

Desperate to stay away from the Hound's jaws, Wulfric wrapped his arms around its neck while his legs squeezed against its body. In response, the Hound bashed him against the side of the mountain. When that failed to dislodge the Ulf, the incensed creature raged again. "Face me, and let me take your soul to the Abyss!"

Wulfric knew that if he released his grip, he would be doomed. "I shall not be goaded by the likes of you, hellspawn! It is *I* who shall send *you* to the Abyss this day!"

THE TOMB OF THERAGAARD

The black sky erupted with a flash of lightning followed by a crack of thunder. A storm had moved over the mountain. The beast's lungs labored, and Wulfric's taunt went unanswered. Wulfric butted his head against the Hound's cracked skull and watched with satisfaction as blood and brain oozed out of the ruined cavity. He did not stop until the creature fell forward and its legs collapsed beneath it.

Wulfric shifted his hands to seize the beast's lower jaw and twisted the creature's neck. Muscles and bones snapped, and the beast's labored breathing stopped.

Wulfric counted a hundred heartbeats before releasing his grip. He retrieved his sword, and with one great thrust, he plunged the blade into the beast's heart, making sure that one fewer child of the Abyss roamed Medias.

The storm rolled overhead, and lightning cracked.

"Back to the Abyss, foul creature. Let your hellspawn brothers know that the Berserkers of Clan Ulf are not to be reckoned with!"

Weary and bloody, Wulfric stumbled away from the dead Hound of Fenrir. As he cleaned his wounds, he was puzzled as to why he felt no happiness. Then he remembered what his mother had told him as a child: "One cannot feel joy unless it can be shared."

With his mother's words in mind, he went about taking the pelt from the Hound of Fenrir.

There would be much cause to celebrate when he returned to his village and many people with whom to share his happiness.

Chapter 34
Clan Ulf on Fire

The Ragnar scout dipped his hands into a pile of soot and proceeded to cover every bit of his exposed flesh. Although his skin was hidden from the glare of the moonlight, nothing could mask the hatred in his eyes, which yearned to see the village of Clan Ulf burn to the ground and its arrogant inhabitants cast savagely into the afterlife. His calloused hand drew a foot-long dagger that was also blackened with ash. The scout could not wait to test its keen edge on the soft flesh of an Ulf warrior. Behind him, a Ragnar force lay hidden atop a ridge, awaiting his signal to start the slaughter. Soon murderous swings from newly forged swords and axes would rain down on the craven Ulf.

The scout's eyes focused up at the village on the hill. The arrogant Ulf had left their gate open and had but one lone warrior standing sentry.

On his stomach, the scout crawled. About him, the tall grass swayed, but only as if disturbed by a gentle breeze. Undetected, he reached the ditch that surrounded the walled village, near the open iron gate. The moon illuminated the sentry. The Ulf warrior stood on the bridge that spanned the ditch. The man yawned and stretched. He wore a fur cap and bearskin cloak, and he had a broad axe tied to his wrist by a thong.

From the pocket of his leather trousers, the scout removed a glass vial. Weighing the object in his hands, he took aim and threw it behind the guard—glad to be rid of the magic given to him by the foreign wizard Dementhus.

When the vial shattered, the guard spun around, now fully alert. From the broken vessel a blackness billowed like a cloud, and a darkness more impenetrable than night shrouded the gate. The spreading void caused the sentry to recoil.

THE TOMB OF THERAGAARD

That lapse in duty was all the scout needed to make for the bridge that spanned the ditch. With the sentry's back to him, the scout plunged his dagger into the Ulf man, penetrating a spot between the man's ribs and likely into his heart. The scout twisted the dying man around, then sliced his throat. Blood fountained from the man's nearly decapitated neck and spilled onto the bridge. The scout then kicked the large man into the ditch below.

The Ragnar scout stepped through the sphere of darkness (holding his breath) and walked into the village. Not a soul was about. He stepped back inside the sphere of darkness, feeling for the gate. He hacked at the iron hinges with his coronium-forged dagger. Much to his amazement, the weapon easily cut through the old iron, and the sphere of darkness did not let any of the sound from his hacking escape. Dementhus had said such would be the case, but the scout had not believed him. He would not doubt the foreigners again.

The scout shoved the gate from its moorings. It would never function again.

After the sphere of darkness dissipated, the scout pulled out a whalebone whistle and emptied his lungs into it. He did not have to wait long before the ground beneath him rumbled. He smiled to himself at the thought of the upcoming slaughter, and he readied his dagger again.

✠ ✠ ✠

"I can see the green hill," I tell Mother, jumping up and down. "I can see Father. There, on the very summit. He is coming home!"

I am longing to feel Father's warm embrace, his soft beard against my cheek. He has been gone for so long!

Mother holds my hand tight. "No, Kara, you are mistaken. Your father can't come home. He can never come home."

"You lie," I spit as I pull my hand away.

I turn from Mother, and I race on my tiny legs toward the green hill. However, no matter how far or how fast I run, Father gets no closer. By the time I reach the crown of the hill, he is gone. I collapse to my knees and furiously pound the ground with my tiny fists, angry that the world has lied to me again.

"Why did he have to die?" I cry, Mother now beside me on the lonely green hill.

"He died so we can live. But now you must get up, Kara!"

I shake my head wildly. "No!"

"Get up!" Mother demands.

The sun fades from the sky, and Mother's face twists and contorts as the light turns to shadow. I look below and see fire begin to climb the green hill.

Mother screams, "Get up now!"

As smoke assaulted her nostrils, Kara jolted awake. She looked about her dark hut, then took notice of the sounds of combat coming from the distance. Kara jumped out of bed and donned her leather jerkin and fur-lined boots. She grabbed two full quivers and strung her longbow before racing outside. The Ulf village was under assault, and without hesitation, she was ready to defend her adopted clan.

With the same desperation she had experienced in her dream, Kara raced up the hill upon which the Ulf village rested. After seeing a swarm of brawling Berserkers at the gate, she approached from the east. As easily as an acrobat, she jumped the ditch, scaled the wall, and dropped into the village below. She ducked an axe blow headed her way, then turned her bow toward her attacker. Her quick reflexes saved the man, because she recognized the warrior as one of Clan Ulf's graybeards. She lowered her bow and shouted to the old man, "Hold, it's me, Kara!"

The man looked at her with wild eyes, unable to form words.

She hooked her bow over her shoulder and grabbed hold of the old man's gnarled hands. "What has happened? Who has attacked us?"

The grizzled warrior had a tired, grim face. "We have been attacked by the scoundrel Ivor of Ragnar. Many of our bravest warriors are now dead, and the few who remain make their last stand before the gate. The women and children are gathering beyond the great longhouse. You should be with them."

"I am not a child, nor a helpless woman," protested Kara. "I am a warrior!"

As if to prove her point, Kara released the man's hands and notched an arrow.

"Stay where you can be protected," pleaded the old man. "You cannot help them."

THE TOMB OF THERAGAARD

"We shall see about that!" vowed Kara as she brushed past the graybeard and headed toward the sound of combat.

As she made her way forward, anger, shock, and dismay mixed inside Kara's veins. Not a single hut she passed had escaped the torch; even the jarl's longhouse was now hopelessly engulfed. Smoke shrouded her movements but also blinded her from potential threats. She needed to get to a safe place, from which she could see the men fighting and launch her arrows. As she advanced, tears stained her face.

Kara mounted the roof of the tannery, the only intact structure she could find near the gate. Once she was concealed, her eyes spied upon the battle below.

Alric stood tallest among the last of the bloodied Ulf warriors. The outnumbered men formed a tight circle as Ragnar warriors, in strange, green-tinted armor, encircled them, recklessly throwing themselves at the Ulf warriors with the confidence of men who knew their adversaries were doomed.

Kara bent to one knee to steady herself on the sloped roof and targeted the cluster of Ragnar men. *I shall make them pay for their arrogance*, she vowed.

Her first arrow hit a man in the back. Kara cursed as the peculiar armor knocked her arrow harmlessly aside. Hits to an armored shoulder, chest, and groin had the same results. She drew in a deep breath and took more care with her aim. Her next shots pierced bare hands, punctured exposed thighs, and lanced a few unprotected heads.

Despite her success, no ground was gained for the Ulf warriors, as eager invaders flooded through the overrun gate to replace their dead. The enemy, Kara realized gloomily, were being aided by other Berserker clans; in fact, she spotted the sigils of other clans painted on armored chests.

The number of Ulf warriors soon dwindled to a dozen beleaguered men. Alric shouted to keep them together and to fight to their dying breath. The brave Ulf responded by attacking the Ragnar with renewed energy. Inevitably, however, even the great warrior Alric grew weary.

A horn blast interrupted the combat, and the Ragnar men parted as an enemy graybeard pushed his way through the blood-covered invaders and over the bodies of the dead. Kara reasoned the man had to be Ivor, the wretched leader of the Ragnar. The men on both sides stopped fighting; Kara lowered her bow and listened when the man spoke.

"Declare your fealty to me," threatened Ivor, "or watch the rest of your people burn!"

Alric stepped forward and pointed the tip of his two-handed sword at Ivor's head. "I shall sever your rotten head from your shoulders, Ivor. We shall never surrender to you."

As Kara listened to the two jarls, her body trembled in rage. She would send Ivor to the Abyss for what he had done to her adopted clan. Ivor's head was uncovered and made for a tempting and easy target.

Her heart pounded in her chest, and sweat poured down her forehead as she drew the bowstring back. As she took aim at Ivor's bloated face, the sinew bit into her flesh. She pulled back on the string until it threatened to snap. She wanted enough power to ensure that the arrow would fly true.

A rustling on the thatched roof distracted her. She turned around, but too late, as a gauntleted fist smashed into the side of her head.

Chapter 35

A Duel to the Death

Ivor's eyes bulged nearly out of their sockets. Facing the man who killed his firstborn, after his having envisioned the moment for many years, was gloriously satisfying. To see Alric covered in the blood and ash of his clan was something even beyond what he had ever dreamt of. Still, Ivor wanted more. "Alric! I shall have my vengeance for the death of my son!"

Alric looked upon Ivor with an emotionless face. "Your son was cruel and cowardly. He waylaid innocent women and children, and he paid for it with his own blood. I gave him a better death than he deserved: single combat." Alric spread his arms to the death and destruction that had already devastated his village. "Has your hate simmered all these years only to boil over into another act of cowardice: attacking us as we sleep? If vengeance is what you seek, then let this fight be between you and me. Call off your dogs, and we shall fight to the death."

Ivor threw off his bearskin cloak, revealing green armor underneath. He nodded his head and spoke to his captains. "Should I fall, return to our village, and leave this place forever." Then he turned back to Alric and sneered. "Should I claim victory, though, know that nothing shall remain of Clan Ulf. We shall burn it to the ground, kill those who resist, and take prisoners of the rest."

Alric spat upon the ground beneath Ivor's feet. "Your craven acts this day will be long remembered. Your descendants shall bear this black mark in the afterlife. Let us fight."

The Ulf king stormed toward Ivor, bringing his two-handed blade to bear against the snarling Ragnar jarl. The blade rang hard against Ivor's pauldron but did not penetrate the green metal.

233

Ivor let loose mocking laughter as he stepped back unharmed, save for a bruised shoulder. "You shall die forgotten," he taunted, "and without a place for your bones to rest."

The jarls exchanged blow after blow, neither gaining ground. Curses and threats passed between their warriors as they cheered for their respective leaders.

After a few probing stabs, Ivor charged at Alric with a swing to his head. Alric, despite his fatigue, ducked the overhead blow. The sword missed its target and sliced into an unlucky Ragnar, splitting him from shoulder to groin. An audible gasp could be heard from the Ulf warriors at the sharpness of the blade.

Blood dripped down Ivor's weapon as he removed it from the twitching corpse. Alric took the opportunity to gather as many breaths as he could.

Ivor smirked at the fatigued Ulf leader. "Are you going to dance all night, or are we going to fight?"

"We fight!" Alric charged at Ivor, and the two met with a thunderous clash as their swords collided. The two exchanged blows, blocking and parrying their greatswords like others would one-handers.

The Ulf jarl's wrists swelled from the repeated blows, and his body spilled blood from a dozen small cuts. Alric tried but could not penetrate the mysterious armor that Ivor wore. He risked a stab at the Ragnar's head but missed. Ivor counterattacked with a speed impossible from an iron blade. Alric could not move in time and fell to his knees. Then Ivor's blade severed Alric's left arm at the elbow, and the Ulf jarl's sword fell to the mud.

The superior numbers of the Ragnar thwarted attempts by the Ulf warriors to rush to the defense of their leader. Ivor advanced for the kill.

Drawing his dagger, the Ulf jarl surprised Ivor with a stab at his knee through a joint between the unnaturally defiant armor.

Ivor cursed as he fell to his knees, avoiding a grievous injury. He shouted to his men. "Finish him and his men. This duel has ended!"

"Your dishonor will not be forgotten!" were Alric's last words on Medias.

After the Ragnar men ravaged the Ulf leader, Ivor knelt down to whisper into the dead man's ear. "You are no longer. Ulf is no longer. The family of Alric is no longer."

THE TOMB OF THERAGAARD

The Ragnar horde swarmed around the survivors. Outnumbered and in a defenseless position, the Ulf men were savagely hacked into bloody chunks. After it was over, Ivor addressed his horde of men.

"Capture all who remain inside: the old men, women, and children. Do not harm them, for we need slaves, and our God needs sacrifices. Burn this village to the ground. I don't want any sign of the Ulf clan left on Medias!"

Ivor's only regret was that his surviving son was not there to see the destruction of the Ragnar's greatest foe.

Chapter 36
The Expedition

His hands and feet were numb, and when icy gusts blew down the face of the mountain, his skin burned as if aflame. Gidran cursed the bleak lands of the barbarians, longing for the golden deserts of his homeland. Here, there was no cloak thick enough to keep out the biting winds, no oasis from which to seek refuge from the cold—nothing but miles and miles of unforgiving mountainous terrain and white death. He was not surprised that this land had birthed the hardy Berserkers.

Crayvor, the beardless son of the jarl, headed the twelve-man expedition up and around the mountain, but it was Gidran who knew the location of the entrance to the ancient fortress. Progress was slow, for the landscape had changed in the centuries since the time of the Golem, and it was from the Golem's memories that he had gleaned the route to take. Rockslides, erosion, and the ever-changing weather patterns made it difficult for the shaman to guide the company with complete certainty. They had walked and climbed for days, and now the nearly identical twin peaks of the mountain loomed directly overhead.

To Gidran's great surprise, the members of Clan Ragnar, despite their living in the mountain's shadow, were unfamiliar with the upper reaches of the split peak. Crayvor explained that the Ragnar believed the entrance to hell was close by. Gidran scoffed and surmised that the Ragnar had been fed a false narrative by the archmagus Antigenesus to keep them away from his fortress. Crayvor disagreed.

"Those who have survived the journey to the summit reported the smell of sulfur and told of glowing caves venting heat like a kiln," explained Crayvor. "Those who tried to explore inside the caves died within moments."

THE TOMB OF THERAGAARD

The pace of the expedition had slowed significantly. Gidran believed it was because of fear and not fatigue. When the men had slowed to a crawl, Crayvor called the expedition to a halt and began to harangue them. "Move, you dogs! We burn precious daylight. Anyone who lags behind shall be left for the frostwolves."

One warrior, a youth with a thin brown beard and narrow eyes named Thrax, threw his axe at the feet of Crayvor. "I shall go no farther! Do you wish to bring doom upon our clan? We ascend to the place our ancestors warned us never to go! To the gates of hell itself!"

As Crayvor looked down at the axe at his feet and then at the youth who had thrown it, Gidran could see murderous flames burning behind the eyes of the jarl's son. Crayvor picked up the weapon and licked the snow from its edge. "We are on a mission for my father. A mission that will make our clan the most powerful force on the continent. And yet you dare challenge me?"

Thrax, unwisely in Gidran's opinion, did not back down. "Yes. I would rather die here on the slope than up there, where fell beasts await to drag us to the Abyss!"

"Then, so be it!"

With that, Crayvor launched the axe back at the impudent fool, but not at his feet. The axe edge sunk deep into the Ragnar's skull. The youth was dead the moment his bloody body collapsed into the snow. Gidran was impressed with the decisiveness and ruthlessness of Crayvor. *These Ragnar will make great servants of Terminus!*

Crayvor retrieved the coronium axe, wiped the gore off it, and stuck it under his bearskin cloak. He spat upon the corpse. "I value this weapon more than I do you," he said. Then he jerked his chin up toward the twin peaks. "We go higher, as Gidran commands we must!"

No one else questioned the jarl's son, and the party ascended at double their previous pace.

After they reached the base of the summit, an image from the Golem's memories flashed into the shaman's mind. "Stop! We are getting near! Give me a moment."

As the shaman attempted to reconcile his vision with the current landscape, Crayvor ordered the fastest Ragnar man to scout the area ahead. The sun had just set when the scout came back with a dire warning on his lips. "I saw a great winged creature circling the sky between the peaks! It did not spot me, but I remained hidden until it flew to one of the peaks and disappeared into the black sky. We must flee while we still can!"

Crayvor grabbed the excited scout by the shoulders. "Show some spine, and describe this creature to me!"

The man regained some of his former Ragnar bravado. "From wingtip to wingtip, it must measure at least six men across. It has a large predatory beak, which looked strong enough to crush a man's skull. Its talons were sharp, shaped like those of a hawk, and able to grasp a white bear if it were so inclined. I have never before seen such a colossal bird!"

"What do you make of this, Gidran?" asked Crayvor.

The shaman ended his ruminations and stood where Crayvor and the others crouched. "Many creatures, some older than the mountain itself, remain from the last time the gates to the Abyss were flung open. This beast may be one of them. Most of these creatures are allies of the Mountain God, but some, who have lingered too long on Medias, believe they no longer have a master. We must proceed with caution, for we have no means of killing such a creature. Our only chance lies in staying unobserved." The troubled expression on the Ragnar faces gave Gidran pause. He needed these fools to help him find the entrance. "We are getting close to our destination, of that I am certain! Have faith that the God of the Mountain will protect us!"

Other than the resolute Crayvor, the Ragnar glared at Gidran dubiously.

Gidran pointed down the steep slope to the lands below. "Stop and look upon the valleys and plains. If we succeed, we shall conquer every land you see and beyond!"

The conviction with which Gidran spoke emboldened the Ragnar, who now raised their axes in salute. Crayvor stood with his men and gestured back up to the peaks. "We continue on."

Despite their fear, the Ragnar traveled steadfastly toward the crater between the peaks, where Gidran informed the expedition he believed the entrance to the fortress lay.

They made it only halfway to their destination before the winged beast returned. Upon Crayvor's shouted orders, the company dove into the snowdrifts to hide themselves from the giant predator. One man, overwhelmed by fear, ignored the command and fled back down the mountain. The great bird changed its course and flew directly toward the spooked Ragnar.

THE TOMB OF THERAGAARD

Before the beast struck, though, it hovered over the expedition, its flapping wings causing ice and snow to swirl in the air. As Gidran whispered a prayer to Terminus, he strangely felt no connection to the beast. If the creature had any loyalties to the Dark God, they had waned over the centuries.

The terrifying bird let out a deafening squawk, and a thunderous rumbling came from farther up the mountain. Gidran was unsure of the source until cries of "Avalanche!" spread among the Ragnar. Gidran had only enough time to shield his head before being buried in snow. As the world became dark and quiet, he prayed to Terminus.

The weight of the crushing snow held him completely immobilized, and the shaman fought the urge to panic. Fortunately, he discovered that his body was awkwardly bent forward, with his arms pressed against his chest. Providence had granted him one favor: A small void had formed around his head. He used what breath he had to pray for Terminus to intervene. Gidran waited with serenity inside his frozen tomb as all awareness of the world above had ceased.

What seemed like hours passed before he sensed anything. Finally, his ears heard the muffled sound of the scraping of ice. Someone was digging down.

Praise be to Terminus!

With a new hope rising in his heart, the shaman resumed his praying as loud as he could. The sound of the digging intensified. He then felt his left foot come into contact with air, and soon thereafter, he felt a hand upon his ankle.

The rescuer cleared more snow, but it was Gidran's faith that gave him the energy to climb out. It was Vaard, the man who had panicked, who found him. For some reason, the beast had spared his life.

The shaman looked around the changed landscape and quickly realized that only he and his rescuer were free from the snow. Fighting to catch his breath, Gidran gestured to the area a few feet beside the hole from where he had emerged. "Crayvor was right beside me when the avalanche hit! Dig here as if your own life depended upon it."

Using their weapons to break up the ice and their hands as spades, the two men worked together to find Crayvor. Gidran was the first to feel his still-warm flesh.

"Hurry, I have him," shouted Gidran to the lucky Vaard.

After the jarl's son was finally pulled from the snow, his teeth chattered uncontrollably behind blue lips. Gidran watched, impressed, as Crayvor flexed his frozen limbs and staggered to his feet. When Crayvor's eyes fell on the rescuers, his face grew sullen. "Are we three the only survivors? We must look for the others!" Crayvor scanned the dark sky. "The great bird is gone. We must hurry!"

Though Crayvor continued to plead for help, Gidran faded from the mortal world as the presence of the Dark God once again warmed his soul. The shaman was directed by this spiritual energy to look up at the changed landscape. When he finally answered Crayvor, he spoke as one in a dream. "They no longer matter. Those men have given their lives for the cause. Look now, below the lip of the crater."

Crayvor fell into silence and looked up the mountain: The avalanche had exposed an expanse of black ice and pumice just below the crater's lip and, more importantly, an unnatural, rectangular opening, which led straight into the side of the mountain.

"Is that … is that the entrance?" gasped Crayvor.

The shaman put his arm around the bewildered Ragnar. "Yes. The avalanche was sent by the God of the Mountain to reveal this door to us."

Crayvor made another plea. "But the beast is gone, and the entrance is now known to us. We still have time to search for the others. If they found a pocket of air, they may yet live!"

Gidran scolded the jarl's son. "We were not spared their fate and given this opportunity by blind luck. Sacrifices have to be made. We risk blaspheming the Mountain God by robbing Him of these men's souls!"

The shaman followed Crayvor's eyes as they looked down the mountain to where the bodies of the others lay buried. When Crayvor met his gaze, the youth was stone-faced. "If that is what the Mountain God wishes, so be it, but we have to make sure this is the true entrance and not a false hope. I cannot come back to my father without being as certain as death that we have accomplished our mission."

"I understand," agreed Gidran.

The shaman had no doubt the massive entrance was exactly what he had claimed it to be; however, he understood the importance of proving that to Crayvor. He was also well aware of the danger of approaching the fortress of one of the greatest archmagi to have ever lived. Without Dementhus and his knowledge of such matters, he did not think it wise to

THE TOMB OF THERAGAARD

stand within a hundred yards of the enigmatic corridor in the side of the mountain, so he formulated a plan. In conspiratorial tones, he spoke into Crayvor's ear. "Perhaps our lucky friend who was spared both the avalanche and the winged menace should be the one to first venture inside."

Crayvor agreed. "Vaard, take the lead, and guide us to the entrance."

The young man, perhaps buoyed by his recent good fortune, smiled broadly and seemed oblivious to the potential danger that awaited him. "It would be an honor."

Two sets of eyes followed the scout's progress up the slope. Crayvor moved to follow, but Gidran placed a hand on his shoulder. "Keep your distance," the shaman warned.

Vaard reached the threshold of the corridor and stopped. He poked his head inside briefly, then shouted down to the others. "The corridor goes a hundred feet. At its end, I see a golden door fifty feet high and a dozen wide."

That the massive corridor and the door it concealed were both large enough to enable the Golem to pass did not go unnoticed by the shaman. "This is the entrance that the God's avatar used when returning to the fortress. It should be safe for us to advance to the threshold."

After Gidran and Crayvor covered the distance to Vaard, Crayvor ordered the young man, "Go to the end of the tunnel and examine the door. Tell us if you see a handle or markings of any sort."

Vaard nodded enthusiastically. Only light from the stars entered the tunnel, so Vaard pulled a torch from his backpack and lit it before proceeding. When the scout reached the door without incident, he stopped to report his findings. "I see no handles or markings." Vaard tentatively reached out and touched the door's surface. "The door is smooth and warm to the touch. It looks metallic, but it feels like stone. I shall try to push it open."

Gidran thought about advising against that course of action but held his tongue, for he wanted to see what would happen. Just as the scout leaned on the door, Gidran and Crayvor were blinded by a bright flash and deafened by a thunderous boom. Both observers were blown out of the entrance.

When the smoke cleared, Gidran saw that a magical trap had reduced Vaard to a smoldering corpse. "It appears his luck has run out," said Gidran.

"Apparently."

"Do you have the proof you need?" asked Gidran.

Crayvor's ashen face was answer enough.

Chapter 37
The Flames in Which They Burn

Wulfric had slept like the dead, awakening to a crimson and gold dawn. The pelt of the Hound of Fenrir had kept him warm despite the blood-freezing temperatures near Crag's summit, but it was the thought of being reunited with Kara and his clanmates, and especially his father, that caused his spirit to soar.

He eschewed breakfast and instead made his way down the mountain with a renewed purpose, his pains long forgotten. Buoyed by his victory, Wulfric flew down Crag, then into the surrounding hills and valleys. With each step he took toward home, the imagined look of pride on his father's face and the warmth of Kara's embrace became more real. The young Ulf did not want to slow his pace, but when he spotted a pair of tracks coming from the south and heading toward his village, he paused to investigate.

Wulfric went to his knees to examine the fresh prints. The tracks had smooth soles on the boots, an indication the two visitors were likely from Arkos. He also discovered, traveling parallel to the prints, indentations in the snow that could be caused only by the use of a walking stick. Kayen carried a walking stick, and Wulfric had seen him leave a similar trail.

Brother Kayen may have found a wayward brother and is returning to Clan Ulf! Perhaps if I am quick enough, I can surprise them before they reach the village. Not even the wandering missionary knows the shortcuts I know. Kayen shall be the first to see I have survived the Trial and wear the Fenrir pelt!

Wulfric raced through the snow and headed toward the stony ridge east of the trail. He cut around a copse of dense trees, splashed through a nearly frozen creek, and scaled a small ravine. He then situated himself on the slope that looked down at the path that led to his village. He saw no tracks or signs of Kayen and his companion. The big Ulf wedged himself behind a rock and waited, giving himself time to catch his breath. His stomach rumbled, reminding him that he had not eaten since his fight with the hellspawn.

The sun was close to setting when he spotted two figures approaching from the south. He recognized Kayen instantly by his crooked shepherd staff. The man walking next to him was wearing a fur-lined, gray traveling cloak and towered over the missionary. It took the Ulf's eyes a moment to overcome his disbelief; it was Tryam! *What was he doing outside the abbey? This will be a better surprise than I could've hoped!*

He dug his hands deep into the snow, formed a ball, packed it tight, and with a grin on his face, launched his first attack at Kayen. The frozen projectile lobbed down from the ridge and smashed off the cleric's fur-trimmed cowl. Wulfric slid on his belly and went farther north to launch his second attack. Once he was hidden, he peered below. As Kayen brushed the snow off his cloak, he looked somewhat displeased. Tryam, however, was glancing nervously about. *He really needs to lighten up!*

The next snowball was aimed at Tryam. The well-thrown projectile hit the youth on the side of the head. Tryam jumped in front of Kayen, taking a protective stance. Wulfric noted a rare look of anger on the young acolyte's face and decided that it might not be wise to torment his friends any further. He scuttled his plan to let out a howl and charge at the pair as if he were the Hound of Fenrir itself.

Wulfric stood from his hiding spot and shouted. "It is only me! Do not fret." He slid down the side of the snow-covered ravine head first.

Relieved faces looked at him in astonishment.

"Wulfric!" The two scolded in unison.

Kayen took a poke at him with his staff. "You thunder-headed fool! You should know not to frighten visitors in your land. Especially at dusk!"

To apologize was foreign to Berserkers; instead, to release the tension, Wulfric laughed. "I thought Tryam was going to spit fire. Besides, this is no time to be angry. Do you not see what I wear?" Wulfric stood to show the results of his hunt, the Abyssal Hound's head worn like a crown, its hide like a cloak. "It is a pelt from a Hound of Fenrir!"

"A Hound of Fenrir? You killed a creature from the Abyss?" Kayen was aghast. The missionary examined the pelt thoroughly. Afterward, he shook his head. "You are lucky to be alive. I had no doubt you would succeed on your rite of passage, but I'd thought you would be bringing home the pelt of a white bear, not this. How did you slay a Hound of Fenrir?"

Wulfric acted out his adventure as he told of his pursuit of the white bear and then his fight against the Hound. After he was done, Tryam's jaw was slack. The young acolyte, having forgotten the snowball incident already, grasped Wulfric's forearm. "That's remarkable!" the youth exclaimed. "A deed worthy to be told before the hearth for many years. You have honored your father, and even Kara will have to admit to being impressed."

Wulfric was glad that his prank had been forgiven, and he slapped his old friend on the back. "I heard about your adventures at the tournament. Kara and I are proud of you. Even I have not ridden a mammoth … yet! And your battle at the end, while you were injured, is worthy of the legends of old!"

Evidently, Tryam was still uncomfortable with his failure; Wulfric noticed his friend changed topics quickly. "How do you know Brother Kayen?"

The missionary stepped between the two youths. "I have been traveling to Clan Ulf for half a decade. I have known Wulfric since he was twice as foolish as he is now."

Wulfric had to agree with Kayen. "That is so. Speaking of foolish deeds, how did you get Tryam out of the abbey? That sour-faced prune Monbatten treats Tryam worse than a dog."

The middle-aged missionary poked his staff at Wulfric again. "Abbott Monbatten can be reasoned with if you know how. He is no different from a stubborn Berserker."

As the talk of the abbot reminded Wulfric of his last encounter with Kayen, a shadow fell across his face. "Did you find your lost brothers?"

Kayen nodded his cowled head solemnly. "I did, but with grave results. The party was ambushed by two Berserkers, and my friend Brother Emil was killed in a senseless violent act. It was thanks to Tryam and one of the Engothian escorts that a massacre was prevented."

Wulfric could not hide his shock, and he stood with mouth agape. "Attacked by Berserkers? Those cowards are not members of my clan, I am certain! What happened to those scoundrels?"

"I killed them."

Tryam spoke the words without emotion.

THE TOMB OF THERAGAARD

Wulfric could sense the impact the deed had upon his friend. He recalled his own first dark encounter with killing. The face of the drunken man who'd made an attempt on his father often entered his thoughts, even though he never doubted the justice of his actions. "Be glad you did," said Wulfric. "Those craven dogs would have killed the lot of you. I wonder where they came from and what they were after."

Tryam shook his head. "Brother Emil offered them all we had, just to make them leave us in peace. They rejected that and tied us up. I think they wanted prisoners."

"Prisoners? Berserkers do not make slaves of others. Did you see any markings on their clothes, any sign of their clan?"

"They wore armor and weapons with a greenish tint. One of them had a tattoo on his face of a grasping fist."

Wulfric knew of no clan that had armor or weapons as described, but he knew well the symbol of the grasping fist. "This is foul news. The grasping fist is a symbol of the Ragnar. They live north of here, deeper in the mountains. I cannot imagine why any of their warriors would range this far south."

The dark news coincided with the darkening of the sky and a chill wind from the Coronas. Tryam shivered. "How far are we to your village? I'd like to be inside their walls before dark."

"Not far now. We shall reach it as the sun sets," assured Wulfric. "I shall lead the way."

An uneasiness came over the young Ulf. It was an emotion he did not experience often. Wulfric drew his sword. He would ask his father about the attack. He would know what was happening and how to respond. Wulfric always took great comfort from his father's sage words.

The three walked in silence, the only sound was that of the wailing winds. When they crested a ridge a few miles outside the village, they could see a cloud of thick black smoke rising from the north. Kayen gasped. "Black smoke is a sign of thatched roofs ablaze! And by the amount of smoke ..."

Wulfric's beating heart drowned out the missionary's remaining words. His thoughts turned to Tryam's story of the treacherous Ragnar. Rage overwhelmed him. He held his sword in a death grip and charged up the ridge. He did not wait for his companions to catch up.

Legs pumping, Wulfric crested the ridge and beheld the Milfaar Forest and the valley of his people. Looking toward his village, he saw smoke and flames crowning the hill upon which it rested. At a sprint now, Wulfric raced toward the conflagration, fear and anger battling for supremacy in his thoughts.

When he reached the base of the hill, the smell of burning pitch mingled with that of burning flesh. Despite all the outward signs of battle, his ears could not pick up the slightest sound of combat. Now, more slowly, he ascended the hill.

"Father?" "Kara!" Wulfric shouted for anyone he could think to name, but all of his calls went unanswered.

Wulfric crossed through the ruined gate and entered the village. Blood and gore covered the ground, and a funeral pyre, stacked ten feet high, smoldered just beyond. Wulfric fell to his knees in dismay, again calling out for his loved ones.

Ripping his eyes from the macabre scene, Wulfric forced himself to his feet, then headed toward his father's longhouse. The short walk through the village told him it was unlikely that a single member of Clan Ulf or a single structure had been spared, and so it was for his family's dwelling, now a pile of embers.

Futile rage erupted from Wulfric, and he unleashed a booming roar to the sky, calling for the blood of the invaders. *I should have been here to defend my people!* He slashed at the air with his sword and pounded the ground with his feet. He needed to unleash his anger or risk losing his mind. The Ulf raced out the gate to begin the hunt for the enemy, but a whack across his chest from Kayen's crooked staff stopped him cold.

"You can't chase them all by yourself!" scolded the missionary.

Wulfric angrily knocked the staff aside, but Kayen's words cleared his mind. He would not chase the killers just yet. "Kara. She lives outside the village. She might not have been here. I have to check her hut." He broke past the cleric and started off again.

"Wait!" This time it was Tryam. He was holding something in his hand. In the dark, Wulfric could not see what it was.

"I have no time for games," Wulfric lashed out.

Tryam took a step forward, and the light from the funeral pyre revealed what was in his hand: the shaft of an arrow, a red arrow.

"So, she was here." Wulfric's heart sank, and he dropped his sword. "She was here," he repeated.

After taking a moment to recover, Wulfric retrieved his sword from the muck. "I must still check her hut, though my heart weighs heavy, knowing

THE TOMB OF THERAGAARD

it unlikely she hides there." He ran a hand through his sweat-soaked hair. "Check for survivors within the village. If you find my father's body, do not disturb it until I can see his face again."

Without further discussion, he left the others and made his way down the hill and into the gloom of the silent and imposing trees. He felt more fear now than he had facing the Hound of Fenrir.

The Milfaar Forest showed no sign that the battle had reached into its domain. *If only she retreated to her home, she may still be safe.*

When he made it to Kara's hut, it looked undisturbed. He did not bother to knock or call her name. Inside, there was no sign of the young Ulf; only her scent lingered.

Wulfric left the forest, knowing he would never again look upon those hallowed bowers with the same youthful eyes. When he made his way back to the village, Kayen was waiting outside the wall.

Wulfric felt devoid of emotion. "The hut was empty."

"Do not give up hope just yet. Hurry, come with me!"

Wulfric's emotions returned in a rush at the missionary's promising words. He pursued Kayen around the top of the hill, the old missionary following tracks that led north, in the vague direction of the Ragnar village. Although Kayen was not as experienced a tracker as Wulfric, he pointed out an unusual line of footprints, indicating that a column of people had been led away. "If they have taken prisoners, as they tried to do with Tryam," the missionary explained, "there's a chance some of your people may still be alive."

Wulfric agreed. "I must give chase at once. To seek vengeance upon the Ragnar, discover the fate of Kara, and rescue the prisoners may be beyond what is possible, so I shall not ask either of you to come with me."

Tryam emerged from the shadows cast by the inferno, to stand by the side of his friend. "I am with you until the end."

"As am I," said Kayen, putting his arms around them both. "We shall do this together. We shall discover Kara's fate and that of the others. But I must caution that justice for this atrocity can come only from Aten."

Wulfric looked in the direction of the Ragnar village, deep within the foreboding Corona Mountain Range. "I thought I had lost everything, but I now realize that is not true. I have two friends who would risk their lives to share a dark path, at the end of which is almost certain doom."

Chapter 38
Pursuit into the Coronas

Monbatten was correct. The world was a darker and colder place than Tryam had ever imagined. He had lost his own family but had been spared any vivid memories. But now he had witnessed cruelty and death on a scale that was unimaginable. *A whole village of people murdered? Kara dead?* He did not want to think it possible.

When his fury had calmed, Wulfric examined the evidence left behind by the invaders for clues to their number. He concluded that the Ragnar force to be no more than a hundred. A small enough force, he said, that his clan should have been able to repel them. Troubling was the number of broken axes and shattered blades, evidence he combined with Tryam's observations of the weapons and arms of the two Berserkers who had attacked Brother Emil's expedition that the Ragnar blacksmiths had forged a more powerful metal.

Before they departed the Ulf village, Brother Kayen performed a service for the dead. Though they found no sign of Wulfric's father, none doubted that he was among the dead. Kayen honored Alric with his final words.

"The jarl had been more than a leader, more than a father. He'd been an example of honor, loyalty, duty, and faith. It is my somber duty but also a privilege to welcome him into Aten's embrace."

Wulfric was eager to leave but not before placing a sword in Tryam's hand. "You will need a weapon."

Tryam looked to Kayen for guidance.

"You are not a member of Saint Paxia. Not yet. Take the weapon, but don't think that means you must use it. Pray on the matter."

In silence, the party left behind the remains of Clan Ulf.

THE TOMB OF THERAGAARD

✠ ✠ ✠

On the third night of their journey, Wulfric spotted a slumped form on the ground. It was a male Ulf. The young barbarian rushed ahead to examine the body. "Alas," said Wulfric, as he closed the man's frozen eyes. "This graybeard, Oliek, was a long-time friend of my father."

Kayen knelt before the corpse, unbound its hands and feet, and said a prayer. When he was done, the missionary shook his head in disgust. "They made him suffer with a sword thrust through the stomach. A man may live a long time with such a wound."

On the evening of the fourth day, Wulfric held up their pursuit so he could hunt for wild game; their food supply had at last run out. He returned a short time later, two rabbits in his hands. Kayen started a fire, and the three huddled under the shadow of a leafless, twisted oak.

In the lurid light, they spoke in quiet tones.

"Why would the Ragnar attack your village?" It was a question Tryam had longed to ask, but he'd had to wait for the proper moment.

Wulfric spat out a piece of gristle before responding. "My father and the leader of the Ragnar, a man named Ivor, had a feud going back many years."

"Was this feud bitter enough to warrant this cowardly assault?"

The fire reflected in Wulfric's eyes. "It should not have been, but it must have. Years ago, there was a dispute over hunting grounds between our two clans. Ivor sent his eldest son to stake a claim on land that we Ulf had been hunting on for generations. Instead of honorable combat, Slaavor and his men massacred women and children fishing along the disputed border. My father would not be intimidated by, nor let stand, such a brutal act, and he led a party to find the killers. When he did, my father killed Ivor's son in honorable combat. The Ragnar retaliated in the years following, sending out war parties, but we overwhelmed them each time. My father had thought them sufficiently cowed and did not think it necessary to attack them in full force." He slowly shook his head as he stared blankly ahead. "Something must have emboldened Clan Ragnar—an alliance, perhaps."

The fire sparked and crackled.

Kayen leaned into the fire. "Tryam, the Berserkers who attacked you, they wore armor and wielded strange green-tinted weapons, isn't that so?"

"Yes. The axe's blade was keen and unusually light, as was the armor. I wish we had taken them back to show Lord Dunford, but Roderick refused to believe that 'savages' could have metal stronger than Engothian steel."

Kayen stroked his brown beard. "The coronium ore that Dunford hoards turns a greenish tint when forged into metal. As far as I know, however, only the Ancients knew how to forge such a soft metal into strong armor and sharp weapons. The possibility exists that a knowledgeable wizard may have rediscovered the secret to manipulate the ore."

The speculation caused Wulfric to jump to his feet and throw his remaining bits of food into the fire. He pounded his right fist into the palm of his left hand. "If the Ragnar have aligned with a wizard, they are even more dishonorable than I could've imagined. Berserkers do not deal in sorcery!" He spat on the ground. "I've had enough rest. We must continue!"

The Ulf stormed off into the darkness.

Kayen and Tryam kicked dirt into the fire and gathered what limited supplies they had left. Wulfric was almost out of sight before they were ready to follow.

✠ ✠ ✠

A conundrum greeted the party in the morning light, when the tracks they were following split. Wulfric traced both paths for a bit, then returned to give his assessment.

"Two men came down from the mountains and intercepted the group we have been tracking." Wulfric gestured toward a circular collection of footprints. "A discussion occurred and a decision made. A new group formed and headed back into the mountains, while the rest continued their way toward the Ragnar village."

"Which should we follow?" pressed Tryam anxiously.

Before Wulfric could respond, Brother Kayen answered: "The obvious choice is to follow the larger group toward the village. We know at least some of the prisoners went with them." He scratched his beard thoughtfully. "But the obvious path is not always the correct one. The smaller group may comprise Clan Ragnar leaders."

Wulfric was quick with his decision. "Stay here. I shall follow the smaller group deeper into the mountains. I want to see where this group heads."

THE TOMB OF THERAGAARD

With a seemingly endless supply of energy, Wulfric rushed off after the smaller group. Kayen suggested they take time to rest, but it was not long before Wulfric returned with what Tryam thought was hope in his eyes.

"I have our answer." With that, Wulfric opened his palm and revealed a leather necklace with a carved whalebone as its centerpiece.

Kayen eyed the jewelry. "Wasn't that your mother's?"

"Yes, it was," answered Wulfric excitedly. "On the night before I left to undergo the Trial of Blood, I gave this necklace to Kara to show my intentions to bond with her." He held the whalebone to his chest. "We must be off as soon as possible! Kara is alive, I know it! Let's gather our strength and be off for the final push."

Wulfric had also brought back a small fox to eat. Brother Kayen started a fire while Wulfric skinned the animal. Tryam did his best to eat as much of the tough meat as he could. He did not know when they would eat again. He wanted to ask Wulfric about his proposal to Kara, but he dared not speak of her until they found her safe.

After the meal, they packed their supplies and sharpened their weapons. The path they followed steered away from the valleys and plains and climbed higher into the Corona Mountain Range. The terrain was rocky, steep, and filled with hazards. Tryam was unused to the altitude and became short of breath and light-headed very quickly. When Kayen saw him stumbling, he made the party stop.

"Drink water and chew on this." Kayen handed him a handful of leaves.

Despite his age and plump physique, Kayen had shown greater stamina and more ease with climbing than Tryam had. The young acolyte was embarrassed by his weakness, and he felt guilty for having slowed them down. Kayen saw the concern in his face.

"I have wandered through and over these mountains for years and have come away stronger for it. Your body must grow accustomed to the elevation. You are young; your body will adjust."

Heeding his advice, Tryam chewed the bitter green leaves and drank deeply from his flask. "Thank you, Brother. I feel better already."

✠ ✠ ✠

It was dusk of the next day when Wulfric finally allowed Tryam and Kayen to rest. Every part of Tryam ached. He found it difficult to ease his body into a position on the ground where he could feel comfortable. The party ate the rest of the fox and rested until midnight, when Wulfric, who had kept watch alone, awoke them and spoke of his plans.

"The killers have chosen a more gradual route through the Coronas. I believe they are headed to the summit of one of the nearby mountains. We shall take a more direct and treacherous route to gain ground. If either of you want to turn back, do so without shame."

"We shall keep up," assured Kayen.

Tryam nodded his head. "If we falter or hold you back, you can continue on by yourself, but give us a chance to prove ourselves."

Grim-faced, Wulfric nodded.

The first obstacle they encountered was a sheer cliff wall with a deep chasm yawning before it. During the day it would have been a challenge to leap, but at night, with only the light of the stars to find a landing, Tryam thought it madness to attempt, but he was resolute to try.

"Observe carefully as I make my jump," instructed Wulfric. "The ledge on the other side is narrow and slick with ice," he cautioned. "If you slip, you will fall to your death."

With a running start, the young Ulf rushed toward the chasm. With his arms acting as pendulums, he easily leapt the eight-foot-wide gap and landed with stable legs on the narrow ledge opposite, avoiding a collision with the cliff face on that side.

From the far side of the divide, Wulfric encouraged Tryam to jump. "I can grab you if you fall short. Hurry!"

Kara's face entered Tryam's mind, along with the memories of her encouraging words during his training sessions. "I am coming," he replied stoically.

Tryam took a deep breath and stretched his limbs. He gazed up at the night sky. The multitude and brightness of the stars transfixed him. He was stunned by the beauty of what he saw and felt privileged that Aten had granted him life. He would not waste this gift. Without further hesitation, he imitated Wulfric's technique and leapt over the crevasse. He felt his feet hit the small ledge, but unlike the big Ulf, he slipped. His head crashed into the cliff face, and his body bounced back. Wulfric reached out and grabbed his cloak before he fell into the chasm.

Wulfric patted Tryam on the back. "That was perfect," he said. Then he stepped to the edge of the crevasse. "Brother Kayen, you're next."

THE TOMB OF THERAGAARD

Perfect? It took Tryam a few moments before he felt steady enough to turn around.

The missionary appeared calm. "I am more ... let's generously say ... *stout* than you two young men," he answered back. "Let me ease my burdens first."

Kayen removed his backpack and threw it over the chasm to Wulfric. He then tossed his staff to Tryam. "I would toss you my cross to lighten the weight," quipped the missionary as he gazed into the seemingly bottomless depths of the crevasse, "but I fear I may need it."

Wulfric hung himself half off the edge and beckoned Tryam to do likewise. "Try to jump between Tryam and me. We shall grab you if you jump short."

"*If*—yes," Kayen grumbled.

With his right hand braced against the cliff face, Tryam leaned his body forward, his left hand ready to grab the missionary. On his lips was a prayer to Aten.

Kayen exhaled deeply, hiked up his brown robes, took a few steps back, then ran forward. At the edge of the gap, he jumped but did so too soon. As he flew, he was off balance. He landed short and let out an un-monkish curse as he fell backward. Tryam grasped at the sleeve of his robes, while Wulfric snatched the missionary's hand. Together they pulled him up and onto the narrow ice ledge.

"That was close," said Tryam, his body more numb from fear than from the cold.

"I thought for a second I would be in Aten's presence," gasped Kayen as he reclaimed his staff and backpack. "Where do we go from here, now that we and our wits are on this side of that accursed crevasse?"

"Now the dangerous part," said Wulfric, pointing toward the cliff face itself.

As he craned his neck up the vertical fifty-foot wall of ice, Kayen let out a whistle. "I hope you have a plan to get me up there that doesn't involve me sprouting wings."

With a gleam in his eye, Wulfric replied, "I always have a plan. I can climb this with ease, but I doubt that either of you can. If I had a rope, I could lift the both of you. Instead, as I climb, I shall cut steps into the cliff face. You can use those notches as hand- and footholds. It will be like climbing a ladder."

"A ladder that is vertical and where one misstep plunges you into a bottomless chasm!" grumbled Kayen. "But if this can get us closer to Kara, I am willing." He cinched the belt of his robes around his waist and strapped his staff to his back. The missionary then spoke to Tryam. "Are you ready, son?"

The cliff face loomed over Tryam's head like an executioner's axe. He gulped but did not back down. "I am ready."

The ease with which Wulfric scaled the cliff amazed Tryam. He did not take a straight path but instead chose a meandering ascent, being careful to install handholds and footholds only in firm rock. As he progressed, the young Ulf chopped deep cuts into the frozen rock face with the small knife he had used to skin his kills. When he reached the top, the nimble Ulf pulled himself up over the lip.

Tryam took Kayen's backpack and strapped it over his own shoulder. "Want me to carry your staff as well?" Tryam feared the middle-aged missionary did not have enough upper body strength to pull himself up, even with the help of Wulfric's steps.

"Not this time. What it burdens me in weight, it makes up for in the comfort it gives me. I've had this staff for many years, and we plan on leaving this world together." Kayen pointed to the waving Ulf up above. "Wulfric grows impatient. You had best go first. I doubt I shall ever learn the skills required to scale a wall like Wulfric, but I should be able to emulate the climbing style of a cloistered acolyte."

From up above he heard Wulfric offering advice. "Stick close to the face of the mountain. Get a good hold with your hand, and then take a step. Move one limb at a time! And whatever you do, don't look down!"

Tryam placed his right boot into the first step and reached with his left hand for the first handhold. *I do this for you, Kara!* The young acolyte progressed handhold to foothold up the cliff face. But after what seemed like hours' worth of exertion, he lost the feeling in his fingers and toes and struggled to hold onto the cliff. He also encountered a problem he had not foreseen: The cold from the ice-covered rocks was causing his entire body to shiver. From below, he heard Kayen shout. "You are almost there! Keep going."

In his determination not to look down, Tryam had forgotten that he could look up. When he did, he saw that Wulfric was only a few feet above him. Encouraged by how far he had come, he climbed the last few feet

THE TOMB OF THERAGAARD

with renewed energy, but he could not relax until he felt Wulfric's strong hand grasp his forearm. The Ulf pulled him up onto the ledge.

Exhausted and unable to move, Tryam lay on his back, the stars overhead reflecting in his eyes. All he could do was give thanks to Aten as he heard Wulfric encouraging Kayen up the cliff face.

"Tryam did it easily. You should have no problem."

Easily?

Tryam had gotten his breath back just as Kayen landed beside him. He was thankful he was spared watching the missionary ascend, but he vowed not to underestimate Kayen's stamina; the missionary appeared as calm and as fresh as he had at the bottom of the cliff.

"How did you climb it so fast?" asked Tryam, still on his back.

"Aten gives his servants strength when in need."

Kayen unstrapped his staff and helped Tryam to his feet. The young acolyte sheepishly returned Kayen's backpack, and he stretched his back and legs. Wulfric urged them forward, and their journey resumed.

The view from atop the cliff offered a glimpse at what Wulfric believed was the end of their journey: a twin-peaked mountain near the horizon. Twinkling stars flashed between the peaks like embers floating over a dying fire. Something about the mountain caused Tryam's spine to chill. It appeared out of place from the hundreds of other peaks that surrounded it.

"We must go on," ordered Wulfric.

✠ ✠ ✠

After a few hours of climbing over the rock-and-snow-covered terrain, Tryam noticed Wulfric's eyes following shadows near the twin-peaked mountain's summit. The young acolyte felt his stomach churn. "What do you see?"

"I see the mountain that borders the Ragnar valley and a line of men seeking its summit." The Ulf pointed for Kayen's benefit. "There, near the crater between the peaks. It has to be those we seek. Let's double our pace."

Wulfric once again guided them over and around obstacles Tryam would have never been able to pass. Into the early-morning hours they climbed, taking a direct route to the enigmatic peaks. When under their shadows, the ground changed from a snow-covered surface to clumps of frozen black dirt mixed with porous, lightweight rocks that Kayen identified as pumice. The sagacious missionary noted that, unlike the other peaks, this mountain was the result of a great eruption of lava. Wulfric called the party to a halt, and they huddled behind a boulder that had fallen from the ancient volcano ages before. With daylight fast approaching, it would not be long before they would be exposed to anyone looking down from above.

Wulfric peeked out from behind the rock and confirmed that they were only a hundred yards from the Ragnar men. Tryam noticed Wulfric's demeanor change when he looked again. "Wulfric, you look like an eagle when it has spotted its prey. What do you see?"

"There are fourteen in total, and one of them is Kara."

Wulfric drew his blade, but Kayen stayed his hand. "Patience! Don't rush them like a reckless hero leaping into a dragon's lair. Not yet. Kara is alive, for now." He stroked his beard anxiously. "What are they doing? What else can you see?"

With eyes burning from primitive rage, the Ulf reluctantly sheathed his sword. He took another chance look at his enemies. "The Ragnar are near the lip of the crater. They stand before a cave." He hesitated a moment. "Not a cave, for the entrance is too regular. It is as if someone carved a corridor into the side of the mountain." His body shook with rage. "I see a wizard! Those traitors! He wears a band around his bald head and flowing red robes."

"What about Kara?" questioned Tryam, who could no longer hold his tongue. "Is she okay?"

"A big man is holding her. He is a foreign warrior the likes of whom I've never seen before. She is bound but otherwise okay. I see no others from my clan."

"What is the color of the gemstone on the wizard's headband?" asked Kayen.

"He wears a white diamond."

"A white diamond!" blurted Kayen. "We must be extra cautious. This is no neophyte wizard, but one strong enough to kill us all with a single spell." He gripped his staff. "What are they doing now?"

Wulfric edged dangerously close to the front of the boulder. "The wizard is examining the corridor as if looking for hidden dangers. He is now deliberating with a Ragnar warrior." The Ulf tightened his grip on the pommel of his sword. "The man is Crayvor, the Ragnar jarl's remaining son! They are entering the cave. We must follow!"

Tryam saw the Ragnar, in single file, cautiously making their way into the enigmatic corridor. He watched until their outlines disappeared into the darkness of the entrance. Tryam wished he could have glimpsed Kara, but it had not been possible.

"We go now!" cried Wulfric as he rushed up the slope, the others unable to stop him.

Tryam and Kayen followed on his heels. The Ulf stopped on the right side of the corridor. Tryam did likewise. The young acolyte peered over Wulfric's shoulder and down the tunnel. He could see nothing, so he nudged into the big Ulf to describe what was happening.

"They are too focused on what lies ahead. It is safe to cross the threshold," encouraged Wulfric, "and stand on the other side."

Eager to spot Kara, Tryam rushed to do as Wulfric suggested. Down the corridor, one marauder had lit a torch, and light now glistened off the tunnel's polished black walls. Thinking of ambushing them, Tryam noted their arms and armor, and he watched to see how well they kept a rear guard. Alas, they were disciplined; a scout stood watch and every few moments would glance behind. In any case, Tryam did not think they could fight so many armed men at once. *Especially not with a wizard at their disposal.*

The corridor extended a hundred feet, sloping down at a slight angle. It ended at a massive golden door. The excited voices of the Ragnar men echoed down the tunnel. The bald wizard was speaking.

"Stand back and give me room. I must have absolute quiet."

The chatter ceased, and the wizard stepped toward the door. A moment later shouts of anger erupted, distracting the mage, and one of the Ragnar men went to his knees after a loud cry of agony.

Kara! Tryam spotted the Ulf girl.

In a desperate attempt to stop the mage, she had head-butted her captor and then kicked another of the Ragnar warriors in his groin. The giant warrior who had held Kara quickly recovered from the head butt and brought the slight Ulf girl to her knees. The incident happened so fast that Wulfric had not had time to move, and he cursed as the Ragnar men swarmed around her.

Kara seemed full of vigor, though Tryam saw dried blood in her hair. *Knowing Kara, the blood is likely not her own!* Tryam wondered why she had been singled out. *They must have something sinister planned for her. A mate for Crayvor perhaps?* Tryam vowed to make sure that did not happen.

After the Ragnar men secured Kara, the wizard stepped closer to the gargantuan gold door. Tryam had never seen a wizard besides Myramar and had never seen one cast a spell before. He found himself fascinated and with great curiosity watched as the mage spread his arms. The wizard spoke, but the words uttered held no meaning for Tryam, despite his uncanny familiarity with ancient tongues.

As the wizard made intricate gesticulations with his hands, perspiration glistened on his head. Tryam felt his own hair stand on end as if lightning were about to strike. The wizard was still for just a moment, then pulled from his robes a quarterstaff topped with a clear crystal. He restarted his incantations, and soon thereafter, a white glow shrouded him from an unseen source.

The wizard spoke more magical phrases. After the words, the light that shrouded him flowed into the crystal tip of the quarterstaff. The jewel throbbed audibly.

The wizard then ordered the Ragnar to step back, and he leveled his staff at the door. On his command, a green beam of energy erupted and struck the portal. The ground beneath Tryam's feet shook.

The door cracked opened, and a rush of air escaped, knocking a few of the Ragnar to the ground. The air also kicked up a cloud of dust, shrouding much of the tunnel. When the shock wave dissipated, Kara, the wizard, and the Ragnar men had already passed through the door.

"We must follow!" cried Wulfric. "Move quickly!"

The Ulf roared down the tunnel, ignoring the pleas for caution from both of his companions. However, by the time Wulfric reached the end of the corridor, the golden door had already slammed shut.

"Touch nothing!" warned Kayen, just as the Ulf was about to pry the door open with his sword.

Kayen pointed at a desiccated corpse on the ground. "That is what happens when you don't have a wizard to do your bidding."

Tryam had not seen the corpse, and neither had Wulfric, who'd almost stumbled over it.

The Ulf paced, his frustration growing with each footstep. "Kara was this close! We must get inside!" Wulfric emphasized his frustration by smashing his fist against the rock wall of the corridor.

Kayen stepped in front of Wulfric. "We shall. But we need to go back to town, tell the Engothian knights what happened, and enlist the aid of

Myramar. The town mage is a kind and generous man. He will help us get Kara out of this place."

Wulfric shook his head angrily. "If I can't save Kara now, I must go to the Ragnar village, find the rest of my people, and free them. I cannot go on a quest to return just Kara when so many others may still be imprisoned."

Kayen stroked his beard. "We cannot linger here, that is for certain. We shall scout out the Ragnar village. But if there is no way to free your people by ourselves, you must agree to enlist help from Arkos."

"Aye," spat Wulfric, whose eyes stared angrily at the golden door.

Chapter 39
A Sleeping Giant

The descent down the mountain was less taxing than the trip to the summit had been, but their pace was slowed, since the party had to be extra vigilant of roving Ragnar war parties. On a break, when the sun was setting behind thickening clouds, Kayen broke the silence the three had fallen into. "I've been to dozens of Berserker villages but never to the Ragnar. I was warned that the Ragnar distrust anyone not of their clan and are protective of their lands." He waved his staff to the west. "Wulfric, have you ever been to the Ragnar village before?"

Wulfric, clad in his wolf pelt hide, stood silhouetted in the red light of dusk, his eyes hunting for any Ragnar. When he answered Kayen, his voice was strong and defiant. "I was at the village many winters ago, when my father brought back the jarl's dead son. The Ragnar refused to settle the dispute honorably and shouted feeble threats. They feared the Ulf and dared not attack us. They had no defenses, and their village was spread thinly over a deep valley. They were an insular clan."

Kayen scratched his beard, which Tryam understood to mean he was searching for ideas. "When in sight of the village, we must hide until we find where the prisoners are being held."

By midnight, they reached the base of the mountain. They decided the best plan would be to approach at night, when most of the Ragnar would be in slumber. Wulfric allowed only a short rest.

As the moon appeared from behind clouds shaped like wispy black dragons, Tryam viewed a man-made marvel that left him speechless. Cut into the side of the mountain was a colossal amphitheater. He had read about such architectural wonders in his books, but they had not prepared him for finding one here in the frozen wastes.

THE TOMB OF THERAGAARD

"What is this place?" asked Tryam as he gawked at the wonder. "It must date from the time of the Ancients!"

"You would be correct," agreed Kayen. "I have seen ruins of amphitheaters near Antium that closely resemble this. I am not sure what the Ragnar would use it for."

"I do," answered Wulfric. "The Ragnar stage fights to the death—the only clan among my people to do so." Wulfric spat upon the ground in disgust. "They believe in blood sacrifice, and they worship a cruel god they call the Mountain God." He frowned. "This place troubles me. Let's be away."

As the party descended down the rows of the icy theater, clouds moved in to block the moonlight, covering the arena in a blanket of darkness.

"I think we can risk more light," decided Kayen as he removed the cross of Aten from beneath his robes. The missionary whispered a prayer, and the cross glowed a soothing blue. Kayen held his cross aloft like a torch and whispered to the others. "Stick close."

Each step the party took echoed inside the empty arena, proving just how well the Ancients had designed the amphitheater to carry sound. Tryam saw many signs of recent use; torn hide cloaks, smashed tankards, and rotting food littered the aisles. However, it was on the stage where a new mystery lay: Scaffolding supported a large block-and-tackle system.

"What do we have here?" questioned Kayen as he stepped onto the stage, the light from his cross removing shadows from the strange structure. The missionary halted and gestured down at his feet. "Be careful. A deep pit is before the rigging!"

Cautiously, Wulfric and Tryam made their way to the stage. Tryam went to the edge of the deep pit Kayen had spotted. He looked into the hole but could see only ice and mud at its bottom. "Why would they have dug such a massive pit? It looks to be at least fifty feet deep!"

A chill beyond that of the air caused Tryam to shiver. *What unholy endeavor happened here?*

Brother Kayen examined the scaffolding that surrounded the pit and looked at one of the large pulleys with particular interest. "Based on the size of the equipment, whatever they pulled out of the ground was extremely heavy."

It was something else that had captured Wulfric's interest. "I don't know what happened here, but look down into the valley. See the smoke that rises? That is where the Ragnar village lies."

Columns of thick smoke curled into the black sky. Tryam thought back to the doomed Ulf village. "Is the village on fire? Has someone attacked?"

"That's smoke from a forge. Or in this case, perhaps a dozen forges," the missionary explained. "I have seen such a sight before, when a nation is preparing for war."

The ominous news unsettled Tryam. *Do the Ragnar seek something more than revenge on just one clan?*

"The pit is empty. There is nothing more we can learn here. We need to go to the village." Wulfric unsheathed his sword and held it ready. "We are not far now. I long to see at least one more survivor from my clan."

Kayen placed his cross back around his neck and under his robes.

From the pit ran massive ruts toward the valley, apparently caused by whatever conveyance had been used to transport the object that had been exhumed. As they retraced their steps, the darkness gave the party cover. Along the way, Tryam noticed evidence of mining operations: Dozens of holes, lit with torches, dotted the face of the twin-peaked mountain that buttressed the Ragnar village. Hammer and pick falls echoed into the night.

They marched alongside the muddy ruts down into the wooded valley. When the Ragnar village finally came into view, Wulfric called the party to a halt. Kayen and Tryam rested while Wulfric scanned the vicinity for wandering Ragnar. When he was sure it was safe, he focused his attention on the village itself.

"The Ragnar had no walls when I was here last. Now they have a massive palisade and newly constructed barracks!" Wulfric's hand tensed around the hilt of his sword. "Other Berserkers have joined them. I see the sigils from a handful of other clans." His voice trembled with rage. "We shall not have an easy time gaining entry. I see no stockade or jail. The prisoners could be anywhere."

Kayen placed his hand on the Ulf's broad shoulders. "The tracks from the conveyance lead to a massive tent outside the walls. Perhaps that is where the prisoners were taken. At the very least, we should find out what it was they dug up."

Wulfric considered the missionary's words and nodded. "They went through a lot of trouble to dig that pit. I shall guide us to the tent to take a look."

Piles of ore, stacks of wood, and other raw materials littered the muddy ground between where they had been resting and the colossal canvas tent.

THE TOMB OF THERAGAARD

Tryam watched as Wulfric stood and sought cover behind a large pile of slag. The hulking Ulf then signaled the others to follow as he scouted for another spot to hide their advance.

Proceeding in this fashion, Wulfric, Kayen, and Tryam crept to a stack of freshly axed timber a dozen yards from their destination.

"Stay here," whispered the brooding Ulf. "I shall approach the tent alone."

"Let me go with you," pleaded Tryam. "If you encounter resistance, I can help."

Wulfric agreed without debate.

"Let Aten be with us," said Tryam, smiling, as he fumbled for his weapon.

Wulfric returned Tryam's smile, but the Fenrir pelt he wore made his appearance predatory. He extended his hand, and the two grasped forearms. Together they sprinted to the dark and ominously quiet tent. With his anxiety building, Tryam waited for Wulfric's next move.

Wulfric did not seek the entrance flap but instead pulled out his knife and made a small rent in the canvas with the tip of its blade. Red light, such as that from that of a low-burning brazier, bled out. He knelt down, split the tear with his fingers, and peered inside the tent. Then he gasped and spoke in a voice loud enough to alert anyone close by: "A giant slumbers inside!"

Tryam put his hand around the Ulf's mouth and whispered into his ear: "Quiet! A giant? That can't be." The myth of giants was common among the Berserkers. Thunder from clouded peaks was said to be their footsteps and lightning their magic. Tryam was sure that superstition had to be overriding his friend's judgment. His heart still raced, though, as he went to check for himself. "Let me look."

When Tryam saw the giant warrior lying on a bed of logs, he almost reacted as Wulfric had. However, he forced himself to scan the monstrous man in greater detail. As he did so, he became more skeptical about its mythological origins. "No, it is no giant. It does not breathe. It does not move. Its skin appears to be made from black metal. It is a statue. But look!" Tryam stepped away and shoved Wulfric back before the slit. "See at the monster's feet? Standing there are old men, women, and children. Could they be from your village?"

"It is them! I see Thrane and Kole!" He looked from prisoner to prisoner. "They are not shackled, so why do they not move? They stare blindly as if sleepwalking. What is this sorcery?"

Further speculation ended when the sound of the gate opening some one hundred yards away reached their ears. "Move," ordered Wulfric.

The two hastened back to Kayen. The missionary wanted to learn what they had found, but before they could report what they had seen, a large force of armored men headed out from the gate. Then Tryam spotted the man leading the Ragnar, and he exclaimed in an excited whisper, stifling with difficulty its volume, "That's Brother Gidran!" Tryam struggled to keep his emotions in check. "He was the visiting monk who wanted to explore the church's vaults! He claimed he was there on a mission with a mage from the Wizard's Council."

Tryam did not think it was possible for Kayen to stroke his beard more vigorously. "What in the Abyss is going on?" mused the missionary. "This is well beyond a dispute between clans."

The three ducked as the Ragnar warriors, under orders from Gidran, tore down the tent. As the canvas was removed and the black metal giant was revealed, Kayen gasped. Gidran led the battered and bewitched prisoners out. To the collective horror of the three observers, once the rest of the tent had been dismantled, they saw an exposed stack of frozen and mutilated corpses.

Wulfric cursed at the grisly sight and then squeezed Kayen's arm as he pointed to the surviving prisoners. "Those are my people. We must free them!"

The missionary stared into Wulfric's eyes. "Yes, we must. But do you note how the prisoners are spellbound? Even if we were to free them, they would remain as empty vessels and not leave with us. We need the help of a wizard to break this magical bondage. It is the only way."

Wulfric's face turned red as he let out a string of whispered curses. He gripped his weapon and added. "We must do something. Every day that passes, more of my clan are lost!"

Kayen held firm. "We cannot throw our own lives away in a rescue attempt that would surely fail. Come, let us return to Arkos as hastily as we can and seek help!"

Wulfric growled. "Why should they help us?"

"I believe I know what that giant metal warrior is," replied Kayen, "and if I am right, all of Arkos could be at risk. It is imperative that we inform Lord Dunford what we have seen here."

Chapter 40

Doors Deep

Dementhus had no memory of stepping across the threshold of the great archmagus's fortress. He was too consumed in the glory of magical exaltation. *Praise be to the Dark God for guiding me here!*

When his senses returned, he realized he stood inside a pitch-black chamber, the only sound the nervous movements of the Ragnar men in the expeditionary party.

"Don't light a torch or take a single step unless I command it!" warned the Necromancer. "An ancient wizard once dwelt here. A man who served your Mountain God. The wizard's power rivaled that of Necromedes the Thrice-Reborn!"

From the darkness, a booming voice responded. "You heard the wizard. Do as he commands. This is his realm, his rules."

Dementhus recognized Crayvor's voice. The youth carried with him the authority of his father, but that did not stop the Ragnar from clucking like nervous hens among themselves. Crayvor warned them again. "Be quiet, or I shall rip your wagging tongues from your slack-jawed mouths!"

Dementhus stood tall and closed his eyes, blocking out all distractions. He concentrated on establishing a connection to the fortress—feeling for the magic buried within its stones. Once the magic was revealed to him, he stepped forward, following the energy trail to a small pedestal, chest high, fifteen feet in from the golden door. With his magic sight, he could see carved into the top of the pedestal an indentation shaped like a hand. He placed his withered hand within the indentation and channeled magic from his body into it.

As the magic poured into the pedestal, it spread throughout the chamber via a network of interconnected runes. Perhaps in response, orbs embedded in the ceiling pooled with light. Moments later, Dementhus noted that the air was fresher and the temperature in the chamber was warming. He was amazed by the efficiency with which his magic was transformed. At the moment, he was at a loss to comprehend how this was accomplished. *If I am awed by the machinations of the fortress's internal mechanisms, what chance do I have of reactivating the Golem?*

Now that they had light, the Ragnar appeared less anxious. The only one still struggling was the Ulf girl captive. Dementhus smiled at her futile attempts to escape from Abbaster's giant hands. *With such spirit, she will make an excellent ceremonial sacrifice to the Mountain God.*

"Come," ordered Dementhus. "We begin our quest to learn the secrets of this fortress. Secrets that can aid the Ragnar in conquering the north and beyond."

Steps past the modest entrance chamber led to an octagonal room, which Dementhus estimated to be ninety feet from end to end. The floor was covered in mosaic tiles, and on the walls hung velvet tapestries. The artwork on the hangings depicted dramatic scenes of a wizard performing various acts of heroism. One particularly elegant piece showed a wizard summoning a creature of fire in a battle against the armies of the kingdom of Bhuron, a former foe of Antium.

In the center of the room was a square platform, on which rested a gold statue of a wizard, the same wizard depicted in the artwork. Dementhus took cautious steps forward to examine the likeness.

The gold-plated statue was twice the scale of a normal man. In exquisite detail, the likeness formed a handsome, middle-aged mage with a skullcap and a long, pointed beard. Placed in one hand was a crystal sphere, representing Medias, now cracked and clouded. In his other hand, the wizard held a wand, from which a platinum bolt flashed. *This must be Antigenesus.*

On each corner of the platform was a pillar supporting a transparent, geometrically shaped container. Inside each bathtub-sized vessel was an example of one of the four foundation elements: A cube accommodated a black rose growing in rich, dark soil; an octahedron held a miniature tornado; water rippled inside a twenty-sided icosahedron; and on the last pillar, fire burned within a tetrahedron.

Dementhus was once again astounded by the elegant and powerful displays of magic. "See here, Abbaster. Antigenesus was a master elemental wizard!"

THE TOMB OF THERAGAARD

The brute strode from shape to shape, carrying the captive Ulf girl with him, but his dour countenance never changed.

His simple mind cannot comprehend the power this demonstration reveals!

The Necromancer urged the Ragnar men to step forward. The dozen men of the expeditionary force were more fearful than curious at the display, and most hesitated to venture close. *It is fortunate that I require their steel and not their brains.*

Having learned all he could from the platform, Dementhus moved on to the rest of the eight-sided room. Doors were located only on the north, west, and east walls. Each had writing over its lintel. Dementhus had believed that the fortress entirety was divided into two sections: one peak of the mountain containing Antigenesus's living quarters, library, laboratories, and lens complex; the other peak for visitors, supplies, and the living quarters of the warriors he commanded. The doors, however, seemed to indicate that the fortress was segmented into three sections.

Above the eastern door were the words *Superius Nul Vanus*, which Dementhus translated as "the Grand Hall," implying that the door led to Antigenesus's living complex and laboratories. Above the western door he read, *Intorium Loculator Cassell*, "the Inner Castle," referring to the fortress portion of the complex, where there was likely an entrance lower on the mountain that soldiers would have used and that could accommodate the slumbering Golem.

Much to his astonishment, he could determine neither the meaning nor even the language of the writing above the northern door. The prospect of what untold secrets might lie down that path was unfathomable, but he had to focus on his goal. "We shall take the western passage," he said.

He had no intention of allowing any Ragnar men into the eastern section's laboratories. If they realized the Golem was not a god but only an automaton of the archmagus, their religious fervor would come to an abrupt and violent end. The Necromancer's top priority was locating the entrance at the bottom of the mountain, where he could bring the Golem inside to study. Once that was accomplished, he would explore the other sections on his own.

With a knowing nod to Abbaster, the wizard indicated that one of the Ragnar should take the lead. Dementhus did not know what traps might be set inside the fortress, and he was curious to see one in action—but only from a safe distance.

267

When an eager Ragnar man stepped forward, Abbaster directed him to the western door. The man took swift, confident strides forward, but he stopped before touching it and looked back at the wizard for instruction.

"These doors work like any other in the civilized lands," said the wizard. "Simply push on the handle."

Dementhus held his breath as the Ragnar man turned and then pushed on the ivory handle. The door opened inward effortlessly and without triggering a trap. Disappointed not to see another display of the fortress's ancient magic, Dementhus nodded his approval to the man. "Well done."

Past this threshold was a broad, carpeted passage. The walls and floor consisted of black marble, and the same orbs that had given light to the other chambers illuminated their path. Dementhus wondered if the small amount of magic he channeled to the pedestal was enough to light the entire complex or if he had merely tapped into an energy reserve.

At the end of the passage were two equally sized blue doors. Above the left, written in the common tongue, was the word *Lower*, and above the right was written *Upper*.

"We take the left door," ordered Dementhus. "We need to find an entrance closer to the village."

This door was significantly smaller and less ornate than the others encountered so far. It was made of painted iron, and rust clung to its edges. Dementhus commanded the door to be opened, and three Ragnar raced to obey.

Each man pulled on the rusted handle, but each time, despite their straining until their faces turned red and their muscles quivered, the metal door did not budge. Dementhus was about to cast a spell and blast the door open when the largest of the Ragnar, a man even more massive than Abbaster, stepped forward. For the big man, the door opened with ease. A Ragnar scout moved past the massive barbarian and poked his head inside.

"The passage slopes downward. The air is warmer and moist."

Dementhus nodded. "This is the way. Lead on."

As the tunnel descended, it narrowed to fifteen feet across. Although less frequent, the ceiling globes still offered sufficient light to illuminate the way. Dementhus noted that the flooring and walls changed from the more lavish marble above to corridors carved out of compacted ash. After more than a hundred feet, the passage ended at a door.

Crayvor, encouraged by Dementhus to take the lead, pushed the stout iron door open. The hallway that was revealed split into three directions:

THE TOMB OF THERAGAARD

One continued southward, where a set of brass doors gleamed in the dim light; the eastern passageway came to an abrupt end after a dozen yards; and the western corridor continued sloping downward.

Curiosity got the better of Dementhus. "We shall see what lies beyond these brass doors. We may stumble upon artifacts left behind."

The wizard took the lead and pushed open one of the doors himself. A cracked marble table dominated the oblong-shaped room. The shattered marble ended Dementhus's hope that the complex had been left unspoiled. Beyond the table was a floor-to-ceiling, curved window, which offered a magnificent view of the surrounding snow-capped mountain peaks and valleys.

"Is this more wizardry, or is that truly a window?" questioned a broad-shouldered Ragnar with an odd-shaped head, a trace of fear in his voice.

The bald wizard let out a belly laugh. "A little of both. The ancient wizard was a master manipulator of elements. This is a window, but it is crafted from stone rather than glass."

The simple man shrugged his shoulders.

The room reminded Dementhus of a council chamber. Perhaps Antigenesus met with visitors in this very room. Further speculation was pointless, however, and the Necromancer conceded, "Time to move on. There is nothing of value here."

He led the Ragnar out of the room and, disregarding the other brass doors, off to the western passage, which appeared to lead down the mountain and to a possible alternative entrance. The corridor gradually bent northward, then leveled out after fifty feet. Another sixty feet along this passage were two rooms. Against his better judgment, he gave a nod of approval to Crayvor to allow the Ragnar to inspect them. They were getting restless.

Disappointed Ragnar faces told Dementhus that the rooms were empty. Besides burnt tapestries, broken chairs, and other refuse, there was nothing inside. The purpose of the rooms was not readily discernable.

The corridor turned westward, where two more rooms, evenly spaced apart, appeared along the northern side. Crayvor, perhaps eager to find an ancient weapon, insisted on inspecting the rooms. The first one was little more than a closet and was completely empty, almost as if it had been cleaned. The second room contained an oddly assembled debris pile that glittered as if filled with gold or jewels.

"Might there be something valuable in this?" asked Crayvor.

Before Dementhus could answer, the jarl's son poked his longsword into the sparkling refuse. With the quickness of a whip, a tentacle snapped from the pile and struck out at Crayvor, reaching for his arm. The warrior's quick reflexes saved his limb, but the tentacle latched onto his sword and ripped it free from his hand. "By the God!" roared Crayvor as he drew his dagger.

The other Ragnar, hearing their leader's cry, wanted to come to his aid, but Dementhus, using his quarterstaff, forced them to remain outside, only allowing Abbaster to pass. The brute threw the Ulf girl into the throng of Ragnar, and with his twin scimitars at the ready, he hacked at the tentacle, but his blade bounced off the creature's rubbery skin.

The monster's serpentine head rose from the pile, its eyes glittering like jewels, its mouth ringed with pointed teeth puckering open. Four new tentacles sprouted from its snakelike body, probing and grabbing at its two attackers. Crayvor slashed with his dagger, but like Abbaster's scimitars, that weapon had no effect, save to keep its owner out of the creature's grasp.

The wizard grabbed Abbaster by the shoulder and shouted into his ear. "Give me one of your weapons!" The bewildered look on the brute's face forced Dementhus to explain further. "I shall enchant one of your blades so you may pierce its flesh!"

With a single motion, Abbaster turned and tossed his weapon, handle first, into Dementhus's velvet-gloved hand. The Necromancer pulled a potion from one of his deep pockets and emptied its contents onto the blade's edge. He spoke a word of magic, and the scimitar glowed red. Dementhus repeated the words, channeling more energy into the weapon, until the scimitar glowed as bright as a torch.

The Ragnar men raised their voices in alarm and shouted their leader's name. When the wizard turned away from his spellcasting, he saw that Crayvor was in the grasp of two tentacles, while a third had wrapped around Abbaster's neck, pulling the big brute off his feet and dragging him toward the creature's grotesque mouth.

Out of time, Dementhus ended the spell. With an adroitness that seemed to surprise the Ragnar, Dementhus tossed the enchanted scimitar back to Abbaster. The warrior caught the enchanted blade and struck at the tentacle that held him by his throat. This time the edge sliced deep into the creature's flesh. A broad grin split the big man's face as the tentacle

THE TOMB OF THERAGAARD

fell from around his neck. He slashed at the beast with the ferocity of a sandstorm, its glowing steel a blur. "I shall send this beast to the pits myself!" he added for emphasis, after slicing through the tentacles that had been holding Crayvor.

With no tentacles to support itself, the stalk-like body of the monster collapsed back into the pile of debris, its black blood pooling on the cluttered floor. Abbaster, the fury of battle still within his veins, plunged the glowing blade into the beast's mouth as Crayvor retrieved his own sword and added slashes to its torso. The creature slithered and hissed until Abbaster decapitated its ugly head.

"What kind of devil was that?" Crayvor asked between gasping breaths.

"It is a creature that lurks in the darkest of dungeons, feasting on fools looking for treasure," lectured Dementhus. "We must not delay any further."

The Necromancer shoved his way past the Ragnar and led the party back down the corridor. After ten feet, the passage ended at a landing, where a staircase, carved from a lava tube, spiraled deeply down the mountain. "Now we descend."

Fatigue was starting to take its toll on the Necromancer, even as the Ragnar men took the steps down with enthusiasm. His limbs ached from both the magical and physical exertions he had already endured. Every hundred steps they encountered a new landing that led to more tunnels deep within the mountain. Dementhus took those opportunities to rest and quaff his potions while telling the others he needed to meditate and search for traps.

"This place reminds me of the catacombs beneath the ancient pyramids of home," observed Abbaster. "If Terminus wills it, we could turn this into a great cathedral and training ground for His forces upon Medias. Do you have any idea how much deeper these passages descend?"

Dementhus nodded his weary head. "I'd estimate another half mile. Then we should reach the base of the mountain." He pointed a gloved finger at Abbaster. "You are right to remind me of the Dark God's role here. I am sure Terminus intends for us to transform this abandoned fortress into a stronghold for Him in the north. Gidran must establish a temple here, so that we can properly convert all the Berserkers to the one true faith."

Abbaster nodded his head while he sharpened his scimitars.

The wizard's estimation of the size of the complex increased, the deeper they descended. At one landing, he thought he heard the roar of an underground river; at another, he glimpsed a vast cavern with a waterfall. It was quickly understood that the fortress was too large to explore in a single day or even in a month's worth of days.

"We shall make camp here, on the landing," announced Dementhus, fatigue now too much to overcome without risking recklessness. "Do not wander, do not stray, for in the inky blackness around us may lie traps that could bring the mountain down on our heads."

The spooked Ragnar looked displeased with Dementhus's decision to spend the night, but none dared protest.

As Dementhus reclined against the nearest wall to rest, Abbaster took command. "Gather 'round, keep an eye on the prisoner, and distribute the food."

But it was Crayvor who tried to lighten the mood. "Fear not, fools. This fortress is ours. We but only have to claim it. We feast tonight and drink!"

Dementhus fell quickly into a deep sleep.

Chapter 41
Off the Path

"Come here," whispered Grollo in conspiratorial tones, as the veteran Ragnar warrior moved away from the other Ragnar.

Halfdan narrowed his eyes as he followed. "Didn't you hear the wizard?" His friend was always trying to get him into trouble and had succeeded many times.

"Bah," dismissed the larger Grollo with the wave of a beefy hand. "When we descended to this level, I saw something. It is just down that corridor over there. If we move in stealth, no one will be the wiser. Think of what secrets this dark abode hides!"

The wizard slumbered near the back wall of the landing. Beside him was the foreign warrior Abbaster, who was discussing with Crayvor matters related to the growing army. The other Ragnar men of the expeditionary party were spread out on the floor, sleeping after a big meal. The only others awake were the two men in charge of standing watch over the pretty Ulf girl captured during the raid on the Ulf village.

"What did you see? I care not for gold," scoffed Halfdan, "but I would not mind a night with that girl! Maybe I could convince Crayvor to let me take her for my mate!"

Grollo chuckled, then rubbed a bump on his forehead, which he had received during the girl's most recent escape attempt. "It would be safer interrupting Dementhus in the midst of one of his conjurings than to deal with that one." The big warrior sobered quickly, then pulled Halfdan closer. "It is not treasure I seek but weapons the Ancients may have left behind when this place was abandoned long ago."

Halfdan looked about. They now stood directly under a pool of light from one of the omnipresent hanging globes. He dragged Grollo to the dark corridor that held the larger man's interest. "This place is cursed! One room held a monster! What exactly was it that your greedy eyes saw?"

Grollo removed his helmet and scratched his head. His dull-eyed expression did not inspire confidence, but he was the single bravest man Halfdan knew. "I saw, in silver, the mark of crossed swords. I believe an armory lies down this passage!"

Halfdan pressed his hands over the big man's lips. "Quiet, fool!" Halfdan shoved Grollo down the corridor and away from the sight of the others. "Take me to what you claim to have seen."

The light diminished the farther down they explored. The orbs in the ceiling in this section were burnt and cracked as if destroyed intentionally. When they could no longer see the light from the landing, Grollo lit a torch.

"See!" exclaimed the bigger man, pointing down next to their feet. "A helmet with crossed swords."

The markings on the floor meant nothing to Halfdan, but perhaps his friend had more knowledge of the customs of the Ancients. "After you," insisted Halfdan.

"Of course," said his friend, laughing. "I do not fear shadows."

Halfdan followed the broad shoulders of Grollo as they entered a part of the fortress that he guessed had not been explored in centuries. On the walls hung ancient tower shields decorated with the insignia of a dozen different companies, now rusted and useless. Side rooms dotted the hallway. Grollo stuck his torch and head inside each one. Together they discovered dusty bunks, empty weapon racks, deserted muster rooms, and even an arena. Grollo found a usable bronze helmet but threw it away in disgust when he could not fit it over his large head.

"How much longer do we risk being away?" inquired Halfdan as his frustration now exceeded his curiosity.

Grollo ignored him and stood in the middle of the underground arena, staring at the ceiling, which was painted to resemble a starry night. Inspired, he moved his bulk over the sandy floor and slashed his torch about as if it were a sword. Eventually he tired of that and said in resignation, "Perhaps we should go."

THE TOMB OF THERAGAARD

When Grollo turned to leave, Halfdan noticed something on the floor that had been revealed by the big man's awkward maneuvers. "What's that?"

"Your whore of a mother," shot back Grollo instinctively.

"No, you ugly bastard. Move more of the sand away."

With his slowly blinking eyes, the big man looked down at his large feet. "Huh?"

Halfdan shoved the big man aside and pointed at the silver image already partially uncovered. "Look, you oaf!" He removed more of the sand to reveal the holy cross of Aten.

Grollo scratched his armpit. "So what?"

In the center of the cross was a bronze ring. Halfdan pulled on it, but it would not budge. "Something is down there. The cross must be a warning of some kind."

"I bet that is where they keep the good stuff, not the rusted junk we have seen," guessed Grollo, passing Halfdan his torch. "Move away." Grollo, his back as broad as a mammoth's backside, bent down and grasped the bronze ring with his ham-hock fists. He strained until something clanked, as if iron had snapped. When he tried pulling again, the silver hatch cover opened with ease and revealed a glowing room below.

"What makes it glow?" asked Halfdan, unable to see past Grollo.

"I dunno." The big man went to his knees to duck his head inside. He whistled and started to chuckle.

"Well, what is it?" pestered Halfdan.

"You'll see soon enough."

Halfdan took a step to the hatch, but Grollo blocked him with a fleshy arm. "Me first."

The eager Ragnar swung his bear-sized legs into the hole, but his larger-than-average torso threatened to present a problem.

"If you get stuck," warned Halfdan, "I would not think twice about leaving you behind."

The lure of whatever Grollo had seen overrode his better judgment, and the big man wedged his body into the enigmatic glowing chamber. Halfdan knelt down and stuck his head inside to watch his friend's progress.

Inside was a black stone chamber, barren save for two curiosities: glowing glyphs printed on the floor and an impossibly large war hammer on a wall, hung like a prized possession.

"Will you take a look at that!" gushed Grollo. "A weapon suitable for the king of jarls, and only I am large enough to wield it!"

"Don't let Ivor hear you say that," cautioned Halfdan.

"Ha! He will make me a general when he sees what I have found," boasted Grollo. "He'll crown me the jarl of the next clan we conquer."

The gleam from the glyphs painted Grollo silver, and he hesitated stepping over them to get to the weapon. Halfdan goaded the usually incautious Ragnar. "The wizard who put those words there is long dead." He growled to emphasize his impatience. "Grab the hammer, so we can leave this place."

The lure of the weapon likely more than the taunts impelled Grollo's hand, and the big man stepped onto the painted glyphs. When he was not immediately vaporized, he laughed. "Ah ha!" he proclaimed as he reached up to grab the tree-trunk-sized war hammer. "I shall name it Clansmasher!"

"Oh, I like that," said Halfdan.

Even with his enormous strength, Grollo struggled to lift the ancient hammer from the hooks that suspended it. "Need any help?" teased Halfdan.

"Not from your wee arms," snapped Grollo.

With the benefit of a few curses, Grollo removed the war hammer, but even with his massive arms, he struggled to hold it. However, the smile on his face showed he did not care how much it weighed. "We are as close as a bonded couple, Clansmasher and I."

"Get your fat backside out of there. We still have time to look for a weapon more my size."

Grollo's chuckle echoed in the small chamber. "A golden toothpick, perhaps?"

The glow from the glyphs faded, and the room turned dark.

"Just move out of there," said Halfdan, worried.

A moment later, through the hatch came the great war hammer and Grollo's grinning face as the big man pulled his massive frame back onto the floor of the underground arena.

Halfdan wrapped his hands around the war hammer's shaft and tried to heft it, but he could not get the weapon above his waist. He settled for examining its anvil-sized head. Shaped like a roaring lion with a flowing mane, it had the look of iron but the weight of gold. Halfdan was sure magic was hidden inside.

Grollo chuckled again. "Put that down, puny. Ya might hurt yourself."

Halfdan reluctantly dropped the artifact.

The big man kicked the hatch closed and the sand back over the painted cross of Aten. He then motioned Halfdan to stand clear before taking the weapon in his hands. "Watch a real warrior!"

With bulging muscles, sweat covering his body, he grabbed the hammer and lifted it, first to his waist, then up to his shoulder. That alone was a feat few men could achieve. When he went to swing the hammer, Halfdan applauded.

Grollo turned on the sandy floor and swung the hammer above his head. He made three complete circles before his muscles gave out, and the heavy hammer thudded to the arena floor. Grollo wiped sweat from his brow. "I need more practice, that's all. Now let's find your toothpick."

"We should get back," decided Halfdan. "This place is too large. It's like a forest with trails badly marked. Now that—" A slight rumble stopped Halfdan mid-sentence. "Did you hear that? It sounded like distant thunder."

Grollo, still smirking from his success, grabbed the torch back from Halfdan and shook his head. "That was my stomach growling," he joked.

A tremor moved the sand, and even the obtuse Grollo took note. "It sounds as if it comes from the chamber below!"

Before Halfdan could advise against it, Grollo moved back to the center of the arena, opened the hatch, and stuck his head inside the chamber.

"I see nothing." A pause. "No, wait, there is something!"

When the big man pulled his head back out, his face was as white as a snow-capped peak.

Halfdan had never seen his friend so alarmed. "What is it?"

The big man threw Halfdan his torch, then grabbed the war hammer. "I don't know, but whatever it is, it's angry."

Halfdan wielded his axe. "What? Tell me!"

Grollo slowly backed away from the hatch, and Halfdan did likewise. Halfdan pressed his courageous friend, "Should we not flee?"

Grollo, face grim, raised his hammer. "Not until I test my new weapon on this creature."

What emerged from the chamber was something wholly foreign to the two barbarians. Up from the hatch came a swirling vortex of wind, inside of which was the hazy image of a well-muscled man. The vortex quickly caused the sand in the arena to whip around and temporarily blind Halfdan.

"It has arms and legs!" shouted Grollo as the creature advanced, the winds forcing the two Ragnar far away from any exit. "That means it can be killed."

With the audacity only a fool could muster, Grollo swung the hammer at the creature's blurry head. When the weapon struck the outer fringes of the swirling entity, however, the hammer was ripped from his hands, and the large man thrown to the floor.

Halfdan went to reach for his friend, but the thing was quicker. It hovered over the behemoth-sized man and sucked him into the vortex.

"Help!" cried Grollo as he was thrashed about like a rabbit in the jowls of a wolf. "Free me!"

As the thing struggled with Grollo, Halfdan edged toward the exit. "I shall get the others! Our wizard friend will know what to do!"

"No! Don't leave!"

Sorry, my friend.

✠ ✠ ✠

Wither and die, wither and die. The words rattled around Dementhus's head as the pain in his extremities continued to hinder his sleep. The potions he'd once relied on to numb the pain from the spread of the necrotic tissue were no longer effective. *I shall not let my body betray me! There must be another answer. Nothing must stop me from achieving my destiny to conquer, to reign, to unlock the mysteries of the astral plane!*

In the world between being awake and being asleep, the Necromancer thought he heard a cry of alarm. *Has the girl escaped again?* But by the time he was fully awake, he could see that the girl was still in the hands of her Ragnar keeper, and he could tell that the cries were more indicative of terror than of alarm. In a flash, Abbaster was by his side, twin scimitars drawn.

"A creature of wind attacks!" informed Abbaster.

"Save us, wizard," cried the Ragnar men who surrounded him, all with wild, pleading eyes.

With the aid of his staff, Dementhus stood and stared in disbelief at the center of the landing, where a tornado twisted along the floor with a half dozen screaming Ragnar warriors in its grasp. Inside the tornado,

THE TOMB OF THERAGAARD

Dementhus could see the body of a creature of air—a creature he understood was one of the ancient guardians of the fortress.

Crayvor rushed to the wizard's side. "We tried to stand and fight, but our weapons are useless."

"Bravery and steel cannot win all battles," replied Dementhus. "I alone must defeat this enemy of the Mountain God."

With his staff tip now glowing white, the Albus wizard reached out with his magic to speak to the air guardian. *Stop! Obey me!*

Unfortunately, the enigmatic and ancient magical creation was unreceptive to Dementhus's commands.

The wizard then spoke words of magic, and a blast of energy rushed out from his staff and slammed into the vortex. The face on the figure of energy grimaced, but whatever discomfort the guardian creature suffered was shared by its Ragnar prisoners, and Dementhus was forced to stop his attack.

Listen to me! I am your master. Retreat to your lair. Retreat!

While speaking the language of wizards, Dementhus was also examining the magic that Antigenesus had used to create the air guardian. If the ancient archmagus were still alive, the Necromancer would have had no hope of countering this spell, but the magic had waned during the ensuing centuries, and Antigenesus was now dust.

"Hurry!" implored Crayvor.

Instead of blasting magic into the creature, Dementhus decided on another tack: He would drain the guardian of its fuel. He recalled the symbols, phrases, and hand gestures of the spell necessary to do so. "Stand aside," he warned.

After he cast the spell, a bubble formed around the vortex, trapping the air guardian inside. Once the bubble was stable, Dementhus channeled magic into the sphere, and it began to harden and shrink. Inside, the guardian and its shield of swirling winds was becoming less energetic, as the air it needed for fuel was slowly being suffocated.

Dementhus channeled more energy, and the air guardian fell to its ephemeral knees. The Ragnar men it had held in its grasp came flying loose. Some crashed hard to the floor, others flew into the sphere, cracking bones in the process, but they all would live.

When the bubble shrank again, the air guardian collapsed to the ground, its mouth mimicking one who is suffocating.

Dementhus did not stop his spell until the apparition disappeared into the very air itself.

"Well done," Abbaster said, returning his scimitars to the red sash about his waist.

"It was a pity to have to destroy such a guardian," lamented Dementhus. "It could have been a powerful ally." With the rush of magic fading, the wizard looked for Crayvor, letting his anger show in his face. "Who disturbed this creature? What fool risked our mission?"

A Ragnar warrior rushed forward and fell before the wizard's feet. "I beg for forgiveness. It was my friend and I. We—"

Crayvor cuffed the man on the ear, then dragged him to his feet so that Dementhus could look into the man's eyes. "He is yours to punish," declared the jarl's son, spitting each word as if they stained his tongue.

In a rare moment of benevolence, the Necromancer spared the fool's life. "Where did you go? What did you disturb?"

The Ragnar warrior pointed down the dark hallway that led from the landing. "My companion heard something coming from the dark and feared we would be waylaid while we slept. We thought it best we go alone, in case what we'd heard was but a rat."

"Halfdan lies!" snapped Crayvor as he cuffed the man on the ear again.

Dementhus halted the attacks with a glare. "Let this man make amends by showing us where he went and how he unleashed the guardian."

"Yes, master wizard," croaked the grateful Ragnar. "I shall at once!"

Halfdan stood tall, then turned toward the hallway. Dementhus followed, allowing only Abbaster and Crayvor to come along.

Dementhus had little interest in this part of Antigenesus's fortress, but he was curious as to why the great archmagus had left an air guardian behind. *What was it protecting?*

Navigating the corridors and rooms that led to bunks and deserted armories left the wizard frustrated at the waste of time, but when they reached an indoor arena, his eyes were drawn to a massive war hammer lying on the sandy floor. The weapon emitted waves of magical energy.

"It was here where we were attacked," said Halfdan. "The thing erupted from that trap door, and that is where we found the great hammer."

From the shadows came the moans of a wounded Ragnar. Halfdan pointed to his friend, lying on the floor. "Grollo! You live!"

The hulking Grollo groaned as he struggled to his feet.

THE TOMB OF THERAGAARD

While Crayvor and Halfdan moved to help the injured man, Dementhus pulled Abbaster aside and pointed to the hammer. "That was what the guardian protected."

Abbaster eyed the weapon greedily. "What does it do?"

"I shall not be sure until I have time to examine it, but I doubt that even someone as strong as you could wield it."

"Perhaps it is Terminus's will that I do."

The magical emanations coming from the weapon showed the hallmark traits of necromancy.

"Perhaps," replied Dementhus dryly.

CHAPTER 42
THE BARGE

In the morning, the expedition set off again in search of an entrance lower on the mountain. After a dozen landings, the massive central stairway terminated into an unadorned cave. The cave was a natural formation, but even here the ever-present glowing spheres lit their way.

"Ahead!" urged Dementhus as he downed the elixir that aided his decaying extremities.

A path clogged with debris stopped their advance. "Quickly, men. Clear away this rubble. We must move on."

Led by Crayvor, the Ragnar rushed to obey the wizard's command. They made short work of the obstruction, carrying stones half their size away with ease.

Beyond the blockage was another vast, octagonally shaped room, which matched the one atop the mountain. In the center, printed on tiles, was a map of the complex. Unfortunately, as Dementhus soon discovered, water from the area behind the partially collapsed west wall had pooled over the tiles and had eroded most of the details—save one, which Dementhus intended to investigate as soon as possible.

"Crayvor, take your men down and explore the southern passage. I believe that is where another entrance to this fortress lies." He beckoned with his staff. "Abbaster, come with me."

When the Ragnar men were out of sight, Dementhus and Abbaster made their way to the door opposite the collapsed wall. The door glittered gold, and upon it was engraved a barge.

Abbaster paused before the door and studied the depictions upon it, but his eyes lacked the spark they had when he was fighting, and he stared dully back at the wizard. "I do not understand the way of wizards. A boat in a mountain?"

"If what I saw upon the map is accurate, it makes perfect sense. Be still as I meditate, so we may end unhelpful speculation."

Dementhus placed his hands on the door and felt for the presence of magic. Using his mind's eye, he saw the opening mechanism. "Stand back," he cautioned as he stepped inside a nook to the left of the door. He felt inside the alcove for a lever, and his velvet-covered hand grasped a brass rod. Pulling the handle down, he watched in anticipation as the ancient door slowly but gracefully receded into the ceiling above. *Remarkable!*

Beyond the opening was a large domed chamber, in the middle of which was a great pool. Sitting in this artificial harbor, bathed in cool white light from orbs hanging down from above, was a barge with brass railings and a shining oak deck.

Unable to contain his glee, Dementhus patted Abbaster on the back. "This is how we transport the Golem to Antigenesus's laboratory! We are so close to achieving our goal I can almost feel Terminus's gaze upon us now!"

"Aye," affirmed Abbaster.

Crayvor came running up to Dementhus and interrupted their mutual excitement. The young Ragnar paused and gaped at the ship.

"What is it?" Dementhus prodded, annoyed by the barbarian's superstitious awe.

Crayvor blinked, remembering what he had come to say. "You were right. We found another entrance. Our village is only a half day's journey from here."

Dementhus nodded his bald head. "As I said you would. Now is the time to make preparations. The Mountain God must return home. Before we move the God's avatar to this barge, we have much work to do."

"And the prisoner?" asked Crayvor. "What shall we do with her?"

"She will be kept in this fortress. She is to be the God's first sacrifice upon His rebirth."

Chapter 43

The Summoning

Gidran was deep in prayer when a scout from Dementhus's expeditionary party came rushing into his hut. Covered in sweat and between gasping breaths, the scout informed the shaman that Dementhus had gained access to the fortress. Not only that, but the driven Albus wizard had found a lower entrance, very near the valley of the Ragnar, and wanted the Mountain God delivered to him immediately.

The news did not surprise the shaman. Terminus had whispered to him earlier in the evening that something wondrous had occurred.

"Have you informed Ivor?"

"Yes, he has gathered a party of men, but they await your presence."

The shaman donned his animal furs and exited the hut he used as a place of worship. It was past midnight, and the sky was roiling with black clouds. The activity around the Ragnar village never ceased. Even at this hour, preparations for war were underway. Near the gate of the newly raised village wall, Gidran spotted the men gathering. The jarl himself was nowhere to be seen, however.

As Gidran walked through the cheering crowd, the Ragnar men cleared a path for him. They did not love him, but they did respect and fear him. Their enthusiasm was in part due to the recent destruction of their rival clan. He was gladdened that their bloodlust, instead of being sated, had only been whetted. Gidran had to raise his voice to be heard. "We must prepare the Mountain God for travel back to His fortress. Follow me!"

The Golem still slumbered on its conveyance outside the wall. Dementhus had ordered Gidran to remove the Golem's tent days earlier. Gidran suspected the Necromancer had done so out of fear of the shaman's connection with the Golem; Dementhus did not want Gidran to commune with the magical entity in private. In truth, his bond with the Golem troubled the shaman far more than it provided him a source of strength or ambition. He had detected a consciousness, but of a type he had never encountered before. It was not a man, not a beast, and not like any creature from the outer realms.

Near the Golem's feet sat the Ulf male prisoners too weak to work in the mines or too old to be adopted into the Ragnar. Dementhus had found it necessary to ensorcell the defiant Ulf members, since Berserkers did not adapt well to captivity. The spell made them docile and receptive to commands; however, they were far too few to move the Golem's sled up to the lower mountain entrance, where the barge awaited. The Ragnar would have to lend their aid.

Before Gidran could order the men into position, someone grabbed him. It was Ivor. He reeked of the bitter beer his warriors liberally quaffed. "Magnificent, it is a wonder to behold! To think, all this time, our God was below our feet, waiting to be rediscovered."

Gidran nodded to the jarl. "The Corona Mountains will tremble with each step the Mountain God takes. All the clans of the north will worship Him from bended knee!"

A young warrior broke through the rank of Ragnar men and interrupted the leaders. "Rettiwalk, what concerns you?" asked Ivor. Rettiwalk bore a face frowned with grave worries.

"I spotted tracks near where the God slumbers. I followed them back to the amphitheater. From there they lead away from our valley. They are from outsiders, I—"

"Show us," interrupted Ivor.

The scout led Ivor and Gidran to the prints. Gidran watched as the jarl inspected the slight impressions in the mud. "He speaks the truth," concluded Ivor. "Outsiders have been to our village. I shall send trackers to hunt them down."

"No!" interjected Gidran. "Let me handle this matter. We cannot spare more men at the moment. We must get the Mountain God moved to the fortress."

The jarl looked at the shaman and arched his eyebrows. "My friend, you may have the best of intentions, but I cannot believe you can track better than one of my scouts."

"I claim no wilderness skills such as your men possess," admitted Gidran. "However, through my bond with the Mountain God, I have means with which to track down the intruders. Have faith! All I require is the help of one of your scouts."

The shaman watched the jarl as he weighed his options. If Ivor agreed, it would prove to Gidran that their alliance with the Ragnar was strong. After only a moment of hesitation, the jarl nodded his gray head. "Do as you must. Rettiwalk will serve you. I shall lead the men as we move the God to His fortress!"

As Ivor retreated to the Golem, Rettiwalk stepped before Gidran and boasted, "I know every path into and out of these lands. I can help you find these intruders, and I can teach you much about surviving in the frozen mountains and valleys."

Gidran dismissed the offer of help. "I track by a different method. Fetch me a torch."

Rettiwalk, his eagerness tempered by Gidran's response, nevertheless was quick to obey and returned a few moments later with a sputtering iron lantern.

"Come closer," urged Gidran. "Lower the light to the ground, and I shall show you my method."

The light exposed the frozen mud by Gidran's feet and the impressions left by the unwelcome interlopers. Gidran could not imagine any fool brave enough to wander into the Ragnar camp unless they were survivors from Clan Ulf seeking revenge. The shaman bent down and followed the tracks. After traveling some distance, he declared, "Ah, I have found what I was looking for."

Next to a footprint was a single strand of hair. Gidran pinched the follicle between his fingers and held it up to the lantern. "All I need to track these men is this."

The Ragnar scout let out a hearty, spontaneous laugh. "Sorry, friend, but through one hair? By the God, I think you are mad!"

Gidran gently chuckled. "Through the power of the Mountain God, my son, all things are possible."

Rettiwalk sobered.

The sound of the giant cart rolling through the mud interrupted their conversation. Gidran watched the Ulf prisoners, along with a cadre of hulking Ragnar, as they pushed the wooden construct in the direction of the lower reaches of the twin-peaked mountain. Satisfied that Ivor had all the help he needed, Gidran turned away and ordered Rettiwalk to follow as he headed back to his hut inside the village. Most of the Ragnar were too occupied with the God's departure to notice their return.

The table inside his hut was cluttered with artifacts of the Dark God. Gidran retrieved two items: a small bronze bowl and an ivory-handled dagger. The shaman stripped to the waist.

Rettiwalk's eyes widened upon seeing the scars on Gidran's body. The shaman ignored his reaction and ushered the youth back outside. He led Rettiwalk beyond the palisade to a secluded area behind a small clump of trees. He wanted neither prying eyes nor ears to note his activities.

Ignoring the bitter cold that assaulted his scarred flesh, Gidran placed the bowl on the ground and held the dagger in his right hand. The Ragnar scout looked on with the simplemindedness of a child. "The tracks lead down to the amphitheater," he pointed out, "and then out of our valley. Why are we here?"

"Calm yourself, Rettiwalk. You are about to witness a miracle. Relax, breathe deeply, and do not shout or interrupt me in any way. "

The Ragnar youth nodded.

The quiet of the woods helped the shaman to clear his mind as he spoke the words of Terminus in low, guttural tones. As the prayer proceeded, he accentuated the words with slashes to his chest, cupping the oozing blood with his free hand and directing it into the bowl at his feet.

After the bowl had filled with blood, Gidran ceased his chanting and fell to his knees. He now carved a symbol into the flesh of his chest. The symbol he drew, a triangle inside a circle, was to be a gateway from the mortal plane to the spirit realm of the Abyss.

The pain of the knife's edge parting flesh was nearly intolerable, but the closeness Gidran felt to Terminus enabled him to continue. Once the symbol was drawn, he packed his other wounds with mud.

The shaman laughed at the absurdity of what he was now asking of the Dark God, and he was sure Rettiwalk was convinced he was mad. The audacity of his plan shocked even himself, but he had grown stronger in his faith during his long journey with Dementhus.

Gidran resumed chanting, and as he did, the blood inside the bowl congealed and then simmered. From the surging smoke of the cooking blood a humanoid form took shape.

"Oh, thank you Terminus, savior of mankind, most powerful of all beings!" exalted the shaman as the sigil on his chest burned into his flesh. Terror had paralyzed Rettiwalk, his primitive mind incapable of comprehending the scene before him.

As the entity slurped Gidran's blood, its appearance became more distinct: that of a shambling man eight feet tall, with limbs of malleable black flesh. The being took a lurching step forward, and a void of a mouth yawned open from its malformed head. A sepulchral voice hissed into the air and demanded, "Why have you summoned me?"

It is beautiful, as are all things from the Abyss!

Gidran was now on his feet. He pulled from his pocket the hair he had found and pressed it into the creature's flesh. "This is from an enemy of Terminus. Hunt down this infidel, and feed on his soul. Kill any who stand in your way. Only then will you be able to return to where you came!"

"You dare command me?"

A thick, fleshy arm reached for Gidran's throat. The shaman stood his ground, and the scar on his chest glowed red. The grotesque arm snapped back. "It is not I who command you," responded Gidran. "It is Terminus!"

The blob of a creature quivered in rage. "As you wish, my lord. But I must feed from mortal flesh now, or I shall recede back into the shadows from where I was summoned."

"I know, fiend. That is why I have brought you your supper."

Gidran grabbed the paralyzed Ragnar scout and threw him at the Daemon's feet. Rettiwalk had no time to flee, fight, or raise an alarm. He twisted and crumpled as the fleshy arms of the Daemon whipped around his body, smothering him. The man convulsed, and his body decayed as if withered by a century's worth of time.

After it had feasted, the Daemon dropped the desiccated corpse. "I am ready to do your bidding, liege."

"Then hurry. Dawn approaches."

The Daemon glided off on its shadowy legs, passing near the shaman. As it did so, Gidran felt the cold of the grave. The Abyssal creature would hunt down its prey and feed, both because it had been commanded to do so and because it enjoyed such a task. As he watched the creature disappear into the night, the shaman felt part of his strength go with it.

I am weary. So weary.

THE TOMB OF THERAGAARD

As he looked upon the corpse on the ground, though, Gidran laughed with lightheaded dizziness. He laughed until he collapsed from lack of breath. The body of the Ragnar scout would never be found, for what remained was only dust.

After resting, the shaman picked up his bowl and licked clean the blood left inside. As he stumbled back into the Ragnar village to slumber, he felt no pain, only exhaustion.

Chapter 44

The Hideout

"Wulfric, I am exhausted. We should rest. We need to have a measure of strength to defend ourselves should we have cause."

Tryam agreed with Brother Kayen. After making their decision to return to Arkos, they had marched for three days without sleep. They'd eaten sparingly and only on the move. It would take four more days to be in sight of the white walls of Arkos, but they would not survive that long if they continued at this exhausting pace.

Wulfric shrugged his broad shoulders. "Perhaps you are right. I shall gather wood for a fire and scrounge us some food."

Something other than fatigue was weighing on Tryam's mind. The young acolyte waited until Wulfric was out of earshot before he shared his feelings with Kayen. "I sensed a presence last night. It was similar to the feeling I experienced under the abbey's vaults but different and more troubling. Something hostile, malevolent."

Kayen leaned his staff against a tree and placed his backpack on the muddy ground. As he watched the orange sun fall toward the western horizon, he stroked his beard. Then he glanced warily about the darkening forest. "I am glad you told me of your concerns; however, you should not have waited so long. Do you sense anything now?"

"No. Nothing."

Kayen beckoned Tryam to sit beside him. "I want you to try something."

Tryam imitated the missionary and rested his sword against a nearby tree before sitting on his backpack. "What is it you want me to do?"

"Something I have longed to show you. The paladins of old spoke a devotion called the Warding Prayer. Those brave warriors oftentimes traveled to bleak places controlled by the minions of hell. In such places, it was sometimes necessary to seek out spirits from other realms, to see if they were friend or foe, to see where they were hidden." He slapped Tryam's back. "I want you to try it. I think you may have the rare ability to peer into places that others cannot."

Thoughts of the paladin Saint Lucian came into Tryam's mind. He recalled the saint's words, his deeds, and his faith, but also the suffering he'd had to endure. Lucian had often been tormented by the voices of the dead, haunted by men he'd killed and by the loved ones he'd lost. "I shall try, but the ancient days were filled with great men. Their like has not been seen in hundreds of years!"

"True, but there are paladins to this day who can recite the prayer just as they did. We may not celebrate men today like they did in the past, but that does not make today's paladins lesser men because of it. Remember, time has a way of polishing tarnished men into perfect gleaming heroes." He reached into his robes. "Now watch and listen."

Kayen stood and then hovered over Tryam, the cross of Aten now out of his robes and displayed on his chest. "I shall say a verse. Then I want you to repeat it. Once you have the entire prayer committed to memory, I shall show you how to use it to invoke Aten's blessing. Here is the first verse." The missionary then recited in the ancient language of Antium.

> By Aten's grace upon this night
> Do I, Your humble servant, petition You.
> Prevent this blight of evil that I see,
> Grant me vision to aid mankind.
> Without Your light, I am blind ...

Tryam listened to the prayer, absorbing the ancient words and their meaning. The language was poetic and, as with most prayers that Tryam admired, invoked thoughts of selflessness and humility.

"Do you think you have you mastered it?"

Tryam nodded. "It is a beautiful prayer for such an ominous task."

Kayen concurred. "Indeed. Now, as you recite the verses, Aten's grace will flow into your body. Close your eyes, and let your mind reach out and explore your surroundings with sight like that of an eagle."

The cold air mixed with Tryam's warm breath. When he spoke, the words felt comfortable and familiar. He closed his eyes. Whether Aten's grace was inside his body he could not be certain.

Neither was he sure how to explore his surroundings with his mind. He started by picturing Kayen standing before him; then he expanded his field of view to the small circle of trees around them. He repeated the verses as his mind pictured a larger and larger area. He imagined Wulfric bending down to retrieve a piece of wood. He pictured their footprints receding up and down the lowland plains. But there was nothing else, nothing that would indicate he had any ability to see what others could not.

Frustration grew. Tryam was tempted to quit, but then he recalled a quote of Saint Lucian. *"Faith is the key to unlocking one's mind."*

Tryam let Aten's love fill his thoughts, let the wonder of His creations enter his mind. He detected a change. He was no longer pretending to view the world. He was out of his body, and he saw the world as a bird looking down from the sky. He recognized the clump of trees where his physical body was sitting. He could see the path through the rugged terrain they had already passed.

He swooped down to ground level, flying over fallen trees, muddy slopes, and rocky hilltops. He dipped below a frost-covered ridge, and that is when he saw it: a black shadow against the dark of night. Evil radiated from the fell creature. The amorphous black being sniffed the air and pawed at the ground. The thing turned its malformed head and rushed across the gloomy landscape on legs made of pulsating flesh.

Tryam shot to his feet but kept his eyes closed. "I see it! A dreadfully evil thing!"

Kayen grasped Tryam's shoulders. "I did not think it possible you could master the prayer so soon! Describe what you observe!"

"I see a creature of shadow! It roams across the Berserker wastes. It knows we are here. It follows our path!"

Tryam fell to his knees in despair.

Kayen pulled Tryam back to his feet. "How far away?"

The young acolyte feared the creature could sense his presence, so he broke away from Aten's embrace. When he opened his eyes, he saw Kayen's bearded face and furrowed brow. "Brother, I am sorry. If only I'd had more faith, I would not have turned away and I'd be able to tell you more, but I believe it is only a two-day journey from here. It hunts us."

"What is hunting us?" Wulfric had returned and spoke with alarm. The Ulf dropped the kindling and looked at the two with wide eyes while drawing his blade.

THE TOMB OF THERAGAARD

Kayen placed his arm across Wulfric's back to calm him. "A monster has been sent against us. However, the creature is still a day or more away." He moved away to give Wulfric space. "Let's eat and rest. It will not catch us tonight. Based on Tryam's description, it is a creature of the shadows, and from my experience, such a creature cannot travel during the light of day."

Wulfric became agitated by Kayen's words, slamming his sword back into his leather belt. "A creature that travels only at night? More sorcery?"

The missionary shook his head. "Not sorcery, but the work of the devil. Something from the Abyss stalks us. How or why it knows of our existence, I don't know." As he sat back down on his backpack, Kayen stroked his beard. "I can't imagine this creature's pursuit of us to be a coincidence. It must have been called from the spirit realm to seek us out."

"Brother Gidran! It has to be his doing," interjected Tryam. "We were such fools to allow him into the abbey."

Kayen shook his head. "The responsibility for that was Father Monbatten's, not yours, but I do not lay blame for Brother Gidran's deception at anyone's feet. Evil has always found a way to present a beneficent face, at least at first," consoled Kayen. "He used your and your brothers' goodwill against you."

"What do we do?" growled Wulfric. "How do we fight such a thing?"

Kayen raised his hands to quiet the Ulf. Then he stood and calmly started working with his flint to start the fire. "Let me think about the situation while we cook the last of our dinner. When the time is right, Aten will provide us with guidance."

Before settling down by the fire, the young warrior looked about the woods with narrow eyes. "How do we know we are being followed? I have seen nothing."

Kayen gutted the rabbit, placed it above the flames, then seated himself before responding. "Tryam has an ability that enables him to sense such things. Just as some men are more attuned to the astral plane and become great wizards, some have a closer relationship to the spirit realms."

"Believe me, Wulf. I can't explain exactly how I know, but something is tracking us," warned the young acolyte, who could not shake the cold even with the aid of the fire. "It is out there."

After the hasty meal, Tryam prayed that his faith would be stronger in the morning.

Tryam awoke as dawn's light was creeping over the Corona Mountains. He was refreshed, calm, and closer to God.

The party broke camp, and once again, it was Wulfric who took the lead, setting a tireless pace as they moved farther away from the mountains toward the lower foothills. Tryam understood that his friend carried the added burden of the horrors of the preceding few days and was inspired by the young Ulf's determination.

Thick gray clouds at dawn begat a soaking rain by noon. The snow-covered hills disappeared, replaced by dreary muddy plains. Tryam recognized landmarks from his previous trip. They were getting close to home.

A dark night followed the gray day. A glance from Kayen prodded Tryam to recite the Warding Prayer again. The young acolyte went over the prayer in his head, then repeated the words aloud as they walked.

"What language is that?"

Those were the first words Wulfric had spoken since morning.

Kayen answered for Tryam. "The language of Antium. The mother tongue of all the languages of the Western Kingdoms." He pointed at Wulfric. "I should teach you. You are sharp of wit."

"Right now, my only concern is reaching Arkos. Are we still being hunted?"

Tryam desperately wanted to answer Wulfric's question. When he completed the second verse, a wave of dread crashed over him. He fell to his knees, his soul ripping from his body. His eyes roamed far above and flew toward the evil presence that stalked them. As the young acolyte drew nearer, the dread intensified, and the smell of sulfur and rotting flesh filled his nostrils.

Below, along the dark landscape, the black thing ran. The shadow creature turned up to the heavens, and blood-red eyes stared at Tryam, boring into him as if to steal his untethered soul.

"No!" shouted Tryam, breaking free of the prayer. When he opened his eyes, he was back beside his companions.

"Where is it?" asked Kayen, pulling Tryam to his feet. "What did you see?"

The young acolyte sought for the words to say. "I smelled its fetid stench, but it also sensed me. Out of fear I broke contact." He shook his head to clear his mind of the creature. "But you must listen. It moves quickly, incredibly so. It is still in the foothills. I am afraid I cannot say precisely where, but it will overtake us sometime tomorrow night."

The Ulf brandished his sword as if to fight the beast right there and then. "Then we shall not reach Arkos before this creature catches up to us. But worry not, I killed one hell-beast. What is another?"

The indomitable spirit of his Ulf friend heartened Tryam, and the feeling of despair that had so overwhelmed him faded quickly. "Brother Kayen, tell us what we can do to send this Daemon back to hell!"

The missionary laughed and held onto his crooked shepherd's staff to keep himself upright. "I am not sure what has gotten into the both of you, but I suspect it is has to do with the enthusiasm and overconfidence of youth! However, since we know we cannot run from this beast, let's make camp here. I shall tell you both over dinner what we can do to survive, for I have spent long moments in contemplation."

Kayen sat on his backpack to encourage the others to start a fire. Wulfric gathered scraps of wood and clumps of tall grass, while Tryam prepared the leftover rabbit meat for cooking. They hastily made a fire.

After the meal, Kayen revealed from underneath his robes the cross of Aten. "This was given to me when I joined the order of monks known as the Imacolata." He placed a hand over his heart. "We of the Order of the Imacolata are dedicated to preserving the knowledge of how to combat creatures from the Abyss. This was necessary, because after the War of the Broken Spire, when the great archmagi were ultimately defeated in their quest to become gods themselves, one of Aten's Aemon generals refused to return to the spirit realm. This Aemon had another name, but He is now known as Terminus." He lowered his head a moment. "Terminus joined with the devils from hell to start what we now refer to as the Abyssal War. When the Daemons first appeared, they conquered with ease. The Imacolata prayed to Aten, and with the help of the paladins, Aten's mortal warriors, they pushed the Daemons back into the Abyss. The forces of Aten sealed Terminus beneath the city of Antium—but not without great cost."

Wulfric kicked the campfire, causing embers to fly into the black sky. "The deeds of men long dead do not interest me. What wisdom do you have for us now?"

Kayen's eyes flared. "The cross I wear around my neck was forged long ago with the hands and prayers of monks who dedicated their lives to the Church.

Its power is based on faith." He moved the cross to let the light from the fire shine on its metal. "See the carvings on the edge? They read 'Defending the faithful, from threats mortal and Abyssal, from within and without.'" Kayen let the cross dangle heavily against his chest. "When the time comes and the dark creature is upon us, I shall use this cross to defeat it."

Wulfric clenched his fists, and his eyes reflected the fire's light. "A cross? I prefer steel blades to a holy relic. I have come to Aten only recently, and my faith wavers with the horrible events I have seen unfold, but I do have faith in you, Brother. You must vow you will not let this hellspawn kill me before I have had my revenge on the Ragnar!"

"I promise to do so or die in the attempt," pledged Kayen.

Tryam echoed the missionary. "We are with you to the end. Remember that."

✠ ✠ ✠

The next morning brought heavier rains and darker clouds. They would be in sight of Arkos and under the protective light of the ward tower in two days, but that would be too late. Tryam was grateful for Brother Kayen, who kept their minds occupied with stories from the days of the Ancients and of the men who stood up against staggering odds. The young acolyte was tempted to ask Kayen about his father, but he could not find the right spot amid the stories to interject that query. An odd sense of melancholy filled his heart when he spotted, between the folds of two adjoining clouds, the red glow of the setting sun. A day, like all days, that would never come again. A day he wanted to remember because of the companionship of the two people at his side.

Kayen had become the party's leader, and it was he who halted the group for the night. "I have been praying on this situation. Wulfric, before it gets too dark, can you find us a defensible position, one in which we can see in all directions?"

As Wulfric surveyed their immediate surroundings, he ran his fingers through his thick blond hair. "We should turn east. Get away from the plains and back toward the foothills."

Leaning on his staff, Kayen looked in that direction. "Very well. We shall take our chances there."

With the setting sun at their backs, Wulfric led the party into the higher lands. It took the Ulf an hour before he found a small hill with

THE TOMB OF THERAGAARD

a forested crown he thought would be defensible. To Tryam's untrained eye, the hill looked no different from the dozens of other small hills nearby, but he did not question Wulfric's instincts.

After Kayen whispered a prayer, the cross of Aten around his neck began to emit a soft blue light. The missionary held the cross aloft, illuminating an area fifteen feet around the party.

Together they climbed up the small hill as Wulfric now took back the lead. Kayen stayed on his heels, while Tryam guarded the rear of the party. After a short time wandering through the brush, Wulfric stopped and knelt down to examine something on the ground. "This is curious: a broken arrow shaft. Someone has been here before." The Ulf continued up the hill, moving with purpose. "I recognize a trail! An old footpath, crudely hidden."

"Do you mean somebody is here now?" Tryam could not imagine who would dwell in this remote part of the north.

"Not likely," answered Wulfric. "This trail is very old, as was that arrow shaft."

Near the summit, the Ulf halted. "This is an excellent spot for a trap. We are almost to the top, but we cannot observe what lies ahead."

The party followed the spiraling trail until they reached the hilltop. The crown of trees ended at the start of a relatively flat summit, where, at the center, there appeared a mound of large rocks. Kayen stepped close to the unusual formation and let the holy light of the cross illuminate the stones. "This is not a natural mound. Someone moved these rocks. Wulfric, come take a look."

The Ulf bounded up to the squat mound, roughly ten feet high. His examination led him to a stone along the base that appeared out of place. "Let's see what is underneath this." Using all his might, the Ulf pulled the stone away, revealing a dark cavity below. "As you suspected, Brother!"

Wulfric stepped back to enable the holy light to shine into the darkness. Kayen then stuck his head inside. As he reported his observations, the missionary's voice slightly echoed: "I see steps, crudely made. Either the builders did them in haste, or perhaps it was built in very ancient times. It could be an ancient burial site, but we shall not know until we explore further."

"I should go first," Wulfric argued, nudging Kayen aside. "Based on the arrow head and the tracks, I think this was some bandits' lair. When they could no longer obscure the trail that leads into and out of this hideout, they likely abandoned it."

"I shall go first," Kayen countered, gently moving Wulfric aside. "The bandits are long gone, but Daemons are known to slumber in dark places."

"There may be traps," returned Wulfric, as he backed Kayen away from the steps.

While the two argued, Tryam drew his sword and made for the steps into the bandit lair. He sensed nothing evil about the place and saw this as an opportunity to take the initiative.

The stairs proceeded down some twenty feet and led into a room carved out of the hill itself. Kayen's light above was just enough for Tryam to see that the chamber was unoccupied. He shouted to the two above. "If you are done arguing, you can come down."

Curses echoed down into the chamber as Wulfric and Kayen now fought to be by the young acolyte's side.

In the center of the roughly square room was a fire pit filled with charred wood and ash. In the corner sat a small table with two rickety chairs. A tin plate with now-desiccated food had been left on the table, and a large mirror with silver trim, perhaps looted from Arkos long before, was along the back wall.

"Look here," said Wulfric. "No doubt about it. Bandits were here."

Tryam's face blushed as the Ulf pointed to an obscene chalk drawing scribbled on the floor.

"Focus, gentlemen," scolded Kayen.

Tryam surveyed the room and found one thing about the hideout puzzling. "This seems like a bad spot to be if attacked. This place has only one exit. The bandits would be trapped."

Wulfric shook his head. "Bandits may be crude, but they are also clever. I have a hunch." He took down the mirror, and behind it was a passageway. "They have an escape tunnel. I bet this leads to an exit somewhere nearby. We should explore it."

Before Wulfric could duck his head inside, Kayen stopped him. "We wasted too much time arguing. Tryam, how close is the beast?"

The thought of the Daemon immediately dampened Tryam's curiosity about the tunnel. "Give me a moment," he replied, taking deep breaths.

The young acolyte knelt near the fire pit and closed his eyes. After a few recitations of the Warding Prayer, his soul departed from his body. As his spirit sailed into the night, he did not find it difficult to locate the

Daemon. Evil excreted like sweat from the creature, who was part shadow, part rancid flesh.

The creature was tearing over the terrain and toward their current location at a speed that was not possible for a natural beast, far faster than it had been traveling before. Tryam, once again sensed its eyes upon him. He had not the skill to keep the beast at bay. There was nothing more he could discern, so he broke the connection and opened his eyes. With alarm he reported, "We have only an hour, maybe less."

Kayen ducked his head into the tunnel, shining the light down the dark passage and sniffing the air. He disappeared from view but returned a moment later. "We don't have time to follow this tunnel, but I have a plan. Join me back outside."

The missionary led Wulfric and Tryam out of the hideout and to the top of the hill. He examined the stone structure as one does a puzzle. When he was finished, he told them his plan. "I intend to lure the creature inside the hideout. I want you two to hide on top, over the entrance. From this vantage point, you should be able to see it approach. I shall stay inside, and you will yell down to me when it is upon us."

"We can't let you fight it alone!" Tryam could not keep the concern out of his voice as it rose in volume and pitch. "Let me stay with you."

Wulfric was equally defiant. "We should fight this Daemon together!"

In a stern voice, Kayen replied: "I don't intend to cross swords with the creature! Now listen. When the beast comes, I shall lure it inside. I have methods that I can use to ensnare the Daemon. If I do it correctly, I shall immobilize it." He pointed to two pillars that acted as supports above the door. "After the beast has entered the hideout and I have placed my enchantment on it, I shall shout to you two above. I want you to use your combined strength to remove one of these stanchions that hold the capstone in place. Once that stone falls, it will seal the entrance."

"Then you will escape out the back!" Wulfric finished. "But why not try to kill the creature? After all, I defeated the Hound of Fenrir."

"With all due respect, Wulfric, this being is far more dangerous than the Hound was. The Hounds are a result of mortal flesh mingling with that of the Abyss. This creature is made entirely of flesh not bound to this plane."

Tryam did not like the major gamble in Kayen's plan. "But Brother, how do we know the escape route has not collapsed? You may be trapped in the hideout with the beast!"

"There are always risks in combat. In any case, we don't have many options. Get in position. Remain quiet and out of the way. I don't want the hellspawn to sup on either of you before it tries to take a bite out of me. Do not say the Warding Prayer again, for the creature may focus only on you. I shall be in the hideout, meditating to build up my strength. Understood?"

The two youths nodded their heads. The missionary, staff in one hand, the cross of Aten in the other, then disappeared down into the hideout with no further commands.

Tryam and Wulfric grimly mounted the rock pile and lay on the cold stones made smooth by centuries of wind and rain. Their bodies were hidden from anyone save a passing bird of prey. Tryam used his mortal eyes to seek out the Daemon. The roof offered a view of the entire landscape that surrounded the hill, and if it had been light, they would have had no problem spotting travelers making their way north to the Berserker lands, or south to Arkos. No doubt, that was one of the reasons bandits had chosen this place as a base of operations.

A half hour later, Wulfric whispered to Tryam, "I am going to stretch my legs a bit." The Ulf stood up and took a quick look around the small hill. "I still see no sign of the beast."

Safe for the moment, Tryam stood up and joined his friend. He was reminded of the anxiety he used to get back at the abbey while looking out over the Frostfoam Sea, awaiting a massive storm to reach the island's shore. To get his mind off of the Daemon, he asked about the history of the area. "I was wondering, what kind of bandits would be in these parts?"

"My clan has seen many sellswords come here from the continent, looking for adventure. It could have been a group of them. Most mean to rob those who dig for rich metals in the mountains. My father told me that before your Lord Dunford arrived, these lands were crawling with brigands looking for easy loot, and they preyed on Berserker and Engothian alike."

"It sounds like the Lord Commander Dunford has done some good."

"As long as you remember the commander's primary concern is to keep the coronium mines open and the gold flowing back to Engoth, yes. He cares little for my people. I would …"

Wulfric paused, and for a moment, Tryam thought his friend was too angry for words. When he looked over, however, he saw the Ulf's eyes bulging, and when his friend resumed speaking, he did so in a whisper.

THE TOMB OF THERAGAARD

"I think I see it approach. It is as if a shadow were rippling through the dark." Wulfric dragged Tryam to the lip of the roof and pointed to a dark form moving between the start of the trees that led to the hideout.

"I shall tell Brother Kayen." Tryam jumped off the roof and hurried down the stairs into the hideout. He found Kayen, the cross of Aten on the floor before him, swinging his staff, as if preparing his limbs for battle.

"It is here, at the base of the hill!" cried Tryam with great anxiety. "We have only minutes!"

The missionary relaxed his body, wiping sweat from his brow with the sleeve of his brown robes. Incredibly, he smiled. "So, it is time. Do not fret. I shall bind the beast in place by the power of Aten. Unable to feast on souls, it will slowly wither. Aten willing, I shall meet up with you and Wulfric someplace nearby. Now get back to the roof, and do as I instructed."

"Are you sure you don't want me to help?"

"Unless you have mastered the mysteries of binding Daemons, there is nothing you can do. Hurry now, before the creature is upon us!"

Reluctantly, Tryam exited the hideout, fearing it might be the last time he would ever see Brother Kayen alive.

Back on top of the mound, Wulfric was growing agitated. His sword was still in his hand, and his eyes tracked the approaching Daemon as it made its way up the hill. Tryam heard his friend urging on the beast in low tones. "Come, you foul ally of the Ragnar!"

"Put your weapon away. That is not how we shall win the fight this day," scolded Tryam. "Stay hidden from its eyes."

Wulfric reluctantly acceded to Tryam's request, and the two young men hid themselves from view by lying flat on the rock.

The Daemon was at the hilltop even sooner than Tryam thought possible. The young acolyte held his breath as sulfurous gas drifted into his nostrils. He struggled to keep his body still, fighting the physical revulsion he felt in the Daemon's presence.

The manic movements the hellspawn had used to stalk them were now replaced by a deliberate and careful investigation of the hilltop in an eerie imitation of man. Tryam noticed that its shape had become more corporeal: It had manlike arms and legs, but it had the head of a boar with a mouth full of razor-sharp teeth. The beast's flesh was as black as the Abyss itself. It had no weapon, but it did have clawed hands and feet to match its deadly mouth. It sniffed the entrance to the hideout with its elongated snout.

301

As the thing drew closer, the scar on Tryam's chest burned, and the pain intensified. A now-familiar rage built inside the young acolyte. He did his best to keep still and swallow the inexplicable hate that threatened to vomit up.

A deathly quiet engulfed the hilltop. Tryam could not even hear his own breathing. The creature headed toward the hidden youths but stopped when a strange sound, like that of a flute, came from inside the hideout. The Daemon, twice the size of a man, turned back to the steps. The sweet melody intensified in sound, and the Daemon got more animated. A moment after that, it turned its malignant bulk down the crude narrow steps and started to descend. The rage left Tryam when the Abyssal creature disappeared from view.

The young acolyte expected to hear shouts from Kayen, but they did not come. Tryam whispered over to Wulfric, who had not moved a muscle. "Why has Brother Kayen not called us to seal the entrance?"

Wulfric was about to answer when the stones beneath them trembled and quaked strong enough to knock them from their perch and to the ground.

"That is all the signal we need!" shouted Wulfric over the tumult that now erupted from the hideout.

The youths rushed to the stanchion.

Deep-throated growls escaped from the gloom inside the hideout. Terror momentarily paralyzed Tryam.

"Tryam, push with all you have!"

Wulfric's command snapped Tryam back to the task at hand. Veins bulged on both of their faces as they grunted and dug their heels into the ground, pushing against the stubborn pillar.

"Push!" implored Wulfric as the sounds inside the hideout became more alarming. Tryam swore he heard the cries of the dead coming from inside.

The stanchion moved, and the ground beneath gave way. As the stone roof cracked and teetered, Wulfric tossed Tryam aside. The young acolyte was clear when the roof collapsed and buried the stone steps under a ton of rock. After the dust had settled, an otherworldly silence followed. Tryam could not help but feel he had just entombed his friend and mentor.

Tryam stared at the sunken mound and asked in a whisper, "What do we do now?"

THE TOMB OF THERAGAARD

"We hide until daybreak in case the hellspawn was not contained. At dawn, we seek Kayen out." He pointed into the dark. "I saw the perfect place to hold out for the night. Come, follow me."

The decisive leadership shown by Wulfric calmed Tryam, and he followed his friend. After making their way halfway down the hill, Wulfric went off trail and circled through the dense trees toward the south face. This area was rockier and more treacherous to scale. The night sky offered no light, and Tryam stumbled and fell numerous times, trying to keep up.

"I spotted this when we approached the hill," explained Wulfric, who was standing outside the entrance to a small cave. "By the smell, some creature made this its lair, but it's empty now."

"Are you sure?" Tryam asked dubiously.

"Remember, you are with the killer of a Hound of Fenrir!" joked the Ulf. "I fear no natural beast. We wait here until daybreak. I shall stand watch at the cave mouth. Perhaps you can recite a prayer for Brother Kayen."

Tryam settled into the back of the cave, disappointed when he saw no evidence that Kayen's escape tunnel exited there, and went to his knees. He said prayers for Brother Kayen. His sense of fear was replaced by one of duty. Instead of sleeping, he chose to join Wulfric in his vigil.

As they stood watch, even the slightest sound brought hope that Kayen had returned to seek them out. Each time, though, as the disturbances turned out to be rodents moving about or dead leaves blowing in the wind, they were disappointed. The hours passed slowly as they huddled against the rocks.

✠ ✠ ✠

Outside, dawn's light steadily began to replace the mournful night hours. Tryam was surprised to find that he had dozed off. Wulfric, with his bright blue eyes, looked as rested as ever. Once the red light of morning was on the tips of the peaks of the Corona Mountains, the Ulf stood and stretched his legs. "It is time to see what has happened."

No longer afraid to be detected by the Daemon, Wulfric shouted, "Kayen!" as he led the way around the side of the hill.

They searched under rocks, behind bushes—any place where an exit tunnel could be hidden. They made their way methodically back toward the hilltop.

"Kayen!" Tryam repeated the desperate call as they scrambled up and around the hill. His heart sank with every unreturned answer. "The tunnel might go deep underground and terminate miles from here," agonized the young acolyte.

"That would be unlikely," scoffed Wulfric as he quickened his pace. "Look for any loose boulders or any large object that might have been placed over the exit. Brother Kayen might have trouble emerging from his end."

When they reached the hilltop, the mound was silent, impenetrable, and as foreboding as a tomb. They did not linger. It was noon when Wulfric called the search to a halt, so they could discuss other options. Tryam's hands were bloodied from flipping rocks and digging into crevices, and he sat down for an uneasy rest.

"I do not know how much longer we should stay," said Wulfric. "We have to get back to Arkos."

"Perhaps the tunnel leads to that yonder hill?" Tryam suggested, with more hope than conviction. "Or more darkly, perhaps Brother Kayen is injured."

"Or maybe he is standing behind you, waiting for you to bring him water!"

The two whirled around, nearly falling over themselves at the sound of the new voice.

Tryam stood motionless, disbelieving his eyes as he saw Brother Kayen before them, covered in dust and grime, his robes disheveled, leaning on his crooked walking staff but alive and whole.

"I said, bring me water!" The voice was stern but with a hint of amusement as Tryam and Wulfric scrambled to find their waterskins.

"What happened?" Tryam asked after the missionary had downed the entire contents of both skins. "Is the Daemon bound?"

"After a lengthy battle, I was able to trap the Daemon on this plane. It struggled, but Aten yet holds sway on this realm. As the hours passed, it weakened as a fish does when caught on a hook. The Daemon faded and returned to the hell from which it came."

Kayen pulled out the cross of Aten from underneath his robes and kissed it. "Praise be to Aten. I am weary and must rest. Fighting the Daemon drained much of my strength, and navigating the tunnel would have been difficult even if I'd had light."

THE TOMB OF THERAGAARD

"Where did the tunnel emerge?" Wulfric asked as he helped the missionary to a sitting position.

"There were many branches down the escape route, but I think they all led to the same exit. The Daemon drained not only my strength but also the light of Aten from my cross, so I was in complete darkness. I eventually emerged from a cleverly concealed overhang at the base of this hill."

With that, the missionary lay down against the rocks and closed his eyes.

"What happened to your beard?" asked Tryam.

Kayen opened his eyes and looked down at his short beard. A shot of gray now ran down the middle. "If this is the only price for such a victory, then I am eternally grateful to Aten!"

Chapter 45
Banging Heads into Walls

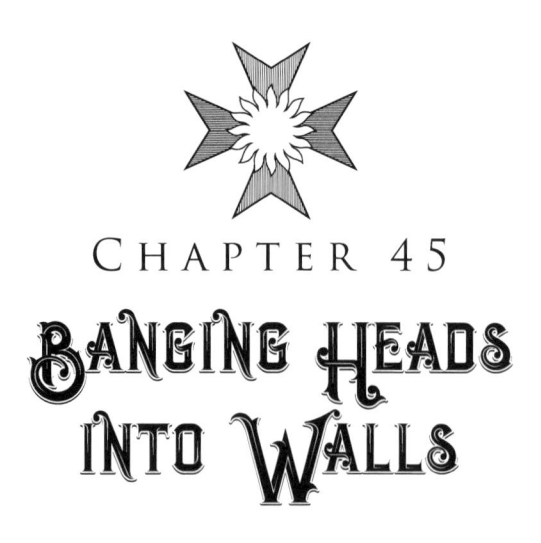

The midday sun reflected off the frost-covered stones of the walls of Arkos. Tryam had long seen the walls as an oppressive barrier, but now he welcomed their sight like a wayward traveler did familiar land.

The closer he came to reaching Arkos, however, the more he mulled over the changes that had happened to the comfortable world he had come to know. He had found out how far and how powerful the tendrils of the Abyss could grasp. A cry from Wulfric snapped Tryam from his distressing ruminations.

"The portcullis is down, and the gate is closed! The gate is never closed during the day. What do you suppose is happening?"

"Something foul, no doubt," replied Kayen, stroking his now brown and gray beard.

The ill omen hastened their steps as they hurried to the gate.

Tryam looked at the gatehouses, both crowned with ballistae that looked to have seen better days, for any sign of the guards. It took a few shouts from Wulfric's booming voice to get a guard to emerge. An armored knight peered down from the crenellated ramparts between the gatehouses and shouted down a challenge. "Who are you, and what is your purpose here?"

Kayen stepped in front of the Ulf. "Our business is with Lord Dunford. Allow us entry at once. We have come with urgent news."

The knight, whose narrow eyes gave him a naturally suspicious face, gave a quick scan of the three. "Who is it that wishes to bring news to our commander?"

THE TOMB OF THERAGAARD

"I, Brother Kayen of the Order of the Imacolata; Tryam, an acolyte of the Abbey of Saint Paxia; and Wulfric, son of Alric, heir to Clan Ulf. Now open these gates!"

Seemingly satisfied with the answer, the guard made a gesture to an unseen subordinate. "I did not recognize you, Brother Kayen," said the guard. "You seem changed from last we met, but it is good to see you back. We have a need for monks. There has been a murder in town, and people have gone missing. Lord Dunford has ordered the gates closed, so that the killer cannot escape."

People missing? A murder? Was the entirety of Medias slipping into madness? Tryam hoped everyone at the abbey was safe.

Unseen gears groaned, and the portcullis lifted. Kayen led the group inside the gate, where they had to wait for a set of iron-reinforced wooden doors to swing open, a second layer of protection usually never employed. The party entered the eerily quiet Arkos.

A man passed them, head down. Tryam stood in his way to get his attention. "Sir, where is everyone? At this hour, the streets should be teeming with people."

At first refusing to respond, the dirt-covered man—probably a miner, Tryam reasoned—answered after looking at the faces of the three determined men. "These are dark times, son. Only fools or those on urgent business are in the streets. I'm off to the tavern, so I guess that makes me a thirsty fool."

With that, the miner continued on his way.

"Come. Let's make our way to the mage tower," urged Wulfric. "It is not too distant. We need to secure Myramar's help."

"Yes, we must, but I know Myramar. He is a good man, but something of a recluse, and certainly not an adventurer," explained Kayen. "We would be better off securing Lord Dunford's support first. He can put pressure on Myramar to help us."

Wulfric clenched his fists. "Very well, you know the way of *civilized* men better than I, but we must hurry."

Upon reaching the keep, located just before the harbor, Kayen displayed his cross of Aten and told the knight atop the battlements he had urgent news for the fortress commander. The knight agreed to escort the party to the commander himself.

The inner fortress was a three-story structure with thick walls that housed the barracks for the officers and the office of the commander.

Tryam could not shake the memory of the last time he had stood there, waiting to bring the news to Lord Dunford of Brother Emil's death.

The three were led up carpeted stone steps to the third floor. At the top of the stairs and across the landing was a door with a boldly carved sigil on its face: the golden lion of Engoth. The knight approached the door and knocked three times before pushing it open and ushering the three muddy travelers inside.

Before them, seated at his desk, was the lord commander of the Engothian knights. He did not immediately look up from the parchmentwork before him. Tryam felt the heat of a large fireplace in the southwest corner of the immaculately clean room and began to feel self-conscious of his well-traveled appearance.

The escort knight coughed, then did a brisk salute. "Lord Commander, Brother Kayen says he has urgent business with you."

Tryam could tell by the deferential tone in the knight's voice that he feared having to interrupt his lord.

The yellow-headed and red-bearded hulk of a man lifted his piercing blue eyes up from the parchments and charts spread across the desk and said dryly, "Leave us, then."

The knight turned on his heels and hastily exited the room, closing the large oak door behind him.

Dunford's eyes had shown a flash of recognition when he saw the young acolyte, and from the scowl the commander made, it was clear that he was none too pleased to have Tryam in his presence again.

"Take a seat," offered Dunford.

There was only one chair before the commander's desk, but it was understood that Dunford was addressing Brother Kayen.

"If it's okay, I'd rather stand," replied Kayen as he stepped up to the desk and leaned on his crooked staff. Tryam and Wulfric moved to flank him.

Tryam examined the commander's face but could read nothing but annoyance. Dunford's priorities were on the pile of charts, maps, and ledgers on his desk.

"Fine." Dunford put down the parchment he was holding and leaned back on his red-cushioned chair. He crossed his arms impatiently. "Do you have information on the murder that has shaken Arkos?"

"Of that ill news, I am afraid we do not. What we have to say goes beyond a single murder, however. Not too far from here, in the reaches just

THE TOMB OF THERAGAARD

north of the Arkos mines, there has been a great slaughter. A brutal attack committed by the same people who killed Brother Emil. Clan Ulf has been destroyed, and those of its people who were not killed outright have been taken prisoner. They need your help."

Tryam watched for any change in the commander's expression, but not a single hint of compassion could be found on the bearded face.

"Help? How? Launch an invading force in the north and bring the whole of Berserkerdom against us? I am sorry, that will not happen."

Upon hearing Dunford's answer, Wulfric pounded his fist on the desk, causing the parchments to scatter. "I told you he would not help us! He cares only about his precious metal!"

Tryam restrained the enraged Ulf, and Brother Kayen adroitly covered for Wulfric's outburst. "Excuse my young friend. He is a member of Clan Ulf. It is his duty to free his people, and it is our moral imperative to help him."

This time a hint of compassion flashed from the commander, who straightened up in his chair. "I am truly sorry, son, but I have to think of this town's needs and safety first. Yes, that includes the coronium mines." He crossed his arms over his barrel chest. "How would the Berserkers react if they saw a company of knights taking sides in a dispute between clans?"

Before Wulfric could respond, Kayen countered the commander's argument. "But this was no ordinary dispute. We followed the captives to the Ragnar valley. The Ragnar are preparing for war on a massive scale."

Dunford rose to his feet and walked toward the window behind his desk. He thrust open the shutters, and a cold rush of air blew into the room. Outside, Tryam could see the Corona Mountain Range, where the sun colored the snow-capped peaks gold. Dunford thrust a finger outside. "The only reason the town of Arkos exists is because of the mines out there, and it has taken me over a decade to secure our operations. The Berserkers have battled one another for generations. They did so before the fall of Antium. We cannot risk drawing the attention of their axes by taking sides in a war. This is not the first time one clan has destroyed another. Isn't that so?"

Kayen reluctantly agreed to that point, but he added, "Clan Ragnar is unifying the various clans under a single banner, and they are succeeding because they are being aided by foreigners. One is a cleric of Terminus who must be held in high regard by the Dark God, for he summoned a creature

309

from the Abyss against us. The other man is an Albus wizard whose power even you should be able to appreciate. But most horrifying of all: At the Ragnar village, we saw they had exhumed a weapon from ancient times, a black metal warrior some fifty feet in height. Arkos will surely be their next target!"

"Did you see this metal warrior fight?" asked Dunford.

"No, it was unmoving, But if that Albus mage could restore it to operation …"

Dunford walked over to warm his hands by the fire and scrunched his face in annoyance. "I care not for a dusty old relic some wizard fancies or for rampaging Berserker clans who fight among themselves! Attack Arkos? Ridiculous. We have walls, a keep, and an armed garrison of knights. If this is about magic, speak to Myramar. If an Albus mage is here on Glacia, I am sure he knows why." The commander shook his head as he let what Kayen said play in his head. "Your news is troubling, I admit, but before I commit my men to battle, I must have more evidence that the town is under threat. Give me that evidence, and I shall listen; otherwise, bother me no more."

Kayen bowed to the commander and said calmly, "Very well, we shall talk to Myramar, and perhaps with his aid, we shall return to you with enough evidence to change your mind."

"You are dismissed," barked Dunford.

Before leaving the commander's office, however, Wulfric glared at Lord Dunford and warned, "If you do not act, it will be Arkos that burns, your warriors killed, and your people enslaved. You cannot hide behind your desk any more than the town can hide behind its walls."

Chapter 46
Unexpected Visitors

Frustrated from weeks of futile research and frightened of the growing decline in Myramar's sanity, Telvar was considering heading off into the mountains after the rogue mage with just the meager amount of information he had. *I am no Albus mage, but I am sure I can find Antigenesus's fortress. As far as traversing the Berserker wastes, if those brainless barbarians can survive, I should have no problem.*

The young wizard's nose was pressed against the pages of a book entitled *The History of Upper Continental Medias* when a rapping from the tower's door jolted him upright.

Has Dementhus returned?

Telvar ran down the steps of the tower, holding up his long black robes so as not to trip. Myramar had not left the subterranean laboratory in weeks, but he did not want to risk the chance the old wizard would answer the door first and refuse him access to the Albus mage.

When Telvar reached the first floor, he assured himself with a sigh of relief that Myramar was nowhere in sight. The young wizard activated the spyglass and peered out. Telvar sighed again upon seeing a middle-aged monk, a young but brawny acolyte, and a giant of a Berserker.

Damn the God! What do these fools want?

He was considering ignoring the visitors and returning to the library when the sound of rapping returned, this time with more urgency and volume. *They probably want gold for some hopeless cause and won't leave until I respond!* The wizard struggled to remember which ridiculous winter festival was around the corner.

Telvar flung the door open, stood in the face of the middle-aged monk, and casually brushed hair away from his wizard band, letting the red gem sparkle in the light. "Sorry, we are not allowed to give money to charity. It is against the Wizard Council rules, I am afraid. Good evening." Telvar went to close the door, but the brute of a barbarian stuck his booted foot in the doorway. The wolf-pelt hide he wore matched the wolf-like stare he gave.

The middle-aged monk stepped forward. "My name is Kayen. I am a missionary and a monk from the Order of the Imacolata. We have an urgent matter to discuss with Myramar, and we shall not leave until we do so."

"I am afraid Myramar is indisposed. Good day." With all the force he could muster, Telvar started again to close the door, only to be defeated by the Berserker's foot.

Telvar sighed in resignation. "Myramar is performing dangerous experiments, so unless you want to risk unleashing enough magical energy to level the entire town, you will have to tell me this urgent business."

Kayen smiled pleasantly but cast a gaze toward his Berserker companion. The warning was not lost on Telvar, who was mildly amused by the implied threat. The bearded missionary cleared his throat. "I have sought counsel from Myramar previously, but I don't recall seeing you before."

"I am the acting tower mage and Myramar's assistant." *"Assistant" sounds better than "apprentice."* "Come in, but leave those two outside." *Let that barbarian glare someplace else.*

"We are together," the Berserker said as his hand hovered over the hilt of his sword.

"Yes," the missionary interrupted. "These are my companions: Wulfric, my friend from the northlands, and my fellow brother in Aten, Tryam."

The Berserker's skull is likely too thick for reason and common sense. Telvar reluctantly backed away from the threshold and let the door open. "Very well, come inside. But *touch* nothing."

Escorting the three into the grand entrance hall, the young wizard led them to the room's only chairs. Telvar sat in the velvet-cushioned one Myramar favored when talking to visitors, while Kayen sat on the matching chair opposite from him. The missionary's two companions stood by the fireplace, their scowling and scrutinizing faces on Telvar at all times. The young wizard was not sure what this urgent business could be, but he suspected it had to do with a goat that changed color unexpectedly or a chicken they'd discovered that did arithmetic.

"How can I be of assistance?" Telvar postured himself, with fingers steepled, as he had seen other wizards do when in counsel.

"Clan Ulf, this young man's clan, has been destroyed by another Berserker clan, the Ragnar," began the missionary, gesturing toward the Ulf youth. "Some of his people were taken prisoner, including Wulfric's mate, Kara. We tracked them to a twin-peaked mountain. There we saw a wizard—"

The word *wizard* sent a shock down Telvar's spine, and he leapt to his feet. "A wizard? Describe him."

"He wore red robes, bald of head. We saw him only from a distance. He wore a white diamond band."

It has to be Dementhus. "What did the Albus wizard do?"

"He spoke words of magic, and a door in the side of the mountain opened. We tried to follow, but the door closed before we could pass. We did not dare try to open the door ourselves."

"A wise move on your part." Telvar moved closer to the missionary to make sure he would hear everything the man had to say. "What else did you see?"

"After a debate, we decided to search for any Ulf prisoners in the Ragnar village. We followed a path that took us to the Ragnar's sacred amphitheater. There we saw something extraordinary. Where the stage should have been was a deep pit, as if something massive had been recently exhumed. Whatever had been extracted was taken to their village, for it left behind a massive trail. Before we reached the village, however, we saw forges burning, enough to blacken the sky with smoke. We continued to follow the tracks until they led us to a tent near the Ragnar's newly completed palisade walls. It was in the tent where we discovered what they had dug up."

"Yes?" demanded Telvar, not waiting for the missionary to catch his breath.

The missionary arched his eyebrows. "A relic from ancient times—a colossal black metal warrior, undoubtedly crafted by magic."

Telvar paced to and fro, his feet trying to keep up with his thoughts. "'Black metal,' you say? You said 'colossal,' but can you be more specific on how large it was? Did it have any markings?"

The missionary conferred with the other two before agreeing on what they'd seen. "It must have been fifty feet in height. It had red markings along its body, like tattoos."

A weapon? Could it be? Telvar stopped his pacing. "I fear it might be an ancient Golem, a metallic imitation of life. The great archmagus Antigenesus created this artifact in defiance of the Church."

Both Kayen and Telvar were arriving at conclusions. Kayen soberly realized that this young assistant wizard was confirming the suspicion he had been harboring since seeing the giant warrior at the Ragnar village.

For his part, Telvar could hardly believe what he was hearing: *By blind luck, these fools have stumbled onto what I have been seeking. If Dementhus can activate the ancient Golem, he will be almost invincible! Is that what he was after? It has to be!* To appear more in control, he folded his hands behind his back. "Can you take me to this mountain?"

The young acolyte stepped forward and spoke for the first time. "If you can guarantee you can get us inside, we shall make sure you get there in one piece."

"Of course, I can get inside. I am a wizard." *But how?*

The Ulf cast a scornful look his way. "There is more. We saw my people. They were being held captive in the Ragnar village. We could not free them, because the Albus mage has them ensorcelled by magic." He walked up to Telvar and put a finger on his chest. "You are only an apprentice, not the tower mage. We need *his* help, not that of an assistant."

Telvar took a deep breath, then exhaled slowly. "The truth of the matter is that Myramar is in ill health and has not left his laboratory in weeks. He would not survive the journey to this mountain. That is why I am here, to take over his responsibilities. My name is Telvar. I can assure you, I am your only option. If you can get me to this village safely, I can remove the enchantments on your people—that is, if they still live."

The response seemed to appease the Ulf and his companions, if not totally convince them.

"There is another obstacle," cautioned Brother Kayen. "The Ragnar are building a Berserker army. You must convince Lord Dunford that Arkos is in danger and that he must send out a force to stop the Ragnar before it is too late!"

If Dementhus is in league with these Ragnar brutes and uses the Golem against Arkos, Lord Dunford will be helpless to prevent the town's destruction. "Upon our safe return, I shall report to him what I have found. I cannot guarantee what actions he will take."

THE TOMB OF THERAGAARD

The missionary rose from his chair to stand by his companions. "Can't we speak to Myramar? Surely, he could convince Lord Dunford to aid us."

The three sets of desperate eyes staring at him compelled Telvar to reveal more information. "Since I have agreed to go on this endeavor, I should explain something. I believe the Albus wizard you encountered is the same one who was in this very tower not too long ago. His name is Dementhus. He is a powerful spellcaster and is on the Wizard Council. Whether intentionally or not, Myramar may have aided him. Either way, ever since his encounter with this rogue wizard, Myramar has grown erratic. Until we have seen what is going on with our own eyes, it would be unwise for us to bring this information to him."

"Do you think this Dementhus may have been involved in the murder in Arkos?" Kayen questioned.

Images of Myramar and the corpse entered Telvar's mind. "Unlikely. I think it more probable that Dementhus has agents in Arkos." Telvar took note of the time. "We should leave as soon as possible, but I must prepare for the journey first. You three stay on this floor. Do not even think of exploring any further. The kitchen is just beyond that door. Take as much food as you need, and get as much rest as you can. We shall leave at first light."

"What if Myramar should see us?" quizzed the Ulf.

"Run from the tower, and do not look back!"

Telvar bowed curtly to the three, then moved swiftly up the stairs.

Once inside his chambers, he took one long last look at the spell to Antigenesus's fortress, which he had recovered from the hidden compartment. In his attempt to decipher the incantation, he had tacked some pages to the wall and spread out others over his desk. Weeks of research and study had gotten him nowhere in deciphering the intricate unlocking spell.

I've wasted enough time with this! Telvar swiped the spell pages from the wall, then gathered the loose pages from the desk. He crumpled the mess into a ball, then stuffed the parchments into his mattress.

Despite his promise, Telvar had no idea how he would get inside the fortress. *I shall come up with a solution on the way.* Of that, he had no doubt.

✠ ✠ ✠

Packed with a fully charged quarterstaff, bags of fresh reagents, a variety of potions, his spell book, and the warmest clothes he possessed, the young, dark-haired mage was almost ready to depart. There was but one task remaining: He would have to inform Myramar of his absence.

He could explain his leaving in several ways, but the truth could not be one of them. His lie had to have only one effect: It had to be convincing enough not to arouse his demented master to anger. *But dare I speak to the old wizard at all?* Telvar composed a brief letter and made his way down to the grand entrance. It was an hour before dawn, and the three visitors were sound asleep on the floor. He was impressed that the Berserker had restrained himself from breaking any furniture.

Telvar grabbed a torch and proceeded down the steps to the subterranean laboratory. He could detect the smells and strange lights seeping from underneath its door. He made his way there and slid the parchment he held in his hand under it.

Before the young wizard could turn away, the door flung open. The quickness with which Myramar appeared at the threshold caused Telvar to nearly jump out of his skin. The old wizard closed the door behind him to keep Telvar's eyes away from whatever he'd been doing inside. Myramar had the look of a man with very little sleep: bloodshot eyes, gaunt features, ruffled clothes, and tangled hair.

"What's this, then?" Myramar picked up the letter. "I told you I was not to be disturbed!"

"Sorry, m-master," stammered Telvar. "That is why I did not knock. I was trying not to disturb you."

The old wizard's breath was foul. "Are you going to tell me what is in this letter, or do I have to rip the information from you?"

With concerted effort, Telvar suppressed his fear and slowly bowed. "Sorry, master. The tower is out of reagents. I wrote the letter telling you I would be gone for a couple of weeks to replenish our supplies." *Will the old man buy it?*

"Leave it to the son of a merchant to be troubled over the inventory. Very well, but be back in two weeks, or I shall not let you back in the tower."

"Of course, my master."

Telvar did not finish bowing before the old man went back into his laboratory and slammed the door shut. Whoever Myramar had been before, he was no longer. *Someone else lives behind those eyes.*

The young wizard could not wait to leave the tower to find answers.

Chapter 47
The Confession

Gidran was pleased to see axes hacking away at the plaster walls, obliterating the frescoes placed upon them years before. Elsewhere, sharpened spades ripped away the tiles of the decorative mosaics on the ancient church floor, obscuring forever the faces on the saints of Aten.

Shaped like a cross, the small church was located in a nook along the south wall near the resting place of the great barge. The shaman felt uneasy in the close confines of the recently exhumed temple, and he relished each act of defilement.

The church was an enigma. *Why would an archmagus allow his soldiers a place of worship at the very same time that he was openly declaring war against Aten?* When the shaman had asked Dementhus about the church, the Necromancer speculated it had likely been created after the archmagus's demise. That the construction had likely been spearheaded by Theragaard was understood but not directly acknowledged.

It was another matter of more immediate importance that darkened Gidran's mood: The Daemon he had sent to find the intruders was overdue.

The shaman ordered the Ragnar workers to leave. They dutifully gathered their tools and carried the shattered icons out in canvas sacks. In solitude, Gidran stripped off his animal furs and prostrated himself, bare-chested, before the scorpion idol of Terminus that now topped the altar, where once a plain cross of Aten had rested. He sought for the Daemon and asked for Terminus's guidance to find it. When the dark light warmed his soul, he scanned the material realm through the Dark God's all-seeing eyes. The Daemon lurked in no shadows, however, nor did it slumber in any cave. Inexplicably, something—or someone—had expelled the beast back to the Abyss. The shaman had no choice but to tell Dementhus he had failed to find the intruders.

Once again, as if sensing Gidran's thoughts, the Necromancer appeared unexpectedly. The low light from the sputtering candles obscured any sign of emotion on the wizard's face. His eyes, however, gleamed as from one on the brink of madness. For the first time, the shaman noticed how warm the temple had become. "Dementhus, I was about to seek you out."

As the mage stepped closer, Gidran noticed that he was actually smiling. "What is the matter? Is this temple not to your liking?" The laugh that followed carried little joviality.

"Now that the Ragnar have removed the images of Aten's saints, it is more than adequate. It is another matter that troubles me."

The wizard stepped farther inside the temple and made his way to the desecrated altar. "Proceed," the mage said coolly.

"When we were preparing the Golem to be moved to the mountain, the prints of three outsiders were found in the mud. You were still away from camp, so I took the opportunity to summon a creature from the Abyss to hunt down the intruders. I was expecting the hellspawn to achieve its goal quickly, but I miscalculated. Whoever these three spies were managed to evade and perhaps even vanquish my Daemon servant."

The news did not cause Dementhus's expression to change, but he spent a few moments before responding. "I am displeased that you took so long to inform me of this. Nevertheless, as troublesome as this may be, setbacks such as this are to be expected. We have had too much good fortune for such little hardship. This must be another obstacle Terminus tasks us to overcome."

The wizard circled the altar, placing his velvet-gloved hands upon the scorpion idol. "As to the identity of these intruders, perhaps your expedition to the abbey's crypts raised suspicions. Only a monk of Aten could banish a creature back to the Abyss. Certainly, a Berserker witch doctor could not."

The shaman shook his head. "The clerics at the abbey were uncommonly timid. I doubt they would have the courage to come to the wastes in order to seek me out. It must be someone else, perhaps one aided by the spirit of Theragaard still lingering in this waste." He let out a deep breath. "Who knows what other secrets lie hidden in these vast mountains?"

Hearing the name of Theragaard brought a scowl to Dementhus's face. "Tell Crayvor what has happened, and have him lead a search party. I have faith in that young man. Also, command him to utilize the network of Ragnar scouts to keep an eye on all likely paths between Arkos and this fortress. These scouts will create a web in which we shall trap any force, no matter how small, that attempts to sneak upon us again."

The wizard turned to exit the temple but then paused and gave Gidran a long stare. "Don't make me lose faith in you. Never do such an undertaking again without my knowledge."

Gidran bowed deeply. "Yes, for that I apologize. In my quest to lighten your burdens, I have instead burdened you more. You will never again have cause to doubt my loyalty to you. I shall tell Crayvor immediately to seek these blasphemers who dare meddle in Bafomeht's plans."

When the Necromancer left the temple, Gidran unleashed the breath he had not realized he'd been holding, and he understood it would be unwise to fail Dementhus again.

Chapter 48

Another Point of Departure

"Where are your mounts?" asked the novice wizard in a voice already near exasperation.

The party had just assembled outside the mage tower, and Tryam was already uneasy with their new companion. *Can we trust Kara's life, the lives of the other captured Ulfs, and perhaps even the entire town of Arkos to an apprentice wizard? He is confident, but is it all bluster?*

"I cannot carry this heavy backpack all the way up a mountain," continued the wizard.

"We have no mounts," admitted Kayen, "though it would be more expeditious if we did."

The wizard sighed, which Tryam realized was the young man's favorite way of expressing himself. "Then, you … Wulfgar, was it? … you must carry my backpack until we procure horses."

"Wulfric," the Ulf corrected before slipping the bulging backpack over his shoulder. "Would you like me to carry anything else?" he asked through clenched teeth.

"I don't think so, but do not fear. If anything gets heavy for me, it will come your way."

To make his load more balanced, Wulfric shifted the wizard's backpack.

"Careful with that!" screamed Telvar. "God knows what would happen if the potions shatter and mix!"

Wulfric's death glare went unnoticed by the wizard.

THE TOMB OF THERAGAARD

The only item Telvar now held was a metal staff with a ruby tip. He wore expensive-looking but practical leather boots and a black cloak over his black robes with their innumerable pockets.

"About the mounts," interrupted Kayen. "I am afraid none of us have any money," he added apologetically.

The sigh returned. "Of course! Why would I think two monks and a Berserker would? I have enough. Follow me."

After they exited the warm tower grove, a brutal cold blast of wind reminded Tryam that winter had arrived in full. Telvar led the party a short distance down the narrow, deserted streets to one of the town's stables.

At this early hour, Tryam imagined few people were awake and doubted anyone at the stable would be. Telvar banged on the door of the stable master's house. He banged until a shutter opened and the glow of a lantern emerged from inside. Soon thereafter, a man dressed only in woolen underclothes shouted from inside. "We are closed. Begone, or I shall call the town guards."

Telvar stepped away from the door and took a step toward the window, enabling the glow from the man's lantern to shine off the red gem on his wizard band. "A wizard has business at all hours of the day. We need four horses, the best ones you have. And we need them now!"

Tryam was aghast at the young wizard's bravado, but he had to admit that it was effective. The old stable master, bothering to put on only a cloak, emerged from the dwelling and ran to open the stable doors, apologizing as he did so.

As he went from horse to horse, examining them from teeth to hooves, the wizard tsked and shook his head.

Is he trying to bargain, or does he truly not like the selection? Tryam wondered.

"If we were not pressed for time, I would walk away now and consider myself better for it!" complained the wizard. "These animals are ill-footed for the shallow valleys of the lower Tamar, let alone for the mountain paths where we need them to go!"

Tryam whispered into Kayen's ear: "Do you trust this Telvar?"

While stroking his beard, the missionary observed Telvar from afar and carefully pondered his response. "Surprisingly, I do. I cannot explain why, but I believe Aten has put him in our path for a reason. I can tell you he is correct about the horses, though I am not sure we should be wasting time to haggle."

Wulfric leaned into the conversation and added, "If he shows us the slightest hint of deception, I shall make sure it will be his last mistake."

With each disparaging comment made by the wizard, the redder the stable master's face became. "You will find no horse better on the mainland!"

After a series of insults, offers, and counteroffers, the bartering was completed. Telvar smiled as if he were the victor, while the old stable master looked defeated and hurried back to his warm house, clasping Telvar's coins in his bony hands.

The group mounted with alacrity and left the stable behind. Tryam, with only limited experience on horseback, was surprised how natural riding came to him. He had no trouble keeping up with the others.

Once they reached the north wall, Tryam heard the wizard shout, "What's the meaning of this?"

The north gate was still closed.

"No one is allowed in or out unless given permission by Lord Dunford," came a reply from a sleepy knight atop the ramparts.

"This is absurd. Don't you know who I am?" fumed Telvar. The wizard lowered his fur-covered cowl and displayed his wizard band.

"No," the shadowed guard shouted down in response, starting a melee of words that included some strong language from Brother Kayen.

The ruckus aroused another knight. From atop the roof of the left gatehouse, a familiar profile emerged. While the others pleaded their case with the obstinate officer, Tryam ambled his horse over and yelled to get the other knight's attention. "Gavin, it is I, Tryam!"

"What are you doing here?" Gavin's eyes shifted between the captain of the gate guards and the party below.

"We need the gates opened immediately. The Berserkers who attacked us have destroyed my friend Wulfric's village and have taken his mate, Kara, as prisoner. We are on a mission to bring her back. By Aten's will, please let us pass!"

After a moment of hesitation, he replied, "The captain will have my head, but I shall do it!"

The young knight disappeared inside the gatehouse.

"Get ready to ride," Tryam warned the others, receiving bewildered looks in response.

THE TOMB OF THERAGAARD

A moment later, the wooden doors swung open, and the portcullis started to rise. Above, the captain threw his helmet down in frustration.

"Never delay a wizard!" Telvar taunted as he spurred his horse ahead.

The others followed. The last thing Tryam heard as he headed out of town were curses being shouted and Gavin's name being called.

Chapter 49
Alive and Alone

Only a hint of light angling through a small slot atop the room's single door brightened her cramped, dusty cell. Kara's wrists and ankles were tightly bound in manacles linked by four chains hammered into the floor. Her mouth was still gagged. Small cuts and bruises covered her body, but it was an itch on her back, *which would not go away*, that was driving her mad.

After all that had happened, Kara was surprised to still be alive. When she'd been separated from her Ulf companions, she expected her fate would be something foul. When the Ragnar's foreign cleric had told her she was to be a sacrifice to the Ragnar mountain god, she'd laughed in his face. "Your god will choke on my soul first!" When he'd told her she would be in this cell until the god could be moved to the mountain, she'd laughed in his face again and teased, "What kind of god can't make the mountain come to him?"

With nothing to do in the lonely cell, Kara nodded off.

In her sleep, she dreamt of reuniting with Wulfric and then of getting revenge against the Ragnar. When she awoke, she could not tell how much time had passed, for the light that filtered through the door came not from a natural source but rather from an orb hanging from the ceiling in the hallway, and its illumination never varied. Her extremities tingled with pain because the blood flow to her hands and feet had been restricted by the tight manacles. She wiggled and stretched to ease the torment. Her mouth was dry, and her stomach ached, but the itch was gone.

If I stay here any longer, I fear I shall go mad!

She scanned the room, looking for a way out. The floor was smooth stone, and the door iron-banded. As far as jail cells went, she felt pleased that they feared her enough to put her in a very secure one.

She decided to test how well she could move in her irons. After many failed attempts, Kara learned how to stand. The chains were heavy, so she could do so only in stages. First, she would sit up, then get to her knees, then jump to her feet. She practiced many times, until she could do it in a matter of seconds. Each time she did the maneuver, more feeling returned to her hands and feet.

Standing on the tips of her toes, she could see out the small window; however, the view was unhelpful, revealing only a dim hallway and the open cell across the way. In a fit of rage, when she saw that the other cell had a small bucket that hers lacked, she stamped her feet.

Kara experimented with walking while shackled until her muscles grew stiff. She collapsed to the ground in a heap.

I need a weapon for when the jailers return. If they return.

Hours of straining her jaw muscles paid off when she finally was able to chew through the leather gag over her mouth, though she had swallowed some of the old animal hide in the process. She thought of crying out for help but decided the only ones likely to respond would be the dishonorable Ragnar.

Another day or more, she presumed, passed in isolation. Boredom, thirst, hunger, anger, and frustration warred within her, until the rattling of a key sent her body into a heightened state of awareness. She lay down on her side and made sure the gag appeared to be still stuffed in her mouth. She feigned sleep.

After a struggle with the ancient locking mechanism, someone entered the room and dropped a tin plate near her head. She smelled cooked meat. A hard kick to the back of her legs caused her to moan through her gag. A deep voice spoke.

"You had best eat if you know what's good for you." The man then tore the ruined gag from her mouth and shoved her face closer to the plate.

All that time wasted, chewing through that bad-tasting leather!

When Kara did not immediately react, another kick sent her over to her stomach, and she let out a low moan.

"I said, eat," bellowed the man.

When Kara still did not react, he knelt down and pulled on her long blond hair, bending her head backward.

As tears fell down her face from the pain, she could feel the man's warm breath on her neck.

"Eat!" he shouted again.

With the patience of a natural-born predator, she waited until the man's lips were almost touching her ear before she launched into action. She snapped open her eyes, whipped her head around, and took aim at the man's neck with her teeth, biting deep into his throat.

Blood spurted into her mouth and ran down her neck. The Ragnar jailer released her hair, and her head bounced off the floor. Kara spat a large chunk of flesh out of her mouth.

The jailer groped at his neck, trying to stop the flow of blood with his hands. Kara had seen enough neck wounds to know he would not survive long.

After a few heartbeats, the man fell to his knees, his green metal helmet toppling from his head. Another moment after that, he fell forward, his death mask a mixture of shock and anger. Kara rolled away from the pooling gore and waited until the man's breathing stopped before moving again. Once his soul was gone from his body, Kara took a visual inventory of his belongings. She focused on the key and dagger tied to the belt about his waist.

Kara stretched her fingers to pluck the keys, then used them to unlock her restraints. She rubbed feeling back into her hands and feet; then she snatched the dagger. She was glad there was no reflective surface nearby, because she was sure she looked a bloody mess. With revenge on her mind, the young Ulf headed out of the cell.

A long look down both sides of the hallway showed no other Ragnar in sight. An idea struck her, and she stepped back into the cell to put on the dead warrior's fur pelt and green helmet.

With her disguise complete, Kara mulled over her next step. She badly wanted revenge on the Ragnar, but she also wanted to find Wulfric. When the Ragnar had attacked the village, he was undergoing the Trial of Blood on the sacred Crag Mountain. *He must still live!* She had to escape and find him, tell him what happened, and let him know that many of his clan had been taken prisoner. *I also need to find where they took my bow and arrows.*

Exiting her cell, she passed eight others, four on each side of the corridor. All were empty. The narrow passage went another dozen feet before leading into a circular room with a round marble desk. A chair, positioned to face the hallway of cells, sat unoccupied.

Precision and artistry had been used in the creation and design of the floors, ceilings, and doors in this room. Even the lights in the ceiling were marvels the likes of which Kara had never seen before. She could not comprehend wasting such efforts on a prison. *What mad dungeon is this?*

The circular room had three exits. She dimly recalled that it was the north exit the Ragnar had dragged her through. Kara walked around the desk and opened the curved wooden door that was seamlessly recessed into the wall. Beyond, a ten-foot-wide corridor led to the fortress's central staircase.

Kara remembered the stairs quite well from the long trip down to the bottom of the mountain, a trip led by a crazed wizard whose skull she'd like to adorn her hut. She peered up the stairwell and listened for any sign of the wizard or one of his minions. She did not see or hear anything, and she decided that going down would be the more logical path anyway.

Her stomach growled so loud she imagined it echoed up and down the mountain. *I should have taken that meat before I escaped!*

Kara stopped at the next landing to rest. This floor had one exit from the stairs, a corridor heading into darkness. As she paused to adjust her oversized helmet, the sound of boots on stone drifted out of the passage. *I have to find out who is near.*

As she went down the new passage, Kara clung to the shadows. After thirty feet, the corridor opened into a vast octagonal chamber, the middle of which was an open pit. On this level, a catwalk ringed the pit below. Kara spotted a Ragnar man patrolling the catwalk, wearing the now-familiar greenish armor. The man was keeping watch over the pit below. Kara pulled out her dagger and held it close to her chest.

Keeping to the shadows, the Ulf girl crept to the room's entrance. From here she was in a better position to see into the pit. Men and women, covered in grime, lurched about in a cavernous chamber some thirty feet below, some carrying ore, others shovels or pickaxes. She recognized many of the faces. *My Ulf family! I have to free them!*

Kara flipped the dagger in her hand and tested its weight. She had to admire the Ragnar blacksmith's work. She turned her attention back to the lone watchman. She was puzzled as to why only one man was on guard; surely, the Ulf, no matter age or infirmity, would fight against their captors. One or a hundred guards, it did not matter—she could not leave until she attempted to free her adopted clan.

To all those Ulf warriors who have passed to the next realm, give me strength!

Kara watched as the guard yawned, stretched, scratched himself, and spat into the pit. While the Ragnar man began his leisurely circumnavigation of the catwalk, she retreated into the corridor and hid herself in the shadows. When he reached the room's entranceway, his back was to her.

I shall give you something to pique your interest!

The dagger flew out of Kara's hand in a flash and sank into the big man's neck. The guard turned around and looked at her with bulging eyes. From where the blade protruded came a geyser of blood. He died on his feet after stumbling toward her for a few steps.

Kara retrieved her weapon, scrambled to the catwalk, and looked over the railing. She scanned the pit for other guards but again saw none. Of the Ulf prisoners she saw, they shuffled into and out of dark tunnels, carrying or digging for ore. She yelled into the pit to get their attention. "Hey! Up here! It's me, Kara!"

No one turned to look.

She yelled louder, but not a single eye glanced in her direction. *How can they not hear me?*

Kara looked around the catwalk for a way down and spotted alcoves recessed into the wall. She explored the nearest one and saw that inside were stairs spiraling down. She listened with a cocked ear but heard nothing but the sounds of the miners at work. She rushed down the steps.

The closest prisoner was a dozen feet away. Kara rushed up to the woman and tapped her on the shoulder. The woman turned slowly and looked at Kara with glazed eyes.

Kara recognized the old woman as Lilia, a leather worker.

"It's me, Kara! You remember, we bartered many times."

No response.

Kara removed her helmet and exposed her golden hair. "Don't you recognize me now?"

Only a vacant stare from Lilia.

She must still be in shock, the poor woman.

Kara went to another dirt-covered prisoner, a middle-aged woman she recognized as Sanra. Sanra was a weaver and had always been kind to her.

"We can escape! I can find us a way out. Follow me!" pleaded Kara.

No response.

Kara went from person to person, even slapping and dragging an old man to the alcove, but to no avail—no sign of recognition, no sign of wanting to be freed. *This can't be happening! They must be drugged or under a spell!*

Kara grew desperate. She grabbed a shovel and came up behind a broad-shouldered Ulf she did not recognize. She raised the spade high overhead. *Maybe they need the sense knocked back into them!*

She took aim at the back of the man's head.

"Your last chance before I smack you. Let's get out of here!" The man did not turn to acknowledge her. "I warned you!"

The shovel descended toward the man's skull but was ripped from her hands before it made contact. Kara whirled around, her dagger in her hand in an instant.

At first, she thought she was staring at a giant mound of sand, then she saw the outline of limbs and a gaping mouth. A city-raised girl would be frozen in fear, but she was a Berserker and would not be cowed by any beast, natural or unnatural. She took a defensive crouch as she'd been trained to do since youth, and she examined her opponent.

The *thing* was eight feet tall and as wide as two men. It had no eyes or ears, and it moved about the floor like mud sliding down a hill. It looked impossible to defeat with only a dagger, but she had no place to flee to.

Kara plunged her weapon into the sand monster's torso to see if the green metal weapon could injure it. She thrust with all her weight, and the dagger slid into the monster's body with ease. Too easily: Her arm sank into the pseudo-flesh up to her elbow. When she tried to pull the knife free, she discovered that her arm was stuck, as if buried in mud.

The sand and rock limbs of the monster embraced her and drew her close to its yawning mouth. Kara struggled to break free but could barely breathe, let alone fight the strange muscles powering the creature.

"Don't you know you aren't supposed to kill me? Your god needs a sacrifice!"

The creature only squeezed tighter.

As her head was directed into the creature's maw, pieces of its dirt-like flesh poured into Kara's mouth. The last thing she remembered before losing consciousness was the feel of sand in her throat.

Chapter 50
Ocean of Blood

Dementhus struggled to push open the double doors of the conference room. In the past few weeks, his use of magic had accelerated the decay in his hands and feet. Ignoring the pain, he strode briskly inside. His eyes were drawn to the semicircular window and the view of the setting sun. It was getting late, and he noted shadows climbing the sharp peaks of the neighboring mountains. The end of another day reminded the Albus mage that time was moving inexorably forward. It made him angry. Constant interruptions had taken away from his exploration of Antigenesus's fortress and his attempts to reanimate the Golem.

Since the last time he was there, someone had replaced the smashed marble table with another of polished black stone. Ivor sat, arms folded, across from the door. Dementhus noticed how out of place the Ragnar leader looked, dressed in primitive bearskins inside a fortress built by a culture far more advanced than the jarl could possibly comprehend. Even the green coronium breastplate the jarl wore was a crude imitation of the armor worn by the Ancients.

"Greetings, Jarl Ivor." Dementhus bowed deeply as a sign of respect. "What do you think of this place?"

Ivor's response did not surprise Dementhus.

"The fortress may be as big as the mountain itself, but it is only as strong as those who defend it."

"I suppose you are right. What do you need that demands my presence?"

The jarl rose from his chair, turned his back to Dementhus, and looked out the window on the setting sun. "The glory of our first victory fades. My men need to fight again, need to kill again. Is the Mountain God ready to lead us to our next victory? Clans have heard of our God come to life and, in their fear, may conspire against us."

THE TOMB OF THERAGAARD

"His avatar is being restored even as we speak, but the obstacles facing us now do not merit His physical presence. He commands you to take up arms and subjugate the first Berserker clan that refuses to yield to your authority." Dementhus waited until Ivor faced him before continuing. When he met the jarl's eyes, he said, "You have seen how well your new weapons have worked. They alone should give you the advantage over any Berserker foe. The Ulf clan was only the first bloody step on your march to conquer all of Glacia. The Mountain God will grow stronger with every drop of blood spilled, and when He is needed, He will march forth as the tip of your spear!"

The gray-headed Ragnar king nodded his head slowly as if weighed down by the task before him. "I understand and will make preparations for our next campaign," he responded. "Is there anything else the Mountain God wishes from us?"

"Yes, there is. You are to start collecting the bodies of the fallen and bring them back to the Ragnar valley. Make a great tent, then stack them like felled logs inside it."

Ivor's features were hidden in shadow, and Dementhus could not make out the jarl's expression. "I assume you mean those of our enemies."

"No! All of the dead. Friend and foe alike."

"If that is what the God commands, then it will be done. My people will not be happy, however, to see their kin treated as such without explanation."

"Their feelings in this matter are of no concern to the God of the Mountain. Only when it is appropriate will the Mountain God's machinations be revealed. No sooner." Dementhus changed the subject to refocus the jarl's attention back to the task at hand. "Have you an idea as to which clan to attack next?"

Ivor nodded. "I have sent emissaries to our neighbors. A few have joined our cause and now stand with us. However, some have rejected our friendship. Clan Gnoll, in their arrogance, refused to even meet our envoy. They shall be the first clan to feel our wrath. Our army will march at dawn to punish them, and we shall paint the winter snow crimson."

"Good! Good!" commended Dementhus. "That will please our God!"

The Necromancer waited until the warrior's footsteps no longer echoed in the deserted fortress before chuckling to himself. He turned to the window and watched the last rays of the sun sink below the horizon. He wondered how much blood would spill for the Prophet Bafomeht's ambition.

An ocean of blood if need be.

Chapter 51
The Red Cloud

On only his third trip beyond the walls of Arkos, Tryam had expected Wulfric to lead the horses on the same path through the lower plains. Instead, the Ulf headed northeast, to the Corona Mountains themselves. With horses, he argued, they could afford to take a more direct route to their destination. They would also avoid any Ragnar scouts monitoring the known paths. No one disagreed.

The brash young wizard's insistence on using mounts had made the journey through the lower foothills remarkably quick. The horses seemed particularly adept on the rocky hills. Only one member of the party appeared in discomfort: Telvar himself, who insisted on switching horses on two occasions after making a variety of complaints about the mount he had selected.

The most hazardous part of this journey had been the brutal weather. There was no hope of escaping the whipping winds that cut into any exposed flesh. Under normal circumstances, only a starving Berserker on the hunt would have even considered traveling in those conditions.

The company rode while the winter sun made its brief appearance, ate when the last rays of the sun touched the western horizon, and then enjoyed only a brief respite before starting all over again while the sky was still black.

Surprisingly, gathering and preparing food was not a problem, even in the harsh conditions. Wulfric could hunt in any weather, and Telvar had shown a bit of his power by being able to start a fire, even with only frozen wood available.

Tryam enjoyed their brief meals, for it provided time for talk and a chance to learn more about their new companion. "How can you make fire without flint?" he asked.

THE TOMB OF THERAGAARD

It was dark, but he was sure Telvar rolled his eyes. "A ten-year-old novice can make a fire. The process is easy, but it makes one hungry. Pass me that piece of meat." Telvar pointed to the choicest piece Kayen had prepared.

Tryam did as asked, then edged near the wizard, hoping to engage the young man in conversation. When he sat down beside him, the wizard glanced at him with a furrowed brow. Undeterred, Tryam asked, "How long have you studied magic?"

"I was twelve when I convinced my parents that my calling was to be a wizard. This was no easy feat, since they are merchants and as thickheaded as Berserkers when it comes to understanding how magic works. They wanted me to take up the family business." He shook his head in disbelief. "Can you believe that? Me, with the talents I have, behind a counter taking orders from commoners?" He laughed bitterly. "If it had not been for their shortsightedness, I might have begun my training at the Veneficturis at age five, and by this time, I would have a tower of my own. I certainly would be far away from such a grim, godforsaken land as this!"

"This 'godforsaken' land is the land of my forefathers," growled Wulfric, taking a menacing step toward the oblivious wizard.

"Sorry to hear that," replied Telvar between mouthfuls, "but one cannot choose where they are born, nor who will be their family. You can always leave this gloomy land, however. They do have places they call cities."

Tryam quickly changed the subject before an argument started. "What of the mountain? How shall we get inside? The door had no handles."

"Magic. But unless you know something about casting a spell," said Telvar, dismissively, "it would be pointless for me to explain further."

"What if this Dementhus has control over the Golem? What then?" The question came from Kayen, who had spent most of the time on the journey with his own thoughts.

"It is one thing to take possession of such an artifact, it is quite another to use it. I doubt that even an Albus wizard could do so on his own," Telvar said confidently. "At the least, it would take months of research and preparation."

"We find him, we kill him, and we save Kara. That is the plan." Wulfric towered over the seated wizard, his arms crossed over his chest. The Fenrir pelt he wore appeared as if ready to come to life and strike.

The wizard laughed. "It is difficult to kill an Albus wizard. We must try to reason with him first. I am sure he does not care about the Berserkers or a single hostage of theirs."

"He is an ally of the Ragnar. The blood of my people is on his hands. He shall die." Wulfric's words were harsh, but his voice was calm.

"As I said, it is not easy to kill an Albus mage!" He wagged his finger in the air. "However, of this I am certain: Dementhus has gone against the orders of the Wizard Council. He shall be brought to justice, but I am not sure if we are the ones who will be able to deliver him."

Wulfric ignored the wizard's response and walked away from the campfire. Tryam excused himself and followed. He caught up to the Ulf and turned him around. "Don't let the wizard's words injure you."

"I care not what the wizard says. As long as he gets us into the mountain, he can say anything he wishes."

"I don't think he understands what you have lost or what is at stake. He sees this only as an adventure."

Wulfric was brushing the snow from his horse's hooves when something in the distance caught his attention. He pointed. Painted red by the sinking sun, a bulbous cloud was racing down the Coronas, enveloping the tall peaks as it headed in their direction. Wulfric's eyes widened in alarm. "We'd better get going. I've seen storms like this before. These mountain storms can bring several feet of snow in just a few hours."

The concern in Wulfric's voice caused Tryam to fill with anxiety. The Ulf rushed back to the fire. "Pack up!" he barked "Let's get going."

"What's the matter," asked Kayen.

"I've just started my meal!" grumbled Telvar.

"A storm is coming," snapped Wulfric. "A monster one."

Kayen stood up to look toward the mountains. As lightning arced through the red cloud, the missionary let out a whistle. "We need to find shelter."

"Are you mad? We should stay here and make camp!" Telvar stood and spat out the rest of his meat. "We can't risk blindly looking for shelter. Night is almost upon us!"

Tryam was comforted, watching Kayen stroke his brown and gray beard; the missionary was formulating a plan. "I know a place," said Kayen. "Not too far from here. A ruin."

THE TOMB OF THERAGAARD

Wulfric, now seated upon his horse, shook his head. "If you are thinking of the same place as I am, then I disagree. We would be safer braving the storm right here. The ruin is haunted."

"Haunted? Utter nonsense. If this ruin has four stout walls and a roof," opined Telvar, heading for his horse, "I would follow our dear missionary into the house of the devil himself!"

Kayen smirked at Telvar's endorsement. He stepped up to the agitated Wulfric and held the reins of his horse. "Wulfric, I can deal with anything that may lurk in the ruins."

Wulfric looked down at the missionary. "My people have been to that cursed place recently and spoke of hearing the moaning of the dead." The Ulf scanned the sky again. "But if you can tame a Daemon, then I suppose a few ghosts should not pose a problem. Let us be off, then." He pulled the reins free and led his horse away at a gallop, not waiting for the others to follow.

Tryam secured his backpack and jumped on his horse. He could not imagine what kind of ruin would exist in such a desolate part of the world, and with Kayen already mounted and following on Wulfric's heels, he had no chance to ask. The young acolyte waited until he was sure the wizard was ready to follow before urging his own horse forward.

The dark red cloud that had been on the far-off mountain peaks was now above their heads. Lighting came from within this cloud, and bolts crackled in the sky.

Gently falling flakes quickly changed to a blinding rage of wind-whipped snow. The blowing snow became so intense that Tryam could see only a dozen feet ahead. An hour passed, and he feared his hands, practically frozen to the reins, would suffer from frostbite. His mount was faring little better. He heard its labored breathing and watched the beast's legs struggle through the deep snow. He was not sure how much longer either of them could last. He prayed to Aten.

The last Tryam had known for sure that was that Wulfric was still in the lead, followed by Kayen, and then the wizard. Tryam hoped the wizard was keeping pace with Kayen, because he could see only one horse tail in front of him. When that horse came to an abrupt halt, Tryam was certain Telvar had lost his way. However, soon thereafter, a glow emerged in the blinding snow. It was Kayen and his cross. Beside the missionary was Wulfric, his wolf pelt covered in snow. They were on foot. *Have we arrived?*

335

Over the howling winds, Kayen yelled, "We must go the rest of the way on foot. The horses will soon fail us. They are not meant for such conditions."

Resolute, Tryam dismounted and grabbed his backpack. He helped the wizard do likewise and added the potion-filled backpack to his own burden. In a weakened state, Telvar actually thanked him through chattering teeth.

"We are close. I know where the ruin is. I shall guide you!" Wulfric had to shout to be heard, since it was now hard to hear or see beyond a few feet.

Tryam linked arms with Kayen, who grabbed hold of Telvar. The three walked together, using Wulfric's deep footsteps through the snow as a guide, the glowing cross their only light.

"My hands are frozen. I cannot cast a spell," lamented Telvar. "I still have magical reserves in my staff, however, if we need it."

The snow was piling on the wizard's pale face. Tryam knew that if they did not find shelter soon, no amount of magic could save them from the blizzard. Kayen began reciting a prayer, Tryam joined in, while Telvar cursed his fate.

When the lighting cracked anew, it revealed a structure ahead. It was a square building, twenty feet high, seemingly alone in the bleak highlands. There were no windows that Tryam could see, and the top of the building was open to the elements with teeth-like crenellations. Wulfric raced ahead, and the others followed as best they could.

Kayen approached the structure with his cross raised high, casting its blue light on the building's exterior. The walls were made from sturdy bricks, similar to the walls of the abbey, and constructed with similar expert craftsmanship that left only the slightest seams between the stones. Tryam sensed no malevolence emanating from the old ruin. If anything, he felt a loneliness about the place, as if it were somehow aware it had been long abandoned.

"We must find a way inside," said Kayen.

The company walked around the building's perimeter. Tryam estimated each side to be roughly forty feet across, giving the ruin a squat appearance. On the north wall, a crack in the brickworks offered a way in. Kayen entered first, squeezing his frame through the opening. After a few moments, he returned and urged the others to come inside. Telvar rushed ahead, almost knocking Wulfric out of the way. Tryam thanked Aten for helping guide them to a haven from the storm.

THE TOMB OF THERAGAARD

Visions of what might be inside such a strange place filled Tryam's head. *A great library? A treasure hoard?* Once he made his way inside and looked around, he was disappointed, however. The room was littered with broken timbers, chunks of cracked bricks, and a sizable amount of snow and ice.

"One of you board up that hole," ordered Telvar, his face pale, his lips blue. "I think it is colder in here than it is outside."

Tryam dropped the two backpacks he carried and placed them in the center of the room, being extra gentle with the wizard's potions. With the help of Wulfric's strong back, they placed a broken table top against the hole and used two thick ceiling timbers to wedge it into place.

"We need fire, and quickly," the wizard said as he rubbed his hands together. "Gather some of the wood lying around."

After the wizard set the kindling ablaze, this time by combining two potions, Kayen placed his cross underneath his robes. The four then gathered around Telvar's handiwork, the smoke filtering up through the ceiling beams. Strange shadows played on the walls as their bodies warmed back to life.

The wind made a soft moan as it seeped through the boarded-up breach, making Tryam feel an even greater sense of melancholy about the ruin. He had to break the silence. "What is this place?" he asked through chapped lips.

"This is an old beacon tower," answered Kayen. "It was part of a warning system for the original inhabitants of Arkos. The last surviving one in a series of towers."

Tryam was confused by Kayen's answer. "Warning from what?"

"The Heim."

"The Heim?" asked Wulfric.

Kayen placed his shepherd's staff across his knees. "Also known as the Hill men. What the Ancients called your people, Wulfric."

The wizard huffed his disagreement. "I know some history of this area. The old beacon towers stood some sixty feet tall. This place is surely something else. An old hunter's lodge, perhaps."

"Most of the tower lies beneath us," insisted Kayen, "buried under centuries of accumulated snow." He stood and walked to a patch of ice in one corner of the room and tapped it with the butt end of his staff. "Below are the stairs leading down." He pointed to the opposite corner, where a pile of debris had been stacked. "And those are the steps leading to the roof, where I bet you would find an ancient cauldron."

Telvar shrugged his shoulders. "I guess it is possible," he admitted.

"If this is just a beacon tower, why do the Berserkers think this place is haunted?" asked Tryam.

"Hunters have tracked beasts to this area," said Wulfric. "They have reported hearing wailings from the dead coming from inside and have seen the tower top flare with fire." He glared at Telvar. "We are not superstitious simpletons some would have you believe. I speak the truth." The wizard remained unconcerned with the Ulf's indignation, however.

Kayen walked back to the fire. "Wulfric, I have learned to trust the wisdom of your people. We shall set watches tonight, and I shall take the first one."

"I shall take the second," offered Tryam.

"And I the third," said Wulfric.

With three sets of eyes upon him, Telvar took notice. "I need to study my magic. That is, if you want me to have enough strength to get us into that mountain!" The wizard pulled an old book from his backpack and buried his nose in its text.

"As you must," replied Kayen with a hint of exasperation as the others began to make preparations for a long night.

Chapter 52
Eternal Loyalty

Dreams swept through Tryam's slumbering mind as soon as he drifted into unconsciousness.

He dreamt he was alone, hopelessly lost in the blinding snow, walking through drifts up to his thighs. He marched, his limbs frozen, until he could no longer move, nearly entombed in a mausoleum of snow. He was doomed. The world was turning black.

Tryam was awaiting death when a glow in the sky ahead offered hope. He pried open his eyes, which ice had frozen shut. It was the beacon tower.

The ancient ruin now stood its full sixty feet of height, no sign of age upon it. A flame from the bronze cauldron that crowned its top flared like a second sun. Reflected in the light were golden statues standing vigil at each corner of the crenellated battlements, their swords brandished as if to warn anyone who dared approach.

Tryam heard urgent whispers coming from inside the building. He strained to hear what they were saying ...

"Up! Up! The young sleep like the dead. It is your turn to watch!"

Kayen stood over him, shaking him awake. Tryam fought to clear the vision from his mind. "Sorry, Brother. I was lost in a dream." The young acolyte wiped his eyes and lumbered to his feet. He felt more tired now than before his rest.

The missionary put his staff down beside the fire and prepared to sleep. He closed his eyes—but not before he reported on his watch. "I neither saw nor heard a soul either alive or dead. I peeked outside through a crack in the barricade and saw that the storm still rages. We shall be stuck here a while. Pray for those innocents who may lie in its path."

As if to add emphasis to the missionary's grim weather report, thunder rattled the old stones of the ruin.

"Rest easy, Brother Kayen," said Tryam.

It did not take long for the young acolyte to walk around the forty-foot-square room. The only difficulty was walking in the darkness, with so much rotting wood strewed on the floor. After a few circumnavigations, Tryam noticed the fire was growing dim, and he placed another piece of broken wood on the sputtering flames.

Bored, Tryam examined the breach. The timbers and tabletop were still solidly in place. Peering through a crack between two pieces of wood, Tryam looked out at a hellish frozen world of blowing snow and ice. As Brother Kayen had requested, he prayed for any poor souls who might still be out in the storm's clutches.

Turning back to the fire, he looked over his compatriots. The wizard had fallen asleep hunched over a book. *A book of spells?* He looked otherwise hale after risking frostbite earlier. Wulfric was asleep, but his face was not at ease. *Is he dreaming of Kara or of revenge?*

Tryam attempted to imagine what this room, their haven from the storm, would have looked like when it was in use. Nothing besides broken furniture offered a clue, and not enough of that had survived.

He continued to look around the room. In the one corner, the stairwell down was hopelessly blocked by thick, dark ice. The stairs up, however, had only a small amount of debris blocking access. *I bet I can get to the roof.*

As quietly as possible, the broad-shouldered young acolyte cleared away the trash. Once his work was done, he gazed upon steps that spiraled up to an intact but rusting iron hatch. *I shall take only a quick peek.*

Tryam advanced on tiptoes. Once on the top step, he pushed on the hatch, but it would not yield. On closer inspection, he realized that ice on the metal hinges was locking it in place. He used a hatchet to methodically chip away the ice, doing so without waking his companions. After a time, he pushed on the hatch again. It now moved.

No alarm sounded, nor did any sign of danger become apparent, encouraging him to continue. Using his tall but lean frame, he pushed on the hatch until he could feel the accumulated snow slide off its lid and the hatch lock into an open position. After all this work, Tryam did not want to settle for just a peek, so he climbed up to the roof. To keep the sounds of the winds from disturbing his companions, he closed the hatch, using a bronze ring attached to its top.

The snow swirled, and the wind raged around him, but the high, crenellated walls blocked most of the storm's ferocity. In the center of the roof, taking up a sizable portion of the floor space, was a giant cauldron. Unlike in his dream, the bowl was ceramic rather than bronze, and it contained only ice and snow rather than a golden flame. Tryam walked to the north and looked out, but he could not see very far into the darkness and the storm. He remembered his dream of the golden statues and examined the four corners. He was disappointed to find no trace that they had ever existed outside of his vision.

The young acolyte checked the view from all sides of the tower; the result was the same: nothing but snow and black sky.

Feeling a sense of unease about the place, Tryam dropped to his knees, closed his eyes, and recited the Warding Prayer. It was not long before he settled into a state of calm, and the words of the prayer became more than just memorized text but an embodiment of the power of faith. When he reached a point where all his anxieties and doubts faded away, an unexplainable force urged him to open his eyes. When he did, movement drew his attention. Tryam hurried to his feet as a figure was emerging from the hatch.

The shadowy form had no physical substance, but it mimed opening the portal. The figure was clad in shimmering spectral armor in the style of ancient warriors. A second ghostly figure followed, this one carrying a large spectral amphora. The second spirit handed the heavy burden to the first apparition and then, after stepping through the hatch, stood with his companion atop the roof.

The two, holding the amphora between them, walked to the ceramic cauldron. Together they emptied its contents. Tryam was sure he smelled fuel oil, though he saw nothing material pour from the vessel. The two spirits then turned from the cauldron and walked back to the hatch. Before disappearing down the steps, one warrior turned to Tryam and beckoned him to follow. The young acolyte's heart raced as he recalled the incident under the crypts. He swallowed hard and inched his way to the hatch, but he stopped and waited until the two spirit knights disappeared below.

"This is not happening," he uttered under his breath. "This is not real."

Tryam closed his eyes, shook his head, then opened his eyes again. His sense of peace was gone, and the sounds of the storm had returned.

He ran to the hatch and pulled on the bronze ring. He descended the steps and closed the hatch behind him. He was fast enough to observe the spectral knights making for the stairwell down to the floor below where his companions slept. The ice clogging those stairs was no obstacle for the spirits. Tryam waited until the knights faded from view before moving forward to investigate. He walked to the stairwell, put his own feet on the ice, and tested its strength. To mortal men, it was hopelessly blocked.

He sensed no malevolence from the apparitions, only a compulsion that he must follow. He had to alert the others, who had remained asleep and unaware.

"Wake up, everybody. Wake up!"

Wulfric was the first to respond. The Ulf leapt to his feet, his sword in hand. Kayen was not far behind, his shepherd's staff at his side. They both wore quizzical looks.

Telvar, however, looked irritated and lazily rolled onto his back. When he saw nothing out of the ordinary, he sighed. "What is the matter now? Did our young acolyte see a creepy-crawly?"

"Sorry, master wizard, but your slumber must wait." Tryam took a deep breath and attempted to remove the excitement from his voice. "I saw two spirits."

Telvar groaned and let out another sigh. "Not this again. This place is *not* haunted. Just ask the missionary."

"Before this missionary passes judgment, he would like to hear what happened," said Kayen. "Go ahead, Tryam. Tell us what you saw."

Tryam related the story of the spectral knights to his companions. Wulfric shook his head knowingly. "Then my clan was right. This place *is* haunted!"

"Yes, but why?" pondered Kayen. "Spirits linger on this realm only when there is a reason." He stroked his graying beard. "It must mean something."

"They wanted me to follow," lamented Tryam, "but I see no way I can."

The wizard rushed to his feet and wrapped his thick black robes around him. "Has everyone gone mad? What good can come from following the dead? For what purpose can this be but to disturb and anger whatever is hidden below? Such folly!"

"Don't listen to the wizard," injected Wulfric. "I shall find a way through the ice."

The big Ulf shouldered his way past Telvar and stormed to the stairwell. He began chopping at the ice with the pommel of his sword.

"We should make an attempt," said Kayen, giving his blessing to the effort. He added the butt of his staff while Tryam used a sharp stick.

The three tried as hard as they could, but progress was slow going. The wizard held his hands to his head as would one suffering from a strong headache. "As much as I would love to listen to this racket for the next two weeks, may I suggest an alternative that would quicken the process?"

Tryam exchanged quizzical looks with his companions.

Telvar pointed to the staff he held in his hand. Tryam had attempted to inspect the staff before, but the wizard had always been protective of it. In the light of the fire, the staff appeared to be made from a dark metal. Iron clamps held a clear gem at the staff's tip. He was disappointed in how plain it appeared to be.

"I can summon fire, remember?" snapped Telvar. "Fire melts ice."

"By all means," Kayen said, ignoring the mage's condescension. "Let the wizard do his work."

"Stand aside, let me pass, let me pass," said Telvar as he walked to the stairwell and nudged Wulfric out of the way.

Foreign words escaped from the young mage's mouth—multisyllabic phrases that disappeared from Tryam's memory as quickly as he heard them. Father Monbatten had preached against the use of magic and had good arguments: The Ancients had been destroyed because of the conflict between wizards, Aten, and the Abyss. Still, magic intrigued Tryam.

The gem at the tip of Telvar's staff glowed red. The wizard seemed pleased and thrust the quarterstaff, gem first, into the ice. A red fog filled the air as the snow and ice that had blocked the stairwell for centuries began to disappear in a matter of minutes. When the gem's glow began to lessen, the wizard uttered more magical words, and the gem grew bright again.

After the stairwell was clear, the wizard wiped his brow with his robes, his eyes lit with satisfaction. "Now you can go down there and get yourselves killed by whatever unholy monsters we have just disturbed."

Kayen grabbed a piece of burning timber from the campfire and carried it like a torch. "We shall proceed with caution, young man. In any event, you and Wulfric should stay here. If something unfortunate were to happen, it would not be wise for all of us to be trapped below."

Wulfric protested with a scowl, but Telvar seemed relieved.

"You truly believe there is something to this besides a young acolyte's overactive imagination?" queried Telvar.

"I do," said Kayen. Without further discussion, with torch in one hand, staff in the other, he made his way down the damp steps. Tryam followed closely behind, unafraid and incredibly curious.

The orange glow of the torch reflected off ice crystals that floated in the air. Frost covered everything on this new level, which included long rectangular tables, a desk, and a row of barracks-style bunk beds. Circular windows in the middle of each of the four walls, which once must have offered a spectacular view of the surrounding area, were now blocked by solid plugs of ice. Tryam coughed as frigid air filled his lungs. It had been many years since people had disturbed this area. There was no sign of the ghostly knights, but there were more stairs leading down.

"Do you see them?" asked Kayen.

"No. But I would like to spend a moment here."

Tryam ran his hands over the moldy blankets and looked under the bunk beds. At the desk, he cracked the frost from the drawers and opened them to see what was inside. He found frozen quills and warped parchment with illegible text; however, from inside the bottom drawer, he pulled out a piece of jewelry. Tryam held it to the light of Kayen's torch. It was a silver locket on a silver chain. He pried open the small trinket, which resembled a sea shell. On the inside of one half was a painting of a beautiful young woman with raven hair; an inscription in the old tongue was written on the other half. At Kayen's prodding, he read the words aloud: "'Though on the Frontier, I am happy, as I know my heart remains with you.'"

"There is no doubting your mastery of the ancient languages, but there is naught here but sad relics. We must keep going," urged Kayen.

Tryam returned the locket to where he had found it, reflecting on the souls that undoubtedly had passed into Aten's grace centuries before.

The stairs to the next level were fortunately free of ice; however, the effect of the crushing snow around the structure was starting to show: The walls bowed slightly inward, and loose plaster from the ceiling littered the ground. As Kayen spread the light from his torch around this new floor, Tryam noted a large table in the center, surrounded by high-backed chairs. The furniture looked reasonably preserved. On the walls, worn tapestries clung loosely from brass bars.

"This must have been the muster room," observed Kayen. "Too bad these tapestries are moldy and faded, for they appear to be maps of the surrounding area. Tryam, do you sense anything?"

Tryam closed his eyes, then reopened them after reciting the first stanza of the Warding Prayer. "We must continue down," he reported.

Kayen nodded.

The original ground floor was in far worse condition than the other levels. The stairs leading down into the room were choked with stones, which Kayen had difficulty getting past. A great brass door, which had been the tower's true entrance, was lying on the ground crumpled, as if it had been kicked in by a giant; it was half buried beneath an avalanche of dirt and ice. The air was colder, the chamber, claustrophobic. Tryam lent a hand to Kayen as they walked through the clutter.

When Tryam turned his head to scan a dark corner, a cold rush went down his spine: A spectral knight was motioning him to follow.

"A spirit is here," he whispered. His words were almost lost in the confined space.

Kayen waved the torch about. "I cannot see him. Tell me what is happening."

"He is beckoning me down to the cellar. Now he descends below! We may have to move stones to follow."

The two men stepped over the debris to the blocked steps. Kayen wedged his torch in a crack in the wall, and the two worked to clear the way down. After they toiled till near exhaustion, the path was finally free.

"I believe you alone must follow," said Kayen, wiping sweat from his brow.

Tryam wanted to disagree but could not. Alone, he went down into the gloom.

The stairs were wooden but still in reasonably good order; the only menace were large cobwebs that had grown during the centuries since any living thing had crossed the basement's threshold. Light from Kayen's burning timber ended at the base of the steps, but the young acolyte did not need the torch to see where he was meant to go.

The cellar was twice the size of the other floors and in almost pristine condition. The entire underground had been dug from bedrock; both floor and walls were hardened stone. When Tryam stepped past the pool of torchlight, he saw the first spectral knight. The spirit stood before a stack of oil-filled amphorae. The knight's companion was beside him, an empty vessel in his hands.

To Tryam's shock, the beckoning spirit spoke: "Theragaard, we have been loyal servants—lo, these many years. We have kept faithful watch to make sure these lands were protected from the dark. Is it not time that we join our brothers in never-ending sleep?"

The spectral knight removed his helmet and, with the aid of his companion, lay down on the ground, propping his back wearily against the wall. Both knights looked to be aging a year for every moment that now passed. The once-vigorous knight Tryam had seen atop the tower was now a dying old man. He spoke again: "Do I have your blessing, sir?"

The young acolyte had neither the heart to tell the spirit he was not Theragaard nor the courage to ask why the spirits had showed themselves to him. Tryam knelt beside the man. "You have been a faithful and loyal warrior. Yes, you may rest. The both of you."

The spirit reached up to grab Tryam's hand, but the spectral appendage had no substance. "Thank you, sir. It was our honor to serve by your side. We shall now take our leave and enter the final sleep."

With that, the spirit's eyes closed, and the shimmering light that had illuminated the ethereal body faded away. After a moment all that remained was dust. His companion saluted Tryam before he too joined his companion in a final death.

Tryam wiped a tear from his eye as he pondered the bond these warriors had with their commander. He also wept as, once again, fear had overridden his faith. *I wasted the time I had with the spirits.*

Now in complete darkness, Tryam called up to Kayen. "It is done. You may come down."

The orange glow of the torch gradually filled the basement. Tryam gathered the knights' ashes and placed them in a battered ancient helmet he found nearby. When Kayen reached his side, he explained what had occurred. "These two men's loyalty to their commander would not permit themselves to leave this world." Tryam rose to his feet. "Brother Kayen, they mistook me for their commander, a man named Theragaard. Could that be the same Theragaard whom I have read about in ancient history books, the great paladin? His name was also whispered to me in the vaults."

"Almost certainly. Theragaard was tasked to hunt down the last rogue archmagus."

THE TOMB OF THERAGAARD

"Antigenesus!" jumped in Tryam. "The same wizard who Telvar said created the Golem we discovered!"

"Exactly. When the Order of Saint Paxia arrived in Arkos, they destroyed all evidence of Theragaard's existence, and in their fanatical devotion to peace, they destroyed all that remained of his castle." The missionary stroked his beard. "These men"—he indicated the remains Tryam now held in his hands—"lingered for a specific purpose. It was not simply loyalty to their long-dead commander. They knew that the shadow of Antigenesus would darken Medias again."

Kayen's words caused Tryam to shudder. "Brother, let us find a better place for these men to rest."

"As Aten would have it," said Kayen, nodding.

Tryam located a secluded alcove near the stairs and placed the ash-filled helmet inside. Kayen knelt before the alcove, drew out his cross, and said a prayer over their remains for a safe journey to Aten's embrace.

"Now they are free," concluded Kayen.

The young acolyte looked about the dark cellar, and he thought of the events that had led him there. "Although I failed to ask these men their purpose in contacting me, I can't help but feel there is something else I was meant to discover. Something more tangible."

"That may be," agreed Kayen. "Let us examine this place."

Dusty shelves, barrels, overflowing racks, and assorted boxes made the cellar a labyrinth. As they explored the room, they discovered enough supplies to equip a company of men. Tryam was astounded. "Look at all these weapons. I see arrows, spears, swords, poleaxes. Unbelievable!"

"Interesting," said Kayen, dusting off a throwing axe. "We—"

The sound of Wulfric shouting from above interrupted Kayen's next thought. "Ragnar men are approaching!" the Ulf warned.

Kayen and Tryam exchanged shocked expressions.

"Go. You're faster than I." Kayen handed Tryam the burning timber, now almost reduced to an ember. "I can use my cross to light my way back."

Heart pounding in his chest, Tryam met Wulfric in the muster room. Wulfric held his own torch, his face grim. Telvar was by his side, with a frown and furrowed brow.

"Brother Kayen is coming," said Tryam. "What is the matter?"

"Come to the top floor," said Wulfric. "You need to see this."

The Ulf led Tryam to the roof. Outside, the storm had subsided, and the sky had brightened with the early light of dawn. Wulfric pointed straight out to the north. "Look there, where the base of that mountain meets the highlands."

Tryam placed his hand over his eyes and looked toward the snow-covered, rolling hills. Contrasting with the white of the ground was a line of dark-armored men. They moved surprisingly swiftly, given the snow they had to trudge through. The men were advancing toward the tower without varying from their path. Tryam counted an even dozen. "Ragnar? Are you sure?"

"Yes, they wear greenish armor, and I can see the sigil of the grasping fist. At their current pace, they will reach the tower in about an hour."

"How did they find us?"

"Does it matter?" the wizard interrupted, gesturing wildly with his staff. "We have to leave now. Our only hope is to outrun them!"

Wulfric grasped the pommel of his sword and leaned into the wizard's face. "We cannot hope to outrun a war party of Ragnar unless you can cast a spell that will sprout us wings."

The two exchanged curses and insults as they debated the best course of action, but the path given to Tryam from Aten was clear. "Wait! Listen!" The young acolyte had to yell to get their attention. "I discovered something down below."

The wizard leaned on his staff and rolled his eyes. "A ghost army, perhaps?"

"Not an army but an armory. In the basement there are arrows, spears, throwing axes, even oil. I was led by spirits to that spot so we could make use of these ancient supplies. Aten is with us!"

"I'd prefer Aten take a sword and stand beside us," snapped Telvar, but he paused for a moment and added in a more reasonable tone, "You said oil?"

"Yes, oil—and lots of weapons. Follow me!"

Tryam took the lead and started back down the beacon tower but stopped when they met Kayen on the way up. He filled Kayen in on the situation with the Ragnar.

As everyone talked over one another, the missionary raised his hands. "Gather round. Let us discuss how best to defend ourselves. We must not waste the time we have."

They decided to assemble in the muster room. Telvar used his magic to ignite an oil lamp that hung down from the ceiling, breathing life into the ghostly place. The four men each took a seat at the table.

THE TOMB OF THERAGAARD

After a few suggestions from Wulfric to bring the battle to the Ragnar, the wizard rose from his chair and paced the room. Sweat poured down his face. "Perhaps I can scare off these barbarians. They would be fools to assault a mage from Engoth! These northern brutes are a superstitious lot; they would most likely flee from the simplest cantrip."

With a red face and bulging neck veins, Wulfric countered in an exaggeratedly calm voice. "They are in league with a wizard, one much more powerful than you, and they have sent a Daemon after us already. They are very determined to kill us or anyone who stands in their way, and they will not be deterred by your simple tricks!"

The wizard ran his hands through his hair. "A bloodthirsty war party, an ancient Golem, a rogue wizard, and now a Daemon? What have I stumbled into?"

"*We* defeated the Daemon," returned Wulfric, "and *we* shall defeat the Ragnar."

Kayen cleared his throat, and all discussion ceased. "Being inside this tower, we hold the advantage, even though we are outnumbered three to one. However, if the Ragnar break through the breach, there is no way we can fight them all off."

Wulfric pounded the table, and a smile appeared on his face. "We can fortify the barricade we already have in place. When they break through, which they will eventually, Tryam and I shall skewer those who make the attempt."

The wizard sat back in his chair and steepled his fingers. He was ready to compromise, and he added to the battle plan. "While you two delay them from below, I shall harass them from above. With the help of the oil Tryam found, I intend to give them a warm reception. I shall require your help, Brother Kayen."

They went over the details in haste and soon went about their assigned tasks. Tryam and Wulfric made multiple trips from the basement to the breach room, carrying as many items as they could in overflowing arms, Telvar returned to studying his spell book and inspecting the gem on the tip of his quarterstaff, and Kayen organized the supplies and prayed for their success.

When they were finished, the Ragnar were almost upon them.

Tryam, dripping with sweat, leaned against the newly fortified breach, and caught his breath. They had done all they could to prepare, but would it be enough? he wondered.

Chapter 53

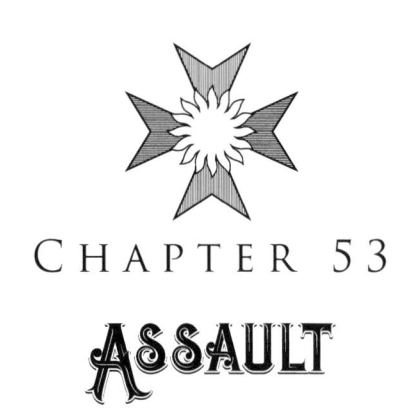

Assault

From atop the beacon tower, Wulfric watched three men separate from the Ragnar war party. The young Ulf, hungry for revenge, alerted Kayen and Telvar. "I think they mean to parley, or perhaps they wish to see who and how many of us we are. Either way, this shall not take too long. Prepare yourself."

Wulfric was in no mood for words. He hefted an ancient throwing spear, recovered from the cellar, and threw it at the approaching warriors' feet. The men wisely halted their advance. When one of them spoke, Wulfric recognized the voice as that of Crayvor, the son of the coward Ivor. Rage simmered inside the brooding Ulf.

"Has the snow blinded me, or is that Alric's pup, Wulfric? I did not expect our network of scouts to ensnare the Ulf jarl's son!" Crayvor laughed in what appeared to be genuine surprise. "I was not at the battle that saw your village destroyed, but I'd assumed the Alric line was dead. This is a fortunate day, for soon you shall join your father and the rest of Clan Ulf in the gray afterlife. Had you been wise, though, you would have fled from here and put all thoughts of kin and clan behind you."

"Crayvor, you cur, I am a pup no longer. I wear the pelt of a Hound of Fenrir and shall soon have your hide as well!" Wulfric stepped to the ramparts to reveal the fur-hide pelt.

"Brave words from someone who hides atop a tower! Are others with you as well? If I were a betting man, I would say you cower with the two others who skulked about my village and spied upon our God. If you surrender yourself, I shall let them live as slaves of the Ragnar. If you resist, they will be tortured before your eyes, their suffering on your conscience."

THE TOMB OF THERAGAARD

"Your words mean nothing," answered Wulfric. "If you wish blood to be shed, let's have at it, but it will be your blood staining the snow red, not ours!"

"Don't you understand? All is lost. Your village is ash, your clan is dead, while our God lives!"

Wulfric had said all he had wanted to say. *They will learn how far these ancient weapons can fly!*

The enraged Ulf grabbed another spear and hurled it at Crayvor's head, then threw two more in quick succession, one for each of Crayvor's companions.

The Ragnar jarl's son easily used his sword to deflect the projectile, but the others were not as quick as their leader. Both of Crayvor's henchmen cried out in agony as they fountained blood from wounds that left them dying in the snow.

Crayvor cursed, then hurled another challenge to Wulfric—this time for single combat. Wulfric ignored the Ragnar man's offer and spoke to his two companions on the roof. "We are done talking. I go to defend the breach. Harry them from above for as long as you can!"

✠ ✠ ✠

Tryam prayed to Aten as he knelt before the barricade. He stood when he heard the parley between the war party and Wulfric through the boards covering the breach. The young acolyte took a deep breath as he awaited the battle to start. He did not have to wait long. The wails of two dying Ragnar preceded the sound of Wulfric's hurried steps coming down from above. He looked at his friend for leadership, but at the moment, Wulfric was focused only on vengeance.

✠ ✠ ✠

"Help me with the oil!"

Kayen had to shout to get the young wizard's attention. The missionary had known a few wizards in his life and recognized the band around Telvar's head as that of a Rutilus, or the Red, the first stage in a wizard's career. Kayen was impressed with the dark-haired mage's confidence, but it was obvious the young man had yet to face the horrors of combat. *Aten, help us!*

"Yes, of course."

The wizard awkwardly grabbed the opposite handle of the amphora and helped the missionary drag it to where the others had been set, along the back of the south-facing battlement. Exhausted from their work before the battle, the two men now assessed the weapons they had placed in the cauldron. Kayen selected two spears, while the wizard eschewed the heavy projectiles and instead produced, from his robes, three throwing daggers—expensive ones, which he had made clear he intended to retrieve once the battle was over.

"They will be upon us before too long," urged Kayen. "We have to act quickly." He strode to the north wall and peered out from behind the battlements. "The Ragnar have spread out. They are trying to encircle the tower! Attack!"

The novice mage readied a dagger, but he was hesitant to move close enough to the wall to get an enemy in sight. Kayen remembered his own first taste of combat nearly twenty years earlier, and he understood the fear.

Holding a spear as Wulfric had instructed, the missionary walked to the west wall and took aim at an eager warrior who had bolted ahead of his comrades. With a grunt, Kayen hurled the projectile over the battlements at the attacker below. He missed badly. Taking his second spear, he took more time to aim. The throw was truer but without effect; the projectile deflected off the man's armor.

Where is our wizard?

After an encouraging wave from Kayen, Telvar edged his way to the battlements. The wizard took aim and threw his three daggers in quick succession. He was surprisingly accurate, but only one of the three struck exposed flesh; the other two clanked off the man's green-tinted armor.

"Damn!" Telvar cursed as the wounded Ragnar continued onward. "The thickheaded Berserker should be up here throwing the spears and axes."

"He defends the breach! And now is not the time to argue battle plans!"

Kayen returned to the cauldron to rearm but was stopped by the sound of metal on stone. He looked around. The reasoning of the Ragnar for encircling the tower became clear when the missionary saw grappling hooks collide with the top of the crenellations. He abandoned the weapons cache and focused on the amphorae. "Now is the time for the oil!"

Together, the two grabbed a container of oil and dragged it to the east, where a hook, trailing a thick rope, had already been secured into the stone. Without aiming, the two overturned the vessel, and the oil poured down the side of the tower. Curses from below indicated that they had hit their mark.

"Out of the way," commanded the wizard, who now had his staff at the ready.

Words of magic came from the young man's mouth, and the gem on the top of his staff glowed red. Telvar leaned over the wall and angled the staff down. Kayen stood beside him to observe. Another phrase of magic sent a burst of fire from the staff toward the oil-soaked Ragnar below. Kayen cringed when the man, just getting ready to climb up, burst into flames like a struck matchhead. The desperate man beat at the fire but was cooked inside his green armor. The other Ragnar backed away from the wall.

Telvar was pleased with his spell and taunted them. "I breathe fire as a dragon! Assail us, and feel the heat of hell upon you!"

Kayen grabbed Telvar's sleeve and pulled him away from the wall. "Save your energy. Your taunts will not deter them. See, more advance upon us! We must defend the west wall at once!"

The two struggled to move another vessel into position, nearly spilling the load before balancing it on the wall. Telvar let out a shout as a Ragnar warrior's hand gained purchase on the crenellation before them.

"Hurry!" implored Kayen. "Get into position."

The wizard wiped sweat from his brow, then moved to help Kayen tilt the amphora. Half of its contents poured onto the climbing Ragnar, but the agile man jumped over the wall and knocked the container to the ground, shattering the clay vessel and spilling the rest of its contents. The warrior unsheathed his sword and grinned like a man presented with a plate of freshly prepared meat.

Kayen prepared to step in front of the wizard, but before he could move, Telvar took aim with his staff and unleashed another stream of fire. Kayen barely had time to get out of the way before flames engulfed the Ragnar attacker.

Any taunts Telvar had ready for the doomed man were stuck in his throat, because the Ragnar warrior stumbled forward, despite the flames, and lunged his sword at the wizard's head. Kayen reacted swiftly and struck the sword out of the man's hand with his shepherd's staff. He followed that assault with a crack to the back of the man's head. The Ragnar's burning body fell lifeless to the ground.

"I count that kill as mine," said Telvar between gasps.

"Step away!" warned Kayen, ignoring the boast. "Unless you want to join him in the afterlife."

Flames spread from the dead Ragnar to the spilt oil. Telvar seemed oblivious to the danger about him. "Move back," warned Kayen again, pushing Telvar out of the pool of oil in which he stood. He then yelled into the stunned wizard's ears. "The fire hastens our plans. I estimate we have time for one more go-round before we must retreat down the hatch."

Telvar nodded.

The two lifted an amphora and dragged it up to another crenellation. Kayen scanned below, where he observed three Ragnar readying to throw a hook.

With the wizard's help, they moved the amphora into position and poured out the vessel's contents. Below, thick oil drenched one Ragnar, but his companions escaped untouched. Telvar, his energy apparently flagging, had to concentrate a moment before he blasted more fire from his staff. When he did, the oil-slicked Ragnar, like the two others before him, was quickly consumed by the fuel oil and magic.

"Three down," boasted Telvar with restored confidence.

"This is no game," scolded Kayen, now worrying that the young wizard might become too cavalier. "The situation is most dire. Look, two more hooks have made purchase behind us!"

✠ ✠ ✠

Tryam ignored the sounds of combat coming from the roof and watched with alarm as the Ragnar hacked away at the wooden barricade before him with surprising ease. Wulfric slapped him on the back and handed him a poleaxe. When gray light filtered through the breach, the Ulf smiled confidently and said, "It is almost time."

The two stood on opposite sides of the breach. Screams of agony and the smell of burning flesh drifted down from above and made Tryam dreadfully aware that death had already made its presence known.

When a Ragnar's head flashed through a hole in the barricade, Tryam was so startled that he hesitated and missed his opportunity to strike. The young acolyte cursed and grasped the awkwardly long poleaxe tighter in his hands. Wulfric grimaced at the lapse but followed it with an encouraging smile. "Remember," reminded the Ulf, "this is for Kara."

THE TOMB OF THERAGAARD

A voice from outside asked for a volunteer to crash into the barricade. Another voice replied with the eagerness of a guileless youth. Shortly thereafter, the timbers shook from a colossal impact. The Ragnar warrior recklessly charged into the barrier, but in the process, he caught his armor in the splintered wood. Tryam could see the horror in the Ragnar's eyes as he struggled to free himself. The young acolyte was closer to the man than Wulfric was. He took aim at the man's head and then struck. Mercifully, the spiked end of the brutal poleaxe ended the Ragnar's life quickly. Wulfric, with no joy in his eyes, nodded his approval.

Outside, the command came for another volunteer. A larger Ragnar charged the barricade, this time shield first. More sections of wood came loose, but this Ragnar's fate matched that of the earlier volunteer as Wulfric thrust his weapon straight through the man's shield and impaled the stunned warrior through his chest. The Ragnar's companions ripped his body away.

Wulfric spat in disgust. "Crayvor, you coward. We have sent two Ragnar to the Abyss. Why do you send others to do your work? Show your face, and let's see if your mountain god can save you from my wrath!"

✠ ✠ ✠

We are trapped!

"Aten, preserve us," uttered Kayen under his breath.

The oil from the spilled amphora had spread to the oil containers stacked along the south wall, igniting a bright hot inferno. Kayen attempted to lead Telvar to the hatch, but a Ragnar warrior, who had mounted the west wall, now stood between them and their only way of escape.

Kayen, staff before him, stood his ground and tried to get Telvar to join in a unified front. The wizard had inhaled too much smoke, however, and was struggling to remain conscious.

Perhaps fearing that the flames might do in his adversaries before he could prove his mettle, the Ragnar brute attacked. He slashed at the wizard with his sword and made contact with his shoulder. Telvar let out an anguished howl as he crumpled to the ground. Kayen stood over the wizard and answered the blow with a powerful strike of his walking staff to the aggressive Ragnar's head. He watched in satisfaction as the man staggered back. *I will be hard pressed to defend Telvar and myself.* A curse came to his lips, followed by a prayer.

✠ ✠ ✠

Wulfric intensified his verbal assault on Crayvor. "Come on, coward! My steel awaits you!"

Tryam, in a moment of madness, almost wished the Ragnar would break through the breach so that combat could begin and he could unleash his nervous energy. A cry of pain from the top of the tower stopped those thoughts.

"That sounded like the wizard," said Wulfric grimly. "They need help. Go to them. I shall hold the breach. I shall stay and fight Crayvor!"

"Are you sure this is wise?"

The Ulf nodded his head.

Tryam dropped his poleaxe in favor of a short sword, then dashed up the stairs and to the hatch. When he stepped onto the roof, an unexpected blast of heat nearly fried his eyebrows off. He coughed and waved his hands in front of his face to see through the thick smoke.

This was not part of the plan. There should be no flames atop the tower!

He focused his eyes through the haze and saw the back of a Ragnar man. The warrior was striking at Kayen, who was on his knees using his staff as a shield. Beside Kayen was the fallen wizard, injured but alive.

"Ragnar, you coward!" Tryam taunted. "Over here!"

The Ragnar turned and slashed at him in whip-like fashion. Tryam parried the blow, but the impact caused him to stumble back and almost fall down the open hatch. He had never seen an opponent react so quickly.

A glance toward Kayen and the fallen mage showed that the missionary had taken advantage of Tryam's distraction to attend to Telvar. Kayen held the cross of Aten to the wizard's injured shoulder, and a faint blue light emitted from the cross.

Instead of fighting, Tryam concentrated on blocking the raging Ragnar's blows as he maneuvered himself toward the others. It was a desperate gambit he hoped would pay off.

✠ ✠ ✠

Wulfric tossed aside his poleaxe and brandished his new weapon: a stout short sword designed to kill in close quarters. It was ancient, perhaps older than the tower itself, but it was free of rust or nicks, light of weight, and deadly sharp. Meanwhile, a flurry of axe strikes from the Ragnar had destroyed the rest of the barricade. Wulfric stepped away from the flying splinters and tested his sword's balance. When the breach was wide enough, two Ragnar men stepped through. The invaders wore greenish black armor and had murder in their eyes.

A third Ragnar entered. It was Crayvor. The coward smiled upon seeing Wulfric surrounded. The smile was not of a Berserker who understood the honor of combat but that of a jackal hoping to feast on the dead.

✠ ✠ ✠

Time and again, the large Ragnar warrior came at Tryam, but the young acolyte's defensive posture frustrated the veteran attacker, whose strikes were getting ever more reckless as, step by step, Tryam maneuvered toward his two companions.

Once Tryam was close enough to see Kayen through the swirling smoke, he launched his first counterattack, using all his pent-up nervous energy in the stab. The blow forced the Ragnar to stumble into the beacon tower's cauldron. Tryam quickly followed up with a thrust aimed at the man's back, but the blade deflected off the Ragnar's green-black armor. He would have to aim his next stab more carefully.

As the invader stumbled back to his feet, Kayen gestured wildly and pointed. "Another warrior has scaled the wall!"

Doom appears to be closing in from all sides.

✠ ✠ ✠

"Only three versus one? You will need more men than that to slay me," mocked Wulfric. "You Ragnar are thin-blooded and weak-spined!" The Ulf warrior gripped his sword in his right hand and palmed a dagger in his left. He spoke to Crayvor's henchmen. "Which one of you curs wants to die first?"

One warrior stepped forward and proclaimed, "I want the honor of slaying this whelp of a jarl who hid in the mountains as his clan was destroyed!"

"So be it," answered Wulfric and with that flung the hidden dagger at the brazen Ragnar. The dagger sank deep into the man's throat, silencing him forever.

Wulfric did not wait to see the man die but turned and slashed at the other scout, pushing him against the wall and knocking the man's helmet off.

In a surge of Berserker strength, Wulfric grabbed the stunned Ragnar and threw him to the ground. Wulfric used the pommel of his sword to brain the dazed Ragnar. Thoughts of his burnt village fueled his rage.

"Impressive," admitted Crayvor from the shadows. "You possess some of your father's skills."

Panting and with blood dripping down his Fenrir pelt, Wulfric looked like the primeval Daemon wolf whose hide he wore. As he rose from the slain Ragnar's body, he glowered at Crayvor.

The Ragnar jarl's son responded by drawing a second gleaming metal blade. He glared back at Wulfric. "And now it is one warrior versus another. I cannot help but think I look upon the last of a kind."

"If I die, I die as my ancestors died before me: in honorable combat." Wulfric leveled his sword and beckoned Crayvor toward the center of the room.

Crayvor obliged and lunged at Wulfric with his two gleaming green metal weapons.

✠ ✠ ✠

Defeating two enemies at once required more practice and skill than Tryam possessed, particularly since he lacked a shield or a second weapon. Fortunately, the close quarters—the fire on one side, the cauldron in the center, and the nearby wall—prevented both of the Ragnar warriors from attacking simultaneously. Nonetheless, Tryam was losing ground as the two Ragnar took turns to attack. He also had to be careful, for he was only a step away from tripping over his companions.

"Move out of the way, you oaf!"

The irritated voice came from Telvar. Tryam was pleased to hear the young wizard's voice despite its tone and their circumstances. He had only a moment to move before the sound of rushing air and the feeling of a chilling blast of cold raced by his ear. A groan from the lead Ragnar followed Telvar's spell as ice formed over the man's hand and he dropped his sword.

The wizard can summon ice as well as fire?

Kayen followed the spell with a crack of his staff on the stunned Ragnar's jaw. The man wobbled woozily. Tryam's sword struck the man's

THE TOMB OF THERAGAARD

frozen wrist, which shattered like broken glass. Kayen finished off the Ragnar with a crack against his skull, giving him a swift death.

The wizard was now on his feet, the crystal on his staff glowed ice blue. "I count that kill as mine! That makes four."

✠ ✠ ✠

Wulfric stalked Crayvor around the campfire. The young Ulf's pent-up rage had been unleashed on the first two Ragnar, but his desire for vengeance for his father, for Kara, and for his people still smoldered. "Your death shall be quick, but your worthless soul shall suffer for eternity." The words came out like a growl from Wulfric's mouth.

Crayvor laughed. "Your death shall be anything but quick. I shall make a spectacle of you."

Wulfric jumped the campfire and slashed at Crayvor. The Ragnar used both of his blades to block Wulfric's attack, and they crashed into the wall from the force of the impact.

The two sons of jarls traded sword strikes that would shatter lesser men's bones. Slashes were met by parries, which forced counterattacks answered with deadly thrusts. The two were equally skilled with the blade, the battle saw no one gaining an advantage, and little damage was inflicted.

If I can't take him with steel, I shall take him down with my thews!

Wulfric dropped his sword and grabbed Crayvor's wrists. Wulfric's strength overwhelmed Crayvor, forcing the Ragnar man to release his coronium blades.

Now weaponless, both men reached for each other's throats before rolling onto the ground. Veins bulged in necks and threatened to burst as they fought to get each other in a death grip. Wulfric sensed the campfire nearby and rolled Crayvor toward it. The flames flared high, and Crayvor screamed in agony when they licked his clothing. Crayvor, however, broke free and scrambled to his feet.

"Harag, Jarth, Athal!" The desperate Crayvor howled to the heavens as would a wolf calling for its pack. When no one answered his cry, Crayvor made a dash for his weapons. Wulfric anticipated the move and pounced on the Ragnar's back. When Wulfric flipped Crayvor over, the man's eyes had a look of panic—darting back and forth for help that was likely too late to matter.

Wulfric seized Crayvor's throat with his two mighty hands and squeezed with all of his strength. Crayvor's face turned red, then blue.

As scenes of his burnt village replayed in his mind, Wulfric continued to squeeze.

Crayvor's struggling arms grew weaker.

☩ ☩ ☩

The heat from the burning oil had cracked the stones under the cauldron, and now the top floor of the tower was buckling. Oblivious to the raging fire, the lone Ragnar kept up his assault.

Perhaps thinking the older monk the quickest to eliminate, the warrior made a jab at Kayen's midsection. Tryam could see the sword pierce the missionary's robes but not his flesh. Kayen used the miss to hook the man around the neck with his staff. With the Ragnar hooked and unable to defend himself, Tryam thrust his sword under the man's breastplate and deep into his torso. The warrior unhooked Kayen's staff and jumped back, the sword still in his belly. He staggered and fell into the flames, clutching at Tryam's sword. He died in the inferno.

"We must be away!" shouted Kayen over the flames. "The fire advances!"

Tryam looked through the haze of smoke and fire for other Ragnar but saw none. The heat was so intense he smelled the hair on his head burning. It was time to abandon their position and retreat to the breach level. "It looks clear. Let's hurry. Wulfric needs our help."

After Tryam retrieved his sword from the burning man's corpse, the wizard remarked, "Well aimed. That kill counts for you."

"Aye," lamented Tryam.

Over Kayen's objections, the young acolyte insisted on being the first to descend the hatch. He did not know if Wulfric still lived or how many of the Ragnar had breached the barricade. The only way he knew how to prepare himself was with another prayer.

After he descended the steps, it took a while for Tryam's eyes to adjust to the change of light level. When they did, the young acolyte was momentarily paralyzed with shock. Two Ragnar men lay dead in pools of blood on either side of the scattered campfire. A third man looked to be under attack by a white wolf. Tryam was poised to strike before he realized the beast was merely Wulfric's bulk under the Fenrir pelt. The Ulf's hands were about the supine man's neck. The Ragnar's face was blue, his body motionless.

"Wulf, the man is dead," said Tryam, afraid to interrupt yet knowing he must.

After a long moment, Wulfric finally acknowledged his presence. The Ulf relaxed his grip and stood up. "He was no man. He was Crayvor, the son of the coward Ivor." Wulfric wiped his hands on his tunic. "My father will rest easier," he stated flatly, "but we have a lot more to do before my people are avenged."

Chapter 54
Back to the Mountain

"Crayvor is dead."

Wulfric repeated the words and then sank to his knees. Sweat soaked his hair, and his skin was unusually pale.

Tryam stepped over the corpse and helped his friend to his feet, easing Wulfric away from the gaze of Crayvor's discolored, bulging eyes. "Your father would be proud. You have honored him with your bravery."

Wulfric shook off Tryam's arm. "I am not done. I need to slay Ivor and free Kara and the rest of my people, if they still live. And then stop the mad wizard and his plans before the Ragnar enslave any other clan."

The farther Tryam led Wulfric away from Crayvor, the more his friend looked and sounded like his normal, Ulf self. Wulfric slapped Tryam on the back. "Well done, all of you. For the bravery you have shown here, you are all now honorary members of the Ulf clan. That includes you, wizard, whether you like it or not."

Kayen bowed his head and said, "I am honored."

Three sets of eyes then turned to Telvar. The wizard strutted about the room, still energized from the battle. "Thank you for the honor, I suppose. This was quite extraordinary. What brutal savages! I was almost skewered, but I kept my head and was able to best them. Perhaps I am destined to be a war mage?"

"How is your wound?" asked Tryam, hoping the memory of the injury would make the mage more appreciative of his good fortune.

The wizard leaned his staff against a wall and felt his left shoulder with his right hand. Blood stained his black robes, and a rent was torn in his otherwise undamaged clothes. As he massaged and moved his arm, he

THE TOMB OF THERAGAARD

showed no sign of pain. "My shoulder feels uninjured." The wizard retrieved his staff and addressed the cleric. "Brother Kayen, how did you do that?"

The missionary dismissed the question with a wave of his staff. "I was a battlefield surgeon for many years."

The wizard looked unsatisfied with the answer.

"Is anyone else injured?" Kayen gave Tryam and Wulfric a thorough inspection with his skilled eyes. When he detected no serious injuries, he suggested, "We should take the bodies outside, as well as any supplies we need, and do so hastily. Due to the fire damage, the ceiling may fall down."

They salvaged four sets of breastplates, and each man got one, but not before Wulfric obliterated its grasping-fist insignia. He also took possession of one of Crayvor's swords, and he placed the other coronium weapon into Tryam's hands. Tryam was amazed at the lightness of the blade. Telvar retrieved his three expensive throwing daggers from outside.

The morning spent, they used the rest of the day to eat and rest. With the help of a heavy snowfall near dusk, the fire atop the tower extinguished itself, and the black smoke that had once darkened the sky above dissipated into the night.

Kayen, Wulfric, and Tryam ventured back inside the beacon tower to inspect the structure. After they put a few fallen beams back into place, the trio were satisfied that the ceiling would not collapse, at least not this night. When the back end of the storm began to blow through, staying inside was their best bet. They agreed to set up a watch, but Telvar claimed his shoulder still needed time to heal, requiring extra sleep. No one grumbled, since the other three expected him to find an excuse.

During his shift, Tryam recited the Warding Prayer. He sensed nothing but peace. Not wanting to be idle, he cleaned up the tower, throwing the scorched and broken amphorae into the cauldron on the roof.

Before his watch ended, the storm finally passed, and the young acolyte was granted a breathtaking view of his surroundings. The stars glinted above like distant lanterns held by unseen hands, and the dark blue of the sky reminded him of the waters on the edge of the Frostfoam Sea. To the north, the peaks of the Corona Mountains were alight with the red glow of the rising sun. He could not help but be frightened by the prospect of entering their domain once again. He had survived one trip—but another? The thought of Kara trapped inside one of these stone goliaths, under the control of a mad wizard, brought him beyond angry and scared. How could

Aten allow such cruelty in a land filled with such beauty? Was the cruelty necessary to appreciate the beauty?

Near the end of his watch, Tryam descended back to the breach room and decided to cook breakfast. The smell of the food woke the others.

After the meal, Kayen said a prayer for the two loyal spirits who had guided them to the stockpile of weapons. Once finished, the party packed and headed out. Tryam believed there was more to his encounter with the spirits, but his faith was not strong enough to enable him to gather more from it.

With renewed urgency, the party of four traveled north on foot (they found that the Ragnar had slain their mounts). With his unerring sense of direction, Wulfric took the lead, while Tryam guarded the rear. Walking through the deep snow was difficult. They had to take each step with care, and the energy it cost to extract a leg from waist-high snow was great. Telvar struggled the most, and as a result, he abandoned his heavy breastplate.

Wulfric turned the party in a direction higher up the mountains, where he said the snow would not be as deep. After a half day's ascent, he was proven correct: They were able to march at a quicker pace on much firmer ground.

As they climbed into the embrace of the Coronas, the winds grew harsher, the nights colder, and the terrain more treacherous. Tryam found that at some points the ground they climbed over consisted only of snow-covered boulders. The wizard's fire skill proved lifesaving, for many times there was little or no shelter, save for a lonely pine or a small outcropping of rock.

The higher elevation afforded them a more expansive view of the north. When dawn broke, Tryam scouted ahead of the party, who were eating breakfast; he scanned the horizon for the path. When he spotted the twin-peaked mountain among the forest of tall peaks, he was so excited he startled the others by shouting, "Look, we are almost there!"

The rest of the party did not react with the same enthusiasm. Tryam was puzzled until Brother Kayen explained: "The distances and scales of the mountains deceive you. At least a week's journey lies ahead of us—if all goes well."

In the wake of the missionary's disappointing words, Tryam's excitement froze, and his head hung low at the prospect of even more days of dangerous traveling.

Wulfric slapped him on the back and offered words of encouragement. "Fear not. Nothing will stand between us and my beloved. No mountain is too far away to reach or too high to climb."

THE TOMB OF THERAGAARD

As the party hiked from ridge to ridge, they spotted numerous snowshoe prints, a sure sign that specially equipped Ragnar scouting parties were about. Wulfric speculated the men were searching for them, for more prisoners, or for Crayvor's party.

Days passed in grim, cold silence.

Wulfric reminded them that the closer to the twin-peaked mountain they journeyed, the closer they came to the valley of the Ragnar itself. Although the village was obscured from their view, signs of Ragnar ambitions were not. Streaming like insects to and from the hive, lines of men, often carrying aloft the spoils of war, headed into and out of the valley from a dozen different directions. Seeing the enormity of the Ragnar operations left a pit in the bottom of Tryam's stomach. *How can we ever hope to stop this madness?*

Once the twin-peaked mountain finally loomed over their heads like a two-headed giant, Telvar sighed in relief, and Tryam expressed gratitude that their journey was nearly over. Wulfric showed no sign of comfort, however, and was quick to remind them of the many challenges that lay ahead. "Now we make for the summit, the most difficult part of our journey. We shall approach from the face opposite the Ragnar valley. We still have three days left of climbing to endure."

Tryam prayed the weather would hold, and he praised Aten when it did. Once they reached the twin-peaked mountain's crown on the afternoon of the third day, the four weary travelers huddled under an overhanging rock and discussed the next phase of their ascent.

"Where was it you saw the entrance?" inquired the wizard.

"Just below the crater," recalled Kayen. "Between the peaks on the western side of the mountain."

The wizard stood up and looked to where Kayen had indicated; then he lay back down without saying another word. Tryam detected doubt on the face of the usually confident mage and wondered if such a young man could truly match wits with the rogue mage they pursued.

Wulfric must have seen the same doubt. "Wizard, can you get us in?"

Telvar paused a moment, then answered: "There are many intricacies involved in magic, especially magically warded doors. If you review the teachings of—"

Wulfric interrupted. "I am not interested in a treatise on magic. You have to get us inside. That is the only reason we brought you here!"

"Yes, I can open the portal!" the wizard replied with his usual bravado. "We should make our attempt at night, however, when it is easier for me to connect to the astral plane. Before I do so, I shall require rest."

At dusk, after a much longer rest than the party had been accustomed to, they began the final leg of their journey. By midnight, they had gotten within sight of the crater between the twin peaks. As before, the hikers took shelter behind a large boulder and then turned their attention to the enigmatic tunnel carved into the side of the mountain.

What they found awaiting cast doubt on their plans. Tryam was the first to speak. "There must be twenty warriors guarding the entrance. We cannot possibly get past them!"

Wulfric's face was difficult to read in the dark, but Tryam could see his friend's body tense. Turning to the wizard, the Ulf snarled, "What do we do now?"

"Fret not. I anticipated this might be the case. I hope you did not expect us to come strolling to the main door as if we were calling on a neighbor for tea. I suspect another entrance is located at the base of the mountain."

As he stood up to loom over the wizard, the Ulf's bulk blocked the sky. He pointed down the mountain. "The Ragnar village lies below. We cannot enter that way."

After his first plan had been exposed as embarrassingly unfeasible, Telvar scrambled to make up another plan that would convince the others. "Do you think that a mage such as Antigenesus would leave himself only two entrances to his complex? Look up. There are two peaks to this mountain yet to be explored."

"And?" Wulfric prodded, crossing his arms across his broad chest.

"I suggest we make our way to one peak and look for another door." Telvar stepped away from the boulder and craned his neck to examine the nearly identical mountaintops. "Which one I cannot say, but surely there must be another entrance higher up—a smaller door, long forgotten, perhaps used by the wizard to study the stars or as an escape route in dire need."

Kayen joined the mage in examining the mountain. "Without knowing for sure which peak to choose, may I suggest the one on the right? The slope is gentler and the terrain more forgiving."

"Agreed," said Telvar without hesitation.

"There is one problem with exploring either of the peaks," cautioned Wulfric. "The Ragnar have a legend of a giant winged monster that protects the mountain. This creature is said to pluck anyone who intrudes into its domain and drop him to his death in the valley below."

"Wonderful," Telvar said and then sighed. "Is there nothing in this accursed place that does not want us dead?"

Chapter 55
The Summit in Shadow

The path toward the summit was not as gentle as it had appeared from the vantage point of the crater. The slope was covered with sharp, loose stone and left no room for any false steps. Despite the danger, Tryam was exhilarated to note that they were now above the lowest-lying clouds. At this height, there was no vegetation, no signs of life, no protection from the elements.

As their guide, Wulfric found the most forgiving paths, but even then, it was very slow going. After they had walked through midday and well into evening, the Ulf ordered a halt. "Our journey has taken longer than expected. We should not venture on these dangerous slopes in the dark. I see a landing just ahead. We should chance a break."

Wulfric's suggestion was met with welcomed sighs of relief.

The wizard hastened to the ledge, unleashing a series of curses as he sat down. "Thrice I have nearly fallen to my death. A rest will enable me to restore my wits and my magic."

Tryam's hands were raw, and his body ached from the awkward positions he'd been forced to assume when climbing. He was also glad for the rest. "Perhaps we should eat. I know I am hungry."

The landing was little more than a twenty-foot-wide square flat rock that jutted from the side of the mountain; it was surrounded by boulders. Once Brother Kayen was safely on top, Tryam walked to the edge and looked down. Any fears of being spotted by someone from below were erased. They were so far above the level of the crater, he doubted that even the most eagle-eyed Ragnar could spot them. He looked toward the abbey, but at this distance, all he could see were the snow-covered plains. He tried to remember what he would have been doing now if he had never left the abbey. *Likely cleaning dishes and scrubbing the kitchen floor.* The sky was growing dark as the pale winter sun set in the west.

After a hasty meal of cold meat, Telvar buried his head in his book, while Tryam and Wulfric rested their achy limbs. Brother Kayen, acting as their watch, explored the perimeter of the landing, poking with his shepherd's staff at the boulders at the back of the ledge.

"This rock formation is very peculiar," the missionary reported. "This landing was intentionally cleared. To move such large boulders would take enormous strength ... or magic. We may have stumbled upon an entrance!"

Telvar secreted his spell book away and was fast to his feet. He stood beside Kayen and examined the gray boulders for himself. Tryam was impressed by the thoroughness with which the young mage studied every detail of the rocks. When pressed for a reason, Telvar explained, "A wizard has to be thorough, or he could end up dead when stumbling on the doings of another wizard." Nevertheless, for all his thoroughness, he could not find any magical explanation for the rock formation.

A peculiar smile played on Wulfric's face. "You rely too much on magic. Come this way!"

The Ulf leapt on, then jumped over, the rocks that lined the back of the landing. Inspired by some unknown discovery, he bounded ahead and out of sight.

"Wait!" cautioned Kayen. "There could be hidden dangers!"

"I shall get him," vowed Tryam without thinking, as he raced up the same boulders. He spotted Wulfric farther up the mountain, weaving his way up to another geological anomaly: a clearing, containing a ring of megalith-sized stones.

After Telvar echoed Kayen's words of caution, Tryam stopped his pursuit and waited for the two of them to join him.

The stench was the first thing that Tryam noticed when he stood before the ring of symmetrically spaced rocks, each some thirty feet high. It reminded him of the smell of the mammoth he had ridden in the tournament, that of a wild beast. Wulfric awaited them, but he had not yet entered the circle.

"I sense great magic!" blurted Telvar in a voice pitched with excitement. He gestured mysteriously with his hands and then reported, "It is emanating from the rocks themselves!" Telvar poked Wulfric with his staff. "Stand aside, so that I may enter the ring."

Batting away the mage's metal rod, Wulfric growled, then said to Telvar, "I shall go first. The rest of you, stay put."

Wulfric, sword drawn, stepped between two of the mammoth stones. As the big Ulf entered the ring, Tryam heard the sound of crunching. Wulfric reported with alarm, "The floor is littered with bones. I see completely cleaned carcasses of beasts and men alike. We have to get away from here now. This is a nest!"

"Do not panic," scolded Telvar, shouldering his way past Tryam and into the ring. "I must investigate these stones."

The wizard moved from monolith to monolith, oblivious of the skulls and other bones beneath his feet. He uttered words of magic while tracing with his fingers the runes that were carved into the rock.

Kayen repeated Wulfric's warning. "This surely must be the lair of the winged beast the Ragnar fear."

"This is not a nest for some brainless animal," huffed the wizard. "No natural methods can explain this formation. This ring of stones was created by Antigenesus, I am sure. We may have stumbled upon a portal that could take us anywhere!"

"Would it take us inside the fortress?" asked Wulfric.

"No," admitted Telvar. "Only to where another portal has been established. Other such portals have been found throughout Medias."

Wulfric spat upon the ground. "Then, we shouldn't waste time here!"

"Stop arguing, you fools," interrupted Kayen. "A path leads from these stones to a cave just ahead. A cave that must lead into the mountain. I think we have found another entrance."

Before they decided any action, however, a black shadow moved across the dark sky.

"As I warned," cried Wulfric, "the beast returns to its lair!"

Tryam pressed the oblivious wizard against the closest stone. With the wizard momentarily immobilized, the young acolyte scanned the sky. What he saw mesmerized him.

High above circled a great bird, the creature's leathery wings spanning nearly forty feet. Its head had a sharp, hooked beak like that of an eagle, while strong talons like those of a hawk flexed beneath its torso. Its tail was reptilian and barbed, while its eyes were like those of a predatory cat.

It circled once, then dove to the ring of stones. Kayen was blown to the ground by the beast's beating wings.

Tryam started for his mentor.

"Don't be a fool!" yelled the wizard, restraining him.

Tryam shrugged the surprisingly strong wizard from his shoulders, but it did not matter: The giant bird was too fast. Helplessly, Tryam watched as the creature, in a single, smooth motion, plucked the cleric up in its massive talons.

As the great bird lifted clear of the ring of stones, it swept over Tryam's position. The young acolyte watched as Kayen struggled to pry open the talons with his staff. Failing that, the missionary removed the cross of Aten from his robes and threw it toward Tryam. Kayen called down, but his words were lost in the noise of the beating of the leathery wings. Tryam caught the cross and looked up in time to see the winged beast disappear with Kayen into the black sky.

Wulfric rushed over to Tryam, and they exchanged horrified expressions.

"He is gone," Tryam gasped.

"We must retreat before it returns for us," implored Telvar. "To the cave! It is our only chance!"

It was now Tryam who was reluctant to leave the circle of stones.

Wulfric shook him by his shoulders. "There's nothing you could have done to save him, and there is nothing we can do now to rescue him."

"You're right," acknowledged Tryam. "Brother Kayen would not want us to risk our lives foolishly."

Taking a last look to the heavens, Tryam said a prayer for his mentor. When he was done, he placed the cross of Aten around his neck and over his breastplate. "Let's find that entrance," he said with a heavy heart. "And let's rescue Kara."

Chapter 56

Heads Shall Roll!

As he made for the Ragnar encampment, Gidran urged his warhorse to speed faster over the icy rocks of the ravine. The shaman was not sure how Ivor would react to the news that Crayvor, his eldest surviving son, was dead. *How much has the jarl drunk from Dementhus's fountain of promised power? Will the Ragnar king blame Dementhus and turn against Terminus's call?*

Gidran was more curious than concerned about the jarl's reaction, for he knew that whatever the result, it was all part of Bafomeht's plan.

The news of Crayvor's death had come to Gidran from a scouting party. Searching for the overdue men, they had followed smoke in the sky that ultimately led to a ruin. There they found Crayvor's body along with the other members of his band. Fire, spear, and sword had taken the men's lives. There was no sign that any of the enemy had been killed. The evidence was clear and disturbing: Crayvor had come across a small but skilled band of warriors, who defeated not only a Daemon but now one of the most accomplished Ragnar warriors. *Who are they, and how dangerous a threat do they represent?*

Dementhus had assured him on many occasions there was no one in the north who could thwart their plans: The Berserkers were too primitive, the knights in Arkos cared only about protecting their mines, the monks of Saint Paxia were helpless pacifists, and the tower mage was under the control of the amulet. When pressed about the power of Theragaard, Dementhus conceded that his tomb should be destroyed but that the monks at the Arkos abbey were content to have his spirit stay buried. Still, Gidran had his doubts. The pain in his leg from the attack of the stone

THE TOMB OF THERAGAARD

Aemon guardians of the tomb still lingered, and the failure to find and destroy the intruders was troublesome. *There is some hidden power at work.*

The concept of maps was foreign to the Ragnar. Gidran was guided to the Ragnar army's encampment by more rudimentary means: by following the havoc that the army had wrought on the surrounding Berserker villages. He started with the Gnoll clan and followed the scars of war from there. When he exited the ravine, he was granted a remarkable view. Before him was the Ragnar army in full, swollen to ten times the size of the entire Ragnar village. More than a dozen of the Berserker clans had bent their knee to Ivor instead of raising steel against him. Smoke drifted like a fog about their latest conquest, and the smell of war filled Gidran's nostrils. It was the smell of victory and of death.

The warriors he passed upon entering the camp looked up at him with eyes bloodshot from drink. Some of the newly recruited warriors reached for their weapons, but those who recognized him as the man who had spoken to their God fell to their knees. Whether they recognized him or not, Gidran's cruel and confident gaze kept all at bay.

Halting his horse, Gidran leaned down and grabbed a Ragnar man by the shoulder. "Where is Ivor? I bring word from the Mountain God."

The bloodstained savage sobered quickly. "He is with Jarl Akrack in the longhouse in the center of the village. They are discussing how the spoils should be divided." A toothless smile spread over the man's cruel face. "If you hurry, there might be a woman waiting for you."

Gidran spurred his horse toward the smoking ruins that had once been a thriving Berserker community. Outside the village, wagons full of corpses stood, waiting to be delivered to Dementhus.

The palisade walls had collapsed, allowing Gidran a straight path to the longhouse. Inside the village, wounded old men, screaming women, and crying children wandered aimlessly, their features masked by blood and mud. He spotted the scorched longhouse and dismounted by the entrance. Two guards at attention recognized him and, without a word, allowed him access.

Inside the wooden hall, the lighting was low and the air stale. A small fire smoldered at the far end, while tables on either side of the rectangular room were occupied with victorious warriors enjoying the fruits of battle with drink, women, or both. Near the fire, on two thrones made from thick oak, sat two gray-bearded men. Their thrones had been placed facing each other, with a table filled with meat and frothy beer between. As he got closer, the shaman could hear them speaking in jovial but low tones. The man on the right was Ivor; the other man, reasoned Gidran, had to be Akrack. *War must agree with Ivor, for he looks years younger.*

Ivor looked up from his conspiratorial talk with his counterpart, and his eyes widened in recognition. The Ragnar jarl gestured toward the shaman with a meaty drumstick. "This is the priest I spoke of! The man in communication with the Mountain God." Then he addressed the shaman directly. "Gidran, find yourself a throne and join us. I have gathered so many thrones these last few weeks, I have more and then some to spare." A broad grin split the man's face as he laughed at his own boast.

Gidran kept his face neutral. He decided the best way to inform Ivor of Crayvor's death was quick and direct. "I have grim news. Crayvor is dead. He was killed in a skirmish at an old beacon tower. Killed by the men we suspect were spying on our village and the Mountain God."

If the news caused any grief or anger to the Ragnar jarl, it was lost on Gidran. "He died in battle," Ivor replied, "and for his people. What more can one ask? I shall have more sons." He took a bite out of his drumstick and washed the meat down with beer. "As far as the band of intruders, we shall deal with this nuisance when my army turns toward Arkos with the Mountain God at its head. Sit and join us as we talk of the future."

The nonchalant reaction of Ivor to his news surprised the shaman, who recalled how the jarl had expressed an abiding rage over the death of his firstborn son years earlier. *The destruction of the Ulf and his subsequent victories must have numbed Ivor from the loss of more of his offspring.* Gidran respectfully bowed. "I must return to the Ragnar village. The Mountain God has summoned me to His presence for further prayers and sacrifices. Before I depart, however, Dementhus tasked me to learn the progress of the war."

Ivor moved his bulk forward on the throne and shouted into a shadowy room at the back of the longhouse. "Klain! Fetch me the sack!"

A man, hobbled by drink, soon emerged, dragging a large burlap sack before Ivor.

"Empty it," commanded Ivor.

Klain uncinched the sack and dumped the contents. Six severed heads rolled out.

"I collect the heads of the jarls who defy me. You may take these to Dementhus to show him our progress."

Chapter 57
Caged Wolf

Kara pushed through the throng of Ragnar. "Spineless cowards! Honorless curs! You bend the knee to a wizard!" The insults did not aid in her escape, but speaking them aloud made her feel better. After she'd been dragged back to her now-refortified pen, she continued her taunts until night came and the Ragnar returned to their war preparations.

Inside her prison, she tested every inch of the iron cage for another way out. When she could not find a flaw, she lay dejectedly on the muddy ground and fell into an uneasy sleep. The blank stares from the ensorcelled Ulf haunted her dreams.

Days passed in her pen inside the Ragnar village, but she was not sure how many; a cloud fogged her head, an aftereffect she suspected from her encounter with the sand creature. While she was fortunate it had not devoured her, it was still no ally. It had deposited her at the feet of its master, the mad wizard who had dragged her through the labyrinthian mountain fortress. The wizard then banished her to the village. Despite her situation, she was not ready to stop fighting. *I shall not give up!* She would just have to be patient.

From her vantage point, nestled between a row of forges and newly fabricated barracks, she listened with eager ears to the words spoken between anvil strikes and shouted commands. She heard of other Berserker clans attacked, of jarls bending the knee, and more wild claims of the Ragnar god's return. She could see evidence of the Ragnar victories, for through the barracks strode warriors bearing the marks from the Tessak, Kree, and Bearg clans.

But what of this god? That the Ragnar had not killed her caused her to wonder if the tales were true: that she was to be sacrificed to this being. She

375

had to admit watching a god feast on a living person would be something to behold, but only if you were not the one being eaten.

On a gloomy, frost-blanketed morning, Kara found herself staring up at the crinkled face of an elderly Ragnar woman. The old woman held a bowl of meat stew and extended it through the bars of the former wolf pen. "Eat, child. My gift to the one who will soon make our God live again."

Kara's stomach growled. She grabbed the proffered bowl while flashing a snarl. "I eat not to please the Ragnar but so that I have the strength to get my revenge!" Before the woman turned away, Kara grabbed her wrist. "Can't you see that what your jarl is doing is wrong? He burned the Ulf village to the ground, slaughtered all who opposed, and now attacks all of his neighbors!" She squeezed the old woman's wrist harder. "I have seen his allies. He follows the orders of men from outside our lands!"

"You are wrong. It is the Mountain God, not His emissaries, Who directs us!" She smiled toothlessly. "Your spirit is strong! Think of the honor it will be to have your fiery blood satiate His hunger!"

Kara tried to reason with the woman, but she was just as ensorcelled as the Ulf had been—they by the wizard, the old woman by the promise of their god's return. Killing their god would be the only way to end the spell—but how? She wished she had listened better when Tryam had spoken of Aten, but she didn't think he ever mentioned anything about one god attacking another or if a god could have a weakness. "Be off!" Kara scolded, releasing her hold. "You tread a path to certain doom!"

The next night, after waking from a vivid nightmare, she sensed something ominous was about to happen. Her premonition was proven correct when she was dragged out of her pen at dawn and placed at the feet of the hulking, scarred brute named Abbaster. The man reeked of evil.

"The time has arrived," he said while clenching the pommels of his twin scimitars. "I come to take you to back to the emissary, and it is he who will prepare you for your final journey." He beckoned a Ragnar to come forward. The Ragnar carried her bow, quiver, and crimson arrows. "I have even preserved your weapons," explained Abbaster, "so that when the Mountain God drains your soul, everyone can delight in the death of a beautiful Berserker warrior."

"Like hell they will," cursed Kara. She surprised her handlers by head-butting Abbaster. The brute fell to the muddy ground while a gash was opened up on her forehead. The handlers grappled with Kara and pinned her to the ground. One made to subdue her with the butt end of a dagger.

"Careful," Abbaster cautioned as he rose to his feet. "We would not want to kill her before she fulfills her destiny." He brushed mud from his bearskins, then towered over the supine Kara. "Don't fret, girl, a reunion awaits. Before you are sacrificed, I shall take you to my sanctuary and show you what remains of your Ulf brethren."

Kara's eyes flashed with hatred. With blood pouring down her face, she vowed, "Whatever evils you have visited upon my kin you shall have returned threefold!"

Chapter 58

In the Cave

Without Brother Kayen's calming influence and sage advice, the tension between Telvar and Wulfric grew. Tryam feared their bickering would lead to a deadly misstep.

"We must proceed with caution!" the wizard explained for the third time. "Traps could be anywhere. We may even head into an ambush!"

"If you are afraid to lead," snarled Wulfric, "then give me your staff to light the way, and end your babbling."

"I shall not part with it. A wizard's staff is as an appendage. Would you relinquish your sword?"

"You'd have to rip my arm off first, trickster!"

"Be quiet!" snapped Tryam, shocked at his own outburst. The two ceased their argument and now directed hostile glares in his direction. "Mere moments have passed since Kayen's death," he continued. "We have not even mourned his passing, yet have we already forgotten his leadership? Brother Kayen sacrificed his life for this mission. Let's not betray him by allowing petty bickering to divide us." He paused a moment for his frustration to subside. "Wulfric, Telvar has said he can get us into this fortress. Let him prove himself, even if it means we 'proceed with caution'!"

"Yes," said Telvar triumphantly. "Stand aside, both of you, and let me show you my mastery of magic. This"—the wizard pointed toward the cave entrance—"is my realm, just as the frozen wastes outside is the dominion of the Berserkers."

Huffing, Wulfric stepped aside to allow the black-robed Rutilus mage access to the cave. As Telvar advanced, he examined everything from floor to ceiling with the aid of his glowing staff. On the floor, a footpath was still visible, though it was eroded from untold centuries. "This is the way," Telvar concluded.

The tunnel's width varied sometimes, allowing only one person at a time to proceed. The slow pace of movement allowed time for the wizard to pontificate about the ring of stones they had abandoned. "It must be a gateway. Since the fall of Antium, only a couple have ever been found. Alas, only those on the Wizard Council know their locations. Perhaps—"

Wulfric suddenly reached forward and grasped the mage by the collar. "Look ahead, you fool! You need to keep your eyes focused on what is in front of you!"

Telvar gulped. He had been lost in conversation and had not noticed that the passage had widened and that a chasm now yawned before them. After catching his breath, the wizard observed calmly, "Centuries of freezing and melting ice must have collapsed this section of the path! The gap must be hundreds of feet deep and at least eight feet wide."

"More like ten," guessed Wulfric, as he made his way forward to inspect the footing before the chasm. "We have enough room to get a running jump. It should be simple to make it to the other side. I shall show you."

Tryam and Telvar moved aside to accommodate Wulfric's bulk in the narrow passage. The Ulf, still loaded down with armor and equipment, stepped back ten paces from the chasm, then raced headlong toward the edge. He jumped mere inches before the chasm but landed softly on the other side, with feet to spare. Once across, he walked down the passageway ahead a fair distance and was soon lost from view.

Anxious moments passed.

"That slackwit intends to leave us here," fretted Telvar.

"No, he won't," assured Tryam. The young acolyte shouted into the gloom. "Wulfric, what do you see? Is everything all right?"

When the light from the wizard's staff shone on Wulfric's returning face, Telvar and Tryam saw a big smile playing under the Ulf's bright blue eyes. He spoke across the chasm to the others, his voice echoing down its depths. "I found a doorway not that far away. It does not look as imposing as the other entrance we found beneath the crater. It may be possible to smash it open if we need to. Come, hurry over."

Encouraged by the good news, Tryam threw his backpack and sword across to Wulfric as he prepared for his jump. He kept the cross of Aten around his neck out of respect for Brother Kayen. The acolyte then followed

Wulfric's lead. He stepped back ten paces down the narrow passage, then turned to face the chasm. He ran as fast as he could and launched himself at the last possible moment. He landed with ease on the other side.

Alone now, the wizard looked down into the depths of the chasm, shook his head, and sighed.

"Throw us your staff. It will make the jump easier," encouraged Tryam, but the wizard was in no mood to do so.

"My staff does not leave my hand. Stand back."

Anxiously, Tryam waited alongside Wulfric. If the wizard fell to his death, they had little chance of defeating the rogue wizard. Telvar appeared to be in good physical shape, but his flowing robes were filled with reagents, and Tryam worried that the wizard might stumble. "Perhaps you should empty your pockets first? Remove your robes?"

The wizard glared at Tryam and did not bother replying. To calculate the steps his slightly shorter legs would need to get up to speed, he did a practice run. Wulfric fidgeted and folded his arms across his breastplate. Irritated by the Ulf's impatience, Telvar snapped, "I'm sorry if I am boring you."

The wizard once more moved twenty steps back down the passage. He tightened the belt around his black robes; then, after a few deep breaths, he started his run. When his feet hit the lip of the chasm, he used his staff to propel himself forward. Tryam gasped, however, when he saw the wizard flounder midair, with the staff tangled in his black robes.

Telvar landed short, slamming his chest against the edge of the chasm. With flailing arms, he grasped for his staff but missed; he watched helplessly as it flipped through the air, banged off of Wulfric's head, and sailed down the corridor beyond.

The wizard next thought about his own safety and sought to hold onto the ledge. "Grab me, you halfwits!" he cried out. After a moment of hesitation, Tryam and Wulfric rushed to the ledge and lent a hand to the precariously hanging wizard.

The incident reminded Tryam of Brother Kayen and his near-identical situation in the mountains. Telvar, however, was not as gracious to his rescuers. "If you oafs had been this slow in combat, you would be dead ten times over. Now lift me up!"

Tryam helped Telvar to his feet and then said, "Rest a moment while I get your staff."

THE TOMB OF THERAGAARD

"No!" said Telvar, bumping the acolyte out of the way. "Don't touch it. You might accidentally discharge the magic stored inside."

"There should be no fear of that," roared Wulfric as he rubbed his head. "If there were any magic to discharge from your precious staff, it would have done so after it bounced off my head!"

"Then we shall be fortunate," snipped Telvar, "if your thick skull did not damage the crystal."

After the wizard retrieved his staff, he kept going down the passage. Wulfric and Tryam followed closely behind. The tunnel ended in a carved-out antechamber, at the end of which was a smooth metal door with no hinges. Despite Wulfric's claim, Tryam was dubious they could smash the door in.

"This is where you prove your worth, wizard," challenged Wulfric.

Chapter 59

The Guardians and Escape

The door was four feet wide, seven feet tall, gold in color, and with no visible carvings, handles, runes, hinges, or knobs. As he searched for a solution to open it, Telvar ignored the throbbing pain in his ribs from his almost fatal leap across the chasm, and he dismissed the grunts and stares from the Ulf he regarded as a blockheaded barbarian. *If what my naïve companions told me is true, Dementhus has already removed the spell from the main door to the fortress.*

On the trip to where they now were, Telvar had convinced himself that Dementhus's act of dispelling the magic on the main door would have lifted the locks covering all other access ways into Antigenesus's fortress. He had spent a great deal of time studying the unlocking spell, but he'd been unable to master its intricacies. Though he was confident in his mastery of elemental magic, the spell also called upon other realms of magic, realms he had not yet studied. Given this, he had abandoned the effort and proceeded on the assumption that Dementhus would have solved the riddle. That was not to conclude, however, that magic of some kind was not required to open this door. In any event, the spell to unlock the fortress was too complicated, and he now had no other choice but to hope he was correct.

Telvar swept his staff around the neatly carved chamber that surrounded the door. The light erased the shadows in the corners but revealed nothing but ordinary rock; however, he was certain there was more to this room than he could see. After careful consideration of his options and their

THE TOMB OF THERAGAARD

limited time, he decided on a course of action. "I need absolute quiet," he cautioned.

The wizard faced the door, closed his eyes, and spoke the incantation to link to the astral plane. When he opened his eyes, he observed runes carved into the metal on each corner of the door. The strange symbols were difficult to interpret, but each one contained within it a sign for the element of stone. *Were these added to give the door extra strength?* He could not see any sign that the door had been locked by a spell. He concluded that only a minimal amount of magical force would be needed to lift it open. *I was right! Dementhus has done all the work for me! The fool.*

"Stand back and arm yourselves," warned Telvar as he strengthened his connection to the astral plane. "We do not know what awaits us on the other side."

Words of magic escaped from his mouth, and the gem on his staff glowed blue. He pointed the staff at the door and uttered a command. Blue ribbons of magical energy arced to the door.

After a moment, rumbling shook the ground; then, with a lurch, the door started to inch upward and recede into the ceiling above. Telvar smiled confidently and looked with amusement at the surprised face of the Ulf. However, the door's progress was ponderously slow. "Let me quicken the pace," he said confidently.

The young mage increased the flow of energy, but a moment later, he realized his mistake. He had not been monitoring the reaction of the enigmatic runes; three of them now flared red in activation. *There had been a trap, and I missed it!*

While he desperately scanned for the trap's trigger, he heard a large thud coming from behind. A door, hidden in a recess, had fallen from above, sealing the three inside the antechamber. He ignored the commotion raised by his two companions. There was no time to try to decipher the runes. All he could do was continue channeling energy, hoping the door ahead would open more quickly. He was interrupted by an urgent warning. "Something is coming through the wall!"

It was Tryam's voice. Telvar now knew enough about the young acolyte to know he did not panic easily. The wizard paused his channeling and looked over his shoulder. A form was indeed stepping through the wall. *A stone guardian!*

Telvar was too fascinated by the magic to be afraid. "Keep the guardian occupied while I continue to work my magic!"

Tryam heard the wizard's order, but it did not help the situation. *How does one occupy a being made of stone?*

Off to Tryam's right, his Ulf friend roared. "Wizard, if we survive this, I shall have your head! Get that accursed door open!"

The being that had emerged from the wall headed for Telvar's unprotected back. Wulfric charged after it. "I hope these coronium weapons are sharp and strong enough to pierce this monster," he added before his blade struck the being's back and caused a storm of sparks to erupt on impact.

The distraction saved Telvar as the guardian turned to face its attacker. Tryam could now see the magical guardian's features more clearly. The seven-foot-tall stone man sported a granite head with a frozen snarling face and a body chiseled with well-defined muscles. *If it was designed to intimidate its adversaries, its creator was successful.*

Tryam stepped in close to the monster to aid Wulfric and struck with his blade at the thing's square jaw. The blow, which would have instantly killed a mortal opponent, removed only a small chip of stone. In response, the guardian attacked the young acolyte with a balled granite fist, striking him in the chest. Tryam flew backward, his now dented coronium breastplate and the padding beneath saving him from cracked ribs.

As Tryam lay helpless on the ground, Wulfric hacked at the creature's broad back. The guardian's attention turned again back to the Ulf. The young acolyte struggled to his feet, then struck at the creature's thick right arm. When his sword struck the stone appendage, the vibrations from the impact nearly shook the blade out of his hand. "This is hopeless!" Tryam yelled when he saw no visible damage.

The wizard then jumped into the combat and aimed his staff at the guardian. "Stand aside," he ordered as a beam of yellow light erupted from the staff's gem and struck a granite leg. The silent guardian flinched from the magical attack, and its left leg lost its shape as it turned to mud. "Attack!" the wizard encouraged. "I can't aid you again. I must finish the door spell, or this antechamber shall be our tomb."

The guardian stumbled and fell toward Wulfric, bear-hugging him as the two fell to the ground. The sound of Wulfric's breastplate buckling sickened Tryam, who tried to imagine the pain. It was now his turn to

THE TOMB OF THERAGAARD

distract the magical monster. He aimed for the creature's withered leg. It took two whacks to splatter the appendage.

The stone guardian loosened its grip on Wulfric to face the new threat from Tryam. The Ulf slipped out from under its mass, then jumped on its back, using his weight to keep it from rising. "Attack its shoulder with all your might!" cried Wulfric, out of breath.

Tryam hacked at the creature's rounded shoulder with his blade. The coronium metal cleaved off sizable chunks of the guardian's weakened body.

Wulfric kept the stone fighter pinned to the ground. After what seemed an eternity, Tryam severed the guardian's arm at its shoulder. Lacking two limbs, it had no hope to stand.

Wulfric jumped off its back. "Now we work together! Strike at its other arm!"

Like lumberjacks felling a tree, the two traded blows until the arm cleaved off the granite torso.

"Now the head!" barked Wulfric.

The thick stone neck yielded after several more blows. The guardian ceased moving when its head split from its body.

Wiping sweat from his brow, Wulfric declared, "That was close. It seems we have survived this trap." Turning back to look at Telvar, he asked, "How goes the door, wizard?"

The door had risen only a few inches.

This is taking too long!

It was only seconds after their victory that the wall to their left began to ripple.

"Another guardian?" gasped Tryam in dismay.

"You had better hurry, wizard!" Wulfric warned, checking his blade for nicks. "We are about to have another visitor!"

Telvar reacted with indignity. "Your ceaseless complaining is breaking my concentration."

With a mixture of fascination and horror, Tryam watched as the new guardian emerged. This being gleamed in blue marble, its chiseled features resembling a nude athletic female. In its right hand, it bore a gleaming metal spear. Once again, Wulfric stepped up to save Telvar from attack.

The blue marble creation thrust its spear at Wulfric, who adroitly dodged the strike. Tryam moved in to attack. The guardian whirled around and thrust its spear at the young acolyte's midsection. Tryam sidestepped the impaling strike, but he gasped at the speed of the attack.

After the creature's failed strike on Tryam, marble chunks flew into the air when Wulfric connected with his coronium steel. "Its skin is weaker!" reported the Ulf through haggard breaths.

The blue woman responded with two quick strikes: one aimed at Wulfric's head and another aimed at his thigh. Had he been any less skilled, either would have been killing blows.

As he watched the marble woman battle Wulfric, Tryam whispered a prayer to Aten for guidance. He stayed his sword arm, waiting until he could inflict the most damage. Stepping over the fallen granite man, he took aim at the living statue's neck and used both hands to swing the coronium blade. When the sword's green metal sank halfway into the creature's neck, his heart was lifted.

The marble woman turned back to Tryam and attacked again with its spear. Tryam parried the first thrust, but the creature followed with a series of attacks that quickly overwhelmed him; only his armor saved his life. "Get it off me!" he yelled.

Wulfric jumped to his aid by leaping on the guardian's back. Muscles bulged as the Ulf twisted the thing's partially severed neck; marble crunched under the strain. The guardian reacted to the attack by backing into the wall, crushing Wulfric against the hard surface. He howled in fury.

Tryam hacked away at the creature's spear until his coronium blade snapped the weaker metal. Soon after, Tryam saw the blue head come off in Wulfric's hands. The creature fell to the ground and remained motionless.

"Why is the door not open?" an exasperated Wulfric asked as he stepped over the second guardian and rushed to the door.

Telvar was still speaking words of magic and did not respond. The door had risen only a foot above the floor, and the blue light coming from the wizard's staff looked in danger of going out. He looked to be in a trancelike state.

The antechamber rumbled again. Tryam stood beside Wulfric, and the two prepared for another guardian. This time, however, it was the ceiling that rippled with magic. What emerged frightened the strong-willed young acolyte.

"Aten, save us!" cried Tryam.

"What horrors are these!" spat Wulfric in dismay.

THE TOMB OF THERAGAARD

Above their heads, an obsidian hand reached out from the rippling rock ceiling—a hand the size of a walrus's head.

"We are leaving now!" yelled Wulfric.

He ducked under the groping black hand and rolled across the chamber to retrieve the first stone guardian's severed head. He crawled back to the door and wedged the head under the narrow opening at the bottom. "If we squeeze, we should be able to fit."

Tryam was dubious.

Telvar's eyes fluttered open and into focus. He was about to protest until his gaze caught the obsidian guardian emerging from the ceiling. "Great Necromedes's ghost!" he gasped.

The largest of the guardians so far jumped down from whatever magic realm had birthed it and landed in the middle of the antechamber. The being looked as if it had lava for blood, as red, fiery veins coursed throughout its black body.

"You might be right, Berserker. Follow my lead!" Telvar blasted one last burst of blue magic at the door before throwing his staff under the gap and then diving head first after it and into the unknown area beyond.

"Figures he would go first," seethed Wulfric. "I can't wait to get through, just so I can get my hands around his neck!"

The obsidian monstrosity advanced.

The last burst of energy had lifted the door a couple more inches. Tryam looked at his barrel-chested friend and shook his head. "Remove your breastplate, or you will never get under!"

Wulfric nodded as he kept one eye on the guardian. Tryam had already removed his armor, but he watched helplessly as Wulfric's crushed breastplate refused to come off. To add more desperation to the situation, Telvar's voice called from the other side with an urgent warning. "Hurry, you fools! The magic will soon dissipate, and when it does, the door will slam shut. The stone head will not hold it open."

"Does he think we are having a feast?" Wulfric asked, exasperated.

Tryam tugged at the Ulf's crushed armor, but the buckles were hopelessly bent.

"Look out!" cried Wulfric.

Fists of lava flew toward Tryam's head, and the young acolyte fell to his knees.

387

"Leave! Save my clan! Save Kara!" said Wulfric as he drew his broadsword. "I shall give you time to escape."

Tryam refused to abandon his companion. "No! We need you, and Kara needs you! Let's face this monster together!"

A gargantuan fist slammed the ground between the two young men, causing the antechamber to quake beneath their feet. Tryam and Wulfric dove in opposite directions to avoid the fist and the chunks of molten stone that flew off the creature's bulbous body. When Tryam got back to his feet, the monster was between him and Wulfric, with the Ulf nearest the door.

Wulfric raised his sword but hesitated. The guardian grinned with hellfire and punched him in the chest with a bare fist, the force slamming him against the magical door and to the ground. When he again stood, his broken breastplate fell to the floor.

"Thanks be to Aten! Go!" shouted Tryam. "You are free from your armor!"

Stunned, Wulfric felt his chest.

"Go!" encouraged Tryam. "I shall follow right after!"

It was obvious to both that they could not defeat the lava guardian without the aid of Telvar. And since the wizard was unlikely to reenter the antechamber willingly, they had no choice but to retreat. After dodging two more swipes of the fiery hot fists, Wulfric dove head first under the door.

Tryam was now alone, with only his coronium longsword with which to fight. The acolyte faced a creature that spanned nearly the entire width of the claustrophobic room, blocking his escape path to the door. He slowly backed up, keeping his eyes on the creature, even as he prayed to find a way around it.

The guardian did not wait to be attacked. It bounded forward and swung a giant fist at the cornered youth. Tryam tripped over the marble guardian and fell to the ground. The mishap was fortunate, though, since the lava-dripping fist missed his head as he fell backward.

"Hurry! Move! Come on!" He heard his companions imploring from the other side of the door.

Aten, what am I to do? The creature towered over him, and the heat it radiated almost burned his flesh. In a desperate move, Tryam tucked and rolled between the lava guardian's legs. A fist again came after him, but Tryam was too fast and suffered only minor burns as he whipped under it.

"Get up," encouraged Wulfric. "You're almost there!"

THE TOMB OF THERAGAARD

Tryam stood and raced for the door. He dove head first, his sword arm outstretched. The rocky ground tore into his robes, and the friction stopped him short. *Aten, no!* With a fatalistic calm, he awaited the destructive force of the guardian. Instead, he was jarred back to life when a pair of hands grabbed each arm and pulled him the rest of the way under the door.

Once Tryam was all the way through, Wulfric kicked the granite head out from under the door, and the wizard spoke a word of magic. The door slammed shut.

"We are all safe, thank Aten," Tryam said, gasping for air.

"That was extraordinary," the wizard declared, as if commenting on a peculiar incident he had read in a book. "There were four runes on that door. We had triggered only the first three. I wonder what the fourth guardian would have been."

"You want to open the door and find out?" asked Wulfric, whose numerous cuts and bruises added to his disdain for the wizard's antics. "I would love to give you the opportunity to study it firsthand!"

"Sadly," retorted Telvar, "the only way we could open that door now is to use your thick head as a battering ram."

"Enough," erupted Tryam. "Save the fighting for our enemies." His eyes probed the darkness. "Where are we?"

A small orb embedded in the ceiling was the only light. The corridor they now found themselves in was ten feet wide and stretched into the darkness an unknown distance. The walls and floors were of a seamless black material. No other doors could be seen.

"We are, my young, naïve monk," began Telvar, "in the late archmagus Antigenesus's trap-ridden lair. Antigenesus was one of the most powerful and innovative wizards to have ever lived. His power was indescribable, and his creations have survived him by centuries. Unfortunately, we have no map, no allies, and little magic. For the moment at least, we are blind and essentially helpless."

"We have our faith," Tryam pointed out as he brought Kayen's cross out from under his robes. He touched its smooth surface and read the inscription to himself. *Defending the faithful, from threats mortal and Abyssal, from within and without.* "With that, all things are possible."

Telvar laughed. "If you say so, but I prefer magic. And if you want to have a chance of ever leaving this place, you need to let me rest, so I can regain my vigor. You can take the time to pray."

"I shall." Tryam ignored the wizard's bluster and countered, "You sound as if you worship this Antigenesus."

"Bah," dismissed Telvar. "I respect him, because he was a powerful and accomplished wizard. You can respect someone without worshipping them. Is there no mortal you hold above others for what they accomplished?"

"I do. Saint Lucian."

"Never heard of him. He could not have been that important."

"He was a brave and just man," retorted Tryam. "A paladin who used his power to help others. He sacrificed himself to save the souls of the innocent. He did not use his gifts for selfish reasons."

"Well, everybody has heard of Antigenesus. Only a few gloomy monks remember Saint Lucian. What does that tell you?"

"It tells me that people worship selfish powerful wizards over humble men."

Telvar laughed again. "I need my rest. This philosophical discussion has made me weary."

Not wanting to venture farther into the archmagus's lair without the wizard's help, Tryam and Wulfric let Telvar rest, and they set up camp where they stood. No sound of any kind could be heard, either from the other side of the door or from down the dark corridor.

Tryam felt his eyelids grow heavy, and despite his uneasiness, he slipped into a deep sleep. He dreamt of Saint Lucian.

Sometime later, a gentle nudging woke Tryam. Wulfric's white wolf pelt momentarily startled the acolyte. "It is time to go," whispered the young Ulf warrior, his voice dripping with sarcasm. "The mage is *ready*."

Tryam shook the sleep from his head. His body and mind were refreshed, and all of his aches were gone. The cross of Aten around his neck was warm, almost hot against his skin. *Was this healing a gift from Aten?* As was his habit from his years of living in the abbey, he said a brief morning prayer and gave thanks for seeing another day.

The wizard looked as refreshed as Tryam felt, and the young acolyte sensed an eagerness in him that bordered on obsession. Telvar urged them deeper into the fortress.

So black was the hallway that even now, with the aid of Telvar's staff, the party nearly missed a doorway only twenty paces from where they had entered the fortress. The door was painted black and made of wood. After some curious hand gestures and whispered words, Telvar pushed the

THE TOMB OF THERAGAARD

door inward with the butt of his staff. The sound of flowing water filled Tryam's ears.

"Go ahead, Wulfric," encouraged the wizard, who stood to the side of the door. "Now do your part."

The Ulf warrior, fearless, brushed past the wizard and into the room. Tryam followed close behind. Both had weapons drawn.

Dominating the center of the spacious circular room was a fountain, which contained a marble statue of a dryad, a mythical woodland elf, leaning provocatively against a stone tree with large jade leaves. Water falling from the ceiling made it appear as if it were raining and the dryad were seeking shelter. Positioned around the fountain were benches, and the painted walls around the room gave the illusion that they were in a dense green forest.

"I would not touch the water until I examine it," cautioned the wizard as Wulfric strode to the fountain.

"This archmagus was not above poisoning his guests?" questioned Wulfric, backing away.

"We don't know the purpose of this room. It may just be what it appears." The wizard placed his hand under the artificial rain and cupped a palmful. He sniffed the water, then took a small taste, swishing the liquid in his mouth before swallowing. "Refreshing and as pure as a mountain stream. I would recommend we fill our waterskins."

"Maybe we should wait to see how you feel in a few hours," suggested Wulfric.

"You would be disappointed. My constitution is unusually strong." Telvar took another sip. "Are all Berserkers so frightened of magic?"

Wulfric cursed, then brushed the wizard aside. The big Ulf dipped his flask into the fountain and took a sip of his own. Tryam followed, and when he tasted the cold water, he found it very pleasing.

"Enough of this. Let's continue," growled Wulfric as he roughly pulled Telvar from the room. "We have to find Kara and kill the rogue wizard."

The three continued down the corridor. After another twenty paces, they spotted another room, this time on the opposite side of the hallway. An iron-bound door blocked entry. Telvar pushed on the door with his staff, but it would not budge. A glance was all Telvar needed to encourage Wulfric and Tryam to lean into the door. It was not locked, and it opened inward after they used enough exertion to loosen the rusty hinges. Before

Wulfric stepped two feet inside, however, Telvar ordered him to stop. "I sense magic here. Powerful magic."

The only thing Tryam could see was a room that resembled an art gallery, like those said to be in Secundus. Paintings of various landscapes lined its curved walls. "Where is the magic? The paintings or something else?"

A sigh escaped from the wizard's mouth. "Yes, the paintings. I do not believe they are just paint on canvas." As Telvar moved about the room with care, his green eyes darted from one picture to the next.

"Then, what are they?" asked Tryam, feeling a bit unnerved.

"If I am correct, the images we gaze upon are of real places on Medias as they are right now. And as time flows and molds, the world depicted in the paintings changes accordingly. If we were to stay here and observe, we could watch seasons pass, trees grow from seed to mighty oak, and even empires rise and then wither into ruin."

Wulfric laughed at the wizard's extraordinary claims. "I've seen nothing change."

Tryam was equally dubious. He walked over to a picture of a swirling mass of red, black, and gray. "Where is this? It looks terrifying."

"As well it should," answered Telvar. "That is the remains of the jewel of humanity, the once-great capital of the world, the eternal city of Antium. Since the end of the Abyssal War, a perpetual cyclone swirls around the old ruin. Some say the storm is there to protect us from discovering the Ancients' secrets. Others say it is there to keep away those who might want to free the trapped spirit of Terminus, who is buried under the city."

"Does anybody live there?" asked Wulfric.

"No mortal lives there; that is for certain," replied Telvar. "Over the centuries, the Wizard Council has sent several expeditions to the great city, looking for lost magic. None has ever returned."

Tryam looked away from the horrifying image and walked over to a more pleasing one. "This one is so beautiful. Where is it?"

The painting depicted a great cathedral, like those from the time of the Ancients, its domed roof submerged under brilliant emerald waters. The building looked intact, though the bell tower had collapsed, and a school of fish swam through its exposed beams.

"An old church," dismissed Telvar in a huff. "Nothing more."

THE TOMB OF THERAGAARD

Tryam had doubts about the wizard's conclusion. *This place has to be significant!* Though he could not explain why, the place looked familiar, as if he had read about it in a book.

"We have dawdled enough looking over a dead man's artwork," grumbled Wulfric. "Let's move ahead."

"As I said, we do not have a map of this fortress. It would be foolhardy for us to rush anywhere unless we know where we are going," rebutted the wizard. "It is possible we could find something in one of these side rooms that could aid us."

The Ulf clenched his fist over the pommel of his sword, and the wizard conceded, "But we have lingered in this particular room long enough."

Telvar led the company out of the room. When they passed another side room, Wulfric poked his head inside, declared it unimportant, and rushed the wizard forward before he could protest.

They continued down the dark corridor, deeper into the heart of the fortress. Tryam felt the weight of the mountain closing in around them. The corridor continued without side passages for a great while. Telvar kept a quick pace and always led with his staff before him. When the wizard's pace slowed, Tryam looked past his companions to find out why. What he saw made him sweat even more. Ahead, a flickering orange light danced as if a fire burned.

"I sense more magic," warned Telvar ominously. "Wait while I check for danger."

The wizard advanced to the light, which emanated from beyond an archway. He stepped through the portal with his staff held before him.

After a moment of tense anticipation, the wizard returned and beckoned them inside. Tryam breathed again for the first time in many a heartbeat.

Ahead was a fifty-foot-square room with broad stairs leading both up and down. As decoration, in the center of the room was a pulsating rock formation. Wulfric warily approached the rock.

"Do not fear," said the wizard. "The stone is not as hot as it appears."

Wulfric reached out a hand and placed it on the rock. "What he says is true," he admitted.

Tryam touched the glowing stones and felt their coolness. *Antigenesus was not afraid to flaunt his magical abilities.*

"The question now is, Which way should we choose?" mused Telvar as he poked around the stairs with his staff, first peering up, then looking down.

"The choice is simple: We go down," stated Wulfric. "Kara is a prisoner and would be placed in the dungeons. No wizard would allow a captive so close to all this opulence."

"A surprisingly sagacious deduction," conceded Telvar. "Typically, prisoners are kept far away from the mage's quarters. Antigenesus's laboratories are likely higher up the mountain, the dungeons below—or perhaps even in the other peak."

Wulfric did not acknowledge the rare compliment and instead headed down the stairs and into the unknown without comment.

As the young acolyte descended, he clutched the cross of Aten. All his thoughts turned to the missing Ulf girl. *Kara, we are coming for you.*

Chapter 60
The Shambling Mound

Astounding! Truly breathtaking! Even the air feels charged with magic! After the party had only descended two floors, Telvar called for a halt. A series of rooms along this landing's south wall intrigued him enough to endure Wulfric's wrath for requesting the delay.

The landing was adorned with statues and murals, exquisitely carved and painted, but it was the runes carved in red above a series of rooms that piqued the wizard's curiosity. The runes indicated elemental magic, though he cursed his inability to understand them entirely. "These may be important," he declared, as he thought of the Golem and the laboratories where it would have been created.

"We have no time to search dusty storerooms looted long ago," snarled Wulfric, who was poised to descend to the next level.

The Ulf's limited imagination irritated the wizard. Telvar appealed to the warrior's more martial instincts: "We may stumble upon a weapon of great power. It is likely that we shall have to fight to free Kara. Do you have a weapon that could defeat an Albus mage?"

Wulfric huffed but left the stairs to stand by the door with his sword ready. Telvar smiled and stood by his side. "We shall take only a quick peek," assured the wizard.

Using the butt end of his staff, Telvar pushed open the plain black door. Inside, bright light from a silver chandelier pooled down, illuminating a ten-foot-square room. The wizard jumped back when his eyes laid upon a lumpy stone-and-sand guardian shambling under the light. The magical mound lurched toward the intruders with tentacle-like limbs, but its reach stopped short, as if restrained by an invisible leash. "Stand back!" warned the wizard.

Telvar pointed at the floor beneath the creature. "It cannot cross the red borders of the painted octagon. We are safe as long as we do not enter its limited dominion."

"Yet another unholy creature!" gasped Tryam. "This Antigenesus was obsessed with creating perversions of life."

Telvar was amused by the dour youth's misplaced outrage. "It is only magic. Powerful magic, but it pales in comparison with the mighty Golem. This is a simple elemental guardian, given awareness, not life, with magic from the astral plane. It can hurt us only if we were to remove the magical spell that binds it in place."

The young acolyte scowled and clenched his cross.

Telvar tested his theory by stepping inside the room, being careful to stay outside the octagon's borders. When the guardian did not strike, the wizard circled the creature, taking mental notes on its construction.

"Unless we can use this creature to kill Dementhus, we should leave," said Wulfric.

Telvar dismissed the Ulf warrior's opinion with a wave of his hand. "What you behold is a wonder of achievement. I did not have time to examine the stone guardians at the door, as you did."

"Examine? We almost died!" snarled Wulfric. "You can't possibly tame this abomination."

"I *might* if I can understand how it works. It would make a powerful companion. It undoubtedly would be a greater physical threat than you are and would be much more agreeable." Telvar opened a channel to the astral plane and peered at the creation with his mind's eye. So engrossed was he in observing the flows of the elemental magic that he did not notice how the light from the chandelier was dimming, until he heard Wulfric's warning.

"You might want to change your opinion on its usefulness, wizard. Something is happening!"

The silver chandelier! Telvar had forgotten about the strange light. "It is not the octagon that binds this guardian in place, but rather the light!" Telvar raised his staff and pointed it at the dimming magical bulbs, but before he could channel energy into the chandelier, the sand-and-stone guardian broke free. With one swipe of a tentacle, it batted the staff out of his hand and knocked him to the ground.

The impact had also knocked the wind out of him. He tried to move himself away from his attacker, but he was trapped against the back wall of the room. He felt blood trickling down his mouth. "Help me, you fools!" cried Telvar in genuine terror.

The wizard's two companions acted swiftly by launching an attack that turned the creature's focus away from him. Telvar watched helplessly as their swords sunk harmlessly into the sandy torso. *They need my magic.* Telvar searched for his staff and saw it near Wulfric's feet. "Kick me my staff!" shouted Telvar over the sound of combat.

With a face red with fury, the Ulf warrior kicked the staff toward the back wall. However, before Telvar could reach it, the staff bounced and landed halfway under the sand beast's body. "Damnable luck!" cursed the wizard.

I must rely upon the last of my personal reserves of magic.

Words of a spell came to Telvar's mind, a spell he'd been eager to try after having mastered it shortly before his arrival in Arkos. He spoke the words of the spell and channeled the rest of the magic from his body through his hands. A gust of wind blasted from his fingertips and into the guardian. He rejoiced when sand filled the room as the elemental guardian began to blow apart from the unnatural windstorm.

Taking no time to gloat, Telvar dove for his staff and wrenched it free from under the thing's now-wobbly stumps. He glanced up in time to see that his spell had run its course; the sand and rock that had been blown away was now returning to make the guardian whole again. He also saw that it had lured the young acolyte into its arms and had started to engulf him.

Time for me to rescue the warriors again!

Emboldened by the challenge, Telvar stood before the guardian, clutching his staff in both hands. He spoke words of magic, connected to the astral plane, and channeled energy directly into the jewel atop his staff. Falling to his knees, he pointed the staff at the silver chandelier. After a spoken command, a beam of energy blasted from the staff into the dark bulbs. With wide, hopeful eyes, the young wizard watched as the chandelier began to shine again and the pool of light grow beneath it.

As the light compelled it back into the center of the room, the rock-and-sand being stomped its lumpy legs. Reluctantly, it seemed, it released the young acolyte, who was covered in gritty sand. Telvar slipped past the creature and pushed Wulfric and Tryam outside the room's threshold. Once they were clear of the room, he exited as well and slammed the door shut behind him.

"Fascinating. What a marvel!" exclaimed Telvar, nearly out of breath but thrilled with the experience. "I think I could control it if I were given time to work out how."

"We are done with this foolishness!" spat Wulfric as he patted the choking Tryam on the back. "We have to find the dungeons now!"

With no comeback ready on his lips, Telvar nodded his acceptance. "Very well. But we learned a valuable lesson: Take nothing we see here for granted."

Chapter 61
An Old Acquaintance

Tryam drank deeply from his waterskin. The water cold and crisp, and it cleansed the coarse sand from his throat, but the young acolyte was uneasy having to thank the archmagus and his magical fountain for this amenity. *This whole fortress is a display of magical horrors. Antigenesus's legacy was written in blasphemy.* Tryam would be glad to be back in the open air once again and under Aten's benevolent gaze.

The party traveled down a dozen or more landings before the stairs terminated into a large black chamber. The fortress was larger than Tryam had imagined. *We could search for days within this labyrinth before finding Kara! And where is Dementhus?* Telvar did not seem to be troubled over the possibility that they might stumble into the rogue wizard. He was convinced the Albus mage was higher up the mountain's peak. The young acolyte was not persuaded, however. The longer they lingered in this place, the darker the shadows around every corner appeared to be.

"I see no exit. Have we gone too far?" Wulfric directed his question to the wizard.

Telvar walked the perimeter of the landing, tapping on the walls with his staff as he went. "Don't be so hasty," said the wizard smugly. "Not all doors are meant to be seen. Here, I think." Telvar pushed on a section of black stone, and as he did so, an area of wall pushed inward, receding into a slot and revealing a curved hallway. "Just as I thought," he added.

The corridor was narrow, made for only one abreast, and sloped downward. The wizard led his companions inside its dark confines. After a few dozen yards, the passage ended at an archway covered by a tapestry. Telvar searched around the hanging, mumbling words of magic. Satisfied with whatever he had done, Telvar motioned for the others to be silent before he moved the tapestry aside and stepped into the room beyond. Tryam followed behind Wulfric, who was always within arm's length of the wizard.

This new chamber was the largest open area they had seen since stepping inside the mountain. Rectangular in shape with rounded ends, the room was well over a hundred feet long. Tapestries depicting scenes of a wizard in combat lined the north and south walls, including the wall from which they had just emerged. At the west tapered end stood a thirty-foot door with writing above the lintel, while at the opposite end of the massive chamber was a pile of burnt wood and scorched stones.

"This is the Grand Hall! It has to be!" Telvar's voice echoed in the cavernous room. "See those words above the entrance, *Superius Nul Vanus*? We are in Antigenesus's Grand Hall!"

"What does that mean for us?" whispered Wulfric, his eyes searching the shadows.

"It means"—Telvar waved his staff in the air—"that from here, we can go to anyplace in this fortress."

"Then, let's find the dungeons!" Wulfric stalked toward the room's main door and appeared about ready to burst through it when something on the ground caught his attention. "I see muddy tracks and drops of blood!"

Telvar directed the light from his staff to the ground. The muddy prints headed to a tapestry-covered alcove along the south wall.

"Those are Kara's boots! I would bet anything on it!" cried Wulfric. "We must follow!"

"Wait!" cautioned Telvar. "Before you blunder ahead and get us all killed, use your tracking skills, and explain everything you see here on the ground."

Wulfric stopped, frustration showing on his grimaced face, but Telvar's words were wise.

"I see three distinct sets of prints." The Ulf warrior knelt down and pointed with his sword at the smallest set of tracks. "These belong to Kara, for they are her size, and I recognize the pattern left by the bindings."

"What about the other prints?" asked Telvar.

"I see one set of very large footprints. The man must tower over even most of my race. The treads on his boots look foreign to me. The third set of prints must be from the rogue wizard; they are soft-soled, and they smear, as if the walker has a limp."

THE TOMB OF THERAGAARD

"So," Telvar surmised, "we know we are dealing with at least two individuals besides Kara: an Albus mage and his hulking bodyguard."

The young warrior's face showed less anger when he stood. "That's right. And we shall defeat both of them to get Kara back. The blood drops would indicate she is hurt. We cannot waste any more time."

Telvar led the way to the alcove, but before proceeding very far, he stopped to caution, "It is unwise to sneak up on a wizard at the best of times, so please follow my lead. Agreed?"

Wulfric pushed aside the tapestry with his sword. "Agreed. Now enough talk."

The Ulf followed as close to Telvar as one page in a book follows another, ready for any encounter. Tryam wished he still had his breastplate, but he felt comforted having Kayen's cross around his neck. Before following the others, the young acolyte uttered a prayer for his mentor.

The corridor sloped up, a mirror image of the passage they had taken into the Grand Hall. Tryam was uneasy about going back toward the mountaintop. *But if that is where Kara is being held, then so we must return.*

At the end of the corridor was an open archway, beyond which lay an empty circular room fifty feet in diameter, with four exits shrouded in black. Telvar poked his head into the room, the gem atop his staff glowing white. After he swept the air with his staff, he whispered, "The way is clear."

Wulfric stepped into the room and searched the ground for the footprints and blood trail. Telvar aided him by lowering his glowing rod to the ground. Tryam glanced at the domed ceiling, bare walls, and black floor, making sure nothing lurked in the gloom. Scorching along the ceiling indicated that something grim had happened there many years before. He recited the Warding Prayer, but he sensed nothing.

After only a brief time, Wulfric spotted the trail. "This way," he grunted, gesturing to the open archway to the south.

The south passage was a ten-foot-wide corridor that abruptly turned eastward after a dozen yards. Down this hallway, doors appeared at regular intervals: black doors with intricate runes painted on them in red. The company bypassed the doors and methodically made their way down the corridor until an overpowering odor filled their nostrils. Telvar stopped and whispered into the gloom. "I smell death. Be on guard."

Tryam was not sure if it was his imagination or the result of his reciting the Warding Prayer, but he could feel warmth coming from

Kayen's cross. He gripped the pommel of his sword as Telvar used his nose to determine from which room the reek of death originated. After a thorough sniffing, the dark-haired wizard stood before a door twenty feet down the hallway along the south wall. The wizard stepped aside to let Wulfric move into position. Tryam prayed they would not find Kara in this dark and foul place.

Wulfric hesitated.

No sound came from behind the door. Either nothing stirred inside, or the enigmatic black door concealed any noise from their ears. With no other option left to them, Wulfric pushed on the handle and entered the room. Tryam stood by his side.

The acolyte was acquainted with the reek of death from his time in the abbey's infirmary, but this stench left no doubt that the Abyss played a part in its creation. As he surveyed the room, his eyes watered. Once his vision cleared, he saw the cause of the malignant odor of death. In the center of the octagonal room was a bloated corpse on a metal table. Iron shackles were around the dead man's limbs. The corpse was that of an older male. Strange tattoos covered his naked body, and his belly was slashed open. Tryam was relieved it was not Kara, but he wondered if it was one of Wulfric's clansmen.

"Necromancy."

The word hissed from the wizard's mouth.

"The magic to bring the dead back to life?" asked Tryam.

"Yes," confirmed Telvar.

Wulfric spat upon the ground.

The young acolyte fought the urge to bolt from the room. *Evil is here.* He looked at the bloated corpse on the table. "Is this poor man still alive, or is he dead?"

Telvar poked the corpse's ruined stomach with his staff. In response, the corpse's eyes opened, revealing hollow cavities. The undead man's mouth moaned hauntingly. Adding to the horror, the corpse thrashed about, sloshing foul-smelling entrails out onto the table. He lacked any sign of his former humanity.

"He is neither," answered Telvar. "When someone is brought back from the dead, only their rudimentary intelligence follows. Their soul is said to be trapped. Mages are taught what necromancy is, but we are forbidden from practicing the dark art. However, this is now the second time I have

THE TOMB OF THERAGAARD

come across a scene such as this. I fear that my own mentor, Myramar, is now dabbling in this forbidden magic."

"I knew this man," said Wulfric, interrupting Telvar's dark words. "This was Breyn. He was one of my father's most trusted graybeards. How do we destroy this abomination? I cannot let him be defiled like this."

"Fire," answered Telvar. "But let me examine these potions first. I may learn secrets that could help us defeat Dementhus."

Racks of multicolored potions in all manner of containers lined the walls around the body. Wulfric grew impatient watching the wizard pick up, smell, and sometimes pocket potion after potion. He snarled and marched up to the bloodstained slab, and with a quick and efficient stroke, he used his sharp-edged coronium weapon to sever the head from the quivering torso of the body that was once his fellow Ulf. The attack did not stop the horror from thrashing about, however. Even the head still lolled its tongue as it rolled along the ground.

"I said fire," clucked Telvar as he wagged his finger at Wulfric.

The wizard was oblivious to Wulfric's anger and returned to the racks of potions, looking as unhurried as a fruit shopper inspecting melons at the agora. Tryam intervened before Wulfric did anything rash. "We mustn't waste time. The trail grows cold."

The wizard put down the dusty flask he was sniffing and turned back to face the young acolyte. "Wasting time? I am attempting to understand how Dementhus has animated the dead. When we return to Arkos, we might find the city under assault from an undead horde. If I can see what reagents are used in the spell, I can gain a better understanding of how to defeat it."

A growl came from Wulfric's throat.

"Very well, just a few more moments," pleaded Telvar, as he began storing potions haphazardly in his voluminous robes.

Wulfric took the time to retrieve the severed head from the floor, place it next to the torso, and then cover the body with a discarded tapestry he found, giving Breyn's unfortunate soul some semblance of dignity. Meanwhile, Tryam blessed the former graybeard with Kayen's cross.

Telvar reluctantly gave up his examinations, ran his fingers through his dark hair, and adjusted his wizard band. "Just too much," he muttered under his breath. "Too much."

Before leaving the room, the wizard poured a potion on the undead man's severed bits of flesh. He then spoke words of magic, and a small flame

403

shot from his staff to the table. The flesh burned and spread with unnatural haste. Tryam closed the door on the horror, and the party continued their trek eastward, following the trail of blood and mud.

The corridor ended at a grand spiraling staircase, the most elegant and artfully constructed Tryam had seen so far.

"See these ivory railings and gold-inlaid steps? They were likely procured from different ends of Medias." Telvar spoke in a manner that was bordering close to admiration. "At the height of Antigenesus's powers, nothing was beyond his reach!"

The steps wound upward, the trail of the three leading still higher into the complex. On the next level, the grand staircase pierced the center of a dimly lit octagonal room, with four archways leading in each of the cardinal directions. Telvar and Wulfric busied themselves trying to pick up Kara's trail, while Tryam searched the room. He could hear his companions arguing in whispered tones about what was a footprint and what wasn't.

The two were tracking footprints heading eastward, but the dark southern archway caught Tryam's interest. Rubble was strewn about the passage, as if it had suffered some sort of catastrophic event localized to that area. But it wasn't only curiosity he felt; he sensed something else, as if a spirit were nearby. Tryam spoke to the others, who were still arguing. "I feel drawn to this area. I can't explain. Keep looking for Kara's trail. I shall be only a moment."

"Shout if you need us," cautioned Wulfric, "and we shall come running."

"But don't shout too loud," warned Telvar, "or Dementhus will get there before we do."

Whispers in the dark—that is what was drawing the young acolyte to this area. It was a sensation reminiscent to what he'd experienced in the vaults under the abbey. He recited the Warding Prayer, and Kayen's cross glowed a gentle blue.

After roughly fifty feet of ruined hallway, the path led to another archway. The thick wooden door that had once stood before the entrance was splintered, twisted, and cracked, leaving only a small opening into the room beyond.

Tryam used the cross of Aten to light the inside of the cavity, but he could see nothing except more debris. Without wasting more time debating whether it was a good idea or not, he wedged his big frame through the gap.

THE TOMB OF THERAGAARD

Centuries of dust was disturbed when he forced his way inside, causing a coughing fit. After he cleared his lungs, Tryam swept Kayen's cross before him. The room was in ruins. Not one of the four walls was intact, and large portions of the ceiling had collapsed, exposing the mountain's natural ash and rock. Amid all the rubble, the light of Aten caught a glint of silver. *What is that?*

Tryam searched for a way through the rubble. A few bumps and scrapes later, using his long reach, he was able to free the object from under the debris. *A silver statuette?* He turned the puzzling object over in his hands. The more he examined the relic, the more puzzled he became. *This is no magical bauble or artwork dedicated to the archmagus and his ego, but rather a holy relic to honor the dead!*

The statuette depicted a monk on bended knee. On the base of the sculpture was a phrase in the language of ancient Antium: "For those who remove the shadows from this world —Captain Theragaard."

"Theragaard!" said the young acolyte aloud. *That was the name I heard whispered in the vault. That was the name the spirits in the beacon tower called me. That was the name of the man who defeated the archmagus!*

"*Theragaard ... must live again.*"

Tryam recalled those words from the whispers under the abbey. He prayed before the statuette. He needed to seek out the spirits of those buried in this chamber. He would not be afraid.

The young acolyte recited the Warding Prayer. He did so until he heard ghostly whispers in his ear.

"*Return to Arkos ... seek out the tomb ... commune with him ... You must hurry ... There isn't much time ... Hurry. There isn't much time ...*"

"I cannot! I am not worthy of such a task!" anguished Tryam in the dark. "Help me!"

The voices faded into the dark like the last rays of light at summer's end. Further attempts to communicate proved fruitless.

Sweat poured down Tryam's body; his worn robes were soaked. Exhausted, he made his way back. He had no idea how long he had been away from the others, but judging by the concerned looks on Wulfric and Telvar's faces when he reentered the octagonal room, it must have been a while.

"There you are, monk! We called out to you, but you did not respond. Never get out of earshot," scolded the wizard. "We must make haste. We've located the trail."

Telvar expressed no curiosity as to what had compelled Tryam to search the rubble or what he might have found. Wulfric's furrowed brow and raised eyebrows, however, showed that *he* was aware something had happened. As Telvar hurried toward the eastern passage, Wulfric said, "You look troubled. Did you find anything other than dust?"

Tryam was reluctant to tell his friend what had happened. "We have to find Kara and get back to Arkos immediately. There is something I must do that could save us all, though I do not know if I am ready."

Wulfric nodded his head in support, but Tryam knew he did not truly understand.

The eastern corridor was very similar in layout and design to that of the crumbled southern passage, and it led to an archway with an open door. Runes in red were carved over the lintel. Telvar mouthed the words but did not seem to know their meaning. "I do not like this," expressed the wizard. "We are headed into a darker place."

"As if the rest has been pleasant!" shot back Wulfric.

The archway led into a rectangular room that had been stripped of all its furnishings. The room appeared cruder in design than the other parts of the complex, as if it had been built in haste—or for a darker purpose, with no need for pleasing aesthetics. Its walls were of simple carved granite. Instead of glowing orbs providing light, torches held in rusting iron sconces illuminated the area. An alcove in the far wall showed steps curving upward.

"These torches did not light themselves!" observed Wulfric—the implication lost on no one. "Keep close. Blood will likely be spilled soon."

With Telvar's tacit approval, Wulfric, his coronium weapon in hand and his white wolf pelt casting a predatory shadow, took the lead and walked up the cold flat steps of the alcove. Every footfall echoed up the narrow stairwell. The wizard, in his overstuffed robes, had dimmed his staff and looked calm, as if his mind were someplace else. Three quarters up the winding steps, the sounds of torture could be heard from the level above. Wulfric started to rush his way to the top, but Telvar grabbed his shoulder. "Don't hurry to your own death. We have surprise on our side. Let us not waste it."

Wulfric grudgingly conceded and took the steps more cautiously. The stairs ended in an archway with a gloomy gray stone corridor beyond. Torches lined the way, but they cast only a pale orange light. The party stepped past rooms, all dark, as they made for the lit room at the end of the corridor, from where emanated the sounds of a whip cracking and screams.

THE TOMB OF THERAGAARD

As they approached the open door, they could see the shadowy movements of a figure inside, causing the three men to halt and Tryam's heart to miss a beat. The whip cracked twice more, but this time no screams followed.

Wulfric crept in the shadows and rushed to one side of the opening, while Tryam, making as little sound as possible, took the other. The Ulf warrior peered inside the doorway, then raised a single finger to indicate that there was only one enemy in the room.

Telvar whispered into Tryam's ear. "You two charge the man and keep him occupied. I shall blast him with fire from a distance."

Tryam nodded, then communicated the plan to Wulfric using pantomime.

Wulfric twirled his blade while Tryam said a silent prayer to Aten. When all were set, Tryam counted down from three fingers to one on his left hand. When the last finger dropped, the three rushed inside.

Tryam dashed into the room on Wulfric's heels, ready to strike a measure of justice on the torturer. Their adversary was in the north corner of the room; beside him was a table upon which rested bloodied instruments of torture. The monster of a man, whose bulk belied his quickness, spun around and threw a dagger at Tryam's head before the acolyte could cover the distance between them. At first, Tryam thought the brute had missed his target, but when he heard Telvar scream and the sound of a metal staff clank to the ground, he understood he had not been the target.

Two scimitars were in the bare-chested man's hands before Wulfric and Tryam could engage him. A smile more fitting a Daemon appeared on the man's face as he said, "Fresh meat for my blades. Barbarian scum, you shall die first!"

After a feint with a blade, the swarthy man kicked Wulfric, sending him reeling backward. Tryam, who was a second behind, took aim at the man's midsection, but the brute easily blocked his attack.

"A boy monk with a sword, a slow-witted Berserker, and a child mage." The man howled with laughter. "Are you the intruders Gidran has been seeking?"

At the mention of Gidran's name, Tryam's mind flashed back to the time he had unloaded supplies onto the dark monk's ship. "Abbaster!" blurted Tryam in recognition. "To think I played a hand in helping you. Before this day is done, you will kneel before Aten!"

The remark amused the brute. Wulfric and Tryam, their surprise strategy negated, stood side by side as the large man kept them out of reach, his scimitars a wall of deadly steel. "Aten is dying, Terminus is rising. It is you who shall be kneeling before the resurrected Mountain God!"

Wulfric responded with a heedless attack on the giant. He paid for his rashness by suffering a slash to his thigh, which brought him to his knees. Tryam was unprepared to counterattack, but he managed to parry a scimitar swipe aimed at his friend's head.

The brute fell upon the two young men with an avalanche of metal and muscle. The three traded blows, but only Abbaster was landing any cuts.

Wulfric's eyes blazed with fire, and he roared with every blow. Tryam attempted to coordinate his attacks with Wulfric, but the Ulf warrior was beyond reason. Tryam did his best to aid his friend, but he was being edged out of the melee. Counting on Wulfric's ability to handle himself in single combat, the young acolyte took a step back to see what had happened to Telvar. He spotted the brash young mage on his hands and knees, cradling a bloody arm.

The wizard turned him back. "Go help Wulfric. I cannot cast any spells. I am useless."

Tryam cursed and stepped back into the battle. In his brief absence, Abbaster had cornered Wulfric.

The young Ulf was in serious jeopardy, his face drenched in sweat and blood spilling down cuts along his arms and legs. Tryam needed to give his friend just one opportunity that could turn the course of battle. A thought came to his head.

Tryam clenched the cross of Aten and said the Warding Prayer. Keeping the cross in his left hand, he slashed at Abbaster's exposed shoulder, getting the big man's attention. The brute swung around and swatted the weapon away, but not before Tryam thrust the cross in his face. Blue light erupted and flashed into the swarthy man's eyes. Abbaster recoiled as if struck by fire, raising one arm to cover his face.

Wulfric took immediate advantage of Tryam's ploy and swung his coronium weapon at the big man's unprotected legs. The coronium sword sliced clear through the man's thigh, severing the limb above the knee. Abbaster fell backward with a look of shocked horror on his face. His scimitars dropped from his hands.

THE TOMB OF THERAGAARD

"You were right," said Wulfric. "You will not kneel down to Aten. You shall grovel to him on your belly! I am Wulfric, son of Alric, heir to Clan Ulf! Tell me where my people are, where my bondmate Kara is!" Wulfric drew his dagger, stabbed deep into the man's guts, and twisted.

The doomed man grinned with bloody teeth. "Your people are dead, fodder for the great wizard's experimentation. Your wench is with the wizard Dementhus. Her quivering flesh is waiting to be sacrificed to the Mountain God. You may slay me, but you have not stopped our mission. The armies of the Ragnar have conquered almost all of the clans west of the Coronas. Before the new moon rises, they will sweep down from the mountains toward Arkos and wipe out the Engothians! You all shall—"

Abbaster never finished his grim forecast. Wulfric's sword sliced through the thick muscle and bone of the man's neck. The brute's body writhed and twisted for a moment but finally was still.

Both exhausted youths exchanged worried glances.

"How did you get the cross of Aten to flash the brute?" asked Wulfric between deep breaths.

Tryam looked dumbfounded at the cross in his hand. "I honestly don't know. I just knew I could."

"If you are both done savoring your victory," came Telvar's weakened voice from behind them, "would you please help me?"

"By the heavens!" cried Tryam as he rushed over to the supine wizard.

Taking the wizard's arm in his hands, Tryam examined the wound. It was a serious cut, but not life threatening. The thick robes the wizard wore had prevented the dagger from penetrating deeper into the flesh. Tryam thoroughly cleaned the wound with water, tore a piece of cloth from the cuff of the wizard's robes, and wrapped it around his bleeding forearm. "You will be fine," he assured Telvar.

When Tryam was finished with the wizard, he stood and looked to see if Wulfric had any wounds that needed tending, but his friend had already entered the next room. In the confusion of battle, the young acolyte had overlooked an open doorway on the north wall. When Tryam stepped to the next room's threshold, a slack-faced Wulfric was just returning.

"Dead. They are all dead."

The somber words preceded an overpowering stench of death. Wearily, Tryam entered the side room. Chained to the wall of the circular chamber were five Ulf males. All showed signs of severe torture, and all were most definitely dead. Tryam wanted to turn away, but he could not.

"I knew all of them," lamented Wulfric. "We are too late. One of them by only a matter of minutes."

Unable to suppress tears from his eyes, Tryam stepped before each man and gave a final blessing. "Their souls shall rest in peace. Praise be to Aten that they show no sign of necromancy."

Wulfric paced the room, running his fingers through his hair. "Kara is not among the dead. Could what that foul man said be true? Is she to be sacrificed to the Ragnar god?"

Tryam watched Wulfric's sorrow turn to frustration and then anger as his friend smashed the table that held the instruments of torture.

The wizard repeatedly tapped the butt end of his staff on the floor until Wulfric took notice. "That fiend said she was with Dementhus and was to be sacrificed to their mountain god. If that is the case, she would be taken to the lens room, where the Golem would also be." Telvar, though pale, seemed to perk up as he spoke. "The blood trail led here, but she was not tortured, as were these men. She was likely only ensorcelled, in order to make her more compliant. I did not see any tracks elsewhere, so there must be a hidden exit from this room." The wizard began tapping on the walls with his staff. He paid particular attention to one spot, and he struck it repeatedly. "Extinguish the torches. I need to examine this area with my magic."

Wulfric removed the torches from the walls and threw them to the ground. Tryam then stepped on the flames. Once the room was dark, the wizard spoke the enigmatic words of magic. Tryam listened intently, but again the words disappeared from his memory soon after they entered his ears.

Telvar cautioned Wulfric and Tryam to stand still. The confident mage spoke another magical phrase, and his staff glowed bright white. This time when he went to tap the wall, the staff went through the solid stone. Tryam gasped in surprise, much to Telvar's amusement.

"Here it is!" said the wizard triumphantly. "Follow me."

"Through a wall?" Wulfric looked at the wizard in disbelief.

"This is only an illusion. Cleverly crafted, but an illusion nonetheless. I shall show you."

The wizard stepped into the wall and disappeared.

"I trust not the ways of mages, but if I must follow, I shall" said Wulfric as he stepped into the wall. Tryam instinctively held his breath and closed his eyes as he, too, passed through the illusory wall. A slight charge ran through his body, but he was otherwise unaffected.

On the other side of the wall was a small tunnel carved from the mountain rock. The smell of fresh water inexplicably filled the air. Tryam heard Telvar's voice echoing from farther ahead. "Remarkable. Truly remarkable."

Tryam and Wulfric rushed down the tunnel, at the end of which they saw the wizard standing next to an underground canal. Telvar was inspecting a small barge tied to a post near the water's edge.

"How can this be?" marveled Tryam. "A river inside a mountain? Another illusion?"

Telvar shook his head. "Not everything is an illusion. This is very real and another example of Antigenesus's mastery over the elements. The question you should ask is, Can we use this to get where we need to go?"

Tryam walked over to the solidly built barge. The craft was just big enough for four men to stand comfortably in, but the canal itself looked as if it could accommodate much larger craft. The barge had no rudder, pole, oars, or obvious means of control. It was unlike any boat Tryam had seen before.

"This does not seem like a wise idea. Who knows what traps may lie upon the water, where we shall have little way of escaping?" said Wulfric, perhaps spooked by the thought of having to rely on magical transportation.

"Nothing we have done in the last couple of weeks has been a wise idea," snapped Telvar as he stepped aboard the craft.

Wulfric hesitated a moment, long enough for Telvar to notice his apprehension. The wizard mockingly jumped up and down on the barge, to show it had substance. "This is the only way we can reach the lens room. Make haste!"

"After we rescue Kara, so help me . . ." grumbled Wulfric into Tryam's ear as he stepped aboard the craft.

Tryam untied the mooring line but was dubious that even Telvar, who had showed his skill in magic thus far, could get the barge to move without oars.

The wizard sat cross-legged and retrieved a thick leather-bound book from his backpack. It was not his usual spell book. Curious, Tryam

411

approached Telvar and saw that the book had complex geometric shapes carved into its cover. He attempted to peek at the book's contents, but Telvar turned his back away protectively. "This may take a moment," he cautioned, then added, "Do not pester me."

After a time, Telvar rested the book on the barge and spoke words of magic, repeating a set of phrases over and over again. He then added hand gestures to the phrases. Nothing seemed to work; the barge remained in place, nestled against the edge of the canal.

"Should I whittle a paddle?" cracked Wulfric.

Telvar ignored the Ulf and started the process over. Tryam used the time to bandage the wound on Wulfric's thigh and attend to other, smaller cuts. After drinking water, the young acolyte dozed off. He awoke when he heard an excited shout come from the wizard.

"I think I may have a solution. Get ready." The wizard strode to the front of the barge and uttered a single-syllable word.

Much to Tryam's surprise and relief, the barge stirred beneath them. Slowly at first, then more swiftly. The barge was heading upstream.

"What did you say?" inquired Tryam.

The wizard frowned. "All I said was, 'Return.' I can only hope it returns us to the right place."

Chapter 62
Meeting in the Blue Room

The barge settled in at a pace worthy of a fast-moving riverboat as it pushed through the dark waters of the mountain canal. Providing light along the waterway were more of the ever-present orbs suspended from the cavernous roof. They passed many landings similar to the one at their departure point, but the barge never changed its course.

Despite being aware of the scale of the fortress, Tryam was still not prepared for what he saw when the barge reached its destination. The magical craft slowed when it rounded a bend and entered a chamber massive enough to accommodate an army of Golems. The barge slipped into a pool the size of a small harbor and drifted toward a pier as if guided by a master seaman. In the harbor, moored before a series of broad steps leading higher into the mountain, was another barge, but one much larger, with brass railings and a coated oak decking.

"Wouldn't you say that craft is large enough to accommodate the Golem?" asked Telvar.

The mage's words echoed into the chamber's shadows. When the wizard spoke again, he did so in a whisper. "We are at the lens complex. It has to be, for we have reached the peak. Any misstep now will be our doom."

The barge came to a full stop alongside its giant cousin. Wulfric was the first to jump off, followed by Telvar, then Tryam. With only one path to follow, up the giant steps, Wulfric took the lead, his sword at the ready.

As they ascended the steps, Tryam noticed damage to the chamber that the shadows had hidden. It appeared as if giant statues had once lined both sides of the chamber, their broken plaster and twisted iron bodies testifying to their having encountered a great destructive force; only their bronze bases remained intact. Even the marble steps they walked upon were cracked and scorched from exposure to intense heat.

Tryam mounted the gargantuan steps, which he was certain had been built for the Golem's legs. As he struggled up each one, his heart beat fast, and sweat poured down his face. The higher he climbed, the farther along the broad path ahead he could see. A pulsating green light was visible, and a tingling sensation surrounded his body. When he reached the top of the steps, he could see that the broad hallway ended about a hundred yards away. The green light blinded all to what was beyond that.

"Look, more mud tracks!" Wulfric pointed his sword at a series of stains on the smoky white marble. "This way!"

Archways lined both sides of the hallway, most of them blocked by rubble. Wulfric raced into the darkness, following the trail that led to a room from which a blue light pulsed.

Cursing Wulfric's rashness, the wizard bolted after him and physically restrained him before he could rush headlong into the room. "Let me investigate before you set off an alarm that could bring the whole fortress upon us!"

"No, we are close to Kara. I can tell."

Wulfric rushed past the wizard and disappeared into the room with the glowing blue light. When no shouts of alarm erupted, Tryam thanked Aten. Instead, to his great amazement, he heard Wulfric's joyful cry: "Kara! It's Kara!"

Tryam rushed past Telvar and charged into the room.

For all the wonders Tryam had seen on this journey, from the golden sunsets to the snow-crowned mountain peaks, nothing filled his heart with more delight than the sight of Kara. Wulfric was draped over her like a warm blanket. So tight was the embrace, it took Tryam a moment to notice glowing blue shackles restraining her to the wall.

Tryam rushed to Kara's side. She was covered in sweat, and her body hung loose in the restraints. "Wulfric, give me a moment to examine her." His Ulf friend, after a long embrace, reluctantly stepped aside. Tryam checked her over. "No broken bones and only a deep cut on her forehead.

She is, however, likely in need of water. She will recover if we can get out of here."

"Here, sweet Kara, take a sip from my flask," said Wulfric, adding, "I shall never let you out of my sight again."

Kara struggled to lift her head, but after downing a big gulp, she replied, "You had better not." Her eyes sparkled briefly before she closed them again.

"Help me get her down!" cried Wulfric.

His fumbling with the cuffs about Kara's wrists and ankles caused her to jolt back awake. She let out a scream, then laughed. "Does a wolf eat me?"

"Fear not. I wear the pelt from a Hound of Fenrir! I succeeded in the Trial of Blood and was returning home. What I found sent me to the brink of madness: the village in ashes and you missing!" Wulfric kissed her on the lips. "As I succeeded in my Trial, so shall I get vengeance on the Ragnar and the wizard who have done this to you, my father, and my people!"

Kara returned his kiss and appeared energized by Wulfric's words. "You killed a Hound of Fenrir? After we are free from this accursed place, I must find out how." She kissed him again. "I knew you would return to the village as a man and our hero, and I knew you would find me. Together, we shall kill the wizard and every last one of his yellow-spined men! We shall have our vengeance!" As she spoke, more of the true Kara showed on her face. When she tried to move her arms and legs, she frowned. "I need to be free at once!"

Wulfric drew his blade and said, "Close your eyes."

Kara smiled and said, "I trust you."

Wulfric slashed at the glowing blue metal around her ankle. His aim was true, but the coronium blade bounced off the restraint, leaving it unscathed and Wulfric stunned. Cursing, he tried a few more swings, but to no avail.

"Hurry!" implored Kara.

When Wulfric stopped out of frustration and fatigue, Tryam made an attempt, but he met with equal disappointment. "We need Telvar's help," he concluded.

It was the first time in a while that Tryam had thought about the wizard. He found Telvar just outside the room, staring intently at the glowing green light and cocking his ear toward the strange noises coming from farther down the hallway. The mage was so focused he did not see Tryam approach.

"We have need of your magic! We cannot remove the restraints."

The call for his magic brought Telvar's focus back to his compatriots. "Coming," he answered, turning away from the green rays.

Kara squirmed when Telvar entered. "Get him away from me! I don't like wizards!"

Gently touching her shoulder, Wulfric tried to calm Kara down. "It's okay. We know him. He has helped us find you. But do not worry, he is no wizard—only an apprentice."

Telvar bowed quickly. "I am actually a powerful wizard but not as powerful as the wizard we shall soon encounter. We must not dawdle." The young Rutilus mage pushed Wulfric aside with his staff and then began examining the four glowing restraints, one at a time.

"Can't you do this any faster?" asked Wulfric.

"No! Unless you have an object hard enough to shatter magically augmented steel," returned Telvar.

While the wizard continued to study the restraints, Tryam and Wulfric filled Kara in on what had happened since their last meeting, including the sad news about losing Brother Kayen. Kara then told them of her adventures in the fortress and what had happened at the Ulf village. She said how the Ulf men had fought bravely despite facing overwhelming odds. She then spoke softly as she told the story of Alric's final battle, as relayed to her from the other Ulf captives. "Alric was the bravest among the Ulf. Wulfric, you would be proud of your father. He died as a warrior, defending his people until his last breath. He never gave Ivor the satisfaction he was seeking."

"I expected nothing else," grieved Wulfric.

As the wizard puzzled over the restraints, Tryam's anxiety grew. Wulfric would not budge from Kara's side, so the young acolyte acted as their lone lookout. He stepped to the exit and peered around the corner toward the green glow at the end of the hallway. Something sinister was happening in that chamber—he was sure of it. He also suspected that Telvar knew exactly what the glowing light portended. If they could stop Dementhus before he brought the Ragnar mountain god to life, Arkos would stand a chance against the Ragnar and their armies. But Tryam had his doubts they could do this on their own. *Theragaard, please help us!*

THE TOMB OF THERAGAARD

Turning back toward the happenings in the room, Tryam heard the mage speaking words of magic. As the incantation progressed, the gem at the tip of his staff changed color. Tryam felt as if he were watching a painter mixing colors on a palette. When the gem matched the color of Kara's restraints, Telvar ceased his spell.

"Ah, I think I have it!" exclaimed Telvar. "Now brace yourself, young lady. If I don't have it exactly right, this may hurt."

"I don't care how much it hurts," Kara responded bravely. "I just want them removed."

"By your command." The wizard slowly tapped the now-blue gem to the blue restraint over Kara's left wrist. When the two bits of magic touched, sparks flew in the air, and the restraint snapped open.

"Hey!" exclaimed Kara. "I am almost free!"

One by one, Telvar removed the remaining restraints. Wulfric caught Kara before she fell to the floor, and he embraced her in a true bear hug. After a time, Kara let Wulfric go and gave Tryam a hug. After rubbing her wrists and ankles, she said, "I need a weapon. We have blood to spill."

Before anyone could move, Kara rushed to a table in the corner of the room. "They were to dress me in my warrior's attire before sacrificing me to their dumb god, so they left all this behind." Kara picked up her bow and hugged it to her chest. She even kissed one of her red arrows before strapping the quiver to her back and testing the bow's sturdiness. Unsatisfied, she tightened the string.

"Are we ready to find Dementhus and end this nightmare?" asked Tryam.

Wulfric and Kara nodded their heads with matching grim faces. The wizard, still breathing heavy from his spellcasting, was more cautious. "The Golem and the Albus mage are close. As Tryam can sense the spirits of the departed, I can sense the presence of great magic. The lens room and the gem have to be what lies at the end of this broad corridor." He leaned on his staff. "I suggest you sharpen your swords and say your prayers, for once we leave this room, there will be no going back."

"Do we have a plan?" asked Tryam.

The laugh that reflexively erupted from Telvar was not one born from joy. "Our only hope is that we can surprise the wizard and that one of us lives long enough to get in the killing blow. At this point, there is no way we can make him see the error of his ways, especially now that he is on the verge of activating one of the most powerful artifacts ever created. The green light, I am sure, is powerful magic being channeled at this very moment into the Golem."

A grave look came over Wulfric, who moved to stand before the wizard. "The time is upon us. Are you willing to use what magic you have against a fellow spellcaster, even at the risk of your own life?"

Pointing to the wizard band atop his head, Telvar stated, "When I chose the life of a wizard, I took an oath. An oath to uphold the rules of the Wizard Council. Dementhus has clearly violated this oath, and I mean to stop him before he causes even more harm to the reputation of our members. As for dying, I shall do what needs to be done, but I have no intention of dying this day!"

If prayer had ever been more important in his life, Tryam could not think of a time. While Wulfric helped Kara with her weapons and Telvar meditated, Tryam went to his knees and clutched Kayen's cross to his chest. He said the only prayer he thought appropriate, a prayer not for power nor for victory but for guidance, and he was rewarded with a feeling of calm. He was ready to accept Aten's will for whatever might come.

Chapter 63
The Gem

With a singular purpose, the group, led by Telvar, headed toward the ominous green light at the end of the broad hallway. Ahead, a strong, acrid smell filled the air, and a low-pitched hum sounded so forcefully that Tryam's chest vibrated. Above the rumble was a voice chanting. Tryam recognized the words as being from the uniquely ephemeral language of magic.

The hallway ended not at a door but at another set of colossal marble steps, which led up to the heart of a cavernous chamber, the hollowed-out top of the mountain peak itself. Giant pillars, holding the ceiling in place, disappeared into the dark above.

The four ascended the steps in unison. Upon reaching the top step, Tryam held his breath in slack-jawed wonder at what he saw. Before him was the Golem in repose on a slab of crimson marble. A bald, red-robed wizard, his back to the party, stood beside the Golem. Held in the mage's outstretched arms was a staff. Atop the staff was a large spherical crystal that focused a glimmering green beam of light down onto the metallic warrior's placid face. Tryam scanned the ceiling high above for the source of the light, and he spotted, embedded in the rock, a smooth, clear lens, a dozen times the size of the lens at the Arkos mage tower. Telvar whispered that a powerful illusion and the inventiveness of ancient engineers was keeping the lens hidden from the outside world.

"Dementhus is feeding the Golem energy," whispered Telvar, "undoubtedly a very complicated undertaking. He may be too preoccupied to be aware of us just yet. We are fortunate the monstrosity has not been animated."

Wulfric, the pelt of the Hound of Fenrir firmly in place over his body, was eager to strike but looked to the wizard for advice. "How should we attack?"

"From two directions at once while he is still focused on the spell! Tryam will follow me, while you take Kara. Watch for my signal. Then attack with the ferocity of your people!"

The two Ulfs nodded their understanding and held hands before splitting off to the right. Tryam followed Telvar off to the left. The young acolyte grasped his sword with shaky hands. When he stood beside the young wizard, he looked past the Golem and beheld the largest gem he had ever seen. The crystal was the size of a mammoth, and it pulsed with energy. It sat in the center of the room, held in place upon the ground by a golden ring. It was this pulsing that created the overpowering hum. Cracks along the gem's surface spilled light, giving the impression that the stone was dangerously unstable. "What in heaven is that?" asked Tryam pointing to the gem.

"That is the heart of this ancient fortress. While most wizards prefer to build towers to house their lens and gem, Antigenesus needed a mountain. Inside that gem is stored a vast amount of magical energy. It was likely damaged when the bond between gem and wizard was severed at the time of Antigenesus's death. Dementhus seems to have made some rudimentary repairs." Before Tryam could ask further questions, Telvar nodded his head in the direction of the others. "Wulfric and Kara are in position. When they charge the wizard, you do the same. I have a spell in mind and a backup plan should this fail."

Backup plan? Tryam had no inspired stratagem other than to slash his sword at Dementhus's undefended back. From the corner of his eye, he observed Kara pulling back on her bowstring, red arrow ready, and Wulfric tensing his leg muscles. With all eyes on the wizard, Telvar signaled the start of the battle with a downward wave of his staff.

A prayer to Aten on his lips, Tryam hurtled himself toward the red-robed sorcerer. The young acolyte's blade reached Dementhus at the same time as Wulfric's eager sword. Wulfric let loose a war cry, and both young men slashed their weapons down at the exposed back of the apparently defenseless wizard. Dementhus did not react as the weapons closed, and his deep-voiced incantations were unchanged. Tryam watched his own weapon fall toward the wizard unopposed.

THE TOMB OF THERAGAARD

Just as his sword was about to bite into the rogue wizard's flesh, a flash of light flared in Tryam's face, and a bolt of energy slammed into his chest. The bolt blew the sword from his hand and knocked him backward a dozen feet. Wulfric landed beside him in a heap. As he struggled to his knees, the young acolyte gasped for breath. He looked up in time to see Kara's and Telvar's attacks. A blast of fire from Telvar's staff struck out at the wizard, but it too failed to penetrate the barrier. Kara's arrow bounced off the same invisible shield.

Their presence was finally acknowledged by the mad wizard, who casually turned toward the four attackers. He lowered his staff in the process, which caused the beam of light that had been redirected from the lens to the Golem to take its natural path into the unstable gem. The great Albus wizard smiled, and he raised his eyebrows in amusement.

"Are these the intruders Gidran has so clumsily tracked and failed to eliminate? You are just children!" mocked Dementhus in an otherworldly, melodious voice. "God of the Mountain, arise and feast on these young souls! Feast!"

The ground beneath Tryam's feet rumbled as the Golem rose from the crimson slab. Tryam's heart sank, and his hopes were crushed as if the mountain itself had fallen on them. *We are too late! The Golem lives!*

The obsidian warrior with red tattoos rose to its more-than-fifty-foot height. Its movements were uncannily human and its blank face, fear inspiring.

"Run!" shouted Wulfric as the Ulf grabbed Tryam by the collar.

Wulfric raced back to Kara, then led the three back to the marble steps. Tryam looked for Telvar but could not see where he had fled.

The sound of metal scraping on stone filled the chamber. As they ran, Tryam looked left and right for the source but could not find it until Kara pointed to the dark recess of the ceiling. She cried a warning. "A metal curtain is dropping on us!"

Tryam saw the steel barrier falling with incredible speed. The three tried to stop but still collided with the metal curtain, which now blocked them from escape. Tryam thanked Aten that, at least, they had not been crushed by it.

"We are trapped!" spat Kara, as she kicked futilely at the metal curtain. "Curse these wizards!"

No one in the group had time to do anything but react as the Golem was upon them with just two of its massive strides. The metal warrior swatted its black fist at the cornered three, missing Kara by only inches and then smashing into the floor with the sound of a thousand hammers striking a thousand anvils.

"Ha, you missed," taunted Kara as she ran to Wulfric's side. "You will have to move faster to catch us!"

Tryam was amazed at the colossus's speed: The metal man moved as if made from flesh. "Split up!" he shouted. "We have to bide time for Telvar. He said he had a backup plan." *If he is still alive.*

Wulfric and Kara moved to the right side of the chamber. The Golem turned in pursuit. Tryam watched with awe as his friends dodged the goliath's fists while diving under tables, brushing past vats of boiling liquids, and leaping over other assorted materials, just to keep one step ahead. Tryam used their diversion to backtrack to where he'd last seen Telvar. As he stumbled his way in the strobing light, the young acolyte felt someone grab him by the collar and drag him back toward a rack of putrid-smelling potions. Thinking Dementhus was upon him, he made a move to attack, but he stopped when he recognized Telvar's red wizard band. "I almost tackled you! Never sneak up on a warrior!"

"Oh, so our young monk is now a warrior?"

"Enough!" shouted Tryam in exasperation. "Do something! The Golem is hunting the others!"

"Be quiet and listen," whispered Telvar in his ear. "I am not sure where Dementhus is. He may have departed so as not to be trampled by the Golem. In any event, he left the lens active, and the energy it gleans from the heavens is now channeling directly into the gem."

Tryam's blank look caused the wizard to sigh. "That means," he continued, "that the gem is absorbing magic with no regulation. If we can destroy the gem, we can sever its link to Dementhus."

"But what of the Golem?"

"Deprived of the gem's energy, Dementhus will lose his control over it."

Telvar handed the young acolyte his staff. "You must run to the gem and thrust this into one of the pulsating cracks. If the gem is split wide enough, the energy stored inside will shatter the jewel. I can't tell how long it will take to crack, but after you plunge the staff into the crystal, run as if Necromedes the Thrice Reborn were after you!"

"I understand, but run to where? The curtain has sealed us in!"

THE TOMB OF THERAGAARD

"While you are shattering the gem, I shall seek to raise the curtain. I think I have enough power to do so. At least enough for us to pass under it and leave the Golem trapped here. Now go!"

The pulsating waves of magical energy streaming down from the lens combined with the tremors caused by the Golem's footsteps made it seem as if the end of the world were upon them. Tryam poked his head up from behind the potion rack and looked for the best path to the glowing, multifaceted gem. Fortunately for him, the Golem had been lured to the other side of the chamber in its pursuit of Wulfric and Kara. In the process, the magical monster was overturning bookcases, smashing tables, and throwing all manner of objects into the air. Tryam was heartened to see an occasional red arrow bounce off the inhuman foe. Ominously, however, Tryam could not spot the red-robed wizard anywhere. Tryam kissed his cross, clutched Telvar's staff in his right hand, and stepped out from behind the potion rack. He would have to cover fifty paces to get to the fractured gem. His first step was hesitant, but when no doom fell upon him, he ran for the gem as fast as he could over the trembling floor.

With only twenty paces to go, a shadow appeared on Tryam's flank. So focused was he on the gem, he did not see the Necromancer appear from behind the red marble table where the Golem had rested. Tryam stopped and reflexively reached for his sword before he realized that he had lost it earlier. He resorted to menacing the bald wizard with Telvar's staff. The threat did not work, for Dementhus only laughed.

"You do not look like a wizard." The rogue Albus mage's voice was deep and strong, the voice of a leader. His head tilted slightly. "How have you come this far? You are just a boy."

"Aten has guided me." Tryam kept his voice level, revealing no fear. "You shall pay for the death you have brought to the Ulf clan."

"If I had the time, I would torture you until you turned away from your god. But instead, I shall show you mercy." Dementhus's eyes gleamed, revealing the cruelty of the man. The Albus mage then raised his arms as if imitating a snake strike. Around his hands, balls of green energy formed. Tryam felt his hair stand on end.

Without a weapon, Tryam did not know what to do besides lunge at the wizard and hope to disrupt the spell. When the young acolyte rushed ahead, Dementhus responded by launching the glowing green balls. Tryam braced for the impact.

But before the green spheres of magical death made contact, a gust of wind slammed into his body. Tryam twisted in the air as he watched, incredulously, as the green spheres flew harmlessly into the darkness, even as his own body flew toward the gem.

The young acolyte landed face first into the side of the pulsating giant crystal. The proximity to the gem and its volatile energy caused his teeth to rattle and his stomach to churn. As he gathered his remaining wits, he understood what had happened. *That wind was Telvar's doing! He saved my life.*

Unfortunately, the force of the impact had also knocked the staff from his hands, and he had not seen where it went. As the light from the gem blinded him, he fumbled for the staff. He cried out in frustration: "Aten, guide my hands in my time of need!"

A scream of pain from Kara brought Tryam's attention back to the Golem. He looked away from the blinding gem and saw, from the gloom, the metallic warrior emerging and heading toward where he had last seen Dementhus. The Golem held in one hand a struggling and angry Wulfric and in the other a writhing and cursing Kara.

With added urgency, Tryam resumed the search for the staff. Providence guided his hand as the young acolyte felt the thin metal staff after only a few heart-pounding moments. He took the staff and fought against the waves of energy pouring from the gem in order to stand as close to one of the cracked facets as possible. Blinded, Tryam whispered another prayer to Aten as he raised Telvar's staff high over his head. He could only hope Telvar was correct.

"No!" shouted Dementhus from behind, his voice echoing in the cavernous room.

As he felt Telvar's staff plunge inside the gem, Tryam smiled with the comfort of Aten's grace.

The world became silent and peaceful. For a moment, at least.

Chapter 64

ARDRAH

Tryam closed his eyes and basked in the peace of the moment.
Then everything changed.

An explosion of light and heat erupted from the gem. Tryam flew into the air and landed hard against one of the chamber's support pillars. When he could breathe again, he was shocked to find that he was still alive and still grasping Telvar's staff.

Around the young man was a scene in complete chaos. Where the once-brilliant gem had rested was now the epicenter of a series of violent destructive waves of magical energy that were violently shaking the entire mountain. Ceiling stones had already fallen, and the marble pillars spaced about the chamber were crumbling one after another. Tryam's eyes burned, and his throat was scorched from vaporized crystals.

High above, the tower lens wobbled and now hung precariously from the metal framework that held it in place. The energy that once was focused down from the lens in a tight beam was now erratic and sprayed destructive force wherever it shone.

Tryam searched for the impossibly black Golem in the inconsistent lighting of the chamber. When he spotted the metal warrior, it was on its knees, still holding in its hands a squirming Kara and a fuming Wulfric.

Before Tryam could make his way to help his friends, another destructive wave of energy erupted from the great gem. As the wave spread, it caused more chaos. The wave slammed into the metal support of the lens above, and the structure groaned and then tore apart. The lens slipped free and fell toward the Golem and its two Ulf hostages.

"Watch out!" screamed Tryam futilely.

Kara and Wulfric could only cover their heads as the hundred-foot-wide lens smashed onto the Golem's back and shoulders. The sound of the impact was loud enough to deafen. When Tryam recovered, he could see that the force of the impact had knocked the Golem to the ground; it was now buried beneath a mound of broken glass. Of Kara and Wulfric there was no sign. *Please Aten, let them still be alive!*

Without regard to his own safety, Tryam headed out into the open and toward the fallen Golem. Aten had been with them again, for he found his friends free of the Golem's grasp. In fact, the metal warrior had unintentionally shielded them from the jagged glass shards.

As she kicked at the Golem's motionless hand, Kara smiled. "How do *you* like it!" she taunted.

When the cracked gem rumbled again, Tryam pulled Kara away from the gargantuan appendage. "Another wave of destruction is about to be unleashed!" he shouted as he urged the two Ulfs in the direction of the metal curtain. "This way!"

Wulfric grabbed Kara's hand and followed Tryam's lead. They made it only halfway, diving behind one of the few intact pillars when the next wave hit.

This time, the destructive wave caused parts of the mountain itself to spill into the chamber from above. Kara shrieked while Wulfric covered her head. Tryam prayed until the wave dissipated, thanking Aten when it was over and they were still alive.

"How do we get out of here?" cried Kara over the chaos.

"Telvar was to raise the curtain, but it has not budged, and he is nowhere in sight! We must find him! He is our only hope of escape!"

The flashing lighting in the chamber made it difficult to see what was shadow and what was substance. "I last saw him over there," explained Tryam as he headed toward where the potion rack had once stood. "But this is also close to where I last saw Dementhus." He looked around nervously. "We must hurry. The next shock wave will come soon!"

Tryam found the potion rack—or what was left of it. The three searched the debris-covered ground, sifting through large piles of cracked marble and stone. They dared not call Telvar's name, for fear of alerting Dementhus.

"We are in danger of lingering too long," warned Wulfric. "The ceiling supports are failing. We have to find another way out of here. I am sorry."

Tryam scanned the nightmarish scene and came to the same conclusion. "Head to the far end of the chamber. We may find a back door."

The magnitude of the shock waves had increased with each successive blast from the gem. If that pattern held, Tryam doubted that the chamber could survive another one.

"Give me that back, you fool!" snapped a voice from the dark.

As a hand reached out to grasp the staff from him, the young acolyte reflexively took a fighting stance. When he saw it was his black-robed companion and not the red-robed Dementhus, his body relaxed. Tryam was shocked to see Telvar and gladly handed the staff over to the dust-covered young man.

"Your escape plan?" inquired Tryam.

"Impossible. I am afraid the power needed to raise the curtain was beyond my abilities," admitted Telvar. He looked back to the epicenter of the energy waves. "We survived the gem's initial fracturing, but it still appears to be acting as a cap over what must be an enormous reserve. Something I did not anticipate. The shock waves will increase in power until the gem is finally destroyed and the reserves are unleashed. We've been very lucky so far."

"I don't feel lucky," said Wulfric as he clung to Kara. "How in the Abyss do we get out of here?"

"Do you have a spell that could help?" Tryam asked Telvar hopefully.

The young wizard examined his staff. The gem that rested atop the magical wand was cracked and dark. When he answered, Tryam sensed, for the first time, none of Telvar's bravado. "I am afraid not. I have spent all of my energy."

"Maybe you can wake up the Golem and have him do *our* bidding. He could bash a way out of here," suggested Kara, with her typical indefatigable enthusiasm. "Did you see him almost crush me?"

Wulfric seemed dubious. "I don't think Telvar can duplicate Dementhus's command of the Golem. Can you?"

"Of course not, you fools!" barked Telvar, his voice rising in pitch as he struggled to keep his composure. "You do realize, don't you, that if we cannot find a way out of here, we are all doomed?"

"As long as we draw breath," said Tryam as he pulled out Kayen's cross, "we have hope."

Telvar sighed.

Another mass of energy formed around the ruined gem. "Get ready," warned Tryam. "Another blast is about to erupt!"

The four moved from the pillar and ran to the back wall of the chamber, the farthest point from the exploding gem. A moment later, magic belched from the crystal, causing another deafening and powerful wave of destruction. As one pillar after another tipped over, tons of dirt, stone, snow, and ice poured inside the chamber. The mountain peak itself was collapsing.

As the wave of death headed their way, Wulfric roared in frustration. He embraced Kara in his massive arms. "To lose you again after having just found you!"

"At least, we have doomed the Ragnar," offered Telvar as consolation. "Without the Albus mage and their false god, they will lose their ambition and their war."

Even as the world closed in around him, Tryam did not despair. He used both hands to hold onto Kayen's cross as he said a prayer to Aten.

The avalanche of dirt and ice collided with the pillar nearest them, but instead of snapping, the pillar tipped and fell their way.

"Look out!" cried Tryam.

The flow of rock and ice knocked the immense pillar over as if it were a twig in a flood, and the hard marble slammed into the back wall. From the impact, a hole opened, and a rush of fresh but bitterly cold air poured into the chamber. Tryam could see the dark sky outside, filled with brilliant white stars.

"I don't believe it. Hurry!" Tryam shouted in joy at their fortune. "This way!" His shout roused the others as he jumped on the fallen pillar that stood half in the chamber and half outside of it. The roof above them was the only part of the lens room still intact.

Wulfric grabbed Kara while Tryam helped Telvar climb on top the marble column. The four used the pillar as a ramp and headed for the opening, but before they could make it all the way out, a new shock wave erupted from the fractured gem. As that wave reached them, all four fell down and hugged the pillar. The force unleashed caused the entire marble stanchion to be ejected out of the chamber and to slide down the snow-covered mountain like a colossal sled.

Everything that Tryam attempted to say to the others was swallowed by the noise of the collapsing mountaintop and the avalanche that was now cascading down the side of the ruined peak. The young acolyte had a firm grasp on Telvar, who in return had a firm grasp on Wulfric. Kara was blanketed by the hulking Ulf warrior's body. Tryam was sure that it was only by the divine hand of Aten that all four still lived.

As snow, rocks, and chunks of ice crashed around them, the pillar slid down the mountain at an ever-increasing speed. There was no opportunity to jump to safety. Above, another shock wave erupted, the largest one yet. Tryam was so relieved to be free of the death trap of the lens chamber, he did not notice the danger ahead until Wulfric shouted a warning.

"We head for the crater between the peaks!"

The snow beneath the pillar changed to coarse stone, then chunky pumice. As the terrain changed, the acceleration of the pillar slowed, but it was not slowing fast enough to stop it from heading to the lip of the crater at a still-incredible speed.

Wulfric, in the front of the pillar, had a better view of what was ahead. He acted as if he had a plan. "Everyone, jump on my signal!"

When the pillar reached the crater's lip, it lifted in the air as if launched from a ramp. When it reached its apex, Tryam heard Wulfric shout, "Now!"

Tryam flew off the marble stone and into the air. He landed in a snowdrift right next to Telvar. The young acolyte helped the wizard to his feet and was ecstatic to see that Wulfric and Kara had landed, unharmed, nearby. The marble pillar continued down the mountain slope as it now tumbled and again gained speed. Tryam breathed a sigh of relief—but it was short-lived.

"This place looks familiar," said Wulfric in an ominous tone.

Tryam was about to argue, but then he looked back up the slope and saw the man-made entrance into the mountain. Still on guard was a company of Ragnar men, who turned away from the exploding peak to look down at the four unexpected visitors. The stunned warriors reached for their weapons.

This is not possible! Of all the places on this mountain to land!

"Our fortune has changed again," said Telvar. "My magical energies are depleted. How can we defeat the Ragnar without magic?"

"We cut them down by axe and blade," Wulfric said, drawing steel.

"By yourself?" Tryam asked. "You are the only one with a weapon."

"I still have my arrows, but I lost my bow," lamented Kara.

The wizard sighed. "My daggers—here, take them." Telvar pulled the sharp weapons from his robes and handed one to each of them. "I want them back, so use them wisely."

The well-armed Ragnar numbered more than twenty and showed cruel smiles under metal visors. After shaking off their bewilderment at both the mountain peak's explosions and the appearance of the party, the fur-covered and green-armored warriors started for their position.

"Their intentions are clear. They will soon attack! We should flee!" pleaded Telvar.

"We are done running!" blasted Wulfric.

Even if Wulfric had been willing, the deep snow made retreat unfeasible. Telvar held his staff in two hands ready to bludgeon any who approached. Kara grasped a dagger. Wulfric stood at the vanguard, his coronium blade gleaming in the starlight.

"My friends," said Tryam, clutching his cross. "Remember the words of Saint Lucian: 'Hope is not lost, as long as we have our faith.'"

Wulfric started a countdown, keeping the group informed on how many feet away were the Ragnar. When the number was under a hundred, Kara made the mood gloomier. "I think this day just got a lot worse!" she said. "Look to the sky!"

A shadow blacked out the stars, and a rush of foul air passed overhead.

"The winged death!" cried one of the Ragnar men.

The odor was unmistakable. The creature that had killed Brother Kayen had returned.

"Dying by this creature's talons would make for a much more exciting end to our tale, wouldn't it, Wulfric?" joked Kara.

"I prefer to die with a sword in my hand," answered Wulfric. "But be careful of what you wish. This is the creature that killed Brother Kayen."

Kara's voice was low and sounded small. "Oh, I did not know."

"Perhaps there is hope," interrupted Telvar. "The creature harries the Ragnar. Let us make haste down the mountain before it turns to face us."

The winged beast circled, then dove at the Ragnar. Each time it did, it carried off a man in one of its hawk-like talons and then either flung helpless Berserker down to the icy plains below or tore him apart. The Ragnar men rallied, throwing spears and shooting arrows, but their attacks were futile against the swift-moving creature.

"I agree with Telvar," implored Tryam. "Let's make haste while the monster is distracted."

"This way, then," Kara suggested. She found her way to firmer ground. "Hurry! Unless you want to be eaten by a giant chicken!"

As the screams of the Ragnar filled the night, no one needed additional incentive to flee. It was only when the screaming stopped that they risked a look back.

"Now it will come for us," stated Telvar matter-of-factly.

The primeval bird flew over their position, circling lower and lower.

"Get ready," shouted Wulfric as he raised his sword.

Kara stood protectively beside the wizard, her dagger in hand. Telvar had his eyes closed, as if trying to bring a memory back from oblivion.

Tryam abandoned his dagger and took out the cross of Aten. *If anything can send this Daemon back to hell, it will be this blessed object.* He uttered the Warding Prayer, and the cross of Aten glowed a soothing blue. He held the cross aloft as the creature descended.

"Brace yourselves, everyone!" cried Wulfric.

The scent of the beast fouled Tryam's nostrils, and the force of the leathery wings whipped the snow into a blinding frenzy. The young acolyte prayed harder and stared into the dark eyes of the creature.

Perhaps in response to the holy light, the great bird slowed and then stopped its descent. Its talons did not strike, nor did its beak try to peck. Instead, the creature hovered over the four frightened companions before turning in midair and then, inexplicably, coming to a landing some fifty yards away.

"Ha!" cried Kara triumphantly. "The big chicken was frightened by the sight of true warriors!"

"Wait! Do not celebrate too soon," warned Wulfric. "A figure is dismounting from the flying Daemon's back."

"Maybe he wants to parley," said Kara. "Let me speak to him. I can think of a lot of insults to say to a coward who lets a chicken do all his fighting."

Telvar coughed to clear his throat. "If he wants to speak, then it is I who should talk with him. I have spoken to many noblemen. The man may be persuaded to let us go."

"No one parleys, for I know who approaches." Wulfric broke into a grin. "Look to his beard, my nearsighted friends!"

Tryam stared with wide eyes at the brown-and-gray-bearded man who walked with a crooked shepherd's staff. The young acolyte's limbs nearly faltered. "Brother Kayen!"

The party did not wait for Kayen to meet up with them but instead rushed to him. Kara let out a gleeful scream and was the first to reach the haggard missionary. Kayen hugged Kara and then shook hands with Tryam, Telvar, and Wulfric in turn.

"You found Kara!" was the missionary's first words as he hugged her again. "I knew Aten would protect her." Kayen pointed up the mountain. "I heard and saw the explosions above. Your doing, no doubt. But how?"

Kara raced to explain. "A giant gem exploded and took down the whole mountain! I saw it with my own eyes! It didn't explode by accident, Tryam stabbed at it with his spear—"

"My staff, actually," interrupted Telvar.

"Staff, whatever. It was hard to see, because I was in the mountain god's hands at the time!" bursted Kara. "Can you believe that?"

"No, I can't," said Kayen. "When we have time, you must tell me what happened in greater detail."

"Hey," blurted Kara. "They told me you were dead!"

"Apparently Aten does not require my presence just yet," quipped the missionary.

"How did you tame the beast?" asked Wulfric.

"What's the bird's name?" inquired Kara.

"Where have you been?" added Tryam.

Kayen put up his hands. "I don't have time to explain. We must make haste from here."

"Are we riding the bird?" asked Kara.

"Yes," Kayen acknowledged. "But she is a bit temperamental."

Kara's squeal of excitement reverberated up and down the mountain.

"Dementhus is dead, the Golem buried. Why retreat in haste?" queried Wulfric.

"We must make certain those things are so," answered Kayen as he made his way back to the giant bird.

The closer that Tryam came to the creature, the less apprehension he felt. He sensed no maliciousness from bird, though there was an otherworldly presence about her. And the bird's strong odor reminded him of the mammoth he had ridden in the tournament rather than the stench of death, sulfur, and decay he had experienced with the Daemon. Her eyes had an intelligence behind them that belied its menacing, primeval appearance.

"Don't be nervous. Find a spot and hold on," encouraged Kayen. "She is an Aemon who was tasked to guard the mountain."

"An Aemon here on Medias?" gasped Tryam. "Why did she attack us at the ring of stones?"

"She'd been abandoned by the men of Arkos, the very people she protected. Alone these centuries, she lost her way, forgetting her purpose here on the mountain. Fortunately, I was able to convince her, after a time, that we are not burglars." Kayen patted the beast's neck. "In any event, we must make haste to both confirm that Dementhus is dead and the Golem destroyed. Once that is accomplished, we shall fly south to speak to Lord Dunford."

"What a sad tale!" exclaimed Kara. "Does she have a name?" She stroked the beast's hooked beak.

"Yes, dear Kara. It is Ardrah. Now quickly, get on her back before a blast triggers another avalanche."

Wulfric and Tryam positioned themselves on Ardrah's left and right wing, respectively, while Kara and Kayen straddled the beast's midsection. Telvar hesitated.

"Perhaps I could walk the rest of the way?" the mage mumbled.

"No, you are coming with us!" Wulfric reached down and grabbed Telvar by his collar, plucking the indignant wizard off his feet and placing him onto the bird's back. As the wizard struggled to hold on, the Ulf let out his first genuine laugh in weeks.

With a gesture of his hand, Kayen commanded the Aemon: "To the sky!"

The great bird straightened her body; then her wings began to flap. As the bird gently lifted off the mountain, Tryam held on more tightly. Seemingly with Kayen's guidance, the bird circled back to the entrance below the lip of the crater. No Ragnar men were in sight. The beast climbed higher still, toward the mountain peak, from where the party had been ejected. Tryam was shocked to see the destruction they had caused.

Kayen leaned forward as if whispering to the Aemon. The beast swerved and then sped toward the peak, where multicolored light exploded in random intervals from the ruined summit. Eruptions of stone and soil corresponded with each flash, as though material were being ejected from a volcano.

Without warning, a focused beam of light flashed from the chaos below and slammed into the great bird's torso. Ardrah jerked violently in reaction, and Tryam had to hang on to the leathery wing with all his strength to keep from falling off.

As the bird faltered, the world spun, and the young acolyte caught a glimpse of movement on the ruined mountain peak. It was the unmistakable black gleam of the Golem's skin. *The great artifact has survived!*

Another beam shot out from the darkness and blasted into Ardrah's left wing, dangerously close to Wulfric's head. The bird cried out in pain, and Tryam felt her quiver. He looked for the source of these attacks and observed a man in red flowing robes standing behind the Golem, a staff in his hand. It was the Albus mage.

Over the squawks of the injured Aemon, Telvar cried out in shock: "Dementhus and the Golem live! We must flee at once! Before he strikes us down."

Ardrah fought the pain bravely, even as her flesh burned. Kayen calmed the Aemon with a few words, and the great bird regained her equilibrium. With only one wing functional, Ardrah dipped below the arc of Dementhus's attacks and fled to the other side of the mountain, above the valley of the Ragnar.

"Pass me my cross, Tryam," Kayen shouted from his perch near the beast's head.

Tryam, oddly reticent, removed the cross he had grown so comforted by and placed it reverently in the missionary's outstretched hand. Kayen pressed the cross to the beast's torso and said a prayer. The cross glowed blue, and soon after, Ardrah was able to spread and flap her injured wing. Kayen then placed the cross around his own neck. "Thanks be to Aten, she will live."

"She is so brave," added Kara, patting the beast.

"What do we do now?" fumed Wulfric. "We must defeat this Dementhus and his evil pet, but even bringing a mountain down on their heads was not enough!"

"Do not fret," answered Kayen. "You have done all you could to defeat this menace—all of you have. The truth is that we need more help, and I believe we shall find it in Arkos. But before we make for home, I must show you all something."

THE TOMB OF THERAGAARD

Spurred on by Kayen's commands, the bird lowered its beak and headed toward the Ragnar valley. Tryam recognized the outdoor amphitheater, the multitude of forges, and the growing town and its palisades. What he could not make out was the moving black mass that stretched out beyond the village.

"Behold the army of the Ragnar," Kayen said stoically.

Rising to his knees, Wulfric moved precipitously close to the edge of the bird's wing. "That's impossible! Nearly every Berserker clan this side of the Corona Mountains must have united behind Dementhus!"

"That is not the worst of it," injected Telvar. "Look to the green and yellow flames. Look at the great tent."

"You speak in rid—" Wulfric stopped abruptly. "It can't possibly be."

"It is," answered Telvar. "Dementhus is a necromancer. In that tent, where the green and yellow smoke billows, he has birthed an army of the undead."

Their presence in the sky did not go unnoticed. Below, like a swarm of ants, men followed Ardrah's shadow against the stars and raised arms in their direction. A few launched bow shots, but they fell far short. Kayen did not wait for the Ragnar to attack with coordination, so he coaxed Ardrah higher into the sky and away from the eyes and missiles of the army. She flew fast and sure until the formerly twin-peaked mountain faded into the blackness of the horizon.

The great Aemon labored to stay aloft, and it was evident that she could not travel for much longer with all the passengers. Tryam was grateful. She had saved the party and had taken them far from danger. He had never before seen an Aemon, and he'd believed that none remained on Medias. When the time was appropriate, he would have to ask Brother Kayen about these demigods of light.

Once over the plains north of Arkos, Kayen guided Ardrah to a landing on the frozen ground below. When the party disembarked, Kara kissed the bird's beak. "I am sorry I called you a chicken," Kara said sweetly as she bid the great bird farewell. Even Telvar showed respect to the creature by bowing before her with a flourish.

Silently, the group watched as the Aemon tucked in her wings and then leapt back into the air. Soon thereafter, her leathery wings spread, and she gained altitude.

With the destruction of her nest, Tryam wondered where the guardian of the mountain would go and what she would do.

Chapter 65

Birth

After the crystal had first erupted, Dementhus feared for his life, but when the release of energy did not ignite the reserves, he was certain the fracturing of the gem had been a departing gift from Antigenesus. The subsequent destructive waves of energy were the purest, most potent magic the Necromancer had ever encountered. *So refined must the ancient lens be, it captured the first light of creation!*

In the face of such powerful magic, he had protected himself by diving beneath the slab that had supported the Golem. Dementhus then made his mind and body a living receptacle, hoping to fill his own reserves with this pure magic. He absorbed as much as he could, but then it was too much. The energy that found its way to him poured over and through his body, threatening to boil the very flesh from his bones. He had called out to Terminus for help. *Save me!*

Someone responded.

I am here.

The voice came from within Dementhus's own mind.

"Who are you? What are you?"

The wizard's questions were answered when the black hand of the Golem lifted the shattered table top from off his body.

I was called Rax Partha, but now I am the God of the Mountain.

The pain in the wizard's legs made it feel as though he were standing in molten lava, yet he had to rise and look upon this new being.

It had taken Dementhus weeks to revive the Golem after it had been transported to the lens room. After looking through the dead archmagus's laboratories, he had gathered the potions and raw materials that remained from its original construction and studied the artifact with great care. He had fused many of the cracks in the great gem, realigned the ancient lens (which had been pointing to the sky of five hundred years earlier), and poured magic into the slumbering metal warrior, so much so that the construct radiated the heat of the forge. But as much energy as he had given the Golem, it still had not answered to his commands.

It was only with the discovery of a dusty spell book, replete with schematics of the great artifact, that Dementhus had learned the artifact's secrets. Most important to the Golem's reanimation, the book described the nature of the crimson tattoos carved into the metal skin of the Golem: They were receptacles for elemental magic. The Albus mage had now gone to work in great haste.

Under the black metal skin was a complex network of artificial veins and arteries, which fed into metal organs as in a human body. With his new understanding of the crimson runes, Dementhus had fed the metal warrior the elements its body had lacked. Once it was nourished, the wizard smiled, since he was now able to give the construct simple commands: "Sit," "Stand," "Protect," "Kill," and to "Feast" upon the souls of the living to restore itself.

The Golem that stood before him after the gem's destruction was different, however. *The magic unleashed from the erupting gem, magic from the creation of the universe, must have seeped into its metal skin and enhanced the nascent consciousness that had communed with Gidran!*

The Mountain God shielded the Necromancer from the next destructive wave belched from the cracked gem.

"Whom do you serve?" Dementhus questioned.

I serve you.

Dementhus smiled through cracked lips. His body was burned, his weakened limbs almost useless, but if this was the price Terminus asked of him, it was a price he was glad to pay.

When he saw the winged creature fly overhead, Dementhus had the Golem retrieve his staff. Using the magic stored within its gem, twice Dementhus blasted the Aemon, but the great bird escaped before he could kill it and the riders it bore. *Not a problem. It is only a matter of time before the people of Arkos pay for their defiance.*

"We must be away at once. The reserves of energy stored inside this mountain are powerful enough to destroy us."

I understand.

The Golem lowered his hand to the shaking ground, and Dementhus used the last of his strength to step onto its palm. "Take me to the Ragnar village!"

As you command.

Chapter 66
Hell's Fires

With empty stomachs and heavy hearts, the party trudged through the freshly fallen snow on the last leg of their journey to Arkos. After the failure to kill Dementhus and stop the Golem, Tryam's hopes now rested entirely on Theragaard and the help the long-dead paladin could provide. He would have to return to the vaults under the abbey and commune with the great paladin, whose spirit, for perhaps this exact moment, still lingered on the material plane. The others would have to convince Lord Dunford of the menace that was sure to come sweeping down from the Coronas with the power of a thousand arctic storms.

When the party took their rest at midday, Kara was still upset about Ardrah. "We should not have left her like that," she fumed. "She saved our lives! Where will she go? She has no home."

Brother Kayen put a hand on Kara's shoulder, but she shrugged it off. "Ardrah stood as guardian over that mountain for centuries," he said. "Her duty to Aten has now ended. She will find a new home: a safe place, where she can heal her wounds."

Kara's compassion, after having seen such cruelty, brightened Tryam's mood. "I share your concerns, Kara," he said, "but Brother Kayen is correct. Ardrah will be okay. Aten will provide."

After a quick meal, the party assembled and made the final, thankfully peaceful, push to Arkos. It wasn't until they were within sight of the town's walls that the solace was broken.

"That doesn't look right." Kara's voice rose in excitement. She rushed ahead and hopped up and down, pointing south. "It looks bad—really bad."

THE TOMB OF THERAGAARD

The setting sun splashed the horizon in glorious red; however, a dark plume of black smoke marred its beauty. As his eyes followed the smoke down to its source, Tryam's heart filled with fear; a fire was raging in the walled town. *Has the Ragnar army overtaken us? No, that is not possible!*

"What burns?" asked Telvar, his voice higher than usual. "Use those keen Berserker eyes and tell me, girl!"

Kara shaded her eyes and stared ahead. "Smoke comes from the center of town."

Telvar gasped.

Kara then added hesitantly, "I think the mage tower is ablaze."

"That can't be!" cried Telvar.

The strain in the wizard's voice was evident to all. Telvar broke free from the party and raced toward the north gate.

"We can't let him get too far ahead," Kara said. "He needs our help!"

"Now who is the fool rushing into danger?" huffed Wulfric.

By the time they stood within sight of the north gate, Tryam was nearly breathless. Telvar had slowed and was leaning heavily on his staff.

"Hail the guards," Kayen ordered. "We don't want them firing arrows upon us. An unexpected party coming from the north at nightfall while a fire rages in town could cause them to act before thinking."

Wulfric, the loudest of the party, shouted up to the guard towers. He was met with silence. When the party arrived before the shadow of the north gate, they found the towers unmanned and the portcullis open.

"What is this madness?" cried Kayen. "The gates are never undefended, even during periods of peace."

"What difference does it make?" shouted Telvar. "I have to get to the tower at once!" The panicked mage rushed through the open portal. The others followed.

Beyond the gate, the town of Arkos was in chaos. Carts carrying goods away from the center of town choked the narrow streets, while mothers in doorways clung tightly to their bundled-up children. Squadrons of knights rushed about on horseback, shouting for the citizens to stay inside. Blanketing the entire area was ash from the fire, which floated to the ground like gray snow.

The young wizard weaved his way through the congestion and headed toward the mage tower. When the rest of the party caught up, a cloaked and armored warrior was blocking Telvar with a gauntleted hand from proceeding any farther. Behind the guard, Tryam could see a swarm of

Engothian knights protecting the gate that led into the tower grounds. At this distance, Tryam could see that it was not the tower itself that burned but the wondrous trees and plants of Myramar's grove. However, the flames were growing in intensity and were licking the sides of the tower's once-pristine white stones and turning them black.

"I must get inside!" Telvar demanded. "I am Myramar's apprentice," he declared to one of the knights.

The warrior shook his head and said, "No one is allowed past me. Upon orders of Lord Dunford."

Telvar brandished his staff.

The knight drew his sword.

The words of a spell came to Telvar's lips.

Brother Kayen separated the two obstinate men with his crooked shepherd's staff. "Enough! If you tell us what is happening, sir, Telvar might be able to help."

When the knight sheathed his sword, he also removed his helmet to wipe the sweat off of his brow.

It's Gavin!

Tryam stepped forward so that the knight could see his face. "Gavin, it is I, Tryam. We speak the truth. We can help!"

A weary smile brightened the soot-stained face of the young knight. "I see you rescued Wulfric's bondmate. The extra-duty shifts I earned for letting you out of the gate were well worth it."

Tryam smiled briefly and nodded his head toward Kara. "We are in your debt, but we discovered something terrifying along the way. An army of Berserkers heads to Arkos, led by a rogue wizard, a necromancer. He commands a fifty-foot-tall metal warrior and a horde of undead. He means to destroy us all."

The smile vanished from the young knight's face. "I shall tell you what happened while you were gone. Myramar went mad. He was caught bringing corpses back to his tower. He may have even murdered the people himself. Lord Dunford came to confront the old wizard, but he refused to speak and instead started the grove ablaze to turn the knights back."

Telvar, whose face was red, stepped up to the knight and spoke inches before his face. "I can stop Myramar if you let me through!"

Gavin glanced at the five, then back at the raging inferno, and then back again at the five. "Of course, go ahead. But the captain will likely try to stop you before you get past the gate."

THE TOMB OF THERAGAARD

Telvar rushed past the knight and headed toward the bronze gate that led into the tower grounds. Tryam noticed that the cracked gem atop his staff glowed brilliant white. *He has some magic left after all.*

"Thank you, again," said Tryam as he shook Gavin's hand. "You would not believe what we have witnessed. Arkos is in mortal danger. This business with Myramar is only the beginning. We have to help our friend and then tell Lord Dunford what awaits. Do you have any weapons for us?"

Gavin nodded, then returned his helmet to his head. "Follow me."

The young knight took the party around to the command tent, which was located a safe distance away from the tower grounds. Near the tent was a cart stacked with an array of weapons.

Before Gavin could even utter a word about the weapons, Kara dove into the cart and came out with a brand-new longbow in her hand. "Now I have a bow to go along with my arrows!" she said, beaming. When she stood, the flames behind her made her golden hair glow as if in bright sunshine. Tryam was reminded of the frescoes painted of heroes and was glad she was on their side that day.

"I shall keep Crayvor's blade. It is light, sharp, and quick, and I do not believe it has tasted enough Ragnar blood," stated Wulfric. "However, I shall pick a blade for you, Tryam. What about you, Brother Kayen?"

"I am sticking with my staff. I am too old to learn any other means of defense."

Kara disagreed. "You are not *that* old, though you are grayer than I remember. After this, I think you should take up the longbow. I shall teach you!"

Wulfric placed a well-balanced blade in Tryam's hand. The young acolyte gripped the sword and took a few practice swings. "This will do nicely," said Tryam.

"Let's help Telvar take down this wizard!" challenged Kara as she jumped off the cart. "I have a grudge against necromancers."

Through the choking smoke, the four companions headed to the bronze gate, where a half-dozen knights stood guard. Telvar had not made it far in their absence and was engaged in a heated argument with the knights' captain. The young wizard was gesturing with his staff and pointing at the wizard band around his head. "Again, let me make this perfectly clear, so that even someone as mentally deficient as you can understand. I am Myramar's apprentice. I can help stop this madness. Let me pass!"

441

"I have never seen you before," the knight argued. "Why should I believe you?"

"We are with the tower wizard," said Kara pushing her way to Telvar's side. "We are all apprentices. My friends and I." Kara pointed back to the rest of the party. "You have to let us inside."

The knights broke into laughter before one grabbed Kara by the shoulder and pulled her back from the gate. "You are just a silly Berserker girl," the captain scolded. "Now get out of here before you get killed."

Telvar was quicker than even Wulfric to come to Kara's defense. "Let her go, or I shall turn you all into armor-plated tree frogs!" Emphasizing his threat, he turned his glowing staff in the knight's direction. "These people are with me. They have information that must be told to Dunford, and I must get to Myramar!"

"It would be wise to do as he asks," added Kayen. "I have seen him do worse things after far less of an insult."

The captain spat upon the ground but then ordered the gate to be opened, adding, "I do so only because I recognize you, Brother Kayen." To his men he said, "He saved many of us from that hellspawn in the mines a few months back."

Kara shook her fist at the captain as she and the others followed Telvar into the grove.

The heat of the inferno increased with each step they took toward the tower. And the air that swirled about the flames contained a mixture of the sweet fragrance of blooming flowers with the pungent scent of burning sap. Now more than ever, Tryam felt the urge to visit the cool crypts under the abbey, but he could not abandon his friends. Not now.

"How do we kill this wizard?" Kara asked with an impish look on her face.

"Let's not speak of killing quite yet," Telvar answered as they made their way down the stone-hewn path that led to the tower proper. "Myramar was a good man, even though a difficult master. I want to speak with him first, if possible." He shuddered. "But I fear my master has been bewitched. He was given an amulet from Dementhus that I believe contains a powerful Daemon. If Brother Kayen can remove the Daemon's influence over Myramar, he may yet be saved."

Kayen looked aghast. "You tell us this now? We might have been able to stop him sooner if you had told us when we first met!"

THE TOMB OF THERAGAARD

The young wizard frowned. "I thought I could handle this myself. But now that I've seen the power and evil of Dementhus firsthand, I fear I might have miscalculated."

"*Might* have miscalculated?" sneered Wulfric. "Look at this blaze!"

As he glanced through the inferno, Tryam shielded his eyes. The fire was not entirely natural: Most of the plants and trees had long since been devoured, yet flames still spiraled into the sky. "Let's not argue now," pleaded the young acolyte. "We have each made mistakes on this journey. Let's focus on what we can do now."

A squadron of men stood before the tower's door, shielding a group of engineers assembling a small battering ram. Tryam recognized Lord Dunford from his thick yellow beard, barrel chest, and gold-enameled armor. The commander's head was craned toward the tower's balcony, located on the top floor. Tryam followed the man's gaze and spotted Myramar peering down at them, a deranged look on his face. The mad wizard showed himself only briefly before stepping back inside the tower.

From Dunford's shadow, a robed figure emerged. Tryam felt his spine grow cold. It was Father Monbatten.

When the abbot saw the party, his face scrunched into severe wrinkles. He moved to intercept and stood before them. "Brother Kayen? Tryam? Why are you here? Why are you not with the Berserkers?" The abbot then saw a reflection of the fire gleaming off Tryam's blade, and his scowl intensified. "What are you doing with that sword in your hand? Have you forsaken your vows of pacifism already?" He pointed a gnarled finger at the grove's entrance. "All of you, go back, This is a fight for the Engothian knights. Let them handle this battle."

Kayen stood his ground and clasped Tryam on the shoulder. "This is a fight against evil, and we are here to stop it. Myramar has been seduced by a Daemon, and we—including Tryam—are here to help end this madness. The time for words has passed. We must prepare to fight."

Father Monbatten shook his head, and he theatrically brought his hands up to cover his face. "Tryam, I have failed as your teacher. It was a mistake for me to have allowed your innocent spirit to be corrupted by Brother Kayen's lies and talk of the glories of war."

"You have not failed me," responded Tryam. "Through you, I have learned the glory of Aten and that each of us must serve Him in our own way. Yours is through teaching and prayer, mine will be to confront evil with the skills with which I have been blessed." He tried to grasp the abbot's hand but was rejected. "Please listen to us. An army is coming, an army of Berserkers—and *undead* led by a necromancer. This sorcerer has exhumed in the mountains a Golem from the time of the Ancients. Tell the monks at the ward tower to light the beacon!"

"This is madness," mocked Monbatten. "Stop this talk at once, and come with me!"

Monbatten offered his hand, expecting Tryam to give up his sword. The young acolyte shook his head. "I cannot abandon my friends. I cannot turn from the path Aten has laid before me."

Father Monbatten closed his eyes and uttered a prayer. When he again spoke to Tryam, his face was as cold as a statue's. "You have chosen the path that your father trod, a path to violence and death." The abbot turned his back to Tryam and made to leave the grove. Before disappearing into the smoke, however, he turned and warned, "You have chosen your destiny, as I have chosen mine. May Aten spare you your father's fate!"

The abbot's ominous warning stung Tryam.

"What happened to your father will *not* happen to you," said Kayen, his eyes staring directly into the young acolyte's. "I know this."

"I would feel better if you would tell me what evil befell my family, but I know this is not the appropriate time." Tryam forced thoughts of the past from his mind and looked back to the knights. Telvar was now speaking animatedly with Lord Dunford. "It appears that our friend needs help again."

"Sir," Telvar began, "It is I, Telvar, Myramar's apprentice—"

Dunford cut him off. The commander's face was red, and his eyes bulged. "Where have you been? Myramar has gone mad and threatens to burn the entire town to the ground! We have to get inside and bring him to justice."

Telvar bowed deeply before the golden-armored nobleman and spoke in his most respectful tone. "Apologies. I was on a mission to get answers to Myramar's sickness. I regret I did not return before the situation escalated to this level. If given the chance, I think I can cure him."

"Cure? You talk of cures? He needs to answer for his crimes. He is a murderer!" Dunford shook his great bearded head. "I cannot trust a mere apprentice to handle this situation. Captain, haul this so-called mage out of here! We have work to do!"

Before any action could be taken against Telvar, an Engothian knight shouted a warning, and all eyes looked to where he pointed. The tower mage had returned to the balcony.

THE TOMB OF THERAGAARD

Myramar leaned over the railing, his orange robes billowing around him. He held a glowing staff in his hands, while an amulet dangled from his neck flamed red. The band that all wizards were required to wear around their heads was missing.

Even from fifty feet below, Tryam could see the wide, wild eyes and madness on the old wizard's face. Myramar shouted down to the knights, but not in Engothian. Tryam recognized the guttural language as that of the speech of the Abyss, and he was disturbed that he could understand the language so easily.

"What does he say?" Dunford asked aloud.

Kayen translated the words. "He says he intends to bring forth the enemy to our very gates."

Dunford looked to the party for answers. "What enemy?"

"The one we warned you about!" snapped Wulfric.

Myramar abruptly retreated from the balcony. Moments after that, the tower vibrated ever so slightly.

"He is repositioning the lens!" Telvar shouted in explanation.

Tryam was not sure what the warning meant, and from the confused looks of the others, he could tell he was not alone.

To the unasked question, Telvar explained: "He intends to unleash the fury of the lens on Arkos!"

The lens that crowned the tower swiveled and then tilted, aiming toward a point to the northwest. A humming began, which Tryam now understood to be a buildup of magical energy. The ground beneath their feet rumbled.

"What can we do to stop it?" asked Lord Dunford.

"Nothing," lamented Telvar.

A blast of light flashed from the lens and arced across the night sky, splashing onto the side of the ward tower. That tower, built by craftsmen from the time of the Ancients, resisted the initial shock; the beam persisted, however, and the focused stream of energy pressed against the stones, causing the entire structure to sway.

A monk rushed from the tower to pray before the great blue crystal at its apex. The power of the beam was too great, however, and like the stones of a bursting dam, the tower erupted in an explosion of timber, gem shards, and pulverized granite. As debris flew into the sky, cries of disbelief rang out from the knights.

Brother Kayen gave voice to the implications resulting from the destruction of the ward tower. "The walls of Arkos are now the only thing that stand between us and the army of Dementhus."

The sound of the ward tower's destruction was still ringing in Tryam's ears when Dunford responded with orders for his men to start breaking down the mage tower's oak door with the battering ram. Telvar begged Dunford to let him try to open the door, but the commander simply shook his head. "I am weary of magic. It is time for steel."

Four knights rolled the wheeled battering ram into position before the door. Once the small siege engine was unlocked, knights on either side swung the iron ram to build momentum. It was Kara's scream that brought everyone's focus back to the balcony. Myramar had returned, his large staff directed at the knights below.

"The wizard attacks!" cried Kara. "Back away!"

"Men, do as she says!" commanded the captain of the Engothian engineers.

The members of the squad jumped back from the war machine as a bolt of energy from Myramar's staff smashed into the battering ram. The ram exploded, sending iron and wood shrapnel everywhere as unnatural flames spontaneously erupted around the tower door.

Kara scolded Lord Dunford. "You should have let Telvar try!" She took out her bow and aimed it toward the balcony, even though she was at an impossible angle to hit Myramar. She took two shots before giving up. "We have to do something!"

"All of you," said Dunford, pointing at Kara and her friends, "stand back, or we cannot protect you." The commander turned to his assembled men. "Bring the hooks and scaling ladders!"

Myramar, once again, retreated from the balcony.

Another squadron of men stepped forward. Despite their bulky armor, the knights assembled a pair of ladders with swift and efficient coordination. Once complete, the ladders looked just tall enough, in Tryam's eyes, to come within reach of the balcony. Other engineers stood next to the ladder makers, with throwing hooks attached to long lines of cable. Tryam doubted these men could throw hooks high enough to reach the balcony, and his doubts were confirmed when he saw knights wheel in a small ballista from which the hooks could be launched. *Lord Dunford's men think of everything!*

THE TOMB OF THERAGAARD

It took four attempts with the ballista to get two hooks attached to the balcony ledge. Everyone kept a watchful eye for Myramar to return—especially Telvar.

Meanwhile, other knights raised the ladders and leaned them against the curved tower wall. Engineers then hammered long iron spikes into the stone apron that surrounded the tower, in order to secure the ladder to the ground.

With two ladders and two hooks ready to go, Dunford ordered the engineers away and for his warriors to gear up and prepare to scale the tower. Telvar warned the commander of the danger of this assault. "This is suicide! This is madness! Myramar has not spent all of his magical reserves. He is luring you closer!"

The commander rebuffed the wizard. "We have no other option."

With shields strapped to their back, the burdened assault force began to climb. Tryam noticed the concern in Dunford's eyes at the slow pace of their ascent; however, when the first knight put his hand on the balcony rail, Tryam thought they might succeed. The hope was quickly dashed when Myramar, now a vision of pure evil with bulging eyes and a snarling face, returned to the balcony.

The mad wizard bellowed words of magic, and the gem on his staff glowed bright white. Myramar waited until the first knight had his foot on the balcony before he unleashed a stream of electricity from the jeweled staff. The bolt struck the climber in the chest, causing him to lose his balance and plummet over the railing. The knight hit the stone apron with a sickening thud.

Myramar was not done. The electric energy arced to the next knight on the ladder and then the knight nearest him. The bolt arced all the way down to those holding the ladder in place. Shouts of the dying and the smell of cooked flesh caused Tryam to retch.

"Commander," begged Kayen, "you must order your men back!"

Tryam watched Dunford's eyes as they looked on in horror at the carnage done to his men; those eyes showed strain and anger. The commander was quick to regain his composure and to process the situation. "Back! Back! Clear away from the tower! Everyone!"

Caught between the burning grove and the threat of Myramar above, the knights were short on areas to regroup. Lord Dunford saw the confusion and was quick to get the warriors in formation, creating a protective circle around Tryam and his companions. "We shall rally outside the tower grounds and contain the wizard inside the grove," announced Dunford in a somewhat defeated tone.

Before the knights could retreat, Myramar's voice thundered down from the balcony. Again, the old mage spoke the tongue of evil, but this time, Tryam could not make sense of the words, for they spoke of invoking the power of the Dark God and the servants of Terminus.

In apparent reaction to the mad tower mage's commands, the flames in the grove diminished, but before the knights could retreat, green and yellow smoke rose from the scorched ground and quickly spread around them like a dense fog. The odor of the gas was a noxious mixture of sulfur and rancid meat.

"He is raising the dead!" explained Telvar after having sniffed the air. "My master must have placed the dead in the grove as some twisted jest."

First one, then two, then a dozen forms clawed their way up from the smoking soil of the grove. In moments, the brainless creatures, now too many to count, began to lumber their way to the embattled knights, oozing decayed flesh, reaching out with claw-like hands and snapping with toothy maws. Dunford consulted with two sergeants and then positioned the men to confront the new threat.

Tryam felt a tug on his robes. It was the young wizard. "I can get inside the tower. In fact, I know I can. Come with me."

In the confusion, it was easy for Tryam, Kara, Wulfric, Kayen, and Telvar to break away from the knights' protection and walk to the flame-shrouded tower entrance. Telvar pointed his staff and uttered words of magic. A blast of frosty air came forth and blew out the flames. The mage strode to the entrance.

"Protect Telvar while he works," ordered Kayen.

Kara, Kayen, and Wulfric stood shoulder to shoulder, their backs to the wizard. No one knew which posed the greater threat—Myramar above or the foul undead in the grove.

After a few minutes of peace, bolts of lightning arced from Myramar's staff above and struck inside the green and yellow fog. The toxic mist muffled the screams of the Engothian knights fighting the undead within.

As Telvar still worked on opening the door, Wulfric watched the balcony with frightened eyes. The Ulf warrior was growing impatient. "Hurry, before we are fried to death!"

"Or ripped apart!" added Kara. "I think that would be worse, don't you think?"

In what seemed almost an eternity, but likely only a few seconds, Telvar triumphantly reported his success. "He never changed the entry word!

THE TOMB OF THERAGAARD

Either it's an oversight, or perhaps some of Myramar still fights against the Daemon. Inside, hurry!"

As the others rushed through the door, Tryam stood back. He took one last look at the greenish mist and shuddered as a wave of evil chilled his soul. He could barely see the knights as they fought against the unholy undead. *Aten, please help them!*

It took only a moment to realize something was amiss inside the tower, as shouts found their way quickly to the young acolyte's ears. Tryam, instinctively now, drew his sword and raced inside. The sound the door made as it closed behind him reminded him of a lid closing on a coffin.

"A guardian! Myramar has left an elemental guardian!" Telvar was explaining with more than a hint of panic in his voice. "You must dispose of it with utmost haste. I have almost no magic left."

Tryam looked past the others and into the tower's great hall, where an amorphous tan-colored blob oozed its way forward. In its pseudopod arms, it held four rusty swords.

"Disgusting!" remarked Kara, holding her nose. "Why couldn't he have made it smell better?"

The guardian was twice the size of the mammoth Tryam had dealt with in the tournament. It lumbered forward, crushing couch and chairs, to get to the party.

"Surround it!" commanded Wulfric. "We can't let it corner us and crush us against the wall."

Kara made a dash to the left, in order to stand on steps up to the next level. Kayen moved to the right, his staff at the ready. Wulfric ran past the guardian, jumped over a chair, and stood guard by the door to the kitchen at the back half of the room. Tryam stood his ground near the front door, once again shielding Telvar. The young acolyte was impressed with their collective coordination.

The first wound to the guardian came from Kara, who sunk an arrow up to its feathers into the creature's blob of a backside. A foul-smelling clear liquid pussed out, but the creature showed no sign of pain. Kara, however, was quick to show her excitement. "Take that!"

The creature did not react to Kara's taunt. Instead, it engaged the others with its crude weapons. Tryam ducked a wild swing from one pseudopod and returned with a slash along the creature's flank. The sword opened a long gash, and more of the strange being's innards oozed out, but the injury was insignificant in comparison to its mass.

449

"How can we kill this thing?" Tryam asked Telvar as he struggled to free his blade. "It is as if we were attacking a whale with toothpicks."

"It will stop only when its magic has been exhausted. Keep slashing at it. I need to rest." As Telvar stood back, watching the others, he leaned on his staff with its cracked jewel. "My impending confrontation with Myramar will require all my strength."

"I have limitations as well," conceded Kayen, who was adroitly fending off a sword-wielding pseudopod with his walking staff. "I fear I cannot pierce this creature's hide!"

Kara laughed at Kayen's predicament but offered her encouragement. "You can bruise it, though. Keep whacking at it!"

The guardian, perhaps sensing Brother Kayen's weakness, oozed toward him. The missionary was pressed against the wall by the creature's rubbery flesh. "I fear I cannot even do that, dear Kara!" he cried.

"I am on my way, Brother," vowed Tryam, leaving Telvar's side.

The ground beneath the young acolyte's feet was sticky from the creature's blood, but he was able to maneuver around its bulk and execute a strike that severed a pseudopod that had been waving a sword in Kayen's face. Tryam was pleased to see the rusty sword fall harmlessly to the ground along with a sizable chunk of the creature's flesh, but the guardian appeared no more upset than it had from the damage inflicted by Kara's arrow.

Wulfric, who was battling against two swords added, "I shall rip this thing to shreds. Have no fear, Brother! It is massive but slow, and its hide is easy to pierce."

"I have an idea," Kara said from her perch on the staircase.

The others shouted in unison, "No!"

Kara dismissed their concerns. "Just watch!" With that, she launched herself from the stairs and landed on the blob's back. She stood, albeit unsteadily, and grinned. "It can't reach me from here!" She began to stab the creature repeatedly with her dagger.

Wulfric roared with laughter and doubled his attacks. The Ulf warrior lopped two more pseudopods from the guardian and then jumped atop the blob to stand beside her.

"Those fools are made for each other," snapped Telvar. "This creature could crush them easily."

As if to prove the young wizard's point, the beast lurched forward and knocked Kayen hard against the wall of the tower. Tryam slashed his way to Kayen and sliced off the leading edge of the blob before it could envelop the shaken missionary.

"Attack faster!" urged Tryam. "It is upon us!"

With whatever sense organs it had, the guardian detected its advantage and pressed its mass against the two warriors of Aten. Tryam took the time to lift Kayen to his feet, but when he tried to swing his sword again, he lacked the room to do so.

"We are coming!" assured Wulfric from above.

The two Ulfs stabbed their way forward. So ferocious were their attacks that the skin of the creature weakened and gave way beneath their feet. The two fell *inside* the guardian, and they disappeared from sight.

"Wulfric! Kara!" gasped Kayen.

Tryam changed tactics and used small stabs to rip into the blob's body. The creature reacted by rolling over the young acolyte, its mass swallowing him whole.

Tryam held his breath and stabbed with all his fury. As he grew more desperate, the scar on his chest burned, and the strange foreign rage within him began to exert itself. He gave into the anger and drew strength from it. He viciously stabbed away until the front end of the guardian deflated like a punctured water bladder. So blinded with rage was he, it took Kayen's firm grasp to stay his sword as Wulfric and Kara spilled out of the rent and were deposited on their feet.

As the rage inside died down, Tryam gasped for breath.

"Thank you, Brother Kayen," gasped Tryam. "I was momentarily lost in fury."

The frown on Kayen's face showed his concern and perhaps disbelief, but he did not comment.

"I think I swallowed some of it," Kara said, breaking the tension, as she and Wulfric extricated themselves from the goo. "Yuck!"

Wulfric went to attack the guardian again, but the creature backed up from the party, quivered in place, and then collapsed, seeping the last of its essence onto the floor until it lost its form completely.

"If you are done fooling around, we have to continue upstairs," huffed Telvar. "Before we confront Myramar, I need to replace the crystal on my staff."

Wulfric looked to Tryam, pleading with his eyes to let him take a swing at the imperious young wizard. Tryam simply shook his head no.

"Lead the way," said Kayen, stepping in before an argument erupted.

Telvar moved up the staircase. He led the party past the second floor and stopped at the third-floor landing. "Wait here," he whispered.

A single corridor bisected the third floor. Rooms with iron-bound wood doors lined both sides. Telvar dashed into the nearest one. He returned with a confident look on his face and a new red crystal atop his staff. He spoke a word of magic, and the gem glowed bright crimson.

"What is our plan?" asked Kayen. "You told us Myramar was bewitched. If he is possessed, how was it done?"

"A gem called an Anima Crystallum," answered Telvar.

Kayen nodded his head. "I am familiar with that term. The gems were created back in antiquity and were used only by the most evil of men. Dark clerics and mad sorcerers would lure beings from other realms to ours and then trap them inside the crystal."

"Yes," concurred Telvar. "Unfortunately, Myramar was not as familiar as you are with an Anima Crystallum. Dementhus offered the gem as a gift for my master to study. Myramar became obsessed with finding out the amulet's secrets. The more he studied the crystal, the more he became ensorcelled by it. I am certain the being inside the amulet is a powerful Daemon that has now exerted its will over my old master."

As all eyes turned to him, Kayen stroked his graying beard. When Wulfric and Kara started to overwhelm him with questions, he raised his hands. "As Telvar needs rest to restore his magic, I need the clarity given to me by my faith. Everyone, please give me a moment."

The missionary went to his knees and prayed. Tryam could not make out the words of the prayer, but he was certain it was not the Warding Prayer. At the prayer's conclusion, the cross around Kayen's neck glowed bright blue. Kayen grabbed the cross with his right hand, his staff in his left, and stood. "I have battled Daemons before, but none that have fused their soul to a wizard. We shall once again need Aten's aid."

"You will have my bow," said Kara.

"And my steel!" offered Wulfric.

"And my magic," added Telvar.

Chapter 67
The Final Lesson

"The young wizard squeezed the cold metal staff in his hands, comforted by the power it represented. "I know of no traps set inside the tower," he told the others as he led them to the fourth floor, "but I still advise caution. I don't know what my master has conspired to do in my absence."

The stairs emerged in the center of the fourth floor. Four closed black doors stood evenly spaced around the circular landing. Beside each door flicked golden flames in silver sconces. Telvar strained to hear for any sign of his master's machinations, but all was quiet.

"Which door leads to the balcony?" asked Wulfric.

Telvar paused for a moment, trying to recall which door it was. Myramar had permitted him in this part of the tower only once before. He hazarded a guess. "That door leads to the balcony, the last place we saw Myramar. Once it is open, the battle will begin. And as Brother Kayen has said, we shall have to bring all the weapons we have against him: physical, spiritual, and magical. Ready yourselves!"

Kara notched an arrow, and Wulfric took a practice swing. Telvar did not doubt the two Ulfs' willingness to fight, but how effective they would be was another matter; the fight against Dementhus had not inspired confidence.

The two holy men, meanwhile, whispered prayers, while Telvar himself went over a few spell ideas in his head. *I wish I had more energy than the little stored that is in my crystal! Brother Kayen has experience fighting Daemons. I hope I can assist him in some manner.*

The entire tower began to vibrate again. "The lens is being repositioned," said Telvar. "Myramar means to unleash another strike against the town! We must attack now!"

"We are ready," assured Brother Kayen.

Telvar rushed to the door and placed his hand upon its jeweled knob. He looked back one last time to make sure everyone was ready. Encouraged by their respective nods, he opened the door.

The room revealed was wedge-shaped. Telvar rushed inside, ready to cast a spell. He pushed through the dark curtains that led to the balcony. The words to the spell died on his lips, however, when he found that Myramar was not there—or anywhere else inside the room.

"Where is he?" raged Wulfric.

"A good question," said Telvar, mystified.

About the room were statues of the past tower masters, poised as if casting a spell. Telvar briefly mistook one that resembled Myramar as a foe and pointed his staff at it, much to his embarrassment and Wulfric's amusement. The others spread out in search of the tower mage, but the room was too small and lacked any shadows in which Myramar could hide.

Telvar returned to the balcony, and the others followed. Below, the green and yellow smoke had grown thicker, obscuring the fighting between the knights and their undead adversaries. Only the sounds of desperate commands, the clashing of steel, and the screams of the dying hinted at what was happening. Telvar looked to the top of the tower and saw that the lens now pointed toward the Engothian knights' keep. "We have to get to the lens room! That's where Myramar must be."

"No need, foolish apprentice. I am right here."

The voice was Myramar's, but it also hinted at something else, something ancient. The tower mage, in orange robes and the amulet still about his neck, stood before a sliding door recessed along a wall, now revealing steps going upward, steps that had been hidden before. Myramar was leaning on his staff. His cruel visage, his confident stance, and especially his penetrating eyes differed greatly from the old man Telvar had known as his master.

Telvar lost his concentration. The harsh words he had planned to say disappeared in the face of this threat. Instead, he made a desperate plea to his mentor, who he hoped still struggled against the will of the Daemon. "You have been duped, beguiled, my master. The amulet you wear about your neck contains a spirit from the Abyss. The spirit has rendered you mad, has made you turn against the town. It has made you destroy and murder!"

"Mad?" scoffed Myramar. "No. I am in full command of my senses, and I intend to take my rightful place as the ruler of Arkos. Does it matter

THE TOMB OF THERAGAARD

if the amulet was my conduit to this newfound wisdom and magic? What does matter is the power I now wield." He flashed his yellow teeth. "It will be a pity to kill you, but I fear I must." Myramar raised his staff, its crystal a brilliant white, and pointed it at Telvar and his companions.

In desperation, Telvar shouted to the others: "Attack!"

Kara was the first to get off an attack, but the crazed wizard casually batted her red arrow away with his staff. Wulfric followed Kara's bowshot and charged Myramar, sword held high; he lunged within feet of the mad mage, but he was not fast enough. Myramar spoke a word of magic. Telvar understood the command. The ground beneath Wulfric melted and then froze around his legs, trapping him within the floor.

Telvar's former master's command of transmutation frightened him. The young wizard brushed off his fear, however, and focused his mind on his staff, as he linked himself to the energy-storing jewel at its tip. As he drained the jewel, the rush of magic filled his body, and he took comfort in its embrace. *He tested my fire skills. Now I shall test his!*

Hoping for a quick, fatal blow, Telvar, staff outstretched, summoned the fire element and hurled it at Myramar as a stream of fire. But the mad tower mage raised his hands and muttered a word of magic; in response, a wall of water appeared before him. The water absorbed the flame strike, leaving nothing but steam.

"I see the pupil thinks he has learned to control his fire!" mocked Myramar. "We shall see how his control compares with mine!"

Telvar closed his eyes and held them fast. Fire was his strongest element; if he wanted to challenge his master, he would need to summon an even greater amount. He made the connection to the realm of magic and again sought the fire element. When he saw it with his mind's eye, he reached for it but was rebuffed. The being with a bestial face had returned. Telvar was now sure it was the face of the Daemon inside the amulet about Myramar's neck.

As he could sense the fire elements being turned against him, the young wizard struggled to break free from the connection. He sweated as if his body were being dangled over a great inferno. The Daemon, shrouded in flames, held him fast to the astral plane, smiling with black teeth as it did so. No matter how hard Telvar concentrated in breaking the spell, he could not return to the material world. *I will never give up! I will die for my magic!*

Telvar used every trick, every bit of knowledge, and every bit of willpower to break free. It was only at his wit's end that he realized what he had to do.

Although the fire element was blocked from his grasp, he could still reach for other powers. Imitating his former master, he summoned water, sending a geyser at the Daemon. A steam cloud enveloped the monster, and its mental grasp on the young wizard faltered. Telvar rushed to terminate his connection spell, and when it succeeded, he fell to his knees from exhaustion.

When he opened his eyes on the material world, he saw Kara held fast in a blanket of frost and Wulfric still trapped in the floor. Kayen and Tryam stood before Myramar, holding the shining cross of Aten between them, while the old tower mage was directing a gale-force wind in an attempt to push the holy men off the balcony.

Kayen shouted toward Telvar above the roar of the magical blast: "You must continue your attack! Whatever you did made the Daemon visible, and its corporeal body withered when touched by Aten's light!"

Telvar gripped his staff and concentrated on the last bits of magic stored in its gem. He drained the energy from the crystal, and his mind flushed with power. Unfortunately, in his haste, he had not prepared himself properly, and his body now burned with pain. When he turned to look at Myramar, he realized that he couldn't see; the sudden rush of magic had rendered him blind. And even with this desperate action, the magic he held within himself was not enough for another flame strike.

With no other option, Telvar focused again on the astral plane. The young wizard pictured every symbol, every nuance, needed to get the connection to reopen. He imagined his hand upon a giant brass handle, tugging with all his strength on a door the size of a castle wall. As he focused more clearly, he grew bigger, as if he were becoming a legendary Titan of old. He grew until the brass handle was but a toy and the door like that of a dollhouse. As a giant, he opened the connection with ease.

But before he could reach into the astral plane for power, the Daemon once again stood before him, now in all its horrific fullness. The being had the head of a horned goat, the torso of a thick-chested giant, and a serpent's coiled body for limbs. The beast cracked its black lips into a grotesque smile and spoke through jagged black teeth.

"This is Myramar now." The voice was deep, soothing, and mesmerizing.

"Where?" asked Telvar, his mind fighting against the beast's overpowering will. "Where is my master?"

As if in a dream, the goat-headed devil slowly opened its hand. Dwarfed in the giant palm was the same amulet Myramar wore on the material

THE TOMB OF THERAGAARD

plane. "Go ahead." The being spoke as if it were encouraging a child to confront his fears. "Don't be afraid. See what I have."

Telvar examined the amulet. Inside was a swirling mist of white and gray. "What is that?"

"Myramar's soul!" answered the being, laughing, before ramming its goat horns into Telvar's head.

The attack severed Telvar from the astral plane, and the young wizard crashed to the very real floor in the material world. He was woozy, but when he opened his eyes, he was relieved to find that his sight had been restored.

Telvar staggered to his feet, blood seeping from a wound to his forehead. He noticed that the wizard band around his head had snapped and fallen to the floor. "Go back to the Abyss!" he shouted at Myramar.

Without the connection to the astral plane, it was impossible to cast another flame strike. Instead, the young wizard brought forth to memory a simple cantrip. He reached into his pocket and grabbed handfuls of two reagents: powdered glass and volcanic ash. He combined the two substances in his hands and spoke words of magic. Telvar then threw the reagents at Myramar. When the reagents fell around the old wizard, a mist of mirrored crystals surrounded the demented tower mage.

Telvar shouted to Brother Kayen. "Press your attack! The cloud shall reflect and enhance the light of Aten!"

Kayen and Tryam needed no further encouragement, and they began to make headway toward Myramar. The spell, like many Telvar knew, was very simple but, the young wizard hoped, very effective. *It is likely our only hope!*

When the blue light from the cross of Aten shone into the cloud of tiny reflective particles, the tower mage was bathed as if in blue flames. The gale-force wind from Myramar's staff lessened immediately, and the tower mage writhed in pain.

Kayen and Tryam inched closer.

The light that fell upon Myramar's flesh began to reveal the old wizard's true shriveled form; gone was the wild-eyed, vigorous madman. Once the light became blinding, Myramar dropped his staff, and his hands began to tear at the amulet around his throat.

Telvar, devoid of magic, watched helplessly as the amulet began to swell in size, its red light battling with that of the blue.

"The Daemon emerges from the jewel!" shouted Kayen in alarm.

The chain holding the Anima Crystallum around the old wizard's neck suddenly snapped, and the amulet fell to the floor with a heavy thud. Larger and larger the bauble grew, as brighter and brighter the light within it shone.

Once the jewel swelled to thrice the size of a man, it shattered with the sound of hundred cracking mirrors.

Emerging from the magical crystal in a twisted mimicry of birth was the horned head and broad shoulders of the Daemon Telvar had seen in the astral plane. Myramar slumped to the floor beside it.

"Everyone, attack!" urged Kayen, as he took sole possession of the cross of Aten. As he advanced on the Daemon, the missionary then repeated lines of a prayer in an ancient language Telvar could not comprehend.

Kara broke free from her ice prison and began plugging the Daemon with her red arrows. Most bounced off its strange, glistening skin, but a few caused deep, penetrating wounds.

Wulfric pulled his legs free from the warped floor and teamed with the young acolyte to flank the slithering entity, which was now wholly on the material plane.

Telvar raced to Myramar's side to check on his old master. Bending down, he looked upon a man wrinkled and withered far beyond his natural years. He cradled the old man's head in his lap and tried to wake him. "Master!"

The old wizard's eyes fluttered open. He struggled to consciousness and grabbed Telvar's hand. "I was a fool, my boy. Forgive me. I was too trusting and confident of my own sagacity." His wrinkled hand fell to his chest. "We are still connected. I can feel its corrupted soul still inside my body. I must stop him."

"Stop? How?" asked Telvar. Myramar's intentions showed in the old man's now-quivering eyes. "No, master, you can't. We can defeat him! Brother Kayen has dealt with Daemons before."

The old man shook his head. "He has not faced a Daemon like this. Help me to my feet. I have one last bit of magic left in me. I know his true name. With that I can lure him to me."

Lifting the old man to his feet, Telvar tried one last attempt to stop his master. "There has to be another way. There has to!"

"It is too late. I must pay for my misjudgment." Myramar pushed Telvar aside and placed his arms in front of himself, poised as if to cast a spell. "Auroth!" the old wizard shouted at the Daemon. "It is time for you to return to the charred ditches of hell."

THE TOMB OF THERAGAARD

Telvar was shocked to see that during his brief conversation with Myramar, Auroth now held Tryam and Wulfric by their throats and Brother Kayen was wrapped within the Daemon's serpentine legs. At the sound of its true name, Auroth turned, faced Myramar, and roared like the animal it was.

Words of magic flowed from the old tower mage's mouth. Telvar could not decipher the spell, which sounded like a mixture of magic along with the words of a dark cleric of Terminus. Black smoke formed around Myramar's hands.

Throwing Telvar's companions roughly aside, Auroth slithered to Myramar and coiled its limbs around him. Telvar reached for his dagger and tried to pierce the snake-like appendages, but they were too tough.

"Stand clear," Myramar warned, his words coming between short breaths as Auroth's coils crushed his chest. "Forgive me, Telvar, for I have failed as your master. Let what I do now stand as my last lesson to you."

Overwhelmed with shame at his inability to help his master, Telvar could only watch as the battle between Myramar and the Daemon proceeded without him. The black smoke from the old man's spell grew to envelop Auroth. Myramar, his face now turning blue, shouted to Brother Kayen. "Now! Pray to Aten!"

The missionary did as he was asked, and the cross of Aten again glowed bright. When the light of Aten reached the struggling pair, it ignited the black cloud and engulfed both beings in flames of red and black. Telvar watched, horrified, as Myramar embraced the Daemon instead of attempting to escape.

Words of magic came from the old wizard's burning lips. Telvar recognized the spell as powerful elemental magic. That magic created a vortex of wind, which swept through the room and then launched the entangled pair into the air and over the balcony.

The young wizard rushed to the railing just as the sickening sound of crunching bones reached his ears. Below, the smoke parted, revealing Myramar's broken body on the tower's stone apron. The Daemon, a dozen feet away, was sinking into the ground, thrashing its coils, and cursing in the Dark Tongue as flames devoured its flesh. Moments later, the Daemon disappeared entirely, its link to the material plane broken with the ending of Myramar's life.

The green and yellow smoke slowly returned to mask the horror.

"It is over," said Telvar glumly. "They are both gone."

"He sacrificed himself to save us all. The Daemon was powerful, extremely so. I was faltering." Kayen's words did not comfort Telvar.

The others gathered around the young wizard and said words of praise for Myramar's selfless deed, but Telvar knew that more trouble was in store for them. He separated himself from the others. "It is important that I gain control over the tower. A mage tower without a master is a dangerous thing. Even now the lens is poised to release a deadly blast of energy at the Engothian keep."

"How do you control a building?" Kara asked skeptically.

"With magic," answered Telvar.

When Kara responded with shrugged shoulders and a blank look, Telvar withheld the sigh he wanted to exhale. Instead, he explained further: "Each mage tower contains a gem like the one we destroyed in Antigenesus's laboratory. If the gem has no master, it can become unstable. I must assert my will over this tower's jewel."

"Can you gain control of this tower?" asked Kayen. "Is your will stronger than that of the gem?"

"If you had asked me this before our quest, I might have answered no. But after all I have seen and overcome recently, I now believe I can assert my will over the gem." He made to adjust his wizard band before remembering that the band had snapped. "Even so, taking over a tower in the best of circumstances is not an easy task. Many wizards have died trying."

"Once you get control of the tower, could you use its power to make my arrows magical?" inquired Kara.

"Without a doubt," said Telvar, smiling.

"Can we help you with this task?" asked Tryam.

"No. I have to do this alone. With the amount of energy stored in the gem, I am uncertain I can protect you if I were to fail." Telvar made for the stairs that Myramar had revealed when he'd appeared to them, the hidden stairs that led to the gem. "The rest of you must leave at once and seek out Lord Dunford. If he still lives, tell him what has happened and what awaits Arkos. He has to listen to you now."

Wulfric reached out to Telvar, and the two grasped forearms. "We have been at odds, but always with the same goal. I wish you luck, friend."

"I am not one for sentimentality," Telvar said, backing away, "so I say to you all: Leave now, and let me do my work!"

As he headed up the hidden stairs to the lens room and his ultimate challenge, the wizard did not turn back to bid farewell.

Chapter 68
The Binding Spell

Upon seeing the lens room, Telvar was underwhelmed. Everything his eyes examined—the walls, the floor, the gem, and even the precisely crafted lens—all of it was exceedingly ordinary. Elegant, perhaps, but lacking the grandeur he had envisioned for the first tower of his career. It certainly paled in comparison with the lens room of Antigenesus, though the young Rutilus wizard knew that that comparison was entirely unfair.

The roof of the tower was domed, with one section occupied by the clear crystal lens. The mechanism that rotated the dome was old but certainly not the original, for it relied on the use of mundane gears rather than magic. The mechanical construct distracted from the mystique of the room, whose walls and floors were decorated in the runes and symbols of thaumaturgy.

Telvar stepped up to the heart of the mage tower: its gem. The crystal was a multifaceted, red-colored stone two feet in diameter that rested on a marble pedestal in the center of the room. The young wizard sensed the magic coming from deep inside the jewel. He circled the crystal, mesmerized and fascinated by the energy fluctuations inside. However, the longer he continued his probing, the less fascinated and more troubled he felt. *The gem is already unstable!* A glance at the lens above showed that it too was pulsating wildly with energy.

After long moments of hesitation, Telvar cursed himself for his indecisiveness. "It is time for me to claim you as mine!"

The young wizard had memorized the binding spell long before he had arrived in Arkos. Most young wizards dreamt of getting a tower of their own and practiced the spell as soon as they could get their hands on a copy.

The binding spell was similar to the spell used to commune with the astral plane, where one's mind reached outside the body, but this spell required part of the wizard's own essence, a price so high a wizard could control only one tower at a time.

As the words of magic came to his lips, Telvar recalled his first year at the Veneficturis and how one of the spell masters had caught him studying the binding spell. The old Crocus wizard had mocked him, through sprays of spittle, saying that a merchant's son would never get a chance at a tower of his own. *What I would say to that shriveled prune now!*

The words of the spell left his lips without further hesitation. As he gauged the gem's response to his mental probing, he made hand gestures and changed voice inflections. This was to be a test of wills, a test of his ability to handle the magical energies inside the gem. Outside sources of magic, such as from the astral plane, could not help him.

The battle for control of the tower could take hours, even days. Telvar made preparations for a long struggle.

Chapter 69

Negotiations with the Commander

By the time Tryam and the others exited the tower, the green and yellow smoke had dissipated. Tryam was shocked and disheartened at the desolation revealed. Myramar's garden was a charred, smoking landscape littered with the broken bodies of knights and the dismembered, rotting corpses of their undead assailants. The tower's once pure white stones were now stained black.

Lord Dunford, his golden armor dented and slick with gore, was overseeing the examination of Myramar's body, while behind him a squadron of knights was organizing the care for the injured. Tryam took some solace when he noticed Gavin was among the survivors.

Nothing of the undead force remained. The young acolyte speculated the victory over the undead had as much to do with the Daemon Auroth returning to hell as it did the swords under Dunford's command.

The party made their way to the fallen Myramar. The knights had lost nearly a dozen men, and the weight of their deaths was imprinted on the commander's pale face as he looked over the body of the tower mage. Kara let out a gasp and turned her head away from the twisted and burnt corpse that lay at Dunford's feet, Wulfric cursed the Daemon's handiwork, and Brother Kayen knelt before the body and made the sign of Aten, hoping to speed Myramar's soul to heaven.

The Arkos commander regarded the party with narrow eyes. "Myramar is dead, and so are his undead allies. How did this"—Dunford pointed at the corpse—"happen?"

"It was Telvar's doing!" snarled Wulfric, stepping up to Dunford's face. "He got us in the tower, and together we helped Myramar fight off the Daemon that had taken control over his mind. If you had not delayed us, some of these knights would still be alive."

"Careful, barbarian," the knight nearest Dunford said while placing his hand on the pommel of his sword. "You are speaking to a lord."

Wulfric responded by grabbing the pommel of his own blade.

The sound of Kayen's staff tapping against the stone apron got both men's attention. "Enough of this bluster. Lord Commander, hear us out. Dark powers conspire to attack our town. This is but the first—"

Dunford cut Kayen's words short. "A costly victory. I lost eleven good men, with many more injured. We mourn their loss, but I am thankful this crisis is over. Does this Telvar still live?"

"Well," responded Kara, "the tower hasn't blown up yet."

"What does that mean, girl?" Dunford motioned his men as if to rally them to action.

Kayen waved his arms to stop the knights from marching toward the tower door. "She means only that it is a difficult and dangerous proposition to secure a mage tower once its master has died. We have the utmost faith in Telvar, and so should you. The young wizard should not be disturbed at the moment, but I must caution you again: This is *not* the end of the crisis but only the beginning! Dementhus, the Albus sorcerer who enslaved Myramar, has gathered an army of Berserkers. They also have with them a Golem from the time of the Ancients. They are marching on Arkos now." He gently laid a hand on Dunford's armor. "The last time we spoke, you asked for evidence to back up our call for action. Look about, and see the evidence for yourself."

Kayen's voice was calm and—to Tryam, at least—convincing.

"An army headed here?" an exasperated Dunford asked. "To what end?"

"Does evil ever need a purpose," responded Kayen, "other than to kill or to impose its will on others?"

Doffing his helmet, Dunford ran his gauntleted hand through his thick mane of blond hair. "What would you have me do? Raise an army from miners and their families? Perhaps Abbot Monbatten would allow his monks to take up the sword?" As he paced back and forth, his face turned red. "I have no other forces to command, and no reinforcements can arrive from Engoth while the harbor is locked in ice."

Wulfric stepped in to scold the commander. "You had the chance to seek allies among the Berserker clans, but now they have been swallowed up by this unholy alliance of a necromancer and the Ragnar!" His voice rose with each word, and his face turned red in obvious rage. "Send out men to look for Berserkers who flee from the Ragnar. They would be the best fighters you could have!"

Tryam watched as the commander tried to make sense of what he was hearing. *He must feel as a ship captain does upon learning the vessel he commands is doomed to sink.*

"I shall man the walls and double our patrols, but I shall not risk the safety of the town or our mining operations on a war between Berserker clansmen," said Dunford. "There is nothing of value in this town for an Albus wizard or for a Berserker clan. Besides, no Berserker army can break through our walls, now that their agent in Arkos has been stopped."

"We thank you for taking those precautions," Kayen said, heading off any further words from Wulfric. "We shall leave you to your grim task."

Kayen grabbed Wulfric about the arm and led the party back to the bronze gate and out of the grove. The group huddled around the missionary.

"The precautions he takes will not be enough," asserted Tryam. "He cannot hide behind these walls. Does he not understand what a Golem can do? Lord Dunford needs to prepare the people of Arkos for what is about to happen."

"He is as mad as Myramar!" added Wulfric through grinding teeth.

Kayen stroked his beard thoughtfully but then shrugged his shoulders in exasperation. "Perhaps the wall can hold for a time, until Telvar can devise a plan to deal with Dementhus and the Golem." His words were, for the first time, hollow and unconvincing.

The voices in the crypts. The spirits at the beacon tower. The shrine in the mountain. Now is the time for Theragaard to step forward and make a stand against the darkness. "Respectfully, Brother," said Tryam, "Telvar cannot stop the Golem by himself. I believe I know a way that Aten can aid us, but I cannot tell you how precisely. I have been guided down a path that I have been reluctant to follow, but it is one I must follow. The first step I need to take is to return to the abbey and speak with Father Monbatten. I must tell him that I intend to leave the Order of Saint Paxia."

On hearing of his decision, Kara let out a cry of triumph. "Please, let me go with you. If he gives you any trouble, I shall knock some sense into him." She smashed her fist into her palm.

Tryam could not help but smile at her enthusiasm. "Thank you, Kara, but I do not think I shall need to resort to violence!"

Kara kicked the ground in disappointment. "After you tell the old prune your decision, then what are you going to do?"

"I shall seek out something in the crypts that may aid us in the fight against Dementhus."

Wulfric jumped at Tryam's words. "An ancient weapon?"

"No, lad," interrupted Brother Kayen. "I believe he seeks the tomb of Theragaard!"

Tryam nodded his head solemnly. "Yes. Three times I was called to Theragaard, and three times I failed to answer the call. I shall return to the vaults under the abbey and commune with his spirit—*if* it is Aten's will."

"Who is Theragaard?" asked Kara. "A great wizard?"

"No," replied Kayen. "He was a great warrior of old."

"A dead guy is going to help us?" she asked incredulously.

Kayen burst out with a belly laugh. "So to speak, child, but not just *any* dead guy. Someone who defeated the Golem once before."

"As a ghost?" Kara thought about the idea for a moment, then jumped up and down enthusiastically. "This might work!"

Chapter 70
The Invocation of the Golem

The Golem's heavy footfalls thundered down the mountain and into the valley below. Dementhus stood on its open palm, perched like a prophet at the pulpit, with his red robes flowing around him, a hand firmly on his long black metal staff. It was time to reveal the Mountain God to His eager worshippers.

Only now, as the pale winter sun rose and the Ragnar village came into focus, did Dementhus realize how long he had been absent from Ivor's warmongering. The Golem's shadow stretched down the sides of the valley and touched the outskirts of the army's encampment. Dementhus calculated that the number of fighting men had swelled to over a thousand. To get their undivided attention, he would need to make a spectacle of his arrival.

Dementhus spoke in the language of magic. At his command, dark clouds lumbered down from the mountains on howling winds to smother the early sun.

Tiny forms began to stir in the village, as ants do when their nest is disturbed. The Albus mage did not want the Ragnar to merely stir at his arrival; he wanted them in a panic.

Despite his now almost useless physical body, a new spell was quickly on the sorcerer's lips. Thunder boomed in response to his command. The Ragnar looked to the sky, but they did not panic. To frighten the hearty Berserkers, he would need to do more.

Dementhus pointed his staff at the clouds and summoned more magic, shouting words into the sky. With a clap and flash, red bolts of lightning struck the village and the surrounding encampment. As men and women ran for cover and the bolts killed indiscriminately, he laughed in delight. Chaos reigned inside and outside the Ragnar village. He may lose a few dozen Ragnar, but he would ensure their devotion.

The Albus mage urged the black metal Golem to close faster on the village.

A blast from a walrus-tusk horn stationed atop the palisade walls cut through the din of the magical storm. In response, a company of men exited the gate. Dementhus spied Ivor at the company's head, instructing the panicked men to get in formation. Gidran was by his side.

When he was within a hundred yards of the palisade, the sorcerer began to diminish the storm's intensity. He then halted the Golem and instructed it to reveal itself to the Ragnar.

"Come to me, My warriors! Come and kneel before your God. Kneel before Me!"

The words were neither spoken by lips nor entered into awaiting ears; they were spread by the power of magic and heard directly inside the minds of the Ragnar.

The Ragnar, Ivor and Gidran among them, reverently made their way to the Mountain God. By the time the storm ended and the pale sun returned, thousands thronged on bended knees before Dementhus and the metal goliath.

Speaking from his pulpit, Dementhus looked over the sea of barbarians and smiled. *They are mine to command!* "The time has come for the Ragnar—those by birth and those by conquest—to ascend to their rightful place among the great peoples of Medias. As your God's chosen emissary, I tell you that He commands all to prepare for our first *true* test."

"What test is this?"

The question came from Gidran, who was playing his part as the spiritual advocate for the Ragnar. To answer, this time it was the true voice of the Mountain God that rang through the valley, forceful as an erupting volcano and as deep as the sea.

"We must destroy Arkos and the foreigners, who are a blight on this continent! We shall slay. We shall conquer. We shall spread to all ends of Medias!"

At the sound of the voice of their long-silent God, the crowd rose to their feet and surged forward. The Golem lowered Dementhus to the ground; he then made his way to the pale and awed jarl. The Necromancer used the last of his physical strength to pull the man away from the others. "Let the Ragnar revel in their God," he shouted into Ivor's ear. "We have important things to discuss."

The stunned jarl, basking in the Golem's aura, resisted Dementhus, but he eventually turned away from the Golem and took plodding steps back to the palisade gate. Only when the two were alone did he find his words. "We saw the disturbance atop the mountain and thought the God was angry. Now we know it was His rebirth. The spilt blood of our victories has sated our God's thirst!"

"Yes, it has. However, His appetite is great," cautioned Dementhus. "We have much more work to do."

"Yes, of course." The jarl, whose teeth were sharpened to points, smiled awkwardly, as one does in a daze. "We have the Mountain God on our side. Everything is possible now. No enemy is too great to overcome, but should Abbaster not join us?" Ivor looked about the shadows, as if the brute would appear. "He has been away from the men for far too long."

"Abbaster is dead," informed Dementhus. "I found his decapitated corpse in the ruins after the God's rebirth."

"He was to be our general!" cried Ivor, his countenance changing to shock and anger.

"The general shall be you! It was destined that a Ragnar should lead the army anyway. But fear not. Abbaster still has a part to play. Our first blessing from the Mountain God has been Abbaster's resurrection. Our big friend will command the undead army, which is to be the tip of the spear when we attack Arkos."

"Abbaster returns from the dead to command the undead forces? Fitting, perhaps. I have witnessed the strength of the Mountain God, and if He wishes such to be possible, I shall not question it." The jarl looked at the Ragnar forces that encircled the Golem. "I shall assemble the men and supplies. We shall make for Arkos at once. But when will this undead army be ready?"

As his body tingled with the pure magic he had taken from Antigenesus's exploding gem, Dementhus smiled. "Soon. Very soon."

Chapter 71

Rallying the Brothers

With the harbor frozen, the only way to get from the mainland to the abbey was by foot. Tryam did not need to use the secret entrance, nor did he want to. He wanted his arrival to be seen and the message he was to deliver to be heard by all.

At this late hour, the docks were deserted, and the mariners on foot patrol were nowhere to be found. Tryam stepped onto the frozen harbor and began the cold trek across the ice to the abbey.

When he reached the island, he looked up to the church as a stranger would. Sorrow filled his heart as he realized how isolated the monks were from the outside world. This solitude insulated them from the suffering of others. *It is no wonder the people of Arkos have never truly embraced the order.*

The young acolyte soon found himself in front of the ruined portcullis. Tryam looked at the defaced ancient gate and pictured in his mind what it must have looked like in the time of Theragaard; then he wondered, *Can this gate be repaired and the breaches in the walls fixed?*

Torchlight caught his eyes. Farther ahead, on the winding path through the ruins, a funeral procession was underway. It was the dead from the ward tower. Tryam hurried to catch up.

By the time he joined his brothers, the procession had made it to the abbey's graveyard. The bodies of four monks, covered in clean linen, had been placed before a statue of Saint Annen, the patron saint of departed clergy. He arrived in time to hear the end of Father Monbatten's eulogy.

"The tentacles of violence have reached our haven here in Arkos. Our brave brothers, who dedicated their lives to preserving the light of Aten, have been thrown into darkness. As their souls ascend from this accursed

THE TOMB OF THERAGAARD

world we call Medias, let us remember our vows and pray for those whose actions have led to the death of four of our brothers. Let us not seek revenge, but rather peace."

Prayers followed as the brothers of Saint Paxia bid final farewell to the dead. Tryam was intimately familiar with each deceased brother, and he grieved for them. Designated monks prepared the bodies for placement in the tomb reserved for those men who had served as guardians of the ward tower.

When the grim ritual was complete, Tryam followed the abbot to his chambers inside the rectory, neither one wanting to disturb the sanctity of the dead with the unpleasant conversation that was to come. Monbatten fell heavily into his chair. His eyes, under his beetling brows, scrutinized Tryam as if he were a mystifying puzzle. "I hope you are here to beg for forgiveness. We have lost four members of our order this sorrowful night. The bodies that lie in that tomb are still warm."

"I am aware of that, Father," responded Tryam. "Their deaths trouble me as much as they do you."

"That Brother Kayen is involved in this chaos I am not surprised. He is always seeking trouble."

"We were trying to help!"

The abbot shook his head in disgust. "I hear that the crisis has ended and that the tower mage has been killed. Is this the case?"

Tryam strode boldly up to the abbot's desk. "Yes, Myramar is dead, but a greater threat looms! There shall be no peace in Arkos as long as the forces of darkness go unopposed. You cast aspersions on Brother Kayen, but it was the visiting monk Gidran, whom we welcomed into this church, and his ally, the rogue wizard Dementhus, who are behind this mayhem."

Monbatten silenced Tryam with a dismissive wave of his hand. "Why are you here? I thought you had made it quite clear that you do not intend to honor your promise to join the order when you brandished that foul blade in my face. The journey to the Berserkers was supposed to show you the harsh realities of life outside these walls, not encourage you to become a Berserker yourself!"

Tryam took a deep breath, swallowing his anger. "When I left these walls, I had every intention of coming back and taking the oath to become a full member of the Order of Saint Paxia, but when Brother Kayen and I found the Berserker village we were to visit destroyed and my friend Kara kidnapped, my priorities changed. Aten put us in a position where we were the only ones who could rescue Kara and try to save those taken prisoner."

"Why did you not seek my guidance?" snapped Monbatten, rising from his chair.

"Because I knew your answer already. You would have advised me to abandon the quest to find Kara and to leave her to her fate." Tryam relaxed, confident that what he was saying was the truth. "I beg you to listen to me now. Arkos will soon be under siege. Without violating any of its tenets, the Order of Saint Paxia can play a role in the town's defense. Make this abbey a haven for those fleeing the Ragnar army! Defend Aten against this horde!"

"If what you say is true, we shall, of course, open our gates for any refugees seeking shelter, but we cannot hope to defend the town from the evil that descends upon it. Our part shall be to pray for peace."

Tryam stared the abbot down. "You can do more than pray. Tell me, why did the order obliterate Theragaard from the history of this island?"

Blood rushed to Monbatten's wrinkled face, and the abbot clenched his fists. "Why do you bring up *his* name now? Theragaard is dead, and so is his philosophy. We built over his legacy of blood with one of peace."

"I shall tell you why. Three different times, I was guided to Theragaard by spirits whose loyalty even death could not diminish. The first time was under the crypts in this very abbey, the second time was when we took refuge inside an abandoned beacon tower, and the third time was when I ventured inside the fortress of the dead archmagus Antigenesus and stumbled upon a ruined temple. All of these spirits, in their own way, urged me to seek out Theragaard! I believe it will only be with Theragaard's help that victory over this evil can be achieved!"

Monbatten started to speak but stopped as his face scowled.

Tryam straightened his back and continued in clear, precise words. "I intend to go down to the catacombs and pray before the tomb of Theragaard for his guidance. I shall not sit back and watch others die. My destiny has been shown to me. I cannot become a member of the order. I am a warrior of Aten, and if my fate is to suffer as my father did, then so be it."

"I shall stop you!" threatened Monbatten. "I shall not allow you back into those crypts!"

The young acolyte refused to acknowledge Monbatten's words. Instead, he turned on his heels and exited the abbot's chambers with his conscience clear.

THE TOMB OF THERAGAARD

I know what I have to do.

Before he descended into the vaults, he had to give his brothers an explanation for his actions and leave a warning of the darkness to come. In a fit of inspiration, Tryam ran to the bell tower. Using his full weight as leverage, he tugged furiously on the rope that hung down from the top of the tower. The bell clanged loudly and echoed throughout the entire abbey grounds. It was not long before the monks, unaccustomed to any deviation from their regimented life, gathered outside in the predawn light to see what was amiss.

"What is this madness?" asked Lathan, an old and close advisor to the abbot. "Young Tryam, have you lost your wits?"

"Found my wits is more like it," responded Tryam, more glibly than he had intended.

As the monks tried to figure out what was going on, the air was filled with a cacophony of voices. Tryam stood before them and waved his arms to get their eyes focused on him. "Brothers, listen to me, for it was I who summoned you here. This has been a tragic night; we lost four of our brothers. But I speak to you now in order to prevent more horrors."

"*Our* brothers?" Lathan pointed his beaked nose and gnarled finger in Tryam's direction. "Father Monbatten told us you turned your back on your brothers!"

Like-minded monks shouted more accusations.

"Hear me out!" implored Tryam. "That is all I ask! What Brother Lathan has said is partially true. I have decided not to become a member of the Order of Saint Paxia, but I am not turning my back on any of you. I am following a path shown to me by Aten."

A mixed reaction followed his declaration, with most of the monks shaking their heads in disbelief.

"What path is there to follow but that of Saint Paxia?" asked one brother.

When Tryam did not answer immediately, the crowd became rowdier. He had never seen them so agitated. When he heard accusations that his actions had led to the destruction of the ward tower, he had doubts of his own.

Perhaps this was a mistake.

"Let him speak!" It was one of the younger monks, a man named Dorsat, who stepped through the throng of clergy. "Let him have his say.

Tell us, Brother. What is this other path? Why do you believe you are now on the correct course?"

"Thank you, Brother Dorsat." Tryam stepped into the center of the crowd and made eye contact with as many of the members as he could. "Three times I have had contact with spirits from the ethereal plane, and each time, I was directed to take the path I now choose. These spirits urged that I commune with Theragaard, the warrior whose castle lies buried under this abbey. Forces of evil are on the march, and *some* of us will be called to take up arms to defend the faithful. I believe I am one of those people. "

Cries of disbelief spread throughout the gathered monks. Dorsat hushed them into silence. Undaunted, Tryam continued. "You saw what happened in town today. That was but the first stage of a much larger attack. Myramar did not go insane. He was possessed by a Daemon! A Daemon in league with a rogue wizard and Brother Gidran, the same man we let into our abbey."

The cries of disbelief changed to ones of shock.

"But that is not all," added Tryam, his voice becoming more emphatic. "An army of Berserkers even now thunders down the mountains, led by a magical metal warrior the height of one of the legendary hill giants!"

Some of the members of the Order of Saint Paxia fell to their knees and prayed.

"We are likely to have a week or less to prepare," he continued, "and I have many tasks I beg of you."

Arguments replaced fear.

"Tasks that will not violate your oaths!" clarified Tryam.

When Lathan clapped his hands, the monks quieted down. "What are these tasks?" he asked with a snarl, his tone filled with doubt.

"I do not ask you to take up the sword, as I do. Instead, rebuild the portcullis, fix the holes in the wall that encircles the island, and most importantly, prepare the cloister for civilians escaping Arkos."

Brother Caydan, who'd worked with Tryam in the infirmary, stepped forward. "I shall aid any of those in need of healing, and I shall set up a ward for injured warriors." He turned toward a couple of his companions. "Brothers Ajon and Lymaz, you have long aided me in my healing arts. Will you join me?"

Both men nodded their heads.

THE TOMB OF THERAGAARD

"I shall take charge of reconstructing the island's defenses," offered Dorsat. "In my youth, I learned much of mason work from my father." He rubbed his hands together nervously. "But what will you be doing?"

"Something I should have done months ago," responded Tryam. "I shall contact the spirit of Theragaard and seek his guidance."

"His spirit has not been venerated for centuries. It would be difficult to contact him even if his spirit yet lingers on this plane." The words of caution came from Gamrow, the most devout of all of Monbatten's followers.

"I have to try. My sword alone will have little impact on the battle to come, but if guided by Theragaard, I might help turn the tide." He bowed his head before his brothers. "I must go now. Please be at peace, and let Aten be with you always."

Tryam stepped back from the others. He had faith that his brothers would do as they said. He turned away and headed for the wine cellar and to the entrance to the crypts below.

Chapter 72
War of Wills

Sweat soaked Telvar's worn black robes as he cautiously absorbed the energy from the tower gem. The crystal was only a Rutilus, the most rudimentary of all the tower stones, yet Telvar felt himself losing this battle. He asserted his will more forcefully, but the gem reacted to his commands for energy like a stubborn child.

More like a rebellious child actually: A bolt of energy escaped from the gem and struck the wall behind him, causing small chunks of stone to fall about the room.

Damn this gem to the Abyss! It tests me like my master did!

As if to prove his point, the gem unleashed elemental magics in quick succession—a fire strike, a blast of ice, then hurricane winds—forcing Telvar to counter each attack.

The battle for control over the gem was turning into a prolonged war, not the quick skirmish Telvar had hoped, but he was seeing a path to victory. The longer the ambitious young wizard stayed connected to the gem, the better he understood its identity. Each gem was unique and possessed qualities that could be uncovered only by a careful understanding of its internal structure—its personality, as some wizards called it. He also sensed, with some disquietude, his late master's presence still residing in the gem.

The unsettling nature of this discovery was replaced by fear on another front, as the energy stored in the lens above began to shake the entire mage tower. Myramar had charged the lens with enough power to destroy the Engothian keep two times over. *I have to win this contest now!*

THE TOMB OF THERAGAARD

With the precision of a jeweler, Telvar began to cleave his master's energy from the gem, releasing it harmlessly into the air as he did so. Once that delicate process was over, the young wizard sighed with relief. *My first taste of success. Now I must insert my own magic, sacrifice a part of myself.*

The wizard's mind wandered for just a moment from the binding spell, and the gem took advantage. Images flashed into Telvar's head: the fire at school, the bestial face of Auroth. The gem knew his failures and his fears. Or so it thought.

Your first mistake! I have moved past those failures; nothing can stop me!

The young wizard fought back, channeling his energy into the gem. His legs were wobbly, and his arms ached from their constant manipulations, but he did not let up. Far above, the lens shook violently. Ceramic tiles that covered the domed ceiling fell, and the mechanism used to rotate the lens began to shake apart. Time had run out; he had to do something.

Telvar rushed to the levers of the lens control panel. With half his attention still focused on the binding spell, he guessed which lever did what and pushed an ivory knob forward. The lens angled upward. He tried to rotate the roof, but the metal gears were jammed. He would have to hope that he changed the angle enough, so that the energy released from the lens would miss the keep and dissipate harmlessly into the air.

Now, with a small part of his own magic transferred, Telvar called upon the gem to do his bidding and to release the unstable magic in the lens.

When the gem complied, the young wizard immediately realized his mistake. The air in the lens room was still filled with wisps of Myramar's dispersed magic. Moments later, the lens flared, and the loose, unrestrained energy ignited. The air around Telvar flashed as if in a lightning storm, slamming him to the ground. He sealed his mind off from the magical onslaught and covered his head. So desperate was his need, he even asked Aten for help.

When the conflagration ended, Telvar came to his feet, pleased to see that he was still alive and that the lens was still intact. From the lack of any explosion in town, it also appeared that he had saved the Engothian keep from destruction. *Another feat of mine that will go unheralded!*

Telvar walked back to the gem and refocused on the binding spell. He peered inside the red jewel, ready to be its master. *You are mine!*

Chapter 73

A Day for Diplomacy

"I shall split your skull in twain!" promised a battle-scarred and thickly bearded Berserker veteran, his jagged axe pointed at the head of a smirking Engothian knight.

"Not before I slice your gullet, you filthy barbarian!" the bold but unwise young knight responded, drawing his blade but keeping it by his side.

Wulfric jumped between the two obstinate warriors and shoved them apart. Both the large Berserker and the fit knight landed hard on their backsides. "And if you don't shut up, I shall kill the both of you!"

Being a mediator was the most onerous job Wulfric had ever been asked to perform. He would sooner wrestle a white bear if asked again. The young Berserker expected his people to be headstrong but never this unwilling to listen. The Engothians, he discovered, were not much more amenable, but at least they were accustomed to making bargains without bloodshed.

Wulfric let out a roar, forestalling any further hostility. The respective factions dragged the two men back to their groups.

"I want to break something! Gimme a head or two to smash!" added Kara, her face turning red. "They do not understand what awaits us! We have to work together, or we shall all die!"

Wulfric hugged Kara, lifting her off her feet, letting her go only after her fury died. "I shall find a solution," he proclaimed, "even if it kills them!"

The band of raging Berserkers and the squad of belligerent knights seethed under the shadow of the palisade of the Engothian mine outside Arkos. In the days since the party had returned from the once-twin-peaked mountain, waves of Berserker refugees had flooded the plains to Arkos.

THE TOMB OF THERAGAARD

They represented members from a dozen different clans, united by their hatred of the Ragnar and by the fear of the army that was gathering in the dark valleys of the Coronas.

Under pressure from Brother Kayen, Lord Dunford had allowed the wandering Berserkers to take refuge inside the mine fort, but only if they agreed to aid in its defense. Over the past few days, however, the Berserker numbers had swelled and overwhelmed the knights' resources.

Wulfric fumed at the Engothians' overconfidence. Despite the stories told by the refugees, Lord Dunford had stopped sending patrols into the Berserker lands. He claimed it was because those patrols had seen no evidence of an army, but Wulfric suspected it was really because the commander still assumed that the fighting was only a squabble among Berserker clans and because he feared getting caught in the middle. In fact, the town's level of alertness was back to what it had been before Myramar had transformed his mage tower into an enemy installation.

Gavin broke away from his fellow knights, a look of exasperation on his face. The young warrior had been Wulfric's only ally among the Engothians. When he spoke, he confirmed Wulfric's doubt about their progress. "I am sorry. No one will listen to your concerns. I fear that if we do not get a confirmation about the threatening Ragnar army, the commander may kick your kin back into the plains."

Wulfric wished Tryam were there to help mediate, but his friend had not yet returned from the abbey. Brother Kayen had assured Wulfric that Tryam was not being held against his will, but the Ulf warrior did not trust that old crow Monbatten. If his friend did not return before the Ragnar army arrived, he would tear down the abbey walls to find him.

"Gavin, bring the two leaders forward," requested Wulfric. "We have to get them away from the rabble."

"That might be a good idea," agreed Gavin.

After some cajoling, the two respective leaders agreed to Gavin's request and stood before Wulfric. Bannett, in his polished armor, was the squad captain representing the Engothians, while Makkong of the Redbone clan, a ragged looking young Berserker with teeth sharpened into points, represented the Berserker warriors.

Before Wulfric could begin, however, Bannett was in his ear. "This is madness. The fort cannot support the number of Berserkers we have now. The smell alone is too much!"

In spite of Bannett's being a leader of men, Wulfric was shocked at the man's insulting pettiness. "Would you prefer the smell of burnt roofs and corpses?" Wulfric's response was harsh but accurate. The incredible arrogance of the foolish knights made them blind to the reality of the overwhelming forces they were soon to face.

"Why should I defend these cowards who have no respect for my people?" Makkong asked, gesturing wildly with his axe.

Gavin interrupted. "I have a suggestion that may be agreeable to both sides."

"Why should I listen to a squire?" began Bannett.

"I like him," countered Makkong, probably just to spite Bannett. "I shall listen."

Bannett removed his helmet and rested it casually on his hip, as if the whole ordeal bored him. "Okay, what is *your* solution, squire?"

"There is truth to what Captain Bannett is saying. The fort simply cannot support the total number of warriors currently being housed. I suggest that some, as per the current arrangement, stay here to help guard the fort, while another group come to Arkos and guard the east gate. Should an attack happen, we do not have enough knights to guard both gates. The Berserker women and children can stay in the abbey."

Hearing what Gavin proposed, each side erupted in charges and countercharges, but Wulfric heard no reasonable argument why the arrangement couldn't work.

"For how long?" Bannett asked after the squawking ceased.

"One month. If the enemy does not come, we shall make other arrangements," said Gavin. "Perhaps we can look for a permanent residence for the Berserkers elsewhere."

As both leaders pondered the situation, the two factions settled into quiet rage. It was Makkong who spoke first. "If this is the best chance I have of securing a home for my people and for revenge against the Ragnar, then I accept."

The Berserker stretched out his arm to Bannett. The knight paused for only a moment before the two gripped forearms. Bannett smiled smugly but said with apparent sincerity, "If the Ragnar army arrives, I could not think of a greater ally to have."

"If Brother Kayen were here," said Kara, who hugged both Wulfric and Gavin, "I think he would say we witnessed a miracle."

"The miracle will be if Lord Dunford endorses this truce," fretted Gavin.

"An uneasy truce is better than nothing," stated Wulfric. "Do you need help at Arkos? Kara and I need something to do."

Gavin smiled. "You're both welcome to stand guard at the north gate, unless you would rather be with your Berserker cousins here."

"I want to be as close to Tryam as possible. I don't trust the monks at the abbey, and I worry about our wizard friend Telvar too, I suppose. We have not heard from either in many days."

"Wherever we make our stand," said Kara, "I want to make sure we deal the Ragnar the deadliest blow possible!"

Wulfric cast his gaze toward the north. The sky was blue and the temperature moderate, but a storm was approaching. He felt it. He grabbed his sword pommel tight and Kara tighter. "We shall, Kara. We shall."

Chapter 74

Gathrey

The warhorse surged forward at Gavin's urging. Clumps of muddy snow flew from its heavy hooves as a frosty mist plumed from the beast's nostrils. The young knight and his three comrades raced toward the border of the Berserker lands in a frantic search for one of their own.

"Keep your wits about you," he shouted over the sound of the hooves.

The men at the north gate respected him and had put their faith in his leadership, despite his being only a newly minted recruit. He had earned their respect during the fight at the wizard's grove against the undead. When the others panicked, he had led the charge against the almost unstoppable creatures and had saved the lives of many men. As a result, he had been named captain of the gate. Now, for the first time, he was experiencing the burden of command, for it had been his decision to send patrols farther north than Lord Dunford had requested. Gavin was convinced that an invading army was headed to Arkos.

I shall not let them lose faith in me now. We must find Gathrey!

Gavin debated whether the man had gotten careless or he had been the victim of something much more sinister. It had been nearly two weeks since Tryam had warned the knights of the invasion. *If an army is coming from the north, they could be at Arkos any day.*

The moon slumbered beneath thick winter clouds. Shadows twisted the familiar landscape into a foreign land with hidden dangers. One false move, and a rider could lose his balance and his life. Gavin sped his warhorse faster, deeming it worth the risk.

When dawn broke, a red line creased the clouds to the east, and the shadows on the ground receded. It was Deljay, the most expert rider of the group, who cried out in alarm at morning's light: "A horse wanders the plains with a man slumped in its saddle!"

Gavin spurred his horse ahead, and the men followed. It soon became clear that the horse Deljay had spotted was an Engothian warhorse and that the injured man was Gathrey. As Gavin closed the gap to the rider, he shouted the man's name, but there was no response. He rode up beside the wayward horse and grabbed its reins. A low moan and a slight movement of the man's head showed that Gathrey still lived.

"Help me free him from his saddle," commanded Gavin as he jumped from his horse.

Deljay dismounted and helped ease the unconscious rider down to the snow-covered ground. Gavin lifted the man's visor and saw blood oozing from his eyes, nose, and mouth. Deljay pressed a waterskin to Gathrey's lips, but the knight was too weak to swallow.

Gathrey's armor was scratched and dented. A large rent in the battered armor showed exposed flesh. Gavin was aghast when he observed bite marks.

"What happened?" Gavin pressed the man, fearing he might expire before revealing his adversaries. "Who attacked you?"

After Deljay wiped Gathrey's face with a damp cloth, the wounded man's eyes focused. Gathrey mustered up his remaining strength and, between gasps of pain, gave his report with the dignity and professionalism Gavin had come to appreciate from his fellow knights. "A black sea of the undead approach. They move fast, unnaturally so. I first came upon what I thought was a drunken Berserker in the wastes, but it was only the first, a wanderer who had gotten ahead of the main horde. It pulled me off my horse …"

As a coughing fit overcame Gathrey, his face became as white as the snow he rested upon. When Gavin dried the blood from Gathrey's lips, the man bravely continued: "I fought the creature off, hacking first its arms and then its legs from its body, but it would not die! The undead thing bayed mournfully, drawing more of its kind. I had to retreat."

His eyes fluttered.

"How far away?" Gavin asked gently.

Gathrey's eyes focused one final time. "A day's march north. We are too late."

With that, the man's eyes closed, and his breathing stopped.

A mixture of grief and horror shook Gavin. It was only after he looked up at his men, who were awaiting orders, that he could stand and take control once again. "Load him back on his horse. We take him home. We must warn those at the mine fort and then head straight for Arkos. The invasion force is coming."

Gavin moved to remount his horse when he felt something grab his ankle. He looked down and saw Gathrey's hand grasping his boot. *Does the man still live?*

Foam lathered out of Gathrey's open mouth, and the man's face contorted unnaturally. It was the same look the undead had had at the wizard's grove.

"This is not possible," gasped Deljay. "He has become one of the undead!"

This did not happen back at the grove. "There is powerful necromancy at work here!" warned Gavin as he shook his boot free from Gathrey's grasp.

The knights surrounded their former companion, each of them reluctant to be the first to strike. The undead knight held no such reservations, however; it threw off its helmet and shrieked into the gray dawn sky. Its next move was to grasp Deljay. Gavin aimed his blow to where Gathrey's armor had already been breached. His attack connected, but the creature did not seem to care as his sword hacked off bits of its flesh.

Deljay fell to the ground, with the wriggling undead man on top of him. "Get it off me!" Deljay cried as the ghoul tried to rip open his visor with its bloody hands.

Taking his axe from his saddlebag, Gavin stood over the entangled combatants. He swung at the neck of his former knight. He continued to swing until Gathrey's head flew from the undead man's shoulders. Deljay flung Gathrey's torso aside. The others watched in horror as that headless torso continued to thrash about.

"What unholy sorcery!" Deljay gasped. "There is a whole army of these creatures headed our way? Nothing can save us!"

Gavin did not argue with Deljay's assessment. "Leave the corpse here. We ride now!"

Grim-faced, the four riders left the dismembered body of their comrade to writhe on the ground, spilling its innards upon the pure white snow. It took a long time for the odor to clear from Gavin's nostrils.

Chapter 75

The Last Game

"Mine is so much better than yours!" squealed Kara as she swooned over her ballista, caressing its refurbished metal parts. "It really needs red paint, but look at it shine!"

When Wulfric ignored her remark, she stamped her foot and repeated, "Look at it!"

Wulfric reluctantly extracted himself from his ballista and made his way across the walkway that connected the two gatehouses to inspect Kara's handiwork. Kara had insisted that she defend the western gatehouse because she was right-handed. Wulfric had not argued the logic and simply stationed himself at the other gatehouse.

Though defending the north gate had proven uneventful so far, Wulfric knew that life with Kara would never prove so. They had spent the past six days getting the two ancient weapons in working order after decades of neglect. The ballistae were from the time of the Ancients, and their craftsmanship could not be duplicated. The weapons were made of sturdy polished wood strengthened with bronze plates and held together with thick iron nails. All the pieces fit with exacting precision, and the process to restore them had been painstakingly slow. During that time, Kara had threatened to skin his hide on only two occasions.

"It looks adequate." Wulfric said in a neutral tone. In reality, he was mightily impressed with Kara's work.

"Adequate?" Kara punched Wulfric on the shoulder. "I could launch a projectile two miles with this beast. Maybe even pierce your thick skull!"

Wulfric roared in laughter.

Kara kicked his shins.

"Okay, stop!" he pleaded. "It is the greatest ballista I have ever seen … apart from mine."

Kara growled, then shook her hands at the sky. Her face had turned a bright red; then, like a passing storm, her anger waned, and her expression turned sullen. She stepped away from her ballista and wandered to the battlements, where she leaned on a merlon between crenellations and looked north, toward the land of the Berserkers.

Wulfric came to stand beside her and placed his arm around her shoulders. "I was only joking."

She shrugged him away. "I have something to tell you that you will not like."

Wulfric's mind raced like a wolf tracking the plains, trying to think of what he had done wrong. When he couldn't think of anything obvious, he cautiously pressed. "Do not fret. What is it?"

"I lost your mother's necklace."

The necklace! Wulfric forgot that he had recovered her gift. Now he pondered how best to reveal, without getting punched, why he had neglected to tell her. "I don't care about an old bit of jewelry. All I care is that I you found you."

The glimmer in Kara's blue eyes was still missing. "By this time, we were to be married and starting our lives together. Now we have no home, we are surrounded by people who don't want us around, and we await an army that will bring certain death."

"Then we have to hold onto this moment—us together—right now! This moment in time is all we are guaranteed." Wulfric grabbed her shoulders and stared into her eyes, wishing for that special light to return. "As soon as we deal with the Ragnar, I shall have Brother Kayen wed us. After they are vanquished, we shall leave this place. We have no more ties here. You said you wanted to see the world; I shall take you to see every corner of it! I have won the pelt of the Hound of Fenrir and passed the Trial of Blood. I am a man, and you are my woman!"

He kissed her, and she kissed him back. When he looked into her eyes again, their glimmer had returned. Above, the gray clouds began to darken, signaling an end to another winter's day.

"I wish I could see the stars," lamented Kara. "They inspire me so." She took Wulfric's hands. "I want to know all the world's secrets and visit all the distant shores beyond the Frostfoam Sea! Take me there!"

THE TOMB OF THERAGAARD

"I shall," assured Wulfric.

Movement and the sound of hooves caught Wulfric's attention, and he released her. When he examined the shadows on the plains, he was disturbed by what he observed. "Gavin returns. However, I count five horses but only four riders. This is an ill omen."

"What could have happened? You don't think—"

Kara did not need to finish her thought. Wulfric paced the ramparts until Gavin and his men stopped before the closed portcullis. Wulfric shouted down. "State the password."

"Death to the Ragnar," responded Gavin.

Wulfric raced down two floors of the gatehouse to the winch mechanism, where he strained his muscles to do a job that was meant for three. After he heard the horses pass, he turned the large winch in the opposite direction until he heard the portcullis fall back into place. The young Berserker then raced down to meet the patrol. He arrived in time to find Gavin giving instructions to his men. The patrol listened intently, then took their horses, full gallop, into Arkos. Gavin, however, stayed behind, the reins of the riderless horse in his hand.

"Is he dead, then?" asked Wulfric.

Gavin dismounted and removed his helmet. "Dead twice over." The youth wore a weary face.

"Twice?" gasped Kara, arriving in time to overhear Gavin's disturbing comment.

"When we found Gathrey, he was drawing his last breaths. By strength of will, he endured long enough to report on what had attacked him: He had been waylaid by an undead Berserker, a straggler from a great horde. After completing the report, he died before my eyes—or, at least, I thought he'd died. After his soul had departed, his body spasmed back into life. We dispatched it, but it still twitched, even after I severed the head. The necromancy that comes is much more powerful than what we found at the grove. We have only hours to prepare for what is coming. The horde moves faster than ordinary men. I've sent the others to warn Lord Dunford."

"What will the commander do?" Kara asked. "Will he send us help along the walls? Right now, only six people guard the north gate!"

"I think so, Kara," answered Gavin. "By now, he has to know your warnings were correct."

"Even someone as thick-headed as he?"

"Yes." Gavin let a smile appear on his worried face. "I think so."

At that moment, a gentle snow began to fall, and a stiff breeze blew through the metal bars of the portcullis. Wulfric thought about his friends Tryam and Telvar. He had heard nothing from Tryam since they separated at the wizard's grove, and the only sign that Telvar lived had been a blast of energy released harmlessly into the sky from the mage tower. The two were not just friends of his; they were stout defenders. They would soon be needed.

Gavin remounted his horse. "I must find what my commander has to say. Stay here, light all the torches, and man those ballistae! I fear those ancient weapons shall see a lot of work tonight." The young knight saluted and then headed off into the sleeping town and its blissfully unaware citizens.

After lighting the torches, Wulfric led Kara to the top of the western gatehouse, and together they looked out toward the north. Neither could spot any signs of the enemy, but both knew they were out there. Kara paced. *I need her to stay focused on the task at hand.* "It looks as if we got these ballistae finished just in time. How many bolts do we have?" asked Wulfric.

Kara turned away from the darkness. "Let me check."

New bolts could not be forged quickly, but fortunately, a pile of the ancient projectiles had been found in a nearby warehouse. Kara counted the pile and stopped at a hundred. "I have over two hundred," she estimated. Looking across the causeway to Wulfric's pile, she said, "You have perhaps a hundred and a half again."

Wulfric smiled. "We have enough bolts to send a mass of these devils back to the Abyss!" The big Ulf warrior held one of the heavy iron shafts in his hands. "We need only a glancing blow to tear each of these unholy abominations to bits." He dragged Kara close and kissed her on the lips. "It is time to test your weapon, and I shall do the same."

"Yes!" Kara screamed, as she raced to arm her ballista. Any fears she harbored seemed to be lost in the excitement.

Wulfric headed across the causeway to his own ballista and settled into the weapon's chair. "Take a few shots. Test your range."

Kara yelled back. "See that snow-covered stone along the horse trail?"

The shadows made everything look like a snow-covered stone. "No," answered Wulfric.

"About two hundred yards north and east, shaped like Lord Dunford's head."

Wulfric saw the curious, block-shaped boulder. "Aye."

"First one to hit the rock wins!"

Kara was quick to her trigger and launched her shot. Wulfric watched helplessly as her projectile arced out over the plains. It landed a dozen yards short and twenty paces to the left. Kara cursed loudly.

"Aha! Now it's my turn!" Wulfric was not sure what it was he would win, but he did not want to lose. He loaded his own shot, locked the bolt, swiveled the ballista to what he hoped was the correct angle, and spun the wheel to build up tension. When he unleashed his bolt, it landed a hundred paces beyond the stone—twice as far off as Kara's.

"Ha!" teased Kara with glee. "I go again!"

On her very next attempt, she hit the stone, and sparks flew into the air. She stood up from her chair and did an exaggerated bow. "Acknowledge the superior markswoman!"

Wulfric cursed and refused.

"Do not be disappointed," she said. "I had the advantage. Shooting the ballista isn't that much different from shooting a bow. You just need more practice."

A disruption in town stayed Wulfric's tongue. The fire gongs, placed strategically atop various buildings, began to clang. From his vantage point atop the gatehouse, Wulfric could see knights pouring out of the keep and flooding into the streets. It appeared that Dunford had finally decided the threat was real.

An unscalable rocky shoreline protected Arkos along the south and west, while the northern and eastern frontiers were protected by forty-foot-high walls. Wulfric believed the town was secure from a conventional assault of a band of raging Berserkers, but this was not the army they were about to face.

One contingent of knights moved to the harbor to protect the shoreline, while the rest made their way to the guard towers, which stood at regular intervals along the wall. Gavin marched a company of men to the north gate: his three-man crew along with an additional twenty foot soldiers.

When the men reached the gate, Gavin began to deploy his forces. Knights armed with longbows and swords were ordered up to the parapets atop the walls. Knights with shields and swords were ordered to guard the portcullis from the ground. As a final measure, Gavin ordered the large wooden door, which was the gate's second line of defense after the portcullis, closed and barred. If anyone now wanted to leave the north gate, they would have to use the hidden tunnel in the basement.

Kara looked at the knights with their longbows. "I bet you and I kill more than all of them combined."

"That we shall," agreed Wulfric. "Now, get back to your weapon, soldier!"

"Aye, sir," Kara said with a deep voice punctuated by a crisp salute.

Chapter 76
The First Wave

The black winter night arrived with howling flurries. Wulfric glanced to his left at Kara, who was busy making last-minute adjustments to her ballista. The young Ulf checked his own weapon as a thousand thoughts went through his head: *Where is the main Ragnar force? How far away is the Necromancer and his Golem? Does Telvar now control the mage tower? Where is Tryam?*

The wind changed direction, and with it came the smell of rotting flesh. All along the wall, the uneasy Engothian knights began to point toward the darkness, and cries of alarm made their way up the chain of command. The enemy had arrived.

Wulfric looked to the north and tracked the undeads' progress through the ballista's crosshairs. The horde surged like a mindless mob fueled by an uncontrollable rage. Some awkwardly held weapons; most simply gnashed their teeth and groped with rotting limbs. Relentlessly, they marched, the air now filled with their hellish screams.

Wulfric was not surprised that Lord Dunford did not send out men into the plains to slow the mob's progress. The risk of knights being turned into the undead was too great. This meant, however, that the enemy would get to the walls in mere minutes.

Details were hard to make out from this distance, but based on the different clothes, weapons, and sigils Wulfric counted, the undead seemed to comprise about a dozen different conquered Berserker clans, and they included Ragnar. A glance back to Arkos and the ruined ward tower filled Wulfric with regret. Brother Kayen had said that the light of Aten generated from its blue crystal would have protected the town from this unholy mob.

The time for regrets was over, however; the horde was now in range. All Wulfric could do was fight until he could do so no longer. "Get ready, Kara! Here they come!"

Kara's bright smile filled him with more courage than any inspirational speech ever could. She wasted no time in unleashing a bolt. Wulfric watched the thick-headed missile arc outward, then descend into the horde. He did not see the missile connect but was encouraged with the eruption of severed limbs that resulted.

"Did you see that? They disintegrated!" yelled Kara in pure joy. "Three kills to none. You'd better hurry if you want to catch up."

Wulfric adjusted the angle, direction, and tension on the string of his weapon, then unleashed his bolt at the leading edge of the horde. The bolt shot up at a slight angle, then arced down just above the first wave of undead. Much to his dismay, he removed only the arm of one monster. "Bah!" he groaned over to Kara. "That would have killed a mortal man."

"I've already sent eight to hell!" he heard Kara say in reaction to her second shot.

The horde came closer. Wulfric's next shots came in rapid succession. The two kept up their assault, but the mass of screaming undead kept coming. The Engothian bowmen were useless, the undead unfazed by their missile shots. As far as Wulfric could tell, the knights had no other effective weapon in play to keep the enemy at bay.

"I have over thirty now!" Kara shouted.

"I must have over forty." Wulfric argued.

"You could never count," teased Kara. "Ha! I just got two more!" She was a blur of activity.

It did not take long for the undead to reach the walls and make the angle too severe for the ballista to be useful. Wulfric stepped off the weapon and took the causeway to Kara's position. When he hugged her, she was strapping on her quiver and preparing her bow. She smiled as if discussing a game of bones. "It looks like I win."

"I can even the score. I just have to jump down into them." Wulfric brandished his coronium blade, ran to the rampart, and put his leg atop the crenellation. Kara rushed over and pulled him back.

"I am not losing you so soon before our wedding!" she scolded.

The brawny Ulf pulled Kara to his side, and together they looked down at the raging mass of mindless terror forty feet below. The screaming undead were wholly unorganized. None of the undead appeared to have the wherewithal to scale the walls. Those that attempted to reach through the portcullis had their limbs quickly severed by Gavin's men. Kara targeted individual undead, but her arrows had only a limited effect. Wulfric wished they had burning oil to pour or boulders to throw.

"No! It can't be! That's not possible!"

The intensity of Kara's exclamation caused Wulfric to glance about with dread. He looked out into the mass of the undead and spotted what had caused her so much anguish. The undead were now organizing around a single being in mismatched armor, wielding a hammer the size of a tree trunk. It was Abbaster, the brute who had kidnapped Kara and whom Wulfric had killed once before.

"Kara, he commands them!" Wulfric gasped in horror. "See how they swarm to him as though he were their pack leader. By some black magic, he has returned to this realm and regained his head and the cruel intellect within. We have to get reinforcements!"

"No!" shouted Kara. "You killed him last time; it's my turn now." She rushed to mount her ballista and aimed it toward the undead commander, who was still in range of the ancient weapon. When the bolt was launched, Wulfric followed its trajectory. Her aim was true; however, the monster used its massive war hammer to turn it away. Abbaster, unharmed, moved inexorably forward.

In frustration, Kara cursed mightily. "Someone send him back to hell permanently!" she demanded.

That is exactly what Wulfric intended to do.

Chapter 77

The Return of Abbaster

The mass of undead now led a coordinated attack against the portcullis, their rotting flesh testing the steel of the bars. Along the wall, in a bizarre parody of circus acrobats, the undead climbed atop one another to make for the ramparts. To the east, Wulfric heard his brethren shouting battle cries in the snowy night. The battle for Arkos had begun in earnest.

"Can they reach us?" Concern mixed with revulsion in Kara's query.

The speed with which the horde progressed made it clear to Wulfric that they could, and for the first time, he felt concern for Kara and his own well-being. The few Engothian knights stationed atop the gatehouses retreated, to stand with those guarding the portcullis, leaving Kara and him as the lone defenders on the roof. "Draw your short sword. Prepare for close combat. We shall make our stand here."

Kara slung her bow over her shoulder and drew a thick gladius, which had been strapped to her slender thigh. She smiled brightly. "I am ready."

Wulfric believed her.

The rotting Abbaster commanded the undead with unspoken words as the war hammer it wielded glowed like a tombstone shining in moonlight. Corpses bashed boulders into the base of both gatehouses, causing sections of their walls to crumble under the relentless pounding. The power of dozens of undead limbs pulled on the buckling portcullis. Most surprising was the ease with which the undead scaled the walls. Mortal invaders feared missiles and the reach of sword and poleaxe, but the undead feared nothing. *What is there to fear when one has already died?*

Kara pointed back to Wulfric's abandoned ballista. The first of the undead had climbed to the top of the forty-foot fortification and now swarmed over the weapon, seeking flesh to rip. Once the undead detected the presence of likely victims, they began to stagger their way across the causeway.

"Here they come," said Wulfric.

The two Ulfs briefly held hands, then kissed before taking fighting stances at the mouth of the causeway. Wulfric's blade went uncontested as it slashed at the first group of grasping arms and snapping teeth. Wulfric found it disconcerting to fight an opponent that made no attempt to parry. The undead that did have weapons, such as hammers, axes, and broadswords, used them only for bashing.

Kara protected Wulfric's back, though no undead had yet tried to scale the walls of the western gatehouse. As more undead scaled the eastern gatehouse, however, the two were forced by the sheer number of the ghouls to retreat. Eventually, they were pushed past Wulfric's ballista and close to their only means of escape, the stairs down to the third floor.

"This is madness," shrieked Kara as she plunged her gladius into the brains and bellies of the undead. "There are too many! I have lost count of how many I have turned back to the grave. I don't even have the energy to gloat."

Bathed in gore, Wulfric began to slip on the ground slicked by the undead's innards. He pressed his back against Kara's and shouted into her ear: "We have done all we can up here. Follow me."

He grabbed her hand, and the two dashed for the stairs. On the floor below, the undead had bashed through a portion of the wall and were now scrambling into the gatehouse. Wulfric slashed the legs off one and then the head from another as they continued their descent. On the next floor, an undead Berserker female had impaled itself on the winch that operated the portcullis. Kara severed both of its arms and then its rotting head. "They are everywhere!" she cried.

"Hurry!" implored Wulfric. He grabbed Kara and forced her to cease combat.

The bottom floor had only one exit, an archway leading to the area behind the portcullis. Wulfric rushed to the doorway, with Kara by his side. Outside, the undead were climbing over the gate, as Gavin and the other knights were pressed together, shields locked, attacking as one at any grasping limb or biting head within range. Several knights had had been torn away from the formation, however, and their dismembered limbs now passed among the undead Berserkers like macabre trophies.

With a sound like a thunderclap, a spidering crack spread across the side of the gatehouse above them—undoubtedly, the result of the undeads' boulder assault on its foundation. "This building is about to collapse!" Wulfric shouted. "We can't stay here. We add our swords to those of the Engothians." He kissed Kara, and together, weapons ready, they made their way out from the gatehouse and into the furious melee.

The combat area was only twenty paces wide by fifty paces long, inside of which a dozen knights and an uncountable number of undead now fought. Kara spotted Gavin in the thick of the fighting and shouted in Wulfric's ear: "We must come to Gavin's aid!"

The pair furiously stabbed and slashed their way to the gate captain's side and formed a fighting triangle as teeth, hands, war hammers, swords, and axes attacked from all directions. Dying torches were the only light, and the sound of the baying undead was deafening. Wulfric wondered ever so briefly if they were already in hell.

"They have scaled the wall and are tearing down the gatehouses!" Wulfric had to shout directly into Gavin's ear, to be heard over the bloodcurdling screams.

Between sword strokes, Gavin shouted a response: "We have to push them back. We can't allow them into the city. Help us get them off the gate."

The horde of undead continued to push against the portcullis, which was now noticeably bowed inward. In Wulfric's opinion, it would be impossible to push them back. "We make a final stand. That is all we can hope."

Kara was by his side, her gladius coated in black blood. Wulfric wished he had a shield, to keep the monsters at arm's length, or a shorter sword, with which he could stab more easily. In any event, he was determined to chop limbs until he was dragged from this world and into the next.

Over the sounds of battle came a great rumbling, and all the mortal combatants looked to the western gatehouse. Wulfric reached for Kara, who had her back to the collapsing structure, but an undead Berserker jumped in the way. Before he could chop the undead thing's head off, the building collapsed with the sound of an avalanche.

Dust billowed into the air, bathing the combatants in powdery debris. The pulverized stone blinded Wulfric's eyes and choked his lungs, and the suddenness of the collapse left him momentarily dazed. When he was able to see again, the undead attacker lay at his feet, a chunk of wall having crushed its skull. Of Kara, however, there was no sign. Wulfric shouted her name over the chaos but received no answer.

Gavin stood by the big Ulf's side and shouted into his ear: "Follow me! I saw her fall."

The young knight used his shield as a plow and pushed the undead away from the rubble of the crumbled gatehouse. As Wulfric beheaded those undead in pursuit, he roared like an animal of the plains. Gavin pointed to a form lying on the ground. "Here she is!"

At their feet was a dusty lump; only a hint of golden hair offered a clue as to what lay beneath.

"I shall protect you," vowed Gavin, as he fought off the grasping attackers in the near-total darkness.

Wulfric sheathed his sword and bent down to remove the rubble from Kara's prone form. Only her right leg was trapped. He picked up the large square stone with both hands and hoisted it above his head. With his anger as fuel, he hurled the rock forward, smashing into the middle of the advancing undead that was flowing uncontested over the gate. Wulfric bent down and dragged Kara to her feet. Covered in dust, she looked like a ghost. Once she coughed, her skin began to regain its color. "Are you okay?" he asked.

"I'm all right," she said meekly. "It will take more than a building to stop me from getting revenge." Her crooked smile proved to Wulfric that he was still on Medias and not yet in hell.

Wulfric placed her fallen gladius back into her hand. "Can you fight?"

Kara grabbed the blade and made two quick jabs into the air. "Yes. And with you by my side, we shall win this night."

"Aye! We shall!"

Holding hands for only a few heartbeats, the two Ulf youths stabbed and slashed their way back into combat and by Gavin's side. However, the closer the three came to the portcullis, the more resistance they faced. "This is futile," Gavin said glumly.

A scream of tearing metal assaulted Wulfric's ears, and he looked to see what had happened. A cry of alarm came from the mouths of several of the knights near the front lines. The portcullis was no more.

"Brace yourselves," warned Wulfric, who expected the undead to pour into the gap like water down a drain. Instead, in a macabre version of the military precision of a veteran infantry unit, the undead parted to either side of the missing gate.

In response, Engothian knights rushed to fill the breach and hold the line where the gate had once stood. The brave soldiers began to tremble, however, as something emerged from the darkness.

"An old foe now enters the fray," concluded Wulfric with dread. "Abbaster comes!"

That which had been Abbaster stepped into the line of knights and used its monstrous war hammer like a scythe. Wherever the great hammer struck, armor crumpled and men died. The undead brute made a direct path toward Wulfric.

In anticipation of the combat, a smile cracked Wulfric's face. "Keep back, Kara, and protect my flank. I must confront this devil myself."

Wulfric spoke in a tone that conveyed his seriousness, and Kara responded with a quick peck to his cheek. "No one else here could defeat such a monster. No one else here has killed a Hound of Fenrir!"

The warmth of Kara's kiss lingered even as the aura of the undead thing invaded his senses. Wulfric found it difficult to assess his adversary, since only blank red eyes peered out from its visored helm. One thing was sure: It moved faster and appeared stronger than Abbaster had in life. Perhaps more robust magic had been used to restore the brute, or maybe it was the strange lion-headed hammer it wielded. Whatever the reason, Abbaster appeared to have only gained from death.

With the remaining knights scrambling out of its way, Abbaster had a clear shot at Wulfric. The Ulf warrior, accepting his fate, taunted the creature to gauge its response. "Come at me, servant of evil!"

The undead brute did not respond with words. With a quickness far exceeding nature, Abbaster swung its hammer at Wulfric's head in a sweeping arc. Wulfric ducked under the blow, saving himself by inches from being brained.

"You foul beast! You twisted monstrosity!" Wulfric taunted, then slashed with his coronium blade at its monstrous thighs. The strike was true, and the flesh parted, but no blood spilled.

Abbaster countered with another swing. This time Wulfric caught the edge of the hammer with his hip and was spun around. Once he stopped spinning, he used his momentum to slash Abbaster in its exposed belly beneath the stretched, patchwork armor. A dark black ooze leaked from the

THE TOMB OF THERAGAARD

wound, but if the slash troubled the undead Abbaster, there was no way to tell.

Again, Abbaster countered and hammered the Ulf in his left shoulder, numbing that side of his body and causing him to stagger backward a few steps.

As he tried to regain his balance, Wulfric heard dark speech come from Abbaster's purple lips, and seemingly in response to these commands, the mob of undead began to attack the remaining knights. Then, with an overhand swing of its mighty hammer, Abbaster took aim at Wulfric's head. Wulfric stepped forward; the blow missed his head and instead impacted the back of his legs. He was sure something within them snapped. Wulfric stumbled, and his head collided with Abbaster's bloated belly before he bounced off and landed flat on his back, his sword slipping free from his hands.

When Wulfric was able to regain his bearings, he blinked up in surprise. Above his head was the causeway that connected the two gatehouses. It somehow remained attached to the eastern gatehouse, but more incredibly, atop it was that the black-robed wizard Telvar. The mage was speaking; Wulfric could hear the wizard's words clearly, words that were directed at him.

"Why is that thick-headed fool resting flat on his back? Get up, you daft barbarian!"

"Resting"? That son-of-a-merchant trickster! Wulfric's anger at the wizard helped clear his senses. He rushed to his feet to resume his battle with the undead Abbaster. However, when he went to retrieve his sword, he was shocked to see the blade turning a bright crimson. *What in the Abyss?*

When flames erupted around the edge of his sword, he knew it was the work of magic. Wulfric looked up and saw Telvar deep in concentration, with his staff aglow. The Ulf's face split in a broad grin. *Fire kills the undead!*

In Wulfric's absence, Gavin and the few remaining knights had rushed to stand against Abbaster. They were not faring well against the undead commander's hammer, however. Wulfric stepped back into the fight, glad to see that Kara was also hard at work keeping the undead at bay.

"Let's see how you like this, fiend!" Wulfric challenged anew.

Fire reflected in Abbaster's red, milky eyes, and the undead brute stumbled backward.

Encouraged by the first sign of the undead commander's weakness, Wulfric struck at Abbaster's massive torso.

The rotting brute attempted to block the weapon, but the hammer was too awkward to parry; Wulfric scored a hit that seared its swollen belly. With renewed purpose, Wulfric slashed again and again, seeking every possible bit of exposed flesh. And wherever his fiery blade touched, flames erupted as if the ghastly corpse were kindling.

Abbaster staggered backward even farther, its flesh cooking inside the patchwork armor. With fumbling hands, the undead commander attempted to remove the dented metal but was too clumsy to do so. Wulfric stepped away from the inferno to stand beside Kara.

"It burns like a torch!" Kara said, her eyes wide, her jaw hanging open. "Look. All the knights' blades glow with the same fire as your blade! But how?"

"You can thank the wizard." Wulfric pointed to the walkway overhead, but the mage had vanished. "Alas, he is gone."

"Sure," sulked Kara. "Figures he would leave before he made my gladius aflame."

"Don't worry," assured Wulfric. "I shall protect you."

The smell of the burning Abbaster caused Wulfric's eyes to tear. By the time the brute collapsed, the inferno of undead flesh was almost as bright as a noonday sun. When nothing remained of the brute save charred bones, Wulfric spat, "Back, again, to the Abyss!"

Without their commander, the undead army reverted to its mindless form. The knights, with their flaming swords, rushed to fill the breach again.

Wulfric, his adrenaline fading, staggered back into Kara's arms, the pain in his legs, hip, and shoulder causing him to feel lightheaded. Kara guided the dazed Ulf back to the rubble of the western gatehouse. "I am the one to protect you, it seems," she chided, while she looked for any undead that attempted to leap over the mountain of rubble. He felt her warm lips on his forehead. "We may still die, but at least we outlived that monster."

"Aye," agreed Wulfric.

Before their eyes, the knights used their fiery blades to great effect. Gavin organized his men to act as a unit, and they began systematically torching the undead invaders. They pushed forward, reclaiming the area where the portcullis had once stood. The undead blindly surged toward the gap and into the knights' awaiting blades.

Dozens, then hundreds, fell to the magic swords. Feeling better, Wulfric jumped up on the rubble of the ruined gatehouse to get a better perspective on what was happening elsewhere. Flames from the east gate showed that Telvar had shared his magic with the Berserker allies there. Wulfric could hear his fellow Berserkers' cries of victory.

Kara joined him atop the jumbled stones. Her sparkling eyes looked over the silent plains. "They are all gone. Can you believe it? We won!"

Wulfric looked around at the devastation already inflicted to the town's defenses: the demolished gatehouse, the ruined portcullis, and the bodies of so many defenders. He studied his blade, watching the flames die as the magic ran its course, and pondered on what was to still to come. "We won this first round, but we shall need another miracle to stop the Necromancer and the main force of the Ragnar."

"Not a miracle," corrected Kara. "We need a hero."

Chapter 78

Lord Dunford's Arrival

Grim precautions had to be made to ensure that those who had died in battle remained dead. A contingent of men created a funeral pyre for the fallen knights, and with military precision, the bodies of the dead were stacked upon it and then set afire. Unceremoniously, the bodies of the undead, including Abbaster's ashes, were entombed in a frozen mass grave. The great war hammer was taken to the keep for safekeeping.

"We lost fourteen," reported Gavin gloomily.

The young knight now stood beside Wulfric and Kara atop the crumbled gatehouse. The falling snow began to cover the gore upon the ground, temporarily masking the horror that had just occurred.

"They died on their feet, giving their life for their fellow man," said Wulfric. "Can any of us ask for more when it is our time to pass from this world?"

Gavin nodded his head, but his eyes revealed sorrow inside. Kara started to console the young knight, but there was nothing comforting to say about what had occurred. Instead, as they watched the rising flames from the funeral pyre, the trio stood in silence. Wulfric checked his leg for damage and was surprised to find that he had suffered only a deep bruise. Kara and Gavin reported nothing but scratches and exhaustion.

The solitude following the battle's end did not last long. Echoing from the plains came a long, low note. Wulfric recognized the sound as coming from a hollowed-out mammoth tusk, a method of communication used by several Berserker clans. The disquieting sound was followed by other horns in response. First one, then another, then dozens.

Gavin looked to Wulfric for an answer.

THE TOMB OF THERAGAARD

Wulfric gripped his now-cool blade and pointed north. "The braying of horns means that the main army of the Ragnar approaches."

The rhythmic clopping of hooves on stone turned their attention back to Arkos. A knight alerted Gavin that Lord Dunford was approaching. From inside Arkos, the massive door that stood between the gatehouses was unbarred and opened. Dunford and his mounted officers stormed with great alacrity into the ruined north gate.

Wearing his gold armor with a blue cloak, the commander appeared to Wulfric like a hero out of one of Tryam's books. Even his long blond hair and thick beard gave Dunford a certain larger-than-life bearing. "Who's in charge here?" he demanded. He was off his horse and on his feet surprisingly quickly, considering his age and bulk.

Stepping down from the rubble of the gatehouse, Gavin saluted his commander. "Gavin, sir. These are my men."

The commander's eyes surveyed the damaged portcullis and the ruined gatehouse. "You did well, all things considered. How did you defeat them so quickly?"

Wulfric answered for Gavin. "It was a combined effort of both Berserker and Engothian. But we would have lost were it not for the new tower mage's intervention. Telvar enchanted our weapons to make them flame like torches. Once this fire touched an undead, the creature's flesh burned as if made from whale blubber."

The commander's eyes turned to Wulfric. "Where has the wizard gone?"

"Back to his tower to get more magic, I imagine."

Wulfric stepped from the rubble down to Gavin's side. He did not expect the commander to thank him personally for helping to defend the town, but at the very least, he hoped Dunford would show some appreciation for the help the Berserker refugees had given. None appeared to be forthcoming, however.

Kara was not as forgiving of Dunford's disrespect, and she yelled from her perch on the rubble: "If it wasn't for *us*, this town would be swarming with the undead! You should be ashamed of how you treated Wulfric and the warnings we gave you. Look to your precious mines; they have already begun to burn!"

Kara pointed toward the foot of the Coronas. In the distance, where the small fort and mining operations were located, giant orange flames erupted. Wulfric had an awful idea about what could cause such swift and cataclysmic damage.

The commander's face did not change, even when the flames reflected in his eyes. "I cannot argue with you, girl," he said. "This battle is won, but it appears the fight has just begun." Dunford stepped past where the portcullis had once stood and looked out into the impenetrable darkness of the plains. "It seems as though what was warned to me has proven true. These walls will not hold. We need to come up with a plan to give us time to evacuate the townsfolk back to the keep."

Dunford turned to huddle with his officers, but Wulfric already had plans in mind. "Commander," he interrupted, "I have an idea."

The commander turned his way and cocked an eyebrow.

Chapter 79
Preparations and the Wedding

The madness of Myramar, the ward tower's destruction, the assault by the undead army, and now the obliteration of the Arkos mines shocked the entire populace. Wulfric saw it in the eyes of everyone he passed. It was as if the citizens of Arkos all wore the same mask, one painted with fear and uncertainty.

The town had no mayor, no council, no one to lead them in this crisis other than Lord Dunford. Wulfric was sure that if things had not been so grim, the commander would not have listened to his plan, but Dunford now had no other option than to do what the young Ulf warrior proposed: Fight the enemy as the Berserkers did, as a united community.

The people of Arkos left their homes, ventured into the raging flurries, and huddled together in the town square to hear Dunford's impassioned plea for help. Wulfric joined them and listened with hopeful ears.

"People of Arkos, grave times are upon us. Long have we lived in peace, but that time has ended. Our fortifications, manned by our brave knights, have long kept the barbarians at arm's reach, and the ward tower's light, made bright by the devout monks of Saint Paxia, have long protected us from the Abyssal creatures that roam these lands at night. Now, however, we cannot depend on either, for the walls may not hold against the force that descends upon us, and the ward tower, along with the brave men inside it, has been destroyed." His eyes scanned the crowd of frightened men, women, and children. "An undead force has already attacked and has been repelled. The undead were turned aside by our brave knights, who were aided by Berserkers who refused to yield to the bloodthirsty ways of their brethren, the Ragnar. Soon, though, a fresh army—that of Berserkers—led by a great mage and—if rumor be true—a magical construct, will soon be here. I call upon all of you to take part in the defense of this town. Those strong enough to bear arms come to the armory, and you will be equipped. No matter our fate, it is better to die with a weapon in hand than to cower in fear. For the very young and the very old, and for the women of our community, hurry to the keep and its stouter walls. For those of you with healing skills, make yourself known, for such will be needed."

The crowd was momentarily shocked into silence. The peace they had known all their lives was no more. Then, almost as one, the townsfolk cheered Dunford's name.

Wulfric was encouraged and a bit surprised by the Engothians' determination and their willingness to fight for their homes and for one another—a trait he had not expected to find among civilized people, who tended to look only after their own self-interests. When Wulfric later returned to the wall, he was feeling optimistic, despite their odds. *Perhaps we are not so different.*

In the plains before the north gate, pitch was already being poured into troughs, and a makeshift barricade of steel, stones, and wood was added to slow down the Ragnar's' mortal army. Engothian engineers dragged the portcullis back into place and hammered it into the ground. It would never function again as a movable barrier, but it would be a long time before Arkos was likely to welcome visitors coming from the north.

The rubble of the collapsed gatehouse was stacked, in order to make climbing it a death trap. Kara tried her best to salvage her ballista, but it had been too severely damaged when the gatehouse collapsed beneath it. All she had to show for her efforts were multiple cuts on her hands and a sullen expression. Wulfric tried to console her, but she was having none of it. "I'm fine," she snapped as she gazed forlornly at the smashed wood and dented bronze.

"I think I know something that can make you feel better," said Wulfric.

"I doubt it."

"Before you say that, look behind you."

Kara loved surprises, and despite her best efforts, her face broke into a smile. When she turned her head, all Wulfric saw was a blur of golden hair. She gasped and shouted, "Brother Kayen!" before embracing the haggard-looking missionary.

Brother Kayen deftly escaped Kara's bear hug. "I wish I could cure your ballista, dear Kara, but I am afraid my healing skills are limited to people."

"That's all right," Kara said. "I still have my bow. That's all that matters." She cocked her head to one side. "Where were you? Did you see Tryam? Please don't tell me the monks killed him!"

Kayen laughed in shock. "Dear God, no! They didn't kill him! Though I have not spoken to Tryam since we all parted company, I have heard good news from one of my few friends left at the abbey, a fellow monk named Cordon. Tryam has grown into a man. He confronted Father Monbatten and then made an impassioned plea to his brothers to prepare the abbey for a coming battle. Cordon told me that the monks listened, and despite the abbot's opposition, they did what Tyram had asked."

"Hasn't Tryam been gone a very long time?" asked Wulfric. "I do not know how one speaks with the dead, but if we expect help from this spirit, we are almost out of time. The Ragnar army will be upon us within hours."

"Communing with a spirit is no easy task, especially with one who has not been venerated in centuries. The faith required to do so taxes you in every way imaginable. We shall give Tryam as much time as possible."

Kayen gestured with his shepherd's staff at the repairs to the portcullis. "It seems you did well to defend the town from the first wave. How did you defeat the undead creatures? I was deep in prayer and was not even aware the town was under attack."

"My ballista took out dozens, but it wasn't enough," admitted Kara. "It was Telvar who made our victory possible. He enchanted everyone's blade to make it burn with fire, and each ugly monster lit up like a torch when struck! I wish he would have magicked my blade, but he didn't. I missed out on the fun."

Kayen stroked his beard and nodded his head approvingly. "The young mage lives, then. At least we have that to be grateful for on this gloomy night. Perhaps he has something else prepared for the Ragnar army."

The sound of a knight scrambling up the ruins stopped their conversation. "Sorry for interrupting," said Gavin, reflexively saluting Kayen. "But, Brother, we are shutting and barring the door into Arkos. If you are heading back to the abbey, I suggest you do so now."

"I shall be staying," answered Kayen. "I have my staff to defend with, and I have skills to aid the injured."

Gavin saluted the missionary again. "On behalf of the knights of Engoth, I thank you." He then saluted Wulfric and Kara. "You both should get in position. We shall talk again when this battle is over!"

Wulfric grasped the knight's forearm. "That we shall."

"The Ragnar will never get over these walls!" vowed Kara as she patted her bow.

Gavin smiled, then backed away to stand with his men mustered at the portcullis. Wulfric sensed the knights' nervous energy as they placed more torches around the gate.

Brother Kayen looked to Wulfric and Kara with shared concern. "What is your plan?"

"I shall man the ballista atop the eastern gatehouse," said Wulfric.

"And I shall be by his side," added Kara, "using my bow to take down as many of the Ragnar as I have arrows." She reached out her hand. "Brother, join us! You can knock on the heads of any Ragnar who try to scale the wall. The time to avenge the Ulf clan is upon us!"

Kara charged down the piled stones on her way to the eastern gatehouse.

"I think she is actually enjoying this," said Wulfric. "Not to say I shan't when I bleed the first Ragnar that gets into range."

"Revenge will not bring your clan back," reminded Kayen. "We must stop the Ragnar here and prevent what they did to the Ulf from happening to anyone else."

"Agreed," nodded Wulfric.

Kara, the ballista, and all the remaining bolts awaited Wulfric on the roof of the gatehouse. The young Ulf warrior walked to the ramparts and looked out into the impenetrable dark. He could not see the enemy, but he knew they were coming.

"A dark night, yet beauty shines above!" remarked Kara as the flurries had suddenly ceased.

Wulfric turned back to stare at Kara, who was pointing skyward. The warrior strained his already stiff neck and looked up. High above, a blue star was peeking through the black veil of clouds.

Kara moved out onto the causeway for a better view.

"What are you doing?" fretted Wulfric. "That walkway is about ready to collapse!"

THE TOMB OF THERAGAARD

Kara ignored his concerns. "I want to do it here, *now*, under *that* star while we still have time. We even have Brother Kayen here. It's as if this were meant to be." Kara's eyes sparkled like blue diamonds.

"Do what? Take our vows? The army is fast approaching!" protested Wulfric as he climbed up to be with her.

"Are you afraid to do it in front of Gavin's men?" teased Kara.

"Of course not, it's just—"

"I can't think of a better time or place," agreed Kayen, joining them on the causeway. "Two youths making such a sacred bond under the halo of one of Aten's angels above? Perfect!"

The glimmering light from the star caused Kara's hair to sparkle like polished gold. The young Ulf girl spotted Wulfric staring at her and attempted to remove the dust that still clung to her worn leather and bearskin cloths. Wulfric stopped her. "You look like the angel Valnarr herself! You are right. No more delays. Let us begin our lives as a bonded pair this night!"

A wave of euphoria flooded over Wulfric. So joyous, in fact, that he had to share to all within earshot. "Gather around, my brothers-in arms. I am taking Kara, the warrior princess of the Ulf clan, as my bondmate!"

Confused faces peered up at the causeway from the knights below. Wulfric grabbed Kara and kissed her on the lips. Hoots and whistles immediately erupted from the knights defending the portcullis and then spread to those manning the walls. Brother Kayen, also with a smile on his face, commented, "In the face of such grim odds, I am glad that you two can give these brave defenders this moment of hope."

When the cheering died down, a nervous Kara asked, "Now what do we do?" Her face was bright red.

Wulfric shrugged has massive shoulders.

Brother Kayen stepped between them and answered. "Just do as I say."

The missionary maneuvered himself so he could address the couple, while also enabling his voice to carry down to the knights below and to those stationed along the wall. "I spent a decade with the Berserkers, learning their culture and getting to understand their values. Wulfric, I knew your mother and your father. From where their spirits reside, they look down upon you with pride at the warrior you have become. Kara, I know the strength of the spirit that lives inside you. It is a spirit that warms all others. Together, you make each other whole."

Brother Kayen looked upon the knights gathered below and then said, "We are joined here this night to witness the sacred vows of two young people who embark on a life-altering journey that ends only when one of them draws their last breath."

Kayen touched the couple on their shoulders. "Wulfric, Kara, this moment is precious. Hold it with you forever, for there shall be none like it ever again."

Wulfric looked into Kara's eyes, and she looked into his. Behind her eyes, Wulfric saw the familiar mixture of shadow and sunshine—her anger for what had happened in her past, the joy she took in imagining a better future.

"Take each other by the hand," commanded Kayen. "State your name and your intentions. Kara, you may begin."

The young Ulf girl responded in a strong, clear voice. "My name is Kara. I am an orphan from the Graak clan and an adopted member of the Ulf clan. I intend to be your bondmate, Wulfric. Your soulmate. Your defender, mother to your children, and your companion until either I die of old age or my enemies steal the last breath from my body."

Brother Kayen nodded to Wulfric.

Wulfric experienced a flash of doubt that he or anyone might be worthy of Kara, but his fear faded quickly. "My name is Wulfric. Son of Jarl Alric. I have passed my Trial of Blood, and as is my right as a full member of the Ulf clan, I claim you, Kara, as my bondmate. You are my soulmate and will become the mother of my children. You will remain my companion, and I your champion, until I draw my last breath."

From the depths of his pocket, Wulfric produced the whalebone necklace that had been his mother's. Kara gasped at the sight of it, and she squealed with delight when it was once again placed around her neck.

"How did you find it?" The bride kicked Wulfric in the shin. "Why didn't you tell me?"

"I shall tell you later," whispered Wulfric in her ear.

Brother Kayen raised his arms to quiet the pair. "These oaths have been witnessed by me, your brothers-in-arms, and Aten above. All that is left is the kiss that will make this bond permanent."

The knights below banged swords on shields and stamped their feet. More than a few let out calls urging for a passionate embrace. Wulfric did not want to disappoint. *I shall give them a kiss they will not soon forget!*

Wulfric grabbed Kara and pulled her head to his lips. He kissed her with the full weight of his passion. She responded by wrapping her arms around his neck and her legs around his torso.

The knights whistled their approval.

They embraced until the lonely star above once again retreated under the dark folds of the clouds.

"It is done!" exclaimed Kayen.

Wulfric ignored everything around him but Kara. It was only when the fire gongs rang out in Arkos and the knights below raised their voices in alarm that he reluctantly returned to the material world. "It appears as if now were the time we fight," said Wulfric, stepping protectively in front of Kara. "Since I discovered our village destroyed, I have waited for this moment. My father, *our* people, will be avenged. When the learned men write of this day, they will tell of the blood we spilled and the justice we delivered."

Kara raised her gladius and shouted to the sky. "Yes, *together* we fight, and *together* we shall prevail!"

The Engothian knights responded with raised weapons and battle cries whose volume challenged that of the Ragnar.

Chapter 80
Fight, Part, and Retreat

Kayen drew forth the cross of Aten from around his neck and blessed the newlyweds one final time.

"Will you stay with us?" asked Wulfric.

"Yes, please stay," pleaded Kara.

"I wish I could, but I have been a physician in many conflicts and would best be of use stationed closer to the gate, so that I can aid the wounded." Kayen returned the cross of Aten to beneath his robes and grabbed his staff. "May Aten be with you both! We shall see each other again—of that, I am sure."

"Thank you," said Kara, struggling to hold back tears, "for everything."

"It was my pleasure." Kayen bowed his head, his face calm and confident; then he wordlessly made his way across the causeway and down the steps of the gatehouse.

Along the wall, knights filed into position, as lieutenants barked orders to ensure the men were equipped and combat-ready. On the enemy side, hundreds of small fires now dotted the dark plains.

"They ready their flame arrows," warned Wulfric, as he raced to mount his ballista. "Get your bow ready, and make sure you are prepared to take cover!"

Once seated, Wulfric looked out through the weapon's crosshairs at the assembled black mass of men. By their numbers, it looked as if the Ragnar jarl had accomplished what no Berserker jarl had ever before done: He had united the disparate clans of the Berserker tribe for a common purpose. If there was any consolation to be had, it was that neither the Golem nor the Necromancer were anywhere to be seen.

THE TOMB OF THERAGAARD

No parleys between generals were likely to occur, but before firing his ballista, Wulfric waited to hear the command that would come down from the knights' hierarchy—just in case, by some miracle, the Ragnar tried to negotiate. When the command to fire did come, hundreds of arrows arced into the air and rained down in unison into the massive army of the Ragnar. The greenish black armor turned away most of the shots. Wulfric added his own ballista bolt soon after, while Kara took careful aim with her longbow. The effort felt futile against such a large force, though Wulfric took some satisfaction when his bolt sailed into a mass of men, killing several.

The Ragnar returned fire, but their target was not the men on the wall but the town itself. Flaming arrows sped overhead and landed at random locations throughout Arkos. In addition, trebuchets from the rear of the Ragnar army lobbed giant barrels of tar that exploded on impact. Wulfric had never known Berserkers to employ siege weapons before.

Men in Arkos had been assigned fire patrol, but flames had already begun to wreak havoc. Wulfric had little hope that the fires could be extinguished quickly, if at all.

After its bombardment, the Ragnar army split into two. Like the heads of a hydra, the two appendages moved as separate entities from the main body; one snaked to the north gate, the other veered toward the east gate. Wulfric unleashed the full fury of his ballista, and wherever the bolts struck, blood and limbs erupted. The Ragnar army, fueled by bloodlust, marched on.

A great rush of air swooshed over Wulfric's head, causing him to duck reflexively. Kara cursed, then squealed in delight. "Did you see that?" she shouted, turning to look inside Arkos.

Wulfric stopped firing his ballista long enough to risk a glance. From the Engothian keep, catapults were launching large projectiles at the Ragnar. The impact of the large round boulders caused the ground to shudder and the enemy to die. Wulfric had no time to appreciate the spectacle but was heartened to learn the knights had fire power of their own. "Kara, keep your head to the front and keep shooting. Don't let up!"

"Yes, sir!"

From the cover of the battlements, Kara took aim with her bow and unleashed her own brand of fury, striking where armor did not cover flesh. For every kill, she named a member of the Ulf clan. Her stack of arrows dwindled quickly.

Despite the disruption from the catapults, the enemy armies continued toward their respective gates without interruption. Engothian officers ordered archers to ignite the pitch, and when their arrows struck, the oil-soaked barriers flamed high and hot. Dozens of Ragnar were caught in the resulting firestorm, but the Berserkers behind them soldiered on, unconcerned, stepping over their charred brethren to advance toward the walls. Wulfric speculated that the Ragnar and their allies must have imbibed heavily from the warroot elixir to increase their courage.

Horns, this time from the Engothian side, rang out from the vicinity of the east gate. Wulfric chanced another break to look in that direction. Thundering down the narrow Arkos street came two dozen cavalrymen. He yelled over to Kara in disbelief: "Lord Dunford leads a cavalry charge!"

Kara paused her assault to view the spectacle. "So few against so many?"

The cavalry bolted out the east gate, galloped through a path between the flaming barricades, and crashed fearlessly into one of the two surging Ragnar armies. Wulfric admired the brave men and the equally brave warhorses as he witnessed the knights, armed with lances, cut a bloody swath through the Ragnar vanguard. The cavalry did not stop but stormed through the head of the army and then cleared out again. The discipline in the Ragnar ranks broke, and the men scattered. One head of the hydra was severed. The cavalry returned through the east gate without suffering a single loss.

"I wish they could help us," cried Kara as she returned to her bow. "The Ragnar still head our way."

In front of the north gate, the barricade and pitch-covered obstructions had been eliminated, and the invading army had surged straight up to the bent portcullis. The head of the army spread out from the gate to crash against the entire length of the north wall. Grappling hooks and ladders were brought forth from the rear.

Civilians tasked to pour boiling tar onto the attackers did so, eliminating most of the first wave of Ragnar climbers. However, for every man killed, ten were ready to take their place. One by one, Ragnar men landed atop the walls, and the Engothian sentries were quickly outnumbered.

Near their location, Berserker allies of the Ragnar tied ropes and chains onto the portcullis. Wulfric aimed his ballista as low as he could and shot his last dozen bolts. As effective as the bolts were, they would not save the gate. In a matter of minutes, the iron portcullis was wrenched from its moorings.

THE TOMB OF THERAGAARD

Wulfric jumped down from the weapon, drew his sword, and rushed to Kara. "I have to help the knights. You are a capable swordswoman, but your skill is with the bow. You must retreat to the keep and protect the civilians."

"No!" Kara cried as she stamped her feet like a petulant child. "I stay by your side. Always!"

Wulfric sheathed his sword and grabbed Kara by her shoulders. "I shall join you shortly, but I cannot abandon the knights. They need me, and I need to face the Ragnar with my steel. I shall make a stand here. Then I shall join you at the keep. After that, I vow never to leave your side again!"

Kara met his eyes and examined his grim face. She looked to the town, where fire was spreading, and Wulfric's eyes followed. The keep stood out like a beacon of hope to the frightened Arkosians now making their way to the safety of its thick stone walls. They locked eyes again, Kara's face stoic. "I shall follow those fleeing to the keep. Avenge our clan, but retreat when you can no longer hold the wall. Don't make me come looking for you!"

"Go quickly," ordered Wulfric. "While you still can."

After a brief hug, Kara filled her quiver with the last of her red arrows and started down the stairs of the gatehouse. Wulfric brandished his sword and followed her with swift strides. His heart pounded with each step closer to the combat. At the ground floor, he hugged and kissed Kara for too brief a moment.

"Take care of yourself," Kara said, her eyes misting.

"I shall."

Kara wiped her eyes, then gave him an Engothian-style salute: raising her hand to her forehead as if lifting a visor. Swiftly, she stepped down into the basement, where a concealed tunnel led back into Arkos. The last thing he saw of her was her golden hair whipped into a frenzy by her quick movements.

She has to be safe. She will be safe.

Alone, Wulfric heard his breathing echoing in the dim chamber. He closed the basement hatch and then proceeded to the only other exit in the room: the portal that would take him to the heart of combat. The sounds and smells of war seeped under the door. In one motion, Wulfric lifted the bar, pulled open the door, and stepped into the melee.

In the confined space stood the last stalwarts of the Engothian gate watch. If the invading Berserkers had been more organized, they would have overrun the Engothians with ease, but the brave knights, led by Gavin, had the edge in military discipline and the added fuel of desperation. "Hold the line! Hold the line!" were the orders from Gavin in the center of the combat.

Atop the rubble of the western gatehouse, Kayen was tending to the wounded. Knights, standing as guardians, fought off any Berserkers who attempted to get near, as Kayen applied healing touches to the grievously injured, who were then lowered by rope ladders into Arkos.

The smell of blood reached Wulfric's nostrils, causing his own blood to boil. The big Ulf lowered the cowl of the Fenrir pelt and pushed his way to Gavin's side. Despite the chaos, the young knight nodded his appreciation for another sword added to the cause.

Wulfric aimed recklessly at the first Berserker in range. Already engaged with a knight to Wulfric's right, the Ragnar man was unprepared for Wulfric's thrust to his exposed neck. The man staggered backward with a surprised look on his giant oval eyes as blood pumped out of his body like water from a fountain. The Ragnar seemed to have a limitless supply of replacements, however, and a red-bearded, battle-axe-wielding, wild-eyed man stepped up to take his place.

"Curse you dogs!" Wulfric raged as he hacked and slashed at every opponent within reach. "Your traitorous jarl leads you to ruin!" With every oath, his blows grew stronger, though the words were lost in the screams of the dying.

Wave after wave of Ragnar was turned back, and the confined space became littered with the dead. The melee evolved into a pushing match. In response, Gavin ordered the knights to form a shield wall to protect their dwindling numbers. Wulfric felt himself being forced backward, as he slipped on bloody ground. The fear of being trapped and crushed between the gatehouses was now very real.

"I think now is the time to make our departure!" Gavin shouted in Wulfric's ear. "We have done all we can."

It took the young Ulf a moment to absorb Gavin's words through the rush of blood in his ears. When he saw how few knights remained, he reluctantly agreed. "You give the orders, and we shall follow."

Gavin spread the plan throughout his men. His first command was for Kayen and the injured to enter the gatehouse. When they had safely passed through to the basement exit, he gave the rest of his men the command to retreat.

THE TOMB OF THERAGAARD

Wulfric turned and ran, following on the heels of the unknown knight whom he had fought beside for the past hour. When he passed through the doorway, he looked back: The Berserker horde, surprised by the maneuver, hesitated before giving chase. Gavin stood by the door, urging his men through. The last of the knights was just five feet from the door when a thrown axe caused him to fall. The man reached for Gavin, but it was too late; the Berserkers were upon him. As Gavin barred the gatehouse door, the image of the fallen knight as he was being hacked to bits by the Ragnar would forever be burnt into Wulfric's mind.

Once inside, the knights made their way to the basement and the hidden tunnel into Arkos. When only Gavin and Wulfric remained, the young knight gave the order for their prearranged plan. "Do it now."

In the center of the chamber, the Engothian engineers had erected a vertical beam. After seeing the west gatehouse collapse, Gavin had the idea to replicate the result with the east gatehouse, in order to give the invading Berserker force another obstacle to overcome, should the north gate be breached. The engineers removed the other supports, leaving the weight of all the floors resting on this single wooden beam. Wulfric chopped at the support beam with his coronium weapon. He hacked at it until the beam began to buckle. When he was sure the beam was about to fail, he grabbed Gavin, and the two hurried down the hatch into the basement. A rush of stone and dust followed the pair, and to avoid the last of the debris, Wulfric had to dive.

Once the sound of the tumbling stones and the crying of crushed Berserkers had ceased, Gavin said, "Many Ragnar have scaled the wall and are inside Arkos. We must regroup."

"Let's kill these curs!"

As they neared the exit back into the town, smoke choked Wulfric's throat and caused his eyes to water. Wulfric prepared himself to step into hell itself.

Chapter 81

Welcome Whispers

"Saint Paxia," cried Tryam into the gloom. "Please let me pass!"

During the young acolyte's absence, Abbot Monbatten had placed a coronium seal over the crack in the wine cellar. Stamped upon the seal was the dove-in-flight sigil of Saint Paxia. For days, Tryam had attempted to break the seal with shovel and pickaxe, but to no avail.

After his desperate pleas to the inscrutable saint had gone unanswered, Tryam took his search for a way into the vaults to every crumbling building on the small island. During his wanderings, he'd been heartened to witness the monks heeding his advice and preparing the abbey for the battle that was sure to come. Even a contingent of Engothian engineers had made the trek across the frozen harbor to help repair the old fortifications.

As Tryam made his way through the ruins, a chilling breeze frosted his breath. He feared he would run out of time before he could make a difference in the fight against the Necromancer. When Arkos's fire gongs rang into the night sky, he feared his time was up. He looked out over the harbor and saw no fire, but he knew from the alarm's urgency that something was amiss. *Watchers on the wall must have spotted the invaders. Is our doom upon us? What must I do?*

It was at his most desperate that he was granted clarity of thought. *I must recite the Warding Prayer and seek guidance from the spirit realm.*

Tryam raced from the ruins to the abbey grounds and did not stop until he burst through the church's double doors. The young acolyte rushed past the pews to kneel before the simple altar. Peering down at him from the back wall of the church, like a heavenly choir, were the portraits of

THE TOMB OF THERAGAARD

the former abbots. Their faces were grim and without warmth. Tryam suppressed a shudder.

"Heavenly Father, I beseech You. Let me speak to Theragaard. Let me learn what it is I need to learn. Let me know what it is I need to know. I have traveled great distances, seen such horrors, and gone through much to get here. Please reveal Your will to me, so that I may help the people of Arkos!"

With sweat pouring down his face, Tryam spoke the words of the Warding Prayer. Over and over, he repeated the verses until their meaning became clear, and his mind and body were at peace.

"... *come ... come ... our promised one ... let us show you ... Theragaard ... Theragaard must live again ...*"

Tryam bolted to his feet and suppressed the urge to panic as the whispered words, which carried the echoes of the sepulcher, filled his head. He took deep breaths. *I shall not flee!*

With his faith as a guide, he sought the voices and implored them to speak again. But they remained as silent as the stony faces of the abbots of Arkos.

Tryam stepped up to the plain marble altar, feeling a compulsion to get closer to the sacred area. He walked gingerly around the apse. As he did so, he repeated the Warding Prayer. After making a few trips around its circumference, he noticed something different about the sound of his footsteps when standing on the rug behind the altar. Tryam removed the rug, but he found only gray stones that matched the rest of the floor.

An urge compelled him to study the area more closely.

He knelt down and touched the stones. He noticed an unusually large gap between them, and he stuck his fingers inside the groove. He lifted, and with surprising ease, the slab yawned open, revealing steps leading down into a gloomy depth.

"Bless you, Aten!" praised Tryam.

With trepidation, the young acolyte started down the steps after he replaced the rug and closed the slab behind him to prevent anyone from following.

The stairs descended far below the church, ending at a cold stone wall. Not to be deterred, Tryam pushed on the wall, and the stone swung open, revealing a large chamber. A shaft of pale light came down from above, illuminating a statue of a warrior on bended knee. Behind the statue was a familiar mausoleum.

The tomb of Theragaard!

Tryam rushed ahead and fell to his knees before the tomb. He prayed for Theragaard's soul, for his spirit to live on in this world, for his deeds to be remembered. And Tryam prayed that, if he was worthy, he be granted help to defeat the Ragnar and the Golem.

He did not know how long he prayed, but when he neither felt nor heard Theragaard's presence or Aten's guidance, he bared his soul to the spirit and let it be known he would not be afraid to receive the ancient warrior, even offering his willingness to sacrifice his life to help the people of Arkos.

Still, he heard nothing.

Tryam slumped down onto the cold floor, more exhausted than from one of Wulfric and Kara's training sessions. When he closed his eyes, a warmth covered him like a blanket. The warmth dragged him into a deep sleep.

When he awoke, he was more rested than he had been in months. But when he stood and opened his eyes, he gasped, for he was no longer in the tomb chamber.

He was now outside, standing at the foot of a great fortress, its white stone battlements gleaming in the sun. It was a world of light, in a time before the Arkos abbey.

Then the scar on his chest burned, and the world that had just been light turned cold and dark.

Fiery destruction flared in his eyes, and smoke choked his lungs. He now held a sword, and his body was encased in white-enameled armor. When the smoke cleared, he discovered that he stood atop a mountain. Thundering steps came toward him, causing him to stumble to his knees. It was the black metal Golem that approached.

He wanted to scream in terror, but he found courage in his faith.

The impenetrable blackness of the giant warrior's skin absorbed all light, including Aten's. As the Golem drew near, Tryam raised his sword and prepared to strike. The Golem raised a monstrous sword of its own: a broadsword as big as a tree. It stepped closer, its blank eyes staring down from above, eyes that reflected the malevolent intentions of the Golem's creator.

The great blade descended, and Tryam braced for the impact. But when the blade struck, instead of feeling the pain of metal slicing through

THE TOMB OF THERAGAARD

flesh, he jolted awake as if from a nightmare. When he looked around, he was back before Theragaard's tomb. Tryam stilled himself. A voice now whispered in his ear.

"… *You have shown your compassion … You have faced your fears … You have stood up to the dark … And in doing so, you have proven your devotion to Aten … You are worthy … But now the time foretold is upon us … You must act as my avatar on this realm … but first, return to your companions, and stand with the people of Arkos … Then, when it is time, return here, to my mortal remains … You will know when … Go now*

… hurry, to battle! … You will know when …"

Tryam crossed himself in reverence to both Theragaard and Aten.

I shall not disappoint you, blessed Theragaard. I shall await your call and return. Until then, I rush to stand with my friends—if they still live.

Chapter 82
The Battle for Arkos

After Tryam bolted from the crypt, he emerged to find that, across the harbor, fires raged in Arkos. *A second wave of attacks must be underway!* The young acolyte stopped his mad rush just long enough to retrieve his sword and strap on his helmet.

Fearing he would be too late, he dashed across the iced-over harbor and scrambled up its rocky slope on his way to the keep. There he found the flanking towers of the south gate unmanned and the portcullis open. The entry yard was likewise deserted.

The young acolyte continued forward and passed the stables—occupied by a dozen draft horses agitated by the smell of smoke—and the smithy, guild house, and chapel. Every building had been abandoned by the knights.

Tryam encountered his first Engothian when he approached the inner gatehouse, which divided the keep in half. As he entered the bailey, the smoke-shrouded watchmen showed only a passing interest in Tryam; their eyes were focused on the battles raging atop the town walls in the distance, the sound of which was now in his ears.

The scale of the horror already inflicted by the battle was evident inside the bailey. It looked to Tryam as if the entire populace not involved in combat were camped on the proving grounds. He saw anguished families huddled together, worried wives fretting about missing husbands, and soot-covered children screaming for missing parents. In the center of the chaos, a tent had been erected for the injured. Already a line of bloody and burnt men and women waited on faltering legs for treatment. Tryam was frustrated at the enormity of the problem and did not know how best to help those in need.

THE TOMB OF THERAGAARD

"Tryam! Tryam! Over here!"

The voice that called out was not Aten's but just as welcome. Tryam spotted Kara climbing down the battlements of the imposing inner fortress. Her quiver was slung over her shoulder, her longbow was in her hand. She looked uninjured but troubled. "Kara!" he shouted back.

They waded through the throng of people and met near the main gate, where Kara initiated a hug. "You are alive!" Kara squeezed his limbs as if to make sure he was made of solid matter. "I can't believe it's you!"

After removing his helmet and tucking his sword in his belt, Tryam patted down his own body. "It is I, as far as I know." His eyes sought Wulfric, but the big Ulf was nowhere to be found along the battlements or in the crowd of people. Since he could not imagine why Wulfric would not be by her side, his spine chilled as if bathed in the Frostfoam Sea. "Where is Wulfric?" he asked with dread.

"He is still out there." Kara's voice was frantic. "He was at the north gate, biding time so others could retreat. You have to help him! I would go, but he made me promise to stay here—and as his bondmate, I am honor bound to do so!"

"Bondmate?"

"Yes!" blushed Kara. "We were wed by Brother Kayen right after we defeated the undead."

"The undead? That was the first wave, then." Tryam looked to the ruins of the ward tower. "How were they defeated?"

"Telvar's magic made our blades burn with fire. Except mine, that is! The monsters burned when struck." When a Ragnar projectile landed nearby, Kara clung to his shoulder. "But now we need you. Go out there and help Wulfric!"

"I shall find him and bring him back," assured Tryam. "Take your bow to the battlements and await our return."

The sounds of combat grew louder. In alarm, the Ulf girl held Tryam's arm so tightly he could not leave. "Arkos is falling! Before you leave, tell me: Do we have any hope? Did you find the answers you sought in the abbey?"

"I did, and when the time is right, I shall return to Theragaard's tomb and bring back help." Tryam donned his helmet and gripped the pommel of his sword. "In the meantime, get back to the ramparts and protect those seeking refuge. And above all, take care of yourself!"

523

She kissed him lightly on the cheek, then released his arm. She then saluted, spun around, and raced back through the throng of townsfolk to the inner fortress and its high walls. *Be safe, Kara. Please be safe.*

Tryam exited the keep's main gate, where the wounded were now staggering through. Most of the people suffered from burns, but a few showed cuts that could have come only from edged weapons. There was only one conclusion to draw: *The Ragnar are in the streets.*

Before the gate, a squad of knights milled about without lending a single gauntleted hand to those in need. Tryam was appalled that these trained soldiers appeared overwhelmed by what was happening. With a confidence born from outrage, he approached them and barked out: "At attention, men! The Ragnar have breached the wall! Do you not see the wounds caused by sword and axe? Civilians and some of your brothers-in-arms are still out there!"

The dazed knights looked in his direction, but none moved. Tryam grabbed the nearest man by his arm and forced him to stand at attention. "We have a battle to fight!"

"He's right," said a haggard knight with gray sideburns. "Our captain ain't coming back to give us orders. We've got to do something."

Another knight protested. "Do what?"

"You have to get to the walls as soon as possible," Tryam explained in exasperation. "Prepare yourself for battle." He glanced back at the keep. "I have an idea."

Tryam searched through the throng of disorientated Arkos townsfolk. Thanks be to Aten, he spotted a stable boy and grabbed him by the shoulder. "Go to the stables, untie all the horses that remain, and lead them back here. Make haste!"

The boy looked confused. "Those aren't warhorses. The cavalry has already left the keep."

"In war you must make do with what you have. Now leave, and be quick about it!" Tryam used the urgency in his voice to convey an authority he did not lawfully have.

The boy shook off his confusion and visible fear. "Of course, sir."

When the boy hurried away, a knight resting on one knee looked up at Tryam. "What's your plan, fighting monk?" The knight had not used the appellation as an insult.

"We ride out to the wall and rescue the knights trapped there. Those who are wounded we can put on the back of our horses. Also, we can lead

THE TOMB OF THERAGAARD

any survivors lost in the fire and smoke back to the keep before the gates must be closed."

The squadron of knights listened to the plan and exchanged harsh words before deciding, as a group, to risk venturing out of the keep. Moments later, the stable boy returned with the large draft horses saddled and ready to mount.

Tryam tucked his blade into his belt, climbed up on the closest beast, and turned to the gathered knights. "Mount up and follow!" The young acolyte spurred his horse through the gate, and the seven men in the squad rushed to catch up.

Fires now encroached upon the buildings nearest the keep, and despite his having lived in Arkos for the entirety of his memories, Tryam grew disoriented. To lead the men north, he would have to rely on the scorched mage tower as a guide. When the sound of clashing swords reached his ears, he turned his horse in order to intercept and lead the men on a meandering charge through the narrow streets.

The melee he sought was in front of the burning smithy, where a gang of bearded Ragnar warriors had trapped four men against the hot flames.

Now apparently remembering their training, the knights shifted their horses into a wedge formation. Tryam stepped his own horse back, fearing he would interfere with their maneuvers. The knights drew their weapons and then, from a simple gesture from the lead knight, charged the Ragnar. Tryam followed behind, ready to help as best he could.

Hooves sparked on stones as the squad charged toward the invaders. When the lead knight burst through their ring, the undisciplined Ragnar scattered. The next line of knights in formation used their swords and axes to slash those too slow to retreat. By the time Tryam followed through, there were none left to fight.

"Stay together," the lead knight ordered. To Tryam he said, "Escort these men we have rescued back to the keep. You have done enough. You have given us our purpose."

The young acolyte nodded, then swung his horse around and headed toward the rescued men. When he did so, his eyes lit up in disbelief. "Wulfric! Gavin! Maxius! You live!"

A drained and haggard Wulfric cracked a war-weary smile. "Yes, we live—though no thanks to the Ragnar. The situation is dire. The enemy has overwhelmed the Engothians at the north gate."

"I can lead us back to the keep," said Tryam. "I know the way."

"We were almost done for," interrupted Maxius's father, the proprietor of the burning smithy. "I did not want to abandon my store. Thankfully, this knight and this young Berserker stopped to help us."

Gavin had a gash on his bare forehead and appeared out of sorts, but he filled Tryam in on the details. "We escaped from the gate but soon found ourselves surrounded. Wulfric and I somehow fought our way free. Then we heard shouts here and had to help, but I am afraid Maxius took a direct hit."

Tryam was shocked at how pale and weak Maxius looked. A dark stain underneath the young blacksmith's leather apron showed that he was bleeding badly. To Wulfric, Tryam said, "Lift Maxius up onto my horse. We need to get him to the keep now!"

Maxius collapsed into the arms of Wulfric, who proceeded to lift the burly youth onto the saddle. Tryam held Maxius in place and ordered the others to follow close on foot.

Expanding fires forced Tryam to alter his return path. After a false start, a fortuitous breeze cleared the smoke ahead, and the walls of the Engothian fortress came into view. Tryam thanked Aten and reached the keep without encountering any additional Ragnar. He dismounted and let Maxius's father take over the reins. "Take him to the healing tent," said Tryam. "They can help him."

Tryam, now on foot with his sword at the ready, stood with Wulfric and Gavin at the gate, and the three waited for more evacuees. Long moments passed before they saw another soul headed to the keep. When they did, it was the seven knights from Tryam's charge, but now each knight carried a survivor on his saddle, and behind them followed the last holdouts of Arkos. When no more evacuees were in sight, the keep portcullis was ordered closed.

Back in the crowded parade ground, Tryam yelled into Gavin's ear. "You must evacuate the townspeople to the abbey. This place cannot hold forever, and when it falls, those inside will have no place to flee."

Gavin's face frowned in confusion. "And they would be safer in the abbey?"

"Yes. The cloister has been prepared for evacuees and the wounded. At the very least, it will give us more time, since the Ragnar would have difficulty crossing the frozen harbor to reach the island."

"How do we evacuate everyone? When the order is given, there would be a mad rush."

THE TOMB OF THERAGAARD

"There is a way. From the rocks near the back of the keep, a long-forgotten tunnel extends under the ice to a building in the ruins below the abbey. I used it often and can vouch for its safety. We can move people quickly and without being spotted."

"A hidden tunnel?" The young squire shook his head. "Okay, but it may take persuasion to get the people to leave the safety of these walls for a tunnel under the water."

"You won't need to persuade anyone when the Golem arrives," warned Tryam.

After Tryam showed Gavin precisely where the tunnel entrance was, the young knight turned on his heels and disappeared into the throng of battered Arkos residents. When Tryam turned to locate Wulfric, he spotted him atop the wall near the keep's inner fortress, already in a reunion embrace with Kara. Tryam ascended the steps to the rampart and was greeted warmly by both of his friends. The apocalyptic scene cast their faces in orange and red shadows, but he felt at peace back in their company.

"Did you contact the spirit?" asked Wulfric. "Is he going to help us?"

"He'd better," said Kara. "Especially after all the things we have been through to get to this point. Besides, I imagine being dead is pretty boring. What else does he have to do?"

Despite the dire situation, Tryam could not help but laugh at Kara's comment. "I communed with Theragaard and shall return to his side when the time is right."

"I hope that time is soon. The second gate has fallen." Wulfric gestured toward the east gate, where dozens of screaming Ragnar surged through the broken portcullis. Back at the abbey, Tryam had heard the monks whispering about a contingent of refugee Berserkers guarding the east gate, and now he saw them with his own eyes. However, the Berserker warriors were now in full retreat alongside the Engothian cavalry. It was with the horsemen that Tryam spotted Lord Dunford, his golden armor dented and stained with blood.

As the Ragnar pursued Lord Dunford and the Berserker allies, crossbowmen atop the keep walls were on high alert. Once the enemy was in range, the archers opened fire. Kara added her own bow and shot with deadly accuracy, expressing satisfaction whenever she sent another Ragnar to the Abyss.

When he was within shouting distance, the commander ordered the gate open and the troops to resume the catapult barrage from atop the four corners of the keep. As the projectiles flew into the air, Kara shrieked in delight. Wherever they landed, they brought death. Their supply of shot was limited, however, while the supply of Ragnar streaming through the breach seemed endless.

Down in the inner bailey, Tryam noticed that the number of townspeople languishing on the frozen ground had dwindled. Either they had hid elsewhere, or Gavin had convinced them to evacuate. He hoped it was the latter.

A great rumbling forced Tryam's attention back to the battle. In the north, a mass of darkness, shrouded in a cloud of red and purple smoke, was now at the wall.

A feeling of impending doom fell upon the keep. Soon thereafter, a colossal impact on the north wall sent debris flying high into the air, and a thunderous boom echoed throughout the town.

"A siege engine perhaps?" offered Wulfric, though he did not sound convinced.

Tryam knew otherwise and turned to take the stairs.

"Where are you going?" shouted Wulfric.

"It is the Golem, I am certain. I have to warn the commander! Stay here!"

The young acolyte found Lord Dunford standing with his cavalry men on the parade grounds, preparing the swift and lean horses to make another charge. Tryam approached the commander and shouted his name. If Dunford was surprised to see Tryam, he did not react.

"The Golem approaches!"

Dunford was putting on his riding gloves. "I was at the wall only moments ago. There was no sign of this monstrosity. I saddle up, and we ride once more. We have the element of surprise, and we must use it. They will not expect another charge so quickly after our tactical retreat."

"You do not stand a chance against such powerful magic," implored Tryam. "We have to retreat to the abbey, where the ancient warrior Theragaard will protect us."

Dunford mounted his horse, then looked down at the young acolyte as if he had questionable intelligence. "The walls of this keep are far stronger than those of the abbey. 'The ancient paladin Theragaard'? You have too much faith in fairy tales. My faith is with my men and my sword." The commander abruptly turned his horse toward the gate. Tryam scrambled to get out of its way. "Form on me, men! We ride again!"

THE TOMB OF THERAGAARD

The twenty-strong cavalry unit lined up two abreast and proceeded out of the portcullis in a hurried but orderly fashion. After the gate was closed, Tryam returned to the wall to stand with Wulfric and Kara. Exasperated, Tryam voiced his disgust. "The folly of that man is astounding. He still will not listen. He will not open his eyes. Instead of helping evacuate the people to the abbey, he risks their lives on a foolish charge."

Wulfric was less angered than Tryam and more pragmatic. "It is a desperate maneuver, for sure, but perhaps he feels only bold moves will win the day. The town is already ablaze, so what else does he have to lose? In any case, his charge may buy us time to evacuate the civilians."

I pray Dunford and some of his brave men survive.

Chapter 83

The Golem versus the Cavalry Charge

"The city's defenders have fled like frightened nomads before a sandstorm."

Dementhus heard the words from Gidran's mouth, but he did not need the information the shaman imparted, for he could see through the eyes of the Golem; the two, one a creation of Aten and the other a creation of magic, were now united as one. "Yes," said the Necromancer, scowling, "but not all has gone according to plan. Where is Myramar?"

Myramar's disappearance—or, rather, Auroth's—had been the only troubling part of his otherwise-flawless battle plan. The ward tower had been destroyed per Dementhus's command, but the ensorcelled wizard was to have opened the gates to allow the undead entry into town. Instead, the undead had been burned before the gates, and Abbaster had been destroyed beyond any power to return. "Have you been able to commune with Auroth?" asked Dementhus.

Gidran shivered, despite the thick bearskin clothes he wore. "Of the Daemon I sense nothing."

"Perhaps there was more to Myramar than we had assumed. The old mage must have overthrown the power of the Daemon and aided those young intruders." Dementhus rubbed the top of his bald pate. "No matter. We march for the mage tower and destroy it—and Myramar, too, if he does indeed live. That is our first objective. Once the old wizard is out of our way, we eliminate the Engothian knights and then rip asunder the tomb of Theragaard."

THE TOMB OF THERAGAARD

Dementhus spoke words of magic and raised his staff. The gem glowed, alternating between red and purple, and the light it emitted merged with a black cloud, whose source was the Albus mage's very own mouth. The energetic cloud moved to shroud the Golem. He ceased his spell and commanded the Mountain God: "*March, destroy, kill!*"

The black metal warrior walked with the weight of a mountain but with the fluidity of a man. The Ragnar wisely parted before their God as His titanic steps quickly took Him to the wall. At a dozen feet taller than the wall itself, the God tore into the stone with His metal hands as a man could into the walls of a sand castle. He did not tire. He did not feel pain. In a matter of minutes, the Mountain God had created a hole large enough for ten men to walk abreast.

Ivor, now in full command of the Ragnar army, appeared at Dementhus's side. "My men are ready to storm the keep whenever you give the order. Some have already made it over the wall and wreak havoc even as we speak. The fury of war has overtaken their wits."

Dementhus smiled. *The Ragnar are loyal and cruel. Perfect subjects for the Dark God.* "Wonderful. Take your forces to the keep at once. The God will join you shortly, but first He must destroy the mage tower. Our supposed wizard ally in Arkos has not proven as loyal as your men."

A crooked smile split the bloodstained face of the jarl. "It will be our pleasure."

After the first company of Ragnar passed through the gap, the men who were to follow raised alarms. Dementhus wondered what could frighten his forces, but then he noticed movement in the streets. The Engothians were launching another cavalry charge, a tactic that had already proven very costly to the inexperienced Ragnar forces. *That will not happen again!*

The Necromancer closed his eyes and bridged his mind to that of the Golem's. "*Eliminate this threat.*"

The Ragnar, as brave as any men Dementhus had seen in combat, were not accustomed to the charge of heavily armored men, and they showed genuine fear. However, when they saw their God heading out to meet the threat, they united behind His tree-trunk legs and shouted in unison, "The Mountain God lives! The Mountain God kills!"

The metal warrior took the most direct route to the approaching cavalry, bothered neither by buildings in His way nor by the fire licking His feet. Dementhus laughed in delight as the Mountain God descended upon the cavalrymen. The giant black God swatted, stomped, kicked, and smashed through the fools in their useless gleaming armor. Horses were crushed, men dismembered—and it happened in only a few red moments.

Whether through accident or dark design, the God saved the golden-armored commander for last. Even after the death of everyone in his charge, the doomed man foolishly turned back toward the God instead of fleeing, raised his lance, and charged. The lance shattered against the God's metal knee, and the commander was unhorsed. The defiant Engothian stood before the Mountain God, his insignificant sword before him. The black metal being reached down and grabbed the commander in one massive hand and squeezed. Lord Dunford's innards oozed out from his armor and stained the God's hand crimson.

Berserkers raced to catch up to their God and stormed through the carnage, grabbing weapons and armor from the dead men. Pleased, Dementhus again communed with the Golem: *"Excellent, my friend. Now return to your original task. Destroy the mage tower!"*

The Golem dropped the lifeless commander to the ground and headed back toward the center of Arkos, hungry for more souls.

Chapter 84
Iscandious's Gambit

I shall not surrender this tower. Not after I have risked my life to conquer its gem, and especially not to an Albus mage who has brought dishonor to all wizards! I have to stop this madman! If only I had more time to come up with a plan. Any other wizard would flee back to civilized lands with his wand tucked between his legs, but I am not any other wizard!

Telvar's mind raced over all possibilities. He had used the potions he had looted from Antigenesus's fortress to create a fuel that could easily consume the undead, but he had not had the time to design a defense against the Golem.

What else have I learned?

Seeing the destruction of the ward tower gave him hope that he could severely damage, if not destroy, the Golem if he could charge the lens with sufficient magic. *The being was created by magic, and it can be destroyed by magic.* But when he reached inside the newly mastered gem with his mind, he realized the power stored inside was not enough for another destructive blast. He racked his brain for a way to quickly charge the lens. Could he alter the angle of the lens to drain more energy from the cosmos? Could he channel energy from the astral plane directly to the lens? None of these were workable in the time remaining.

He had learned about the harrowing period after the fall of Antium, when the wizards who survived the purge had struggled to find magic. This epoch was dubbed the Darkening, because the mage towers of the time could not focus on a single magical energy source in the heavens. Some thought this crisis was a curse by Aten, others revenge by the Lords of the Abyss for the imprisonment of Terminus. The more radical sages believed, though never with confirmation, that a creature called Chrondus stood between Medias and the astral plane, blocking all magic left over from the creation of the universe. In any event, during this bleak time, the panicked wizards turned on one another, attacking fellow wizards to steal their energy reserves. Many towers switched hands or were completely destroyed.

One crafty wizard named Iscandious came up with a solution for finding a temporary source of magic after he had been ordered by his king and patron to infuse a blade with the ability to increase the bearer's size and strength to that of a giant. Telvar tried to recall the name of the blade: *Kingreaver? Cleavus?* He cursed himself for getting distracted.

Iscandious had gone to work in secret, his tower secluded somewhere in the Endless Woods. His solution for the lack of magic was to break open the tower's gem and use the energy released to imbue the weapon. Telvar had seen the power of a shattered gem firsthand in Antigenesus's fortress, but its destruction had come about by happenstance.

Despite his misgivings about destroying his own gem, Telvar searched Myramar's magic library (his own magic library now) for any detailed descriptions of Iscandious's Gambit, as it was later called. He found a few dozen commentaries on the incident, but only one wizard, Dartamus, had an opinion on how it had been done. His idea was widely dismissed, but it seemed logical to Telvar. Dartamus speculated on the spell Iscandious had used and the device he had created to assist with focusing the volatile energy released. The spell was so simple that Telvar understood why other wizards tried to discredit Dartamus: They feared that more gems would be destroyed in such a manner. The young wizard sighed. *I have already destroyed one irreplaceable gem. Why not another?*

The Rutilus wizard went to work.

The apparatus required significant time and lots of copper wire and silver. He scrounged the wire from the backs of tapestries. For the silver, he gathered all of Myramar's most expensive dishware from the kitchen. In the lens room, he wove the copper wire through the silver plates; then he strung the whole construct so that it hung from the lens high above to the center of the gem. According to the theory, as Telvar understood it, after the gem was fractured, the magical energy released would slowly and steadily flow up the wire, with the silver plates acting as resistors to ensure that the lens would not be damaged or any magic lost.

THE TOMB OF THERAGAARD

Dartamus's spell required nothing more than a few simple commands, but it demanded a mastery of the tower gem. After having battled with the gem for control, Telvar was confident he now understood its unique properties well enough. He quickly mastered the words and gestures of the spell.

After a period of brief but restful meditation, the young wizard went to the balcony to observe the fighting in Arkos. He was not prepared for what he saw. The town was ablaze, the walls abandoned, the gates demolished. In a cruel irony, he found himself perhaps the last defender of a town he had never felt was his home. However, what was most startling was the sight of the Golem emerging from a fog of purple and red light. The giant warrior had smashed a hole through the wall and had obliterated what looked to be a desperate cavalry charge. Now the black metal being turned its blank eyes toward the tower itself. *The last grains of sands have fallen from the hourglass!*

Telvar hurried back to the lens room and looked over the setup he had created. From this perspective—with wires everywhere, metal scraps on the floor, and a strange contraption strung to the ceiling—he questioned his own sanity. When he felt the tower rumble from the Golem's approaching footsteps, he realized it was the world that was mad.

The rare red gem sparkled in the meager light of the room. The thought of its fate almost brought Telvar to tears. It was more than the act of destroying something unique to the world; it was an act of betrayal. He had fought so hard to assert his will on the gem, he had sacrificed his own magic, and he had established a symbiotic relationship with the jewel. And now he would destroy it?

Telvar reached out to the doomed gem. He found it easily in his mind's eye. The two-foot-wide multifaceted red stone sat on a marble pedestal in his mind as clearly as it did on the material plane. He told it his plans and tried to prepare it, but the gem refused him, turned its back to him, made him feel shame. Telvar showed it the Golem, told it of Dementhus, and described the fate of Myramar. The gem relented. It would not resist.

The words and hand gestures for the spell for Iscandious's Gambit came easily to Telvar, despite the growing distraction from the shock of the Golem's steps. When the spell was cast, the gem vibrated, and a rainbow of colors emanated from its perfectly smooth facets. With the gem prepared, Telvar plunged his staff into its heart. He realized then that he would be destroying not only the gem but likely his staff as well.

When the gem cracked, Telvar let out an audible gasp at its suddenness and force. As soon as the fracture occurred, magical energy erupted and surged to the wire above. The flow, however, was even and under control. The first silver plate melted, and the energy proceeded higher up the wire. Telvar smiled confidently at his handiwork. The next plate snapped a few moments later, and the third one was soon behind. As each successive plate melted faster, alarm bells rang in Telvar's head. He realized his failing too late: He had miscalculated the size of the plates needed to regulate the flow of energy up the wire. The only thing Telvar could do now was hide from the impending explosion and hope the lens did not shatter when the energy reached it.

The eruption of energy was deafening. Heat scorched the young wizard's robes, and a shock wave knocked him to his knees. But as quickly as the explosion came, it abated. He stood up and looked up at the lens. Remarkably, it was intact and, better yet, boiling over with energy.

Below, and not as fortunate, was the gem. Its facets were dull and cracked. Telvar lamented its loss.

A tremor shook the tower and urged the young wizard into action. Using the old mechanism, Telvar eased the lens into position. To connect to the lens, he spoke the words of command, and he focused his thoughts on the Golem. The monstrous magical being came into view.

The stored energy inside the lens threatened to unleash on its own. Telvar could wait no longer. For lack of a better phrase, he uttered, "Born of magic, be destroyed by magic!"

The energy beam shot from the lens, leaving a blinding flash in Telvar's eyes and causing a concussive force wave that threw him off his feet for the second time in minutes. This time when he got up, he climbed on wobbly legs down to the balcony and peered out to see if his gambit had paid off: Where the Golem had stood was a cloud of vaporized debris.

Telvar held his breath and counted as the seconds passed. It did not take long for the pit of his stomach to fill with a sickening feeling as he saw a black form take shape in the crater of destruction. The Golem survived and was resuming its advance.

I should have known the magic would not be enough, but I am glad to show this Dementhus who controls the tower at Arkos!

Before he could consider his next option, the Golem, which was as tall and as stout as the mage tower itself, was before him. Telvar retreated inside and made it to the central staircase before he heard its massive metal fists slam into the tower. As the walls and ceiling collapsed around him, the young wizard was thrown against the guardrail.

Chapter 85

The Defense of the Keep

All eyes had followed Lord Dunford's valiant charge, since all hope for the salvation of Arkos had ridden with him. When the defenders witnessed the Golem's attack and the brutal destruction of the best of the Engothian knights in mere seconds, though, cries of panic spread throughout the keep at the realization that an unimaginable and unstoppable horror would come for them next.

"Horrible!" cried Kara, averting her eyes from the carnage. "Just horrible!"

Wulfric took the frightened girl in his arms.

Prayers for the fallen were on Tryam's lips as he sought guidance from Theragaard. He whispered the Warding Prayer, but no answers were forthcoming.

"The monster heads toward the mage tower!" voiced Wulfric in alarm. "Do you think Telvar still lives? Can he stop this Golem, as he did the undead?"

The top of the tower slowly rotated, bringing the lens to bear on the approaching Golem. Tryam felt a moment of hope as he saw the lens flare. "Telvar attacks!"

Those on the wall pointed to the mage tower, and hope started to build anew. When the Golem stood within a hundred yards of the tower, the lens flashed a blinding white light. The knights cheered in elation as the beam struck the Golem, immediately swallowing it in a shroud of energy.

As Arkos settled into an eerie quiet, all held their breaths.

Slowly, as the winds picked up, the debris cloud that had enveloped the Golem began to dissipate. When the monster emerged unharmed and resumed its relentless path toward the mage tower, cries of fear rang out from the defenders.

"A worthy effort by the wizard," admitted Wulfric glumly. "I give him credit."

The Golem neared the mage tower, its metal fists extended. If it was angry, its placid face did not express it; nonetheless, its intentions were dreadfully obvious.

"I hope he has the sense to flee!" Kara shouted futilely as the Golem reached for the charred tower.

"It is too late, I fear," lamented Tryam.

Black metal fists hammered into the tower with the power of a dozen battering rams. Even from this distance, the sound of the shattering stones was deafening. In just seconds, the once-proud tower, which had long stood as a jewel in the center of Arkos, was pulverized into a dusty pile of chalky stones. Tryam lowered his head and prayed for the wizard's soul.

"There is nothing to stop the Ragnar from reaching the keep," observed Wulfric.

It was not long after the dust from the crumbling tower had settled that streams of Ragnar and their Berserker allies came pouring into the streets, seeking the keep like vultures to a rotting carcass. Leading the charge was a gray-bearded man with a jagged, green-tinted, two-handed sword.

"I see Ivor, the wretched coward!" spat Wulfric. "I wish I could jump down these walls and rip his worthless heart from his sunken chest!" He was seized with fury. His sentiment was shared along the wall by the other displaced Berserker warriors who had now joined in the defense of the keep.

Racing ahead of the Golem, the Ragnar crashed against the keep's main gate and pressed siege ladders against its walls. The Engothians were leaderless atop the ramparts, and the knights on the wall shouted conflicting orders. The Berserker defenders from the east gate had a leader, the blood-soaked Makkong. After a short spat between knights and Berserkers, it was decided that Makkong's Berserkers would stay on to defend the walls, while the Engothians would gather in the bailey to stand before the gate, awaiting its inevitable fall.

Tryam watched the confusion and turned to his friends. "I have been asked by Theragaard to ensure the safety of the townsfolk. Our Berserker allies can man the walls. We should stand with the Engothians on the proving grounds and cover for those fleeing through the tunnel."

From the long look Wulfric cast at the Ragnar mere feet away, Tryam understood his friend was reluctant to leave the spot atop the battlements.

THE TOMB OF THERAGAARD

"All right," the Ulf warrior conceded, "but my steel will taste their flesh soon, or I *will* leap over these walls!"

The proving ground was emptying of townsfolk, much to Tryam's relief. When the young acolyte looked past the inner gatehouse, he saw a line of women and children waiting to pass through the south gate and into the underground tunnel. Tryam sought the knight who had taken charge of the Engothian civilians. When he approached, the knight removed his helmet, and much to Tryam's surprise, it was Roderick. The youth's face was pale. Tryam shook the knight's shoulders. "We need to give the townsfolk time to make it to the abbey."

Roderick nodded his head, but his eyes looked about in confusion. "Yes, the abbey. Gavin told me of your plan. A tunnel under the water? How is that possible?" The young knight's sword and shield shook in his hands. "Will the monks be able to protect us from that ... giant god-thing out there?"

"That thing is no god. It is merely a rogue wizard's weapon that is called a Golem. All you need to know is that the abbey is the safest place we can be. So just make sure you give the people time to get there. Then retreat yourself!"

"Yes, of course. We are Engothians. We shall save our people." With a shaky hand, Roderick put his helmet back on and slammed down his visor.

Tryam returned to Wulfric and Kara's side, where they had lined up with the other Engothian knights. The young acolyte put his hand on Kara's shoulder. "You should go with the townsfolk. Wulfric and I can handle ourselves here."

"Your bow would be worthless in such close quarters," added Wulfric.

"Worthless?" Kara punched Wulfric in the shoulder. "My bow is never worthless." Kara paused a moment, "I have an idea! I shall stand atop the inner gatehouse and provide cover until my arrows run out."

Wulfric looked back to the inner gatehouse, which bisected the keep, and nodded his approval. "All right, but don't stay too long!"

"I never stay anywhere too long!" Kara slapped Tryam on the shoulder and gave Wulfric a long kiss. She turned away, started toward the gatehouse, then turned back to give a wave and a smile. Tryam watched her retreat long enough to see her make it safely to the top of the battlements and notch a red arrow.

At the main gate, Roderick had arranged the knights in formation, shields locked. Tryam dragged Wulfric to his side, and the two filed in line with the other Engothians.

Almost as if outside his body, Tryam watched as the Ragnar invaders began to mount the walls. The Berserker defenders met them eagerly and put hungry weapons to their flesh in a bloody melee. Despite the defenders' success, however, some of the Ragnar men began to crest the walls unopposed. One by one, the Ragnar began to drop into the proving grounds. Since the main gate still held, Roderick moved the knights back to the inner gatehouse to prevent the Ragnar from going unopposed to the south gate and the fleeing townsfolk.

The first few Ragnar warriors, perhaps drunk from bloodlust or warroot, rushed heedlessly into the line of Engothians. Their lack of discipline betrayed their superior arms and armor, and they were quickly overwhelmed. But the more Ragnar men who came over the walls, the more organized they became. Eventually, a line of Ragnar warriors assaulted the front and sides of Roderick's formation, pushing the knights together as they protected the inner gatehouse. Both Tryam and Wulfric were inside the formation not yet fighting. Wulfric roared in anger and frustration, his eyes blood red, awaiting the enemy to come within reach of his grasp. Tryam used his time to focus on the Warding Prayer.

As the battle proceeded, the knights struggled to hold the line. Eventually, through loss and fatigue, Tryam and Wulfric were forced to the front of the formation. Before attacking, Tryam prayed to Aten. He felt calm, a stark contrast to the blind fury, almost a madness, exhibited by the Ragnar. Wulfric stepped up beside him, and they both took turns slashing and stabbing at the waves of invaders. Periodically, Tryam would see a red-shafted arrow take down a warrior standing before them.

Looking for his next opponent, Tryam was surprised to see that there were no more enemies to attack, and he wondered briefly if it were possible that they had defeated the entire horde. However, when cries not of victory but of terror came from those he fought beside, he understood why this was only a lull in the storm. Limned in the light of the Arkos inferno was the silhouette of the Golem, its gigantic stride taking it to the keep's gate.

"Retreat!" ordered Roderick. "We have done all we can!"

As the beleaguered knights and their frightened Berserker allies together fled toward the south gate and the harbor, no one argued.

THE TOMB OF THERAGAARD

"Where is Kara?" asked Wulfric before he and Tryam joined in the retreat.

Tryam scanned the battlements but could not see her. "I don't know. Perhaps she retreated before the knights gave the order?" He called up to the dark gatehouse. "Kara! Kara!"

Wulfric joined in with his own booming voice, but she did not respond.

The Golem's shadow darkened the parade ground.

"We cannot linger," cautioned Tryam.

No sooner had Tryam spoken than the Golem bashed into the keep's thick walls, sending large chunks of stone into the air. After each blow of a mighty metal fist, the piercing wailings of two small children sounded from a source nearby.

Wulfric was the first to spot the children, covered in mud, huddled together, under the awning of the smithy. Abandoning their search for Kara, he and Tryam raced to their side. It was apparent that the children had gotten lost in the evacuation. Each warrior sheathed his sword and lifted a child in his arms.

"We have to get them to the tunnel," said Wulfric, his blue eyes shadowed with anxiety.

"Aye."

As he followed Wulfric out the south gate and then down onto the rocky shore, where the secret tunnel stood wide open, Tryam kept his eyes open for Kara.

"At the very least," Wulfric said, "I would have expected her to stay by the tunnel and wait for us."

"I know."

A cloud of smoke and hot ash moved over the keep. Tryam scanned the battlements, but Kara was still nowhere to be seen. Ragnar had returned to the ramparts in anticipation of the Golem breaching the gate. "We have to seal the tunnel entrance before the Ragnar observe where we went."

Wulfric nodded his head, his expression grim. The Ulf warrior gave one last shout of Kara's name. The two waited for any response, but they heard only the sounds of the approaching enemy. It was time to leave, and they both knew it. Glumly, Tryam guided the children down the long, dark tunnel, and Wulfric slid the concealed door back into place with the sorrow that of sealing a tomb.

Tryam prayed they would find Kara's smiling face awaiting them on the other side.

Chapter 86

The Markswoman

With only one arrow left in her quiver, Kara sought the target that would be the most worthy of the honor. She looked for the Ragnar jarl, but the jackal was not among the warriors who had scaled the walls and pressed the knights below. "Coward," she cursed under her breath.

As she notched the last arrow and trained her eyes on the melee below, she could not help but notice that the number of Ragnar men in the proving ground was thinning out. She was tempted to cheer but then thought better of it and decided to see why the Ragnar were in retreat.

She left her position and walked atop the interconnecting parapets back to the battlements of the inner fortress. When the wind changed direction, smoke choked her lungs and blinded her vision. The sky rained hot ash.

After a few moments, the smoke cleared enough for her to see that the Ragnar men at the portcullis were parting as if to make room for a siege engine. But it was no siege engine that caused the ground to tremble and the walls of the keep to sway. It was the Golem, and it was close.

Kara was tempted to launch an arrow at the thing to prove she was not afraid, but she did not want to waste her last arrow on a futile gesture. She scanned the crowd of Ragnar outside the gate; the eyes of those warriors were focused on the Golem as if in a state of rapture. She could not help but be fascinated by the magical beast herself.

It was so close now, and Kara understood why the Ragnar warriors called it the God of the Mountain: It exuded an aura, almost as one would expect from something divine. Being in its presence again, she was momentarily lost in awe before she slapped herself in the face. *It is only a magical trick!*

THE TOMB OF THERAGAARD

As the Golem stepped through the captivated Ragnar warriors to stand before the keep's main gate, Kara ducked low behind a merlon between two crenellations. Once they were in range, the metal warrior's mighty fists slammed down, over and over again, on each of the flanking towers. The towers flew apart and scattered stone blocks high into the air, killing a few unlucky Ragnar when they crashed back to the ground. The Golem took a moment to clear away the rubble; then it ripped the iron gate from its moorings and flung it over its shoulder as a mortal man could a crumpled piece of parchment.

Kara gasped when she realized how long she had been mesmerized by the Golem. In the time she had wasted, all of the Berserker refugees defending the wall had retreated and the Engothian knights, including Wulfric and Tryam, had retired from the bailey. A sense of dread caused her stomach to stir; she was now alone, with an enemy army and a deranged god between her and escape. She ducked lower on the rampart.

The Golem stepped aside to let the raging mob of Ragnar warriors pour into the keep. As it did so, a flash of red and purple light sparkled through the smoky haze in the rear of the army. The unnatural light had to come from a wizard, and there was only one evil wizard she knew: *Dementhus!*

Kara crawled on her hands and knees toward the keep's northwest corner tower, where a catapult sat abandoned. She crept past the weapon to the battlements and peered below at the assembled invaders. There she found the source of the light: It was the gem atop the staff of the red-robed wizard. The bald man stood behind the Golem like a puppeteer would his puppet.

Mesmerized by the spectacle, Kara spied the wizard advancing in an awkwardly stilted manner, almost as if his legs were about to fail. But there was no doubt about the power of his magic. When the Necromancer commanded, the Golem obeyed. The two were as one. Kara's heart beat uncontrollably as Dementhus walked below her position.

"There, above, a defender!"

The alarm acted as a slap to her face and gave her clarity. She knew what she had to do, and the sound of booted feet told her she had little time in which to do it. *Aten, I know we don't talk very often, but please make my aim true! Please!*

The Golem turned from the ruined gate and took a step in her direction. The metal warrior rose over the keep like a black mountain. As she took aim, her hands trembled, but they stopped when a calm filled her soul as an image of Wulfric rushed into her head. She wiped away tears as she selected her target: the wizard's bald head. "To the Abyss with you!" she shouted as the arrow left her bow.

Perhaps the wizard heard her shout, or it could have been a coincidence, but Dementhus turned to look her way just as the arrow flew through the air. Kara's aim was true, and the projectile sunk deep into the wizard's right eye socket, half of the red shaft emerging from the back of his head.

The wizard stumbled and dropped his staff as his velvet-covered hands reached to dislodge the arrow. Blood and brain matter oozed from the wound. After a few moments of spastic flailing, the wizard's hands dropped to his sides, and the Albus mage fell backward, falling ignominiously onto the snow-and-ash-covered street. Blood pooled beneath his head.

"That was for Clan Ulf!" shouted Kara down to the dead wizard.

She did not savor her victory but instead began to look for an escape. Warriors in green-black armor were approaching from both directions along the parapets. She thought of jumping down into the bailey, but it was already crawling with dozens of warriors. Instead, Kara drew her gladius and gritted her teeth as she waited for the warriors to come. "Here I am, cowards! Fight me!"

As she shouted her taunt, a shadow blotted the sky. "No!" cried Kara as she caught sight of the Golem.

When Dementhus died, the metal warrior had stopped advancing. Now in an obscene mimicry of the Necromancer's collapse, the giant metal warrior began to descend onto her position. She dove under the catapult and covered her head.

The last thing she heard was the goliath crashing into the corner of the keep.

✠ ✠ ✠

The God of the Mountain fell into blackness, the same blackness He had endured during His long, frigid slumber. What He had become was slipping away. What He had gained was almost lost. He cried out to the Necromancer: *Help me!*

An eternity seemed to pass before He heard the imploring commands of the wizard.

THE TOMB OF THERAGAARD

Come to me! Come to me! My physical body is dying.

The Mountain God stirred from under the rubble that threatened to trap Him, as the ice had trapped Him so long before. He rose to His knees but faltered.

You must hurry if we are both to survive!

Pushing away the larger stones, the Mountain God climbed to one knee.

It is almost too late! My link to this world is almost broken.

The Mountain God used the last of His power to stand.

The wizard was nearby. The God took a lumbering step forward before scooping the broken man into His massive black hands.

Chapter 87

Starting Her Journey Alone

A familiar blue-white glow removed the gloom from the end of the tunnel. Tryam, Wulfric, and the two children rushed to enter the light's embrace.

"Brother Kayen!" Tryam cried in disbelief. "I did not expect to see you here."

A pale face greeted the exhausted youths. "I fled just as Lord Dunford made his cavalry charge. Gavin guided me here with the rest of the injured and townsfolk." The missionary's hair dripped with sweat, and he leaned heavily on his staff. "Are you and the children the last ones? Where is Kara?" He peered past them with fearful eyes.

Tryam went cold. "You have not seen her?"

Kayen shook his head. "No, I have not. I can assure you she was not among the evacuees."

"I have to go back to find her!" stormed Wulfric.

The Ulf warrior turned to race back down the tunnel, but Tryam and Kayen grabbed him by the shoulders. "You cannot go back," said Kayen. "You would lead the Ragnar to our very doorstep."

Wulfric pounded his fists against the tunnel walls. "I can't leave her with the enemy. I've got to go back! I shall not let that evil wizard get his hands on her again!"

At that moment, shouts of terror erupted from the evacuees just outside the tunnel's exit.

THE TOMB OF THERAGAARD

"Quickly, out now!" commanded the missionary, shoving the scared children ahead.

Tryam pulled his friend forward, and together they emerged among the ruins below the abbey, where a gray dawn, choked with smoke, greeted them. Along the path that double-backed to the abbey was the trailing end of the line of men, women, and children evacuated from Arkos. Their fingers were pointing back across the harbor at the Engothian keep; all had open-mouthed expressions on their ash-covered faces.

Tryam stepped out from the ruins and looked back to see what had caused the townsfolk of Arkos to react with such shock. At first, he was distracted by the nightmarish glow of the inferno that engulfed the town—the horizon was smeared in red, orange, and black—but then his eyes found the Golem. The black metal behemoth wobbled until it pitched forward and crashed into one of the keep's towers.

While mass panic spread among the Ragnar warriors at the sight of their God's collapse, whispers of hope escaped the lips of the war-ravaged townsfolk across the harbor.

"Is it dead?"

"Are we saved?"

After a long quiet, a rumbling like thunder floated across the harbor as a cloud of dust lifted into the air over the keep. When the dust dissipated, so did all hope that the Golem was gone forever. Slowly it rose to its feet; then it turned and retreated into the town. In its hand, it held a crumpled figure, covered in blood that matched the red robes it wore.

"Is that Dementhus he carries?" asked Tryam.

Wulfric, with his keener eyes, slapped Tryam on the back. "It is. And do you see what impales the wizard's head?"

Tryam strained his eyes, but the distance combined with the smoke and fire made it hard for him to see. "It looks like an arrow. ... Could it be ... ?"

"Yes, a red arrow! Kara lives! With the Ragnar in chaos, I can find her!"

"And I shall go with you," said Tryam.

"I would like to go as well, but I would only be a hindrance to your speed," admitted Kayen. "But if there's a chance Kara can be rescued, do so. Take a couple horses left behind by the Engothian engineers, and fly across the frozen harbor."

Wulfric shook Kayen's forearm. "Thank you, Brother. We shall find her." Then he turned his eyes to Tryam. "We risk riding to our death. Are you sure you want to come? What about Theragaard?"

"I have not yet heard his call. Kara needs us now—of that I am certain."

"Godspeed," offered Kayen as he guided them to two horses tied to a post near a refurbished section of the defenses. The two quickly mounted.

While they galloped down the path to the dock, Tryam spotted the repairs the engineers had done to the defenses. He prayed that the refurbished portcullis and the patched walls could hold off the Ragnar should the army regroup and head to the island.

Ahead, Wulfric with single-minded determination spurred his horse past the dock and onto the ice with the speed of a gale. Tryam said a short prayer to Aten before he too headed across the frozen expanse.

The closer his horse carried him to the inferno, the harsher the smoke assailed the young acolyte's eyes and nostrils. The fire had spread. To his relief, though, the harbor itself was free from the conflagration. Also to his relief, it appeared that the Ragnar warriors had never advanced past the keep.

Ahead, Wulfric had tied his horse to the cleats of the pier closest to the keep and was already creeping forward on foot. Tryam hurried to close the gap; at the same pier, he dismounted and tied his horse next to Wulfric's.

The young acolyte glanced about at the frost-covered caravels locked in the harbor and wondered if any threats lay hidden inside the dark vessels. He suppressed a shudder, unsheathed his sword, and rushed ahead to the brooding Ulf, who prowled back and forth, into and out of the shadows, like a snow leopard—all the while whispering Kara's name. Wulfric, likewise, had his sword unsheathed.

Together now, they made their way through the eerily quiet harbor and followed the path to the keep's south gate. There were no Ragnar along the ramparts. After they had advanced under the unguarded gate, Wulfric signaled for Tryam to be still; he had spotted two Ragnar stumbling out from the stables. They appeared to be arguing over a bottle of wine.

Wulfric sprang into action.

The only advance warning the two warriors had of Wulfric's attack was a glint of fire off his blade. His slash caused a deep gash in the exposed neck of the taller of the two drunken men. The second man, sobering quickly, threw the wine battle at Wulfric and then retreated into one of the stables, drawing a long, thin blade as he did so. Tryam left Wulfric to finish off the injured Ragnar and rushed into the stable to press the attack before the second man could raise an alarm.

As the young acolyte searched for the Ragnar, he stumbled in the meager light of the cavernous building. His opponent took advantage and leapt from a pitch-black stall to stab at his chest. Tryam heard more than saw the attack and sidestepped the thrust, the momentum causing him to roll onto the hay-covered ground. When he looked up at his attacker, he saw the point of Wulfric's sword poking out from under the Ragnar's gorget, and the drunk warrior fell dead at Tryam's feet.

"C'mon, let's go," Wulfric whispered, ignoring the gory scene as he pulled Tryam to his feet.

"Yes, all right," Tryam managed to respond despite the shock.

They clung to the shadows and passed the keep's warehouse, provisioner shop, and chapel, before making it back to Kara's last-known location, the inner gatehouse. No one was on the walls, and only the dead lingered in the bailey. It appeared as though the Ragnar had retreated with their God back to the center of Arkos.

Both men called out for Kara but heard nothing in response. Wulfric disappeared into the gatehouse but emerged with the same glum expression he had when he'd entered.

When Tryam conversed with Wulfric about their situation, he did his best to keep his voice under control. "The flanking towers are rubble, the portcullis is gone, and the northwest tower has collapsed. I see no Ragnar, but we should still be cautious."

Wulfric crept into the bailey. Tryam started to follow but halted. From inside the inner fortress came the sound of raucous laughter and the smashing of objects. The inner fortress had been the knights' headquarters and contained loot that would interest some of the more avaricious Ragnar. The young acolyte could see the orange glow of fire coming out of the top-floor windows, where Lord Dunford's office had been located. He could see an occasional dark shadow passing through the light.

"There are Ragnar nearby," warned Tryam, pointing to the fortification.

"They are too occupied with their own dark pursuits to notice us," dismissed Wulfric as he called Kara's name—a whisper at first, then more boldly as he advanced into the proving grounds.

Snow fell and mixed with hot ash. The wind changed direction again and now carried smoke over the keep. As Tryam gazed through the gaping hole where the main gate had once stood, he struggled to recognize any landmark in Arkos.

Where can Kara be? She would not have followed the Ragnar into the burning town. If she shot the Necromancer from the walls …

Tryam followed his thoughts with his feet and moved to where the Golem had collapsed. He climbed over the large stones that had once been the corner of the keep. As he made his way over the uneven rocks, he called out Kara's name, ever mindful of the Ragnar presence in the inner fortress at his back.

When the young acolyte reached the top of the mound, he saw the remains of one of the keep's four catapults, smashed and partially buried. Under the broken weapon, a dark void had formed. Seeing the cavity gave him hope. He stuck his head beneath the catapult's wheel and called Kara's name once again. In response, he heard a cough and then caught sight of a strand of blond hair. Tryam momentarily froze as he tried to speak. He lifted his head out of the hole and yelled down to Wulfric. "Over here! Someone is trapped in the rubble!" Wulfric abandoned his investigation and rushed to Tryam.

The two combined their strength to lift the stones from the shattered catapult. There was an urgency in their movements, confirming the unspoken assumption that both believed it was Kara below.

As the two sweated and bled to remove the debris, harrowing moments passed. Any sound outside of their ragged breathing caused Tryam to flinch, but he could not stop. Once they found Kara's broken body, he felt as if the weight of the stones had also fallen on him. She lay buried under a pointed rock. A wooden beam spanned her chest, saving her body from being crushed completely.

"We shall have you out in moment!" cried Wulfric. "Stay with us!"

The two stood together and placed their hands upon the jagged stone. The uneven mound of rubble made it hard for them to get leverage. Wulfric's face turned as red as the fire in Arkos, and Tryam strained his muscles to the point of snapping. In a feat of strength only a Berserker could manage, Wulfric got his hands underneath the stone and threw it aside.

Free of the obstructions, Kara groaned but did not speak. Blood dripped from her mouth and nose. Her face was as white as alabaster.

Wulfric sank to his knees and grabbed Kara from under her shoulders, gently lifting her out of the hole. He tried to get her to speak, but she was unresponsive. Not knowing what else to do, he cradled her small body in his massive arms. "Can you do anything for her?"

A brief inspection of Kara's motionless body was enough for Tryam to realize that her grievous injuries were far beyond his healing skills, but he did know someone who could possibly help. "We have to get her to Brother Kayen."

Wulfric glumly nodded his head.

Shouts and the clashing of blades echoed from an upper-floor window of the inner fortress, and a chair was thrown from another. Wulfric and Tryam could hear commands from Ragnar captains in the town, rallying warriors back to the keep. The two would have no time to be stealthy.

Holding Kara as gently as he could, Wulfric raced back to the docks. Tryam followed as fast as his legs could go.

The return trip to the island was a frenzied blur. Tryam had no recollection of how he managed to find his horse, cross the ice, or end up on the other side of the abbey's restored portcullis, where a grim-faced Kayen stood waiting. It was as if the young acolyte had ridden through the realm of nightmares.

Kara rested on the grungy floor of what once, centuries ago, had been a storage room but was now overgrown with weeds, cluttered by moldy amphorae, and covered in fallen plaster. The sight of Kara's beauty among the filth left Tryam feeling gutted. *Someone who shines so brightly should never know such gloom.*

Kayen knelt beside Kara and placed one hand on her forehead. With his other hand, he brought forth the cross of Aten and pressed the holy symbol to her chest. He spoke words of a healing prayer, and Tryam lent his voice.

Wulfric stood in the shadows. He did not move, not even as the light of Aten illuminated the damp room in a warm, blue light.

After what felt like a lifetime in the Abyss, Kayen ended his prayer. The missionary looked up to Wulfric and spoke in a grave tone: "I am sorry. I have done all I that I can. She no longer feels pain, but soon she will pass into Aten's grace."

The blank expression on Wulfric's face did not change as he moved into the light and aided Kayen to his feet. "May I speak to her?"

The shaken missionary nodded his head and was about to lead Tryam out of the room when Kara's eyes fluttered open. She spoke: "Stay."

Her voice was weak, but Tryam saw a flash of life in her placid blue eyes. She continued: "I guess all the gods in heaven can't cure someone who had a mountain fall on her."

"Bless you, child," said Kayen, who looked down on her with the love of a parent, "but I am afraid so."

Kara's eyes locked onto Tryam's. "You will make a great warrior. I can see that. Let nobody stop you. You can make a difference. You have to make a difference, because most people are too afraid to fight for what's right."

The appropriate words of response were lost in Tryam's throat, but after a deep breath, he found a few meager ones. "I shall never be as good a warrior as you. Especially after what you did today." Tryam wished he had something more profound to say, but instead he knelt down and kissed her forehead.

"Did I kill the wizard?" Kara looked to Wulfric, her eyes briefly gaining their former brilliance. "Is he dead?"

Wulfric knelt by her side and held her small, pale hands. "The wizard is dead, the Golem retreats, and the Ragnar are in chaos."

Kara coughed, and blood foamed on her lips. As tears ran down her cheeks, she looked into Wulfric's eyes. "Do you love me?"

"I love you."

Another coughing spasm ravaged Kara, but she was able to recover her voice. "Our days together were few, but they fill me as if they were an eternity. I am glad I shared them with you."

"As am I."

"Will you remember me?" she asked.

"Always," he vowed.

Her eyes started to close. Wulfric shook her shoulders. "Kara, hold on," he begged. "Hold on to this moment."

Kara's eyes opened again, but they had the look of twilight. "It appears as if I must start my journey without you."

"No, no, you won't," pleaded Wulfric. "You can't! Stay here with me!"

Kara closed her eyes for the final time and whispered, "Can't you see? I am already gone."

Tryam watched her final breath leave her body, and an overwhelming sense of loss brought the young acolyte to his knees. He wanted to comfort Wulfric but was frozen with sadness.

THE TOMB OF THERAGAARD

Wulfric held Kara's broken body in his arms before gently laying her back down onto the cold stones. His voice broke the grim silence. "All that she was in this world and all that she could have been is no more."

With the stoic nature bred into all Berserkers, Wulfric rose to his feet. "Brother Kayen, we do not have time to mourn her properly. Would you take her body to the abbey? I must make sure the defenses are in order before the Ragnar arrive. This is where we shall make our last stand, and it is where I shall get my vengeance."

When Wulfric left the ancient storage room, his sword was already in his hand.

Chapter 88

Yearning for Theragaard

The call to be by Theragaard's side came not in whispered words but in the form of a great yearning. Tryam neither had time to grieve for Kara nor accept that he would never see her smile or hear her voice again. That would have to wait. Before it was too late, he had to return to the vaults and commune with the spirit of the great warrior.

"Brother Kayen, it is time. I must return to Theragaard's tomb."

The grieving missionary put his hand on Tryam's shoulder. "Go then, and do what you must do. You have my blessing, and you carry all our hope."

"Thank you, Brother."

As Tryam made his way up the ruins to the abbey, he spotted Wulfric. His friend mourned in the manner of his people: by fighting to preserve their way of life. The young Ulf was organizing the last of the free Berserkers, placing them in strategic spots atop the island's rebuilt defenses. The displaced warriors were eager to mete out death to their beguiled cousins, and they willingly accepted Wulfric's commands.

Farther up the ascending path, Engothian knights stood guard atop the gate on the island's second tier, the last line of defense before reaching the abbey itself. The Engothians had proven resilient despite heavy losses, and they stoically stood by their Berserker allies. It was also here where the more able-bodied townsfolk lent a hammer, pitchfork, or rusty dirk to the effort. How much time Kara's sacrifice had gained for the defenders, Tryam dared not guess.

At the abbey grounds, Tryam observed his brothers thronged about the bell tower. Father Monbatten was noticeably absent. The usually dispassionate and composed monks were engaged in a boisterous and heated argument. Dorsat, his face flush, was the most vocal, but he stepped aside when he saw Tryam rush to query him.

"Are the townsfolk okay? Has something happened?"

The flustered monk waved his arms frantically. "They are safe. The refugees are being well cared for in the cloister."

"Then, what is the matter? I have never seen the brothers so fretful."

"It's the abbot, Gamrow, and some of the others!"

What madness is Monbatten up to now? Tryam crinkled his forehead. "What about them?"

"They were talking foolishness. They plan to meet with the Albus wizard and negotiate!"

"*Negotiate?* What folly! The rogue wizard has been slain!" He suppressed his anger. "Where are they now?"

Dorsat shrugged his shoulders. "The abbot said they needed to head to the vaults first."

"The vaults?" Dorsat's words made Tryam feel as if a mammoth had kicked him in the stomach. *Do they go to defile Theragaard's tomb? I must stop him, but I can't alarm the others!* "Tell the brothers not to worry about Father Monbatten. The abbot has always done what he believed was in the order's best interest. Just make sure the people of Arkos are safe."

Chapter 89
Negotiations for Peace

"Father, where you take us is forbidden!"

"Gamrow, no part of the abbey, including the Netherium, is forbidden to me."

The Netherium's access tunnel was concealed along the back wall of the abbot's very own chambers. Monbatten held his torch aloft inside the cramped space, its flames licking the black stone ceiling. He signaled his twenty most devout followers to hurry their pace down into the vaults.

When the early monks had settled into Theragaard's old fortress, the Netherium was the first place they had sealed away from the outside world. Monbatten knew they had done so for a very good reason. Buried within this subterranean cemetery were the mortal remains of the most malevolent souls that the paladins, under Theragaard's command, had vanquished in their campaign against Antigenesus and his allies from the Abyss. These unholy remains had been buried in blessed soil in order to prevent worshipers from venerating the dead and gaining powers only those who have passed to the afterlife could bequeath.

Whispered fears spread throughout Monbatten's followers. The abbot decided that now was the time to tell them his reasoning for venturing into such a dark place. "It is only because of the unimaginable violence in Arkos that I take this desperate action. I do not do so lightly and only in the pursuit of peace."

The monks quieted down and quickened their pace, reaching their destination without further interruptions.

Monbatten stopped before the door of the Netherium and lowered his torch to examine the entrance more closely. Affixed to the nondescript gray metal door was a ceramic plate on which were carved sigils of Aten and words of the holy script. He looked to his followers. "In order for us to enter, this glyph must be destroyed. Gamrow, my staff."

"Yes, Father."

Monbatten grabbed the shepherd's staff and then stared deeply into the eyes of his monks. Deepening his voice to convey the seriousness of what they were about to do, Monbatten said. "As the fire in Arkos grows, let us pray. As the death and devastation continue, let us pray. Before we do what we must do, let us pray."

The gathered monks bowed their heads and spoke a verse from the Words of Saint Paxia. Monbatten listened rather than reciting the words himself. He needed neither the comfort nor the insight of prayer. He had decided, and he knew he was right.

When the monks ended their prayer, they turned their focus to the abbot and waited, shifting uneasily in place. The tip of Monbatten's staff glowed bright red.

"Remember, what we do is for the benefit of Arkos!" With that, Monbatten turned to the door and, in one dramatic motion, smashed the glyph with his glowing staff.

The falling shards still echoed down the tunnel when he turned the knob and pushed the door inward. A rush of stale air came forth, which reeked of ancient, evil times. The staff lost its brightness.

Monbatten grabbed the torch from Gamrow and walked down dusty steps into the gloom. Where the torchlight burned away the shadows, black tombstones and the Netherium's shape came to light. The room formed a cross, each of whose axes was almost two hundred feet long.

In the center of the Netherium, where the arms of the cross intersected, was a blue-white marble statue of an Aemon, its wings outstretched so that their tips touched the ceiling. The Aemon's placid face looked to the heavens, as its nude feminine form gripped a sword in one hand and a spear in the other.

"That is what we seek," whispered the abbot, who was afraid his voice would disturb the dark spirits imprisoned beneath the tombstones. "It lies at the base of the angel's feet."

"What is it?" asked Frey, his voice quivering.

"Do not fear, my young son," assured Monbatten. "It holds the key to peace."

Monbatten laid the torch across the angel's arms and knelt down before the statue. On the ground rested a two-foot-wide, thirty-foot-long box. A bronze lock was the only adornment on the lead container.

"I shall need all of your help. Do I have it?"

Monbatten need not have asked his followers for help, but he did so to show they were as one.

The monks nodded their heads in silent agreement.

"I ask again. Do I have it?"

This time, the monks affirmed with a robust, unified voice.

No key could unlock the bronze clasp; it would unlock only with the words of a prayer. Monbatten held the cold metal in his hands and demanded silence from his devotees. When he prayed, he did so with his entire body lying prostrate before the Aemon statue. The words echoed off the thick walls of the Netherium, and his gesticulations increased. When sweat mixed with tears on his wrinkled face, the bronze became brittle in his hands. He then showed the monks the power of prayer by making a display of destroying the lock with his bare hands. "Aten has given us His blessing! Frey, help me!"

The abbot made way for the young man. Frey, less agitated and without hesitation, lifted the heavy lid from the long, narrow box. When the sputtering torchlight revealed its contents, gasps and a look of horror spread from one monk to the next. Inside, shining brightly, was a sword over twenty feet long, its metal gleaming as one never stained with blood.

"What is this?" Sweat poured down Frey's face. "A weapon of war? We cannot wield this or allow it into battle!"

"No, we can't, nor shall we," assured Monbatten to Frey and the rest of the monks. "I shall present this weapon as a gift to the commander of the armies who have sacked Arkos. After their leader sees what it is we offer, he will believe our sincerity when we plead for peace. And when the Engothian knights see that the Golem has its weapon returned, they will have no choice but to lay down their arms and cease all hostilities. Even the most warmongering among them will have to understand that to fight—to resist—is madness."

"But what then? Will they leave us in peace?"

Frey's question was echoed by a dozen other monks. Monbatten quieted them with a stern gaze. "Yes, of course they will. We have nothing that the wizard or his Berserker allies covet. Not for much longer, at least. This great sword will help the mighty Golem shatter the wretched tomb of

THE TOMB OF THERAGAARD

Theragaard, and in so doing, it will rid Arkos of the curse that has plagued this land since that warrior's arrival here centuries ago!" Monbatten waved away further questions. "We have no more time for discussion. It will take our collective strength to carry this weapon to Arkos, and we must do so without being spotted by the knights. There is an exit at the rear of the abbey that takes us down the cliff. We can use this path to take us to the frozen waters and travel to the town undetected."

The abbot organized the men into quick action. They covered the gigantic weapon in a shroud, and eight monks carried it from the Netherium to the church grounds. The smoke-choked air hid their movements, as Monbatten led the group to the back of the church, where a wall, a remnant of Theragaard's castle, overlooked the cliff face that protected the back of the island. A hidden door in the thick wall offered access to concealed steps carved into the rock. The stairs traced a zigzag pattern down to the frozen water of the harbor.

"Do not fear," assured the abbot. "This is the way."

With measured movements and coordination, the monks carried their heavy burden down the precipitous, ice-covered steps. When they reached the bottom, several dozen feet below, Father Monbatten granted them a brief respite. A weary Brother Cordon asked Father Monbatten, "How shall we arrange to meet this Ragnar leader?"

"Their leader is a great wizard, not a Berserker," reminded Monbatten. "He will seek us out. Let's move. We must hurry!"

The ice cracked and groaned as the monks shuffled their feet over the slippery surface of the frozen harbor. Once the group cleared the island's profile, Monbatten was dismayed at the sight of the burning town and the devastation the foolish Engothians had caused by resisting the overwhelming force of the wizard. He prayed for peace as he scolded the knights aloud to his devotees. "Foolish warmongers! Bloody fools!"

The abbot guided the monks to a rocky slope north of the last pier. He wondered what the reaction would be from the people of Arkos if they were to spot the order of pacifistic monks carrying a great weapon of war. In order to drag the impossibly heavy great sword over the boulders, they tied a rope about its massive handle. "Pull with all your strength," commanded Monbatten. "Pull as if the flames of the Abyss lick your back!"

The monks did as they were ordered. After a long struggle, where many of the monks who had not lifted anything heavier than a dinner fork suffered cuts and bruises against the sharp rocks, the exhausted brothers of Saint Paxia lifted the titanic sword up and over the bank.

The harbor had thus far been spared destruction, and the gate that separated the harbor from the town was wide open and free of any Ragnar. The abbot sought the Golem through the smoke, but he could neither see nor hear its heavy footfalls. *Has something happened while we lingered in the vaults?* He felt a renewed urgency to find the wizard. "This way. You can rest when salvation comes."

Monbatten, staff now in hand, led his men like a shepherd would his flock. Beyond the scorched archway of the harbor gate, the cries of looting men filled the air, and dark shadows danced in front of burning buildings in the town beyond. "It is the wizard we wish to encounter, not the barbarians. Until we have made contact with him, we must avoid detection."

The burdened monks coughed from the smoke, and their hands, habitually used to nothing sharper than a stylus, bled from contact with the giant weapon.

"Physical pain in this world," reminded Monbatten, "will lead to salvation in the next!"

The Ragnar scavenged about with bloody blades, darting into and out of houses in the area where the miners and their families dwelt. The sounds of murder echoed into the night. As a result, the abbot led the monks more hastily.

"Aten protects us," assured the abbot, as he led his group from building to building, heading north and east, guided partly by instinct but mostly by faith.

He led his followers past the mage tower, now a crumbling pile of scorched stone where dangerous discharges of magic periodically erupted. Monbatten felt no sadness over the tower's demise, because he believed it had always been a blight on the town.

When the group rounded a corner past a pile of dismembered knights, he called his brothers to a halt. Ahead, the Golem was on its knees and almost lost in the shadows. The great being was hunched over the body of a red-robed man.

"The Golem!" exclaimed Monbatten. He smiled broadly, turned to his brothers, and pointed to a tannery nearby. "Take the sword inside this building, and await my return!"

With bold strides, Monbatten approached the bizarre scene, one that looked more akin to something from the time of the Ancients than that of the present. Once he was within a dozen feet of the black metal goliath, he felt his body vibrating from the energy exuded from the magical creation. The black metal skin of the Golem was so lifelike that the abbot shuddered at the mockery of life. He gulped before he prayed to Saint Paxia. He stepped up to face the giant and saw that the body before it was a bald wizard with an arrow impaling his skull. *Is this the man I am to negotiate with? The leader of the Ragnar is no more?*

A cloud of red and greenish smoke was coming from the corpse. The Golem's hands were placed, palm up, before the body, almost as a supplicant beseeching its god.

Monbatten was not sure how long he stood transfixed before the giant being turned to look in his direction. The Golem spoke to him, but not with an audible voice. The words echoed around his brain and forced him to his knees.

Your soul shall quench my thirst.

The abbot pressed his hands against the sides of his head. "No, I beg of you, spare me, and listen to what I have to say!"

The Golem clenched its fists and stood to its full height. The body of the wizard by its feet was now a desiccated corpse.

I need to feed. I need the energy of life to bind my soul to this creation.

Monbatten rose to his feet, using all of his force of will. "You are in a weakened state and do not understand. You do not want to destroy the town and its people. I can help you. I can help you destroy Theragaard's tomb. I can remove the barriers that protect it! That is what you want, isn't it? To get revenge for what Theragaard did to you centuries ago?"

The Golem snatched the abbot in its mighty fist and slowly began to squeeze.

"Wait," the abbot pleaded, "I beseech you! We can be allies!"

I have no need for allies.

"The tomb. You need to destroy the tomb," the abbot said between breaths. "Inside that building I have your sword, the only weapon powerful enough to turn Theragaard's crypt to dust."

The Golem unclenched its blood-encrusted hand, dropping Monbatten to the ground, but it did not respond to him with another mental blast. Instead, the black metal warrior stepped forward, its massive feet pounding the ground with deafening force. The abbot rose to his knees and prayed to Aten to be spared.

The Golem ignored him and headed toward the building where the monks hid. Balled-up metal fists bashed through the front of the tannery, collapsing the entrance and trapping the frightened monks inside. The great sword lay before the Golem, yet it did not move to pick it up; rather, it grabbed two of the monks in its giant hands.

With fear and horror in his quivering voice, Monbatten shouted, "Wait, wait! The sword is yours! Spare my flock! We seek only peace!"

A tremendous mental blast struck Monbatten. *Quiet, monk, or you shall join them. It is neither Aten nor your foolish Saint Paxia whom I obey.*

Monbatten watched the horrified expressions of his followers as, two by two, they were lifted before the Golem's blank face. Green and black smoke shrouded each pair of the doomed men, and after a brief struggle punctuated with ear-piercing and gravestone-rattling screams, the smoke cleared. Nothing remained of each pair of monks except bones in smoldering robes. As the abbot covered his ears from their pleas for mercy, he prayed for the men's souls.

When the last man's body had been drained, the Golem reached into the ruins and emerged with its hand grasping the steel blade. Monbatten prostrated himself before the black entity. "See what I have done for you? All I ask in return is to spare the people of Arkos!"

The Golem responded with a voice deep in pitch and rich in quality, which emanated from its now-working mouth and lips. "I shall spare your life, but you must take me to Theragaard's tomb!"

The abbot stood and thanked the being, which now seemed more man than metal. "I shall remove the barrier that protects that accursed tomb!" Stepping before the Golem, he went on to ask: "I see you have undergone a transformation. You are no longer simply the metalworks Golem created by Antigenesus. Who or what stands before me? I must know."

"I am Dementhus," said the Golem's human voice, which then paused and added, "but more as well."

"This was not part of Bafomeht's plan. This is an abomination!"

Monbatten whirled around to find the source of this new voice.

From the shadows emerged the swarthy shaman Gidran, clad in the clothes of the Berserkers. Monbatten scowled at the man who had deceived him and his brothers and pointed a gnarled finger in his direction. "You are an agent of Terminus. You are the abomination!"

THE TOMB OF THERAGAARD

The shaman's face contorted, his eyes bulged, and his mouth snarled, but he ignored Monbatten and continued his badgering of the giant. "The Golem was to be a weapon for the Prophet and his gift to Terminus!"

"That may have been your plan, but it was not mine!" The entity clenched its fist. "My magic was strong, but my body was failing. I knew I needed to replace it. When this mission was given to me, I knew this was my chance at immortality. To bring the Golem back to life, I sacrificed myself. It is only fair that the Golem repay me in kind. I have obtained my immortality and am now more powerful than any wizard who has ever lived!" It took a step forward. "But I still hunger!"

Gidran turned to flee, but he was too late. The entity snatched up the shaman in its free hand.

"No! You can't do this!" begged the wretched Gidran. "Terminus save me!"

Dementhus would not yield, and Terminus did not intervene. In seconds, the shaman was reduced to ashes. Gidran's remains filtered through the giant black hand and mingled with the soot already in the air.

"Your usefulness has ended," declared the being to the empty bear skins.

Fearing the enigmatic entity might turn on him, Monbatten backed away. As he did, he saw first a few, then a dozen, and then hundreds of Ragnar warriors converging on their Mountain God.

"Come, my children. Do not fear! It is I, the God of the Mountain, Lord of the Berserkers," the entity beckoned with His open hand.

Warriors, led by their gray-bearded jarl, gathered closer, as their fears evaporated in the face of religious awe.

The Mountain God's black skin shimmered like the great void of heaven as He basked in the adoration. To the jarl, the God intoned, "The foreign men are gone! It is now up to you and your people to carry out My wishes. The tomb of the defiler Theragaard must be destroyed! Kill those who resist, spare those who surrender. We head to their abbey."

The jarl stepped forward, his aged face split into a grin. "You heard our God! Slay those who stand in our way!"

Bloodthirsty screams erupted from the war-frenzied men. Their unabashed lust for battle shocked Monbatten as the Ragnar moved like a loosely organized mob toward the harbor. The Golem followed, but at a reduced pace that the abbot could match.

By the time the abbot and the Golem reached the end of the largest stone pier, the gray light of dawn was at their back. Ahead, the Ragnar army had begun the trek across the ice-covered harbor on foot.

Much to Monbatten's dismay, the knights of Arkos had regrouped, and projectiles from the island's ancient fortifications rained down on the advancing mob. The boulders struck the thick ice, smashing through it, taking screaming Ragnar men into the embrace of the freezing water and certain death. The fearless invaders ignored the peril, however, and intent on murder, they continued their charge over the ice. Soon they reached the island's dock. The frenzied Ragnar threw themselves against the rebuilt portcullis there and the defenders who stood atop it.

As the entity stepped onto the ice and advanced toward the island, Monbatten followed. He suspected that the wizard inside the Golem was manipulating the ice, because frost spread wherever the giant's feet landed.

Upon reaching the island's small dock, the Mountain God spoke words in a rumbling deep tone. Monbatten recognized the language as that of magic. The God raised His left hand, and a ball of fire appeared in His palm. The ball grew in size as He repeated the words of the spell.

When the Ragnar men saw their God was with them and had a fireball in His hand, they retreated from the embattled portcullis. With a single motion, the God threw the fiery ball at the gate. The rebuilt stone and iron fortification exploded upon impact, as the globe of magic destruction melted iron and vaporized stone.

Monbatten was awed by Dementhus's power. *It is now only a matter of time before peace reigns. The Engothians must see that to resist means death!*

Of this, Monbatten was sure.

Chapter 90

Retreat

Wulfric stood upon the rampart, sword in hand, meting out death to all Ragnar foolhardy enough to attempt to scale the wall where he stood. The defenses were holding, but when he saw the false Ragnar god returning to the battlefield with a giant steel blade, he knew that the prospect for a successful resistance was now merely an illusion. As he scanned the enemy for the rogue wizard, fearing that he might also have risen from the dead, he saw no sign. *The depraved Necromancer shall never return to this world, thanks to you, dear sweet Kara.* In the rear of the Ragnar force, however, was Monbatten. Wulfric spat in disgust as the man did nothing to stop the Golem and appeared at peace even as the siege of his abbey was about to begin. *Tryam will deal with you.*

A Ragnar captain shouted commands to the men nearest the gate, and his warriors retreated from the battle to make room for the giant black warrior. Wulfric watched in horror as the Golem halted at the docks and stared back at him with eyes almost human. Even at this distance, Wulfric could make out the sound of the construct's voice. Inexplicably, it was speaking words of magic, and a ball of fire was growing in its left hand.

"Retreat from the gates!" cried Wulfric. "Retreat!"

The defenders dove from the fortification. As the young Ulf jumped in the air, a wave of intense heat seared his back, and a concussive force slammed him to the ground. The impact of the magical flaming sphere on the gate was devastating, as metal was melted and stone pulverized.

His ears ringing, his vision blurry, and his head dazed, the bloodied Ulf warrior rose to his feet on the strength of his inner fury; miraculously, his sword was still in his hand. When he looked back to where he had been fighting only a moment earlier, all he saw was a smoldering hole. Through the haze of the magical flames was the black outline of the Golem.

Wulfric emptied his lungs with a challenge loud enough to echo off the Corona Mountains. "Stop hiding behind your false god, and face my steel!"

Kara, prepare for me.

Before any Ragnar swarmed ahead of the Golem to answer him, Wulfric felt multiple hands upon his shoulders. "Leave me be!" he protested as he was dragged up the path to the second tier of defenses. He threatened the use of his coronium blade, until he realized that the man leading his capture was Gavin. The young knight was covered in blood and ash.

"Make for the last gate," pleaded Gavin. "The knights rain death from above on the invaders. Let us make our last stand together."

Furious that his sword would be cheated of its chance to taste Ragnar flesh, yet not so angry that he had lost his reason entirely, Wulfric ended his resistance. "I shall retreat no farther than this wall!"

"There is no place farther to retreat, other than the ocean," Gavin countered with the humor of the doomed. "Let the Ragnar and their god earn their way up the island."

They were not alone in their retreat before the ground-stomping footsteps of the Golem. A few dozen refugee Berserker survivors also made their way up the path to the second gate. As they ran to their fallback position, projectiles from mangonels and ballistae rained down on the Ragnar. Wulfric and the others cheered each boulder and bolt.

Once he was standing with the Engothian knights on the ramparts, Wulfric looked back and saw that the Ragnar and their new ally, Monbatten, did not advance in force but rather hid behind the tree-like legs of the Golem, with its great sword in hand. And judging from the solemn faces of his fellow defenders beside him, no one expected to see another dawn after the black metal warrior attacked.

Wulfric leaned over the ramparts and called out to the Ragnar, a mortal enemy he knew he could defeat, and taunted their craven, gray-bearded tyrant: "I challenge you, Ivor! Come and fight me! As I defeated your son, so shall I defeat you!"

The threats were lost in the sound of the mangonel and the ballista batteries, their granite blocks and iron bolts bouncing harmlessly off the giant metal warrior. Wulfric examined the Golem as he would any opponent but found no weaknesses.

Tryam is our last and only hope.

Chapter 91
Answering Theragaard's Call

The guilt over leaving the overmatched defenders wounded his heart almost as much as the touch of Theragaard's spirit warmed it. As he approached the church atop the island, Tryam blocked the pain from his mind. *What I do, I do for them*, he convinced himself.

When Tryam opened the church doors, the dark, silent emptiness inside made him overwrought with melancholy. Candles that usually illuminated the church in a warm orange glow had melted to nothing, and there was not a single soul sitting in the lonely rows of pews. The painful knowledge of those brothers who would never return to pray inside this haven of peace threatened to overwhelm Tryam with despair.

The young acolyte closed his eyes to his memories and stepped past the altar. He moved aside the rug and lifted the slab it concealed. Familiar whispers urged him into the foreboding gloom.

As he moved down the steps, he did so with the same fervor as one on a pilgrimage. At the passage's terminus, he pressed on the cold stone until it yawned open, revealing the subterranean chamber. A shaft of pale light came down from above, illuminating the statue of the warrior on bended knee. Beyond the warrior awaited Theragaard's tomb. To Tryam's profound relief, the mausoleum was undamaged. The acolyte pushed any thoughts of the machinations of Monbatten out of his head.

"I am here," he whispered into the chamber, unsure how else to make his presence known.

As he awaited an answer, Tryam went to one knee, unintentionally imitating the warrior's pose, and prayed aloud. The moments passed in serenity, all thoughts of the war and the night's tragedies set aside. In time, the sound of his own voice was lost to him, and a new voice emerged—a deep voice, filled with passion.

From the clutches of the past escapes a force for evil that threatens to ravage the present. A lightbringer is needed to banish this horror from Medias. If the light were to fail, kingdoms will fall as the darkness spreads, and men will bend their knees to the evil.

Tryam's heart pounded against his breastbone. Through the strength of his faith, he found the courage to respond: "Tell me what I must do, where I must go, and to stop this malevolence, I shall do all you ask."

Arise.

Tryam got to his feet.

You must cleanse your troubled mind and allow the light of Aten to purify your thoughts. Come forward.

The door to Theragaard's tomb cracked open.

Without fear, the young acolyte took hesitant steps forward. When he passed beyond the threshold, he fell to his knees as shame overwhelmed him.

"I am not worthy. I do not deserve Aten's grace. I heard the call before, and I turned my back on Him. I retreated into darkness."

Today, you have answered.

A blue glow filled the small tomb, revealing a suit of glittering plate armor and a silver longsword atop a stone slab. The items appeared so flawlessly crafted that Tryam doubted they had been forged by mortal men.

Take these.

"I am not worthy of this blessing. I carry inside a rage whose source I don't understand, and I bear a scar in the shape of Aten's cross as one marked by evil," cried Tryam, admitting secrets he had never expressed before. "I cannot be trusted with such power."

Fear not. The rage you carry is not your own. When you were a child, a Daemon sought to use your spirit sight for evil ends. Brother Kayen removed the Daemon, though its presence in your body yet lingers. That is why you know ancient languages and possess certain knowledge you should not possess. Let the scar of exorcism serve as a reminder of the danger of Terminus and of the sacrifice needed to overcome him. Now arise, and let my loyal men perform their last duty upon this mortal world.

THE TOMB OF THERAGAARD

Within the blue light appeared the silhouettes of men-at-arms such as Tryam had seen in the ruined watch tower. The youth stood and removed his travel-stained robes. The spectral hands of Theragaard's men placed the armor on his body, and then they placed the silver sword and shield in his hands.

Now we must face what has to be returned to the past. For its evil has already caused great suffering and has twisted the very soul of Father Monbatten.

"Father Monbatten? What else has he done?"

In his zealotry to appease what cannot be appeased, he has sent twenty of his flock to the awaiting mouth of the Golem. Their souls cry out in torment. Can you not hear?

"My brothers," wept Tryam, falling to his knees and covering his ears.

Arise, for now is not the time to mourn. It is the time to act.

Tryam found the strength to do so. He exited the tomb, ready for battle—the wisdom, the experience, the soul of Theragaard now a part of him.

Chapter 92
Vengeance

The Ragnar mountain god began its attack on the gate, even as the hopeless defenders hurled everything they had down upon its head. Unaffected, the Golem slashed its sword through the stone ramparts as though it were a scythe cutting through wheat. The black metal being advanced over the rubble and headed toward the abbey without the slightest acknowledgment of the defenders it trampled. Monbatten followed in its wake.

The Ragnar army surged through the gap created by the Golem as swords, axes, spears, picks, and hammers sought the flesh of the last defenders.

Wulfric, for the second time that day, had to pick himself off the ground. The last Ulf warrior then stepped in line with his remaining allies (a mixture of knights, townsfolk, and refugee Berserkers) as brutal hand-to-hand combat began in earnest. He whetted his sword on the skull of a man from the Bearg clan while his eyes sought his real target: Ivor.

As he slashed his way through the line of Ragnar men, the young Ulf shouted curses at the jarl: "Come here, you filth! Fight me! It is I, Wulfric, son of Alric!"

The defenders were driven back by the superior numbers of enraged Ragnar and their Berserker allies and were being pushed down the path to the abbey. Time and again, though, a single knight, unknown to Wulfric, rallied the men to form the lines again. The Ragnar took notice of this knight and moved to single him out for death.

"No!" cried Wulfric, as he pushed his way forward.

However, it was too late to save the man. Ivor himself, with his great two-handed coronium blade removed the knight's head, the bloody helmet

THE TOMB OF THERAGAARD

landing at Wulfric's feet. It was then that the helmet's visor ripped away, and Wulfric recognized the stalwart knight as Roderick, Tryam's former tormentor.

With hope to win all but lost, Wulfric focused his attention back to Ivor. The dishonorable Ragnar leader was within range of his voice. "Face me! I am Wulfric, son of Alric, last of the Ulf clan!"

As he fought beside the last defenders, Wulfric continued to antagonize the Ragnar jarl. Eventually, word spread through the enemy ranks that Alric's son lived and was seeking the right of challenge. The Ragnar, with confidence of victory soon at hand, encouraged the spectacle.

"Let him through, and let Ivor thrash him!"

"Feed him to our jarl!"

"Ivor will grind his bones into dust!"

The boasts of the Ragnar men compelled those in front to open a path for Wulfric. The jarl, whose blade was still wet with the blood of Roderick, locked eyes with the younger man and smiled with pointed teeth. He made his way forward. When the Ragnar saw what was happening, a circle formed around the two men.

"Alric's pup has some bite, I see," said the jarl, smirking.

The sight of the man who had wrought so much destruction and had overseen so much pointless killing caused blood to roil in Wulfric's veins. The Ulf warrior charged at Ivor, hot breath misting in the frigid morning air. Rage guided his aim and fury his tactics as his wild overhead swing made for the jarl's head.

The Ragnar roared in delight at the blood sport they had long enjoyed at their icy amphitheater in the mountains. Wulfric ignored their ravings, his focus only on revenge.

The jarl was a veteran of a hundred battles, and he laughed as he sidestepped Wulfric's wild attack. "Boy, you would make your father weep!"

Ivor countered with his great sword and made for a killing slice at Wulfric's neck. The young Ulf, blinded with hate, avoided the sweeping giant blade but had to fall to his knees. A quick follow-up strike forced Wulfric to roll back into the mud.

"He ruts like a pig!" mocked Ivor, poking Wulfric with the tip of his sword.

Rage painted the world in shades of red, as the young Ulf shot to his feet and slashed at the head of the jarl. The strike missed by a wide margin,

571

unbalancing him, and he stumbled into Ivor's longer range. Ivor reversed his sword grip and smashed Wulfric on the back of the head with the pommel of his great sword.

Wulfric felt his senses leave him. He dropped his sword and fell to the ground, rolling onto his back. The only thing keeping him from slipping into unconsciousness was the jarl's mockery.

"You are as pathetic as the rest of your kin," Ivor spat. "It is fitting that you shall die in the mud. Your ancestors, who linger without honor in shallow graves, await you!"

Ivor prowled over Wulfric's supine body, playing to the circle of Ragnar warriors. "Can anyone else still hear Alric's voice echoing off the mountaintops as he begged for his life?"

Wulfric spat out blood as his senses slowly returned. He looked for Ivor through the slits of his eyes. The jarl had his back to him, his arms spread wide as he boasted before the hooting Ragnar. Wulfric tensed his body, then slowly rose to his knees.

Ivor played before his men. "It is time, my Ragnar brothers, to bid farewell to the last of the Ulf."

Before any of the Ragnar in the circle could warn their warlord, Wulfric lunged, shoulder first, into the jarl's back.

The impact drove the arrogant man, face first, hard into the bloodstained ground. Ivor rolled over, but Wulfric pinned the man's arms with his thighs. Wulfric then grabbed Ivor's throat and bashed the jarl's head into the ground, as his hands squeezed with the force of a Hound of Fenrir's jaw.

"It is you who shall meet your ancestors this day! It is you who will see them weep at their thin-blooded, cowardly son!"

As the jarl gurgled a response, the Ragnar men and their allies closed the circle. Wulfric cared not for what they planned to do to him. He would die with the knowledge that he had done one small measure of justice for his people.

Angry Ragnar warriors pinned Wulfric's arms, and bloodstained axes moved toward his head. But before the first blow was struck, the blast of a walrus-tusk horn stayed all hands. Word spread among the combatants: Something was happening with the Mountain God.

Chapter 93
Dementhus Versus Rax Partha

Fear?
Fear!

Dementhus was unused to anxiety hindering his ambitions. The strange emotion crawled over his new metallic skin and down his metal spine. He searched for its source and discovered that it was not his own fear he sensed.

When his mind had first entered the Golem's body, the Necromancer had waged a battle for control with the construct's surprisingly strong, nascent consciousness. His will was much stronger, though, and he had pushed Rax Partha's mind aside, until it lingered only as fading memories do.

However, the closer his new titanic legs took him to Theragaard's tomb, the louder these whispers from the Golem's past became.

Dementhus closed metal eyelids over his metal eyes, but the past played before him as fresh as the time it had once occurred. Images from centuries earlier filled his vision. Scenes of a battle on a mountaintop. The body of a dead archmagus.

Rax Partha, listen to me! Fear not, for we get revenge and will forever rid the world of this accursed Theragaard!

The anxiety faded.

Now when the Necromancer walked, his limbs no longer ached. Now when his hand clenched the giant sword, his grip was stronger than iron.

Dementhus used the strength of his own will to wrest full control back over their commingled consciousness, and he swallowed any lingering fear deep into the pit of his black metal stomach. As he focused his eyes to the present, looming before him was the small stone church that was the heart of the Abbey of Saint Paxia. He stepped inside the church grounds and passed the bell tower.

"The final resting spot of our long-dead nemesis!"

Dementhus spoke the words aloud.

He took one giant step to the church's door and raised back the titanic blade behind his head in preparation for a single destructive strike.

"Be forever lost to the minds of mortal men!"

The sword fell toward the church like a guillotine blade to an awaiting neck. When the sword had reached within a foot of the roof, however, Dementhus felt his metal skin crawl. He tried to abort the attack, but it was too late. A jolt, not unlike that of a lighting strike, blasted Dementhus's new body, and he was knocked backward.

In his new voice, he bellowed his anger as he cursed Aten. In rage, he slammed his fist and struck at the invisible barrier. The light of Aten protected the church, and that holiness caused such pain, it forced Dementhus to his knees.

"Monbatten!" the wizard cried, struggling to stand. "Come to me!"

The abbot approached, his arms extended. "Here I am, Master Dementhus. Alas, Aten's grace abides. I told you, as part of our bargain, that I could remove these barriers. Theragaard's tomb lies in a chamber beneath the altar, and I can take you there. All I ask is that you spare the rest of my order and the townsfolk who have taken refuge in the cloister."

Dementhus leveled his sword at Monbatten's head. "I shall do as I have said. Now remove the barrier!"

The sniveling old monk bowed deeply to Dementhus and hurried his way to the church door. There, the abbot prostrated himself before the iron cross that hung over the lintel and prayed. Tears flowed down Monbatten's face as he beseeched some unknown power to answer his call for peace. *Was it Aten? Was it Saint Paxia?*

A red glow flashed, then faded about the cross.

Rising slowly to his feet, as if weary from physical exertion, Monbatten returned to Dementhus and bent to one knee. "I have done as you asked."

THE TOMB OF THERAGAARD

Dementhus, less than gently, swatted the abbot aside with his giant broadsword and stepped up to the door. Battling the fear from Rax Partha's conquered consciousness, he targeted the church with his gigantic weapon again.

This time he encountered no resistance.

The titanic blade crashed through the arched roof, causing the ancient timbers to shatter and the stone supports to collapse. It had taken only one swing. Dementhus impaled the ground with his sword and stepped into the rubble. With his gigantic metal hands, he dug through the debris in search of the altar. He found it quickly and smashed it with his bare fists. Dementhus then removed the stone flooring underneath.

As the sun began to rise in the east, the passage to the underground vaults was revealed. Dementhus stepped back to retrieve his sword, intending to use it to smash the mausoleum in the chamber below.

"No, it's not possible!"

Monbatten's alarm caused Dementhus to turn around. Rising from the vaults, resplendent in silver armor, was a warrior.

Rax Partha's consciousness reemerged and threatened Dementhus's control. *Theragaard lives!* it cried in terror.

Dementhus found himself speaking the Golem's thoughts. "How can this be?"

First it was fear, but now it was rage that Dementhus suffered from Rax Partha.

Dauntless in the face of the raging Golem, the warrior figure emerged into the brilliant morning light, the silver armor gleaming as a second sun.

Chapter 94

Dawn

Tryam greeted the glorious dawn with his right hand gripping the pommel of Theragaard's sword and his left arm locked into the great paladin's silver tower shield.

As he ascended the ruined steps to face the monster that Dementhus had become, he experienced no fear or shock. What he had not expected was to encounter Father Monbatten, who stood trembling beside the Golem. He heard the abbot's cry of disbelief at his emergence.

"Yes, it is I, Father," Tryam said. "I have come to defeat this threat, while I see you have come to aid it. Why have you betrayed Aten?"

The abbot shook his head vigorously as he stumbled over the rubble of the church to stand where the altar had once stood. Tryam could not help but be reminded of the many times Monbatten had lectured about peace from that very spot, a spot that was now infected with the contagion of evil.

"I have betrayed no one," protested Monbatten. "Least of all, Aten!"

"No? Look around at what you have done!" Tryam spread his arms to the destruction and madness that surrounded them. "And it is not only the physical church that has been lost but also the souls of our brothers you fed to this perversion of life."

The abbot shook his head. "That is not true!"

"I know what you did, for I heard their anguished calls from the spirit realm. You have lost your way and now serve evil!"

Monbatten stepped closer, his face flush, and reached to embrace his acolyte. Tryam stood his ground. The abbot then fell to his knees. "It was a sacrifice! Your brothers laid down their lives to secure peace!"

THE TOMB OF THERAGAARD

Tryam dragged the old man back to his feet with his shield arm. "Against their will? To feed this weapon of war?"

"I beg you! Don't let their sacrifice go in vain. This battle is over. As long as we don't resist, the invaders will leave us in peace. The church can be repaired, and the injured can be healed. Put down that weapon. Drop that shield."

Tryam did neither.

Monbatten took a step back. "You have fallen under the spell of Brother Kayen and the false words he has whispered in your ear. You follow the spirit of a dead warrior whose legacy was violence, death, and destruction. I see I have failed as your teacher." His scowl contorted to make his face unrecognizable as the man who had once been the abbot of Saint Paxia. "But I must now teach you one last lesson. So that peace can return to Arkos, you will be the final sacrifice to the Golem."

The abbot turned his back to Tryam and took his place behind the Golem. That giant, whose metal skin gleamed from the moisture freed by the morning sun, throbbed with magical energy, and the eyes that stared from its no-longer-placid face radiated hatred. Pointing to Tryam, Monbatten addressed the giant: "Destroy him, and you destroy Theragaard—forever banning his soul from the mortal plane." The former abbot of Saint Paxia then turned and headed away from the abbey, never looking back.

The metal warrior raised its gigantic broadsword. "Let this be your last dawn!"

The ancient soul now within Tryam urged him into action, and the young warrior rolled forward and between the Golem's legs. As Tryam tumbled, he slashed at the creature's metal flesh. Sparks flew, and whether from pain or frustration, the Golem, with Dementhus's voice, cried out.

Tryam continued to move forward and into the church's courtyard.

The Golem, as quick as any warrior Tryam had ever seen, turned and launched its attack. Tryam had time only to raise his shield and pray.

The giant blade crashed onto the top of the shield, which absorbed most of the energy; however, the remaining force was strong enough to throw Tryam backward, and he landed on his back twelve feet away, at the base of the bell tower. Recovering quickly, he taunted the Golem as the metal being screamed in frustration.

"Theragaard defeated you once before, and he shall defeat you again!"

The Golem raised its left hand and extended it forward. From black fingertips a green lightning bolt flashed, striking Tryam in the chest. The young warrior collapsed, dropping his shield; his limbs lost their feeling, and a burning sensation flowed up and down his body.

The Golem stepped forward to stand over Tryam's supine form, and the tattoo-like runes carved into its black metal skin glowed red. When it raised its sword, screams of terror erupted from the windows and doorways of the cloister. The head of the great giant turned to the frightened townsfolk holed up inside, and it eyed their souls hungrily. Tryam used the Golem's hesitation to rush to his feet and grab his shield. Before he fled, the voice of Theragaard entered his thoughts. *You must lead the Golem away from here before it feeds again on the innocents.*

The young warrior understood what he had to do.

"You shall never succeed if you do not kill me!" taunted Tryam before ducking around the bell tower. The Golem turned from the petrified townsfolk to Tryam and then back again, torn as to which to destroy first. Tryam continued to run to the steps leading to the crumbling ancient wall that ringed the church grounds.

The Golem, fast but not as nimble, at last gave chase, smashing through the bell tower in its mad rush to grab the fleeing warrior. After stumbling through the rubble, it spotted Tryam perched atop the outer wall, and it charged anew. Now at the same height, Tryam could see the madness in the Golem's eyes as it bore down on him. The Golem collided into the wall, throwing Tryam over the side; the young warrior landed outside the abbey, precipitously close to the edge of the cliff.

As Tryam dodged stones from the crumbling wall, a memory not his own entered his head. He evaded the Golem, which ripped through the debris to get at him, and he ran along the edge of the cliff until he found narrow stone steps cut into the cliff face. As he took the icy stairs as fast as his legs could go, he gave praise to Theragaard.

Above, the Golem, much bigger than the stairs could accommodate, had to leap from tier to tier in order to descend. Relentlessly it pursued.

Tryam stumbled down the last step, landing on the frozen waters of the harbor, exhausted.

You cannot rest! Arise! Arise!

THE TOMB OF THERAGAARD

Theragaard's urgings rejuvenated Tryam's legs. The young warrior slipped his way out over the ice, away from the island, and out into the vast Frostfoam Sea.

The Golem followed, saying in its unique voice, "You have run out of shadows to hide in and tombs to slumber in, Theragaard."

The metal wizard raised its left hand, and flames shot out from its fingertips. Tryam put his shield before him even as a vision from Theragaard for his next course of action played inside his mind

The vision was more troubling than the burning flames that scorched his shining armor.

"No, you can't depart this world. Not yet!" begged Tryam. "You have so much to teach, and I have so much to learn!"

A sacrifice must be made.

"Then let it be me alone!" begged Tryam.

It is Aten's will.

When the flame attack ceased, the young warrior dropped his shield and stood, unafraid, before the throbbing eyes of the mad perversion of life.

The Golem raised its mighty fist to cast another spell.

Now!

With two hands, the young warrior launched the sword of Theragaard at the feet of the Golem. When the sword struck the ice, an explosion of blue light, the visual expression of the soul of the great paladin, encompassed the perverted life-form.

The Golem staggered as blue flames engulfed its black body. The magical entity screamed as one in agony, dropped its sword, and attempted to smother the flames with its hands. But nothing could stop the spread of the holy fire. After a few agonizing moments, the Golem, now stiff and lifeless, the crimson tattoos on its body having faded, fell face first onto the ice, causing a shock wave to spread across the frozen sea. The crack propagated in all directions, including beneath Tryam, who could not stop himself from falling through the ice.

The sting of the arctic water stabbed like knives. Tryam reached for the surface with outstretched arms, but the blue sky above receded from view, as does a ship when sailing toward sunset. The world grew dark, as the heavy armor dragged Tryam down to the murky depths of the Frostfoam Sea.

Even as he struggled for breath, Tryam was more concerned with the fate of Theragaard. As his connection waned, he at first became frightened;

then, as the touch became only as a distant memory, he felt empty and alone. To stop the Golem, the paladin had once again sacrificed himself.

As the spirit of the paladin passed from his body and the mortal realm, Tryam took comfort in knowing he had served Theragaard and had made a difference.

At peace with his decisions, Tryam looked for the Golem, hoping to have proof of its demise. He spotted the black metal monstrosity through the haze of the water: It was sinking much more quickly than he was, and as if guided by Aten's hand, it was descending toward a volcanic vent.

As he watched the immobile monstrosity disappear into the glowing crack at the bottom of the sea, Tryam gave thanks to Aten. *The sacrifice of Theragaard, Kara, the defenders of Arkos, and my brothers in the Order of Saint Paxia have not been in vain. The world is finally free from this horror once and for all.*

The darkness of the void wrapped around Tryam's body like burial robes. He grew tired, and his eyes started to close. He was about to surrender to the eternal solitude of death when a new voice filled his head: the voice of a woman.

Fight! Never give in to the darkness!

Tryam snapped back to consciousness, unsure if the voice was a memory or something from the spirit realm. Theragaard's armor had fallen from his body, and he discovered he was more buoyant. Unburdened, he struggled back toward the surface, eager to hear the voice again. Light above filtered down, offering hope. In a final effort, Tryam reached for the surface and discovered a hand from above was reaching down. Before slipping back to unconsciousness, he grasped the hand.

The last sensation he felt was being pulled upward.

Chapter 95

The Paladin

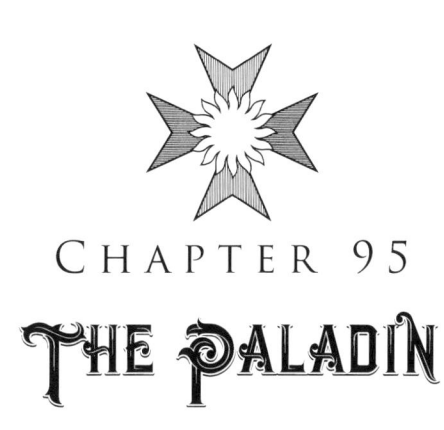

Nightmares of a gray land under a gray sky blossomed into dreams of green lands under golden suns. But it was the sound of a familiar voice that ultimately lured Tryam back to the mortal plane. When his eyes fluttered open, he was greeted by Kayen's smiling face. It took a few moments before Tryam realized where he was: inside the abbey's infirmary. It took a few additional moments to find his voice.

"Dementhus, the Golem, are they …?"

"They are no more," assured Kayen.

Tryam started to rise, but Kayen gently pushed him back down. "Don't make any sudden movements. You nearly froze to death."

"But the Ragnar army still survives. I must rejoin the defenders!"

In another attempt to get off the bed, Tryam fought through the painful tingling sensation in his extremities. Kayen pushed him back down again, but not as gently.

"The Ragnar army has been turned away."

"How?" asked Tryam incredulously.

"Wulfric." Kayen's smile broadened. "He challenged Ivor to single combat. The two battled, and as good overcomes evil, so Wulfric defeated Ivor. The Ragnar descended upon Wulfric to take revenge, but something miraculous occurred to intervene on our young friend's behalf: Their mountain god was challenged by a warrior in gleaming armor and was defeated! Without the cruel leadership of Ivor or the awe inspired by the Golem, the Berserkers panicked and split back into their separate clans. They have retreated to Arkos, and a meeting of the jarls is taking place right now."

"Then, there will be no more fighting?"

Kayen scratched his brown and gray beard. "I hope not. The remaining Berserkers appear to have lost all taste for conquest, and the leaderless Ragnar clan no longer holds sway over them. Wulfric believes he can convince the Berserkers to go back home."

Tryam attempted to absorb what he had just been told. *Is it possible we have won?* "I should have known Wulfric would rise to be a leader among his people, but what price was paid for this peace? All those lives lost. Kara …"

"We must focus on the souls saved and pray that the souls lost are with Aten now."

Tryam's mind was not yet at ease. One more tragic figure was still unaccounted for. "Where is Monbatten? Are you aware of his final, treacherous deeds?"

"Aye, I know what evil he has done. I asked Brother Sam to search for the abbot, but he has disappeared. I doubt if we shall ever see him again."

Tryam was not so sure about that. Another unanswered question yet lingered. He sat upright in bed, shocked it had taken him this long to ask. "Was it you who saved me?"

Kayen laughed. "No, it was not I, though I appreciate your thinking I am strong enough to pull you out of the sea!" Turning serious, he continued. "What happened to you was an act of providence. The man who saved your life is someone whom I have long wanted to introduce to you. Now that Monbatten is gone, I can make this introduction without fear of repercussions."

"Who?" As Tryam asked the question, an uneasy feeling came over him.

The missionary patted Tryam on the chest. "Do not be alarmed, my son. He is a man I have known for many years. He is a paladin in the service of Aten, and his name is Sir Valins von Gihlcrist deClave."

A voice came from the shadows. "If it is easier, just call me Valins."

The speaker stepped into the candlelight, revealing a middle-aged man with thinning light-brown hair. His formal yet friendly smile put Tryam at ease. A jagged scar accentuated his rugged face, and his hazel eyes were lit by a commanding soul. Valins wore a black cloak over a white tunic. On the tunic was embroidered a black and gold cross of Aten. Underneath the tunic, Tryam detected the bulk of armor.

"Sir Valins, I thank you for saving my life. I am forever in your debt."

THE TOMB OF THERAGAARD

As if caught by surprise, the paladin erupted in laughter. "Saving you? It is you I should thank for saving me, the town, and the rest of Medias from the danger of that ancient artifact."

"You are familiar with the Golem?"

"Of course. It is why I am here. I was sent by the order to investigate reports of increased Daemon activity in this region."

"The order?"

"The Order of the Imperium." Valins moved closer to Tryam's bed and threw back the cloak from his right shoulder, revealing an armband depicting a gold lion on a black-and-white-checkered shield.

"So, it is true. You are a paladin!"

Kayen puffed out his chest. "You didn't think I would know a real paladin?"

"I am sorry, Brother. I did not mean for it to sound that way. I just found it hard to imagine I would ever see one in person. After reading all the stories of the paladins from ages past, it is hard to imagine one who is yet flesh and blood."

Valins traced the scar that spanned his face from brow to chin. "I am afraid we are a little too flesh and blood for my liking."

Tryam started to rise again, but this time, it was Valins who laid a forceful hand on his shoulder. "You should sit back down and rest. I have an offer you might be interested in, and you might take it better lying down."

"I am ready," Tryam said with numb lips. "What is your offer, sir?"

"I have spoken with Kayen, and he has revealed to me your ability to see into the spirit realm. I also witnessed firsthand your actions to save this town. It is rare to find a person willing to put the lives of others ahead of themself. It would be a sin for you not to use your skills for the purpose for which Aten gave them to you. Would you be interested in taking the first step to become a paladin?"

Tryam did not hesitate to respond. "I can think of no greater honor and privilege. If I am worthy, I accept the challenge."

"Good. We should leave as soon as the situation here allows for it. Arkos still wobbles over a precipice."

"Yes, and I have one other task I must do."

"What is it?" questioned Valins.

"A companion of mine helped us discover Dementhus's plot—a young wizard named Telvar. He was in the mage tower when the Golem destroyed it. I doubt anyone has had the time to find his body. I feel I owe him that, at least."

"Then let's find your wizard," agreed Valins.

CHAPTER 96

OUT OF THE PIT

The evening sun cast red shadows over the smoldering town. Another act of providence—a midday burst of heavy snow—had arrested the spread of fire, and now only black smoke rose in the sky above Arkos. During the short time that Tryam had been unconscious in the abbey infirmary after having nearly drowned, a temporary truce between the Berserker invading forces, now in council along the north wall, and the Engothian knights, stationed back inside their ruined keep, had been negotiated.

Gavin had taken on the mantle of leadership over the knights. The valiant young warrior had already begun to distribute food from the keep's stores to the shocked townsfolk.

The monks, now with Sam in charge of the order, had offered homeless citizens continued sanctuary in the abbey.

In the matter of a few hours, my entire world has changed! thought Tryam.

Tryam, Kayen, and Valins were on their way to the mage tower. Even from a distance, Tryam could see that it still crackled with dangerous bolts of residual magical energy. The three sought aid in their search for the wizard, but they found none willing to enter the former tower grounds.

There was one person Tryam knew who would lend a hand. He made a plea to Kayen and Valins. "Wulfric is stronger than all of us. He would be a great asset in our search for Telvar. May I seek him out?"

"A wise idea, son," agreed Valins. "Find him, and if he is able to leave his Berserker brethren, ask him to help us. Brother Kayen and I shall start the search without you."

Tryam headed for the north wall. He soon found the Berserkers gathered around the ruins of another tower, the ward tower. He was reminded of the

THE TOMB OF THERAGAARD

last time he had stood there. He'd been with Kara and Wulfric, who helped him load supplies for the winter—supplies the monks would never need. It was near there that he had decided to enter the Engothian tournament. Kara had been so excited. Tryam swallowed the sweet memories, painful in their remembrance; then he crept through the blasted stones to listen to what the jarls and their respective clans were saying.

The Berserkers were using the tumbled stones like seats in an amphitheater. On the bottom of the ruins gathered the war-scarred jarls who had bent their knee to the conquering Ragnar. From the shadows, Tryam observed how each jarl in turn argued either for or against continuing the war on Arkos. Many argued that it was their right to sack the town. Others acknowledged that they had been deceived and beguiled by the tricks of the foreigner Dementhus and the lies of the bloodthirsty Ivor, and it was to their great shame they had been so foolish. Some jarls were challenged by members of their own clans and lost their heads in the process.

When the bloody challenges were over, the Berserkers resumed their summit as the new leaders replaced those deposed. To Tryam's delight, Wulfric was representing Clan Ulf as its only survivor. His Ulf friend spoke as an equal among the assembled jarls, who averaged more than twice his age. Wulfric was a natural leader and a warrior without peer. He was urging the clans to unify as a single tribe, not for conquest but for brotherhood. He called for the conflict with Arkos to cease. Back and forth the discussion went, and as ferocious as Wulfric was in battle, he was equal in argument.

Just as the last rays of light sank beneath the horizon, the leaders came to a consensus. Wulfric prevailed, and the jarls agreed to leave Arkos in peace. Regarding the Ragnar clan, a new jarl was to be determined at a later date, and any punishment was to be decided by the other clans when they returned to their own villages. It was a beginning that gave Tryam hope.

When the Berserkers dispersed, they left behind their coronium weapons as a sign to the people of Arkos that they were ceasing all future conflict.

Wulfric noticed Tryam and scrambled over the stones to greet him. He grasped Tryam's forearm. "I heard what you did against the Golem, and I still cannot believe it! How did you manage to sink it beneath the sea?"

"I had help from Theragaard," replied Tryam, mindful of the sacrifice the paladin had made. "But what you just did here—getting the clans together to end further bloodshed—you did all on your own."

Wulfric shrugged his shoulders. "Though Berserkers are thickheaded, it is fortunate that they are not totally unyielding to reason." The big Ulf released his grip and stepped back. Tryam could see his own reflection in his friend's eyes. "You are still troubled by something," said Wulfric. "What is it?"

Tryam pointed back to the center of town, where the mage tower had once stood. "There is still one member of our party unaccounted for."

Wulfric considered the matter only briefly. "Let's get to work and find his body. We owe him that."

Without further discussion, the Ulf started for the ruined tower, and Tryam followed. As they drew closer, the ominous sounds of discharging magic filled their ears; bolts of energy were lashing out into the now-black sky. Nothing of Myramar's gardens remained, not even the iron fence that had once encircled the area. Tryam spotted Kayen and Valins: The missionary was using his staff to poke inside pockets in the rubble, while the paladin was lifting rocks out of the way. Tryam hailed them.

"Is that one of the Dunford's officers?" inquired Wulfric, pointing at Valins. "I do not recognize him."

"No, that is Sir Valins," answered Tryam. "A paladin sent here to help us."

"A little late, isn't he?"

"Not from my perspective. He arrived just in time to pull me from the icy waters of the Frostfoam."

After brief introductions, the four men resumed the search. It was long into the night—and it was after a few close calls from dangerous magical discharges—when Valins reported something odd. "See here," he said, urging the others to his position. "These stones are cold to the touch, while the others around it are still quite warm."

"Interesting," agreed Kayen.

Wulfric felt the stones and asked, "Could the discharges from the tower be the cause?"

"Perhaps," said Kayen, "but other explanations come to mind. Let's move as many of the cool stones off the pile as we can."

Individually, they lifted the smaller rocks, while collectively they removed the larger ones. After hours of arduous but hopeful work, they had dug a pit fifteen feet deep. The cool stones they had removed were not discharging magic, a fact that intrigued the paladin. Valins surmised that some force had drained the dangerous magic from this particular area.

THE TOMB OF THERAGAARD

"Or someone," added Kayen hopefully.

The deeper they went, the larger the stones became and the harder they were to remove. When the pit was more than twenty feet deep, Wulfric raised his arm to silence the others. "I hear tapping!"

Despite their weariness, they intensified their efforts. They removed stones until they located their last obstacle, a twisted metal staircase. They pried this away, using only their bare hands. Kayen gasped and Wulfric whooped when, under the metal stairs, they revealed a grime-covered face instantly recognizable as Telvar by his perpetual look of annoyance.

Telvar spat dirt from his mouth and complained immediately. "It took you long enough! I can't breathe underground indefinitely!" His eyes looked about nervously. "Don't stand there with your mouths agape. Get me out of here before the Golem returns!"

"Fret not," chided Wulfric. "Tryam has vanquished the Golem, and the battle for Arkos is over. Even now the Ragnar and their allies are withdrawing back to the mountains."

Telvar opened his mouth as if to speak, closed it, opened it again, and then went silent.

Wulfric laughed. "For once, our friend Telvar has been left speechless."

Valins led the effort to free the wizard, who appeared to be uninjured outside of a few scrapes and bruises. Tryam found it disconcerting to see the young man without his staff. After brushing the dirt from his robes, Telvar bowed to the paladin. "You are a paladin, are you not? I recognize your badge of office." Telvar, as was his habit, flashed his charm in the face of people of high social status.

"That I am. My name is Sir Valins von Gihlcrist deClave."

"An honor, sir," bowed the young mage for the second time. Perhaps humbled by the experience, Telvar looked to his companions and bowed to them as well. "Thank you all for freeing me."

"How did you survive for so long?" asked Tryam.

"I was in the stairwell when the tower collapsed around me. I somehow was spared being crushed and found myself trapped but surrounded by magic. I was able to use this magic to provide myself with small amounts of air and water." He glanced about in disbelief. "How did you manage to destroy Dementhus and the Golem? I must know!"

"Soon," promised Wulfric, stepping to the mage's side. "Let us get out of here first. This whole area is unstable."

The three helped Telvar away from the pit. From the vantage point atop the piled stones, Telvar could survey the damage that war had done to Arkos. "It looks as if I am one of the fortunate ones," mused the wizard.

"Aye," said Wulfric glumly, "you are."

Telvar's face went slack, and Tryam saw true sorrow in the wizard's eyes as he asked, "Kara, she is …?"

"Gone? Yes," said Wulfric.

"I wish I had the words of healing and comfort as a monk might have, but I can give you only my simple condolences. I wish there were something I could have done to save her."

"We all do," agreed Kayen.

Before the group departed, Wulfric grabbed Telvar's arm. "There is something you can do for Kara, but it requires going back to the Corona Mountains."

EPILOGUE

HER HOME

After days of silent and arduous hiking, Tryam could see that they were atop the summit of the southernmost mountain in the Corona Range. The view from this vantage point was breathtaking. From here, the golden light that shone on far-off Arkos masked the town's battle scars. Other wounds ran deeper.

It was Wulfric, and he alone, who carried Kara's body as the party searched for a proper burial spot. As Tryam looked upon the bright white snow and dark blue ice, he could not imagine a more fitting resting place for such a beautiful soul.

Wulfric must have agreed, for he stopped abruptly, and without words, he placed Kara before a natural ice shelf only a dozen yards below the mountain's peak. He removed her burial shroud and looked up at the wizard. "We have found her home," he said at last.

Telvar stepped away from the group and made preparations to cast a spell.

Tryam stood by and watched his Ulf friend scoop handfuls of snow to cover Kara's body, leaving only her head exposed. Wulfric brushed Kara's golden hair one final time before enveloping her face beneath a veil of sparkling ice crystals. "Goodbye," he whispered.

With the cross of Aten in his hands, Brother Kayen said a final blessing. Tryam added his voice, as did Valins.

Once the prayer echoed no more, Telvar stepped forward. The wizard, now dressed in clean gray robes, threw a mixture of reagents around Kara. In response, the snow and ice on the shelf began to melt. The melted water did not pool but rather flowed together to surround her body. Telvar spoke more words of magic and gestured with his hands. By some means known only to magic users, the water froze, forming a rectangular tomb of ice.

With the spell finished, Tryam moved closer. The sun filtered down through the crystal-clear ice and rested on Kara's face, giving her the illusion of life. To Tryam, she looked as if she were merely in a deep sleep, dreaming of the life she would share with Wulfric. Tryam sought her spirit but found nothing. *Was it her voice I heard as I sank into the depths of the Frostfoam Sea? If it was, where is she now?* The loss of Kara in this world left him empty. As he looked at Wulfric's expressionless face, he wondered what pain the young warrior hid.

"She will be preserved always," said Telvar with pride, "until the mountain itself crumbles into the Frostfoam Sea."

After long, solemn moments, Wulfric turned his back to the tomb and walked to the edge of the shelf. When Tryam joined him, the Ulf warrior asked, "What do I do now?"

As Tryam gazed with the eyes of youth out over the vast expanse before them, the world seemed limitless. "You can go back to the Berserkers. Be an example to them. Help them recover from the damage the Ragnar caused." When Wulfric harrumphed, he suggested, "Or you can stay in Arkos and help rebuild?"

Wulfric shook his head. "My past is buried here, and I have no wish to wander over the graves of my yesterdays. I mean to leave this cold part of the world and never see the sun rise or set here again."

"Then come with me to Secundus. Sir Valins has a ship, the *Sunseeker*, ready to go."

"So, you mean to join the paladins?"

"If I am worthy, yes."

Wulfric smiled, the first sign of cheer to show on his face in a long time. "I would like to see a city—even though I am sure they are not as fantastic a place as Telvar makes them seem." He gripped Tryam's forearm. "To the *Sunseeker*," he said.

Dramatis Personae

Main Characters

Abbaster	WARRIOR, AGENT OF BAFOMEHT
Dementhus	NECROMANCER, FALLEN ALBUS MAGE
Lord Dunford	KNIGHT COMMANDER OF ARKOS
Gidran	SHAMAN, AGENT OF BAFOMEHT
Kara	YOUNG LADY ARCHER OF ULF CLAN
Kayen	MISSIONARY MONK
Monbatten	ABBOT OF THE MONESTARY
Myramar	OLD MAGE OF ARKOS
Telvar	NEWLY ARRIVED APPRENTICE MAGE
Tryam	YOUNG MONK EAGER FOR ADVENTURE
Wulfric	BERSERKER OF THE ULF CLAN

Additional Characters

Abbaster	warrior agent of Bafomeht, a brute
Ajon	a monk at the abbey, a healer
Akrack	Berserker jarl of a clan allied with the Ragnar
Alikey	a saint, founder of an order
Alric	Berserker jarl of the Ulf clan, father of Wulfric
Amelia	daughter of Kayen, killed in the plague
Annen	Saint Annen
Antigenesus	the last great archmagus
Ardrah	a winged Aemon beast, guardian of the mountain
Arion the huntsman	a blue team member among the knight aspirants
Aten	God Himself
Athal	a Ragnar warrior on Crayvor's expedition
Athelrad	King Athelrad of Engoth

Auroth	the Daemon inside the Anima Crystallum amulet
Bafomeht	the Prophet, the priest king of Lux
Bannett	Engothian knight, squad captain at the miner fort
Braxis	portly blue team member among knight aspirants
Breyn	member of the Ulf Clan that meats horrible end
Caydan	a monk at the abbey, a healer
Chrondus	magical creature between Medias and the astral plane
Claes the farmer	a blue team member among the knight aspirants
Cordon	abbey cook
Crayvor	son of Jarl Ivor of the Ragnar clan
Deljay	an Engothian knight and expert rider
Dartamus	a wizard with knowledge of Iscandious's Gambit
Dementhus	the Necromancer, wizard, an Albus mage
Dolobreth	Prince Dolobreth, character in Tryam's favorite book
Domedian	highest ranked mage in the Western world
Dorn	child of Kayen, killed in the plague
Dorsat	a young monk at the abbey
Dunford	Lord Dunford, commander of the knights at Arkos
Emil	Brother Emil, a venerable monk at the abbey
Fenrir	a great Daemon, father of the Hounds of Fenrir
Frey	a black-haired young monk, a true believer
Fritzal	Father Fritzal, abbot of the Order of Saint Alikey
Gamrow	the most devout monk of the abbey
Gathrey	Engothian knight that meets a terrible end
Gavin	a blue team member among the knight aspirants
Gidran	a shaman agent of Bafomeht, a cleric of Terminus
Gord	Berserker Ulf youth clan, died in his Trial of Blood
Grollo	a veteran Ragnar warrior
Halfdan	a veteran Ragnar warrior
Halldor	Berserker champion of the Ragnar clan
Harag	a Ragnar warrior on Crayvor's expedition
Iscandious	a crafty wizard during the Darkening epoch
Ivor	the gray-bearded jarl of the Ragnar clan
Jarrard	the sergeant at the keep

THE TOMB OF THERAGAARD

Jarth	a Ragnar warrior on Crayvor's expedition
Judithia	an Aemon, one of twin guardians of thonored dead
Kalla	daughter of Kayen, killed in the plague
Kara	young lady Berserker archer adopted into the Ulf clan
Kayen	a missionary monk of the Order of the Imacolata
Klain	a Ragnar warrior
Kole	a villager from Clan Ulf, prisoner of the Ragnar
Korddainer	the illusionist tower mage
Kreegar	Captain Kreegar, an Engothian knight
Krell	smallest blue team member among knight aspirants
Lathan	a monk at the abbey, advisor to Monbatten
Lilia	leather worker from Clan Ulf, prisoner of the Ragnar
Lucian	Saint Lucian
Lymaz	a monk at the abbey, a healer
Makkong	a Berserker warrior from the Redbone clan
Maxius	son of the blacksmith, a red team
Minova	an Aemon, one of twin guardians of honored dead
Monbatten	Father Monbatten, Abbot Monbatten
Muriel	wife of Kayen, killed in the plague
Myramar	the Arkos tower mage
Necromedes the Thrice-Reborn	Creator of Necromancy
Oliek	a graybeard Berserker of Clan Ulf
Paxia	Saint Paxia
Rax Partha	name of the God of the Mountain, the Golem
Rettiwalk	a Ragnar warrior
Roderick	a red-haired Engothian knight
Samuel	elderly monk, confidant of Father Monbatten
Sanra	a weaver from Clan Ulf, prisoner of the Ragnar
Skracks	a blue team member among the knight aspirants
Slaavor	firstborn son of Jarl Ivor of the Ragnar clan
Telvar	young red Mage, Myramar's new apprentice
Terminus	the Dark God, God of All Things

Theragaard . . . . . . one of Aten's greatest warriors
Thrane . . . . a villager from Clan Ulf, prisoner of the Ragnar
Thrax . . . . a Ragnar warrior
Tryam . . . . the young acolyte
Vaard . . . . a Ragnar warrior
Valins . . . . Sir Valins von Gihlcrist deClave, a paladin
Valnarr . . . . an angel revered by the Ulf
Vrooman . . . . quietest blue team member
Wulfric . . . . Berserker of the Ulf clan

Printed in Great Britain
by Amazon